From Cornhill to Grand Cairo
and
The Irish Sketch Book

From Cornhill to Grand Cairo
and
The Irish Sketch Book

by

W. M. Thackeray

CAMBRIDGE SCHOLARS PUBLISHING
classic texts

From Cornhill to Grand Cairo and The Irish Sketch Book, by W. M. Thackeray

This book in its current typographical format first published 2008 by

Cambridge Scholars Publishing

12 Back Chapman Street, Newcastle upon Tyne, NE6 2XX, UK

British Library Cataloguing in Publication Data
A catalogue record for this book is available from the British Library

ISBN (10): 1-84718-816-8, ISBN (13): 9781847188168

CONTENTS

A JOURNEY FROM CORNHILL TO GRAND CAIRO

PREFACE

On the 20th of August, 1844, the writer of this little book went to dine at the — Club, quite unconscious of the wonderful events which Fate had in store for him.

Mr. William was there, giving a farewell dinner to his friend Mr. James (now Sir James). These two asked Mr. Titmarsh to join company with them, and the conversation naturally fell upon the tour Mr. James was about to take. The Peninsular and Oriental Company had arranged an excursion in the Mediterranean, by which, in the space of a couple of months, as many men and cities were to be seen as Ulysses surveyed and noted in ten years. Malta, Athens, Smyrna, Constantinople, Jerusalem, Cairo were to be visited, and everybody was to be back in London by Lord Mayor's Day.

The idea of beholding these famous places inflamed Mr. Titmarsh's mind; and the charms of such a journey were eloquently impressed upon him by Mr. James. "Come," said that kind and hospitable gentleman, "and make one of my family party; in all your life you will never probably have a chance again to see so much in so short a time. Consider—it is as easy as a journey to Paris or to Baden." Mr. Titmarsh considered all these things; but also the difficulties of the situation: he had but six-and-thirty hours to get ready for so portentous a journey—he had engagements at home—finally, could he afford it? In spite of these objections, however, with every glass of claret the enthusiasm somehow rose, and the difficulties vanished.

But when Mr. James, to crown all, said he had no doubt that his friends, the Directors of the Peninsular and Oriental Company, would make Mr. Titmarsh the present of a berth for the voyage, all objections ceased on his part: to break his outstanding engagements—to write letters to his amazed family, stating that they were not to expect him at dinner on Saturday fortnight, as he would be at Jerusalem on that day—to purchase eighteen shirts and lay in a sea stock of Russia ducks,—was the work of four-and-twenty hours; and on the 22nd of August, the "Lady Mary Wood" was sailing from Southampton with the "subject of the present memoir," quite astonished to find himself one of the passengers on board.

These important statements are made partly to convince some incredulous friends—who insist still that the writer never went abroad at all, and wrote the following pages, out of pure fancy, in retirement at Putney; but mainly, to give him an opportunity of thanking the Directors of the Company in question for a delightful excursion.

It was one so easy, so charming, and I think profitable—it leaves such a store of pleasant recollections for after days—and creates so many new sources of interest (a newspaper letter from Beyrout, or Malta, or Algiers, has twice the interest now that it had formerly),—that I can't but recommend all persons who have time and means to make a similar journey—vacation idlers to extend their travels and pursue it: above all, young well-educated men entering life, to take this course, we will say, after that at college; and, having their book-learning fresh in their minds, see the living people and their cities, and the actual aspect of Nature, along the famous shores of the Mediterranean.

CHAPTER I: VIGO

The sun brought all the sick people out of their berths this morning, and the indescribable moans and noises which had been issuing from behind the fine painted doors on each side of the cabin happily ceased. Long before sunrise, I had the good fortune to discover that it was no longer necessary to maintain the horizontal posture, and, the very instant this truth was apparent, came on deck, at two o'clock in the morning, to see a noble full moon sinking westward, and millions of the most brilliant stars shining overhead. The night was so serenely pure, that you saw them in magnificent airy perspective; the blue sky around and over them, and other more distant orbs sparkling above, till they glittered away faintly into the immeasurable distance. The ship went rolling over a heavy, sweltering, calm sea. The breeze was a warm and soft one; quite different to the rigid air we had left behind us, two days since, off the Isle of Wight. The bell kept tolling its half-hours, and the mate explained the mystery of watch and dog-watch.

The sight of that noble scene cured all the woes and discomfitures of sea-sickness at once, and if there were any need to communicate such secrets to the public, one might tell of much more good that the pleasant morning-watch effected; but there are a set of emotions about which a man had best be shy of talking lightly,—and the feelings excited by contemplating this vast, magnificent, harmonious Nature are among these. The view of it inspires a delight and ecstasy which is not only hard to describe, but which has something secret in it that a man should not utter loudly. Hope, memory, humility, tender yearnings towards dear friends, and inexpressible love and reverence towards the Power which created the infinite universe blazing above eternally, and the vast ocean shining and rolling around—fill the heart with a solemn humble happiness, that a person dwelling in a city has rarely occasion to enjoy. They are coming away from London parties at this time: the dear little eyes are closed in sleep under mother's wing. How far off city cares and pleasures appear to be! how small and mean they seem, dwindling out of sight before this magnificent brightness of Nature! But the best thoughts only grow and strengthen under it. Heaven shines above, and the humble spirit looks up reverently towards that boundless aspect of wisdom and beauty. You are at home, and with all at rest there, however far away they may be; and through the distance the heart broods over them, bright and wakeful like yonder peaceful stars overhead.

The day was as fine and calm as the night; at seven bells, suddenly a bell began to toll very much like that of a country church, and on going on deck we found an awning raised, a desk with a flag flung over it close to the compass, and the ship's company and passengers assembled there to hear the Captain read the Service in a manly respectful voice. This, too, was a novel and touching sight to me. Peaked ridges of purple mountains rose to the left of the ship,—Finisterre and the coast of Galicia. The sky above was cloudless and shining; the vast dark ocean smiled peacefully round about, and the ship went rolling over it, as the people within were praising the Maker of all.

In honour of the day, it was announced that the passengers would be regaled with champagne at dinner; and accordingly that exhilarating liquor was served out in decent profusion, the company drinking the Captain's health with the customary orations of compliment and acknowledgment. This feast was scarcely ended, when we found ourselves rounding the headland into Vigo Bay, passing a grim and tall island of rocky mountains which lies in the centre of the bay.

Whether it is that the sight of land is always welcome to weary mariners, after the perils and annoyances of a voyage of three days, or whether the place is in itself extraordinarily beautiful, need not be argued; but I have seldom seen anything more charming than the amphitheatre of noble hills into which the ship now came— all the features of the landscape being lighted up with a wonderful clearness of air, which rarely adorns a view in our country. The sun had not yet set, but over the town and lofty rocky castle of Vigo a great ghost of a moon was faintly visible, which blazed out brighter and brighter as the superior luminary retired behind the purple mountains of the headland to rest. Before the general background of waving heights which encompassed the bay, rose a second semicircle of undulating hills, as cheerful and green as the mountains behind them were grey and solemn. Farms and gardens, convent towers, white villages and churches, and buildings that no doubt were hermitages once, upon the sharp peaks of the hills, shone brightly in the sun. The sight was delightfully cheerful, animated, and pleasing.

Presently the Captain roared out the magic words, "Stop her!" and the obedient vessel came to a stand-still, at some three hundred yards from the little town, with its white houses clambering up a rock, defended by the superior mountain whereon the castle stands. Numbers of people, arrayed in various brilliant colours of red, were standing on the sand close by the tumbling, shining, purple waves: and there we beheld, for the first time, the Royal red and yellow standard of Spain floating on its own ground, under the guardianship of a light blue sentinel, whose musket glittered in the sun. Numerous boats were seen, incontinently, to put off from the little shore.

And now our attention was withdrawn from the land to a sight of great splendour on board. This was Lieutenant Bundy, the guardian of Her Majesty's mails, who issued from his cabin in his long swallow-tailed coat with anchor buttons; his sabre clattering between his legs; a magnificent shirt-collar, of several inches in height, rising round his good-humoured sallow face; and above it a cocked hat, that shone so, I thought it was made of polished tin (it may have been that or oilskin), handsomely laced with black worsted, and ornamented with a shining gold cord. A little squat boat, rowed by three ragged gallegos, came bouncing up to the ship. Into this Mr. Bundy and Her Majesty's Royal mail embarked with much majesty; and in the twinkling of an eye, the Royal standard of England, about the size of a pocket-handkerchief,—and at the bows of the boat, the man-of-war's pennant, being a strip of bunting considerably under the value of a farthing,—streamed out.

"They know that flag, sir," said the good-natured old tar, quite solemnly, in the evening afterwards: "they respect it, sir." The authority of Her Majesty's lieutenant on board the steamer is stated to be so tremendous, that he may order it to stop, to move, to go larboard, starboard, or what you will; and the captain dare only disobey him *suo periculo*.

It was agreed that a party of us should land for half-an-hour, and taste real Spanish chocolate on Spanish ground. We followed Lieutenant Bundy, but humbly in the providor's boat; that officer going on shore to purchase fresh eggs, milk for tea (in place of the slimy substitute of whipped yolk of egg which we had been using for our morning and evening meals), and, if possible, oysters, for which it is said the rocks of Vigo are famous.

It was low tide, and the boat could not get up to the dry shore. Hence it was necessary to take advantage of the offers of sundry gallegos, who rushed barelegged into the water, to land on their shoulders. The approved method seems to be, to sit upon one shoulder only, holding on by the porter's whiskers; and though some of our party were of the tallest and fattest men whereof our race is composed, and their living sedans exceedingly meagre and small, yet all were landed without accident upon the juicy sand, and forthwith surrounded by a host of mendicants, screaming, "I say, sir! penny, sir! I say, English! tam your ays! penny!" in all voices, from extreme youth to the most lousy and venerable old age. When it is said that these beggars were as ragged as those of Ireland, and still more voluble, the Irish traveller will be able to form an opinion of their capabilities.

Through this crowd we passed up some steep rocky steps, through a little low gate, where, in a little guard-house and barrack, a few dirty little sentinels were keeping a dirty little guard; and by low-roofed whitewashed houses, with balconies, and women in them,— the very same women, with the very same head-clothes, and yellow fans and eyes, at once sly and solemn, which Murillo painted,—by a neat church into which we took a peep, and, finally, into the Plaza del Constitucion, or grand place of the town, which may be about as big as that pleasing square, Pump Court, Temple. We were taken to an inn, of which I forget the name, and were shown from one chamber and storey to another, till we arrived at that apartment where the real Spanish chocolate was finally to be served out. All these rooms were as clean as scrubbing and whitewash could make them; with simple French prints (with Spanish titles) on the walls; a few rickety half-finished articles of furniture; and, finally, an air of extremely respectable poverty. A jolly, black-eyed, yellow-shawled Dulcinea conducted us through the apartment, and provided us with the desired refreshment.

Sounds of clarions drew our eyes to the Place of the Constitution; and, indeed, I had forgotten to say, that that majestic square was filled with military, with exceedingly small firelocks, the men ludicrously young and diminutive for the most part, in a uniform at once cheap and tawdry,—like those supplied to the warriors at Astley's, or from still humbler theatrical wardrobes: indeed, the whole scene was just like that of a little theatre; the houses curiously small, with arcades and balconies, out of which looked women apparently a great deal too big for the chambers they inhabited; the warriors were in ginghams, cottons, and tinsel; the officers had huge epaulets of sham silver lace drooping over their bosoms, and looked as if they were attired at a very small expense. Only the general—the captain-general (Pooch, they told us, was his name: I know not how 'tis written in Spanish)—was well got up, with a smart hat, a real feather, huge stars glittering on his portly chest, and tights and boots of the first order. Presently, after a good deal of trumpeting, the little men marched off the place, Pooch and his staff coming into the very inn in which we were awaiting our chocolate.

Then we had an opportunity of seeing some of the civilians of the town. Three or four ladies passed, with fan and mantle; to them came three or four dandies, dressed smartly in the French fashion, with strong Jewish physiognomies. There was one, a solemn lean fellow in black, with his collars extremely turned over, and holding before him a long ivory-tipped ebony cane, who tripped along the little place with a solemn smirk, which gave one an indescribable feeling of the truth of "Gil Blas," and of those delightful bachelors and licentiates who have appeared to us all in our dreams.

In fact we were but half-an-hour in this little queer Spanish town; and it appeared like a dream, too, or a little show got up to amuse us. Boom! the gun fired at the end of the funny little entertainment. The women and the balconies, the beggars and the walking Murillos, Pooch and the little soldiers in tinsel, disappeared, and were shut up in their box again. Once more we were carried on the beggars' shoulders out off the shore, and we found ourselves again in the great stalwart roast-beef world; the stout British steamer bearing out of the bay, whose purple waters had grown more purple. The sun had set by this time, and the moon above was twice as big and bright as our degenerate moons are.

The providor had already returned with his fresh stores, and Bundy's tin hat was popped into its case, and he walking the deck of the packet denuded of tails. As we went out of the bay, occurred a little incident with which the great incidents of the day may be said to wind up. We saw before us a little vessel, tumbling and plunging about in the dark waters of the bay, with a bright light beaming from the mast. It made for us at about a couple of miles from the town, and came close up, flouncing and bobbing in the very jaws of the paddle, which looked as if it would have seized and twirled round that little boat and its light, and destroyed them for ever and ever. All the passengers, of course, came crowding to the ship's side to look at the bold little boat.

"I SAY!" howled a man; "I say!—a word!—I say! Pasagero! Pasagero! Pasage-e-ero!" We were two hundred yards ahead by this time.

"Go on," says the captain.

"You may stop if you like," says Lieutenant Bundy, exerting his tremendous responsibility. It is evident that the lieutenant has a soft heart, and felt for the poor devil in the boat who was howling so piteously "Pasagero!"

But the captain was resolute. His duty was NOT to take the man up. He was evidently an irregular customer—someone trying to escape, possibly.

The lieutenant turned away, but did not make any further hints. The captain was right; but we all felt somehow disappointed, and looked back wistfully at the little boat, jumping up and down far astern now; the poor little light shining in vain, and the poor wretch within screaming out in the most heartrending accents a last faint desperate "I say! Pasagero-o!"

We all went down to tea rather melancholy; but the new milk, in the place of that abominable whipped egg, revived us again; and so ended the great events on board the "Lady Mary Wood" steamer, on the 25th August, 1844.

CHAPTER II: LISBON—CADIZ

A great misfortune which befalls a man who has but a single day to stay in a town, is that fatal duty which superstition entails upon him of visiting the chief lions of the city in which he may happen to be. You must go through the ceremony, however much you may sigh to avoid it; and however much you know that the lions in one capital roar very much like the lions in another; that the churches are more or less large and splendid, the palaces pretty spacious, all the world over; and that there is scarcely a capital city in this Europe but has its pompous bronze statue or two of some periwigged, hook-nosed emperor, in a Roman habit, waving his bronze baton on his broad-flanked brazen charger. We only saw these state old lions in Lisbon, whose roar has long since ceased to frighten one. First we went to the Church of St. Roch, to see a famous piece of mosaic-work there. It is a famous work of art, and was bought by I don't know what king for I don't know how much money. All this information may be perfectly relied on, though the fact is, we did not see the mosaic-work: the sacristan, who guards it, was yet in bed; and it was veiled from our eyes in a side-chapel by great dirty damask curtains, which could not be removed, except when the sacristan's toilette was done, and at the price of a dollar. So we were spared this mosaic exhibition; and I think I always feel relieved when such an event occurs. I feel I have done my duty in coming to see the enormous animal: if he is not at home, *virtute mea me*, &c.—we have done our best, and mortal can do no more.

In order to reach that church of the forbidden mosaic, we had sweated up several most steep and dusty streets—hot and dusty, although it was but nine o'clock in the morning. Thence the guide conducted us into some little dust-powdered gardens, in which the people make believe to enjoy the verdure, and whence you look over a great part of the arid, dreary, stony city. There was no smoke, as in honest London, only dust—dust over the gaunt houses and the dismal yellow strips of gardens. Many churches were there, and tall half-baked-looking public edifices, that had a dry, uncomfortable, earth-quaky look, to my idea. The ground-floors of the spacious houses by which we passed seemed the coolest and pleasantest portions of the mansion. They were cellars or warehouses, for the most part, in which white-jacketed clerks sat smoking easy cigars. The streets were plastered with placards of a bull-fight, to take place the next evening (there was no opera that season); but it was not a real Spanish tauromachy—only a theatrical combat, as you could see by the picture in which the horseman was cantering off at three miles an hour, the bull tripping after him with tips to his gentle horns. Mules interminable, and almost all excellently sleek and handsome, were pacing down every street: here and there, but later in the day, came clattering along a smart rider on a prancing Spanish horse; and in the afternoon a few families might be seen in the queerest old-fashioned little carriages, drawn by their jolly mules and swinging between, or rather before, enormous wheels.

The churches I saw were of the florid periwig architecture—I mean of that pompous cauliflower kind of ornament which was the fashion in Louis the Fifteenth's time, at which unlucky period a building mania seems to have seized upon many of the monarchs of Europe, and innumerable public edifices were erected. It seems to me to have been the period in all history when society was the least natural, and perhaps the most dissolute; and I have always fancied that the bloated artificial forms of the architecture partake of the social disorganisation of the time. Who can respect a simpering ninny, grinning in a Roman dress and a full-bottomed wig, who is made to pass off for a hero? or a fat woman in a hoop, and of a most doubtful virtue, who leers at you as a goddess? In the palaces which we saw, several Court allegories were represented, which, atrocious as they were in point of art, might yet serve to attract the regard of the moraliser. There were Faith, Hope, and Charity restoring Don John to the arms of his happy Portugal: there were Virtue, Valour, and Victory saluting Don Emanuel: Reading, Writing, and Arithmetic (for what I know, or some mythologic nymphs) dancing before Don Miguel—the picture is there still, at the Ajuda; and ah me! where is poor Mig? Well, it is these State lies and ceremonies that we persist in going to see; whereas a man would have a much better insight into Portuguese manners, by planting himself at a corner, like yonder beggar, and watching the real transactions of the day.

A drive to Belem is the regular route practised by the traveller who has to make only a short stay, and accordingly a couple of carriages were provided for our party, and we were driven through the long merry street of Belem, peopled by endless strings of mules,—by thousands of gallegos, with water-barrels on their shoulders, or lounging by the fountains to hire,—by the Lisbon and Belem omnibuses, with four mules, jingling along at a good pace; and it seemed to me to present a far more lively and cheerful, though not so regular, an appearance as the stately quarters of the city we had left behind us. The little shops were at full work— the men brown, well-dressed, manly, and handsome: so much cannot, I am sorry to say, be said for the ladies, of whom, with every anxiety to do so, our party could not perceive a single good-looking specimen all day. The noble blue Tagus accompanies you all along these three miles of busy pleasant street, whereof the chief charm, as I thought, was its look of genuine business—that appearance of comfort which the cleverest Court-architect never knows how to give.

The carriages (the canvas one with four seats and the chaise in which I drove) were brought suddenly up to a gate with the Royal arms over it; and here we were introduced to as queer an exhibition as the eye has often looked on. This was the state-carriage house, where there is a museum of huge old tumble-down gilded coaches of the last century, lying here, mouldy and dark, in a sort of limbo. The gold has vanished from the great lumbering old wheels and panels; the velvets are wofully tarnished. When one thinks of the patches and powder that have simpered out of those plate-glass windows—the mitred bishops, the big-wigged marshals, the shovel-hatted abbés which they have borne in their time—the human mind becomes affected in no ordinary degree. Some human minds heave a sigh for the glories of bygone days; while others, considering rather the lies and humbug, the vice and servility, which went framed and glazed and enshrined, creaking along in those old Juggernaut cars, with fools worshipping under the wheels, console themselves for the decay of institutions that may have been splendid and costly, but were ponderous, clumsy, slow, and unfit for daily wear. The guardian of these defunct old carriages tells some prodigious fibs concerning them: he pointed out one carriage that was six hundred years old in his calendar; but any connoisseur in bric-a-brac can see it was built at Paris in the Regent Orleans' time.

Hence it is but a step to an institution in full life and vigour,— a noble orphan-school for one thousand boys and girls, founded by Don Pedro, who gave up to its use the superb convent of Belem, with its splendid cloisters, vast airy dormitories, and magnificent church. Some Oxford gentlemen would have wept to see the desecrated edifice,—to think that the shaven polls and white gowns were banished from it to give place to a thousand children, who have not even the clergy to instruct them. "Every lad here may choose his trade," our little informant said, who addressed us in better French than any of our party spoke, whose manners were perfectly gentlemanlike and respectful, and whose clothes, though of a common cotton stuff, were cut and worn with a military neatness and precision. All the children whom we remarked were dressed with similar neatness, and it was a pleasure to go through their various rooms for study, where some were busy at mathematics, some at drawing, some attending a lecture on tailoring, while others were sitting at the feet of a professor of the science of shoemaking. All the garments of the establishment were made by the pupils; even the deaf and dumb were drawing and reading, and the blind were, for the most part, set to perform on musical instruments, and got up a concert for the visitors. It was then we wished ourselves of the numbers of the deaf and dumb, for the poor fellows made noises so horrible, that even as blind beggars they could hardly get a livelihood in the musical way.

Hence we were driven to the huge palace of Necessidades, which is but a wing of a building that no King of Portugal ought ever to be rich enough to complete, and which, if perfect, might outvie the Tower of Babel. The mines of Brazil must have been productive of gold and silver indeed when the founder imagined this enormous edifice. From the elevation on which it stands it commands the noblest views,—the city is spread before it, with its many churches and towers, and for many miles you see the magnificent Tagus, rolling by banks crowned with trees and towers. But to arrive at this enormous building you have to climb a steep suburb of wretched huts, many of them with dismal gardens of dry cracked earth, where a few reedy sprouts of Indian corn seemed to be the chief cultivation, and which were guarded by huge plants of spiky aloes, on which the rags of the proprietors of the huts were sunning themselves. The terrace before the palace was similarly encroached upon by these wretched habitations. A few millions judiciously expended might make of this arid hill one of the most magnificent gardens in the world; and the palace seems to me to excel for situation any Royal edifice I have ever seen. But the huts of these swarming poor have crawled up close to its gates,— the superb walls of hewn stone stop all of a sudden with a lath-and-plaster hitch; and capitals, and hewn stones for columns, still lying about on the deserted terrace, may lie there for ages to come, probably, and never take their places by the side of their brethren in yonder tall bankrupt galleries. The air of this pure sky has little effect upon the edifices,—the edges of the stone look as sharp as if the builders had just left their work; and close to the grand entrance stands an outbuilding, part of which may have been burnt fifty years ago, but is in such cheerful preservation that you might fancy the fire had occurred yesterday. It must have been an awful sight from this hill to have looked at the city spread before it, and seen it reeling and swaying in the time of the earthquake. I thought it looked so hot and shaky, that one might fancy a return of the fit. In several places still remain gaps and chasms, and ruins lie here and there as they cracked and fell.

Although the palace has not attained anything like its full growth, yet what exists is quite big enough for the monarch of such a little country; and Versailles or Windsor has not apartments more nobly proportioned. The Queen resides in the Ajuda, a building of much less pretensions, of which the yellow walls and beautiful gardens are seen between Belem and the city. The Necessidades are only used for grand galas, receptions of ambassadors, and ceremonies of state. In the throne-room is a huge throne, surmounted by an enormous gilt crown, than which I have never seen anything larger in the finest pantomime at Drury Lane; but the effect of this splendid piece is lessened by a shabby old Brussels carpet, almost the only other article of furniture in the apartment, and not quite large enough to cover its spacious floor. The looms of Kidderminster have supplied the web which ornaments the "Ambassadors' Waiting-Room," and the ceilings are painted with huge allegories in distemper, which pretty well correspond with the other furniture. Of all the undignified objects in the world, a palace out at elbows is surely the meanest. Such places ought not to be seen in adversity,—splendour is their decency,—and when no longer able to maintain it, they should sink to the level of their means, calmly subside into manufactories, or go shabby in seclusion.

There is a picture-gallery belonging to the palace that is quite of a piece with the furniture, where are the mythological pieces relative to the kings before alluded to, and where the English visitor will see some astonishing pictures of the Duke of Wellington, done in a very characteristic style of Portuguese art. There is also a chapel, which has been decorated with much care and sumptuousness of ornament—the altar surmounted by a ghastly and horrible carved figure in the taste of the time when faith was strengthened by the shrieks of Jews on the rack, and enlivened by the roasting of heretics. Other such frightful images may be seen in the churches of the city; those which we saw were still rich, tawdry, and splendid to outward show, although the French, as usual, had robbed their shrines of their gold and silver, and the statues of their jewels and crowns. But brass and tinsel look to the visitor full as well at a little distance,—as doubtless Soult and Junot thought, when they despoiled these places of worship, like French philosophers as they were.

A friend, with a classical turn of mind, was bent upon seeing the aqueduct, whither we went on a dismal excursion of three hours, in the worst carriages, over the most diabolical clattering roads, up and down dreary parched hills, on which grew a few grey olive-trees and many aloes. When we arrived, the gate leading to the aqueduct was closed, and we were entertained with a legend of some respectable character who had made a good livelihood there for some time past lately, having a private key to this very aqueduct, and lying in wait there for unwary travellers like ourselves, whom he pitched down the arches into the ravines below, and there robbed them at leisure. So that all we saw was the door and the tall arches of the aqueduct, and by the time we returned to town it was time to go on board the ship again. If the inn at which we had sojourned was not of the best quality, the bill, at least, would have done honour to the first establishment in London. We all left the house of entertainment joyfully, glad to get out of the sun-burnt city and go *home*. Yonder in the steamer was home, with its black funnel and gilt portraiture of "Lady Mary Wood" at the bows; and every soul on board felt glad to return to the friendly little vessel. But the authorities of Lisbon, however, are very suspicious of the departing stranger, and we were made to lie an hour in the river before the Sanita boat, where a passport is necessary to be procured before the traveller can quit the country. Boat after boat laden with priests and peasantry, with handsome red-sashed gallegos clad in brown, and ill-favoured women, came and got their permits, and were off, as we lay bumping up against the old hull of the Sanita boat; but the officers seemed to take a delight in keeping us there bumping, looked at us quite calmly over the ship's sides, and smoked their cigars without the least attention to the prayers which we shrieked out for release.

If we were glad to get away from Lisbon, we were quite as sorry to be obliged to quit Cadiz, which we reached the next night, and where we were allowed a couple of hours' leave to land and look about. It seemed as handsome within as it is stately without; the long narrow streets of an admirable cleanliness, many of the tall houses of rich and noble decorations, and all looking as if the city were in full prosperity. I have seen no more cheerful and animated sight than the long street leading from the quay where we were landed, and the market blazing in sunshine, piled with fruit, fish, and poultry, under many-coloured awnings; the tall white houses with their balconies and galleries shining round about, and the sky above so blue that the best cobalt in all the paint-box looks muddy and dim in comparison to it. There were pictures for a year in that market-place—from the copper-coloured old hags and beggars who roared to you for the love of Heaven to give money, to the swaggering dandies of the market, with red sashes and tight clothes, looking on superbly, with a hand on the hip and a cigar in the mouth. These must be the chief critics at the great bull-fight house yonder by the Alameda, with its scanty trees, and cool breezes facing the water. Nor are there any corks to the bulls' horns here, as at Lisbon. A small old English guide who seized upon me the moment my foot was on shore, had a store of agreeable legends regarding the bulls, men, and horses that had been killed with unbounded profusion in the late entertainments which have taken place.

It was so early an hour in the morning that the shops were scarcely opened as yet; the churches, however, stood open for the faithful, and we met scores of women tripping towards them with pretty feet, and smart black mantillas, from which looked out fine dark eyes and handsome pale faces, very different from the coarse brown countenances we had seen at Lisbon. A very handsome modern cathedral, built by the present bishop at his own charges, was the finest of the public edifices we saw; it was not, however, nearly so much frequented as another little church, crowded with altars and fantastic ornaments, and lights and gilding, where we were told to look behind a huge iron grille, and beheld a bevy of black nuns kneeling. Most of the good ladies in the front ranks stopped their devotions, and looked at the strangers with as much curiosity as we directed at them through the gloomy bars of their chapel. The men's convents are closed; that which contains the famous Murillos has been turned into an academy of the fine arts; but the English guide did not think the pictures were of sufficient interest to detain strangers, and so hurried us back to the shore, and grumbled at only getting three shillings at parting for his trouble and his information. And so our residence in Andalusia began and ended before breakfast, and we went on board and steamed for Gibraltar, looking, as we passed, at Joinville's black squadron, and the white houses of St. Mary's across the bay, with the hills of Medina Sidonia and Granada lying purple beyond them. There's something even in those names which is pleasant to write down; to have passed only two hours in Cadiz is something—to have seen real donnas with comb and mantle—real caballeros with cloak and cigar—real Spanish barbers lathering out of brass basins—and to have heard guitars under the balconies: there was one that an old beggar was jangling in the market, whilst a huge leering fellow in bushy whiskers and a faded velvet dress came singing and jumping after our party,—not singing to a guitar, it is true, but imitating one capitally with his voice, and cracking his fingers by way of castanets, and performing a dance such as Figaro or Lablache might envy. How clear that fellow's voice thrums on the ear even now; and how bright and pleasant remains the recollection of the fine city and the blue sea, and the Spanish flags floating on the boats that danced over it, and Joinville's band beginning to play stirring marches as we puffed out of the bay.

The next stage was Gibraltar, where we were to change horses. Before sunset we skirted along the dark savage mountains of the African coast, and came to the Rock just before gun-fire. It is the very image of an enormous lion, crouched between the Atlantic and the Mediterranean, and set there to guard the passage for its British mistress. The next British lion is Malta, four days further on in the Midland Sea, and ready to spring upon Egypt or pounce upon Syria, or roar so as to be heard at Marseilles in case of need.

To the eyes of the civilian the first-named of these famous fortifications is by far the most imposing. The Rock looks so tremendous, that to ascend it, even without the compliment of shells or shot, seems a dreadful task—what would it be when all those mysterious lines of batteries were vomiting fire and brimstone; when all those dark guns that you see poking their grim heads out of every imaginable cleft and zigzag should salute you with shot, both hot and cold; and when, after tugging up the hideous perpendicular place, you were to find regiments of British grenadiers ready to plunge bayonets into your poor panting stomach, and let out artificially the little breath left there? It is a marvel to think that soldiers will mount such places for a shilling—ensigns for five and ninepence—a day: a cabman would ask double the money to go half way! One meekly reflects upon the above strange truths, leaning over the ship's side, and looking up the huge mountain, from the tower nestled at the foot of it to the thin flagstaff at the summit, up to which have been piled the most ingenious edifices for murder Christian science ever adopted. My hobby-horse is a quiet beast, suited for Park riding, or a gentle trot to Putney and back to a snug stable, and plenty of feeds of corn:-it can't abide climbing hills, and is not at all used to gunpowder. Some men's animals are so spirited that the very appearance of a stone-wall sets them jumping at it: regular chargers of hobbies, which snort and say "Ha, ha!" at the mere notion of a battle.

CHAPTER III: THE "LADY MARY WOOD"

Our week's voyage is now drawing to a close. We have just been to look at Cape Trafalgar, shining white over the finest blue sea. (We, who were looking at Trafalgar Square only the other day!) The sight of that cape must have disgusted Joinville and his fleet of steamers, as they passed yesterday into Cadiz bay, and to-morrow will give them a sight of St. Vincent.

One of their steaM—vessels has been lost off the coast of Africa; they were obliged to burn her, lest the Moors should take possession of her. She was a virgin vessel, just out of Brest. Poor innocent! to die in the very first month of her union with the noble whiskered god of war!

We Britons on board the English boat received the news of the "Groenenland's" abrupt demise with grins of satisfaction. It was a sort of national compliment, and cause of agreeable congratulation. "The lubbers!" we said; "the clumsy humbugs! there's none but Britons to rule the waves!" and we gave ourselves piratical airs, and went down presently and were sick in our little buggy berths. It was pleasant, certainly, to laugh at Joinville's admiral's flag floating at his foremast, in yonder black ship, with its two thundering great guns at the bows and stern, its busy crew swarming on the deck, and a crowd of obsequious shore-boats bustling round the vessel—and to sneer at the Mogador warrior, and vow that we English, had we been inclined to do the business, would have performed it a great deal better.

Now yesterday at Lisbon we saw H.M.S. "Caledonia." *This*, on the contrary, inspired us with feelings of respect and awful pleasure. There she lay—the huge sea-castle—bearing the unconquerable flag of our country. She had but to open her jaws, as it were, and she might bring a second earthquake on the city—batter it into kingdoM—come—with the Ajuda palace and the Necessidades, the churches, and the lean, dry, empty streets, and Don John, tremendous on horseback, in the midst of Black Horse Square. Wherever we looked we could see that enormous "Caledonia," with her flashing three lines of guns. We looked at the little boats which ever and anon came out of this monster, with humble wonder. There was the lieutenant who boarded us at midnight before we dropped anchor in the river: ten white-jacketed men pulling as one, swept along with the barge, gig, boat, curricle, or coach-and-six, with which he came up to us. We examined him—his red whiskers—his collars turned down—his duck trousers, his bullion epaulets—with awe. With the same reverential feeling we examined the seamen—the young gentleman in the bows of the boat—the handsome young officers of marines we met sauntering in the town next day—the Scotch surgeon who boarded us as we weighed anchor—every man, down to the broken-nosed mariner who was drunk in a wine-house, and had "Caledonia" written on his hat. Whereas at the Frenchmen we looked with undisguised contempt. We were ready to burst with laughter as we passed the Prince's vessel—there was a little

French boy in a French boat alongside cleaning it, and twirling about a little French mop—we thought it the most comical, contemptible French boy, mop, boat, steamer, prince—Psha! it is of this wretched vapouring stuff that false patriotism is made. I write this as a sort of homily 'a propos of the day, and Cape Trafalgar, off which we lie. What business have I to strut the deck, and clap my wings, and cry "Cock-a-doodle-doo" over it? Some compatriots are at that work even now.

We have lost one by one all our jovial company. There were the five Oporto wine-merchants—all hearty English gentlemen—gone to their wine-butts, and their red-legged partridges, and their duels at Oporto. It appears that these gallant Britons fight every morning among themselves, and give the benighted people among whom they live an opportunity to admire the spirit national. There is the brave honest major, with his wooden leg—the kindest and simplest of Irishmen: he has embraced his children, and reviewed his little invalid garrison of fifteen men, in the fort which he commands at Belem, by this time, and, I have no doubt, played to every soul of them the twelve tunes of his musical-box. It was pleasant to see him with that musical-box—how pleased he wound it up after dinner—how happily he listened to the little clinking tunes as they galloped, ding-dong, after each other! A man who carries a musical-box is always a good-natured man.

Then there was his Grace, or his Grandeur, the Archbishop of Beyrouth (in the parts of the infidels), His Holiness's Nuncio to the Court of Her Most Faithful Majesty, and who mingled among us like any simple mortal,—except that he had an extra smiling courtesy, which simple mortals do not always possess; and when you passed him as such, and puffed your cigar in his face, took off his hat with a grin of such prodigious rapture, as to lead you to suppose that the most delicious privilege of his whole life was that permission to look at the tip of your nose or of your cigar. With this most reverend prelate was his Grace's brother and chaplain—a very greasy and good-natured ecclesiastic, who, from his physiognomy, I would have imagined to be a dignitary of the Israelitish rather than the Romish Church—as profuse in smiling courtesy as his Lordship of Beyrouth. These two had a meek little secretary between them, and a tall French cook and valet, who, at meal times, might be seen busy about the cabin where their reverences lay. They were on their backs for the greater part of the voyage; their yellow countenances were not only unshaven, but, to judge from appearances, unwashed. They ate in private; and it was only of evenings, as the sun was setting over the western wave, and, comforted by the dinner, the cabin-passengers assembled on the quarter-deck, that we saw the dark faces of the reverend gentlemen among us for a while. They sank darkly into their berths when the steward's bell tolled for tea.

At Lisbon, where we came to anchor at midnight, a special boat came off, whereof the crew exhibited every token of reverence for the ambassador of the ambassador of Heaven, and carried him off from our company. This abrupt departure in the darkness disappointed some of us, who had promised ourselves the pleasure of seeing his Grandeur depart in state in the morning, shaved, clean, and in full pontificals, the tripping little secretary swinging an incense-pot before him, and the greasy chaplain bearing his crosier.

Next day we had another bishop, who occupied the very same berth his Grace of Beyrouth had quitted—was sick in the very same way— so much so that this cabin of the "Lady Mary Wood" is to be christened "the bishop's berth" henceforth; and a handsome mitre is to be painted on the basin.

Bishop No. 2 was a very stout, soft, kind-looking old gentleman, in a square cap, with a handsome tassel of green and gold round his portly breast and back. He was dressed in black robes and tight purple stockings: and we carried him from Lisbon to the little flat coast of Faro, of which the meek old gentleman was the chief pastor.

We had not been half-an-hour from our anchorage in the Tagus, when his Lordship dived down into the episcopal berth. All that night there was a good smart breeze; it blew fresh all the next day, as we went jumping over the blue bright sea; and there was no sign of his Lordship the bishop until we were opposite the purple hills of Algarve, which lay some ten miles distant,—a yellow sunny shore stretching flat before them, whose long sandy flats and villages we could see with our telescope from the steamer.

Presently a little vessel, with a huge shining lateen sail, and bearing the blue and white Portuguese flag, was seen playing a sort of leap-frog on the jolly waves, jumping over them, and ducking down as merry as could be. This little boat came towards the steamer as quick as ever she could jump; and Captain Cooper roaring out, "Stop her!" to "Lady Mary Wood," her Ladyship's paddles suddenly ceased twirling, and news was carried to the good bishop that his boat was almost alongside, and that his hour was come.

It was rather an affecting sight to see the poor old fat gentleman, looking wistfully over the water as the boat now came up, and her eight seamen, with great noise, energy, and gesticulation laid her by the steamer. The steamer steps were let down; his Lordship's servant, in blue and yellow livery (like the Edinburgh Review), cast over the episcopal luggage into the boat, along with his own bundle and the jack-boots with which he rides postilion on one of the bishop's fat mules at Faro. The blue and yellow domestic went down the steps into the boat. Then came the bishop's turn; but he couldn't do it for a long while. He went from one passenger to another, sadly shaking them by the hand, often taking leave and seeming loth to depart, until Captain Cooper, in a stern but respectful tone, touched him on the shoulder, and said, I know not with what correctness, being ignorant of the Spanish language, "Señor 'Bispo! Señor 'Bispo!" on which summons the poor old man, looking ruefully round him once more, put his square cap under his arm, tucked up his long black petticoats, so as to show his purple stockings and jolly fat calves, and went trembling down the steps towards the boat. The good old man! I wish I had had a shake of that trembling podgy hand somehow before he went upon his sea martyrdom. I felt a love for that soft-hearted old Christian. Ah! let us hope his governante tucked him comfortably in bed when he got to Faro that night, and made him a warm gruel and put his feet in warm water. The men clung around him, and almost kissed him as they popped him into the boat, but he did not heed their caresses. Away went the boat scudding madly before the wind. Bang! another lateen-sailed boat in the distance fired a gun in his honour; but the wind was blowing away from the shore, and who knows when that meek bishop got home to his gruel?

I think these were the notables of our party. I will not mention the laughing ogling lady of Cadiz, whose manners, I very much regret to say, were a great deal too lively for my sense of propriety; nor those fair sufferers, her companions, who lay on the deck with sickly, smiling female resignation: nor the heroic children, who no sooner ate biscuit than they were ill, and no sooner were ill than they began eating biscuit again: but just allude to one other martyr, the kind lieutenant in charge of the mails, and who bore his cross with what I can't but think a very touching and noble resignation.

There's a certain sort of man whose doom in the world is disappointment,—who excels in it,—and whose luckless triumphs in his meek career of life, I have often thought, must be regarded by the kind eyes above with as much favour as the splendid successes and achievements of coarser and more prosperous men. As I sat with the lieutenant upon deck, his telescope laid over his lean legs, and he looking at the sunset with a pleased, withered old face, he gave me a little account of his history. I take it he is in nowise disinclined to talk about it, simple as it is: he has been seven-and-thirty years in the navy, being somewhat more mature in the service than Lieutenant Peel, Rear-Admiral Prince de Joinville, and other commanders who need not be mentioned. He is a very well-educated man, and reads prodigiously,—travels, histories, lives of eminent worthies and heroes, in his simple way. He is not in the least angry at his want of luck in the profession. "Were I a boy to-morrow," he said, "I would begin it again; and when I see my schoolfellows, and how they have got on in life, if some are better off than I am, I find many are worse, and have no call to be discontented." So he carries Her Majesty's mails meekly through this world, waits upon port-admirals and captains in his old glazed hat, and is as proud of the pennon at the bow of his little boat, as if it were flying from the mainmast of a thundering man-of-war. He gets two hundred a year for his services, and has an old mother and a sister living in England somewhere, who I will wager (though he never, I swear, said a word about it) have a good portion of this princely income.

Is it breaking a confidence to tell Lieutenant Bundy's history? Let the motive excuse the deed. It is a good, kind, wholesome, and noble character. Why should we keep all our admiration for those who win in this world, as we do, sycophants as we are? When we write a novel, our great stupid imaginations can go no further than to marry the hero to a fortune at the end, and to find out that he is a lord by right. O blundering lickspittle morality! And yet I would like to fancy some happy retributive Utopia in the peaceful cloud-land, where my friend the meek lieutenant should find the yards of his ship manned as he went on board, all the guns firing an enormous salute (only without the least noise or vile smell of powder), and he be saluted on the deck as Admiral Sir James, or Sir Joseph—ay, or Lord Viscount Bundy, knight of all the orders above the sun.

I think this is a sufficient, if not a complete catalogue of the worthies on board the "Lady Mary Wood." In the week we were on board—it seemed a year, by the way—we came to regard the ship quite as a home. We felt for the captain—the most good-humoured, active, careful, ready of captains—a filial, a fraternal regard; for the providor, who provided for us with admirable comfort and generosity, a genial gratitude; and for the brisk steward's lads— brisk in serving the banquet, sympathising in handing the basin— every possible sentiment of regard and good-will. What winds blew, and how many knots we ran, are all noted down, no doubt, in the ship's log: and as for what ships we saw—every one of them with their gunnage, tonnage, their nation, their direction whither they were bound—were not these all noted down with surprising ingenuity and precision by the lieutenant, at a family desk at which he sat every night, before a great paper elegantly and mysteriously ruled off with his large ruler? I have a regard for every man on board that ship, from the captain down to the crew—down even to the cook, with tattooed arms, sweating among the saucepans in the galley, who used (with a touching affection) to send us locks of his hair in the soup. And so, while our feelings and recollections are warm, let us shake hands with this knot of good fellows, comfortably floating about in their little box of wood and iron, across Channel, Biscay Bay, and the Atlantic, from Southampton Water to Gibraltar Straits.

CHAPTER IV: GIBRALTAR

Suppose all the nations of the earth to send fitting ambassadors to represent them at Wapping or Portsmouth Point, with each, under its own national signboard and language, its appropriate house of call, and your imagination may figure the Main Street of Gibraltar: almost the only part of the town, I believe, which boasts of the name of street at all, the remaining houserows being modestly called lanes, such as Bomb Lane, Battery Lane, Fusee Lane, and so on. In Main Street the Jews predominate, the Moors abound; and from the "Jolly Sailor," or the brave "Horse Marine," where the people of our nation are drinking British beer and gin, you hear choruses of "Garryowen" or "The Lass I left behind me;" while through the flaring lattices of the Spanish ventas come the clatter of castanets and the jingle and moan of Spanish guitars and ditties. It is a curious sight at evening this thronged street, with the people, in a hundred different costumes, bustling to and fro under the coarse flare of the lamps; swarthy Moors, in white or crimson robes; dark Spanish smugglers in tufted hats, with gay silk handkerchiefs round their heads; fuddled seamen from men-of-war, or merchantmen; porters, Galician or Genoese; and at every few minutes' interval, little squads of soldiers tramping to relieve guard at some one of the innumerable posts in the town.

Some of our party went to a Spanish venta, as a more convenient or romantic place of residence than an English house; others made choice of the club-house in Commercial Square, of which I formed an agreeable picture in my imagination; rather, perhaps, resembling the Junior United Service Club in Charles Street, by which every Londoner has passed ere this with respectful pleasure, catching glimpses of magnificent blazing candelabras, under which sit neat half-pay officers, drinking half-pints of port. The club-house of Gibraltar is not, however, of the Charles Street sort: it may have been cheerful once, and there are yet relics of splendour about it. When officers wore pigtails, and in the time of Governor O'Hara, it may have been a handsome place; but it is mouldy and decrepit now; and though his Excellency, Mr. Bulwer, was living there, and made no complaints that I heard of, other less distinguished persons thought they had reason to grumble. Indeed, what is travelling made of? At least half its pleasures and incidents come out of inns; and of them the tourist can speak with much more truth and vivacity than of historical recollections compiled out of histories, or filched out of handbooks. But to speak of the best inn in a place needs no apology: that, at least, is useful information. As every person intending to visit Gibraltar cannot have seen the flea-bitten countenances of our companions, who fled from their Spanish venta to take refuge at the club the morning after our arrival, they may surely be thankful for being directed to the best house of accommodation in one of the most unromantic, uncomfortable, and prosaic of towns.

If one had a right to break the sacred confidence of the mahogany, I could entertain you with many queer stories of Gibraltar life, gathered from the lips of the gentlemen who enjoyed themselves round the dingy tablecloth of the club-house coffee-room, richly decorated with cold gravy and spilt beer. I heard there the very names of the gentlemen who wrote the famous letters from the "Warspite" regarding the French proceedings at Mogador; and met several refugee Jews from that place, who said that they were much more afraid of the Kabyles without the city than of the guns of the French squadron, of which they seemed to make rather light. I heard the last odds on the ensuing match between Captain Smith's b. g. Bolter, and Captain Brown's ch. c. Roarer: how the gun-room of Her Majesty's ship "Purgatory" had "cobbed" a tradesman of the town, and of the row in consequence. I heard capital stories of the way in which Wilkins had escaped the guard, and Thompson had been locked up among the mosquitoes for being out after ten without the lantern. I heard how the governor was an old -, but to say what, would be breaking a confidence: only this may be divulged, that the epithet was exceedingly complimentary to Sir Robert Wilson. All the while these conversations were going on, a strange scene of noise and bustle was passing in the market-place, in front of the window, where Moors, Jews, Spaniards, soldiers were thronging in the sun; and a ragged fat fellow, mounted on a tobacco-barrel, with his hat cocked on his ear, was holding an auction, and roaring with an energy and impudence that would have done credit to Covent Garden.

The Moorish castle is the only building about the Rock which has an air at all picturesque or romantic; there is a plain Roman Catholic cathedral, a hideous new Protestant church of the cigar-divan architecture, and a Court-house with a portico which is said to be an imitation of the Parthenon: the ancient religions houses of the Spanish town are gone, or turned into military residences, and masked so that you would never know their former pious destination. You walk through narrow whitewashed lanes, bearing such martial names as are before mentioned, and by-streets with barracks on either side: small Newgate-like looking buildings, at the doors of which you may see the sergeants' ladies conversing; or at the open windows of the officers' quarters, Ensign Fipps lying on his sofa and smoking his cigar, or Lieutenant Simson practising the flute to while away the weary hours of garrison dulness. I was surprised not to find more persons in the garrison library, where is a magnificent reading-room, and an admirable collection of books.

In spite of the scanty herbage and the dust on the trees, the Alameda is a beautiful walk; of which the vegetation has been as laboriously cared for as the tremendous fortifications which flank it on either side. The vast Rock rises on one side with its interminable works of defence, and Gibraltar Bay is shining on the other, out on which from the terraces immense cannon are perpetually looking, surrounded by plantations of cannon-balls and beds of bomb-shells, sufficient, one would think, to blow away the whole peninsula. The horticultural and military mixture is indeed very queer: here and there temples, rustic summer-seats, &c. have been erected in the garden, but you are sure to see a great squat mortar look up from among the flower-pots: and amidst the aloes and geraniums sprouts the green petticoat and scarlet coat of a Highlander. Fatigue-parties are seen winding up the hill, and busy about the endless cannon-ball plantations; awkward squads are drilling in the open spaces: sentries marching everywhere, and (this is a caution to artists) I am told have orders to run any man through who is discovered making a sketch of the place. It is always beautiful, especially at evening, when the people are sauntering along the walks, and the moon is shining on the waters of the bay and the hills and twinkling white houses of the opposite shore. Then the place becomes quite romantic: it is too dark to see the dust on the dried leaves; the cannon-balls do not intrude too much, but have subsided into the shade; the awkward squads are in bed; even the loungers are gone, the fan-flirting Spanish ladies, the sallow black-eyed children, and the trim white-jacketed dandies. A fife is heard from some craft at roost on the quiet waters somewhere; or a faint cheer from yonder black steamer at the Mole, which is about to set out on some night expedition. You forget that the town is at all like Wapping, and deliver yourself up entirely to romance; the sentries look noble pacing there, silent in the moonlight, and Sandy's voice is quite musical as he challenges with a "Who goes there?"

"All's Well" is very pleasant when sung decently in tune, and inspires noble and poetic ideas of duty, courage, and danger: but when you hear it shouted all the night through, accompanied by a clapping of muskets in a time of profound peace, the sentinel's cry becomes no more romantic to the hearer than it is to the sandy Connaught-man or the bare-legged Highlander who delivers it. It is best to read about wars comfortably in Harry Lorrequer or Scott's novels, in which knights shout their war-cries, and jovial Irish bayoneteers hurrah, without depriving you of any blessed rest. Men of a different way of thinking, however, can suit themselves perfectly at Gibraltar; where there is marching and counter-marching, challenging and relieving guard all the night through. And not here in Commercial Square alone, but all over the huge Rock in the darkness—all through the mysterious zig-zags, and round the dark cannon-ball pyramids, and along the vast rock-galleries, and up to the topmost flagstaff, where the sentry can look out over two seas, poor fellows are marching and clapping muskets, and crying "All's Well," dressed in cap and feather, in place of honest nightcaps best befitting the decent hours of sleep.

All these martial noises three of us heard to the utmost advantage, lying on iron bedsteads at the time in a cracked old room on the ground-floor, the open windows of which looked into the square. No spot could be more favourably selected for watching the humours of a garrison town by night. About midnight, the door hard by us was visited by a party of young officers, who having had quite as much drink as was good for them, were naturally inclined for more; and when we remonstrated through the windows, one of them in a young tipsy voice asked after our mothers, and finally reeled away. How charming is the conversation of high-spirited youth! I don't know whether the guard got hold of them: but certainly if a civilian had been hiccuping through the streets at that hour, he would have been carried off to the guard-house, and left to the mercy of the mosquitoes there, and had up before the

Governor in the morning. The young man in the coffee-room tells me he goes to sleep every night with the keys of Gibraltar under his pillow. It is an awful image, and somehow completes the notion of the slumbering fortress. Fancy Sir Robert Wilson, his nose just visible over the sheets, his night-cap and the huge key (you see the very identical one in Reynolds's portrait of Lord Heathfield) peeping out from under the bolster!

If I entertain you with accounts of inns and nightcaps it is because I am more familiar with these subjects than with history and fortifications: as far as I can understand the former, Gibraltar is the great British depot for smuggling goods into the Peninsula. You see vessels lying in the harbour, and are told in so many words they are smugglers: all those smart Spaniards with cigar and mantles are smugglers, and run tobaccos and cotton into Catalonia; all the respected merchants of the place are smugglers. The other day a Spanish revenue vessel was shot to death under the thundering great guns of the fort, for neglecting to bring to, but it so happened that it was in chase of a smuggler: in this little corner of her dominions Britain proclaims war to custoM—houses, and protection to free trade. Perhaps ere a very long day, England may be acting that part towards the world, which Gibraltar performs towards Spain now; and the last war in which we shall ever engage may be a custoM—house war. For once establish railroads and abolish preventive duties through Europe, and what is there left to fight for? It will matter very little then under what flag people live, and foreign ministers and ambassadors may enjoy a dignified sinecure; the army will rise to the rank of peaceful constables, not having any more use for their bayonets than those worthy people have for their weapons now who accompany the law at assizes under the name of javelin-men. The apparatus of bombs and eighty-four-pounders may disappear from the Alameda, and the crops of cannon-balls which now grow there may give place to other plants more pleasant to the eye; and the great key of Gibraltar may be left in the gate for anybody to turn at will, and Sir Robert Wilson may sleep in quiet.

I am afraid I thought it was rather a release, when, having made up our minds to examine the Rock in detail and view the magnificent excavations and galleries, the admiration of all military men, and the terror of any enemies who may attack the fortress, we received orders to embark forthwith in the "Tagus," which was to early us to Malta and Constantinople. So we took leave of this famous Rock— this great blunderbuss—which we seized out of the hands of the natural owners a hundred and forty years ago, and which we have kept ever since tremendously loaded and cleaned and ready for use. To seize and have it is doubtless a gallant thing; it is like one of those tests of courage which one reads of in the chivalrous romances, when, for instance, Sir Huon of Bordeaux is called upon to prove his knighthood by going to Babylon and pulling out the Sultan's beard and front teeth in the midst of his Court there. But, after all, justice must confess it was rather hard on the poor Sultan. If we had the Spaniards established at Land's End, with impregnable Spanish fortifications on St. Michael's Mount, we should perhaps come to the same conclusion. Meanwhile let us hope, during this long period of deprivation, the Sultan of Spain is reconciled to the loss of his front teeth and bristling whiskers— let us even try to think that he is better without them. At all events, right or wrong, whatever may be our title to the property, there is no Englishman but must think with pride of the manner in which his countrymen have kept it, and of the courage, endurance, and sense of duty with which stout old Eliott and his companions resisted Crillon and the Spanish battering ships and his fifty thousand men. There seems to be something more noble in the success of a gallant resistance than of an attack, however brave. After failing in his attack on the fort, the French General visited the English Commander who had foiled him, and parted from him and his garrison in perfect politeness and good-humour. The English troops, Drinkwater says, gave him thundering cheers as he went away, and the French in return complimented us on our gallantry, and lauded the humanity of our people. If we are to go on murdering each other in the old-fashioned way, what a pity it is that our battles cannot end in the old-fashioned way too!

One of our fellow-travellers, who had written a book, and had suffered considerably from sea-sickness during our passage along the coasts of France and Spain, consoled us all by saying that the very minute we got into the Mediterranean we might consider ourselves entirely free from illness; and, in fact, that it was unheard of in the Inland Sea. Even in the Bay of Gibraltar the water looked bluer than anything I have ever seen—except Miss Smith's eyes. I thought, somehow, the delicious faultless azure never could look angry—just like the eyes before alluded to—and under this assurance we passed the Strait, and began coasting the African shore calmly and without the least apprehension, as if we were as much used to the tempest as Mr. T. P. Cooke.

But when, in spite of the promise of the man who had written the book, we found ourselves worse than in the worst part of the Bay of Biscay, or off the storm-lashed rocks of Finisterre, we set down the author in question as a gross impostor, and had a mind to quarrel with him for leading us into this cruel error. The most provoking part of the matter, too, was, that the sky was deliciously clear and cloudless, the air balmy, the sea so insultingly blue that it seemed as if we had no right to be ill at all, and that the innumerable little waves that frisked round about our keel were enjoying an *anerithmon gelasma* (this is one of my four Greek quotations: depend on it I will manage to introduce the other three before the tour is done)—seemed to be enjoying, I say, the above-named Greek quotation at our expense. Here is the dismal log of Wednesday, 4th of September: —"All attempts at dining very fruitless. Basins in requisition. Wind hard ahead. *Que diable allais-je faire dans cette galère*? Writing or thinking impossible: so read 'Letters from the Ægean.'" These brief words give, I think, a complete idea of wretchedness, despair, remorse, and prostration of soul and body. Two days previously we passed the forts and moles and yellow buildings of Algiers, rising very stately from the sea, and skirted by gloomy purple lines of African shore, with fires smoking in the mountains, and lonely settlements here and there.

On the 5th, to the inexpressible joy of all, we reached Valetta, the entrance to the harbour of which is one of the most stately and agreeable scenes ever admired by sea-sick traveller. The small basin was busy with a hundred ships, from the huge guard-ship, which lies there a city in itself;—merchantmen loading and crews cheering, under all the flags of the world flaunting in the sunshine; a half-score of busy black steamers perpetually coming and going, coaling and painting, and puffing and hissing in and out of harbour; slim men-of-war's barges shooting to and fro, with long shining oars flashing like wings over the water; hundreds of painted town-boats, with high heads and white awnings,—down to the little tubs in which some naked, tawny young beggars came paddling up to the steamer, entreating us to let them dive for halfpence. Round this busy blue water rise rocks, blazing in sunshine, and covered with every imaginable device of fortification; to the right, St. Elmo, with flag and lighthouse; and opposite, the Military Hospital, looking like a palace; and all round, the houses of the city, for its size the handsomest and most stately in the world.

Nor does it disappoint you on a closer inspection, as many a foreign town does. The streets are thronged with a lively comfortable-looking population; the poor seem to inhabit handsome stone palaces, with balconies and projecting windows of heavy carved stone. The lights and shadows, the cries and stenches, the fruit-shops and fish-stalls, the dresses and chatter of all nations; the soldiers in scarlet, and women in black mantillas; the beggars, boat-men, barrels of pickled herrings and macaroni; the shovel-hatted priests and bearded capuchins; the tobacco, grapes, onions, and sunshine; the signboards, bottled-porter stores, the statues of saints and little chapels which jostle the stranger's eyes as he goes up the famous stairs from the Water-gate, make a scene of such pleasant confusion and liveliness as I have never witnessed before. And the effect of the groups of multitudinous actors in this busy cheerful drama is heightened, as it were, by the decorations of the stage. The sky is delightfully brilliant; all the houses and ornaments are stately; castle and palaces are rising all around; and the flag, towers, and walls of Fort St. Elmo look as fresh and magnificent as if they had been erected only yesterday.

The Strada Reale has a much more courtly appearance than that one described. Here are palaces, churches, court-houses and libraries, the genteel London shops, and the latest articles of perfumery. Gay young officers are strolling about in shell-jackets much too small for them: midshipmen are clattering by on hired horses; squads of priests, habited after the fashion of Don Basilio in the opera, are demurely pacing to and fro; professional beggars run shrieking after the stranger; and agents for horses, for inns, and for worse places still, follow him and insinuate the excellence of their goods. The houses where they are selling carpet-bags and pomatum were the palaces of the successors of the goodliest company of gallant knights the world ever heard tell of. It seems unromantic; but *these* were not the romantic Knights of St. John. The heroic days of the Order ended as the last Turkish galley lifted anchor after the memorable siege. The present stately houses were built in times of peace and splendour and decay. I doubt whether the Auberge de Provence, where the "Union

Club" flourishes now, has ever seen anything more romantic than the pleasant balls held in the great room there.

The Church of St. John, not a handsome structure without, is magnificent within: a noble hall covered with a rich embroidery of gilded carving, the chapels of the different nations on either side, but not interfering with the main structure, of which the whole is simple, and the details only splendid; it seemed to me a fitting place for this wealthy body of aristocratic soldiers, who made their devotions as it were on parade, and, though on their knees, never forgot their epaulets or their quarters of nobility. This mixture of religion and worldly pride seems incongruous at first; but have we not at church at home similar relics of feudal ceremony?—the verger with the silver mace who precedes the vicar to the desk; the two chaplains of my Lord Archbishop, who bow over his Grace as he enters the communion-table gate; even poor John, who follows my Lady with a coroneted prayer-book, and makes his congé as he hands it into the pew. What a chivalrous absurdity is the banner of some high and mighty prince, hanging over his stall in Windsor Chapel, when you think of the purpose for which men are supposed to assemble there! The Church of the Knights of St. John is paved over with sprawling heraldic devices of the dead gentlemen of the dead Order; as if, in the next world, they expected to take rank in conformity with their pedigrees, and would be marshalled into heaven according to the orders of precedence. Cumbrous handsome paintings adorn the walls and chapels, decorated with pompous monuments of Grand Masters. Beneath is a crypt, where more of these honourable and reverend warriors lie, in a state that a Simpson would admire. In the altar are said to lie three of the most gallant relics in the world: the keys of Acre, Rhodes, and Jerusalem. What blood was shed in defending these emblems! What faith, endurance, genius, and generosity; what pride, hatred, ambition, and savage lust of blood were roused together for their guardianship!

In the lofty halls and corridors of the Governor's house, some portraits of the late Grand Masters still remain: a very fine one, by Caravaggio, of a knight in gilt armour, hangs in the dining-room, near a full-length of poor Louis XVI., in Royal robes, the very picture of uneasy impotency. But the portrait of De Vignacourt is the only one which has a respectable air; the other chiefs of the famous Society are pompous old gentlemen in black, with huge periwigs, and crowns round their hats, and a couple of melancholy pages in yellow and red. But pages and wigs and Grand Masters have almost faded out of the canvas, and are vanishing into Hades with a most melancholy indistinctness. The names of most of these gentlemen, however, live as yet in the forts of the place, which all seem to have been eager to build and christen: so that it seems as if, in the Malta mythology, they had been turned into freestone.

In the armoury is the very suit painted by Caravaggio, by the side of the armour of the noble old La Valette, whose heroism saved his island from the efforts of Mustapha and Dragut, and an army quite as fierce and numerous as that which was baffled before Gibraltar, by similar courage and resolution. The sword of the last-named famous corsair (a most truculent little scimitar), thousands of pikes and halberts, little old cannons and wall-pieces, helmets and cuirasses, which the knights or their people wore, are trimly arranged against the wall, and, instead of spiking Turks or arming warriors, now serve to point morals and adorn tales. And here likewise are kept many thousand muskets, swords, and boarding-pikes for daily use, and a couple of ragged old standards of one of the English regiments, who pursued and conquered in Egypt the remains of the haughty and famous French republican army, at whose appearance the last knights of Malta flung open the gates of all their fortresses, and consented to be extinguished without so much as a remonstrance, or a kick, or a struggle.

We took a drive into what may be called the country; where the fields are rocks, and the hedges are stones—passing by the stone gardens of the Florian, and wondering at the number and handsomeness of the stone villages and churches rising everywhere among the stony hills. Handsome villas were passed everywhere, and we drove for a long distance along the sides of an aqueduct, quite a Royal work of the Caravaggio in gold armour, the Grand Master De Vignacourt. A most agreeable contrast to the arid rocks of the general scenery was the garden at the Governor's country-house; with the orange-trees and water, its beautiful golden grapes, luxuriant flowers, and thick cool shrubberies. The eye longs for this sort of refreshment, after being seared with the hot glare of the general country; and St. Antonio was as pleasant after Malta as Malta was after the sea.

We paid the island a subsequent visit in November, passing seventeen days at an establishment called Fort Manuel there, and by punsters the Manuel des Voyageurs; where Government accommodates you with quarters; where the authorities are so attentive as to scent your letters with aromatic vinegar before you receive them, and so careful of your health as to lock you up in your room every night lest you should walk in your sleep, and so over the battlements into the sea—if you escaped drowning in the sea, the sentries on the opposite shore would fire at you, hence the nature of the precaution. To drop, however, this satirical strain: those who know what quarantine is, may fancy that the place somehow becomes unbearable in which it has been endured. And though the November climate of Malta is like the most delicious May in England, and though there is every gaiety and amusement in the town, a comfortable little opera, a good old library filled full of good old books (none of your works of modern science, travel, and history, but good old USELESS books of the last two centuries), and nobody to trouble you in reading them, and though the society of Valetta is most hospitable, varied, and agreeable, yet somehow one did not feel SAFE in the island, with perpetual glimpses of Fort Manuel from the opposite shore; and, lest the quarantine authorities should have a fancy to fetch one back again, on a pretext of posthumous plague, we made our way to Naples by the very first opportunity—those who remained, that is, of the little Eastern Expedition. They were not all there. The Giver of life and death had removed two of our company: one was left behind to die in Egypt, with a mother to bewail his loss, another we buried in the dismal lazaretto cemetery.

* * *

One is bound to look at this, too, as a part of our journey. Disease and death are knocking perhaps at your next cabin door. Your kind and cheery companion has ridden his last ride and emptied his last glass beside you. And while fond hearts are yearning for him far away, and his own mind, if conscious, is turning eagerly towards the spot of the world whither affection or interest calls it—the Great Father summons the anxious spirit from earth to himself, and ordains that the nearest and dearest shall meet here no more.

Such an occurrence as a death in a lazaretto, mere selfishness renders striking. We were walking with him but two days ago on deck. One has a sketch of him, another his card, with the address written yesterday, and given with an invitation to come and see him at home in the country, where his children are looking for him. He is dead in a day, and buried in the walls of the prison. A doctor felt his pulse by deputy—a clergyman comes from the town to read the last service over him—and the friends, who attend his funeral, are marshalled by lazaretto-guardians, so as not to touch each other. Every man goes back to his room and applies the lesson to himself. One would not so depart without seeing again the dear dear faces. We reckon up those we love: they are but very few, but I think one loves them better than ever now. Should it be your turn next?—and why not? Is it pity or comfort to think of that affection which watches and survives you?

The Maker has linked together the whole race of man with this chain of love. I like to think that there is no man but has had kindly feelings for some other, and he for his neighbour, until we bind together the whole family of Adam. Nor does it end here. It joins heaven and earth together. For my friend or my child of past days is still my friend or my child to me here, or in the home prepared for us by the Father of all. If identity survives the grave, as our faith tells us, is it not a consolation to think that there may be one or two souls among the purified and just, whose affection watches us invisible, and follows the poor sinner on earth?

CHAPTER V: ATHENS

Not feeling any enthusiasm myself about Athens, my bounden duty of course is clear, to sneer and laugh heartily at all who have. In fact, what business has a lawyer, who was in Pump Court this day three weeks, and whose common reading is law reports or the newspaper, to pretend to fall in love for the long vacation with mere poetry, of which I swear a great deal is very doubtful, and to get up an enthusiasm quite foreign to his nature and usual calling in life? What call have ladies to consider Greece "romantic," they who get their notions of mythology from the well-known pages of "Tooke's Pantheon"? What is the reason that blundering Yorkshire squires, young dandies from Corfu regiments, jolly sailors from ships in the harbour, and yellow old Indians returning from Bundelcund, should think proper to be enthusiastic about a country of which they know nothing; the mere physical beauty of which they cannot, for the most part, comprehend; and because certain characters lived in it two thousand four hundred years ago? What have these people in common with Pericles, what have these ladies in common with Aspasia (O fie)? Of the race of Englishmen who come wandering about the tomb of Socrates, do you think the majority would not have voted to hemlock him? Yes: for the very same superstition which leads men by the nose now, drove them onward in the days when the lowly husband of Xantippe died for daring to think simply and to speak the truth. I know of no quality more magnificent in fools than their faith: that perfect consciousness they have, that they are doing virtuous and meritorious actions, when they are performing acts of folly, murdering Socrates, or pelting Aristides with holy oyster-shells—all for Virtue's sake; and a "History of Dulness in all Ages of the World," is a book which a philosopher would surely be hanged, but as certainly blessed, for writing.

If papa and mamma (honour be to them!) had not followed the faith of their fathers, and thought proper to send away their only beloved son (afterwards to be celebrated under the name of Titmarsh) into ten years' banishment of infernal misery, tyranny, annoyance; to give over the fresh feelings of the heart of the little Michael Angelo to the discipline of vulgar bullies, who, in order to lead tender young children to the Temple of Learning (as they do in the spelling-books), drive them on with clenched fists and low abuse; if they fainted, revive them with a thump, or assailed them with a curse; if they were miserable, consoled them with a brutal jeer—if, I say, my dear parents, instead of giving me the inestimable benefit of a ten years' classical education, had kept me at home with my dear thirteen sisters, it is probable I should have liked this country of Attica, in sight of the blue shores of which the present pathetic letter is written; but I was made so miserable in youth by a classical education, that all connected with it is disagreeable in my eyes; and I have the same recollection of Greek in youth that I have of castor-oil.

So in coming in sight of the promontory of Sunium, where the Greek Muse, in an awful vision, came to me, and said in a patronising way, "Why, my dear" (she always, the old spinster, adopts this high and mighty tone)—"Why, my dear, are you not charmed to be in this famous neighbourhood, in this land of poets and heroes, of whose history your classical education ought to have made you a master? if it did not, you have wofully neglected your opportunities, and your dear parents have wasted their money in sending you to school." I replied, "Madam, your company in youth was made so laboriously disagreeable to me, that I can't at present reconcile myself to you in age. I read your poets, but it was in fear and trembling; and a cold sweat is but an ill accompaniment to poetry. I blundered through your histories; but history is so dull (saving your presence) of herself, that when the brutal dulness of a schoolmaster is superadded to her own slow conversation, the union becomes intolerable: hence I have not the slightest pleasure in renewing my acquaintance with a lady who has been the source of so much bodily and mental discomfort to me." To make a long story short, I am anxious to apologise for a want of enthusiasm in the classical line, and to excuse an ignorance which is of the most undeniable sort.

This is an improper frame of mind for a person visiting the land of Æschylus and Euripides; add to which, we have been abominably overcharged at the inn: and what are the blue hills of Attica, the silver calm basin of Piræus, the heathery heights of Pentelicus, and yonder rocks crowned by the Doric columns of the Parthenon, and the thin Ionic shafts of the Erechtheum, to a man who has had little rest, and is bitten all over by bugs? Was Alcibiades bitten by bugs, I wonder; and did the brutes crawl over him as he lay in the rosy arms of Phryne? I wished all night for Socrates's hammock or basket, as it is described in the "Clouds;" in which resting-place, no doubt, the abominable animals kept perforce clear of him.

A French man-of-war, lying in the silvery little harbour, sternly eyeing out of its stern portholes a saucy little English corvette beside, began playing sounding marches as a crowd of boats came paddling up to the steamer's side to convey us travellers to shore. There were Russian schooners and Greek brigs lying in this little bay; dumpy little windmills whirling round on the sunburnt heights round about it; an improvised town of quays and marine taverns has sprung up on the shore; a host of jingling barouches, more miserable than any to be seen even in Germany, were collected at the landing-place; and the Greek drivers (how queer they looked in skull-caps, shabby jackets with profuse embroidery of worsted, and endless petticoats of dirty calico!) began, in a generous ardour for securing passengers, to abuse each other's horses and carriages in the regular London fashion. Satire could certainly hardly caricature the vehicle in which we were made to journey to Athens; and it was only by thinking that, bad as they were, these coaches were much more comfortable contrivances than any Alcibiades or Cimon ever had, that we consoled ourselves along the road. It was flat for six miles along the plain to the city: and you see for the greater part of the way the purple mount on which the Acropolis rises, and the gleaming houses of the town spread beneath. Round this wide, yellow, barren plain,—a stunted district of olive-trees is almost the only vegetation visible—there rises, as it were, a sort of chorus of the most beautiful mountains; the most elegant, gracious, and noble the eye ever looked on. These hills did not appear at all lofty or terrible, but superbly rich and aristocratic. The clouds were dancing round about them; you could see their rosy purple shadows sweeping round the clear serene summits of the hill. To call a hill aristocratic seems affected or absurd; but the difference between these hills and the others, is the difference between Newgate Prison and the Travellers' Club, for instance: both are buildings; but the one stern, dark, and coarse; the other rich, elegant, and festive. At least, so I thought. With such a stately palace as munificent Nature had built for these people, what could they be themselves but lordly, beautiful, brilliant, brave, and wise? We saw four Greeks on donkeys on the road (which is a dust-whirlwind where it is not a puddle); and other four were playing with a dirty pack of cards, at a barrack that English poets have christened the "Half-way House." Does external nature and beauty influence the soul to good? You go about Warwickshire, and fancy that from merely being born and wandering in those sweet sunny plains and fresh woodlands Shakspeare must have drunk in a portion of that frank artless sense of beauty which lies about his works like a bloom or dew; but a Coventry ribbon-maker, or a slang Leamington squire, are looking on those very same landscapes too, and what do they profit? You theorise about the influence which the climate and appearance of Attica must have had in ennobling those who were born there: yonder dirty, swindling, ragged blackguards, lolling over greasy cards three hours before noon, quarrelling and shrieking, armed to the teeth and afraid to fight, are bred out of the same land which begot the philosophers and heroes. But the "Half-way House" is passed by this time, and behold! we are in the capital of King Otho.

I swear solemnly that I would rather have two hundred a year in Fleet Street, than be King of the Greeks, with Basileus written before my name round their beggarly coin; with the bother of perpetual revolutions in my huge plaster-of-Paris palace, with no amusement but a drive in the afternoon over a wretched arid country, where roads are not made, with ambassadors (the deuce knows why, for what good can the English, or the French, or the Russian party get out of such a bankrupt alliance as this?) perpetually pulling and tugging at me, away from honest Germany, where there is beer and aesthetic conversation, and operas at a small cost. The shabbiness of this place actually beats Ireland, and that is a strong word. The palace of the Basileus is an enormous edifice of plaster, in a square containing six houses, three donkeys, no roads, no fountains (except in the picture of the inn); backwards it seems to look straight to the mountain—on one side is a beggarly garden—the King goes out to drive (revolutions permitting) at five—some four-and-twenty blackguards saunter up to the huge sandhill of a terrace, as His Majesty passes by in a gilt barouche and an absurd fancy dress; the gilt barouche goes plunging down the sandhills; the two dozen soldiers, who have been presenting arms, slouch off to their quarters; the vast barrack of a palace remains entirely white, ghastly, and lonely; and, save the braying of a donkey now and then (which long-eared minstrels are more active and sonorous in Athens than in any place I know), all is entirely silent round Basileus's palace. How could people who knew Leopold fancy he would be so "jolly green" as to take such a berth? It was only a gobemouche of a Bavarian that could ever have been induced to accept it.

I beseech you to believe that it was not the bill and the bugs at the inn which induced the writer hereof to speak so slightingly of the residence of Basileus. These evils are now cured and forgotten. This is written off the leaden flats and mounds which they call the Troad. It is stern justice alone which pronounces this excruciating sentence. It was a farce to make this place into a kingly capital; and I make no manner of doubt that King Otho, the very day he can get away unperceived, and get together the passage-money, will be off for dear old Deutschland, Fatherland, Beerland!

I have never seen a town in England which may be compared to this; for though Herne Bay is a ruin now, money was once spent upon it and houses built; here, beyond a few score of mansions comfortably laid out, the town is little better than a rickety agglomeration of larger and smaller huts, tricked out here and there with the most absurd cracked ornaments and cheap attempts at elegance. But neatness is the elegance of poverty, and these people despise such a homely ornament. I have got a map with squares, fountains, theatres, public gardens, and Places d'Othon marked out; but they only exist in the paper capital—the wretched tumble-down wooden one boasts of none.

One is obliged to come back to the old disagreeable comparison of Ireland. Athens may be about as wealthy a place as Carlow or Killarney—the streets swarm with idle crowds, the innumerable little lanes flow over with dirty little children, they are playing and puddling about in the dirt everywhere, with great big eyes, yellow faces, and the queerest little gowns and skull-caps. But in the outer man, the Greek has far the advantage of the Irishman: most of them are well and decently dressed (if five-and-twenty yards of petticoat may not be called decent, what may?), they swagger to and fro with huge knives in their girdles. Almost all the men are handsome, but live hard, it is said, in order to decorate their backs with those fine clothes of theirs. I have seen but two or three handsome women, and these had the great drawback which is common to the race—I mean, a sallow, greasy, coarse complexion, at which it was not advisable to look too closely.

And on this score I think we English may pride ourselves on possessing an advantage (by WE, I mean the lovely ladies to whom this is addressed with the most respectful compliments) over the most classical country in the world. I don't care for beauty which will only bear to be looked at from a distance, like a scene in a theatre. What is the most beautiful nose in the world, if it be covered with a skin of the texture and colour of coarse whitey-brown paper; and if Nature has made it as slippery and shining as though it had been anointed with pomatum? They may talk about beauty, but would you wear a flower that had been dipped in a grease-pot? No; give me a fresh, dewy, healthy rose out of Somersetshire; not one of those superb, tawdry, unwholesome exotics, which are only good to make poems about. Lord Byron wrote more cant of this sort than any poet I know of. Think of "the peasant girls with dark blue eyes" of the Rhine—the brown-faced, flat-nosed, thick-lipped, dirty wenches! Think of "filling high a cup of Samian wine;" small beer is nectar compared to it, and Byron himself always drank gin. That man never wrote from his heart. He got up rapture and enthusiasm with an eye to the public; but this is dangerous ground, even more dangerous than to look Athens full in the face, and say that your eyes are not dazzled by its beauty. The Great Public admires Greece and Byron: the public knows best. Murray's "Guide-book" calls the latter "our native bard." Our native bard! *Mon Dieu*! *He* Shakspeare's, Milton's, Keats's, Scott's native bard! Well, woe be to the man who denies the public gods!

The truth is, then, that Athens is a disappointment; and I am angry that it should be so. To a skilled antiquarian, or an enthusiastic Greek scholar, the feelings created by a sight of the place of course will be different; but you who would be inspired by it must undergo a long preparation of reading, and possess, too, a particular feeling; both of which, I suspect, are uncommon in our busy commercial newspaper-reading country. Men only say they are enthusiastic about the Greek and Roman authors and history, because it is considered proper and respectable. And we know how gentlemen in Baker Street have editions of the classics handsomely bound in the library, and how they use them. Of course they don't retire to read the newspaper; it is to look over a favourite ode of Pindar, or to discuss an obscure passage in Athenæus! Of course country magistrates and Members of Parliament are always studying Demosthenes and Cicero; we know it from their continual habit of quoting the Latin grammar in Parliament. But it is agreed that the classics are respectable; therefore we are to be enthusiastic about them. Also let us admit that Byron is to be held up as "our native bard."

I am not so entire a heathen as to be insensible to the beauty of those relics of Greek art, of which men much more learned and enthusiastic have written such piles of descriptions. I thought I could recognise the towering beauty of the prodigious columns of the Temple of Jupiter; and admire the astonishing grace, severity, elegance, completeness of the Parthenon. The little Temple of Victory, with its fluted Corinthian shafts, blazed under the sun almost as fresh as it must have appeared to the eyes of its founders; I saw nothing more charming and brilliant, more graceful, festive, and aristocratic than this sumptuous little building. The Roman remains which lie in the town below look like the works of barbarians beside these perfect structures. They jar strangely on the eye, after it has been accustoming itself to perfect harmony and proportions. If, as the schoolmaster tells us, the Greek writing is as complete as the Greek art; if an ode of Pindar is as glittering and pure as the Temple of Victory; or a discourse of Plato as polished and calm as yonder mystical portico of the Erechtheum: what treasures of the senses and delights of the imagination have those lost to whom the Greek books are as good as sealed!

And yet one meets with very dull first-class men. Genius won't transplant from one brain to another, or is ruined in the carriage, like fine Burgundy. Sir Robert Peel and Sir John Hobhouse are both good scholars; but their poetry in Parliament does not strike one as fine. Muzzle, the schoolmaster, who is bullying poor trembling little boys, was a fine scholar when he was a sizar, and a ruffian then and ever since. Where is the great poet, since the days of Milton, who has improved the natural offshoots of his brain by grafting it from the Athenian tree?

I had a volume of Tennyson in my pocket, which somehow settled that question, and ended the querulous dispute between me and Conscience, under the shape of the neglected and irritated Greek muse, which had been going on ever since I had commenced my walk about Athens. The old spinster saw me wince at the idea of the author of Dora and Ulysses, and tried to follow up her advantage by farther hints of time lost, and precious opportunities thrown away. "You might have written poems like them," said she; "or, no, not like them perhaps, but you might have done a neat prize poem, and pleased your papa and mamma. You might have translated Jack and Jill into Greek iambics, and been a credit to your college." I turned testily away from her. "Madam," says I, "because an eagle houses on a mountain, or soars to the sun, don't you be angry with a sparrow that perches on a garret window, or twitters on a twig. Leave me to myself: look, my beak is not aquiline by any means."

And so, my dear friend, you who have been reading this last page in wonder, and who, instead of a description of Athens, have been accommodated with a lament on the part of the writer, that he was idle at school, and does not know Greek, excuse this momentary outbreak of egotistic despondency. To say truth, dear Jones, when one walks among the nests of the eagles, and sees the prodigious eggs they laid, a certain feeling of discomfiture must come over us smaller birds. You and I could not invent—it even stretches our minds painfully to try and comprehend part of the beauty of the Parthenon—ever so little of it,—the beauty of a single column,—a fragment of a broken shaft lying under the astonishing blue sky there, in the midst of that unrivalled landscape. There may be grander aspects of nature, but none more deliciously beautiful. The hills rise in perfect harmony, and fall in the most exquisite cadences—the sea seems brighter, the islands more purple, the clouds more light and rosy than elsewhere. As you look up through the open roof, you are almost oppressed by the serene depth of the blue overhead. Look even at the fragments of the marble, how soft and pure it is, glittering and white like fresh snow! "I was all beautiful," it seems to say: "even the hidden parts of me were spotless, precious, and fair"—and so, musing over this wonderful scene, perhaps I get some feeble glimpse or idea of that ancient Greek spirit which peopled it with sublime races of heroes and gods;[i] and which I never could get out of a Greek book,—no, not though Muzzle flung it at my head.

CHAPTER VI: SMYRNA—FIRST GLIMPSES OF THE EAST

I am glad that the Turkish part of Athens was extinct, so that I should not be baulked of the pleasure of entering an Eastern town by an introduction to any garbled or incomplete specimen of one. Smyrna seems to me the most Eastern of all I have seen; as Calais will probably remain to the Englishman the most French town in the world. The jack-boots of the postilions don't seem so huge elsewhere, or the tight stockings of the maid-servants so Gallic. The churches and the ramparts, and the little soldiers on them, remain for ever impressed upon your memory; from which larger temples and buildings, and whole armies have subsequently disappeared: and the first words of actual French heard spoken, and the first dinner at "Quillacq's," remain after twenty years as clear as on the first day. Dear Jones, can't you remember the exact smack of the white hermitage, and the toothless old fellow singing "*Largo al factotum*"?

The first day in the East is like that. After that there is nothing. The wonder is gone, and the thrill of that delightful shock, which so seldom touches the nerves of plain men of the world, though they seek for it everywhere. One such looked out at Smyrna from our steamer, and yawned without the least excitement, and did not betray the slightest emotion, as boats with real Turks on board came up to the ship. There lay the town with minarets and cypresses, domes and castles; great guns were firing off, and the blood-red flag of the Sultan flaring over the fort ever since sunrise; woods and mountains came down to the gulf's edge, and as you looked at them with the telescope, there peeped out of the general mass a score of pleasant episodes of Eastern life—there were cottages with quaint roofs; silent cool kiosks, where the chief of the eunuchs brings down the ladies of the harem. I saw Hassan, the fisherman, getting his nets; and Ali Baba going off with his donkey to the great forest for wood. Smith looked at these wonders quite unmoved; and I was surprised at his apathy; but he had been at Smyrna before. A man only sees the miracle once; though you yearn over it ever so, it won't come again. I saw nothing of Ali Baba and Hassan the next time we came to Smyrna, and had some doubts (recollecting the badness of the inn) about landing at all. A person who wishes to understand France or the East should come in a yacht to Calais or Smyrna, land for two hours, and never afterwards go back again.

But those two hours are beyond measure delightful. Some of us were querulous up to that time, and doubted of the wisdom of making the voyage. Lisbon, we owned, was a failure; Athens a dead failure; Malta very well, but not worth the trouble and sea-sickness: in fact, Baden-Baden or Devonshire would be a better move than this; when Smyrna came, and rebuked all mutinous Cockneys into silence. Some men may read this who are in want of a sensation. If they love the odd and picturesque, if they loved the "Arabian Nights" in their youth, let them book themselves on board one of the Peninsular and Oriental vessels, and try one *dip* into Constantinople or Smyrna. Walk into the bazaar, and the East is unveiled to you: how often and often have you tried to fancy this, lying out on a summer holiday at school! It is wonderful, too, how *like* it is: you may imagine that you have been in the place before, you seem to know it so well!

The beauty of that poetry is, to me, that it was never too handsome; there is no fatigue of sublimity about it. Shacabac and the little Barber play as great a part in it as the heroes; there are no uncomfortable sensations of terror; you may be familiar with the great Afreet, who was going to execute the travellers for killing his son with a date-stone. Morgiana, when she kills the forty robbers with boiling oil, does not seem to hurt them in the least; and though King Schahriar makes a practice of cutting off his wives' heads, yet you fancy they have got them on again in some of the back rooms of the palace, where they are dancing and playing on dulcimers. How fresh, easy, good-natured, is all this! How delightful is that notion of the pleasant Eastern people about knowledge, where the height of science is made to consist in the answering of riddles! and all the mathematicians and magicians bring their great beards to bear on a conundrum!

When I got into the bazaar among this race, somehow I felt as if they were all friends. There sat the merchants in their little shops, quiet and solemn, but with friendly looks. There was no smoking, it was the Ramazan; no eating, the fish and meat fizzing in the enormous pots of the cook-shops are only for the Christians. The children abounded; the law is not so stringent upon them, and many wandering merchants were there selling figs (in the name of the Prophet, doubtless) for their benefit, and elbowing onwards with baskets of grapes and cucumbers. Countrymen passed bristling over with arms, each with a huge bellyful of pistols and daggers in his girdle; fierce, but not the least dangerous. Wild swarthy Arabs, who had come in with the caravans, walked solemnly about, very different in look and demeanour from the sleek inhabitants of the town. Greeks and Jews squatted and smoked, their shops tended by sallow-faced boys, with large eyes, who smiled and welcomed you in; negroes bustled about in gaudy colours; and women, with black nose-bags and shuffling yellow slippers, chattered and bargained at the doors of the little shops. There was the rope quarter and the sweetmeat quarter, and the pipe bazaar and the arm bazaar, and the little turned-up shoe quarter, and the shops where ready-made jackets and pelisses were swinging, and the region where, under the ragged awning, regiments of tailors were at work. The sun peeps through these awnings of mat or canvas, which are hung over the narrow lanes of the bazaar, and ornaments them with a thousand freaks of light and shadow. Cogia Hassan Alhabbal's shop is in a blaze of light; while his neighbour, the barber and coffee-house keeper, has his premises, his low seats and narghiles, his queer pots and basins, in the shade. The cobblers are always good-natured; there was one who, I am sure, has been revealed to me in my dreams, in a dirty old green turban, with a pleasant wrinkled face like an apple, twinkling his little grey eyes as he held them up to talk to the gossips, and smiling under a delightful old grey beard, which did the heart good to see. You divine the conversation between him and the cucumber-man, as the Sultan used to understand the language of birds. Are any of those cucumbers stuffed with pearls, and is that Armenian with the black square turban Haroun Alraschid in disguise, standing yonder by the fountain where the children are drinking—the gleaming marble fountain, chequered all over with light and shadow, and engraved with delicate arabesques and sentences from the Koran?

But the greatest sensation of all is when the camels come. Whole strings of real camels, better even than in the procession of Blue Beard, with soft rolling eyes and bended necks, swaying from one side of the bazaar to the other to and fro, and treading gingerly with their great feet. O you fairy dreams of boyhood! O you sweet meditations of half-holidays, here you are realised for half-an-hour! The genius which presides over youth led us to do a good action that day. There was a man sitting in an open room, ornamented with fine long-tailed sentences of the Koran: some in red, some in blue; some written diagonally over the paper; some so shaped as to represent ships, dragons, or mysterious animals. The man squatted on a carpet in the middle of this room, with folded arms, waggling his head to and fro, swaying about, and singing through his nose choice phrases from the sacred work. But from the room above came a clear noise of many little shouting voices, much more musical than that of Naso in the matted parlour, and the guide told us it was a school, so we went upstairs to look.

I declare, on my conscience, the master was in the act of bastinadoing a little mulatto boy; his feet were in a bar, and the brute was laying on with a cane; so we witnessed the howling of the poor boy, and the confusion of the brute who was administering the correction. The other children were made to shout, I believe, to drown the noise of their little comrade's howling; but the punishment was instantly discontinued as our hats came up over the stair-trap, and the boy cast loose, and the bamboo huddled into a corner, and the schoolmaster stood before us abashed. All the small scholars in red caps, and the little girls in gaudy handkerchiefs, turned their big wondering dark eyes towards us; and the caning was over for *that* time, let us trust. I don't envy some schoolmasters in a future state. I pity that poor little blubbering Mahometan: he will never be able to relish the "Arabian Nights" in the original, all his life long.

From this scene we rushed off somewhat discomposed to make a breakfast off red mullets and grapes, melons, pomegranates, and Smyrna wine, at a dirty little comfortable inn, to which we were recommended: and from the windows of which we had a fine cheerful view of the gulf and its busy craft, and the loungers and merchants along the shore. There were camels unloading at one wharf, and piles of melons much bigger than the Gibraltar cannon-balls at another. It was the fig-season, and we passed through several alleys encumbered with long rows of fig-dressers, children and women for the most part, who were packing the fruit diligently into drums, dipping them in salt-water first, and spreading them neatly over with leaves; while the figs and leaves are drying, large white worms crawl out of them, and swarm over the decks of the ships which carry them to Europe and to England, where small children eat them with pleasure—I mean the figs, not the worms—and where they are still served at wine-parties at the Universities. When fresh they are not better than elsewhere; but the melons are of admirable flavour, and so large, that Cinderella might almost be accommodated with a coach made of a big one, without any very great distension of its original proportions.

Our guide, an accomplished swindler, demanded two dollars as the fee for entering the mosque, which others of our party subsequently saw for sixpence, so we did not care to examine that place of worship. But there were other cheaper sights, which were to the full as picturesque, for which there was no call to pay money, or, indeed, for a day, scarcely to move at all. I doubt whether a man who would smoke his pipe on a bazaar counter all day, and let the city flow by him, would not be almost as well employed as the most active curiosity-hunter.

To be sure he would not see the women. Those in the bazaar were shabby people for the most part, whose black masks nobody would feel a curiosity to remove. You could see no more of their figures than if they had been stuffed in bolsters; and even their feet were brought to a general splay uniformity by the double yellow slippers which the wives of true believers wear. But it is in the Greek and Armenian quarters, and among those poor Christians who were pulling figs, that you see the beauties; and a man of a generous disposition may lose his heart half-a-dozen times a day in Smyrna. There was the pretty maid at work at a tambour-frame in an open porch, with an old duenna spinning by her side, and a goat tied up to the railings of the little court-garden; there was the nymph who came down the stair with the pitcher on her head, and gazed with great calm eyes, as large and stately as Juno's; there was the gentle mother, bending over a queer cradle, in which lay a small crying bundle of infancy. All these three charmers were seen in a single street in the Armenian quarter, where the house-doors are all open, and the women of the families sit under the arches in the court. There was the fig-girl, beautiful beyond all others, with an immense coil of deep black hair twisted round a head of which Raphael was worthy to draw the outline and Titian to paint the colour. I wonder the Sultan has not swept her off, or that the Persian merchants, who come with silks and sweetmeats, have not kidnapped her for the Shah of Tehran.

We went to see the Persian merchants at their khan, and purchased some silks there from a swarthy black-bearded man, with a conical cap of lambswool. Is it not hard to think that silks bought of a man in a lambswool cap, in a caravanserai, brought hither on the backs of camels, should have been manufactured after all at Lyons? Others of our party bought carpets, for which the town is famous; and there was one who absolutely laid in a stock of real Smyrna figs; and purchased three or four real Smyrna sponges for his carriage; so strong was his passion for the genuine article.

I wonder that no painter has given us familiar views of the East: not processions, grand sultans, or magnificent landscapes; but faithful transcripts of everyday Oriental life, such as each street will supply to him. The camels afford endless motives, couched in the market-places, lying by thousands in the camel-square, snorting and bubbling after their manner, the sun blazing down on their backs, their slaves and keepers lying behind them in the shade: and the Caravan Bridge, above all, would afford a painter subjects for a dozen of pictures. Over this Roman arch, which crosses the Meles river, all the caravans pass on their entrance to the town. On one side, as we sat and looked at it, was a great row of plane-trees; on the opposite bank, a deep wood of tall cypresses—in the midst of which rose up innumerable grey tombs, surmounted with the turbans of the defunct believers. Beside the stream, the view was less gloomy. There was under the plane-trees a little coffee-house, shaded by a trellis-work, covered over with a vine, and ornamented with many rows of shining pots and water-pipes, for which there was no use at noon-day now, in the time of Ramazan. Hard by the coffee-house was a garden and a bubbling marble fountain, and over the stream was a broken summer-house, to which amateurs may ascend for the purpose of examining the river; and all round the plane-trees plenty of stools for those who were inclined to sit and drink sweet thick coffee, or cool lemonade made of fresh green citrons. The master of the house, dressed in a white turban and light blue pelisse, lolled under the coffee-house awning; the slave in white with a crimson striped jacket, his face as black as ebony, brought us pipes and lemonade again, and returned to his station at the coffee-house, where he curled his black legs together, and began singing out of his flat nose to the thrumming of a long guitar with wire strings. The instrument was not bigger than a soup-ladle, with a long straight handle, but its music pleased the performer; for his eyes rolled shining about, and his head wagged, and he grinned with an innocent intensity of enjoyment that did one good to look at. And there was a friend to share his pleasure: a Turk dressed in scarlet, and covered all over with daggers and pistols, sat leaning forward on his little stool, rocking about, and grinning quite as eagerly as the black minstrel. As he sang and we listened, figures of women bearing pitchers went passing over the Roman bridge, which we saw between the large trunks of the planes; or grey forms of camels were seen stalking across it, the string preceded by the little donkey, who is always here their long-eared conductor.

These are very humble incidents of travel. Wherever the steamboat touches the shore adventure retreats into the interior, and what is called romance vanishes. It won't bear the vulgar gaze; or rather the light of common day puts it out, and it is only in the dark that it shines at all. There is no cursing and insulting of Giaours now. If a Cockney looks or behaves in a particularly ridiculous way, the little Turks come out and laugh at him. A Londoner is no longer a spittoon for true believers: and now that dark Hassan sits in his divan and drinks champagne, and Selim has a French watch, and Zuleika perhaps takes Morison's pills, Byronism becomes absurd instead of sublime, and is only a foolish expression of Cockney wonder. They still occasionally beat a man for going into a mosque, but this is almost the only sign of ferocious vitality left in the Turk of the Mediterranean coast, and strangers may enter scores of mosques without molestation. The paddle-wheel is the great conqueror. Wherever the captain cries "Stop her!" Civilisation stops, and lands in the ship's boat, and makes a permanent acquaintance with the savages on shore. Whole hosts of crusaders have passed and died, and butchered here in vain. But to manufacture European iron into pikes and helmets was a waste of metal: in the shape of piston-rods and furnace-pokers it is irresistible; and I think an allegory might be made showing how much stronger commerce is than chivalry, and finishing with a grand image of Mahomet's crescent being extinguished in Fulton's boiler.

This I thought was the moral of the day's sights and adventures. We pulled off to the steamer in the afternoon—the Inbat blowing fresh, and setting all the craft in the gulf dancing over its blue waters. We were presently under way again, the captain ordering his engines to work only at half power, so that a French steamer which was quitting Smyrna at the same time might come up with us, and fancy she could beat their irresistible, "Tagus." Vain hope! Just as the Frenchman neared us, the "Tagus" shot out like an arrow, and the discomfited Frenchman went behind. Though we all relished the joke exceedingly, there was a French gentleman on board who did not seem to be by any means tickled with it; but he had received papers at Smyrna, containing news of Marshal Bugeaud's victory at Isly, and had this land victory to set against our harmless little triumph at sea.

That night we rounded the island of Mitylene: and the next day the coast of Troy was in sight, and the tomb of Achilles—a dismal-looking mound that rises in a low dreary barren shore—less lively and not more picturesque than the Scheldt or the mouth of the Thames. Then we passed Tenedos and the forts and town at the mouth of the Dardanelles. The weather was not too hot, the water as smooth as at Putney, and everybody happy and excited at the thought of seeing Constantinople to-morrow. We had music on board all the way from Smyrna. A German commis-voyageur, with a guitar, who had passed unnoticed until that time, produced his instrument about mid-day, and began to whistle waltzes. He whistled so divinely that the ladies left their cabins, and men laid down their books. He whistled a polka so bewitchingly that two young Oxford men began whirling round the deck, and performed that popular dance with much agility until they sank down tired. He still continued an unabated whistling, and as nobody would dance, pulled off his coat, produced a pair of castanets, and whistling a mazurka, performed it with tremendous agility. His whistling made everybody gay and happy— made those acquainted who had not spoken before, and inspired such a feeling of hilarity in the ship, that that night, as we floated over the Sea of Marmora, a general vote was expressed for broiled bones and a regular supper-party. Punch was brewed, and speeches were made, and, after a lapse of fifteen years, I heard the "Old English Gentleman" and "Bright Chanticleer Proclaims the Morn," sung in such style that you would almost fancy the proctors must hear, and send us all home.

CHAPTER VII: CONSTANTINOPLE

When we arose at sunrise to see the famous entry to Constantinople, we found, in the place of the city and the sun, a bright white fog, which hid both from sight, and which only disappeared as the vessel advanced towards the Golden Horn. There the fog cleared off as it were by flakes, and as you see gauze curtains lifted away, one by one, before a great fairy scene at the theatre. This will give idea enough of the fog; the difficulty is to describe the scene afterwards, which was in truth the great fairy scene, than which it is impossible to conceive anything more brilliant and magnificent. I can't go to any more romantic place than Drury Lane to draw my similes from—Drury Lane, such as we used to see it in our youth, when to our sight the grand last pictures of the melodrama or pantomime were as magnificent as any objects of nature we have seen with maturer eyes. Well, the view of Constantinople is as fine as any of Stanfield's best theatrical pictures, seen at the best period of youth, when fancy had all the bloom on her—when all the heroines who danced before the scene appeared as ravishing beauties, when there shone an unearthly splendour about Baker and Diddear—and the sound of the bugles and fiddles, and the cheerful clang of the cymbals, as the scene unrolled, and the gorgeous procession meandered triumphantly through it—caused a thrill of pleasure, and awakened an innocent fulness of sensual enjoyment that is only given to boys.

The above sentence contains the following propositions:-The enjoyments of boyish fancy are the most intense and delicious in the world. Stanfield's panorama used to be the realisation of the most intense youthful fancy. I puzzle my brains and find no better likeness for the place. The view of Constantinople resembles the *ne plus ultra* of a Stanfield diorama, with a glorious accompaniment of music, spangled houris, warriors, and winding processions, feasting the eyes and the soul with light, splendour, and harmony. If you were never in this way during your youth ravished at the play-house, of course the whole comparison is useless: and you have no idea, from this description, of the effect which Constantinople produces on the mind. But if you were never affected by a theatre, no words can work upon your fancy, and typographical attempts to move it are of no use. For, suppose we combine mosque, minaret, gold, cypress, water, blue, caiques, seventy-four, Galata, Tophana, Ramazan, Backallum, and so forth, together, in ever so many ways, your imagination will never be able to depict a city out of them. Or, suppose I say the Mosque of St. Sophia is four hundred and seventy-three feet in height, measuring from the middle nail of the gilt crescent surmounting the dome to the ring in the centre stone; the circle of the dome is one hundred and twenty-three feet in diameter, the windows ninety-seven in number—and all this may be true, for anything I know to the contrary: yet who is to get an idea of St. Sophia from dates, proper names, and calculations with a measuring-line? It can't be done by giving the age and measurement of all the buildings along the river, the names of all the boatmen who ply on it. Has your fancy, which pooh-poohs a simile, faith enough to build a city with a foot-rule? Enough said about descriptions and similes (though whenever I am uncertain of one I am naturally most anxious to fight for it): it is a scene not perhaps sublime, but charming, magnificent, and cheerful beyond any I have ever seen—the most superb combination of city and gardens, domes and shipping, hills and water, with the healthiest breeze blowing over it, and above it the brightest and most cheerful sky.

It is proper, they say, to be disappointed on entering the town, or any of the various quarters of it, because the houses are not so magnificent on inspection and seen singly as they are when beheld *en masse* from the waters. But why form expectations so lofty? If you see a group of peasants picturesquely disposed at a fair, you don't suppose that they are all faultless beauties, or that the men's coats have no rags, and the women's gowns are made of silk and velvet: the wild ugliness of the interior of Constantinople or Pera has a charm of its own, greatly more amusing than rows of red bricks or drab stones, however symmetrical. With brick or stone they could never form those fantastic ornaments, railings, balconies, roofs, galleries, which jut in and out of the rugged houses of the city. As we went from Galata to Pera up a steep hill, which newcomers ascend with some difficulty, but which a porter, with a couple of hundredweight on his back, paces up without turning a hair, I thought the wooden houses far from being disagreeable objects, sights quite as surprising and striking as the grand one we had just left.

I do not know how the custom-house of His Highness is made to be a profitable speculation. As I left the ship, a man pulled after my boat, and asked for backsheesh, which was given him to the amount of about twopence. He was a custom-house officer, but I doubt whether this sum which he levied ever went to the revenue.

I can fancy the scene about the quays somewhat to resemble the river of London in olden times, before coal-smoke had darkened the whole city with soot, and when, according to the old writers, there really was bright weather. The fleets of caiques bustling along the shore, or scudding over the blue water, are beautiful to look at: in Hollar's print London river is so studded over with wherry-boats, which bridges and steamers have since destroyed. Here the caique is still in full perfection: there are thirty thousand boats of the kind plying between the cities; every boat is neat, and trimly carved and painted; and I scarcely saw a man pulling in one of them that was not a fine specimen of his race, brawny and brown, with an open chest and a handsome face. They wear a thin shirt of exceedingly light cotton, which leaves their fine brown limbs full play; and with a purple sea for a background, every one of these dashing boats forms a brilliant and glittering picture. Passengers squat in the inside of the boat; so that as it passes you see little more than the heads of the true believers, with their red fez and blue tassel, and that placid gravity of expression which the sucking of a tobacco-pipe is sure to give to a man.

The Bosphorus is enlivened by a multiplicity of other kinds of craft. There are the dirty men-of-war's boats of the Russians, with unwashed mangy crews; the great ferry-boats carrying hundreds of passengers to the villages; the melon-boats piled up with enormous golden fruit; His Excellency the Pasha's boat, with twelve men bending to their oars; and His Highness's own caique, with a head like a serpent, and eight-and-twenty tugging oarsmen, that goes shooting by amidst the thundering of the cannon. Ships and steamers, with black sides and flaunting colours, are moored everywhere, showing their flags, Russian and English, Austrian, American, and Greek; and along the quays country ships from the Black Sea or the islands, with high carved poops and bows, such as you see in the pictures of the shipping of the seventeenth century. The vast groves and towers, domes and quays, tall minarets and spired spreading mosques of the three cities, rise all around in endless magnificence and variety, and render this water-street a scene of such delightful liveliness and beauty, that one never tires of looking at it. I lost a great number of the sights in and round Constantinople through the beauty of this admirable scene: but what are sights after all? and isn't that the best sight which makes you most happy?

We were lodged at Pera at Misseri's Hotel, the host of which has been made famous ere this time by the excellent book "Eothen,"—a work for which all the passengers on board our ship had been battling, and which had charmed all—from our great statesman, our polished lawyer, our young Oxonian, who sighed over certain passages that he feared were wicked, down to the writer of this, who, after perusing it with delight, laid it down with wonder, exclaiming, "*Aut Diabolus aut*"—a book which has since (greatest miracle of all) excited a feeling of warmth and admiration in the bosom of the god-like, impartial, stony Athenæum. Misseri, the faithful and chivalrous Tartar, is transformed into the most quiet and gentlemanlike of landlords, a great deal more gentlemanlike in manner and appearance than most of us who sat at his table, and smoked cool pipes on his house-top, as we looked over the hill and the Russian palace to the water, and the Seraglio gardens shining in the blue. We confronted Misseri, "Eothen" in hand, and found, on examining him, that it *was* "*aut Diabolus aut amicus*"—but the name is a secret; I will never breathe it, though I am dying to tell it.

The last good description of a Turkish bath, I think, was Lady Mary Wortley Montagu's—which voluptuous picture must have been painted at least a hundred and thirty years ago; so that another sketch may be attempted by a humbler artist in a different manner. The Turkish bath is certainly a novel sensation to an Englishman, and may be set down as a most queer and surprising event of his life. I made the *valet-de-place* or dragoman (it is rather a fine thing to have a dragoman in one's service) conduct me forthwith to the best appointed hummums in the neighbourhood; and we walked to a house at Tophana, and into a spacious hall lighted from above, which is the cooling-room of the bath.

The spacious hall has a large fountain in the midst, a painted gallery running round it; and many ropes stretched from one gallery to another, ornamented with profuse draperies of towels and blue cloths, for the use of the frequenters of the place. All round the room and the galleries were matted inclosures, fitted with numerous neat beds and cushions for reposing on, where lay a dozen of true believers smoking, or sleeping, or in the happy half-dozing state. I was led up to one of these beds, to rather a retired corner, in consideration of my modesty; and to the next bed presently came a dancing dervish, who forthwith began to prepare for the bath.

When the dancing dervish had taken off his yellow sugar-loaf cap, his gown, shawl, &c., he was arrayed in two large blue cloths; a white one being thrown over his shoulders, and another in the shape of a turban plaited neatly round his head; the garments of which he divested himself were folded up in another linen, and neatly put by. I beg leave to state I was treated in precisely the same manner as the dancing dervish.

The reverend gentleman then put on a pair of wooden pattens, which elevated him about six inches from the ground; and walked down the stairs, and paddled across the moist marble floor of the hall, and in at a little door, by the which also Titmarsh entered. But I had none of the professional agility of the dancing dervish; I staggered about very ludicrously upon the high wooden pattens; and should have been down on my nose several times, had not the dragoman and the master of the bath supported me down the stairs and across the hall. Dressed in three large cotton napkins, with a white turban round my head, I thought of Pall Mall with a sort of despair. I passed the little door, it was closed behind me—I was in the dark—I couldn't speak the language—in a white turban. *Mon Dieu!* what was going to happen?

The dark room was the tepidarium, a moist oozing arched den, with a light faintly streaming from an orifice in the domed ceiling. Yells of frantic laughter and song came booming and clanging through the echoing arches, the doors clapped to with loud reverberations. It was the laughter of the followers of Mahound, rollicking and taking their pleasure in the public bath. I could not go into that place: I swore I would not; they promised me a private room, and the dragoman left me. My agony at parting from that Christian cannot be described.

When you get into the sudarium, or hot room, your first sensations only occur about half a minute after entrance, when you feel that you are choking. I found myself in that state, seated on a marble slab; the bath man was gone; he had taken away the cotton turban and shoulder shawl: I saw I was in a narrow room of marble, with a vaulted roof, and a fountain of warm and cold water; the atmosphere was in a steam, the choking sensation went off, and I felt a sort of pleasure presently in a soft boiling simmer, which, no doubt, potatoes feel when they are steaming. You are left in this state for about ten minutes: it is warm certainly, but odd and pleasant, and disposes the mind to reverie.

But let any delicate mind in Baker Street fancy my horror when, on looking up out of this reverie, I saw a great brown wretch extended before me, only half dressed, standing on pattens, and exaggerated by them and the steam until he looked like an ogre, grinning in the most horrible way, and waving his arm, on which was a horsehair glove. He spoke, in his unknown nasal jargon, words which echoed through the arched room; his eyes seemed astonishingly large and bright, his ears stuck out, and his head was all shaved, except a bristling top-knot, which gave it a demoniac fierceness.

This description, I feel, is growing too frightful; ladies who read it will be going into hysterics, or saying, "Well, upon my word, this is the most singular, the most extraordinary kind of language. Jane, my love, you will not read that odious book—" and so I will be brief. This grinning man belabours the patient violently with the horse-brush. When he has completed the horsehair part, and you lie expiring under a squirting fountain of warm water, and fancying all is done, he reappears with a large brass basin, containing a quantity of lather, in the midst of which is something like old Miss MacWhirter's flaxen wig that she is so proud of, and that we have all laughed at. Just as you are going to remonstrate, the thing like the wig is dashed into your face and eyes, covered over with soap, and for five minutes you are drowned in lather: you can't see, the suds are frothing over your eye-balls; you can't hear, the soap is whizzing into your ears; can't gasp for breath, Miss MacWhirter's wig is down your throat with half a pailful of suds in an instant—you are all soap. Wicked children in former days have jeered you, exclaiming, "How are you off for soap?" You little knew what saponacity was till you entered a Turkish bath.

When the whole operation is concluded, you are led—with what heartfelt joy I need not say—softly back to the cooling-room, having been robed in shawls and turbans as before. You are laid gently on the reposing bed; somebody brings a narghilé, which tastes as tobacco must taste in Mahomet's Paradise; a cool sweet dreamy languor takes possession of the purified frame; and half-an-hour of such delicious laziness is spent over the pipe as is unknown in Europe, where vulgar prejudice has most shamefully maligned indolence—calls it foul names, such as the father of all evil, and the like; in fact, does not know how to educate idleness as those honest Turks do, and the fruit which, when properly cultivated, it bears.

The after-bath state is the most delightful condition of laziness I ever knew, and I tried it wherever we went afterwards on our little tour. At Smyrna the whole business was much inferior to the method employed in the capital. At Cairo, after the soap, you are plunged into a sort of stone coffin, full of water which is all but boiling. This has its charms; but I could not relish the Egyptian shampooing. A hideous old blind man (but very dexterous in his art) tried to break my back and dislocate my shoulders, but I could not see the pleasure of the practice; and another fellow began tickling the soles of my feet, but I rewarded him with a kick that sent him off the bench. The pure idleness is the best, and I shall never enjoy such in Europe again.

Victor Hugo, in his famous travels on the Rhine, visiting Cologne, gives a learned account of what he *didn't* see there. I have a remarkable catalogue of similar objects at Constantinople. I didn't see the dancing dervishes, it was Ramazan; nor the howling dervishes at Scutari, it was Ramazan; nor the interior of St. Sophia, nor the women's apartment of the Seraglio, nor the fashionable promenade at the Sweet Waters, always because it was Ramazan; during which period the dervishes dance and howl but rarely, their legs and lungs being unequal to much exertion during a fast of fifteen hours. On account of the same holy season, the Royal palaces and mosques are shut; and though the Valley of the Sweet Waters is there, no one goes to walk; the people remaining asleep all day, and passing the night in feasting and carousing. The minarets are illuminated at this season; even the humblest mosque at Jerusalem, or Jaffa, mounted a few circles of dingy lamps; those of the capital were handsomely lighted with many festoons of lamps, which had a fine effect from the water. I need not mention other and constant illuminations of the city, which innumerable travellers have described—I mean the fires. There were three in Pera during our eight days' stay there; but they did not last long enough to bring the Sultan out of bed to come and lend his aid. Mr. Hobhouse (quoted in the "Guide-book") says, if a fire lasts an hour, the Sultan is bound to attend it in person; and that people having petitions to present, have often set houses on fire for the purpose of forcing out this Royal trump. The Sultan can't lead a very "jolly life," if this rule be universal. Fancy His Highness, in the midst of his moon-faced beauties, handkerchief in hand, and obliged to tie it round his face, and go out of his warm harem at midnight at the cursed cry of "Yang en Var!"

We saw His Highness in the midst of his people and their petitions, when he came to the mosque at Tophana; not the largest, but one of the most picturesque of the public buildings of the city. The streets were crowded with people watching for the august arrival, and lined with the squat military in their bastard European costume; the sturdy police, with bandeliers and brown surtouts, keeping order, driving off the faithful from the railings of the Esplanade through which their Emperor was to pass, and only admitting (with a very unjust partiality, I thought) us Europeans into that reserved space. Before the august arrival, numerous officers collected, colonels and pashas went by with their attendant running footmen; the most active, insolent, and hideous of these great men, as I thought, being His Highness's black eunuchs, who went prancing through the crowd, which separated before them with every sign of respect.

The common women were assembled by many hundreds: the yakmac, a muslin chin-cloth which they wear, makes almost every face look the same; but the eyes and noses of these beauties are generally visible, and, for the most part, both these features are good. The jolly negresses wear the same white veil, but they are by no means so particular about hiding the charms of their good-natured black faces, and they let the cloth blow about as it lists, and grin unconfined. Wherever we went the negroes seemed happy. They have the organ of child-loving: little creatures were always prattling on their shoulders, queer little things in night gowns of yellow dimity, with great flowers, and pink or red or yellow shawls, with great eyes glistening underneath. Of such the black women seemed always the happy guardians.

I saw one at a fountain, holding one child in her arms, and giving another a drink—a ragged little beggar—a sweet and touching picture of a black charity.

I am almost forgetting His Highness the Sultan. About a hundred guns were fired off at clumsy intervals from the Esplanade facing the Bosphorus, warning us that the monarch had set off from his Summer Palace, and was on the way to his grand canoe. At last that vessel made its appearance; the band struck up his favourite air; his caparisoned horse was led down to the shore to receive him; the eunuchs, fat pashas, colonels and officers of state gathering round as the Commander of the Faithful mounted. I had the indescribable happiness of seeing him at a very short distance. The Padishah, or Father of all the Sovereigns on earth, has not that majestic air which some sovereigns possess, and which makes the beholder's eyes wink, and his knees tremble under him: he has a black beard, and a handsome well-bred face, of a French cast; he looks like a young French *roué* worn out by debauch; his eyes bright, with black rings round them; his cheeks pale and hollow. He was lolling on his horse as if he could hardly hold himself on the saddle: or as if his cloak, fastened with a blazing diamond clasp on his breast, and falling over his horse's tail, pulled him back. But the handsome sallow face of the Refuge of the World looked decidedly interesting and intellectual. I have seen many a young Don Juan at Paris, behind a counter, with such a beard and countenance; the flame of passion still burning in his hollow eyes, while on his damp brow was stamped the fatal mark of premature decay. The man we saw cannot live many summers. Women and wine are said to have brought the Zilullah to this state; and it is whispered by the dragomans, or l*aquais-de-place* (from whom travellers at Constantinople generally get their political information), that the Sultan's mother and his ministers conspire to keep him plunged in sensuality, that they may govern the kingdom according to their own fancies. Mr. Urquhart, I am sure, thinks that Lord Palmerston has something to do with the business, and drugs the Sultan's champagne for the benefit of Russia.

As the Pontiff of Mussulmans passed into the mosques a shower of petitions was flung from the steps where the crowd was collected, and over the heads of the gendarmes in brown. A general cry, as for justice, rose up; and one old ragged woman came forward and burst through the throng, howling, and flinging about her lean arms, and baring her old shrunken breast. I never saw a finer action of tragic woo, or heard sounds more pitiful than those old passionate groans of hers. What was your prayer, poor old wretched soul? The gendarmes hemmed her round, and hustled her away, but rather kindly. The Padishah went on quite impassible—the picture of debauch and ennui.

I like pointing morals, and inventing for myself cheap consolations, to reconcile me to that state of life into which it has pleased Heaven to call me; and as the Light of the World disappeared round the corner, I reasoned pleasantly with myself about His Highness, and enjoyed that secret selfish satisfaction a man has, who sees he is better off than his neighbour. "Michael Angelo," I said, "you are still (by courtesy) young: if you had five hundred thousand a year, and were a great prince, I would lay a wager that men would discover in you a magnificent courtesy of demeanour, and a majestic presence that only belongs to the sovereigns of the world. If you had such an income, you think you could spend it with splendour: distributing genial hospitalities, kindly alms, soothing misery, bidding humility be of good heart, rewarding desert. If you had such means of purchasing pleasure, you think, you rogue, you could relish it with gusto. But fancy being brought to the condition of the poor Light of the Universe yonder; and reconcile yourself with the idea that you are only a farthing rushlight. The cries of the poor widow fall as dead upon him as the smiles of the brightest eyes out of Georgia. He can't stir abroad but those abominable cannon begin roaring and deafening his ears. He can't see the world but over the shoulders of a row of fat pashas, and eunuchs, with their infernal ugliness. His ears can never be regaled with a word of truth, or blessed with an honest laugh. The only privilege of manhood left to him, he enjoys but for a month in the year, at this time of Ramazan, when he is forced to fast for fifteen hours; and, by consequence, has the blessing of feeling hungry." Sunset during Lent appears to be his single moment of pleasure; they say the poor fellow is ravenous by that time, and as the gun fires the dish-covers are taken off, so that for five minutes a day he lives and is happy over pillau, like another mortal.

And yet, when floating by the Summer Palace, a barbaric edifice of wood and marble, with gilded suns blazing over the porticoes, and all sorts of strange ornaments and trophies figuring on the gates and railings—when we passed a long row of barred and filigreed windows, looking on the water—when we were told that those were the apartments of His Highness's ladies, and actually heard them whispering and laughing behind the bars—a strange feeling of curiosity came over some ill-regulated minds—just to have one peep, one look at all those wondrous beauties, singing to the dulcimers, paddling in the fountains, dancing in the marble halls, or lolling on the golden cushions, as the gaudy black slaves brought pipes and coffee. This tumultuous movement was calmed by thinking of that dreadful statement of travellers, that in one of the most elegant halls there is a trap-door, on peeping below which you may see the Bosphorus running underneath, into which some luckless beauty is plunged occasionally, and the trap-door is shut, and the dancing and the singing, and the smoking and the laughing go on as before. They say it is death to pick up any of the sacks thereabouts, if a stray one should float by you. There were none any day when I passed, *at least, on the surface of the water*.

It has been rather a fashion of our travellers to apologise for Turkish life, of late, and paint glowing agreeable pictures of many of its institutions. The celebrated author of "palm-Leaves" (his name is famous under the date-trees of the Nile, and uttered with respect beneath the tents of the Bedaween) has touchingly described Ibrahim Pasha's paternal fondness, who cut off a black slave's head for having dropped and maimed one of his children; and has penned a melodious panegyric of "The Harem," and of the fond and beautiful duties of the inmates of that place of love, obedience, and seclusion. I saw, at the mausoleum of the late Sultan Mahmoud's family, a good subject for a Ghazul, in the true new Oriental manner.

These Royal burial-places are the resort of the pious Moslems. Lamps are kept burning there; and in the antechambers, copies of the Koran are provided for the use of believers; and you never pass these cemeteries but you see Turks washing at the cisterns, previous to entering for prayer, or squatted on the benches, chanting passages from the sacred volume. Christians, I believe, are not admitted, but may look through the bars, and see the coffins of the defunct monarchs and children of the Royal race. Each lies in his narrow sarcophagus, which is commonly flanked by huge candles, and covered with a rich embroidered pall. At the head of each coffin rises a slab, with a gilded inscription; for the princesses, the slab is simple, not unlike our own monumental stones. The headstones of the tombs of the defunct princes are decorated with a turban, or, since the introduction of the latter article of dress, with the red fez. That of Mahmoud is decorated with the imperial aigrette.

In this dismal but splendid museum, I remarked two little tombs with little red fezzes, very small, and for very young heads evidently, which were lying under the little embroidered palls of state. I forget whether they had candles too; but their little flame of life was soon extinguished, and there was no need of many pounds of wax to typify it. These were the tombs of Mahmoud's grandsons, nephews of the present Light of the Universe, and children of his sister, the wife of Halil Pasha. Little children die in all ways: these of the much-maligned Mahometan Royal race perished by the bowstring. Sultan Mahmoud (may he rest in glory!) strangled the one; but, having some spark of human feeling, was so moved by the wretchedness and agony of the poor bereaved mother, his daughter, that his Royal heart relented towards her, and he promised that, should she ever have another child, it should be allowed to live. He died; and Abdul Medjid (may his name be blessed!), the debauched young man whom we just saw riding to the mosque, succeeded. His sister, whom he is said to have loved, became again a mother, and had a son. But she relied upon her father's word and her august brother's love, and hoped that this little one should be spared. The same accursed hand tore this infant out of its mother's bosom, and killed it. The poor woman's heart broke outright at this second calamity, and she died. But on her death-bed she sent for her brother, rebuked him as a perjurer and an assassin, and expired calling down the divine justice on his head. She lies now by the side of the two little fezzes.

Now I say this would be a fine subject for an Oriental poem. The details are dramatic and noble, and could be grandly touched by a fine artist. If the mother had borne a daughter, the child would have been safe; that perplexity might be pathetically depicted as agitating the bosom of the young wife about to become a mother. A son is born: you can see her despair and the pitiful look she casts on the child, and the way in which she hugs it every time the curtains of her door are removed. The Sultan hesitated probably; he allowed the infant to live for six weeks. He could not bring his Royal soul to inflict pain. He yields at last; he is a martyr--to be pitied, not to be blamed. If he melts at his daughter's agony, he is a man and a father. There are men and fathers too in the much-maligned Orient.

Then comes the second act of the tragedy. The new hopes, the fond yearnings, the terrified misgivings, the timid belief, and weak confidence; the child that is born—and dies smiling prettily—and the mother's heart is rent so, that it can love, or hope, or suffer no more. Allah is God! She sleeps by the little fezzes. Hark! the guns are booming over the water, and His Highness is coming from his prayers.

After the murder of that little child, it seems to me one can never look with anything but horror upon the butcherly Herod who ordered it. The death of the seventy thousand Janissaries ascends to historic dignity, and takes rank as war. But a great Prince and Light of the Universe, who procures abortions and throttles little babies, dwindles away into such a frightful insignificance of crime, that those may respect him who will. I pity their Excellencies the Ambassadors, who are obliged to smirk and cringe to such a rascal. To do the Turks justice—and two days' walk in Constantinople will settle this fact as well as a year's residence in the city—the people do not seem in the least animated by this Herodian spirit. I never saw more kindness to children than among all classes, more fathers walking about with little solemn Mahometans in red caps and big trousers, more business going on than in the toy quarter, and in the Atmeidan. Although you may see there the Thebaic stone set up by the Emperor Theodosius, and the bronze column of serpents which Murray says was brought from Delphi, but which my guide informed me was the very one exhibited by Moses in the wilderness, yet I found the examination of these antiquities much less pleasant than to look at the many troops of children assembled on the plain to play; and to watch them as they were dragged about in little queer arobas, or painted carriages, which are there kept for hire. I have a picture of one of them now in my eyes: a little green oval machine, with flowers rudely painted round the window, out of which two smiling heads are peeping, the pictures of happiness. An old, good-humoured, grey-bearded Turk is tugging the cart; and behind it walks a lady in a yakmac and yellow slippers, and a black female slave, grinning as usual, towards whom the little coach-riders are looking. A small sturdy barefooted Mussulman is examining the cart with some feelings of envy: he is too poor to purchase a ride for himself and the round-faced puppy-dog, which he is hugging in his arms as young ladies in our country do dolls.

All the neighbourhood of the Atmeidan is exceedingly picturesque— the mosque court and cloister, where the Persians have their stalls of sweetmeats and tobacco; a superb sycamore-tree grows in the middle of this, overshadowing an aromatic fountain; great flocks of pigeons are settling in corners of the cloister, and barley is sold at the gates, with which the good-natured people feed them. From the Atmeidan you have a fine view of St. Sophia: and here stands a mosque which struck me as being much more picturesque and sumptuous—the Mosque of Sultan Achmed, with its six gleaming white minarets and its beautiful courts and trees. Any infidels may enter the court without molestation, and, looking through the barred windows of the mosque, have a view of its airy and spacious interior. A small audience of women was collected there when I looked in, squatted on the mats, and listening to a preacher, who was walking among them, and speaking with great energy. My dragoman interpreted to me the sense of a few words of his sermon: he was warning them of the danger of gadding about to public places, and of the immorality of too much talking; and, I dare say, we might have had more valuable information from him regarding the follies of womankind, had not a tall Turk clapped my interpreter on the shoulder, and pointed him to be off.

Although the ladies are veiled, and muffled with the ugliest dresses in the world, yet it appears their modesty is alarmed in spite of all the coverings which they wear. One day, in the bazaar, a fat old body, with diamond rings on her fingers, that were tinged with henne of a logwood colour, came to the shop where I was purchasing slippers, with her son, a young Aga of six years of age, dressed in a braided frock-coat, with a huge tassel to his fez, exceeding fat, and of a most solemn demeanour. The young Aga came for a pair of shoes, and his contortions were so delightful as he tried them, that I remained looking on with great pleasure, wishing for Leech to be at hand to sketch his lordship and his fat mamma, who sat on the counter. That lady fancied I was looking at her, though, as far as I could see, she had the figure and complexion of a roly-poly pudding; and so, with quite a premature bashfulness, she sent me a message by the shoemaker, ordering me to walk away if I had made my purchases, for that ladies of her rank did not choose to be stared at by strangers; and I was obliged to take my leave, though with sincere regret, for the little lord had just squeezed himself into an attitude than which I never saw anything more ludicrous in General Tom Thumb. When the ladies of the Seraglio come to that bazaar with their *cortège* of infernal black eunuchs, strangers are told to move on briskly. I saw a bevy of about eight of these, with their aides-de-camp; but they were wrapped up, and looked just as vulgar and ugly as the other women, and were not, I suppose, of the most beautiful sort. The poor devils are allowed to come out, half-a-dozen times in the year, to spend their little wretched allowance of pocket-money in purchasing trinkets and tobacco; all the rest of the time they pursue the beautiful duties of their existence in the walls of the sacred harem.

Though strangers are not allowed to see the interior of the cage in which these birds of Paradise are confined, yet many parts of the Seraglio are free to the curiosity of visitors, who choose to drop a backsheesh here and there. I landed one morning at the Seraglio point from Galata, close by an ancient pleasure-house of the defunct Sultan; a vast broad-brimmed pavilion, that looks agreeable enough to be a dancing room for ghosts now: there is another summer-house, the Guide-book cheerfully says, whither the Sultan goes to sport with his women and mutes. A regiment of infantry, with their music at their head, were marching to exercise in the outer grounds of the Seraglio; and we followed them, and had an opportunity of seeing their evolutions, and hearing their bands, upon a fine green plain under the Seraglio walls, where stands one solitary column, erected in memory of some triumph of some Byzantian emperor.

There were three battalions of the Turkish infantry, exercising here; and they seemed to perform their evolutions in a very satisfactory manner: that is, they fired all together, and charged and halted in very straight lines, and bit off imaginary cartridge-tops with great fierceness and regularity, and made all their ramrods ring to measure, just like so many Christians. The men looked small, young, clumsy, and ill-built; uncomfortable in their shabby European clothes; and about the legs, especially, seemed exceedingly weak and ill-formed. Some score of military invalids were lolling in the sunshine, about a fountain and a marble summer-house that stand on the ground, watching their comrades' manoeuvres (as if they could never have enough of that delightful pastime); and these sick were much better cared for than their healthy companions. Each man had two dressing-gowns, one of white cotton, and an outer wrapper of warm brown woollen. Their heads were accommodated with wadded cotton nightcaps; and it seemed to me, from their condition and from the excellent character of the military hospitals, that it would be much more wholesome to be ill than to be well in the Turkish service.

Facing this green esplanade, and the Bosphorus shining beyond it, rise the great walls of the outer Seraglio Gardens: huge masses of ancient masonry, over which peep the roofs of numerous kiosks and outhouses, amongst thick evergreens, planted so as to hide the beautiful frequenters of the place from the prying eyes and telescopes. We could not catch a glance of a single figure moving in these great pleasure-grounds. The road winds round the walls; and the outer park, which is likewise planted with trees, and diversified by garden-plots and cottages, had more the air of the outbuildings of a homely English park, than of a palace which we must all have imagined to be the most stately in the world. The most commonplace water-carts were passing here and there; roads were being repaired in the Macadamite manner; and carpenters were mending the park-palings, just as they do in Hampshire. The next thing you might fancy would be the Sultan walking out with a spud and a couple of dogs, on the way to meet the post-bag and the Saint James's Chronicle.

The palace is no palace at all. It is a great town of pavilions, built without order, here and there, according to the fancy of succeeding Lights of the Universe, or their favourites. The only row of domes which looked particularly regular or stately, were the kitchens. As you examined the buildings they had a ruinous dilapidated look: they are not furnished, it is said, with particular splendour,—not a bit more elegantly than Miss Jones's seminary for young ladies, which we may be sure is much more comfortable than the extensive establishment of His Highness Abdul Medjid.

In the little stable I thought to see some marks of Royal magnificence, and some horses worthy of the king of all kings. But the Sultan is said to be a very timid horseman: the animal that is always kept saddled for him did not look to be worth twenty pounds; and the rest of the horses in the shabby dirty stalls were small, ill-kept, common-looking brutes. You might see better, it seemed to me, at a country inn stable on any market-day.

The kitchens are the most sublime part of the Seraglio. There are nine of these great halls, for all ranks, from His Highness downwards, where many hecatombs are roasted daily, according to the accounts, and where cooking goes on with a savage Homeric grandeur. Chimneys are despised in these primitive halls; so that the roofs are black with the smoke of hundreds of furnaces, which escapes through apertures in the domes above. These, too, give the chief light in the rooms, which streams downwards, and thickens and mingles with the smoke, and so murkily lights up hundreds of swarthy figures busy about the spits and the cauldrons. Close to the door by which we entered they were making pastry for the sultanas; and the chief pastrycook, who knew my guide, invited us courteously to see the process, and partake of the delicacies prepared for those charming lips. How those sweet lips must shine after eating these puffs! First, huge sheets of dough are rolled out till the paste is about as thin as silver paper: then an artist forms the dough-muslin into a sort of drapery, curling it round and round in many fanciful and pretty shapes, until it is all got into the circumference of a round metal tray in which it is baked. Then the cake is drenched in grease most profusely; and, finally, a quantity of syrup is poured over it, when the delectable mixture is complete. The moon-faced ones are said to devour immense quantities of this wholesome food; and, in fact, are eating grease and sweetmeats from morning till night. I don't like to think what the consequences may be, or allude to the agonies which the delicate creatures must inevitably suffer.

The good-natured chief pastrycook filled a copper basin with greasy puffs; and, dipping a dubious ladle into a large cauldron, containing several gallons of syrup, poured a liberal portion over the cakes, and invited us to eat. One of the tarts was quite enough for me: and I excused myself on the plea of ill-health from imbibing any more grease and sugar. But my companion, the dragoman, finished some forty puffs in a twinkling. They slipped down his opened jaws as the sausages do down clowns' throats in a pantomime. His moustaches shone with grease, and it dripped down his beard and fingers. We thanked the smiling chief pastrycook, and rewarded him handsomely for the tarts. It is something to have eaten of the dainties prepared for the ladies of the harem; but I think Mr. Cockle ought to get the names of the chief sultanas among the exalted patrons of his antibilious pills.

From the kitchens we passed into the second court of the Seraglio, beyond which is death. The Guide-book only hints at the dangers which would befall a stranger caught prying in the mysterious *first* court of the palace. I have read "Bluebeard," and don't care for peeping into forbidden doors; so that the second court was quite enough for me; the pleasure of beholding it being heightened, as it were, by the notion of the invisible danger sitting next door, with uplifted scimitar ready to fall on you—present though not seen.

A cloister runs along one side of this court; opposite is the hall of the divan, "large but low, covered with lead, and gilt, after the Moorish manner, plain enough." The Grand Vizier sits in this place, and the ambassadors used to wait here, and be conducted hence on horseback, attired with robes of honour. But the ceremony is now, I believe, discontinued; the English envoy, at any rate, is not allowed to receive any backsheesh, and goes away as he came, in the habit of his own nation. On the right is a door leading into the interior of the Seraglio; *none pass through it but such as are sent for*, the Guide-book says: it is impossible to top the terror of that description.

About this door lads and servants were lolling, ichoglans and pages, with lazy looks and shabby dresses; and among them, sunning himself sulkily on a bench, a poor old fat, wrinkled, dismal white eunuch, with little fat white hands, and a great head sunk into his chest, and two sprawling little legs that seemed incapable to hold up his bloated old body. He squeaked out some surly reply to my friend the dragoman, who, softened and sweetened by the tarts he had just been devouring, was, no doubt, anxious to be polite: and the poor worthy fellow walked away rather crestfallen at this return of his salutation, and hastened me out of the place.

The palace of the Seraglio, the cloister with marble pillars, the hall of the ambassadors, the impenetrable gate guarded by eunuchs and ichoglans, have a romantic look in print; but not so in reality. Most of the marble is wood, almost all the gilding is faded, the guards are shabby, the foolish perspectives painted on the walls are half cracked off. The place looks like Vauxhall in the daytime.

We passed out of the second court under *the sublime porte*—which is like a fortified gate of a German town of the middle ages—into the outer court, round which are public offices, hospitals, and dwellings of the multifarious servants of the palace. This place is very wide and picturesque: there is a pretty church of Byzantine architecture at the further end; and in the midst of the court a magnificent plane-tree, of prodigious dimensions and fabulous age according to the guides; St. Sophia towers in the further distance: and from here, perhaps, is the best view of its light swelling domes and beautiful proportions. The Porte itself, too, forms an excellent subject for the sketcher, if the officers of the court will permit him to design it. I made the attempt, and a couple of Turkish beadles looked on very good-naturedly for some time at the progress of the drawing; but a good number of other spectators speedily joined them, and made a crowd, which is not permitted, it would seem, in the Seraglio; so I was told to pack up my portfolio, and remove the cause of the disturbance, and lost my drawing of the Ottoman Porte.

I don't think I have anything more to say about the city which has not been much better told by graver travellers. I, with them, could see (perhaps it was the preaching of the politicians that warned me of the fact) that we are looking on at the last days of an empire; and heard many stories of weakness, disorder, and oppression. I even saw a Turkish lady drive up to Sultan Achmet's mosque *in a brougham*. Is not that a subject to moralise upon? And might one not draw endless conclusions from it, that the knell of the Turkish dominion is rung; that the European spirit and institutions once admitted can never be rooted out again; and that the scepticism prevalent amongst the higher orders must descend ere very long to the lower; and the cry of the muezzin from the mosque become a mere ceremony?

But as I only stayed eight days in this place, and knew not a syllable of the language, perhaps it is as well to pretermit any disquisitions about the spirit of the people. I can only say that they looked to be very good-natured, handsome, and lazy; that the women's yellow slippers are very ugly; that the kabobs at the shop hard by the Rope Bazaar are very hot and good; and that at the Armenian cookshops they serve you delicious fish, and a stout raisin wine of no small merit. There came in, as we sat and dined there at sunset, a good old Turk, who called for a penny fish, and sat down under a tree very humbly, and ate it with his own bread. We made that jolly old Mussulman happy with a quart of the raisin wine; and his eyes twinkled with every fresh glass, and he wiped his old beard delighted, and talked and chirped a good deal, and, I dare say, told us the whole state of the empire. He was the only Mussulman with whom I attained any degree of intimacy during my stay in Constantinople; and you will see that, for obvious reasons, I cannot divulge the particulars of our conversation.

"You have nothing to say, and you own it," says somebody: "then why write?" That question perhaps (between ourselves) I have put likewise; and yet, my dear sir, there are *some* things worth remembering even in this brief letter: that woman in the brougham is an idea of significance: that comparison of the Seraglio to Vauxhall in the daytime is a true and real one; from both of which your own great soul and ingenious philosophic spirit may draw conclusions, that I myself have modestly forborne to press. You are too clever to require a moral to be tacked to all the fables you read, as is done for children in the spelling-books; else I would tell you that the government of the Ottoman Porte seems to be as rotten, as wrinkled, and as feeble as the old eunuch I saw crawling about it in the sun; that when the lady drove up in a brougham to Sultan Achmet, I felt that the schoolmaster was really abroad; and that the crescent will go out before that luminary, as meekly as the moon does before the sun.

CHAPTER VIII: RHODES

The sailing of a vessel direct for Jaffa brought a great number of passengers together, and our decks were covered with Christian, Jew, and Heathen. In the cabin we were Poles and Russians, Frenchmen, Germans, Spaniards, and Greeks; on the deck were squatted several little colonies of people of different race and persuasion. There was a Greek Papa, a noble figure with a flowing and venerable white beard, who had been living on bread-and-water for I don't know how many years, in order to save a little money to make the pilgrimage to Jerusalem. There were several families of Jewish Rabbis, who celebrated their "feast of tabernacles" on board; their chief men performing worship twice or thrice a day, dressed in their pontifical habits, and bound with phylacteries: and there were Turks, who had their own ceremonies and usages, and wisely kept aloof from their neighbours of Israel.

The dirt of these children of captivity exceeds all possibility of description; the profusion of stinks which they raised, the grease of their venerable garments and faces, the horrible messes cooked in the filthy pots, and devoured with the nasty fingers, the squalor of mats, pots, old bedding, and foul carpets of our Hebrew friends, could hardly be painted by Swift in his dirtiest mood, and cannot be, of course, attempted by my timid and genteel pen. What would they say in Baker Street to some sights with which our new friends favoured us? What would your ladyship have said if you had seen the interesting Greek nun combing her hair over the cabin—combing it with the natural fingers, and, averse to slaughter, flinging the delicate little intruders, which she found in the course of her investigation, gently into the great cabin? Our attention was a good deal occupied in watching the strange ways and customs of the various comrades of ours.

The Jews were refugees from Poland, going to lay their bones to rest in the valley of Jehoshaphat, and performing with exceeding rigour the offices of their religion. At morning and evening you were sure to see the chiefs of the families, arrayed in white robes, bowing over their books, at prayer. Once a week, on the eve before the Sabbath, there was a general washing in Jewry, which sufficed until the ensuing Friday. The men wore long gowns and caps of fur, or else broad-brimmed hats, or, in service time, bound on their heads little iron boxes, with the sacred name engraved on them. Among the lads there were some beautiful faces; and among the women your humble servant discovered one who was a perfect rosebud of beauty when first emerging from her Friday's toilet, and for a day or two afterwards, until each succeeding day's smut darkened those fresh and delicate cheeks of hers. We had some very rough weather in the course of the passage from Constantinople to Jaffa, and the sea washed over and over our Israelitish friends and their baggages and bundles; but though they were said to be rich, they would not afford to pay for cabin shelter. One father of a family, finding his progeny half drowned in a squall, vowed he *would* pay for a cabin; but the weather was somewhat finer the next day, and he could not squeeze out his dollars, and the ship's authorities would not admit him except upon payment.

This unwillingness to part with money is not only found amongst the followers of Moses, but in those of Mahomet, and Christians too. When we went to purchase in the bazaars, after offering money for change, the honest fellows would frequently keep back several piastres, and when urged to refund, would give most dismally: and begin doling out penny by penny, and utter pathetic prayers to their customer not to take any more. I bought five or six pounds' worth of Broussa silks for the womankind, in the bazaar at Constantinople, and the rich Armenian who sold them begged for three-halfpence to pay his boat to Galata. There is something naif and amusing in this exhibition of cheatery—this simple cringing and wheedling, and passion for twopence-halfpenny. It was pleasant to give a millionaire beggar an alms, and laugh in his face and say, "There, Dives, there's a penny for you: be happy, you poor old swindling scoundrel, as far as a penny goes." I used to watch these Jews on shore, and making bargains with one another as soon as they came on board; the battle between vendor and purchaser was an agony—they shrieked, clasped hands, appealed to one another passionately; their handsome noble faces assumed a look of woe— quite an heroic eagerness and sadness about a farthing.

Ambassadors from our Hebrews descended at Rhodes to buy provisions, and it was curious to see their dealings: there was our venerable Rabbi, who, robed in white and silver, and bending over his book at the morning service, looked like a patriarch, and whom I saw chaffering about a fowl with a brother Rhodian Israelite. How they fought over the body of that lean animal! The street swarmed with Jews: goggling eyes looked out from the old carved casements— hooked noses issued from the low antique doors—Jew boys driving donkeys, Hebrew mothers nursing children, dusky, tawdry, ragged young beauties and most venerable grey-bearded fathers were all gathered round about the affair of the hen! And at the same time that our Rabbi was arranging the price of it, his children were instructed to procure bundles of green branches to decorate the ship during their feast. Think of the centuries during which these wonderful people have remained unchanged; and how, from the days of Jacob downwards, they have believed and swindled!

The Rhodian Jews, with their genius for filth, have made their quarter of the noble desolate old town the most ruinous and wretched of all. The escutcheons of the proud old knights are still carved over the doors, whence issue these miserable greasy hucksters and pedlars. The Turks respected these emblems of the brave enemies whom they had overcome, and left them untouched. When the French seized Malta they were by no means so delicate: they effaced armorial bearings with their usual hot-headed eagerness; and a few years after they had torn down the coats-of-arms of the gentry, the heroes of Malta and Egypt were busy devising heraldry for themselves, and were wild to be barons and counts of the Empire.

The chivalrous relics at Rhodes are very superb. I know of no buildings whose stately and picturesque aspect seems to correspond better with one's notions of their proud founders. The towers and gates are warlike and strong, but beautiful and aristocratic: you see that they must have been high-bred gentlemen who built them. The edifices appear in almost as perfect a condition as when they were in the occupation of the noble Knights of St. John; and they have this advantage over modern fortifications, that they are a thousand times more picturesque. Ancient war condescended to ornament itself, and built fine carved castles and vaulted gates: whereas, to judge from Gibraltar and Malta, nothing can be less romantic than the modern military architecture; which sternly regards the fighting, without in the least heeding the war-paint. Some of the huge artillery with which the place was defended still lies in the bastions; and the touch-holes of the guns are preserved by being covered with rusty old corselets, worn by defenders of the fort three hundred years ago. The Turks, who battered down chivalry, seem to be waiting their turn of destruction now. In walking through Rhodes one is strangely affected by witnessing the signs of this double decay. For instance, in the streets of the knights, you see noble houses, surmounted by noble escutcheons of superb knights, who lived there, and prayed, and quarrelled, and murdered the Turks; and were the most gallant pirates of the inland seas; and made vows of chastity, and robbed and ravished; and, professing humility, would admit none but nobility into their order; and died recommending themselves to sweet St. John, and calmly hoping for heaven in consideration of all the heathen they had slain. When this superb fraternity was obliged to yield to courage as great as theirs, faith as sincere, and to robbers even more dexterous and audacious than the noblest knight who ever sang a canticle to the Virgin, these halls were filled by magnificent Pashas and Agas, who lived here in the intervals of war, and having conquered its best champions, despised Christendom and chivalry pretty much as an Englishman despises a Frenchman. Now the famous house is let to a shabby merchant, who has his little beggarly shop in the bazaar; to a small officer, who ekes out his wretched pension by swindling, and who gets his pay in bad coin. Mahometanism pays in pewter now, in place of silver and gold. The lords of the world have run to seed. The powerless old sword frightens nobody now—the steel is turned to pewter too, somehow, and will no longer shear a Christian head off any shoulders. In the Crusades my wicked sympathies have always been with the Turks. They seem to me the better Christians of the two: more humane, less brutally presumptuous about their own merits, and more generous in esteeming their neighbours. As far as I can get at the authentic story, Saladin is a pearl of refinement compared to the brutal beef-eating Richard—about whom Sir Walter Scott has led all the world astray.

When shall we have a real account of those times and heroes—no good-humoured pageant, like those of the Scott romances—but a real authentic story to instruct and frighten honest people of the present day, and make them thankful that the grocer governs the world now in place of the baron? Meanwhile a man of tender feelings may be pardoned for twaddling a little over this sad spectacle of the decay of two of the great institutions of the world. Knighthood is gone—amen; it expired with dignity, its face to the foe: and old Mahometanism is lingering about just ready to drop. But it is unseemly to see such a Grand Potentate in such a state of decay: the son of Bajazet Ilderim insolvent; the descendants of the Prophet bullied by Calmucs and English and whipper-snapper Frenchmen; the Fountain of Magnificence done up, and obliged to coin pewter! Think of the poor dear houris in Paradise, how sad they must look as the arrivals of the Faithful become less and less frequent every day. I can fancy the place beginning to wear the fatal Vauxhall look of the Seraglio, and which has pursued me ever since I saw it: the fountains of eternal wine are beginning to run rather dry, and of a questionable liquor; the ready-roasted-meat trees may cry, "Come eat me," every now and then, in a faint voice, without any gravy in it—but the Faithful begin to doubt about the quality of the victuals. Of nights you may see the houris sitting sadly under them, darning their faded muslins: Ali, Omar, and the Imaums are reconciled and have gloomy consultations: and the Chief of the Faithful himself, the awful camel-driver, the supernatural husband of Khadijah, sits alone in a tumbledown kiosk, thinking moodily of the destiny that is impending over him; and of the day when his gardens of bliss shall be as vacant as the bankrupt Olympus.

All the town of Rhodes has this appearance of decay and ruin, except a few consuls' houses planted on the sea-side, here and there, with bright flags flaunting in the sun; fresh paint; English crockery; shining mahogany, &c.,—so many emblems of the new prosperity of their trade, while the old inhabitants were going to rack—the fine Church of St. John, converted into a mosque, is a ruined church, with a ruined mosque inside; the fortifications are mouldering away, as much as time will let them. There was considerable bustle and stir about the little port; but it was the bustle of people who looked for the most part to be beggars; and I saw no shop in the bazaar that seemed to have the value of a pedlar's pack.

I took, by way of guide, a young fellow from Berlin, a journeyman shoemaker, who had just been making a tour in Syria, and who professed to speak both Arabic and Turkish quite fluently—which I thought he might have learned when he was a student at college, before he began his profession of shoemaking; but I found he only knew about three words of Turkish, which were produced on every occasion, as I walked under his guidance through the desolate streets of the noble old town. We went out upon the lines of fortification, through an ancient gate and guard-house, where once a chapel probably stood, and of which the roofs were richly carved and gilded. A ragged squad of Turkish soldiers lolled about the gate now; a couple of boys on a donkey; a grinning slave on a mule; a pair of women flapping along in yellow papooshes; a basket-maker sitting under an antique carved portal, and chanting or howling as he plaited his osiers: a peaceful well of water, at which knights' chargers had drunk, and at which the double-boyed donkey was now refreshing himself—would have made a pretty picture for a sentimental artist. As he sits, and endeavours to make a sketch of this plaintive little comedy, a shabby dignitary of the island comes clattering by on a thirty-shilling horse, and two or three of the ragged soldiers leave their pipes to salute him as he passes under the Gothic archway.

The astonishing brightness and clearness of the sky under which the island seemed to bask, struck me as surpassing anything I had seen--not even at Cadiz, or the Piraeus, had I seen sands so yellow, or water so magnificently blue. The houses of the people along the shore were but poor tenements, with humble courtyards and gardens; but every fig-tree was gilded and bright, as if it were in an Hesperian orchard; the palms, planted here and there, rose with a sort of halo of light round about them; the creepers on the walls quite dazzled with the brilliancy of their flowers and leaves; the people lay in the cool shadows, happy and idle, with handsome solemn faces; nobody seemed to be at work; they only talked a very little, as if idleness and silence were a condition of the delightful shining atmosphere in which they lived.

We went down to an old mosque by the sea-shore, with a cluster of ancient domes hard by it, blazing in the sunshine, and carved all over with names of Allah, and titles of old pirates and generals who reposed there. The guardian of the mosque sat in the garden-court, upon a high wooden pulpit, lazily wagging his body to and fro, and singing the praises of the Prophet gently through his nose, as the breeze stirred through the trees overhead, and cast chequered and changing shadows over the paved court, and the little fountains, and the nasal psalmist on his perch. On one side was the mosque, into which you could see, with its white walls and cool-matted floor, and quaint carved pulpit and ornaments, and nobody at prayers. In the middle distance rose up the noble towers and battlements of the knightly town, with the deep sea-line behind them.

It really seemed as if everybody was to have a sort of sober cheerfulness, and must yield to indolence under this charming atmosphere. I went into the courtyard by the sea-shore (where a few lazy ships were lying, with no one on board), and found it was the prison of the place. The door was as wide open as Westminster Hall. Some prisoners, one or two soldiers and functionaries, and some prisoners' wives, were lolling under an arcade by a fountain; other criminals were strolling about here and there, their chains clinking quite cheerfully; and they and the guards and officials came up chatting quite friendly together, and gazed languidly over the portfolio, as I was endeavouring to get the likeness of one or two of these comfortable malefactors. One old and wrinkled she-criminal, whom I had selected on account of the peculiar hideousness of her countenance, covered it up with a dirty cloth, at which there was a general roar of laughter among this good-humoured auditory of cut-throats, pickpockets, and policemen. The only symptom of a prison about the place was a door, across which a couple of sentinels were stretched, yawning; while within lay three freshly-caught pirates—chained by the leg. They had committed some murders of a very late date, and were awaiting sentence; but their wives were allowed to communicate freely with them: and it seemed to me that if half-a-dozen friends would set them flee, and they themselves had energy enough to move, the sentinels would be a great deal too lazy to walk after them.

The combined influence of Rhodes and Ramazan, I suppose, had taken possession of my friend the Schustergesell from Berlin. As soon as he received his fee, he cut me at once, and went and lay down by a fountain near the port, and ate grapes out of a dirty pocket-handkerchief. Other Christian idlers lay near him, dozing, or sprawling, in the boats, or listlessly munching water-melons. Along the coffee-houses of the quay sat hundreds more, with no better employment; and the captain of the "Iberia" and his officers, and several of the passengers in that famous steamship, were in this company, being idle with all their might. Two or three adventurous young men went off to see the valley where the dragon was killed; but others, more susceptible of the real influence of the island, I am sure would not have moved though we had been told that the Colossus himself was taking a walk half a mile off.

CHAPTER IX: THE WHITE SQUALL

On deck, beneath the awning,
I dozing lay and yawning;
It was the grey of dawning,
        Ere yet the sun arose;
And above the funnel's roaring,
And the fitful wind's deploring,
I heard the cabin snoring
        With universal nose.
I could hear the passengers snorting,
I envied their disporting:
Vainly I was courting
        The pleasure of a doze.

So I lay, and wondered why light
Came not, and watched the twilight
And the glimmer of the skylight,
        That shot across the deck;
And the binnacle pale and steady,
And the dull glimpse of the dead-eye,
And the sparks in fiery eddy,
        That whirled from the chimney neck:
In our jovial floating prison
There was sleep from fore to mizen,
And never a star had risen
        The hazy sky to speck.

Strange company we harboured;
We'd a hundred Jews to larboard,
Unwashed, uncombed, unbarbered,
        Jews black, and brown, and grey;
With terror it would seize ye,
And make your souls uneasy,
To see those Rabbis greasy,
        Who did nought but scratch and pray:
Their dirty children puking,
Their dirty saucepans cooking,
Their dirty fingers hooking
        Their swarming fleas away.

To starboard Turks and Greeks were,
Whiskered, and brown their cheeks were,
Enormous wide their breeks were,
Their pipes did puff alway;
Each on his mat allotted,
In silence smoked and squatted,
Whilst round their children trotted
In pretty, pleasant play.
He can't but smile who traces
The smiles on those brown faces,
And the pretty prattling graces
Of those small heathens gay.

And so the hours kept tolling,
And through the ocean rolling,
Went the brave "Iberia" bowling
Before the break of day—

When a *squall* upon a sudden
Came o'er the waters scudding;
And the clouds began to gather,
And the sea was lashed to lather,
And the lowering thunder grumbled,
And the lightning jumped and tumbled,
And the ship, and all the ocean,
Woke up in wild commotion.
Then the wind set up a howling,
And the poodle-dog a yowling,
And the cocks began a crowing,
And the old cow raised a lowing,
As she heard the tempest blowing;
And fowls and geese did cackle,
And the cordage and the tackle
Began to shriek and crackle;
And the spray dashed o'er the funnels,
And down the deck in runnels;
And the rushing water soaks all,
From the seamen in the fo'ksal

To the stokers, whose black faces
Peer out of their bed-places;
And the captain he was bawling,
And the sailors pulling, hauling;
And the quarter-deck tarpauling
Was shivered in the squalling;

And the passengers awaken,
Most pitifully shaken;
And the steward jumps up, and hastens
For the necessary basins.

Then the Greeks they groaned and quivered,
And they knelt, and moaned, and shivered,
As the plunging waters met them,
And splashed and overset them;
And they call in their emergence
Upon countless saints and virgins;
And their marrowbones are bended,
And they think the world is ended.

And the Turkish women for'ard
Were frightened and behorror'd;
And, shrieking and bewildering,
The mothers clutched their children;
The men sung, "Allah Illah!
Mashallah Bismillah!"
As the warring waters doused them,
And splashed them and soused them;
And they called upon the Prophet,
And thought but little of it.

Then all the fleas in Jewry
Jumped up and bit like fury;
And the progeny of Jacob
Did on the main-deck wake up
(I wot those greasy Rabbins
Would never pay for cabins);
And each man moaned and jabbered in
His filthy Jewish gaberdine,
In woe and lamentation,
And howling consternation.
And the splashing water drenches
Their dirty brats and wenches;
And they crawl from bales and benches,
In a hundred thousand stenches.

This was the White Squall famous
Which latterly o'ercame us,
And which all will well remember
On the 28th September:
When a Prussian Captain of Lancers

(Those tight-laced, whiskered prancers)
Came on the deck astonished,
By that wild squall admonished,
And wondering cried, "Potztausend!
Wie ist der Sturm jetzt brausend!"
And looked at Captain Lewis,
Who calmly stood and blew his
Cigar in all the bustle,
And scorned the tempest's tussle.
And oft we've thought thereafter
How he beat the storm to laughter;
For well he knew his vessel
With that vain wind could wrestle;
And when a wreck we thought her
And doomed ourselves to slaughter,
How gaily he fought her,
And through the hubbub brought her,
And, as the tempest caught her, Cried,
"*George! Some brandy-and-water*!"

And when, its force expended,
The harmless storm was ended,
And, as the sunrise splendid
Came blushing o'er the sea;
I thought, as day was breaking,
My little girls were waking,
And smiling, and making
A prayer at home for me.

CHAPTER X: TELMESSUS—BEYROUT

There should have been a poet in our company to describe that charming little bay of Glaucus, into which we entered on the 26th of September, in the first steam-boat that ever disturbed its beautiful waters. You can't put down in prose that delicious episode of natural poetry; it ought to be done in a symphony, full of sweet melodies and swelling harmonies; or sung in a strain of clear crystal iambics, such as Milnes knows how to write. A mere map, drawn in words, gives the mind no notion of that exquisite nature. What do mountains become in type, or rivers in Mr. Vizetelly's best brevier? Here lies the sweet bay, gleaming peaceful in the rosy sunshine: green islands dip here and there in its waters: purple mountains swell circling round it; and towards them, rising from the bay, stretches a rich green plain, fruitful with herbs and various foliage, in the midst of which the white houses twinkle. I can see a little minaret, and some spreading palm-trees; but, beyond these, the description would answer as well for Bantry Bay as for Makri. You could write so far, nay, much more particularly and grandly, without seeing the place at all, and after reading Beaufort's "Caramania," which gives you not the least notion of it.

Suppose the great Hydrographer of the Admiralty himself can't describe it, who surveyed the place; suppose Mr. Fellowes, who discovered it afterwards—suppose, I say, Sir John Fellowes, Knt., can't do it (and I defy any man of imagination to got an impression of Telmessus from his book)—can you, vain man, hope to try? The effect of the artist, as I take it, ought to be, to produce upon his hearer's mind, by his art, an effect something similar to that produced on his own by the sight of the natural object. Only music, or the best poetry, can do this. Keats's "Ode to the Grecian Urn" is the best description I know of that sweet old silent ruin of Telmessus. After you have once seen it, the remembrance remains with you, like a tune from Mozart, which he seems to have caught out of heaven, and which rings sweet harmony in your ears for ever after! It's a benefit for all after life! You have but to shut your eyes, and think, and recall it, and the delightful vision comes smiling back, to your order!—the divine air—the delicious little pageant, which nature set before you on this lucky day.

Here is the entry made in the note-book on the eventful day:—"In the morning steamed into the bay of Glaucus—landed at Makri—cheerful old desolate village—theatre by the beautiful sea-shore—great fertility, oleanders—a palm-tree in the midst of the village, spreading out like a Sultan's aigrette—sculptured caverns, or tombs, up the mountain—camels over the bridge."

Perhaps it is best for a man of fancy to make his own landscape out of these materials: to group the couched camels under the plane-trees; the little crowd of wandering ragged heathens come down to the calm water, to behold the nearing steamer; to fancy a mountain, in the sides of which some scores of tombs are rudely carved; pillars and porticos, and Doric entablatures. But it is of the little theatre that he must make the most beautiful picture—a charming little place of festival, lying out on the shore, and looking over the sweet bay and the swelling purple islands. No theatre-goer ever looked out on a fairer scene. It encourages poetry, idleness, delicious sensual reverie. O Jones! friend of my heart! would you not like to be a white-robed Greek, lolling languidly, on the cool benches here, and pouring compliments (in the Ionic dialect) into the rosy ears of Neæra? Instead of Jones, your name should be Ionides; instead of a silk hat, you should wear a chaplet of roses in your hair: you would not listen to the choruses they were singing on the stage, for the voice of the fair one would be whispering a rendezvous for the *mesonuktiais horais*, and my Ionides would have no ear for aught beside. Yonder, in the mountain, they would carve a Doric cave temple, to receive your urn when all was done; and you would be accompanied thither by a dirge of the surviving Ionidæ. The caves of the dead are empty now, however, and their place knows them not any more among the festal haunts of the living. But, by way of supplying the choric melodies sung here in old time, one of our companions mounted on the scene and spouted,

"My name is Norval."

On the same day we lay to for a while at another ruined theatre, that of Antiphilos. The Oxford men, fresh with recollections of the little-go, bounded away up the hill on which it lies to the ruin, measured the steps of the theatre, and calculated the width of the scene; while others, less active, watched them with telescopes from the ship's sides, as they plunged in and out of the stones and hollows.

Two days after the scene was quite changed. We were out of sight of the classical country, and lay in St. George's Bay, behind a huge mountain, upon which St. George fought the dragon, and rescued the lovely Lady Sabra, the King of Babylon's daughter. The Turkish fleet was lying about us, commanded by that Halil Pasha whose two children the two last Sultans murdered. The crimson flag, with the star and crescent, floated at the stern of his ship. Our diplomatist put on his uniform and cordons, and paid his Excellency a visit. He spoke in rapture, when he returned, of the beauty and order of the ship, and the urbanity of the infidel Admiral. He sent us bottles of ancient Cyprus wine to drink: and the captain of Her Majesty's ship "Trump," alongside which we were lying, confirmed that good opinion of the Capitan Pasha which the reception of the above present led us to entertain, by relating many instances of his friendliness and hospitalities. Captain G— said the Turkish ships were as well manned, as well kept, and as well manoeuvred, as any vessels in any service; and intimated a desire to command a Turkish seventy-four, and a perfect willingness to fight her against a French ship of the same size. But I heartily trust he will neither embrace the Mahometan opinions, nor be called upon to engage any seventy-four whatever. If he do, let us hope he will have his own men to fight with. If the crew of the "Trump" were all like the crew of the captain's boat, they need fear no two hundred and fifty men out of any country, with any Joinville at their head. We were carried on shore by this boat. For two years, during which the "Trump" had been lying off Beyrout, none of the men but these eight had ever set foot on shore. Mustn't it be a happy life? We were landed at the busy quay of Beyrout, flanked by the castle that the fighting old commodore half battered down.

Along the Beyrout quays civilisation flourishes under the flags of the consuls, which are streaming out over the yellow buildings in the clear air. Hither she brings from England her produce of marine-stores and woollens, her crockeries, her portable soups, and her bitter ale. Hither she has brought politeness, and the last modes from Paris. They were exhibited in the person of a pretty lady, superintending the great French store, and who, seeing a stranger sketching on the quay, sent forward a man with a chair to accommodate that artist, and greeted him with a bow and a smile, such as only can be found in France. Then she fell to talking with a young French officer with a beard, who was greatly smitten with her. They were making love just as they do on the Boulevard. An Arab porter left his bales, and the camel he was unloading, to come and look at the sketch. Two stumpy flat-faced Turkish soldiers, in red caps and white undresses, peered over the paper. A noble little Lebanonian girl, with a deep yellow face, and curly dun-coloured hair, and a blue tattooed chin, and for all clothing a little ragged shift of blue cloth, stood by like a little statue, holding her urn, and stared with wondering brown eyes. How magnificently blue the water was! —how bright the flags and buildings as they shone above it, and the lines of the rigging tossing in the bay! The white crests of the blue waves jumped and sparkled like quicksilver; the shadows were as broad and cool as the lights were brilliant and rosy; the battered old towers of the commodore looked quite cheerful in the delicious atmosphere; and the mountains beyond were of an amethyst colour. The French officer and the lady went on chattering quite happily about love, the last new bonnet, or the battle of Isly, or the "Juif Errant." How neatly her gown and sleeves fitted her pretty little person! We had not seen a woman for a month, except honest Mrs. Flanigan, the stewardess, and the ladies of our party, and the tips of the noses of the Constantinople beauties as they passed by leering from their yakmacs, waddling and plapping in their odious yellow papooshes.

And this day is to be marked with a second white stone, for having given the lucky writer of the present, occasion to behold a second beauty. This was a native Syrian damsel, who bore the sweet name of Mariam. So it was she stood as two of us (I mention the number for fear of scandal) took her picture.

So it was that the good-natured black cook looked behind her young mistress, with a benevolent grin, that only the admirable Leslie could paint.

Mariam was the sister of the young guide whom we hired to show us through the town, and to let us be cheated in the purchase of gilt scarfs and handkerchiefs, which strangers think proper to buy. And before the following authentic drawing could be made, many were the stratagems the wily artists were obliged to employ, to subdue the shyness of the little Mariam. In the first place, she would stand behind the door (from which in the darkness her beautiful black eyes gleamed out like penny tapers); nor could the entreaties of her brother and mamma bring her from that hiding-place. In order to conciliate the latter, we began by making a picture of her too— that is, not of her, who was an enormous old fat woman in yellow, quivering all over with strings of pearls, and necklaces of sequins, and other ornaments, the which descended from her neck, and down her ample stomacher: we did not depict that big old woman, who would have been frightened at an accurate representation of her own enormity; but an ideal being, all grace and beauty, dressed in her costume, and still simpering before me in my sketch-book like a lady in a book of fashions.

This portrait was shown to the old woman, who handed it over to the black cook, who, grinning, carried it to little Mariam—and the result was, that the young creature stepped forward, and submitted; and has come over to Europe as you see.

A very snug and happy family did this of Mariam's appear to be. If you could judge by all the laughter and giggling, by the splendour of the women's attire, by the neatness of the little house, prettily decorated with arabesque paintings, neat mats, and gay carpets, they were a family well to do in the Beyrout world, and lived with as much comfort as any Europeans. They had one book; and, on the wall of the principal apartment, a black picture of the Virgin, whose name is borne by pretty Mariam.

The camels and the soldiers, the bazaars and khans, the fountains and awnings, which chequer, with such delightful variety of light and shade, the alleys and markets of an Oriental town, are to be seen in Beyrout in perfection; and an artist might here employ himself for months with advantage and pleasure. A new costume was here added to the motley and picturesque assembly of dresses. This was the dress of the blue-veiled women from the Lebanon, stalking solemnly through the markets, with huge horns, near a yard high, on their foreheads. For thousands of years, since the time the Hebrew prophets wrote, these horns have so been exalted in the Lebanon.

At night Captain Lewis gave a splendid ball and supper to the "Trump." We had the "Trump's" band to perform the music; and a grand sight it was to see the captain himself enthusiastically leading on the drum. Blue lights and rockets were burned from the yards of our ship; which festive signals were answered presently from the "Trump," and from another English vessel in the harbour.

They must have struck the Capitan Pasha with wonder, for he sent his secretary on board of us to inquire what the fireworks meant. And the worthy Turk had scarcely put his foot on the deck, when he found himself seized round the waist by one of the "Trump's" officers, and whirling round the deck in a waltz, to his own amazement, and the huge delight of the company. His face of wonder and gravity, as he went on twirling, could not have been exceeded by that of a dancing dervish at Scutari; and the manner in which he managed to enjamber the waltz excited universal applause.

I forgot whether he accommodated himself to European ways so much further as to drink champagne at supper-time; to say that he did would be telling tales out of school, and might interfere with the future advancement of that jolly dancing Turk.

We made acquaintance with another of the Sultan's subjects, who, I fear, will have occasion to doubt of the honour of the English nation, after the foul treachery with which he was treated.

Among the occupiers of the little bazaar matchboxes, vendors of embroidered handkerchiefs and other articles of showy Eastern haberdashery, was a good-looking neat young fellow, who spoke English very fluently, and was particularly attentive to all the passengers on board our ship. This gentleman was not only a pocket-handkerchief merchant in the bazaar, but earned a further livelihood by letting out mules and donkeys; and he kept a small lodging-house, or inn, for travellers, as we were informed.

No wonder he spoke good English, and was exceedingly polite and well-bred; for the worthy man had passed some time in England, and in the best society too. That humble haberdasher at Beyrout had been a lion here, at the very best houses of the great people, and had actually made his appearance at Windsor, where he was received as a Syrian Prince, and treated with great hospitality by Royalty itself.

I don't know what waggish propensity moved one of the officers of the "Trump" to say that there was an equerry of His Royal Highness the Prince on board, and to point me out as the dignified personage in question. So the Syrian Prince was introduced to the Royal equerry, and a great many compliments passed between us. I even had the audacity to state that on my very last interview with my Royal master, His Royal Highness had said, "Colonel Titmarsh, when you go to Beyrout, you will make special inquiries regarding my interesting friend Cogia Hassan."

Poor Cogia Hassan (I forget whether that was his name, but it is as good as another) was overpowered with this Royal message; and we had an intimate conversation together, at which the waggish officer of the "Trump" assisted with the greatest glee.

But see the consequences of deceit! The next day, as we were getting under way, who should come on board but my friend the Syrian Prince, most eager for a last interview with the Windsor equerry; and he begged me to carry his protestations of unalterable fidelity to the gracious consort of Her Majesty. Nor was this all. Cogia Hassan actually produced a great box of sweetmeats, of which he begged my Excellency to accept, and a little figure of a doll dressed in the costume of Lebanon. Then the punishment of imposture began to be felt severely by me. How to accept the poor devil's sweetmeats? How to refuse them? And as we know that one fib leads to another, so I was obliged to support the first falsehood by another; and putting on a dignified air—"Cogia Hassan," says I, "I am surprised you don't know the habits of the British Court better, and are not aware that our gracious master solemnly forbids his servants to accept any sort of backsheesh upon our travels."

So Prince Cogia Hassan went over the side with his chest of sweetmeats, but insisted on leaving the doll, which may be worth twopence-halfpenny; of which, and of the costume of the women of Lebanon, the following is an accurate likeness:—[ii]

CHAPTER XI: A DAY AND NIGHT IN SYRIA

When, after being for five whole weeks at sea, with a general belief that at the end of a few days the marine malady leaves you for good, you find that a brisk wind and a heavy rolling swell create exactly the same inward effects which they occasioned at the very commencement of the voyage—you begin to fancy that you are unfairly dealt with: and I, for my part, had thought of complaining to the Company of this atrocious violation of the rules of their prospectus; but we were perpetually coming to anchor in various ports, at which intervals of peace and good-humour were restored to us.

On the 3rd of October our cable rushed with a huge rattle into the blue sea before Jaffa, at a distance of considerably more than a mile off the town, which lay before us very clear, with the flags of the consuls flaring in the bright sky and making a cheerful and hospitable show. The houses a great heap of sun-baked stones, surmounted here and there by minarets and countless little whitewashed domes; a few date-trees spread out their fan-like heads over these dull-looking buildings; long sands stretched away on either side, with low purple hills behind them; we could see specks of camels crawling over these yellow plains; and those persons who were about to land had the leisure to behold the sea-spray flashing over the sands, and over a heap of black rocks which lie before the entry to the town. The swell is very great, the passage between the rocks narrow, and the danger sometimes considerable. So the guide began to entertain the ladies and other passengers in the huge country boat which brought us from the steamer with an agreeable story of a lieutenant and eight seamen of one of Her Majesty's ships, who were upset, dashed to pieces, and drowned upon these rocks, through which two men and two boys, with a very moderate portion of clothing, each standing and pulling half an oar—there were but two oars between them, and another by way of rudder—were endeavouring to guide us.

When the danger of the rocks and surf was passed, came another danger of the hideous brutes in brown skins and the briefest shirts, who came towards the boat, straddling through the water with outstretched arms, grinning and yelling their Arab invitations to mount their shoulders. I think these fellows frightened the ladies still more than the rocks and the surf; but the poor creatures were obliged to submit; and, trembling, were accommodated somehow upon the mahogany backs of these ruffians, carried through the shallows, and flung up to a ledge before the city gate, where crowds more of dark people were swarming, howling after their fashion. The gentlemen, meanwhile, were having arguments about the eternal backsheesh with the roaring Arab boatmen; and I recall with wonder and delight especially, the curses and screams of one small and extremely loud-lunged fellow, who expressed discontent at receiving a five, instead of a six-piastre piece. But how is one to know, without possessing the language? Both coins are made of a greasy pewtery sort of tin; and I thought the biggest was the most valuable: but the fellow showed a sense of their value, and a disposition seemingly to cut any man's throat who did not understand it. Men's throats have been cut for a less difference before now.

Being cast upon the ledge, the first care of our gallantry was to look after the ladies, who were scared and astonished by the naked savage brutes, who were shouldering the poor things to and fro; and bearing them through these and a dark archway, we came into a street crammed with donkeys and their packs and drivers, and towering camels with leering eyes looking into the second-floor rooms, and huge splay feet, through which mesdames et mesdemoiselles were to be conducted. We made a rush at the first open door, and passed comfortably under the heels of some horses gathered under the arched court, and up a stone staircase, which turned out to be that of the Russian consul's house. His people welcomed us most cordially to his abode, and the ladies and the luggage (objects of our solicitude) were led up many stairs and across several terraces to a most comfortable little room, under a dome of its own, where the representative of Russia sat. Women with brown faces and draggle-tailed coats and turbans, and wondering eyes, and no stays, and blue beads and gold coins hanging round their necks, came to gaze, as they passed, upon the fair neat Englishwomen. Blowsy black cooks puffing over fires and the strangest pots and pans on the terraces, children paddling about in long striped robes, interrupted their sports or labours to come and stare; and the consul, in his cool domed chamber, with a lattice overlooking the sea, with clean mats, and pictures of the Emperor, the Virgin, and St. George, received the strangers with smiling courtesies, regaling the ladies with pomegranates and sugar, the gentlemen with pipes of tobacco, whereof the fragrant tubes were three yards long.

The Russian amenities concluded, we left the ladies still under the comfortable cool dome of the Russian consulate, and went to see our own representative. The streets of the little town are neither agreeable to horse nor foot travellers. Many of the streets are mere flights of rough steps, leading abruptly into private houses: you pass under archways and passages numberless; a steep dirty labyrinth of stone-vaulted stables and sheds occupies the ground-floor of the habitations; and you pass from flat to flat of the terraces; at various irregular corners of which, little chambers, with little private domes, are erected, and the people live seemingly as much upon the terrace as in the room.

We found the English consul in a queer little arched chamber, with a strange old picture of the King's arms to decorate one side of it: and here the consul, a demure old man, dressed in red flowing robes, with a feeble janissary bearing a shabby tin-mounted staff, or mace, to denote his office, received such of our nation as came to him for hospitality. He distributed pipes and coffee to all and every one; he made us a present of his house and all his beds for the night, and went himself to lie quietly on the terrace; and for all this hospitality he declined to receive any reward from us, and said he was but doing his duty in taking us in. This worthy man, I thought, must doubtless be very well paid by our Government for making such sacrifices; but it appears that he does not get one single farthing, and that the greater number of our Levant consuls are paid at a similar rate of easy remuneration. If we have bad consular agents, have we a right to complain? If the worthy gentlemen cheat occasionally, can we reasonably be angry? But in travelling through these countries, English people, who don't take into consideration the miserable poverty and scanty resources of their country, and are apt to brag and be proud of it, have their vanity hurt by seeing the representatives of every nation but their own well and decently maintained, and feel ashamed at sitting down under the shabby protection of our mean consular flag.

The active young men of our party had been on shore long before us, and seized upon all the available horses in the town; but we relied upon a letter from Halil Pasha, enjoining all governors and pashas to help us in all ways: and hearing we were the bearers of this document, the cadi and vice-governor of Jaffa came to wait upon the head of our party; declared that it was his delight and honour to set eyes upon us; that he would do everything in the world to serve us; that there were no horses, unluckily, but he would send and get some in three hours; and so left us with a world of grinning bows and many choice compliments from one side to the other, which came to each filtered through an obsequious interpreter. But hours passed, and the clatter of horses' hoofs was not heard. We had our dinner of eggs and flaps of bread, and the sunset gun fired: we had our pipes and coffee again, and the night fell. Is this man throwing dirt upon us? we began to think. Is he laughing at our beards, and are our mothers' graves ill-treated by this smiling swindling cadi? We determined to go and seek in his own den this shuffling dispenser of infidel justice. This time we would be no more bamboozled by compliments; but we would use the language of stern expostulation, and, being roused, would let the rascal hear the roar of the indignant British lion; so we rose up in our wrath. The poor consul got a lamp for us with a bit of wax-candle, such as I wonder his means could afford; the shabby janissary marched ahead with his tin mace; the two *laquais-de-place*, that two of our company had hired, stepped forward, each with an old sabre, and we went clattering and stumbling down the streets of the town, in order to seize upon this cadi in his own divan. I was glad, for my part (though outwardly majestic and indignant in demeanour), that the horses had not come, and that we had a chance of seeing this little queer glimpse of Oriental life, which the magistrate's faithlessness procured for us.

As piety forbids the Turks to eat during the weary daylight hours of the Ramazan, they spend their time profitably in sleeping until the welcome sunset, when the town wakens: all the lanterns are lighted up; all the pipes begin to puff, and the narghilés to bubble; all the sour-milk-and-sherbet-men begin to yell out the excellence of their wares; all the frying-pans in the little dirty cookshops begin to friz, and the pots to send forth a steam: and through this dingy, ragged, bustling, beggarly, cheerful scene, we began now to march towards the Bow Street of Jaffa. We bustled through a crowded narrow archway which led to the cadi's police-office, entered the little room, atrociously perfumed with musk, and passing by the rail-board, where the common sort stood, mounted the stage upon which his worship and friends sat, and squatted down on the divans in stern and silent dignity. His honour ordered us coffee, his countenance evidently showing considerable alarm. A black slave, whose duty seemed to be to prepare this beverage in a side-room with a furnace, prepared for each of us about a teaspoonful of the liquor: his worship's clerk, I presume, a tall Turk of a noble aspect, presented it to us; and having lapped up the little modicum of drink, the British lion began to speak.

All the other travellers (said the lion with perfect reason) have good horses and are gone; the Russians have got horses, the Spaniards have horses, the English have horses, but we, we vizirs in our country, coming with letters of Halil Pasha, are laughed at, spit upon! Are Halil Pasha's letters dirt, that you attend to them in this way? Are British lions dogs that you treat them so?—and so on. This speech with many variations was made on our side for a quarter of an hour; and we finally swore that unless the horses were forthcoming we would write to Halil Pasha the next morning, and to His Excellency the English Minister at the Sublime Porte. Then you should have heard the chorus of Turks in reply: a dozen voices rose up from the divan, shouting, screaming, ejaculating, expectorating (the Arabic spoken language seems to require a great employment of the two latter oratorical methods), and uttering what the meek interpreter did not translate to us, but what I dare say were by no means complimentary phrases towards us and our nation. Finally, the palaver concluded by the cadi declaring that by the will of Heaven horses should be forthcoming at three o'clock in the morning; and that if not, why, then, we might write to Halil Pasha.

This posed us, and we rose up and haughtily took leave. I should like to know that fellow's real opinion of us lions very much: and especially to have had the translation of the speeches of a huge-breeched turbaned roaring infidel, who looked and spoke as if he would have liked to fling us all into the sea, which was hoarsely murmuring under our windows an accompaniment to the concert within.

We then marched through the bazaars, that were lofty and grim, and pretty full of people. In a desolate broken building, some hundreds of children were playing and singing; in many corners sat parties over their water-pipes, one of whom every now and then would begin twanging out a most queer chant; others there were playing at casino—a crowd squatted around the squalling gamblers, and talking and looking on with eager interest. In one place of the bazaar we found a hundred people at least listening to a story-teller who delivered his tale with excellent action, voice, and volubility: in another they were playing a sort of thimble-rig with coffee-cups, all intent upon the game, and the player himself very wild lest one of our party, who had discovered where the pea lay, should tell the company. The devotion and energy with which all these pastimes were pursued, struck me as much as anything. These people have been playing thimble-rig and casino; that story-teller has been shouting his tale of Antar for forty years; and they are just as happy with this amusement now as when first they tried it. Is there no ennui in the Eastern countries, and are blue-devils not allowed to go abroad there?

From the bazaars we went to see the house of Mustapha, said to be the best house and the greatest man of Jaffa. But the great man had absconded suddenly, and had fled into Egypt. The Sultan had made a demand upon him for sixteen thousand purses, £80,000—Mustapha retired—the Sultan pounced down upon his house, and his goods, his horses and his mules. His harem was desolate. Mr. Milnes could have written six affecting poems, had he been with us, on the dark loneliness of that violated sanctuary. We passed from hall to hall, terrace to terrace—a few fellows were slumbering on the naked floors, and scarce turned as we went by them. We entered Mustapha's particular divan—there was the raised floor, but no bearded friends squatting away the night of Ramazan; there was the little coffee furnace, but where was the slave and the coffee and the glowing embers of the pipes? Mustapha's favourite passages from the Koran were still painted up on the walls, but nobody was the wiser for them. We walked over a sleeping negro, and opened the windows which looked into his gardens. The horses and donkeys, the camels and mules were picketed there below, but where is the said Mustapha? From the frying-pan of the Porte, has he not fallen into the fire of Mehemet Ali? And which is best, to broil or to fry? If it be but to read the "Arabian Nights" again on getting home, it is good to have made this little voyage and seen these strange places and faces.

Then we went out through the arched lowering gateway of the town into the plain beyond, and that was another famous and brilliant scene of the "Arabian Nights." The heaven shone with a marvellous brilliancy—the plain disappeared far in the haze—the towers and battlements of the town rose black against the sky—old outlandish trees rose up here and there—clumps of camels were couched in the rare herbage—dogs were baying about—groups of men lay sleeping under their haicks round about—round about the tall gates many lights were twinkling—and they brought us water-pipes and sherbet--and we wondered to think that London was only three weeks off.

Then came the night at the consul's. The poor demure old gentleman brought out his mattresses; and the ladies sleeping round on the divans, we lay down quite happy; and I for my part intended to make as delightful dreams as Alnaschar; but—lo, the delicate mosquito sounded his horn: the active flea jumped up, and came to feast on Christian flesh (the Eastern flea bites more bitterly than the most savage bug in Christendom), and the bug—oh, the accursed! Why was he made? What duty has that infamous ruffian to perform in the world, save to make people wretched? Only Bulwer in his most pathetic style could describe the miseries of that night—the moaning, the groaning, the cursing, the tumbling, the blistering, the infamous despair and degradation! I heard all the cocks in Jaffa crow; the children crying, and the mothers hushing them; the donkeys braying fitfully in the moonlight; at last I heard the clatter of hoofs below, and the hailing of men. It was three o'clock, the horses were actually come; nay, there were camels likewise; asses and mules, pack-saddles and drivers, all bustling together under the moonlight in the cheerful street—and the first night in Syria was over.

CHAPTER XII: FROM JAFFA TO JERUSALEM

It took an hour or more to get our little caravan into marching order, to accommodate all the packs to the horses, the horses to the riders; to see the ladies comfortably placed in their litter, with a sleek and large black mule fore and aft, a groom to each mule, and a tall and exceedingly good-natured and mahogany-coloured infidel to walk by the side of the carriage, to balance it as it swayed to and fro, and to offer his back as a step to the inmates whenever they were minded to ascend or alight. These three fellows, fasting through the Ramazan, and over as rough a road, for the greater part, as ever shook mortal bones, performed their fourteen hours' walk of near forty miles with the most admirable courage, alacrity, and good-humour. They once or twice drank water on the march, and so far infringed the rule; but they refused all bread or edible refreshment offered to them, and tugged on with an energy that the best camel, and I am sure the best Christian, might envy. What a lesson of good-humoured endurance it was to certain Pall Mall Sardanapaluses, who grumble if club sofa cushions are not soft enough!

If I could write sonnets at leisure, I would like to chronicle in fourteen lines my sensations on finding myself on a high Turkish saddle, with a pair of fire-shovel stirrups and worsted reins, red padded saddle-cloth, and innumerable tags, fringes, glass-beads, ends of rope, to decorate the harness of the horse, the gallant steed on which I was about to gallop into Syrian life. What a figure we cut in the moonlight, and how they would have stared in the Strand! Ay, or in Leicestershire, where I warrant such a horse and rider are not often visible! The shovel stirrups are deucedly short; the clumsy leathers cut the shins of some equestrians abominably; you sit over your horse as it were on a tower, from which the descent would be very easy, but for the big peak of the saddle. A good way for the inexperienced is to put a stick or umbrella across the saddle peak again, so that it is next to impossible to go over your horse's neck. I found this a vast comfort in going down the hills, and recommend it conscientiously to other dear simple brethren of the city.

Peaceful men, we did not ornament our girdles with pistols, yataghans, &c., such as some pilgrims appeared to bristle all over with; and as a lesson to such rash people, a story may be told which was narrated to us at Jerusalem, and carries a wholesome moral. The Honourable Hoggin Armer, who was lately travelling in the East, wore about his stomach two brace of pistols, of such exquisite finish and make, that a Sheikh, in the Jericho country, robbed him merely for the sake of the pistols. I don't know whether he has told the story to his friends at home.

Another story about Sheikhs may here be told *à propos*. That celebrated Irish Peer, Lord Oldgent (who was distinguished in the Buckinghamshire Dragoons), having paid a sort of black mail to the Sheikh of Jericho country, was suddenly set upon by another Sheikh, who claimed to be the real Jerichonian governor; and these twins quarrelled over the body of Lord Oldgent, as the widows for the innocent baby before Solomon. There was enough for both—but these digressions are interminable.

The party got under way at near four o'clock: the ladies in the litter, the French *femme-de-chambre* manfully caracoling on a grey horse; the cavaliers, like your humble servant, on their high saddles; the domestics, flunkeys, guides, and grooms, on all sorts of animals,—some fourteen in all. Add to these, two most grave and stately Arabs in white beards, white turbans, white haicks and raiments; sabres curling round their military thighs, and immense long guns at their backs. More venerable warriors I never saw; they went by the side of the litter soberly prancing. When we emerged from the steep clattering streets of the city into the grey plains, lighted by the moon and starlight, these militaries rode onward, leading the way through the huge avenues of strange diabolical-looking prickly pears (plants that look as if they had grown in Tartarus), by which the first mile or two of route from the city is bounded; and as the dawn arose before us, exhibiting first a streak of grey, then of green, then of red in the sky, it was fine to see these martial figures defined against the rising light. The sight of that little cavalcade, and of the nature around it, will always remain with me, I think, as one of the freshest and most delightful sensations I have enjoyed since the day I first saw Calais pier. It was full day when they gave their horses a drink at a large pretty Oriental fountain, and then presently we entered the open plain—the famous plain of Sharon—so fruitful in roses once, now hardly cultivated, but always beautiful and noble.

Here presently, in the distance, we saw another cavalcade pricking over the plain. Our two white warriors spread to the right and left, and galloped to reconnoitre. We, too, put our steeds to the canter, and handling our umbrellas as Richard did his lance against Saladin, went undaunted to challenge this caravan. The fact is, we could distinguish that it was formed of the party of our pious friends the Poles, and we hailed them with cheerful shouting, and presently the two caravans joined company, and scoured the plain at the rate of near four miles per hour. The horse-master, a courier of this company, rode three miles for our one. He was a broken-nosed Arab, with pistols, a sabre, a fusee, a yellow Damascus cloth flapping over his head, and his nose ornamented with diachylon. He rode a hog-necked grey Arab, bristling over with harness, and jumped, and whirled, and reared, and halted, to the admiration of all.

Scarce had the diachylonian Arab finished his evolutions, when lo! yet another cloud of dust was seen, and another party of armed and glittering horsemen appeared. They, too, were led by an Arab, who was followed by two janissaries, with silver maces shining in the sun. 'Twas the party of the new American Consul-General of Syria and Jerusalem, hastening to that city, with the inferior consuls of Ramleh and Jaffa to escort him. He expects to see the Millennium in three years, and has accepted the office of consul at Jerusalem, so as to be on the spot in readiness.

When the diachylon Arab saw the American Arab, he straightway galloped his steed towards him, took his pipe, which he delivered at his adversary in guise of a jereed, and galloped round and round, and in and out, and there and back again, as in a play of war. The American replied in a similar playful ferocity—the two warriors made a little tournament for us there on the plains before Jaffa, in the which diachylon, being a little worsted, challenged his adversary to a race, and fled away on his grey, the American following on his bay. Here poor sticking-plaster was again worsted, the Yankee contemptuously riding round him, and then declining further exercise.

What more could mortal man want? A troop of knights and paladins could have done no more. In no page of Walter Scott have I read a scene more fair and sparkling. The sober warriors of our escort did not join in the gambols of the young men. There they rode soberly, in their white turbans, by their ladies' litter, their long guns rising up behind them.

There was no lack of company along the road: donkeys numberless, camels by twos and threes; now a mule-driver, trudging along the road, chanting a most queer melody; now a lady, in white veil, black mask, and yellow papooshes, bestriding her ass, and followed by her husband,—met us on the way; and most people gave a salutation. Presently we saw Ramleh, in a smoking mist, on the plain before us, flanked to the right by a tall lonely tower, that might have held the bells of some *moutier* of Caen or Evreux. As we entered, about three hours and a half after starting, among the white domes and stone houses of the little town, we passed the place of tombs. Two women were sitting on one of them,—the one bending her head towards the stone, and rocking to and fro, and moaning out a very sweet pitiful lamentation. The American consul invited us to breakfast at the house of his subaltern, the hospitable one-eyed Armenian, who represents the United States at Jaffa. The stars and stripes were flaunting over his terraces, to which we ascended, leaving our horses to the care of a multitude of roaring ragged Arabs beneath, who took charge of and fed the animals, though I can't say in the least why; but, in the same way as getting off my horse on entering Jerusalem, I gave the rein into the hand of the first person near me, and have never heard of the worthy brute since. At the American consul's we were served first with rice soup in pishpash, flavoured with cinnamon and spice; then with boiled mutton, then with stewed ditto and tomatoes; then with fowls swimming in grease; then with brown ragouts belaboured with onions; then with a smoking pilaff of rice: several of which dishes I can pronounce to be of excellent material and flavour. When the gentry had concluded this repast, it was handed to a side table, where the commonalty speedily discussed it. We left them licking their fingers as we hastened away upon the second part of the ride.

And as we quitted Ramleh, the scenery lost that sweet and peaceful look which characterises the pretty plain we had traversed; and the sun, too, rising in the heaven, dissipated all those fresh beautiful tints in which God's world is clothed of early morning, and which city people have so seldom the chance of beholding. The plain over which we rode looked yellow and gloomy; the cultivation little or none; the land across the roadside fringed, for the most part, with straggling wild-carrot plants; a patch of green only here and there. We passed several herds of lean, small, well-conditioned cattle: many flocks of black goats, tended now and then by a ragged negro shepherd, his long gun slung over his back, his hand over his eyes to shade them as he stared at our little cavalcade. Most of the half-naked countryfolks we met had this dismal appendage to Eastern rustic life; and the weapon could hardly be one of mere defence, for, beyond the faded skull-cap, or tattered coat of blue or dirty white, the brawny, brown-chested, solemn-looking fellows had nothing seemingly to guard. As before, there was no lack of travellers on the road: more donkeys trotted by, looking sleek and strong; camels singly and by pairs, laden with a little humble ragged merchandise, on their way between the two towns. About noon we halted eagerly at a short distance from an Arab village and well, where all were glad of a drink of fresh water. A village of beavers, or a colony of ants, make habitations not unlike these dismal huts piled together on the plain here. There were no single huts along the whole line of road; poor and wretched as they are, the Fellahs huddle all together for protection from the other thieves their neighbours. The government (which we restored to them) has no power to protect them, and is only strong enough to rob them. The women, with their long blue gowns and ragged veils, came to and fro with pitchers on their heads. Rebecca had such an one when she brought drink to the lieutenant of Abraham. The boys came staring round, bawling after us with their fathers for the inevitable backsheesh. The village dogs barked round the flocks, as they were driven to water or pasture.

We saw a gloomy, not very lofty-looking ridge of hills in front of us; the highest of which the guide pointing out to us, told us that from it we should see Jerusalem. It looked very near, and we all set up a trot of enthusiasm to get into this hill country.

But that burst of enthusiasm (it may have carried us nearly a quarter of a mile in three minutes) was soon destined to be checked by the disagreeable nature of the country we had to traverse. Before we got to the real mountain district, we were in a manner prepared for it, by the mounting and descent of several lonely outlying hills, up and down which our rough stony track wound. Then we entered the hill district, and our path lay through the clattering bed of an ancient stream, whose brawling waters have rolled away into the past, along with the fierce and turbulent race who once inhabited these savage hills. There may have been cultivation here two thousand years ago. The mountains, or huge stony mounds environing this rough path, have level ridges all the way up to their summits; on these parallel ledges there is still some verdure and soil: when water flowed here, and the country was thronged with that extraordinary population, which, according to the Sacred Histories, was crowded into the region, these mountain steps may have been gardens and vineyards, such as we see now thriving along the hills of the Rhine. Now the district is quite deserted, and you ride among what seem to be so many petrified waterfalls. We saw no animals moving among the stony brakes; scarcely even a dozen little birds in the whole course of the ride. The sparrows are all at Jerusalem, among the housetops, where their ceaseless chirping and twittering forms the most cheerful sound of the place.

The company of Poles, the company of Oxford men, and the little American army, travelled too quick for our caravan, which was made to follow the slow progress of the ladies' litter, and we had to make the journey through the mountains in a very small number. Not one of our party had a single weapon more dreadful than an umbrella: and a couple of Arabs, wickedly inclined, might have brought us all to the halt, and rifled every carpet-bag and pocket belonging to us. Nor can I say that we journeyed without certain qualms of fear. When swarthy fellows, with girdles full of pistols and yataghans, passed us without unslinging their long guns—when scowling camel-riders, with awful long bending lances, decorated with tufts of rags, or savage plumes of scarlet feathers, went by without molestation—I think we were rather glad that they did not stop and parley: for, after all, a British lion with an umbrella is no match for an Arab with his infernal long gun. What, too, would have become of our women? So we tried to think that it was entirely out of anxiety for them that we were inclined to push on.

There is a shady resting-place and village in the midst of the mountain district where the travellers are accustomed to halt for an hour's repose and refreshment; and the other caravans were just quitting this spot, having enjoyed its cool shades and waters, when we came up. Should we stop? Regard for the ladies (of course no other earthly consideration) made us say, "No!" What admirable self-denial and chivalrous devotion! So our poor devils of mules and horses got no rest and no water, our panting litter-men no breathing time, and we staggered desperately after the procession ahead of us. It wound up the mountain in front of us: the Poles with their guns and attendants, the American with his janissaries; fifty or sixty all riding slowly like the procession in "Bluebeard."

But alas, they headed us very soon; when we got up the weary hill they were all out of sight. Perhaps thoughts of Fleet Street did cross the minds of some of us then, and a vague desire to see a few policemen. The district now seemed peopled, and with an ugly race. Savage personages peered at us out of huts, and grim holes in the rocks. The mules began to loiter most abominably—water the muleteers must have—and, behold, we came to a pleasant-looking village of trees standing on a hill; children were shaking figs from the trees—women were going about—before us was the mosque of a holy man—the village, looking like a collection of little forts, rose up on the hill to our right, with a long view of the fields and gardens stretching from it, and camels arriving with their burdens. Here we must stop; Paolo, the chief servant, knew the Sheikh of the village—he very good man—give him water and supper--water very good here—in fact we began to think of the propriety of halting here for the night, and making our entry into Jerusalem on the next day.

A man on a handsome horse dressed in red came prancing up to us, looking hard at the ladies in the litter, and passed away. Then two others sauntered up, one handsome, and dressed in red too, and he stared into the litter without ceremony, began to play with a little dog that lay there, asked if we were Inglees, and was answered by me in the affirmative. Paolo had brought the water, the most delicious draught in the world. The gentlefolks had had some, the poor muleteers were longing for it. The French maid, the courageous Victoire (never since the days of Joan of Arc has there surely been a more gallant and virtuous female of France) refused the drink; when suddenly a servant of the party scampers up to his master and says: "Abou Gosh says the ladies must get out and show themselves to the women of the village!"

It was Abou Gosh himself, the redoubted robber Sheikh about whom we had been laughing and crying "Wolf!" all day. Never was seen such a skurry! "March!" was the instant order given. When Victoire heard who it was and the message, you should have seen how she changed countenance; trembling for her virtue in the ferocious clutches of a Gosh. "*Un verre d'eau pour l'amour de Dieu*!" gasped she, and was ready to faint on her saddle. "*Ne buvez plus, Victoire*!" screamed a little fellow of our party. "Push on, push on!" cried one and all. "What's the matter?" exclaimed the ladies in the litter, as they saw themselves suddenly jogging on again. But we took care not to tell them what had been the designs of the redoubtable Abou Gosh. Away then we went—Victoire was saved—and her mistresses rescued from dangers they knew not of, until they were a long way out of the village.

Did he intend insult or good will? Did Victoire escape the odious chance of becoming Madame Abou Gosh? Or did the mountain chief simply propose to be hospitable after his fashion? I think the latter was his desire; if the former had been his wish, a half-dozen of his long guns could have been up with us in a minute, and had all our party at their mercy. But now, for the sake of the mere excitement, the incident was, I am sorry to say, rather a pleasant one than otherwise: especially for a traveller who is in the happy condition of being able to sing before robbers, as is the case with the writer of the present.

A little way out of the land of Goshen we came upon a long stretch of gardens and vineyards, slanting towards the setting sun, which illuminated numberless golden clusters of the most delicious grapes, of which we stopped and partook. Such grapes were never before tasted; water so fresh as that which a countryman fetched for us from a well never sluiced parched throats before. It was the ride, the sun, and above all Abou Gosh, who made that refreshment so sweet, and hereby I offer him my best thanks. Presently, in the midst of a most diabolical ravine, down which our horses went sliding, we heard the evening gun: it was fired from Jerusalem. The twilight is brief in this country, and in a few minutes the landscape was grey round about us, and the sky lighted up by a hundred thousand stars, which made the night beautiful.

Under this superb canopy we rode for a couple of hours to our journey's end. The mountains round about us dark, lonely, and sad; the landscape as we saw it at night (it is not more cheerful in the daytime), the most solemn and forlorn I have ever seen. The feelings of almost terror with which, riding through the night, we approached this awful place, the centre of the world's past and future history, have no need to be noted down here. The recollection of those sensations must remain with a man as long as his memory lasts; and he should think of them as often, perhaps, as he should talk of them little.

CHAPTER XIII: JERUSALEM

The ladies of our party found excellent quarters in readiness for them at the Greek convent in the city; where airy rooms, and plentiful meals, and wines and sweetmeats delicate and abundant, were provided to cheer them after the fatigues of their journey. I don't know whether the worthy fathers of the convent share in the good things which they lavish on their guests; but they look as if they do. Those whom we saw bore every sign of easy conscience and good living; there were a pair of strong, rosy, greasy, lazy lay-brothers, dawdling in the sun on the convent terrace, or peering over the parapet into the street below, whose looks gave one a notion of anything but asceticism.

In the principal room of the strangers' house (the lay traveller is not admitted to dwell in the sacred interior of the convent), and over the building, the Russian double-headed eagle is displayed. The place is under the patronage of the Emperor Nicholas; an Imperial Prince has stayed in these rooms; the Russian consul performs a great part in the city; and a considerable annual stipend is given by the Emperor towards the maintenance of the great establishment in Jerusalem. The Great Chapel of the Church of the Holy Sepulchre is by far the richest, in point of furniture, of all the places of worship under that roof. We were in Russia, when we came to visit our friends here; under the protection of the Father of the Church and the Imperial Eagle! This butcher and tyrant, who sits on his throne only through the crime of those who held it before him—every step in whose pedigree is stained by some horrible mark of murder, parricide, adultery—this padded and whiskered pontiff—who rules in his jack-boots over a system of spies and soldiers, of deceit, ignorance, dissoluteness, and brute force, such as surely the history of the world never told of before—has a tender interest in the welfare of his spiritual children: in the Eastern Church ranks after Divinity, and is worshipped by millions of men. A pious exemplar of Christianity truly! and of the condition to which its union with politics has brought it! Think of the rank to which he pretends, and gravely believes that he possesses, no doubt!—think of those who assumed the same ultra-sacred character before him!—and then of the Bible and the Founder of the Religion, of which the Emperor assumes to be the chief priest and defender!

We had some Poles of our party; but these poor fellows went to the Latin convent, declining to worship after the Emperor's fashion. The next night after our arrival, two of them passed in the Sepulchre. There we saw them, more than once on subsequent visits, kneeling in the Latin Church before the pictures, or marching solemnly with candles in processions, or lying flat on the stones, or passionately kissing the spots which their traditions have consecrated as the authentic places of the Saviour's sufferings. More honest or more civilised, or from opposition, the Latin fathers have long given up and disowned the disgusting mummery of the Eastern Fire—which lie the Greeks continue annually to tell.

Their travellers' house and convent, though large and commodious, are of a much poorer and shabbier condition than those of the Greeks. Both make believe not to take money; but the traveller is expected to pay in each. The Latin fathers enlarge their means by a little harmless trade in beads and crosses, and mother-of-pearl shells, on which figures of saints are engraved; and which they purchase from the manufacturers, and vend at a small profit. The English, until of late, used to be quartered in these sham inns; but last year two or three Maltese took houses for the reception of tourists, who can now be accommodated with cleanly and comfortable board, at a rate not too heavy for most pockets.

To one of these we went very gladly; giving our horses the bridle at the door, which went off of their own will to their stables, through the dark inextricable labyrinths of streets, archways, and alleys, which we had threaded after leaving the main street from the Jaffa Gate. There, there was still some life. Numbers of persons were collected at their doors, or smoking before the dingy coffee-houses, where singing and story-telling were going on; but out of this great street everything was silent, and no sign of a light from the windows of the low houses which we passed.

We ascended from a lower floor up to a terrace, on which were several little domed chambers, or pavilions. From this terrace, whence we looked in the morning, a great part of the city spread before us:-white domes upon domes, and terraces of the same character as our own. Here and there, from among these whitewashed mounds round about, a minaret rose, or a rare date-tree; but the chief part of the vegetation near was that odious tree the prickly pear,—one huge green wart growing out of another, armed with spikes, as inhospitable as the aloe, without shelter or beauty. To the right the Mosque of Omar rose; the rising sun behind it. Yonder steep tortuous lane before us, flanked by ruined walls on either side, has borne, time out of mind, the title of Via Dolorosa; and tradition has fixed the spots where the Saviour rested, bearing his cross to Calvary. But of the mountain, rising immediately in front of us, a few grey olive-trees speckling the yellow side here and there, there can be no question. That is the Mount of Olives. Bethany lies beyond it. The most sacred eyes that ever looked on this world have gazed on those ridges: it was there He used to walk and teach. With shame and humility one looks towards the spot where that inexpressible Love and Benevolence lived and breathed; where the great yearning heart of the Saviour interceded for all our race; and whence the bigots and traitors of his day led Him away to kill Him!

That company of Jews whom we had brought with us from Constantinople, and who had cursed every delay on the route, not from impatience to view the Holy City, but from rage at being obliged to purchase dear provisions for their maintenance on ship-board, made what bargains they best could at Jaffa, and journeyed to the Valley of Jehoshaphat at the cheapest rate. We saw the tall form of the old Polish Patriarch, venerable in filth, stalking among the stinking ruins of the Jewish quarter. The sly old Rabbi, in the greasy folding hat, who would not pay to shelter his children from the storm off Beyrout, greeted us in the bazaars; the younger Rabbis were furbished up with some smartness. We met them on Sunday at the kind of promenade by the walls of the Bethlehem Gate; they were in company of some red-bearded co-religionists, smartly attired in Eastern raiment; but their voice was the voice of the Jews of Berlin, and of course as we passed they were talking about so many hundert thaler. You may track one of the people, and be sure to hear mention of that silver calf that they worship.

The English mission has been very unsuccessful with these religionists. I don't believe the Episcopal apparatus—the chaplains, and the colleges, and the beadles—have succeeded in converting a dozen of them; and a sort of martyrdom is in store for the luckless Hebrews at Jerusalem who shall secede from their faith. Their old community spurn them with horror; and I heard of the case of one unfortunate man, whose wife, in spite of her husband's change of creed, being resolved, like a true woman, to cleave to him, was spirited away from him in his absence; was kept in privacy in the city, in spite of all exertions of the mission, of the consul and the bishop, and the chaplains and the beadles; was passed away from Jerusalem to Beyrout, and thence to Constantinople; and from Constantinople was whisked off into the Russian territories, where she still pines after her husband. May that unhappy convert find consolation away from her. I could not help thinking, as my informant, an excellent and accomplished gentleman of the mission, told me the story, that the Jews had done only what the Christians do under the same circumstances. The woman was the daughter of a most learned Rabbi, as I gathered. Suppose the daughter of the Rabbi of Exeter, or Canterbury, were to marry a man who turned Jew, would not her Right Reverend Father be justified in taking her out of the power of a person likely to hurl her soul to perdition? These poor converts should surely be sent away to England out of the way of persecution. We could not but feel a pity for them, as they sat there on their benches in the church conspicuous; and thought of the scorn and contumely which attended them without, as they passed, in their European dresses and shaven beards, among their grisly, scowling, long-robed countrymen.

As elsewhere in the towns I have seen, the Ghetto of Jerusalem is pre-eminent in filth. The people are gathered round about the dung-gate of the city. Of a Friday you may hear their wailings and lamentations for the lost glories of their city. I think the Valley of Jehoshaphat is the most ghastly sight I have seen in the world. From all quarters they come hither to bury their dead. When his time is come yonder hoary old miser, with whom we made our voyage, will lay his carcase to rest here. To do that, and to claw together money, has been the purpose of that strange long life.

We brought with us one of the gentlemen of the mission, a Hebrew convert, the Rev. Mr. E-; and lest I should be supposed to speak with disrespect above of any of the converts of the Hebrew faith, let me mention this gentleman as the only one whom I had the fortune to meet on terms of intimacy. I never saw a man whose outward conduct was more touching, whose sincerity was more evident, and whose religious feeling seemed more deep, real, and reasonable.

Only a few feet off, the walls of the Anglican Church of Jerusalem rise up from their foundations on a picturesque open spot, in front of the Bethlehem Gate. The English Bishop has his church hard by: and near it is the house where the Christians of our denomination assemble and worship.

There seem to be polyglot services here. I saw books of prayer, or Scripture, in Hebrew, Greek, and German: in which latter language Dr. Alexander preaches every Sunday. A gentleman who sat near me at church used all these books indifferently; reading the first lesson from the Hebrew book, and the second from the Greek. Here we all assembled on the Sunday after our arrival: it was affecting to hear the music and language of our country sounding in this distant place; to have the decent and manly ceremonial of our service; the prayers delivered in that noble language. Even that stout anti-prelatist, the American consul, who has left his house and fortune in America in order to witness the coming of the Millennium, who believes it to be so near that he has brought a dove with him from his native land (which bird he solemnly informed us was to survive the expected Advent), was affected by the good old words and service. He swayed about and moaned in his place at various passages; during the sermon he gave especial marks of sympathy and approbation. I never heard the service more excellently and impressively read than by the Bishop's chaplain, Mr. Veitch. But it was the music that was most touching I thought,—the sweet old songs of home.

There was a considerable company assembled: near a hundred people I should think. Our party made a large addition to the usual congregation. The Bishop's family is proverbially numerous: the consul, and the gentlemen of the mission, have wives, and children, and English establishments. These, and the strangers, occupied places down the room, to the right and left of the desk and communion-table. The converts, and the members of the college, in rather a scanty number, faced the officiating clergyman; before whom the silver maces of the janissaries were set up, as they set up the beadles' maces in England.

I made many walks round the city to Olivet and Bethany, to the tombs of the kings, and the fountains sacred in story. These are green and fresh, but all the rest of the landscape seemed to me to be *frightful*. Parched mountains, with a grey bleak olive-tree trembling here and there; savage ravines and valleys, paved with tombstones—a landscape unspeakably ghastly and desolate, meet the eye wherever you wander round about the city. The place seems quite adapted to the events which are recorded in the Hebrew histories. It and they, as it seems to me, can never be regarded without terror. Fear and blood, crime and punishment, follow from page to page in frightful succession. There is not a spot at which you look, but some violent deed has been done there: some massacre has been committed, some victim has been murdered, some idol has been worshipped with bloody and dreadful rites. Not far from hence is the place where the Jewish conqueror fought for the possession of Jerusalem. "The sun stood still, and hasted not to go down about a whole day;" so that the Jews might have daylight to destroy the Amorites, whose iniquities were full, and whose land they were about to occupy. The fugitive heathen king, and his allies, were discovered in their hiding-place, and hanged: "and the children of Judah smote Jerusalem with the edge of the sword, and set the city on fire; and they left none remaining, but utterly destroyed all that breathed."

I went out at the Zion Gate, and looked at the so-called tomb of David. I had been reading all the morning in the Psalms, and his history in Samuel and Kings. "Bring thou down Shimei's hoar head to the grave with blood," are the last words of the dying monarch as recorded by the history. What they call the tomb is now a crumbling old mosque; from which Jew and Christian are excluded alike. As I saw it, blazing in the sunshine, with the purple sky behind it, the glare only served to mark the surrounding desolation more clearly. The lonely walls and towers of the city rose hard by. Dreary mountains, and declivities of naked stones, were round about: they are burrowed with holes in which Christian hermits lived and died. You see one green place far down in the valley: it is called En Rogel. Adonijah feasted there, who was killed by his brother Solomon, for asking for Abishag for wife. The Valley of Hinnom skirts the hill: the dismal ravine was a fruitful garden once. Ahaz, and the idolatrous kings, sacrificed to idols under the green trees there, and "caused their children to pass through the fire." On the mountain opposite, Solomon, with the thousand women of his harem, worshipped the gods of all their nations, "Ashtoreth," and "Milcom, and Molech, the abomination of the Ammonites." An enormous charnel-house stands on the hill where the bodies of dead pilgrims used to be thrown; and common belief has fixed upon this spot as the Aceldama, which Judas purchased with the price of his treason. Thus you go on from one gloomy place to another, each seared with its bloody tradition. Yonder is the Temple, and you think of Titus's soldiery storming its flaming porches, and entering the city, in the savage defence of which two million human souls perished. It was on Mount Zion that Godfrey and Tancred had their camp: when the Crusaders entered the mosque, they rode knee-deep in the blood of its defenders, and of the women and children who had fled thither for refuge: it was the victory of Joshua over again. Then, after three days of butchery, they purified the desecrated mosque and went to prayer. In the centre of this history of crime rises up the Great Murder of all...

I need say no more about this gloomy landscape. After a man has seen it once, he never forgets it—the recollection of it seems to me to follow him like a remorse, as it were to implicate him in the awful deed which was done there. Oh! with what unspeakable shame and terror should one think of that crime, and prostrate himself before the image of that Divine Blessed Sufferer!

Of course the first visit of the traveller is to the famous Church of the Sepulchre.

In the archway, leading from the street to the court and church, there is a little bazaar of Bethlehemites, who must interfere considerably with the commerce of the Latin fathers. These men bawl to you from their stalls, and hold up for your purchase their devotional baubles,—bushels of rosaries and scented beads, and carved mother-of-pearl shells, and rude stone salt-cellars and figures. Now that inns are established—envoys of these pedlars attend them on the arrival of strangers, squat all day on the terraces before your door, and patiently entreat you to buy of their goods. Some worthies there are who drive a good trade by tattooing pilgrims with the five crosses, the arms of Jerusalem; under which the name of the city is punctured in Hebrew, with the auspicious year of the Hadji's visit. Several of our fellow-travellers submitted to this queer operation, and will carry to their grave this relic of their journey. Some of them had engaged as servant a man at Beyrout, who had served as a lad on board an English ship in the Mediterranean. Above his tattooage of the five crosses, the fellow had a picture of two hearts united, and the pathetic motto, "Betsy my dear." He had parted with Betsy my dear five years before at Malta. He had known a little English there, but had forgotten it. Betsy my dear was forgotten too. Only her name remained engraved with a vain simulacrum of constancy on the faithless rogue's skin: on which was now printed another token of equally effectual devotion. The beads and the tattooing, however, seem essential ceremonies attendant on the Christian pilgrim's visit; for many hundreds of years, doubtless, the palmers have carried off with them these simple reminiscences of the sacred city. That symbol has been engraven upon the arms of how many Princes, Knights, and Crusaders! Don't you see a moral as applicable to them as to the swindling Beyrout horseboy? I have brought you back that cheap and wholesome apologue, in lieu of any of the Bethlehemite shells and beads.

After passing through the porch of the pedlars, you come to the courtyard in front of the noble old towers of the Church of the Sepulchre, with pointed arches and Gothic traceries, rude, but rich and picturesque in design. Here crowds are waiting in the sun, until it shall please the Turkish guardians of the church-door to open. A swarm of beggars sit here permanently: old tattered hags with long veils, ragged children, blind old bearded beggars, who raise up a chorus of prayers for money, holding out their wooden bowls, or clattering with their sticks on the stones, or pulling your coat-skirts and moaning and whining; yonder sit a group of coal-black Coptish pilgrims, with robes and turbans of dark blue, fumbling their perpetual beads. A party of Arab Christians have come up from their tents or villages: the men half-naked, looking as if they were beggars, or banditti, upon occasion; the women have flung their head-cloths back, and are looking at the strangers under their tattooed eyebrows. As for the strangers, there is no need to describe *them*: that figure of the Englishman, with his hands in his pockets, has been seen all the world over: staring down the crater of Vesuvius, or into a Hottentot kraal—or at a pyramid, or a Parisian coffee-house, or an Esquimaux hut—with the same insolent calmness of demeanour. When the gates of the church are open, he elbows in among the first, and flings a few scornful piastres to the Turkish door-keeper; and gazes round easily at the place, in which people of every other nation in the world are in tears, or in rapture, or wonder. He has never seen the place until now, and looks as indifferent as the Turkish guardian who sits in the doorway, and swears at the people as they pour in.

Indeed, I believe it is impossible for us to comprehend the source and nature of the Roman Catholic devotion. I once went into a church at Rome at the request of a Catholic friend, who described the interior to be so beautiful and glorious, that he thought (he said) it must be like heaven itself. I found walls hung with cheap stripes of pink and white calico, altars covered with artificial flowers, a number of wax candles, and plenty of gilt-paper ornaments. The place seemed to me like a shabby theatre; and here was my friend on his knees at my side, plunged in a rapture of wonder and devotion.

I could get no better impression out of this the most famous church in the world. The deceits are too open and flagrant; the inconsistencies and contrivances too monstrous. It is hard even to sympathise with persons who receive them as genuine; and though (as I know and saw in the case of my friend at Rome) the believer's life may be passed in the purest exercise of faith and charity, it is difficult even to give him credit for honesty, so barefaced seem the impostures which he professes to believe and reverence. It costs one no small effort even to admit the possibility of a Catholic's credulity: to share in his rapture and devotion is still further out of your power; and I could get from this church no other emotions but those of shame and pain.

The legends with which the Greeks and Latins have garnished the spot have no more sacredness for you than the hideous, unreal, barbaric pictures and ornaments which they have lavished on it. Look at the fervour with which pilgrims kiss and weep over a tawdry Gothic painting, scarcely better fashioned than an idol in a South Sea Morai. The histories which they are called upon to reverence are of the same period and order,—savage Gothic caricatures. In either a saint appears in the costume of the middle ages, and is made to accommodate himself to the fashion of the tenth century.

The different churches battle for the possession of the various relics. The Greeks show you the Tomb of Melchisedec, while the Armenians possess the Chapel of the Penitent Thief; the poor Copts (with their little cabin of a chapel) can yet boast of possessing the thicket in which Abraham caught the Ram, which was to serve as the vicar of Isaac; the Latins point out the Pillar to which the Lord was bound. The place of the Invention of the Sacred Cross, the Fissure in the Rock of Golgotha, the Tomb of Adam himself—are all here within a few yards' space. You mount a few steps, and are told it is Calvary upon which you stand. All this in the midst of blaring candles, reeking incense, savage pictures of Scripture story, or portraits of kings who have been benefactors to the various chapels; a din and clatter of strange people,—these weeping, bowing, kissing,—those utterly indifferent; and the priests clad in outlandish robes, snuffling and chanting incomprehensible litanies, robing, disrobing, lighting up candles or extinguishing them, advancing, retreating, bowing with all sorts of unfamiliar genuflexions. Had it pleased the inventors of the Sepulchre topography to have fixed on fifty more spots of ground as the places of the events of the sacred story, the pilgrim would have believed just as now. The priest's authority has so mastered his faith, that it accommodates itself to any demand upon it; and the English stranger looks on the scene, for the first time, with a feeling of scorn, bewilderment, and shame at that grovelling credulity, those strange rites and ceremonies, that almost confessed imposture.

Jarred and distracted by these, the Church of the Holy Sepulchre, for some time, seems to an Englishman the least sacred spot about Jerusalem. It is the lies, and the legends, and the priests, and their quarrels, and their ceremonies, which keep the Holy Place out of sight. A man has not leisure to view it, for the brawling of the guardians of the spot. The Roman conquerors, they say, raised up a statue of Venus in this sacred place, intending to destroy all memory of it. I don't think the heathen was as criminal as the Christian is now. To deny and disbelieve, is not so bad as to make belief a ground to cheat upon. The liar Ananias perished for that; and yet out of these gates, where angels may have kept watch—out of the tomb of Christ—Christian priests issue with a lie in their hands. What a place to choose for imposture, good God! to sully with brutal struggles for self-aggrandisement or shameful schemes of gain!

The situation of the Tomb (into which, be it authentic or not, no man can enter without a shock of breathless fear, and deep and awful self-humiliation) must have struck all travellers. It stands in the centre of the arched rotunda, which is common to all denominations, and from which branch off the various chapels belonging to each particular sect. In the Coptic chapel I saw one coal-black Copt, in blue robes, cowering in the little cabin, surrounded by dingy lamps, barbarous pictures, and cheap faded trumpery. In the Latin Church there was no service going on, only two fathers dusting the mouldy gewgaws along the brown walls, and laughing to one another. The gorgeous church of the Fire impostors, hard by, was always more fully attended; as was that of their wealthy neighbours, the Armenians. These three main sects hate each other; their quarrels are interminable; each bribes and intrigues with the heathen lords of the soil, to the prejudice of his neighbour. Now it is the Latins who interfere, and allow the common church to go to ruin, because the Greeks purpose to roof it; now the Greeks demolish a monastery on Mount Olivet, and leave the ground to the Turks, rather than allow the Armenians to possess it. On another occasion, the Greeks having mended the Armenian steps which lead to the (so-called) Cave of the Nativity at Bethlehem, the latter asked for permission to destroy the work of the Greeks, and did so. And so round this sacred spot, the centre of Christendom, the representatives of the three great sects worship under one roof, and hate each other!

Above the Tomb of the Saviour, the cupola is *open*, and you see the blue sky overhead. Which of the builders was it that had the grace to leave that under the high protection of Heaven, and not confine it under the mouldering old domes and roofs, which cover so much selfishness, and uncharitableness, and imposture?

We went to Bethlehem, too; and saw the apocryphal wonders there.

Five miles' ride brings you from Jerusalem to it, over naked wavy hills; the aspect of which, however, grows more cheerful as you approach the famous village. We passed the Convent of Mar Elyas on the road, walled and barred like a fort. In spite of its strength, however, it has more than once been stormed by the Arabs, and the luckless fathers within put to death. Hard by was Rebecca's Well: a dead body was lying there, and crowds of male and female mourners dancing and howling round it. Now and then a little troop of savage scowling horsemen—a shepherd driving his black sheep, his gun over his shoulder—a troop of camels—or of women, with long blue robes and white veils, bearing pitchers, and staring at the strangers with their great solemn eyes—or a company of labourers, with their donkeys, bearing grain or grapes to the city,—met us and enlivened the little ride. It was a busy and cheerful scene. The Church of the Nativity, with the adjoining convents, forms a vast and noble Christian structure. A party of travellers were going to the Jordan that day, and scores of their followers—of the robbing Arabs, who profess to protect them (magnificent figures some of them, with flowing haicks and turbans, with long guns and scimitars, and wretched horses, covered with gaudy trappings), were standing on the broad pavement before the little convent gate. It was such a scene as Cattermole might paint. Knights and Crusaders may have witnessed a similar one. You could fancy them issuing out of the narrow little portal, and so greeted by the swarms of swarthy clamorous women and merchants and children.

The scene within the building was of the same Gothic character. We were entertained by the Superior of the Greek Convent, in a fine refectory, with ceremonies and hospitalities that pilgrims of the middle ages might have witnessed. We were shown over the magnificent Barbaric Church, visited of course the Grotto where the Blessed Nativity is said to have taken place, and the rest of the idols set up for worship by the clumsy legend. When the visit was concluded, the party going to the Dead Sea filed off with their armed attendants; each individual traveller making as brave a show as he could, and personally accoutred with warlike swords and pistols. The picturesque crowds, and the Arabs and the horsemen, in the sunshine; the noble old convent, and the grey-bearded priests, with their feast; and the church, and its pictures and columns, and incense; the wide brown hills spreading round the village; with the accidents of the road,—flocks and shepherds, wells and funerals, and camel-trains,—have left on my mind a brilliant, romantic, and cheerful picture. But you, dear M—, without visiting the place, have imagined one far finer; and Bethlehem, where the Holy Child was born, and the angels sang, "Glory to God in the highest, and on earth peace and goodwill towards men," is the most sacred and beautiful spot in the earth to you.

By far the most comfortable quarters in Jerusalem are those of the Armenians, in their convent of St. James. Wherever we have been, these Eastern quakers look grave, and jolly, and sleek. Their convent at Mount Zion is big enough to contain two or three thousand of their faithful; and their church is ornamented by the most rich and hideous gifts ever devised by uncouth piety. Instead of a bell, the fat monks of the convent beat huge noises on a board, and drub the faithful in to prayers. I never saw men more lazy and rosy than these reverend fathers, kneeling in their comfortable matted church, or sitting in easy devotion. Pictures, images, gilding, tinsel, wax candles, twinkle all over the place; and ten thousand ostrichs' eggs (or any lesser number you may allot) dangle from the vaulted ceiling. There were great numbers of people at worship in this gorgeous church: they went on their knees, kissing the walls with much fervour, and paying reverence to the most precious relic of the convent,—the chair of St. James, their patron, the first Bishop of Jerusalem.

The chair pointed out with greatest pride in the church of the Latin Convent, is that shabby red damask one appropriated to the French Consul,—the representative of the King of that nation,—and the protection which it has from time immemorial accorded to the Christians of the Latin rite in Syria. All French writers and travellers speak of this protection with delightful complacency. Consult the French books of travel on the subject, and any Frenchman whom you may meet: he says, "*La France, Monsieur, de tous les temps protège les Chrêtiens d'Orient*;" and the little fellow looks round the church with a sweep of the arm, and protects it accordingly. It is *bon ton* for them to go in processions; and you see them on such errands, marching with long candles, as gravely as may be. But I have never been able to edify myself with their devotion; and the religious outpourings of Lamartine and Chateaubriand, which we have all been reading *à propos* of the journey we are to make, have inspired me with an emotion anything but respectful. "*Voyez comme M. de Chateaubriand prie Dieu*," the Viscount's eloquence seems always to say. There is a sanctified grimace about the little French pilgrim which it is very difficult to contemplate gravely.

The pictures, images, and ornaments of the principal Latin convent are quite mean and poor, compared to the wealth of the Armenians. The convent is spacious, but squalid. Many hopping and crawling plagues are said to attack the skins of pilgrims who sleep there. It is laid out in courts and galleries, the mouldy doors of which are decorated with twopenny pictures of favourite saints and martyrs; and so great is the shabbiness and laziness, that you might fancy yourself in a convent in Italy. Brown-clad fathers, dirty, bearded, and sallow, go gliding about the corridors. The relic manufactory before mentioned carries on a considerable business, and despatches bales of shells, crosses, and beads to believers in Europe. These constitute the chief revenue of the convent now. La France is no longer the most Christian kingdom, and her protection of the Latins is not good for much since Charles X. was expelled; and Spain, which used likewise to be generous on occasions (the gifts, arms, candlesticks, baldaquins of the Spanish sovereigns figure pretty frequently in the various Latin chapels), has been stingy since the late disturbances, the spoliation of the clergy, &c.

After we had been taken to see the humble curiosities of the place, the Prior treated us in his wooden parlour with little glasses of pink Rosolio, brought with many bows and genuflexions by his reverence the convent butler.

After this community of holy men, the most important perhaps is the American Convent, a Protestant congregation of Independents chiefly, who deliver tracts, propose to make converts, have meetings of their own, and also swell the little congregation that attends the Anglican service. I have mentioned our fellow-traveller, the Consul-General for Syria of the United States. He was a tradesman, who had made a considerable fortune, and lived at a country-house in comfortable retirement. But his opinion is, that the prophecies of Scripture are about to be accomplished; that the day of the return of the Jews is at hand, and the glorification of the restored Jerusalem. He is to witness this—he and a favourite dove with which he travels; and he forsook home and comfortable country-house, in order to make this journey. He has no other knowledge of Syria but what he derives from the prophecy; and this (as he takes the office gratis) has been considered a sufficient reason for his appointment by the United States Government. As soon as he arrived, he sent and demanded an interview with the Pasha; explained to him his interpretation of the Apocalypse, in which he has discovered that the Five Powers and America are about to intervene in Syrian affairs, and the infallible return of the Jews to Palestine. The news must have astonished the Lieutenant of the Sublime Porte; and since the days of the Kingdom of Munster, under his Anabaptist Majesty, John of Leyden, I doubt whether any Government has received or appointed so queer an ambassador. The kind, worthy, simple man took me to his temporary consulate-house at the American Missionary Establishment; and, under pretence of treating me to white wine, expounded his ideas; talked of futurity as he would about an article in The Times; and had no more doubt of seeing a divine kingdom established in Jerusalem than you that there would be a levée next spring at St. James's. The little room in which we sat was padded with missionary tracts, but I heard of scarce any converts—not more than are made by our own Episcopal establishment.

But if the latter's religious victories are small, and very few people are induced by the American tracts, and the English preaching and catechising, to forsake their own manner of worshipping the Divine Being in order to follow ours; yet surely our religious colony of men and women can't fail to do good, by the sheer force of good example, pure life, and kind offices. The ladies of the mission have numbers of clients, of all persuasions, in the town, to whom they extend their charities. Each of their houses is a model of neatness, and a dispensary of gentle kindnesses; and the ecclesiastics have formed a modest centre of civilisation in the place. A dreary joke was made in the House of Commons about Bishop Alexander and the Bishopess his lady, and the Bishoplings his numerous children, who were said to have scandalised the people of Jerusalem. That sneer evidently came from the Latins and Greeks; for what could the Jews and Turks care because an English clergyman had a wife and children as their own priests have? There was no sort of ill will exhibited towards them, as far as I could learn; and I saw the Bishop's children riding about the town as safely as they could about Hyde Park. All Europeans, indeed, seemed to me to be received with forbearance, and almost courtesy, within the walls. As I was going about making sketches, the people would look on very good-humouredly, without offering the least interruption; nay, two or three were quite ready to stand still for such an humble portrait as my pencil could make of them; and the sketch done, it was passed from one person to another, each making his comments, and signifying a very polite approval. Here are a pair of them[iii], Fath Allah and Ameenut Daoodee his father, horse-dealers by trade, who came and sat with us at the inn, and smoked pipes (the sun being down), while the original of the above masterpiece was made. With the Arabs outside the walls, however, and the freshly arriving country people, this politeness was not so much exhibited. There was a certain tattooed girl, with black eyes and huge silver earrings, and a chin delicately picked out with blue, who formed one of a group of women outside the great convent, whose likeness I longed to carry off;— there was a woman with a little child, with wondering eyes, drawing water at the Pool of Siloam, in such an attitude and dress as Rebecca may have had when Isaac's lieutenant asked her for drink:-both of these parties standing still for half a minute, at the next cried out for backsheesh: and not content with the five piastres which I gave them individually, screamed out for more, and summoned their friends, who screamed out backsheesh too. I was pursued into the convent by a dozen howling women calling for pay, barring the door against them, to the astonishment of the worthy papa who kept it; and at Miriam's. Well, the women were joined by a man with a large stick, who backed their petition. But him we could afford to laugh at, for we were two and had sticks likewise.

In the village of Siloam I would not recommend the artist to loiter. A colony of ruffians inhabit the dismal place, who have guns as well as sticks at need. Their dogs howl after the strangers as they pass through; and over the parapets of their walls you are saluted by the scowls of a villanous set of countenances, that it is not good to see with one pair of eyes. They shot a man at mid-day at a few hundred yards from the gates while we were at Jerusalem, and no notice was taken of the murder. Hordes of Arab robbers infest the neighbourhood of the city, with the Sheikhs of whom travellers make terms when minded to pursue their journey. I never could understand why the walls stopped these warriors if they had a mind to plunder the city, for there are but a hundred and fifty men in the garrison to man the long lonely lines of defence.

I have seen only in Titian's pictures those magnificent purple shadows in which the hills round about lay, as the dawn rose faintly behind them; and we looked at Olivet for the last time from our terrace, where we were awaiting the arrival of the horses that were to carry us to Jaffa. A yellow moon was still blazing in the midst of countless brilliant stars overhead; the nakedness and misery of the surrounding city were hidden in that beautiful rosy atmosphere of mingling night and dawn. The city never looked so noble; the mosques, domes, and minarets rising up into the calm star-lit sky.

By the gate of Bethlehem there stands one palm-tree, and a house with three domes. Put these and the huge old Gothic gate as a background dark against the yellowing eastern sky: the foreground is a deep grey: as you look into it dark forms of horsemen come out of the twilight: now there come lanterns, more horsemen, a litter with mules, a crowd of Arab horseboys and dealers accompanying their beasts to the gate; all the members of our party come up by twos and threes; and, at last, the great gate opens just before sunrise, and we get into the grey plains.

Oh! the luxury of an English saddle! An English servant of one of the gentlemen of the mission procured it for me, on the back of a little mare, which (as I am a light weight) did not turn a hair in the course of the day's march—and after we got quit of the ugly, stony, clattering, mountainous Abou Gosh district, into the fair undulating plain, which stretches to Ramleh, carried me into the town at a pleasant hand-gallop. A negro, of preternatural ugliness, in a yellow gown, with a crimson handkerchief streaming over his head, digging his shovel spurs into the lean animal he rode, and driving three others before—swaying backwards and forwards on his horse, now embracing his ears, and now almost under his belly, screaming "yallah" with the most frightful shrieks, and singing country songs—galloped along ahead of me. I acquired one of his poems pretty well, and could imitate his shriek accurately; but I shall not have the pleasure of singing it to you in England. I had forgotten the delightful dissonance two days after, both the negro's and that of a real Arab minstrel, a donkey-driver accompanying our baggage, who sang and grinned with the most amusing good-humour.

We halted, in the middle of the day, in a little wood of olive-trees, which forms almost the only shelter between Jaffa and Jerusalem, except that afforded by the orchards in the odious village of Abou Gosh, through which we went at a double quick pace. Under the olives, or up in the branches, some of our friends took a siesta. I have a sketch of four of them so employed. Two of them were dead within a month of the fatal Syrian fever. But we did not know how near fate was to us then. Fires were lighted, and fowls and eggs divided, and tea and coffee served round in tin panikins, and here we lighted pipes, and smoked and laughed at our ease. I believe everybody was happy to be out of Jerusalem. The impression I have of it now is of ten days passed in a fever.

We all found quarters in the Greek convent at Ramleh, where the monks served us a supper on a terrace, in a pleasant sunset; a beautiful and cheerful landscape stretching around; the land in graceful undulations, the towers and mosques rosy in the sunset, with no lack of verdure, especially of graceful palms. Jaffa was nine miles off. As we rode all the morning we had been accompanied by the smoke of our steamer, twenty miles off at sea.

The convent is a huge caravanserai; only three or four monks dwell in it, the ghostly hotel-keepers of the place. The horses were tied up and fed in the courtyard, into which we rode; above were the living-rooms, where there is accommodation, not only for an unlimited number of pilgrims, but for a vast and innumerable host of hopping and crawling things, who usually persist in partaking of the traveller's bed. Let all thin-skinned travellers in the East be warned on no account to travel without the admirable invention described in Mr. Fellowes's book; nay, possibly invented by that enterprising and learned traveller. You make a sack, of calico or linen, big enough for the body, appended to which is a closed chimney of muslin, stretched out by cane hoops, and fastened up to a beam, or against the wall. You keep a sharp eye to see that no flea or bug is on the look-out, and when assured of this, you pop into the bag, tightly closing the orifice after you. This admirable bug-disappointer I tried at Ramleh, and had the only undisturbed night's rest I enjoyed in the East. To be sure it was a short night, for our party were stirring at one o'clock, and those who got up insisted on talking and keeping awake those who inclined to sleep. But I shall never forget the terror inspired in my mind, being shut up in the bug-disappointer, when a facetious lay-brother of the convent fell upon me and began tickling me. I never had the courage again to try the anti-flea contrivance, preferring the friskiness of those animals to the sports of such a greasy grinning wag as my friend at Ramleh.

In the morning, and long before sunrise, our little caravan was in marching order again. We went out with lanterns and shouts of "yallah" through the narrow streets, and issued into the plain, where, though there was no moon, there were blazing stars shining steadily overhead. They become friends to a man who travels, especially under the clear Eastern sky; whence they look down as if protecting you, solemn, yellow, and refulgent. They seem nearer to you than in Europe; larger and more awful. So we rode on till the dawn rose, and Jaffa came in view. The friendly ship was lying out in waiting for us; the horses were given up to their owners; and in the midst of a crowd of naked beggars, and a perfect storm of curses and yells for backsheesh, our party got into their boats, and to the ship, where we were welcomed by the very best captain that ever sailed upon this maritime globe, namely, Captain Samuel Lewis, of the Peninsular and Oriental Company's Service.

CHAPTER XIV: FROM JAFFA TO ALEXANDRIA

[From the Providor's Log-book.]

Bill of Fare, October 12th.

Mulligatawny Soup. Salt Fish and Egg Sauce. Roast Haunch of Mutton. Boiled Shoulder and Onion Sauce. Boiled Beef. Roast Fowls. Pillau ditto. Ham. Haricot Mutton. Curry and Rice.

Cabbage. French Beans. Boiled Potatoes. Baked ditto. Damson Tart. Rice Puddings. Currant ditto. Currant Fritters.

We were just at the port's mouth—and could see the towers and buildings of Alexandria rising purple against the sunset, when the report of a gun came booming over the calm golden water; and we heard, with much mortification, that we had no chance of getting pratique that night. Already the ungrateful passengers had begun to tire of the ship,—though in our absence in Syria it had been carefully cleansed and purified; though it was cleared of the swarming Jews who had infested the decks all the way from Constantinople; and though we had been feasting and carousing in the manner described above.

But very early next morning we bore into the harbour, busy with a great quantity of craft. We passed huge black hulks of mouldering men-of-war, from the sterns of which trailed the dirty red flag, with the star and crescent; boats, manned with red-capped seamen, and captains and steersmen in beards and tarbooshes, passed continually among these old hulks, the rowers bending to their oars, so that at each stroke they disappeared bodily in the boat. Besides these, there was a large fleet of country ships, and stars and stripes, and tricolours, and Union Jacks; and many active steamers, of the French and English companies, shooting in and out of the harbour, or moored in the briny waters. The ship of our company, the "Oriental," lay there—a palace upon the brine, and some of the Pasha's steam-vessels likewise, looking very like Christian boats; but it was queer to look at some unintelligible Turkish flourish painted on the stern, and the long-tailed Arabian hieroglyphics gilt on the paddle-boxes. Our dear friend and comrade of Beyrout (if we may be permitted to call her so), H.M.S. "Trump," was in the harbour; and the captain of that gallant ship, coming to greet us, drove some of us on shore in his gig.

I had been preparing myself overnight, by the help of a cigar and a moonlight contemplation on deck, for sensations on landing in Egypt. I was ready to yield myself up with solemnity to the mystic grandeur of the scene of initiation. Pompey's Pillar must stand like a mountain, in a yellow plain, surrounded by a grove of obelisks as tall as palm-trees. Placid sphinxes brooding o'er the Nile—mighty Memnonian countenances calm—had revealed Egypt to me in a sonnet of Tennyson's, and I was ready to gaze on it with pyramidal wonder and hieroglyphic awe.

The landing quay at Alexandria is like the dockyard quay at Portsmouth: with a few score of brown faces scattered among the population. There are slop-sellers, dealers in marine-stores, bottled-porter shops, seamen lolling about; flys and cabs are plying for hire; and a yelling chorus of donkey-boys, shrieking, "Ride, sir!—Donkey, sir!—I say, sir!" in excellent English, dispel all romantic notions. The placid sphinxes brooding o'er the Nile disappeared with that shriek of the donkey-boys. You might be as well impressed with Wapping as with your first step on Egyptian soil.

The riding of a donkey is, after all, not a dignified occupation. A man resists the offer at first, somehow, as an indignity. How is that poor little, red-saddled, long-eared creature to carry you? Is there to be one for you, and another for your legs? Natives and Europeans, of all sizes, pass by, it is true, mounted upon the same contrivance. I waited until I got into a very private spot, where nobody could see me, and then ascended—why not say descended, at once?—on the poor little animal. Instead of being crushed at once, as perhaps the rider expected, it darted forward, quite briskly and cheerfully, at six or seven miles an hour; requiring no spur or admonitive to haste, except the shrieking of the little Egyptian gamin, who ran along by asinus's side.

The character of the houses by which you pass is scarcely Eastern at all. The streets are busy with a motley population of Jews and Armenians, slave-driving-looking Europeans, large-breeched Greeks, and well-shaven buxom merchants, looking as trim and fat as those on the Bourse or on 'Change; only, among the natives, the stranger can't fail to remark (as the Caliph did of the Calenders in the "Arabian Nights") that so many of them *have only one eye*. It is the horrid ophthalmia which has played such frightful ravages with them. You see children sitting in the doorways, their eyes completely closed up with the green sickening sore, and the flies feeding on them. Five or six minutes of the donkey-ride brings you to the Frank quarter, and the handsome broad street (like a street of Marseilles) where the principal hotels and merchants' houses are to be found, and where the consuls have their houses, and hoist their flags. The palace of the French Consul-General makes the grandest show in the street, and presents a great contrast to the humble abode of the English representative, who protects his fellow-countrymen from a second floor.

But that Alexandrian two-pair-front of a Consulate was more welcome and cheering than a palace to most of us. For there lay certain letters, with post-marks of *home* upon them; and kindly tidings, the first heard for two months:-though we had seen so many men and cities since, that Cornhill seemed to be a year off, at least, with certain persons dwelling (more or less) in that vicinity. I saw a young Oxford man seize his despatches, and slink off with several letters, written in a tight neat hand, and sedulously crossed; which any man could see, without looking farther, were the handiwork of Mary Ann, to whom he is attached. The lawyer received a bundle from his chambers, in which his clerk eased his soul regarding the state of Snooks v. Rodgers, Smith ats Tomkins, &c. The statesman had a packet of thick envelopes, decorated with that profusion of sealing-wax in which official recklessness lavishes the resources of the country: and your humble servant got just one little modest letter, containing another, written in pencil characters, varying in size between one and two inches; but how much pleasanter to read than my Lord's despatch, or the clerk's account of Smith vs. Tomkins,—yes, even than the Mary Ann correspondence!...Yes, my dear madam, you will understand me, when I say that it was from little Polly at home, with some confidential news about a cat, and the last report of her new doll.

It is worth while to have made the journey for this pleasure: to have walked the deck on long nights, and have thought of home. You have no leisure to do so in the city. You don't see the heavens shine above you so purely there, or the stars so clearly. How, after the perusal of the above documents, we enjoyed a file of the admirable Galignani; and what O'Connell was doing; and the twelve last new victories of the French in Algeria; and, above all, six or seven numbers of Punch! There might have been an avenue of Pompey's Pillars within reach, and a live sphinx sporting on the banks of the Mahmoodieh Canal, and we would not have stirred to see them, until Punch had had his interview and Galignani was dismissed.

The curiosities of Alexandria are few, and easily seen. We went into the bazaars, which have a much more Eastern look than the European quarter, with its Anglo-Gallic-Italian inhabitants, and Babel-like civilisation. Here and there a large hotel, clumsy and whitewashed, with Oriental trellised windows, and a couple of slouching sentinels at the doors, in the ugliest composite uniform that ever was seen, was pointed out as the residence of some great officer of the Pasha's Court, or of one of the numerous children of the Egyptian Solomon. His Highness was in his own palace, and was consequently not visible. He was in deep grief, and strict retirement. It was at this time that the European newspapers announced that he was about to resign his empire; but the quidnuncs of Alexandria hinted that a love-affair, in which the old potentate had engaged with senile extravagance, and the effects of a potion of hachisch, or some deleterious drug, with which he was in the habit of intoxicating himself, had brought on that languor and desperate weariness of life and governing, into which the venerable Prince was plunged. Before three days were over, however, the fit had left him, and he determined to live and reign a little longer. A very few days afterwards several of our party were presented to him at Cairo, and found the great Egyptian ruler perfectly convalescent.

This, and the Opera, and the quarrels of the two prime donne, and the beauty of one of them, formed the chief subjects of conversation; and I had this important news in the shop of a certain barber in the town, who conveyed it in a language composed of French, Spanish, and Italian, and with a volubility quite worthy of a barber of "Gil Blas."

Then we went to see the famous obelisk presented by Mehemet Ali to the British Government, who have not shown a particular alacrity to accept this ponderous present. The huge shaft lies on the ground, prostrate, and desecrated by all sorts of abominations. Children were sprawling about, attracted by the dirt there. Arabs, negroes, and donkey-boys were passing, quite indifferent, by the fallen monster of a stone—as indifferent as the British Government, who don't care for recording the glorious termination of their Egyptian campaign of 1801. If our country takes the compliment so coolly, surely it would be disloyal upon our parts to be more enthusiastic. I wish they would offer the Trafalgar Square Pillar to the Egyptians; and that both of the huge ugly monsters were lying in the dirt there side by side.

Pompey's Pillar is by no means so big as the Charing Cross trophy. This venerable column has not escaped ill-treatment either. Numberless ships' companies, travelling cockneys, &c., have affixed their rude marks upon it. Some daring ruffian even painted the name of "Warren's blacking" upon it, effacing other inscriptions,—one, Wilkinson says, of "the second Psammetichus." I regret deeply, my dear friend, that I cannot give you this document respecting a lamented monarch, in whose history I know you take such an interest.

The best sight I saw in Alexandria was a negro holiday; which was celebrated outside of the town by a sort of negro village of huts, swarming with old, lean, fat, ugly, infantine, happy faces, that nature had smeared with a preparation even more black and durable than that with which Psammetichus's base has been polished. Every one of these jolly faces was on the broad grin, from the dusky mother to the india-rubber child sprawling upon her back, and the venerable jetty senior whose wool was as white as that of a sheep in Florian's pastorals.

To these dancers a couple of fellows were playing on a drum and a little banjo. They were singing a chorus, which was not only singular, and perfectly marked in the rhythm, but exceeding sweet in the tune. They danced in a circle; and performers came trooping from all quarters, who fell into the round, and began waggling their heads, and waving their left hands, and tossing up and down the little thin rods which they each carried, and all singing to the very best of their power.

I saw the chief eunuch of the Grand Turk at Constantinople pass by--(here is an accurate likeness of his beautiful features[iv])—but with what a different expression! Though he is one of the greatest of the great in the Turkish Empire (ranking with a Cabinet Minister or Lord Chamberlain here), his fine countenance was clouded with care, and savage with ennui.

Here his black brethren were ragged, starving, and happy; and I need not tell such a fine moralist as you are, how it is the case, in the white as well as the black world, that happiness (republican leveller, who does not care a fig for the fashion) often disdains the turrets of kings, to pay a visit to the "tabernas pauperum."

We went the round of the coffee-houses in the evening, both the polite European places of resort, where you get ices and the French papers, and those in the town, where Greeks, Turks, and general company resort, to sit upon uncomfortable chairs, and drink wretched muddy coffee, and to listen to two or three miserable musicians, who keep up a variation of howling for hours together. But the pretty song of the niggers had spoiled me for that abominable music.

CHAPTER XV: TO CAIRO

We had no need of hiring the country boats which ply on the Mahmoodieh Canal to Atfeh, where it joins the Nile, but were accommodated in one of the Peninsular and Oriental Company's fly-boats; pretty similar to those narrow Irish canal boats in which the enterprising traveller has been carried from Dublin to Ballinasloe. The present boat was, to be sure, tugged by a little steamer, so that the Egyptian canal is ahead of the Irish in so far: in natural scenery, the one prospect is fully equal to the other; it must be confessed that there is nothing to see. In truth, there was nothing but this: you saw a muddy bank on each side of you, and a blue sky overhead. A few round mud-huts and palm-trees were planted along the line here and there. Sometimes we would see, on the water-side, a woman in a blue robe, with her son by her, in that tight brown costume with which Nature had supplied him. Now, it was a hat dropped by one of the party into the water; a brown Arab plunged and disappeared incontinently after the hat, re-issued from the muddy water, prize in hand, and ran naked after the little steamer (which was by this time far ahead of him), his brawny limbs shining in the sun: then we had half-cold fowls and bitter ale: then we had dinner—bitter ale and cold fowls; with which incidents the day on the canal passed away, as harmlessly as if we had been in a Dutch trackschuyt.

Towards evening we arrived at the town of Atfeh—half land, half houses, half palm-trees, with swarms of half-naked people crowding the rustic shady bazaars, and bartering their produce of fruit or many-coloured grain. Here the canal came to a check, ending abruptly with a large lock. A little fleet of masts and country ships were beyond the lock, and it led into *the Nile*.

After all, it is something to have seen these red waters. It is only low green banks, mud-huts, and palm-clumps, with the sun setting red behind them, and the great, dull, sinuous river flashing here and there in the light. But it is the Nile, the old Saturn of a stream—a divinity yet, though younger river-gods have deposed him. Hail! O venerable father of crocodiles! We were all lost in sentiments of the profoundest awe and respect; which we proved by tumbling down into the cabin of the Nile steamer that was waiting to receive us, and fighting and cheating for sleeping-berths.

At dawn in the morning we were on deck; the character had not altered of the scenery about the river. Vast flat stretches of land were on either side, recovering from the subsiding inundations: near the mud villages, a country ship or two was roosting under the date-trees; the landscape everywhere stretching away level and lonely. In the sky in the east was a long streak of greenish light, which widened and rose until it grew to be of an opal colour, then orange; then, behold, the round red disc of the sun rose flaming up above the horizon. All the water blushed as he got up; the deck was all red; the steersman gave his helm to another, and prostrated himself on the deck, and bowed his head eastward, and praised the Maker of the sun: it shone on his white turban as he was kneeling, and gilt up his bronzed face, and sent his blue shadow over the glowing deck. The distances, which had been grey, were now clothed in purple; and the broad stream was illuminated. As the sun rose higher, the morning blush faded away; the sky was cloudless and pale, and the river and the surrounding landscape were dazzlingly clear.

Looking ahead in an hour or two, we saw the Pyramids. Fancy my sensations, dear M—: two big ones and a little one—

! ! !

There they lay, rosy and solemn in the distance—those old, majestical, mystical, familiar edifices. Several of us tried to be impressed; but breakfast supervening, a rush was made at the coffee and cold pies, and the sentiment of awe was lost in the scramble for victuals.

Are we so blases of the world that the greatest marvels in it do not succeed in moving us? Have society, Pall Mall clubs, and a habit of sneering, so withered up our organs of veneration that we can admire no more? My sensation with regard to the Pyramids was, that I had seen them before: then came a feeling of shame that the view of them should awaken no respect. Then I wanted (naturally) to see whether my neighbours were any more enthusiastic than myself—Trinity College, Oxford, was busy with the cold ham: Downing Street was particularly attentive to a bunch of grapes: Figtree Court behaved with decent propriety; he is in good practice, and of a Conservative turn of mind, which leads him to respect from principle *les faits accomplis*: perhaps he remembered that one of them was as big as Lincoln's Inn Fields. But, the truth is, nobody was seriously moved...And why should they, because of an exaggeration of bricks ever so enormous? I confess, for my part, that the Pyramids are very big.

After a voyage of about thirty hours, the steamer brought up at the quay of Boulak, amidst a small fleet of dirty comfortless cangias, in which cottons and merchandise were loading and unloading, and a huge noise and bustle on the shore. Numerous villas, parks, and country-houses had begun to decorate the Cairo bank of the stream ere this: residences of the Pasha's nobles, who have had orders to take their pleasure here and beautify the precincts of the capital; tall factory chimneys also rise here; there are foundries and steam-engine manufactories. These, and the pleasure-houses, stand as trim as soldiers on parade; contrasting with the swarming, slovenly, close, tumble-down, Eastern old town, that forms the outport of Cairo, and was built before the importation of European taste and discipline.

Here we alighted upon donkeys, to the full as brisk as those of Alexandria, invaluable to timid riders, and equal to any weight. We had a Jerusalem pony race into Cairo; my animal beating all the rest by many lengths. The entrance to the capital, from

Boulak, is very pleasant and picturesque—over a fair road, and the wide-planted plain of the Ezbekieh; where are gardens, canals, fields, and avenues of trees, and where the great ones of the town come and take their pleasure. We saw many barouches driving about with fat Pashas lolling on the cushions; stately-looking colonels and doctors taking their ride, followed by their orderlies or footmen; lines of people taking pipes and sherbet in the coffee-houses; and one of the pleasantest sights of all,—a fine new white building with *Hôtel d'Orient* written up in huge French characters, and which, indeed, is an establishment as large and comfortable as most of the best inns of the South of France. As a hundred Christian people, or more, come from England and from India every fortnight, this inn has been built to accommodate a large proportion of them; and twice a month, at least, its sixty rooms are full.

The gardens from the windows give a very pleasant and animated view: the hotel-gate is besieged by crews of donkey-drivers; the noble stately Arab women, with tawny skins (of which a simple robe of floating blue cotton enables you liberally to see the colour) and large black eyes, come to the well hard by for water: camels are perpetually arriving and setting down their loads: the court is full of bustling dragomans, ayahs, and children from India; and poor old venerable he-nurses, with grey beards and crimson turbans, tending little white-faced babies that have seen the light at Dumdum or Futtyghur: a copper-coloured barber, seated on his hams, is shaving a camel-driver at the great inn-gate. The bells are ringing prodigiously; and Lieutenant Waghorn is bouncing in and out of the courtyard full of business. He only left Bombay yesterday morning, was seen in the Red Sea on Tuesday, is engaged to dinner this afternoon in the Regent's Park, and (as it is about two minutes since I saw him in the courtyard) I make no doubt he is by this time at Alexandria, or at Malta, say, perhaps, at both. *Il en est capable*. If any man can be at two places at once (which I don't believe or deny) Waghorn is he.

Six o'clock bell rings. Sixty people sit down to a quasi-French banquet: thirty Indian officers in moustaches and jackets; ten civilians in ditto and spectacles; ten pale-faced ladies with ringlets, to whom all pay prodigious attention. All the pale ladies drink pale ale, which, perhaps, accounts for it; in fact the Bombay and Suez passengers have just arrived, and hence this crowding and bustling, and display of military jackets and moustaches, and ringlets and beauty. The windows are open, and a rush of mosquitoes from the Ezbekieh waters, attracted by the wax candles, adds greatly to the excitement of the scene. There was a little tough old Major, who persisted in flinging open the windows, to admit these volatile creatures, with a noble disregard to their sting—and the pale ringlets did not seem to heed them either, though the delicate shoulders of some of them were bare.

All the meat, ragouts, fricandeaux, and roasts, which are served round at dinner, seem to me to be of the same meat: a black uncertain sort of viand do these "fleshpots of Egypt" contain. But what the meat is no one knew: is it the donkey? The animal is more plentiful than any other in Cairo.

After dinner, the ladies retiring, some of us take a mixture of hot water, sugar, and pale French brandy, which is said to be deleterious, but is by no means unpalatable. One of the Indians offers a bundle of Bengal cheroots; and we make acquaintance with those honest bearded white-jacketed Majors and military Commanders, finding England here in a French hotel kept by an Italian, at the city of Grand Cairo, in Africa.

On retiring to bed you take a towel with you into the sacred interior, behind the mosquito curtains. Then your duty is, having tucked the curtains closely around, to flap and bang violently with this towel, right and left, and backwards and forwards, until every mosquito should have been massacred that may have taken refuge within your muslin canopy.

Do what you will, however, one of them always escapes the murder; and as soon as the candle is out the miscreant begins his infernal droning and trumpeting; descends playfully upon your nose and face, and so lightly that you don't know that he touches you. But that for a week afterwards you bear about marks of his ferocity, you might take the invisible little being to be a creature of fancy—a mere singing in your ears.

This, as an account of Cairo, dear M—, you will probably be disposed to consider as incomplete: the fact is, I have seen nothing else as yet. I have peered into no harems. The magicians, proved to be humbugs, have been bastinadoed out of town. The dancing-girls, those lovely Alme, of whom I had hoped to be able to give a glowing and elegant, though strictly moral, description, have been whipped into Upper Egypt, and as you are saying in your mind—Well, it *isn't* a good description of Cairo: you are perfectly right. It is England in Egypt. I like to see her there with her pluck, enterprise, manliness, bitter ale, and Harvey Sauce. Wherever they come they stay and prosper. From the summit of yonder Pyramids forty centuries may look down on them if they are minded; and I say, those venerable daughters of time ought to be better pleased by the examination, than by regarding the French bayonets and General Bonaparte, Member of the Institute, fifty years ago, running about with sabre and pigtail. Wonders he did, to be sure, and then ran away, leaving Kleber, to be murdered, in the lurch—a few hundred yards from the spot where these disquisitions are written. But what are his wonders compared to Waghorn? Nap massacred the Mamelukes at the Pyramids: Wag has conquered the Pyramids themselves; dragged the unwieldy structures a month nearer England than they were, and brought the country along with them. All the trophies and captives that ever were brought to Roman triumph were not so enormous and wonderful as this. All the heads that Napoleon ever caused to be struck off (as George Cruikshank says) would not elevate him a monument as big. Be ours the trophies of peace! O my country! O Waghorn! *Hae tibi erunt artes*. When I go to the Pyramids I will sacrifice in your name, and pour out libations of bitter ale and Harvey Sauce in your honour.

One of the noblest views in the world is to be seen from the citadel, which we ascended to-day. You see the city stretching beneath it, with a thousand minarets and mosques,—the great river curling through the green plains, studded with innumerable villages. The Pyramids are beyond, brilliantly distinct; and the lines and fortifications of the height, and the arsenal lying below. Gazing down, the guide does not fail to point out the famous Mameluke leap, by which one of the corps escaped death, at the time that His Highness the Pasha arranged the general massacre of the body.

The venerable Patriarch's harem is close by, where he received, with much distinction, some of the members of our party. We were allowed to pass very close to the sacred precincts, and saw a comfortable white European building, approached by flights of steps, and flanked by pretty gardens. Police and law-courts were here also, as I understood; but it was not the time of the Egyptian assizes. It would have been pleasant, otherwise, to see the Chief Cadi in his hall of justice; and painful, though instructive, to behold the immediate application of the bastinado.

The great lion of the place is a new mosque which Mehemet Ali is constructing very leisurely. It is built of alabaster of a fair white, with a delicate blushing tinge; but the ornaments are European—the noble, fantastic, beautiful Oriental art is forgotten. The old mosques of the city, of which I entered two, and looked at many, are a thousand times more beautiful. Their variety of ornament is astonishing,—the difference in the shapes of the domes, the beautiful fancies and caprices in the forms of the minarets, which violate the rules of proportion with the most happy daring grace, must have struck every architect who has seen them. As you go through the streets, these architectural beauties keep the eye continually charmed: now it is a marble fountain, with its arabesque and carved overhanging roof, which you can look at with as much pleasure as an antique gem, so neat and brilliant is the execution of it; then, you come to the arched entrance to a mosque, which shoots up like—like what?—like the most beautiful pirouette by Taglioni, let us say. This architecture is not sublimely beautiful, perfect loveliness and calm, like that which was revealed to us at the Parthenon (and in comparison of which the Pantheon and Colosseum are vulgar and coarse, mere broad-shouldered Titans before ambrosial Jove); but these fantastic spires, and cupolas, and galleries, excite, amuse, tickle the imagination, so to speak, and perpetually fascinate the eye. There were very few believers in the famous mosque of Sultan Hassan when we visited it, except the Moslemitish beadle, who was on the look-out for backsheesh, just like his brother officer in an English cathedral; and who, making us put on straw slippers, so as not to pollute the sacred pavement of the place, conducted us through it.

It is stupendously light and airy; the best specimens of Norman art that I have seen (and surely the Crusaders must have carried home the models of these heathenish temples in their eyes) do not exceed its noble grace and simplicity. The mystics make discoveries at home, that the Gothic architecture is Catholicism carved in stone— (in which case, and if architectural beauty is a criterion or expression of religion, what a dismal barbarous creed must that expressed by the Bethesda meeting-house and Independent chapels be?)—if, as they would gravely hint, because Gothic architecture is beautiful, Catholicism is therefore lovely and right,—why,

Mahometanism must have been right and lovely too once. Never did a creed possess temples more elegant; as elegant as the Cathedral at Rouen, or the Baptistery at Pisa.

But it is changed now. There was nobody at prayers; only the official beadles, and the supernumerary guides, who came for backsheesh. Faith hath degenerated. Accordingly they can't build these mosques, or invent these perfect forms, any more. Witness the tawdry incompleteness and vulgarity of the Pasha's new temple, and the woful failures among the very late edifices in Constantinople!

However, they still make pilgrimages to Mecca in great force. The Mosque of Hassan is hard by the green plain on which the Hag encamps before it sets forth annually on its pious peregrination. It was not yet its time, but I saw in the bazaars that redoubted Dervish, who is the master of the Hag—the leader of every procession, accompanying the sacred camel; and a personage almost as much respected as Mr. O'Connell in Ireland.

This fellow lives by alms (I mean the head of the Hag). Winter and summer he wears no clothes but a thin and scanty white shirt. He wields a staff, and stalks along scowling and barefoot. His immense shock of black hair streams behind him, and his brown brawny body is curled over with black hair, like a savage man. This saint has the largest harem in the town; he is said to be enormously rich by the contributions he has levied; and is so adored for his holiness by the infatuated folk, that when he returns from the Hag (which he does on horseback, the chief Mollahs going out to meet him and escort him home in state along the Ezbekieh road), the people fling themselves down under the horse's feet, eager to be trampled upon and killed, and confident of heaven if the great Hadji's horse will but kick them into it. Was it my fault if I thought of Hadji Daniel, and the believers in him?

There was no Dervish of repute on the plain when I passed; only one poor wild fellow, who was dancing, with glaring eyes and grizzled beard, rather to the contempt of the bystanders, as I thought, who by no means put coppers into his extended bowl. On this poor devil's head there was a poorer devil still—a live cock, entirely plucked, but ornamented with some bits of ragged tape and scarlet and tinsel, the most horribly grotesque and miserable object I ever saw.

A little way from him, there was a sort of play going on—a clown and a knowing one, like Widdicombe and the clown with us,—the buffoon answering with blundering responses, which made all the audience shout with laughter; but the only joke which was translated to me would make you do anything but laugh, and shall therefore never be revealed by these lips. All their humour, my dragoman tells me, is of this questionable sort; and a young Egyptian gentleman, son of a Pasha, whom I subsequently met at Malta, confirmed the statement, and gave a detail of the practices of private life which was anything but edifying. The great aim of woman, he said, in the much-maligned Orient, is to administer to the brutality of her lord; her merit is in knowing how to vary the beast's pleasures. He could give us no idea, he said, of the wit of the Egyptian women, and their skill in *double entendre*; nor, I presume, did we lose much by our ignorance. What I would urge, humbly, however, is this—Do not let us be led away by German writers and aesthetics, Semilassoisms, Hahnhahnisms, and the like. The life of the East is a life of brutes. The much maligned Orient, I am confident, has not been maligned near enough; for the good reason that none of us can tell the amount of horrible sensuality practised there.

Beyond the Jack-pudding rascal and his audience, there was on the green a spot, on which was pointed out to me a mark, as of blood. That morning the blood had spouted from the neck of an Arnaoot soldier, who had been executed for murder. These Arnaoots are the curse and terror of the citizens. Their camps are without the city; but they are always brawling, or drunken, or murdering within, in spite of the rigid law which is applied to them, and which brings one or more of the scoundrels to death almost every week.

Some of our party had seen this fellow borne by the hotel the day before, in the midst of a crowd of soldiers who had apprehended him. The man was still formidable to his score of captors: his clothes had been torn off; his limbs were bound with cords; but he was struggling frantically to get free; and my informant described the figure and appearance of the naked, bound, writhing savage, as quite a model of beauty.

Walking in the street, this fellow had just before been struck by the looks of a woman who was passing, and laid hands on her. She ran away, and he pursued her. She ran into the police-barrack, which was luckily hard by; but the Arnaoot was nothing daunted, and followed into the midst of the police. One of them tried to stop him. The Arnaoot pulled out a pistol, and shot the policeman dead. He cut down three or four more before he was secured. He knew his inevitable end must be death: that he could not seize upon the woman: that he could not hope to resist half a regiment of armed soldiers: yet his instinct of lust and murder was too strong; and so he had his head taken off quite calmly this morning, many of his comrades attending their brother's last moments. He cared not the least about dying; and knelt down and had his head off as coolly as if he were looking on at the same ceremony performed on another.

When the head was off, and the blood was spouting on the ground, a married woman, who had no children, came forward very eagerly out of the crowd, to smear herself with it,—the application of criminals' blood being considered a very favourable medicine for women afflicted with barrenness,—so she indulged in this remedy.

But one of the Arnaoots standing near said, "What, you like blood, do you?" (or words to that effect). "Let's see how yours mixes with my comrade's." And thereupon, taking out a pistol, he shot the woman in the midst of the crowd and the guards who were attending the execution; was seized of course by the latter; and no doubt to-morrow morning will have *his* head off too. It would be a good chapter to write—the Death of the Arnaoot—but I shan't go. Seeing one man hanged is quite enough in the course of a life. *J'y ai été*, as the Frenchman said of hunting.

These Arnaoots are the terror of the town. They seized hold of an Englishman the other day, and were very nearly pistolling him. Last week one of them murdered a shopkeeper at Boulak, who refused to sell him a water-melon at a price which he, the soldier, fixed upon it. So, for the matter of three-halfpence, he killed the shopkeeper; and had his own rascally head chopped off, universally regretted by his friends. Why, I wonder, does not His Highness the Pasha invite the Arnaoots to a *déjeuner* at the Citadel, as he did the Mamelukes, and serve them up the same sort of breakfast? The walls are considerably heightened since Emin Bey and his horse leapt them, and it is probable that not one of them would escape.

This sort of pistol practice is common enough here, it would appear; and not among the Arnaoots merely, but the higher orders. Thus, a short time since, one of His Highness's grandsons, whom I shall call Bluebeard Pasha (lest a revelation of the name of the said Pasha might interrupt our good relations with his country)— one of the young Pashas being rather backward in his education, and anxious to learn mathematics, and the elegant deportment of civilised life, sent to England for a tutor. I have heard he was a Cambridge man, and had learned both algebra and politeness under the Reverend Doctor Whizzle, of—College.

One day when Mr. MacWhirter, B.A., was walking in Shoubra Gardens, with His Highness the young Bluebeard Pasha, inducting him into the usages of polished society, and favouring him with reminiscences of Trumpington, there came up a poor fellah, who flung himself at the feet of young Bluebeard, and calling for justice in a loud and pathetic voice, and holding out a petition, besought His Highness to cast a gracious eye upon the same, and see that his slave had justice done him.

Bluebeard Pasha was so deeply engaged and interested by his respected tutor's conversation, that he told the poor fellah to go to the deuce, and resumed the discourse which his ill-timed outcry for justice had interrupted. But the unlucky wight of a fellah was pushed by his evil destiny, and thought he would make yet another application. So he took a short cut down one of the garden lanes, and as the Prince and the Reverend Mr. MacWhirter, his tutor, came along once more engaged in pleasant disquisition, behold the fellah was once more in their way, kneeling at the august Bluebeard's feet, yelling out for justice as before, and thrusting his petition into the Royal face.

When the Prince's conversation was thus interrupted a second time, his Royal patience and clemency were at an end. "Man," said he, "once before I bade thee not to pester me with thy clamour, and lo! you have disobeyed me,—take the consequences of disobedience to a Prince, and thy blood be upon thine own head." So saying, he drew out a pistol and blew out the brains of that fellah, so that he never bawled out for justice any more.

The Reverend Mr. MacWhirter was astonished at this sudden mode of proceeding: "Gracious Prince," said he, "we do not shoot an undergraduate at Cambridge even for walking over a college grass-plot.—Let me suggest to your Royal Highness that this method of ridding yourself of a poor devil's importunities is such as we should consider abrupt and almost cruel in Europe. Let me beg you to moderate your Royal impetuosity for the future; and, as your Highness's tutor, entreat you to be a little less prodigal of your powder and shot."

"O Mollah!" said His Highness, here interrupting his governor's affectionate appeal,—"you are good to talk about Trumpington and the Pons Asinorum, but if you interfere with the course of justice in any way, or prevent me from shooting any dog of an Arab who snarls at my heels, I have another pistol; and, by the beard of the Prophet! a bullet for you too." So saying he pulled out the weapon, with such a terrific and significant glance at the Reverend Mr. MacWhirter, that that gentleman wished himself back in his Combination Room again; and is by this time, let us hope, safely housed there.

Another facetious anecdote, the last of those I had from a well-informed gentleman residing at Cairo, whose name (as many copies of this book that is to be will be in the circulating libraries there) I cannot, for obvious reasons, mention. The revenues of the country come into the august treasury through the means of farmers, to whom the districts are let out, and who are personally answerable for their quota of the taxation. This practice involves an intolerable deal of tyranny and extortion on the part of those engaged to levy the taxes, and creates a corresponding duplicity among the fellahs, who are not only wretchedly poor among themselves, but whose object is to appear still more poor, and guard their money from their rapacious overseers. Thus the Orient is much maligned; but everybody cheats there: that is a melancholy fact. The Pasha robs and cheats the merchants; knows that the overseer robs him, and bides his time, until he makes him disgorge by the application of the tremendous bastinado; the overseer robs and squeezes the labourer; and the poverty-stricken devil cheats and robs in return; and so the government moves in a happy cycle of roguery.

Deputations from the fellahs and peasants come perpetually before the august presence, to complain of the cruelty and exactions of the chiefs set over them: but, as it is known that the Arab never will pay without the bastinado, their complaints, for the most part, meet with but little attention. His Highness's treasury must be filled, and his officers supported in their authority.

However, there was one village, of which the complaints were so pathetic, and the inhabitants so supremely wretched, that the Royal indignation was moved at their story, and the chief of the village, Skinflint Beg, was called to give an account of himself at Cairo.

When he came before the presence, Mehemet Ali reproached him with his horrible cruelty and exactions; asked him how he dared to treat his faithful and beloved subjects in this way, and threatened him with disgrace, and the utter confiscation of his property, for thus having reduced a district to ruin.

"Your Highness says I have reduced these fellahs to ruin," said Skinflint Beg: "what is the best way to confound my enemies, and to show you the falsehood of their accusations that I have ruined them?—To bring more money from them. If I bring you five hundred purses from my village, will you acknowledge that my people are not ruined yet?"

The heart of the Pasha was touched: "I will have no more bastinadoing, O Skinflint Beg; you have tortured these poor people so much, and have got so little from them, that my Royal heart relents for the present, and I will have them suffer no farther."

"Give me free leave—give me your Highness's gracious pardon, and I will bring the five hundred purses as surely as my name is Skinflint Beg. I demand only the time to go home, the time to return, and a few days to stay, and I will come back as honestly as Regulus Pasha did to the Carthaginians,—I will come back and make my face white before your Highness."

Skinflint Beg's prayer for a reprieve was granted, and he returned to his village, where he forthwith called the elders together. "O friends," he said, "complaints of our poverty and misery have reached the Royal throne, and the benevolent heart of the Sovereign has been melted by the words that have been poured into his ears. 'My heart yearns towards my people of El Muddee,' he says; 'I have thought how to relieve their miseries. Near them lies the fruitful land of El Guanee. It is rich in maize and cotton, in sesame and barley; it is worth a thousand purses; but I will let it to my children for seven hundred, and I will give over the rest of the profit to them, as an alleviation for their affliction.'"

The elders of El Muddee knew the great value and fertility of the lands of Guanee, but they doubted the sincerity of their governor, who, however, dispelled their fears, and adroitly quickened their eagerness to close with the proffered bargain. "I will myself advance two hundred and fifty purses," he said; "do you take counsel among yourselves, and subscribe the other five hundred; and when the sum is ready, a deputation of you shall carry it to Cairo, and I will come with my share; and we will lay the whole at the feet of His Highness." So the grey-bearded ones of the village advised with one another; and those who had been inaccessible to bastinadoes, somehow found money at the calling of interest; and the Sheikh, and they, and the five hundred purses, set off on the road to the capital.

When they arrived, Skinflint Beg and the elders of El Muddee sought admission to the Royal throne, and there laid down their purses. "Here is your humble servant's contribution," said Skinflint, producing his share; "and here is the offering of your loyal village of El Muddee. Did I not before say that enemies and deceivers had maligned me before the august presence, pretending that not a piastre was left in my village, and that my extortion had entirely denuded the peasantry? See! here is proof that there is plenty of money still in El Muddee: in twelve hours the elders have subscribed five hundred purses, and lay them at the feet of their lord."

Instead of the bastinado, Skinflint Beg was instantly rewarded with the Royal favour, and the former mark of attention was bestowed upon the fellahs who had maligned him; Skinflint Beg was promoted to the rank of Skinflint Bey; and his manner of extracting money from his people may be studied with admiration in a part of the United Kingdom[v].

At the time of the Syrian quarrel, and when, apprehending some general rupture with England, the Pasha wished to raise the spirit of the fellahs, and *relever la morale nationale*, he actually made one of the astonished Arabs a colonel. He degraded him three days after peace was concluded. The young Egyptian colonel, who told me this, laughed and enjoyed the joke with the utmost gusto. "Is it not a shame," he said, "to make me a colonel at three-and-twenty; I, who have no particular merit, and have never seen any service?" Death has since stopped the modest and good-natured young fellow's further promotion. The death of — Bey was announced in the French papers a few weeks back.

My above kind-hearted and agreeable young informant used to discourse, in our evenings in the Lazaretto at Malta, very eloquently about the beauty of his wife, whom he had left behind him at Cairo—her brown hair, her brilliant complexion, and her blue eyes. It is this Circassian blood, I suppose, to which the Turkish aristocracy that governs Egypt must be indebted for the fairness of their skin. Ibrahim Pasha, riding by in his barouche, looked like a bluff jolly-faced English dragoon officer, with a grey moustache and red cheeks, such as you might see on a field-day at Maidstone. All the numerous officials riding through the town were quite as fair as Europeans. We made acquaintance with one dignitary, a very jovial and fat Pasha, the proprietor of the inn, I believe, who was continually lounging about the Ezbekieh garden, and who, but for a slight Jewish cast of countenance, might have passed any day for a Frenchman. The ladies whom we saw were equally fair; that is, the very slight particles of the persons of ladies which our lucky eyes were permitted to gaze on. These lovely creatures go through the town by parties of three or four, mounted on donkeys, and attended by slaves holding on at the crupper, to receive the lovely riders lest they should fall, and shouting out shrill cries of "Schmaalek," "Ameenek" (or however else these words may be pronounced), and flogging off the people right and left with the buffalo-thong. But the dear creatures are even more closely disguised than at Constantinople: their bodies are enveloped with a large black silk hood, like a cab-head; the fashion seemed to be to spread their arms out, and give this covering all the amplitude of which it was capable, as they leered and ogled you from under their black masks with their big rolling eyes.

Everybody has big rolling eyes here (unless, to be sure, they lose one of ophthalmia). The Arab women are some of the noblest figures I have ever seen. The habit of carrying jars on the head always gives the figure grace and motion; and the dress the women wear certainly displays it to full advantage. I have brought a complete one home with me, at the service of any lady for a masqued ball. It consists of a coarse blue dress of calico, open in front, and fastened with a horn button. Three yards of blue stuff for a veil; on the top of the veil a jar to be balanced on the head; and a little black strip of silk to fall over the nose, and leave the beautiful eyes full liberty to roll and roam. But such a costume, not aided by any stays or any other article of dress whatever, can be worn only by a very good figure. I suspect it won't be borrowed for many balls next season.

The men, a tall, handsome, noble race, are treated like dogs. I shall never forget riding through the crowded bazaars, my interpreter, or *laquais-de-place*, ahead of me to clear the way— when he took his whip, and struck it over the shoulders of a man who could not or would not make way!

The man turned round—an old, venerable, handsome face, with awfully sad eyes, and a beard long and quite grey. He did not make the least complaint, but slunk out of the way, piteously shaking his shoulder. The sight of that indignity gave me a sickening feeling of disgust. I shouted out to the cursed lackey to hold his hand, and forbade him ever in my presence to strike old or young more; but everybody is doing it. The whip is in everybody's hands: the Pasha's running footman, as he goes bustling through the bazaar; the doctor's attendant, as he soberly threads the crowd on his mare; the negro slave, who is riding by himself, the most insolent of all, strikes and slashes about without mercy, and you never hear a single complaint.

How to describe the beauty of the streets to you!—the fantastic splendour; the variety of the houses, and archways, and hanging roofs, and balconies, and porches; the delightful accidents of light and shade which chequer them: the noise, the bustle, the brilliancy of the crowd; the interminable vast bazaars with their barbaric splendour. There is a fortune to be made for painters in Cairo, and materials for a whole Academy of them. I never saw such a variety of architecture, of life, of picturesqueness, of brilliant colour, and light and shade. There is a picture in every street, and at every bazaar stall. Some of these our celebrated water-colour painter, Mr. Lewis, has produced with admirable truth and exceeding minuteness and beauty; but there is room for a hundred to follow him; and should any artist (by some rare occurrence) read this, who has leisure, and wants to break new ground, let him take heart, and try a winter in Cairo, where there is the finest climate and the best subjects for his pencil.

A series of studies of negroes alone would form a picturebook, delightfully grotesque. Mounting my donkey to-day, I took a ride to the desolate noble old buildings outside the city, known as the Tombs of the Caliphs. Every one of these edifices, with their domes, and courts, and minarets, is strange and beautiful. In one of them there was an encampment of negro slaves newly arrived: some scores of them were huddled against the sunny wall; two or three of their masters lounged about the court, or lay smoking upon carpets. There was one of these fellows, a straight-nosed ebony-faced Abyssinian, with an expression of such sinister good-humour in his handsome face as would form a perfect type of villany. He sat leering at me, over his carpet, as I endeavoured to get a sketch of that incarnate rascality. "Give me some money," said the fellow. "I know what you are about. You will sell my picture for money when you get back to Europe; let me have some of it now!" But the very rude and humble designer was quite unable to depict such a consummation and perfection of roguery; so flung him a cigar, which he began to smoke, grinning at the giver. I requested the interpreter to inform him, by way of assurance of my disinterestedness, that his face was a great deal too ugly to be popular in Europe, and that was the particular reason why I had selected it.

Then one of his companions got up and showed us his black cattle. The male slaves were chiefly lads, and the women young, well formed, and abominably hideous. The dealer pulled her blanket off one of them, and bade her stand up, which she did with a great deal of shuddering modesty. She was coal black, her lips were the size of sausages, her eyes large and good-humoured; the hair or wool on this young person's head was curled and greased into a thousand filthy little ringlets. She was evidently the beauty of the flock.

They are not unhappy: they look to being bought, as many a spinster looks to an establishment in England; once in a family they are kindly treated and well clothed, and fatten, and are the merriest people of the whole community. These were of a much more savage sort than the slaves I had seen in the horrible market at Constantinople, where I recollect the following young creature—[vi](indeed it is a very fair likeness of her) whilst I was looking at her and forming pathetic conjectures regarding her fate—smiling very good-humouredly, and bidding the interpreter ask me to buy her for twenty pounds.

From these Tombs of the Caliphs the Desert is before you. It comes up to the walls of the city, and stops at some gardens which spring up all of a sudden at its edge. You can see the first Station-house on the Suez Road; and so from distance-point to point, could ride thither alone without a guide.

Asinus trotted gallantly into this desert for the space of a quarter of an hour. There we were (taking care to keep our back to the city walls), in the real actual desert: mounds upon mounds of sand, stretching away as far as the eye can see, until the dreary prospect fades away in the yellow horizon! I had formed a finer idea of it out of "Eothen." Perhaps in a simoom it may look more awful. The only adventure that befell in this romantic place was that Asinus's legs went deep into a hole: whereupon his rider went over his head, and bit the sand, and measured his length there; and upon this hint rose up, and rode home again. No doubt one should have gone out for a couple of days' march—as it was, the desert did not seem to me sublime, only *uncomfortable*.

Very soon after this perilous adventure the sun likewise dipped into the sand (but not to rise therefrom so quickly as I had done); and I saw this daily phenomenon of sunset with pleasure, for I was engaged at that hour to dine with our old friend J-, who has established himself here in the most complete Oriental fashion.

You remember J—, and what a dandy he was, the faultlessness of his boots and cravats, the brilliancy of his waistcoats and kid-gloves; we have seen his splendour in Regent Street, in the Tuileries, or on the Toledo. My first object on arriving here was to find out his house, which he has taken far away from the haunts of European civilisation, in the Arab quarter. It is situated in a cool, shady, narrow alley; so narrow, that it was with great difficulty—His Highness Ibrahim Pasha happening to pass at the same moment— that my little procession of two donkeys, mounted by self and valet-de-place, with the two donkey-boys our attendants, could range ourselves along the wall, and leave room for the august cavalcade. His Highness having rushed on (with an affable and good-humoured salute to our imposing party), we made J.'s quarters; and, in the first place, entered a broad covered court or porch, where a swarthy tawny attendant, dressed in blue, with white turban, keeps a perpetual watch. Servants in the East lie about all the doors, it appears; and you clap your hands, as they do in the dear old "Arabian Nights," to summon them.

This servant disappeared through a narrow wicket, which he closed after him; and went into the inner chambers, to ask if his lord would receive us. He came back presently, and rising up from my donkey, I confided him to his attendant (lads more sharp, arch, and wicked than these donkey-boys don't walk the pave of Paris or London), and passed the mysterious outer door.

First we came into a broad open court, with a covered gallery running along one side of it. A camel was reclining on the grass there; near him was a gazelle, to glad J— with his dark blue eye; and a numerous brood of hens and chickens, who furnish his liberal table. On the opposite side of the covered gallery rose up the walls of his long, queer, many-windowed, many-galleried house. There were wooden lattices to those arched windows, through the diamonds of one of which I saw two of the most beautiful, enormous, ogling black eyes in the world, looking down upon the interesting stranger. Pigeons were flapping, and hopping, and fluttering, and cooing about. Happy pigeons, you are, no doubt, fed with crumbs from the henne-tipped fingers of Zuleika! All this court, cheerful in the sunshine, cheerful with the astonishing brilliancy of the eyes peering out from the lattice-bars, was as mouldy, ancient, and ruinous—as any gentleman's house in Ireland, let us say. The paint was peeling off the rickety old carved galleries; the arabesques over the windows were chipped and worn;—the ancientness of the place rendered it doubly picturesque. I have detained you a long time in the outer court. Why the deuce was Zuleika there, with the beautiful black eyes?

Hence we passed into a large apartment, where there was a fountain; and another domestic made his appearance, taking me in charge, and relieving the tawny porter of the gate. This fellow was clad in blue too, with a red sash and a grey beard. He conducted me into a great hall, where there was a great, large Saracenic oriel window. He seated me on a divan; and stalking off, for a moment, returned with a long pipe and a brass chafing-dish: he blew the coal for the pipe, which he motioned me to smoke, and left me there with a respectful bow. This delay, this mystery of servants, that outer court with the camels, gazelles, and other beautiful-eyed things, affected me prodigiously all the time he was staying away; and while I was examining the strange apartment and its contents, my respect and awe for the owner increased vastly.

As you will be glad to know how an Oriental nobleman (such as J— undoubtedly is) is lodged and garnished, let me describe the contents of this hall of audience. It is about forty feet long, and eighteen or twenty high. All the ceiling is carved, gilt, painted and embroidered with arabesques, and choice sentences of Eastern writing. Some Mameluke Aga, or Bey, whom Mehemet Ali invited to breakfast and massacred, was the proprietor of this mansion once: it has grown dingier, but, perhaps, handsomer, since his time. Opposite the divan is a great bay-window, with a divan likewise round the niche. It looks out upon a garden about the size of Fountain Court, Temple; surrounded by the tall houses of the quarter. The garden is full of green. A great palm-tree springs up in the midst, with plentiful shrubberies, and a talking fountain. The room beside the divan is furnished with one deal table, value five shillings; four wooden chairs, value six shillings; and a couple of mats and carpets. The table and chairs are luxuries imported from Europe. The regular Oriental dinner is put upon copper trays, which are laid upon low stools. Hence J-Effendi's house may be said to be much more sumptuously furnished than those of the Beys and Agas his neighbours.

When these things had been examined at leisure, J— appeared. Could it be the exquisite of the "Europa" and the "Trois Freres"? A man--in a long yellow gown, with a long beard somewhat tinged with grey, with his head shaved, and wearing on it, first, a white wadded cotton nightcap; second, a red tarboosh—made his appearance and welcomed me cordially. It was some time, as the Americans say, before I could "realise" the semillant J— of old times.

He shuffled off his outer slippers before he curled up on the divan beside me. He clapped his hands, and languidly called "Mustapha." Mustapha came with more lights, pipes, and coffee; and then we fell to talking about London, and I gave him the last news of the comrades in that dear city. As we talked, his Oriental coolness and languor gave way to British cordiality; he was the most amusing companion of the club once more.

He has adapted himself outwardly, however, to the Oriental life. When he goes abroad he rides a grey horse with red housings, and has two servants to walk beside him. He wears a very handsome grave costume of dark blue, consisting of an embroidered jacket and gaiters, and a pair of trousers, which would make a set of dresses for an English family. His beard curls nobly over his chest, his Damascus scimitar on his thigh. His red cap gives him a venerable and Bey-like appearance. There is no gewgaw or parade about him, as in some of your dandified young Agas. I should say that he is a Major-General of Engineers, or a grave officer of State. We and the Turkified European, who found us at dinner, sat smoking in solemn divan.

His dinners were excellent; they were cooked by a regular Egyptian female cook. We had delicate cucumbers stuffed with forced-meats; yellow smoking pilaffs, the pride of the Oriental cuisine; kid and fowls a l'Aboukir and a la Pyramide: a number of little savoury plates of legumes of the vegetable-marrow sort: kibobs with an excellent sauce of plums and piquant herbs. We ended the repast with ruby pomegranates, pulled to pieces, deliciously cool and pleasant. For the meats, we certainly ate them with the Infidel knife and fork; but for the fruit, we put our hands into the dish and flicked them into our mouths in what cannot but be the true Oriental manner. I asked for lamb and pistachio-nuts, and cream-tarts au poivre; but J.'s cook did not furnish us with either of those historic dishes. And for drink, we had water freshened in the porous little pots of grey clay, at whose spout every traveller in the East has sucked delighted. Also, it must be confessed, we drank certain sherbets, prepared by the two great rivals, Hadji Hodson and Bass Bey—the bitterest and most delicious of draughts! O divine Hodson! a camel's load of thy beer came from Beyrout to Jerusalem while we were there. How shall I ever forget the joy inspired by one of those foaming cool flasks?

We don't know the luxury of thirst in English climes. Sedentary men in cities at least have seldom ascertained it; but when they travel, our countrymen guard against it well. The road between Cairo and Suez is *jonché* with soda-water corks. Tom Thumb and his brothers might track their way across the desert by those landmarks.

Cairo is magnificently picturesque: it is fine to have palm-trees in your gardens, and ride about on a camel; but, after all, I was anxious to know what were the particular excitements of Eastern life, which detained J—, who is a town-bred man, from his natural pleasures and occupations in London; where his family don't hear from him, where his room is still kept ready at home, and his name is on the list of his club; and where his neglected sisters tremble to think that their Frederick is going about with a great beard and a crooked sword, dressed up like an odious Turk. In a "lark" such a costume may be very well; but home, London, a razor, your sister to make tea, a pair of moderate Christian breeches in lieu of those enormous Turkish shulwars, are vastly more convenient in the long run. What was it that kept him away from these decent and accustomed delights?

It couldn't be the black eyes in the balcony—upon his honour she was only the black cook, who has done the pilaff, and stuffed the cucumbers. No, it was an indulgence of laziness such as Europeans, Englishmen, at least, don't know how to enjoy. Here he lives like a languid Lotus-eater—a dreamy, hazy, lazy, tobaccofied life. He was away from evening parties, he said: he needn't wear white kid gloves, or starched neckcloths, or read a newspaper. And even this life at Cairo was too civilised for him: Englishmen passed through; old acquaintances would call: the great pleasure of pleasures was life in the desert,—under the tents, with still more nothing to do than in Cairo; now smoking, now cantering on Arabs, and no crowd to jostle you; solemn contemplations of the stars at night, as the camels were picketed, and the fires and the pipes were lighted.

The night-scene in the city is very striking for its vastness and loneliness. Everybody has gone to rest long before ten o'clock. There are no lights in the enormous buildings; only the stars blazing above, with their astonishing brilliancy, in the blue peaceful sky. Your guides carry a couple of little lanterns which redouble the darkness in the solitary echoing street. Mysterious people are curled up and sleeping in the porches. A patrol of soldiers passes, and hails you. There is a light yet in one mosque, where some devotees are at prayers all night; and you hear the queerest nasal music proceeding from those pious believers. As you pass the madhouse, there is one poor fellow still talking to the moon—no sleep for him. He howls and sings there all the night—quite cheerfully, however. He has not lost his vanity with his reason: he is a Prince in spite of the bars and the straw.

What to say about those famous edifices, which has not been better said elsewhere? —but you will not believe that we visited them, unless I bring some token from them.

That white-capped lad skipped up the stones with a jug of water in his hand, to refresh weary climbers; and squatting himself down on the summit, was designed as you see. The vast flat landscape stretches behind him; the great winding river; the purple city, with forts, and domes, and spires; the green fields, and palm-groves, and speckled villages; the plains still covered with shining inundations—the landscape stretches far far away, until it is lost and mingled in the golden horizon. It is poor work this landscape-painting in print. Shelley's two sonnets are the best views that I know of the Pyramids—better than the reality; for a man may lay down the book, and in quiet fancy conjure up a picture out of these magnificent words, which shan't be disturbed by any pettinesses or mean realities,—such as the swarms of howling beggars, who jostle you about the actual place, and scream in your ears incessantly, and hang on your skirts, and bawl for money.

The ride to the Pyramids is one of the pleasantest possible. In the fall of the year, though the sky is almost cloudless above you, the sun is not too hot to bear; and the landscape, refreshed by the subsiding inundations, delightfully green and cheerful. We made up a party of some half-dozen from the hotel, a lady (the kind soda-water provider, for whose hospitality the most grateful compliments are hereby offered) being of the company, bent like the rest upon going to the summit of Cheops. Those who were cautious and wise, took a brace of donkeys. At least five times during the route did my animals fall with me, causing me to repeat the desert experiment over again, but with more success. The space between a moderate pair of legs and the ground, is not many inches. By eschewing stirrups, the donkey could fall, and the rider alight on the ground, with the greatest ease and grace. Almost everybody was down and up again in the course of the day.

We passed through the Ezbekieh and by the suburbs of the town, where the garden-houses of the Egyptian noblesse are situated, to Old Cairo, where a ferry-boat took the whole party across the Nile, with that noise and bawling volubility in which the Arab people seem to be so unlike the grave and silent Turks; and so took our course for some eight or ten miles over the devious tract which the still outlying waters obliged us to pursue. The Pyramids were in sight the whole way. One or two thin silvery clouds were hovering over them, and casting delicate rosy shadows upon the grand simple old piles. Along the track we saw a score of pleasant pictures of Eastern life:-The Pasha's horses and slaves stood caparisoned at his door; at the gate of one country-house, I am sorry to say, the Bey's *gig* was in waiting,—a most unromantic chariot; the husbandmen were coming into the city, with their strings of donkeys and their loads; as they arrived, they stopped and sucked at the fountain: a column of red-capped troops passed to drill, with slouched gait, white uniforms, and glittering bayonets. Then we had the pictures at the quay: the ferryboat, and the red-sailed river-boat, getting under way, and bound up the stream. There was the grain market, and the huts on the opposite side; and that beautiful woman, with silver armlets, and a face the colour of gold, which (the nose-bag having been luckily removed) beamed solemnly on us Europeans, like a great yellow harvest moon. The bunches of purpling dates were pending from the branches; grey cranes or herons were flying over the cool shining lakes, that the river's overflow had left behind; water was gurgling through the courses by the rude locks and barriers formed there, and overflowing this patch of ground; whilst the neighbouring field was fast budding into the more brilliant fresh green. Single dromedaries were stepping along, their riders lolling on their hunches; low sail-boats were lying in the canals; now, we crossed an old marble bridge; now, we went, one by one, over a ridge of slippery earth; now, we floundered through a small lake of mud. At last, at about half-a-mile off the Pyramid, we came to a piece of water some two-score yards broad, where a regiment of half-naked Arabs, seizing upon each individual of the party, bore us off on their shoulders, to the laughter of all, and the great perplexity of several, who every moment expected to be pitched into one of the many holes with which the treacherous lake abounded.

It was nothing but joking and laughter, bullying of guides, shouting for interpreters, quarrelling about sixpences. We were acting a farce, with the Pyramids for the scene. There they rose up enormous under our eyes, and the most absurd trivial things were going on under their shadow. The sublime had disappeared, vast as they were. Do you remember how Gulliver lost his awe of the tremendous Brobdingnag ladies? Every traveller must go through all sorts of chaffering, and bargaining, and paltry experiences, at this spot. You look up the tremendous steps, with a score of savage ruffians bellowing round you; you hear faint cheers and cries high up, and catch sight of little reptiles crawling upwards; or, having achieved the summit, they come hopping and bouncing down again from degree to degree,—the cheers and cries swell louder and more disagreeable; presently the little jumping thing, no bigger than an insect a moment ago, bounces down upon you expanded into a panting Major of Bengal cavalry. He drives off the Arabs with an oath,—wipes his red shining face with his yellow handkerchief, drops puffing on the sand in a shady corner, where cold fowl and hard eggs are awaiting him, and the next minute you see his nose plunged in a foaming beaker of brandy and soda-water. He can say now, and for ever, he has been up the Pyramid. There is nothing sublime in it. You cast your eye once more up that staggering perspective of a zigzag line, which ends at the summit, and wish you were up there—and down again. Forwards!—Up with you! It must be done. Six Arabs are behind you, who won't let you escape if you would.

The importunity of these ruffians is a ludicrous annoyance to which a traveller must submit. For two miles before you reach the Pyramids they seize on you and never cease howling. Five or six of them pounce upon one victim, and never leave him until they have carried him up and down. Sometimes they conspire to run a man up the huge stair, and bring him, half-killed and fainting, to the top. Always a couple of brutes insist upon impelling you sternwards; from whom the only means to release yourself is to kick out vigorously and unmercifully, when the Arabs will possibly retreat. The ascent is not the least romantic, or difficult, or sublime: you walk up a great broken staircase, of which some of the steps are four feet high. It's not hard, only a little high. You see no better view from the top than you behold from the bottom; only a little more river, and sand, and ricefield. You jump down the big steps at your leisure; but your meditations you must keep for after-times,—the cursed shrieking of the Arabs prevents all thought or leisure.

-And this is all you have to tell about the Pyramids? Oh! for shame! Not a compliment to their age and size? Not a big phrase,--not a rapture? Do you mean to say that you had no feeling of respect and awe? Try, man, and build up a monument of words as lofty as they are—they, whom "*imber edax*" and "*aquilo impotens*" and the flight of ages have not been able to destroy.

—No: be that work for great geniuses, great painters, great poets! This quill was never made to take such flights; it comes of the wing of a humble domestic bird, who walks a common; who talks a great deal (and hisses sometimes); who can't fly far or high, and drops always very quickly; and whose unromantic end is, to be laid on a Michaelmas or Christmas table, and there to be discussed for half-an-hour—let us hope, with some relish.

* * *

Another week saw us in the Quarantine Harbour at Malta, where seventeen days of prison and quiet were almost agreeable, after the incessant sight-seeing of the last two months. In the interval, between the 23rd of August and the 27th of October, we may boast of having seen more men and cities than most travellers have seen in such a time:—Lisbon, Cadiz, Gibraltar, Malta, Athens, Smyrna, Constantinople, Jerusalem, Cairo. I shall have the carpet-bag, which has visited these places in company with its owner, embroidered with their names; as military flags are emblazoned, and laid up in ordinary, to be looked at in old age. With what a number of sights and pictures,—of novel sensations, and lasting and delightful remembrances, does a man furnish his mind after such a tour! You forget all the annoyances of travel; but the pleasure remains with you, through that kind provision of nature by which a man forgets being ill, but thinks with joy of getting well, and can remember all the minute

circumstances of his convalescence. I forget what sea-sickness is now: though it occupies a woful portion of my Journal. There was a time on board when the bitter ale was decidedly muddy; and the cook of the ship deserting at Constantinople, it must be confessed his successor was for some time before he got his hand in. These sorrows have passed away with the soothing influence of time: the pleasures of the voyage remain, let us hope, as long as life will endure. It was but for a couple of days that those shining columns of the Parthenon glowed under the blue sky there; but the experience of a life could scarcely impress them more vividly. We saw Cadiz only for an hour; but the white buildings, and the glorious blue sea, how clear they are to the memory!—with the tang of that gipsy's guitar dancing in the market-place, in the midst of the fruit, and the beggars, and the sunshine. Who can forget the Bosphorus, the brightest and fairest scene in all the world; or the towering lines of Gibraltar; or the great piles of Mafra, as we rode into the Tagus? As I write this, and think, back comes Rhodes, with its old towers and artillery, and that wonderful atmosphere, and that astonishing blue sea which environs the island. The Arab riders go pacing over the plains of Sharon, in the rosy twilight, just before sunrise; and I can see the ghastly Moab mountains, with the Dead Sea gleaming before them, from the mosque on the way towards Bethany. The black gnarled trees of Gethsemane lie at the foot of Olivet, and the yellow ramparts of the city rise up on the stony hills beyond.

But the happiest and best of all the recollections, perhaps, are those of the hours passed at night on the deck, when the stars were shining overhead, and the hours were tolled at their time, and your thoughts were fixed upon home far away. As the sun rose I once heard the priest, from the minaret of Constantinople, crying out, "Come to prayer," with his shrill voice ringing through the clear air; and saw, at the same hour, the Arab prostrate himself and pray, and the Jew Rabbi, bending over his book, and worshipping the Maker of Turk and Jew. Sitting at home in London, and writing this last line of farewell, those figures come back the clearest of all to the memory, with the picture, too, of our ship sailing over the peaceful Sabbath sea, and our own prayers and services celebrated there. So each, in his fashion, and after his kind, is bowing down, and adoring the Father, who is equally above all. Cavil not, you brother or sister, if your neighbour's voice is not like yours; only hope that his words are honest (as far as they may be), and his heart humble and thankful.

THE IRISH SKETCH BOOK

CHAPTER I: A SUMMER DAY IN DUBLIN, OR THERE AND THEREABOUTS

THE coach that brings the passenger by wood and mountain, by brawling waterfall and gloomy plain, by the lonely lake of Festiniog and across the swinging world's wonder of a Menai Bridge, through dismal Anglesea to dismal Holyhead—the Birmingham mail,—manages matters so cleverly, that after ten hours' ride the traveller is thrust incontinently on board the packet, and the steward says there's no use in providing dinner on board because the passage is so short.

That is true: but why not give us half-an-hour on shore ? Ten hours spent on a coach-box render the dinner question one of extreme importance; and as the packet reaches Kingstown at midnight, when all the world is asleep, the inn-larders locked up, and the cook in bed; and as the mail is not landed until five in the morning (at which hour the passengers are considerately awakened by a great stamping and shouting overhead), might not 'Lord Lowther' give us one little half-hour? Even the steward agreed that it was a useless and atrocious tyranny; and, indeed, after a little demur, produced a half-dozen of fried eggs, a feeble makeshift for a dinner.

Our passage across from the Head was made in a rain so pouring and steady, that Bea and coast were entirely hidden from us, and one could see very little beyond the glowing tip of the cigar which remained alight nobly in spite of the weather. When the gallant exertions of that fiery spirit were over for ever, and burning bravely to the end it had breathed its last in doing its master service, all became black and cheerless around; the passengers had dropped off one by one, preferring to be dry and ill below rather than wet and squeamish above: even the mate, with his gold-laced cap (who is so astonishingly like Mr. Charles Dickens that he might pass for that gentleman)—even the mate said he would go to his cabin and turn in. So there remained nothing for it but to do as all the world had done.

Hence it was impossible to institute the comparison between the Bay of Naples and that of Dublin (the Bee of Neeples the former is sometimes called in this country), where I have heard the likeness asserted in a great number of societies and conversations. But how could one see the Bay of Dublin in the dark? and how, supposing one could see it, should a person behave who has never seen the Bay of Naples? It is but to take the similarity for granted, and remain in bed till morning.

When everybody was awakened at five o'clock by the noise made upon the removal of the mail-bags, there was heard a cheerless dribbling and pattering overhead, which led one to wait still further until the rain should cease. At length the steward said the last boat was going ashore, and receiving half-a-crown for his own services (the regular tariff), intimated likewise that it was the custom for gentlemen to compliment the stewardess with a shilling, which ceremony was also complied with. No doubt she is an amiable woman, and deserves any sum of money. As for inquiring whether she merited it or not in this instance, that surely is quite unfair. A traveller who stops to inquire the deserts of every individual claimant of a shilling on his road, had best stay quiet at home. If we only got what we *deserved*,—Heaven save us!—many of us might whistle for a dinner.

A long pier, with a steamer or two at hand, and a few small vessels lying on either side of the jetty; a town irregularly built, with many handsome terraces, some churches, and showy-looking hotels; a few people straggling on the beach; two or three cars at the railroad station, which runs along the shore as far as Dublin; the sea stretching interminably eastward; to the north the Hill of Howth, lying grey behind the mist; and, directly under his feet, upon the wet, black, shining, slippery deck, an agreeable reflection of his own legs, disappearing seemingly in the direction of the cabin from which he issues: are the sights which a traveller may remark on coming on deck at Kingstown pier on a wet morning—let us say on an *average* morning; for according to the statement of well-informed natives, the Irish day is more often rainy than otherwise. A hideous obelisk, stuck upon four fat balls, and surmounted with a crown on a cushion (the latter were no bad emblems perhaps of the monarch in whose honour they were raised), commemorates the sacred spot at which George IV. *quitted* Ireland. You are landed here from the steamer; and a carman, who is dawdling in the neighbourhood, with a straw in his mouth, comes leisurely up to ask whether you will go to Dublin? Is it natural indolence, or the effect of despair because of the neighbouring railroad, which renders him so indifferent?—He does not even take the straw out of his mouth as he proposes the question—he seems quite careless as to the answer.

He said he would take me to Dublin 'in three quarthers,' as soon as we began a parley. As to the fare, he would not hear of it—he said he would leave it to my honour; he would take me for nothing. Was it possible to refuse such a genteel offer? The times are very much changed since those described by the facetious Jack Hinton, when the carmen tossed up for the passenger, and those who won him took him ; for the renaming cars on the stand did not seem to take the least interest in the bargain, or offer to overdrive or underbid their comrade in any way.

Before that day, so memorable for joy and sorrow, for rapture at receiving its monarch and tearful grief at losing him, when George IV. came and left the maritime resort of the citizens of Dublin, it bore a less genteel name than that which it owns at present, and was called Dunleary. After that glorious event Dunleary disdained to be Dunleary any longer, and became Kingstown henceforward and for ever. Numerous terraces and pleasure-houses have been built in the place —they stretch row after row along the banks of the sea, and rise one above another on the hill. The rents of these houses are said to be very high; the Dublin citizens crowd into them in summer; and a great source of pleasure and comfort must it be to them to have the fresh sea-breezes and prospects so near to the metropolis.

The better sort of houses are handsome and spacious; but the fashionable quarter is yet in an unfinished state, for enterprising architects are always beginning new roads, rows and terraces: nor are those already built by any means complete. Beside the aristocratic part of the town is a commercial one, and nearer to Dublin stretch lines of low cottages which have not a Kingstown look at all, but are evidently of the Dunleary period. It is quite curious to see in the streets where the shops are, how often the painter of the signboards begins with big letters, and ends, for want of space, with small; and the Englishman accustomed to the thriving neatness and regularity which characterise towns great and small in his own country, can't fail to notice the difference here. The houses have a battered rakish look, and seem going to ruin before their time. As seamen of all nations come hither who have made no vow of temperance, there are plenty of liquor-shops still, and shabby cigar-shops, and shabby milliners' and tailors' with fly-blown prints of old fashions. The bakers and apothecaries make a great brag of their calling, and you see MEDICAL HALL, or PUBLIC BAKERY, BALLYRAGGET FLOUR-STORE (or whatever the name may be) pompously inscribed over very humble tenements. Some comfortable grocers' and butchers' shops, and numbers of shabby sauntering people, the younger part of whom are barelegged and bareheaded, make up the rest of the picture which the stranger sees as his car goes jingling through the street.

After the town come the suburbs of pleasure-houses; low one-storeyed cottages for the most part: some neat and fresh; some that have passed away from the genteel state altogether, and exhibit downright poverty; some in a state of transition, with broken windows and pretty romantic names upon tumbledown gates. Who lives in them? One fancies that the chairs and tables inside are broken, that the teapot on the breakfast-table has no spout, and the table-cloth is ragged and sloppy; that the lady of the house is in dubious curl-papers; and the gentleman, with an imperial to his chin, and a flaring dressing-gown all ragged at the elbows.

To be sure, a traveller who in ten minutes can see not only the outsides of houses, but the interiors of the same, must have remarkably keen sight; and it is early yet to speculate. It is clear, however, that these are pleasure-houses for a certain class; and looking at the houses, one can't but fancy the inhabitants resemble them somewhat. The car, on its road to Dublin, passes by numbers of these—by more shabbiness than a Londoner will see in the course of his home peregrinations for a year.

The capabilities of the country, however, are very very great, and in many instances have been taken advantage of: for you see, besides the misery, numerous handsome houses and parks along the road, having fine lawns and woods; and the sea is in our view at a quarter of an hour's ride from Dublin. It is the continual appearance of this sort of wealth which makes the poverty more striking: and thus between the two (for there is no vacant space of fields between Kingstown and Dublin) the car reaches the city. There is but little commerce on this road, which was also in extremely bad repair. It is neglected for the sake of its thriving neighbour the railroad; on which a dozen pretty little stations accommodate the inhabitants of the various villages through which we pass.

The entrance to the capital is very handsome. There is no bustle and throng of carriages, as in London; but you pass by numerous rows of neat houses, fronted with gardens and adorned with all sorts of gay-looking creepers. Pretty market-gardens, with trim beds of plants and shining glass-houses, give the suburbs a *riante* and cheerful look; and, passing under the arch of the railway, we are in the city itself. Hence you come upon several old-fashioned, well-built, airy, stately streets, and through Fitzwilliam Square, a noble place, the garden of which is full of flowers and foliage. The leaves are green, and not black as in similar places in London; the red-brick houses tall and handsome. Presently the car stops before an extremely big red house, in that extremely large square, Stephen's Green, where Mr. O'Connell says there is one day or other to be a Parliament. There is room enough for that, or for any other edifice which fancy or patriotism may have a mind to erect, for part of one of the sides of the square is not yet built, and you see the fields and the country beyond.

This then is the chief city of the aliens.—The hotel to which I had been directed is a respectable old edifice, much frequented by families from the country, and where the solitary traveller may likewise find society: for he may either use the Shelbume as an hotel or a boarding-house, in which latter case he is comfortably accommodated at the very moderate daily charge of six-and-eightpence. For this charge a copious breakfast is provided for him in the coffee-room, a perpetual luncheon is likewise there spread, a plentiful dinner is ready at six o'clock: after which there is a drawing-room, and a rubber of whist, with *tay* and coffee and cakes in plenty to satisfy the largest appetite. The hotel is majestically conducted by clerks and other officers; the landlord himself does not appear, after the honest comfortable English fashion, but lives in a private mansion hard by, where his name may be read inscribed on a brass-plate, like that of any other private gentleman.

A woman melodiously crying 'Dublin Bay herrings' passed just as we came up to the door, and as that fish is famous throughout Europe, I seized the earliest opportunity and ordered a broiled one for breakfast. It merits all its reputation ; and in this respect I should think the Bay of Dublin is far superior to its rival of Naples. Are there any herrings in Naples Bay? Dolphins there may be; and Mount Vesuvius, to be sure, is bigger than even the Hill of Howth : but a dolphin is better in a sonnet than at a breakfast, and what poet is there that, at certain periods of the day, would hesitate in his choice between the two?

With this famous broiled herring the morning papers are served up; and a great part of these, too, gives opportunity of reflection to the new-comer, and shows him how different this country is from his own. Some hundred years hence, when students want to inform themselves of the history of the present day, and refer to files of

Times and Chronicle for the purpose, I think it is possible that they will consult, not so much those luminous and philosophical leading articles which call our attention at present both by the majesty of their eloquence and the largeness of their type, but that they will turn to those parts of the journals into which information is squeezed in the smallest possible print: to the advertisements, namely, the law and police reports, and to the instructive narratives supplied by that ill-used body of men who transcribe knowledge at the rate of a penny a line.

The papers before me *(The Morning Register*, Liberal and Roman Catholic; *Saunders's News-letter,* neutral and Conservative) give a lively picture of the movement of city and country on this present fourth day of July [1842], and the Englishman can scarcely fail, as he reads them, to note many small points of difference existing between his own country and this. How do the Irish amuse themselves in the capital? The love for theatrical exhibitions is evidently not very great. Theatre Royal—Miss Kemble and the Sonnambula, an Anglo-Italian importation. Theatre Royal, Abbey Street—The Temple of Magic and the Wizard, last week. Adelphi Theatre, Great Brunswick Street—The Original Seven Lancashire Bell-ringers: a delicious excitement indeed! Portobello Gardens—'The Last Eruption but Six,' says the advertisement in capitals. And, finally, 'Miss Hayes will give her first and farewell concert at the Rotunda, previous to leaving her native country.' Only one instance of Irish talent do we read of, and that, in a desponding tone, announces its intention of quitting its native country. All the rest of the pleasures of the evening are importations from Cockney-land. The Sonnambula from Covent Garden, the Wizard from the Strand, the Seven Lancashire Bell-ringers, from Islington or the City Road no doubt; and as for 'The last Eruption but Six,' it has *erumped* near the 'Elephant and Castle' any time these two years, until the cockneys would wonder at it no longer.

The commercial advertisements are but few—a few horses and cars for sale; some flaming announcements of insurance companies; some 'emporiums' of Scotch tweeds and English broadcloths; an auction for damaged sugar; and an estate or two for sale. They lie in the columns languidly, and at their ease as it were: how different from the throng, and squeeze, and bustle of the commercial part of a London paper, where every man (except Mr. George Robins) states his case as briefly as possible, because thousands more are to be heard besides himself, and as if he had no time for talking!

The most active advertisers are the schoolmasters. It is now the happy time of the Midsummer holidays; and the pedagogues make wonderful attempts to encourage parents, and to attract fresh pupils for the ensuing half-year. Of all these announcements that of Madame Shanahan (a delightful name) is perhaps the most brilliant. 'To Parents and Guardians.—Paris.—Such parents and guardians as may wish to entrust their children for education *in its fullest extent* to Madame Shanahan, *can have the advantage of being conducted to Paris* by her brother, the Rev. J. P. O'Reilly, of Church Street Chapel:' which admirable arrangement carries the parents to Paris and leaves the children in Dublin. Ah, Madame, you may take a French title;

but your heart is still in your country, and you are to the *fullest extent* an Irishwoman still!

Fond legends are to be found in Irish books regarding places where you may now see a round tower and a little old chapel, twelve feet square, where famous universities are once said to have stood, and which have accommodated myriads of students. Mrs. Hall mentions Glendalough, in Wicklow, as one of these places of learning; nor can the fact be questioned, as the universities existed hundreds of years since, and no sort of records are left regarding them. A century hence some antiquary may light upon a Dublin paper, and form marvellous calculations regarding the state of education in the country. For instance, at Bective House Seminary, conducted by Doctor J. L. Burke, ex-scholar T. C. D., no less than *two hundred and three* young gentlemen took prizes at the Midsummer examination: nay, Borne of the most meritorious earned off a dozen premiums apiece. A Doctor Delamere, ex-scholar T. C. D., distributed three hundred and twenty rewards to his young friends: and if we allow that one lad in twenty is a prizeman, it is clear that there must be six thousand four hundred and forty youths under the Doctor's care.

Other schools are advertised in the same journals, each with its hundred of prize-bearers; and if other schools are advertised, how many more must there be in the country which are not advertised!

There must be hundreds of thousands of prizemen, millions of scholars: besides national-schools, hedge-schools, infant-schools, and the like. The English reader will see the accuracy of the calculation.

In the *Morning Register*, the Englishman will find something to the full as curious and startling to him: you read gravely in the English language how the Bishop of Aureliopolis has just been consecrated; and that the distinction has been conferred upon him by—the Holy Pontiff!—the Pope of Rome, by all that is holy! Such an announcement sounds quite strange *in English*, and in your own country, as it were: or isn't it your own country? Suppose the Archbishop of Canterbury were to send over a clergyman to Rome, and consecrate him Bishop of the Palatine or the Suburra, I wonder how his Holiness would like *that*?

There is a report of Doctor Miley's sermon upon the occasion of the new bishop's consecration; and the *Register* happily lauds the discourse for its 'refined and fervent eloquence.' The Doctor salutes the Lord Bishop of Aureliopolis on his admission among the 'Princes of the Sanctuary,' gives a blow *en passant* at the Established Church, whereof the revenues, he elegantly says, 'might excite the zeal of Dives or Epicurus to become a bishop,' and having vented his sly wrath upon the 'courtly artifice and intrigue' of the Bench, proceeds to make the most outrageous comparisons with regard to my Lord of Aureliopolis; his virtues, his sincerity, and the severe privations and persecutions which acceptance of the episcopal office entails upon him.

'That very evening,'says the *Register*, 'the new bishop entertained at dinner, in the chapel-house, a select number of friends; amongst whom were the officiating prelates and clergymen who assisted in the ceremonies of the day. The repast was provided by Mr. Jude, of Grafton Street, and was served up in a style of elegance and comfort that did great honour to that gentleman's character as a *restaurateur*. The wines were of the *richest and rarest quality*. It may be truly said to have been an entertainment where the feast of reason and the flow of soul predominated. The company broke up at nine.'

And so my Lord is scarcely out of chapel but his privations begin! Well. Let us hope that, in the course of his episcopacy, he may incur no greater hardships, and that Doctor Miley may come to be a bishop too in his time; when perhaps he will have a better opinion of the Bench.

The ceremony and feelings described are curious, I think; and more so perhaps to a person who was in England only yesterday, and quitted it just as their Graces, Lordships, and Reverences were sitting down to dinner. Among what new sights, ideas, customs, does the English traveller find himself after that brief six hours' journey from Holyhead?

There is but one part more of the papers to be looked at; and that is the most painful of all. In the law reports of the Tipperary Special Commission sitting at Clonmel, you read that Patrick Byrne is brought up for sentence, for the murder of Robert Hall, Esq.: and Chief Justice Doherty says, 'Patrick Byrne, I will not now recapitulate the circumstances of your enormous crime; but guilty as you are of the barbarity of having perpetrated with your hand the foul murder of an unoffending old man—barbarous, cowardly, and cruel as that act was—there lives one more guilty man, and that is he whose diabolical mind hatched the foul conspiracy of which you were but the instrument and perpetrator. Whoever that may be, I do not envy him his protracted existence. He has sent that aged gentleman, without one moment's warning, to face his God; but he has done more: he has brought you, unhappy man, with more deliberation and more cruelty, to face your God, *with the weight of that man's blood upon you.* I have now only to pronounce the sentence of the law:'—it is the usual sentence, with the usual prayer of the judge, that the Lord may have mercy upon the convict's soul.

Timothy Woods, a young man of twenty years of age, is then tried for the murder of Michael Laffan. The Attorney-General states the case;—On the 19th of May last, two assassins dragged Laffan from the house of Patrick Cummins, fired a pistol-shot at him, and left him dead as they thought. Laffan, though mortally wounded, crawled away after the fall; when the assassins, still Beeing him give signs of life, rushed after him, fractured his skull by blows of a pistol, and left him on a dunghill dead. There Laffan's body lay for several hours, and *nobody dared to touch it*. Laffan's widow found the body there two hours after the murder, and *an inquest was held on the body as it lay on the dunghill.* Laffan was driver on the lands of Kilnertin, which were formerly held by Pat Cummins, *the man who had the charge of the lands before Laffan was murdered*; the latter was dragged out of Cummins's house in the presence of a witness who refused to swear to the murderers, and was shot in sight of another witness, James Meara, who with other men was on the road: when asked whether he cried out, or whether he went to assist the deceased, Meara answers, '*Indeed I did not; we would not interfere—it was no business of ours*!'

Six more instances are given of attempts to murder; on which the judge, in passing sentence, comments in the following way:—

'The Lord Chief Justice addressed the several persons, and said—It was now his painful duty to pronounce upon them severally and respectively the punishment which the law and the court awarded against them for the crimes of which they had been convicted. Those crimes were one and all of them of no ordinary enormity—they were crimes which, in point of morals, involved the atrocious guilt of murder; and if it had pleased God to spare their souls from the pollution of that offence the court could not still shut its eyes to the fact, that although death had not ensued in consequence of the crimes of which they had been found guilty, yet it was not owing to their forbearance that such a dreadful crime had not been perpetrated. The prisoner, Michael Hughes, had been convicted of firing a gun at a person of the name of John Ryan (Luke); his horse had been killed, and no one could say that the balls were not intended for the prosecutor himself. The prisoner had fired one shot himself, and then called on his companion in guilt to discharge another. One of these shots killed Ryan's mare, and it was by the mercy of God that the life of the prisoner had not become forfeited by his own act. The next culprit was John Pound, who was equally guilty of the intended outrage perpetrated on the life of an unoffending individual—that individual a female, surrounded by her little children, five or six in number—with a complete carelessness to the probable consequences, while she and her family were going, or had gone, to bed. The contents of a gun were discharged through the door, which entered the panel in three different places. The deaths resulting from this act might have been extensive, but it was not a matter of any moment how many were deprived of life. The woman had just risen from her prayers, preparing herself to sleep under the protection of that arm which would shield the child and protect the innocent, when she was wounded. As to Cornelius Flynn and Patrick Dwyer, they likewise were the subjects of similar imputations and similar observations. There was a very slight difference between them, but not such as to amount to any real distinction. They had gone upon a common illegal purpose, to the house of a respectable individual, for the purpose of interfering with the domestic arrangements he thought fit to make. They had no sort of right to interfere with the disposition of a man's affairs; and what would be the consequences if the reverse were to be held? No imputation had ever been made upon the gentleman whose house was visited, but he was desired to dismiss another, under the pains and penalties of death, although that other was not a retained servant, but a friend who had come to Mr. Hogan on a visit. Because this visitor used sometimes to inspect the men at work, the lawless edict issued that he should be put away. Good God! to what extent did the prisoners and such misguided men intend to carry out their objects? Where was their dictation to cease? are they, and those in a similar rank, to take upon themselves to regulate how many and what men a farmer should take into his employment? Were they to be the judges whether a servant had discharged his duty to his principal? or was it because a visitor happened to come, that the host should turn him away, under the pains and penalties of death? His Lordship, after adverting to the guilt of the prisoners in this case—the last two persons convicted, Thomas Stapleton and Thomas Gleeson—said their case was so recently before the public, that it was sufficient to say they were morally guilty of what might be considered wilful and deliberate murder. Murder was most awful, because it could only be suggested by deliberate malice, and the act of the prisoners was the result of that base, malicious, and diabolical disposition. What was the cause of resentment against the unfortunate man who had been shot at, and so desperately wounded? Why, he had dared to comply with the wishes of a just landlord; and because the landlord, for the benefit of his tenantry, proposed that the farms should be squared, those who acquiesced in his wishes were to be equally the victims of the assassin. What were the facts in this case? The two prisoners at the bar, Stapleton and Gleeson, sprang out at the man as he was leaving work, placed him on his knees, and without giving him a moment of preparation, commenced the work of blood, intending deliberately to despatch that unprepared and unoffending individual to eternity. What country was it that they lived in, in which such crimes could be perpetrated in the open light of day? It was not necessary that deeds of darkness should be shrouded in the clouds of night, for the darkness of the deeds themselves was considered a sufficient protection. He (the Chief Justice) was not aware of any solitary instance at the present Commission, to show that the crimes committed were the consequences of poverty. Poverty should be no justification, however; it might be some little palliation, but on no trial at this Commission did it appear that the crime could be attributed to distress. His Lordship concluded a most impressive address, by sentencing the six prisoners called up to transportation for life.

'The clock was near midnight as the court was cleared, and the whole of the proceedings were solemn and impressive in the extreme. The Commission is likely to prove extremely beneficial in its results on the future tranquillity of the country.'

I confess, for my part, to that common cant and sickly sentimentality, which, thank God! is felt by a great number of people nowadays, and which leads them to revolt against murder, whether performed by a ruffian's knife or a hangman's rope: whether accompanied with a curse from the thief as he blows his victim's brains out, or a prayer from my Lord on the bench in his wig and black cap. Nay, is all the cant and sickly sentimentality on our side, and might not some such charge be applied to the admirers of the good old fashion? Long ere this is printed, for instance, Byrne and Woods have been hanged:[vii] sent 'to face their God,' as the Chief Justice says, 'with the weight of their victim's blood upon them,'—a just observation; and remember that it is *we who send them*. It is true that the judge hopes Heaven will have mercy upon their souls; but are such recommendations of particular weight because they come from the bench? Psha! If we go on killing people without giving them time to repent, let us at least give up the cant of praying for their souls' salvation. We find a man drowning in a well, shut the lid upon him, and heartily pray that he may get out. Sin has hold of him, as the two ruffians of Laffan yonder, and we stand aloof and hope that he may escape. Let us give up this ceremony of condolence, and be honest, like the witness, and say, 'Let him save himself or not, it's no business of ours.'...Here a waiter, with a very broad, though insinuating accent, says, 'Have you done with the *Sandthers*, sir? there's a gentleman waiting for't these two hours.' And so he carries off that strange picture of pleasure and pain, trade, theatres, schools, courts, churches, life and death, in Ireland, which a man may buy for a fourpenny-piece.

The papers being read, it became my duty to discover the town; and a handsomer town, with fewer people in it, it is impossible to see on a summer's day. In the whole wide square of Stephen's Green, I think there were not more than two nursery-maids to keep company with the statue of George I., who rides on horseback in the middle of the garden, the horse having his foot up to trot, as if he wanted to go out of town too. Small troops of dirty children (too poor and dirty to have lodgings at Kingstown) were squatting here and there upon the sunshiny steps, the only clients at the thresholds of the professional gentlemen whose names figure on brass-plates on the doors. A stand of lazy carmen, a policeman or two with clinking boot-heels, a couple of moaning beggars leaning against the rails and calling upon the Lord, and a fellow with a toy and book stall, where the lives of St. Patrick, Robert Emmett, and Lord Edward Fitzgerald may be bought for double their value, were all the population of the Green.

At the door of the Kildare Street Club, I saw eight gentlemen looking at two boys playing at leap-frog: at the door of the University six lazy porters, in jockey-caps, were sunning themselves on a bench—a sort of blue-bottle race; and the Bank on the opposite side did not look as if sixpence-worth of change had been negotiated there during the day. There was a lad pretending to sell umbrellas under the colonnade, almost the only instance of trade going on; and I began to think of Juan Fernandez, or Cambridge in the long vacation. In the courts of the College, scarce the ghost of a gyp or the shadow of a bed-maker.

In spite of the solitude, the square of the College is a fine sight: a large ground, surrounded by buildings of various ages and styles, but comfortable, handsome, and in good repair; a modern row of rooms; a row that has been Elizabethan once; a hall and senate-house, facing each other, of the style of George I.; and a noble library, with a range of many windows, and a fine manly simple façade of cut stone. The library was shut. The librarian, I suppose, is at the seaside; and the only part of the establishment which I could see was the museum, to which one of the jockey-capped porters conducted me, up a wide dismal staircase (adorned with an old pair of jack-boots, a dusty canoe or two, a few helmets, and a South Sea Islander's armour), which passes through a hall hung round with cobwebs (with which the blue-bottles are too wise to meddle), into an old mouldy room, filled with clingy glass-cases, under which the articles of curiosity or science were partially visible.

In the middle was a very *seedy* camelopard (the word has grown to be English by this time), the straw splitting through his tight old skin and the black cobbler's-wax stuffing the dim orifices of his eyes. Other beasts formed a pleasing group around him, not so tall, but equally mouldy and old. The porter took me round to the cases, and told me a great number of fibs concerning their contents: there was the harp of Brian Boru, and the sword of some one else, and other cheap old gimcracks with their corollary of lies. The place would have been a disgrace to Don Saltero. I was quite glad to walk out of it, and down the dirty staircase again: about the ornaments of which the jockey-capped gyp had more figments to tell; an atrocious one (I forget what) relative to the pair of boots; near which—a fine specimen of collegiate taste—were the shoes of Mr. O'Brien, the Irish giant. If the collection is worth preserving,—and indeed the mineralogical specimens look quite as awful as those in the British Museum,—one thing is clear, that the rooms are worth sweeping. A pail of water costs nothing, a scrubbing-brush not much, and a charwoman might be hired for a trifle, to keep the room in a decent state of cleanliness.

Among the curiosities is a mask of the Dean—not the scoffer and giber, not the fiery politician, nor the courtier of St. John and Harley, equally ready with servility and scorn; but the poor old man, whose great intellect had deserted him, and who died old, wild, and sad. The tall forehead is fallen away in a ruin, the mouth has settled in a hideous vacant smile. Well, it was a mercy for Stella that she died first: it was better that she should be killed by his unkindness than by the sight of his misery; which, to such a gentle heart as that, would have been harder still to bear.

The Bank, and other public buildings of Dublin, are justly famous. In the former may still be seen the room which was the House of Lords formerly, and where the Bank directors now sit, under a clean marble image of George III. The House of Commons has disappeared, for the accommodation of clerks and cashiers. The interior is light, splendid, . airy, well furnished, and the outside of the building not less so. The Exchange, hard by, is an equally magnificent structure; but the genius of commerce has deserted it, for all its architectural beauty. There was nobody inside when I entered but a pert statue of George III. in a Roman toga, simpering and turning out his toes; and two dirty children playing, whose hoop-sticks caused great clattering echoes under the vacant sounding dome. The neighbourhood is not cheerful, and has a dingy poverty-stricken look.

Walking towards the river, you have on either side of you, at Carlisle Bridge, a very brilliant and beautiful prospect: the Four Courts and their dome to the left, the Custom House and its dome to the right; and in this direction seaward, a considerable number of vessels are moored and the quays are black and busy with the cargoes discharged from ships. Seamen cheering, herring-women bawling, coal-carts loading—the scene is animated and lively. Yonder is the famous Corn Exchange; but the

Lord Mayor is attending to his duties in Parliament, and little of note is going on. I had just passed his Lordship's mansion in Dawson Street,—a queer old dirty brick house, with dumpy urns at each extremity, and looking as if a storey of it had been cut off—a rasée-house. Close at hand, and peering over a paling, is a statue of our blessed sovereign George II. How absurd these pompous images look, of defunct majesties, for whom no breathing soul cares a halfpenny! It is not so with the effigy of William III., who has done something to merit a statue. At this minute the Lord Mayor has William's effigy under a canvas, and is painting him of a bright green, picked out with yellow—his Lordship's own livery.

The view along the quays to the Four Courts has no small resemblance to a view along the quays at Paris, though not so lively as are even those quiet walks. The vessels do not come above-bridge, and the marine population remains constant about them, and about numerous dirty liquor-shops, eating-houses, and marine-store establishments, which are kept for their accommodation along the quay. As far as you can see, the shining Liffey flows away eastward, hastening (like the rest of the inhabitants of Dublin) to the sea.

In front of Carlisle Bridge, and not in the least crowded, though in the midst of Sackville Street, stands Nelson upon a stone pillar. The. Post Office is on his right hand (only it is cut off); and on his left, Gresham's and the Imperial Hotel. Of the latter let me say (from subsequent experience) that it is ornamented by a cook who could dress a dinner by the side of M. Borel or M. Soyé. Would there were more such artists in this ill-fated country! The street is exceedingly broad and handsome; the shops at the commencement, rich and spacious; but in Upper Sackville Street, which closes with the pretty building and gardens of the Rotunda, the appearance of wealth begins to fade somewhat, and the houses look as if they had seen better days. Even in this, the great street of the town, there is scarcely any one, and it is as vacant and listless as Pall Mall in October. In one of the streets off Sackville Street is the house and exhibition of the Irish Academy, which I went to see, as it was positively to close at the end of the week. While I was there, two *other* people came in; and we had, besides, the money-taker and a porter, to whom the former was reading, out of a newspaper, those Tipperary murders which were mentioned in a former page. The echo took up the theme, and hummed it gloomily through the vacant place.

The drawings and reputation of Mr. Burton are well known in England: his pieces were the most admired in the collection. The best draughtsman is an imitator of Maclise, Mr. Bridgeman, whose pictures are full of vigorous drawing, and remarkable too for their grace. I gave my catalogue to the two young ladies before mentioned, and have forgotten the names of other artists of merit, whose works decked the walls of the little gallery. Here, as in London, the Art Union is making a stir; and several of the pieces were marked as the property of members of that body. The possession of some of these one would not be inclined to covet; but it is pleasant to see that people begin to buy pictures at all and there will be no lack of artists presently, in a country where nature is so beautiful, and genius so plenty. In speaking of the fine arts and of views of Dublin, it may be said that Mr. Petrie's designs for Curry's Guide-book of the City are exceedingly beautiful, and, above all, *trustworthy*: no common quality in a descriptive artist at present.

Having a couple of letters of introduction to leave, I had the pleasure to find the blinds down at one house, and the window in papers at another; and at each place the knock was answered in that leisurely way by one of those dingy female Lieutenants who have no need to tell you that families are out of town. So the solitude became very painful, and I thought I would go back and talk to the waiter at the Shelburne, the only man in the whole kingdom that I knew. I had been accommodated with a queer little room and dressing-room on the ground-floor, looking towards the Green: a black-faced good-humoured chambermaid had promised to perform a deal of scouring which was evidently necessary (a fact she might have observed for six months back, only she is no doubt of an absent turn), and when I came back from the walk, I saw the little room was evidently enjoying itself in the sunshine, for it had opened its window, and was taking a breath of fresh air, as it looked out upon the Green. Here is a portrait of the little window.[viii]

As I came up to it in the street, its appearance made me burst out laughing, very much to the surprise of a ragged cluster of idlers lolling upon the steps next door; and I have drawn it here, not because it is a particularly picturesque or rare kind of window, but because, as I fancy, there is a sort of *moral* in it. You don't see such windows commonly in respectable English inns—windows leaning gracefully upon hearth-brooms for support. Look out of that window without the hearth-broom and it would cut your head off: how the beggars would start that are always sitting on the steps next door! Is it prejudice that makes one prefer the English window, that relies on its own ropes and ballast (or lead if you like), and does not need to be propped by any foreign aid? or is this only a solitary instance of the kind, and are there no other specimens in Ireland of the careless, dangerous, extravagant hearth-broom system?

In the midst of these reflections (which might have been carried much farther, for a person with an allegorical turn might examine the entire country through this window), a most wonderful cab, with an immense prancing cab-horse, was seen to stop at the door of the hotel, and Pat the waiter tumbling into the room swiftly with a card in his hand, says, 'Sir, the gentleman of this card is waiting for you at the door.' *Mon Dieu*! it was an invitation to dinner! and I almost leapt into the arms of the man in the cab—so delightful was it to find a friend in a place where, a moment before, I had been as lonely as Robinson Crusoe.

The only drawback, perhaps, to pure happiness, when riding in such a gorgeous equipage as this, was that we could not drive up Regent Street, and meet a few creditors, or acquaintances at least. However, Pat, I thought, was exceedingly awe-stricken by my disappearance in this vehicle; which had evidently, too, a considerable effect upon some other waiters at the Shelburne, with whom I was not as yet so familiar. The mouldy camelopard at the Trinity College 'Musayum' was scarcely taller than the bay-horse in the cab; the groom behind was of a corresponding smallness. The cab was of a lovely olive-green, picked out with white, on high springs and enormous wheels, which, big as they were, scarcely seemed to touch the earth. The little tiger swung gracefully up and down, holding on by the hood, which was of the material of which the most precious and polished boots are made. As for the *lining*—but here we come too near the sanctity of private life; suffice that there was a kind friend inside, who (though by no means of the fairy sort) was as welcome as any fairy in the finest chariot. W— had seen me landing from the packet that morning, and was the very man who in London, a month previous, had recommended me to the Shelburne. These facts are not of much consequence to the public, to be sure, except that an explanation was necessary of the miraculous appearance of the cab and horse.

Our course, as may be imagined, was towards the seaside; for whither else should an Irishman at this season go? Not far from Kingstown is a house devoted to the purpose of festivity: it is called Salt Hill, stands upon a rising ground, commanding a fine view of the bay and the railroad, and is kept by persons bearing the celebrated name of Lovegrove. It is in fact a sea-Greenwich, and though there are no marine whitebait, other fishes are to be had in plenty, and especially the famous Bray trout, which does not ill deserve its reputation.

Here we met three young men, who may be called by the names of their several counties—Mr. Galway, Mr. Roscommon, and Mr. Clare; and it seemed that I was to complain of solitude no longer: for one straightway invited me to his county, where was the finest salmon-fishing in the world; another said he would drive me through the county Kerry in his four-in-hand drag; and the third had some propositions of sport equally hospitable. As for going down to some races, on the Curragh of Kildare I think, which were to be held on the next and the three following days, there seemed to be no question about *that.* That a man should miss a race within forty miles, seemed to be a point never contemplated by these jovial sporting fellows.

Strolling about in the neighbourhood before dinner, we went down to the seashore, and to some caves which had lately been discovered there; and two Irish ladies, who were standing at the entrance of one of them, permitted me to sketch their portraits, which were pronounced to be pretty accurate.

They said they had not acquiesced in the general Temperance movement that had taken place throughout the country; and, indeed, if the truth must be known, it was only under promise of a glass of whisky apiece that their modesty could be be so far overcome as to permit them to sit for their portraits. By the time they were done, a crowd of both sexes had gathered round, and expressed themselves quite ready to sit upon the same terms. But though there was great variety in their countenances, there wasnot much beauty; and besides, dinner was by this time ready, which has at certain periods a charm even greater than art.

The bay, which had been veiled in mist and grey in the morning, was now shining under the most beautiful clear sky, which presently became rich with a thousand gorgeous hues of sunset. The view was as smiling and delightful a one as can be conceived,—just such a one as should be seen *à travers* a good dinner; with no fatiguing sublimity or awful beauty in it, but brisk, brilliant, sunny, enlivening. In fact, in placing his banqueting-house here, Mr. Lovegrove had, as usual, a brilliant idea. You must not have too much view, or a severe one, to give a relish to a good dinner; nor too much music, nor too quick, nor too slow, nor too loud. Any reader who has dined at a *table-d'hôte* in Germany will know the annoyance of this: a set of musicians immediately at your back will sometimes play you a melancholy polonaise; and a man with a good ear must perforce eat in time, and your soup is quite cold before it is swallowed. Then, all of a sudden, crash goes a brisk gallop! and you are obliged to gulp your victuals at the rate of ten miles an hour. And in respect of conversation during a good dinner, the same rules of propriety should be consulted. Deep and sublime talk is as improper as sublime prospects. Dante and champagne (I was going to say Milton and oysters, but that is a pun) are quite unfit themes of dinner-talk. Let it be light, brisk, not oppressive to the brain. Our conversation was, I recollect, just the thing. We talked about the last Derby the whole time, and the state of the odds for the St. Leger; nor was the Ascot Cup forgotten; and a bet or two was gaily booked.

Meanwhile the sky, which had been blue and then red, assumed towards the horizon, as the red was sinking under it, a gentle delicate cast of green. Howth Hill became of a darker purple, and the sails of the boats rather dim. The sea grew deeper and deeper in colour. The lamps at the railroad dotted the line with fire; and the lighthouses of the bay began to flame. The trains to and from the city rushed flashing and hissing by. In a word, everybody said it was time to light a cigar; which was done, the conversation about the Derby still continuing.

'Put out that candle,' said Roscommon to Clare. This the latter instantly did by flinging the taper out of window upon the lawn, which is a thoroughfare; and where a great laugh arose among half a score of beggar-boys, who had been under the window for some time past, repeatedly requesting the company to throw out sixpence between them.

Two other sporting young fellows had now joined the company; and as by this time claret began to have rather a mawkish taste, whisky-and-water was ordered, which was drunk upon the *perron* before the house, whither the whole party adjourned, and where for many hours we delightfully tossed for sixpences—a noble and fascinating sport. Nor would these remarkable events have been narrated, had I not received express permission from the gentlemen of the party to record all that was said and done. Who knows but a thousand years hence some antiquary or historian may find a moral in this description of the amusement of the British youth at the present enlightened time?

HOT LOBSTER

P.S.—You take a lobster, about three feet long if possible, remove the shell, cut or break the flesh of the fish in pieces not too small. Some one else meanwhile makes a mixture of mustard, vinegar, catsup, and lots of cayenne pepper. You produce a machine called a *despatcher*, which has a spirit-lamp under it that is usually illuminated with whisky. The lobster, the sauce, and near half a pound of butter are placed in the despatcher, which is immediately closed. When boiling, the mixture is stirred up, the lobster being sure to heave about in the pan in a convulsive manner, while it emits a remarkably rich and agreeable odour through the apartment. A glass and a half of sherry is now thrown into the pan, and the contents served out hot, and eaten by the company. Porter is commonly drunk, and whisky-punch afterwards, and the dish is fit for an emperor.

N.B.—You are recommended not to hurry yourself in getting up the next morning, and may take soda-water with advantage.—Probatum est.

CHAPTER II: A COUNTRY-HOUSE IN KILDARE—SKETCHES OF AN IRISH FAMILY AND FARM

IT had been settled among my friends, I don't know for what particular reason, that the Agricultural Show at Cork was an exhibition I was specially bound to see. When, therefore, a gentleman to whom I had brought a letter of introduction kindly offered me a seat in his carriage, which was to travel by short days' journeys to that city, I took an abrupt farewell of Pat the waiter, and some other friends in Dublin: proposing to renew our acquaintance, however, upon some future day.

We started then one fine afternoon on the road from Dublin to Naas, which is the main southern road from the capital to Munster, and met, in the course of the ride of a score of miles, a dozen of coaches very heavily loaded, and bringing passengers to the city. The exit from Dublin this way is not much more elegant than the outlet by way of Kingstown: for though the great branches of the city appear flourishing enough as yet, the small outer ones are in a sad state of decay. Houses drop off here and there, and dwindle wofully in size; we are got into the back-premises of the seemingly prosperous place, and it looks miserable, careless, and deserted We passed through a street which was thriving once, but has fallen since into a sort of decay, to judge outwardly,—St. Thomas's Street. Emmett was hanged in the midst of it. And on pursuing the line of street, and crossing the Great Canal you come presently to a fine tall square building in the outskirts of the town, which is no more nor less than Kilmainham Gaol, or Castle. Poor Emmett is the Irish darling still—his history is on every bookstall in the city, and yonder trim-looking brick gaol a spot where Irishmen may go and pray. Many a martyr of theirs has appeared and died in front of it,—found guilty of 'wearing of the green.'

There must be a fine view from the gaol windows, for we presently come to a great stretch of brilliant green country, leaving the Dublin hills lying to the left, picturesque in their outline, and of wonderful colour. It seems to me to be quite a different colour to that in England —different-shaped clouds—different shadows and lights. The country is well tilled, well peopled; the hay-harvest on the ground, and the people taking advantage of the sunshine to gather it in; but, in spite of everything,—green meadows, white villages and sunshine,—the place has a sort of sadness in the look of it.

The first town we passed, as appears by reference to the Guidebook, is the little town of Rathcoole; but in the space of three days Rathcoole has disappeared from my memory, with the exception of a little low building which the village contains, and where are the quarters of the Irish constabulary. Nothing can be finer than the trim, orderly, and soldierlike appearance of this splendid corps of men.

One has glimpses all along the road of numerous gentlemen's places, looking extensive and prosperous, of a few mills by streams here and there; but though the streams run still, the mill-wheels are idle for the chief part; and the road passes more than one long low village, looking bare and poor, but neat and white-washed: it seems as if the inhabitants were determined to put a decent look upon their poverty. One or two villages there were evidently appertaining to gentlemen's seats: these are smart enough, especially that of Johnstown, near Lord Mayo's fine domain, where the houses are of the Gothic sort, with pretty porches, creepers, and railings. Noble purple hills to the left and right keep up, as it were, an accompaniment to the road.

As for the town of Naas, the first after Dublin that I have seen, what can be said of it but that it looks poor, mean, and yet somehow cheerful? There was a little bustle in the small shops, a few cars were jingling along the broadest street of the town—some sort of dandies and military individuals were lolling about right and left; and I saw a fine court-house, where the assizes of Kildare county are held.

But by far the finest, and I think the most extensive edifice in Naas, was a haystack in the inn-yard, the proprietor of which did not fail to make me remark its size and splendour. It was of such dimensions as to strike a cockney with respect and pleasure; and here standing just as the new crops were coming in, told a tale of opulent thrift and good husbandry. Are there many more such haystacks, I wonder, in Ireland? The crops along the road seemed healthy, though rather light: wheat and oats plenty, and especially flourishing; hay and clover not so good; and turnips (let the important remark be taken at its full value) almost entirely wanting.

The little town, as they call it, of Kilcullen, tumbles down a bill and struggles up another; the two being here picturesquely divided by the Liffey, over which goes an antique bridge. It boasts, moreover, of a portion of an abbey wall, and a piece of round tower, both on the hill summit, and to be seen (says the Guide-book) for many miles round. Here we saw the first public evidences of the distress of the country. There was no trade in the little place, and but few people to be seen, except a crowd round a meal-shop, where meal is distributed once a week by the neighbouring gentry. There must have been some hundreds of persons waiting about the doors; women for the most part: some of their children were to be found loitering about the bridge much farther up the street; but it was curious to note, amongst these undeniably starving people, how healthy their looks were. Going a little farther, we saw women pulling weeds and nettles in the hedges, on which dismal sustenance the poor creatures live, having no bread, no potatoes, no work. Well! these women did not look thinner or more unhealthy than many a well-fed person. A company of English lawyers, now, look more cadaverous than these starving creatures.

Stretching away from Kilcullen bridge, for a couple of miles or more, near the fine house and plantations of the Latouche family, is to be seen a much prettier sight, I think, than the finest park and mansion in the world. This is a tract of excessively green land, dotted over with brilliant white cottages, each with its couple of trim acres of garden, where you see thick potato-ridges covered with blossom, great blue plots of comfortable cabbages and such pleasant plants of the poor man's garden. Two or three years since, the land was a marshy common, which had never since the days of the Deluge fed any being bigger than a snipe, and into which the poor people descended, draining and cultivating and rescuing the marsh from the water, and raising their cabins and setting up their little enclosures of two or three acres upon the land which they had thus created. 'Many of 'em has passed months in gaol for that,' said my informant (a groom on the back seat of my host's phaeton): for it appears that certain gentlemen in the neighbourhood looked upon the titles of these new colonists with some jealousy, and would have been glad to depose them; but there were some better philosophers among the surrounding gentry, who advised that instead of discouraging the settlers it would be best to help them; and the consequence has been, that there are now two hundred flourishing little homesteads upon this rescued land, and as many families in comfort and plenty.

Just at the confines of this pretty rustic republic, our pleasant afternoon's drive ended; and I must begin this tour with a monstrous breach of confidence, by first describing what I saw.

Well, then, we drove through a neat lodge-gate, with no stone lions or supporters, but riding well on its hinges, and looking fresh and white; and passed by a lodge, not Gothic, but decorated with flowers and evergreens, with clean windows and a sound slate roof; and then went over a trim road, through a few acres of grass, adorned with plenty of young firs and other healthy trees, under which were feeding a dozen of fine cows or more. The road led up to a house, or rather a congregation of rooms, built seemingly to suit the owner's convenience, and increasing with his increasing wealth, or whim, or family. This latter is as plentiful as everything else about the place; and as the arrows increased, the good-natured lucky father has been forced to multiply the quivers.

First came out a young gentleman, the heir of the house, who, after greeting his papa, began examining the horses with much interest; whilst three or four servants, quite neat and well dressed, and, wonderful to say, without any talking, began to occupy themselves with the carnage, the passengers, and the trunks. Meanwhile, the owner of the house had gone into the hall, which is snugly furnished as a morning-room, and where one, two, three young ladies came in to greet him. the young ladies having concluded their embraces, performed (as I am bound to say from experience, both in London and Paris) some very appropriate and well-finished curtseys to the strangers arriving; and these three young persons were presently succeeded by some still younger, who came without any curtseys at all; but, bounding and jumping, and shouting out 'Papa' at the top of their voices, they fell forthwith upon that worthy gentleman's person, taking possession this of his knees, that of his arms, that of his whiskers, as fancy or taste might dictate.

'Are there any more of you?' says he, with perfect good-humour; and, in fact, it appeared that there were some more in the nursery, as we subsequently had occasion to see.

Well, this large happy family are lodged in a house than which a prettier or more comfortable is not to be seen even in England; of the furniture of which it may be in confidence said, that each article is only made to answer one purpose:—thus, that chairs are never called upon to exercise the versatility of their genius by propping up windows; that chests of drawers are not obliged to move their unwieldy persons in order to act as locks to doors; that the windows are not variegated by paper, or adorned with wafers, as in other places which I have seen: in fact, that the place is just as comfortable as a place can be.

And if these comforts and reminiscences of three days' date are enlarged upon at some length, the reason is simply this:—this is written at what is supposed to be the best inn at one of the best towns of Ireland, Waterford. Dinner is just over; it is assize-week, and the *table d'hôte* was surrounded for the chief part by English attorneys— the cyouncillors (as the bar are pertinaciously called) dining upstairs in private. Well, on going to the public room and being about to lay down my hat on the sideboard, I was obliged to pause—out of regard to a fine thick coat of dust which had been kindly left to gather for some days past I should think, and which it seemed a shame to displace. Yonder is a chair basking quietly in the sunshine; some round object has evidently reposed upon it (a hat or plate probably), for you see a clear circle of black horsehair in the middle of the chair and dust all round it. Not one of those dirty napkins that the four waiters carry would wipe away the grime from the chair, and take to itself a little dust more! The people in the room are shouting out for the waiters, who cry, 'Yes, sir,' peevishly, and don't come; but stand bawling and jangling, and calling each other names, at the sideboard. The dinner is plentiful and nasty—raw ducks, raw peas, on a crumpled tablecloth, over which a waiter has just spirted a pint of obstreperous cider. The windows are open, to give free view of a crowd of old beggar-women, and of a fellow playing a cursed Irish pipe. Presently this delectable apartment fills with choking peat-smoke; and on asking what is the cause of this agreeable addition to the pleasures of the place, you are told that they are lighting a fire in a back-room.

Why should lighting a fire in a back-room fill a whole enormous house with smoke? Why should four waiters stand and *jaw* and gesticulate among themselves, instead of waiting on the guests? Why should ducks be raw, and dust lie quiet in places where a hundred people pass daily? All these points make one think very regretfully of neat, pleasant, comfortable, prosperous H— town, where the meat was cooked, and the rooms were clean, and the servants didn't talk. Nor need it be said here, that it is as cheap to have a house clean as dirty, and that a raw leg of mutton costs exactly the same sum as one *cuit à point.* And by this moral earnestly hoping that all Ireland may profit, let us go back to H—, and the sights to be seen there.

There is no need to particularise the chairs and tables any farther, nor to say what sort of conversation and claret we had; nor to set down the dishes served at dinner. If an Irish gentleman does not give you a more hearty welcome than an Englishman, at least he has a more hearty manner of welcoming you; and while the latter reserves his fun and humour (if he possess those qualities) for his particular friends, the former is ready to laugh and talk his best with all the world, and give way entirely to his mood. And it would be a good opportunity here for a man who is clever at philosophising to expound various theories upon the modes of hospitality practised in various parts of Europe. In a couple of hours' talk, an Englishman will give you his notions on trade, politics, the crops: the last run with the hounds, or the weather: it requires a long sitting, and a bottle of wine at the least, to induce him to laugh cordially, or to speak unreservedly; and if you joke with him before you know him, he will assuredly set you down as a low impertinent fellow. In two hours, and over a pipe, a German will be quite ready to let loose the easy floodgates of his sentiment, and confide to you many of the secrets of his soft heart. In two hours a Frenchman will say a hundred and twenty smart, witty, brilliant, false things, and will care for you as much then as he would if you saw him every day for twenty years—that is, not one single straw; and in two hours an Irishman will have allowed his jovial humour to unbutton, and gambolled and frolicked to his heart's content. Which of these, putting *Monsieur* out of the question, will stand by his friend with the most constancy, and maintain his steady wish to serve him? That is a question which the Englishman (and I think with a little of his ordinary cool assumption) is disposed to decide in his own favour; but it is clear that for a stranger the Irish ways are the pleasantest, for here he is at once made happy and at home; or at ease rather; for home is a strong word, and implies much more than any stranger can expect, or even desire to claim.

Nothing could be more delightful to witness than the evident affection which the children and parents bore to one another, and the cheerfulness and happiness of their family-parties. The father of one lad went with a party of his friends and family on a pleasure-party, in a handsome coach-and-four. The little fellow sat on the coach-box and played with the whip very wistfully for some time: the sun was shining, the horses came out in bright harness, with glistening coats; one of the girls brought a geranium to stick in papa's button-hole, who was to drive.

But although there was room in the coach, and though papa said he should go if he liked, and though the lad longed to go—as who wouldn't—he jumped off the box, and said he would not go: mamma would like him to stop at home and keep his sister company; and so down he went like a hero. Does this story appear trivial to any one who reads it? If so, he is a pompous fellow, whose opinion is not worth the having; or he has no children of his own; or he has forgotten the day when he was a child himself; or he has never repented of the surly selfishness with which he treated brothers and sisters, after the habit of young English gentlemen.

'That's a list that Uncle keeps of his children,' said the same young fellow, seeing his uncle reading a paper; and to understand this joke, it must be remembered that the children of the gentleman called Uncle came into the breakfast-room by half-dozens. 'That's a *rum* fellow,' said the eldest of these latter to me, as his father went out of the room, evidently thinking his papa was the greatest wit and wonder in the whole world. And a great merit, as it appeared to me, on the part of these worthy parents was, that they consented not only to make, but to take jokes from their young ones; nor was the parental authority in the least weakened by this kind familiar intercourse.

A word with regard to the ladies so far. Those I have seen appear to the full as well educated and refined, and far more frank and cordial, than the generality of the fair creatures on the other side of the Channel. I have not heard anything about poetry, to be sure, and in only one house have seen an album; but I have heard some capital music, of an excellent family sort—that sort which is used, namely, to set young people dancing, which they have done merrily for some nights. In respect of drinking, among the gentry teetotalism does not, thank Heaven! as yet appear to prevail; but although the claret has been invariably good, there has been no improper use of it.[ix] Let all English be recommended to be very careful of whisky, which experience teaches to be a very deleterious drink. Natives say that it is wholesome, and may be sometimes seen to use it with impunity; but the whisky-fever is naturally more fatal to strangers than inhabitants of the country; and whereas an Irishman will sometimes imbibe a half-dozen tumblers of the poison, two glasses will often be found sufficient to cause headaches, heartburns, and fevers to a person newly arrived in the country. The said whisky is always to be had for the asking, but is not produced at the bettermost sort of tables.

Before setting out on our second day's journey, we had time to accompany the well-pleased owner of H— town over some of his fields and out-premises. Nor can there be a pleasanter sight to owner or stranger. Mr. P— farms four hundred acres of land about his house; and employs on this estate no less than a hundred and ten persons. He says there is full work for every one of them; and to see the elaborate state of cultivation in which the land was, it is easy to understand how such an agricultural regiment were employed. The estate is like a well-ordered garden: we walked into a huge field of potatoes, and the landlord made us remark that there was not a single weed between the furrows; and the whole formed a vast flower-bed of a score of acres. Every bit of land up to the hedge-side was fertilised and full of produce: the space left for the plough having afterwards been gone over, and yielding its fullest proportion of ' fruit.' In a turnip-field were a score or more of women and children, who were marching through the ridges, removing the young plants where two or three had grown together, and leaving only the most healthy. Every individual root in the field was thus the object of culture; and the owner said that this extreme cultivation answered his purpose, and that the employment of all these hands (the women and children earn 6d. and 8d. a day all the year round), which gained him some reputation as a philanthropist, brought him profit as a farmer too; for his crops were the best that land could produce. He has further the advantage of a large stock for manure, and does everything for the land which art can do. Here we saw several experiments in manuring: an acre of turnips prepared with bone-dust; another with 'Murray's Composition,' whereof I do not pretend to know the ingredients; another with a new manure called guano. As far as turnips and a first year's crop went, the guano carried the day. The plants on the guano acre looked to be three weeks in advance of their neighbours, and were extremely plentiful and healthy. I went to see this field two months after the above passage was written: the guano acre still kept the lead; the bone-dust ran guano very hard; and composition was clearly distanced.

Behind the house is a fine village of corn and hayricks, and a street of outbuildings, where all the work of the farm is prepared. Here were numerous people coming with pails for buttermilk, which the good-natured landlord made over to them. A score of men or more were busied about the place; some at a grindstone, others at a forge—other fellows busied in the cart-houses and stables, all of which were as neatly kept as in the best farm in England. A little farther on was a flower-garden, a kitchen-garden, a hot-house just building, a kennel of fine pointers and setters;—indeed a noble feature of country neatness, thrift, and plenty.

We went into the cottages and gardens of several of Mr. P—'s labourers, which were all so neat that I could not help fancying they were pet cottages erected under the landlord's own superintendence, and ornamented to his order. But he declared that it was not so; that the only benefit his labourers got from him was constant work, and a house rent-free; and that the neatness of the gardens and dwellings was of their own doing. By making them a present of the house, he said, he made them a present of the pig and live stock, with which almost every Irish cotter pays his rent, so that each workman could have a bit of meat for his support;—would that all labourers in the empire had as much! With regard to the neatness of the houses, the best way to ensure this, he said, was for the master constantly to visit them—to awaken as much emulation as he could amongst the cottagers, so that each should make his place as good as his neighbour's—and to take them good-humouredly to task if they failed in the requisite care.

And so this pleasant day's visit ended. A more practical person would have seen, no doubt, and understood much more than a mere citizen could, whose pursuits have been very different from those noble and useful ones here spoken of. But a man has no call to be a judge of turnips or live stock, in order to admire such an establishment as this, and heartily to appreciate the excellence of it. There are some happy organisations in the world which possess the great virtue of *prosperity*. It implies cheerfulness, simplicity, shrewdness, perseverance, honesty, good health. See how, before the good-humoured resolution of such characters, ill-luck gives way, and fortune assumes their own smiling complexion! Such men grow rich without driving a single hard bargain; their condition being to make others prosper along with themselves. Thus, his very charity, another informant tells me, is one of the causes of my host's good fortune. He might have three pounds a year from each of forty cottages, but instead prefers a hundred healthy workmen; or he might have a fourth of the number of workmen, and a farm yielding a produce proportionately less; but instead of saving the money of their wages, prefers a farm the produce of which, as I have heard from a gentleman whom I take to be good authority, is unequalled elsewhere.

Besides the cottages, we visited a pretty school, where children of an exceeding smallness were at their work,—the children of the Catholic peasantry. The few Protestants of the district do not attend the national-school, nor learn their alphabet or their multiplication-table in company with their little Roman Catholic brethren. The clergyman, who lives hard by the gate of H— town, in his communication with his parishioners cannot fail to see how much misery is relieved and how much good is done by his neighbour; but though the two gentlemen are on good terms, the clergyman will not break bread with his Catholic fellow-Christian. There can be no harm, I hope, in mentioning this fact, as it is rather a public than a private matter; and, unfortunately, it is only a stranger that is surprised by such a circumstance, which is quite familiar to residents of the country. There are Catholic inns and Protestant inns in the towns; Catholic coaches and Protestant coaches on the roads; nay, in the North, I have since heard of a High Church coach and a Low Church coach adopted by travelling Christians of either party.

CHAPTER III: FROM CARLOW TO WATERFORD

THE next morning being fixed for the commencement of our journey towards Waterford, a carriage made its appearance in due time before the hall-door: an amateur stage-coach, with four fine horses, that were to carry us to Cork. The crew of the 'drag,' for the present, consisted of two young ladies, and two who will not be old, please Heaven! for these thirty years; three gentlemen whose collective weights might amount to fifty-four stone; and one of smaller proportions, being as yet only twelve years old: to these were added a couple of grooms and a lady's-maid. Subsequently we took in a dozen or so more passengers, who did not seem in the slightest degree to inconvenience the coach or the horses; and thus was formed a tolerably numerous and merry party. The governor took the reins, with his geranium in his button-hole, and the place on the box was quarrelled for without ceasing, and taken by turns.

Our day's journey lay through a country more picturesque, though by no means so prosperous and well-cultivated, as the district through which we had passed on our drive from Dublin. This trip carried us through the county of Carlow and the town of that name: a wretched place enough, with a fine court-house, and a couple of fine churches: the Protestant church a noble structure, and the Catholic cathedral said to be built after some Continental model. The Catholics point to the structure with considerable pride: it was the first, I believe, of the many handsome cathedrals for their worship which have been built of late years in this country by the noble contributions of the poor man's penny, and by the untiring energies and sacrifices of the clergy. Bishop Doyle, the founder of the church, has the place of honour within it; nor, perhaps, did any Christian pastor ever merit the affection of his flock more than that great and high-minded man. He was the best champion the Catholic Church and cause ever had in Ireland; in learning, and admirable kindness and virtue, the best example to the clergy of his religion; and if the country is now filled with schools, where the humblest peasant in it can have the benefit of a liberal and wholesome education, it owes this great boon mainly to his noble exertions, and to the spirit which they awakened.

As for the architecture of the cathedral, I do not fancy a professional man would find much to praise in it: it seems to me overloaded with ornaments, nor were its innumerable spires and pinnacles the more pleasing to the eye because some of them were out of the perpendicular. The interior is quite plain, not to say bare and unfinished. Many of the chapels in the country that I have since seen are in a similar condition; for when the walls are once raised, the enthusiasm of the subscribers to the building seems somewhat characteristically to grow cool, and you enter at a porch that would suit a palace, with an interior scarcely more decorated than a barn. A wide large floor, some confession-boxes against the blank walls here and there, with some humble pictures at the 'stations,' and the statue, under a mean canopy of red woollen stuff, were the chief furniture of the cathedral.

The severe homely features of the good bishop were not very favourable subjects for Mr. Hogan's chisel; but a figure of prostrate weeping Ireland, kneeling by the prelate's side, and for whom he is imploring protection, has much beauty. In the chapels of Dublin and Cork some of this artist's works may be seen, and his countrymen are exceedingly proud of him.

Connected with the Catholic cathedral is a large tumble-down-looking divinity college: there are upwards of a hundred students here, and the college is licensed to give degrees in arts as well as divinity; at least so the officer of the church said, as he showed us the place through the bars of the sacristy-windows, in which apartment may be seen sundry crosses, a pastoral letter of Doctor Doyle, and a number of ecclesiastical vestments formed of laces, poplins, and velvets, handsomely laced with gold. There is a convent by the side of the cathedral, and, of course, a parcel of beggars all about, and indeed all over the town, profuse in their prayers and invocations of the Lord, and whining flatteries of the persons whom they address. One wretched old tottering hag began whining the Lord's Prayer as a proof of her sincerity, and blundered in the very midst of it, and left us thoroughly disgusted after the very first sentence.

It was market-day in the town, which is tolerably full of poor-looking shops, the streets being thronged with donkey-carts, and people eager to barter their small wares. Here and there were picture-stalls, with huge hideous-coloured engravings of the Saints; and indeed the objects of barter upon the banks of the clear bright river Barrow seemed scarcely to be of more value than the articles which change hands, as one reads of, in a town of African huts and traders on the banks of the Quorra. Perhaps the very bustle and cheerfulness of the people served only, to a Londoner's eyes, to make it look the more miserable. It seems as if they had no *right* to be eager about such a parcel of wretched rags and trifles as were exposed to sale.

There are some old towers of a castle here, looking finely from the river; and near the town is a grand modern residence belonging to Colonel Bruen, with an oak-park on one side of the road, and a deer-park on the other. These retainers of the Colonel's lay, in their rushy-green enclosures, in great numbers and seemingly in flourishing condition.

The road from Carlow to Leighlin Bridge is exceedingly beautiful: noble purple hills rising on either side, and the broad silver Barrow flowing through rich meadows of that astonishing verdure which is only to be seen in this country. Here and there was a country-house, or a tall mill by a stream-side: but the latter buildings were for the most part empty, the gaunt windows gaping without glass, and their great wheels idle. Leighlin Bridge, lying up and down a hill by the river, contains a considerable number of pompous-looking warehouses, that looked for the most part to be doing no more business than the mills on the Carlow road, but stood by the roadside staring at the coach as it were, and basking in the sun, swaggering, idle, insolvent, and out-at-elbows. There are one or two very pretty, modest, comfortable-looking country-places about Leighlin Bridge, and on the road thence to a miserable village called the Royal Oak, a beggarly sort of bustling place.

Here stands a dilapidated hotel and posting-house: and indeed on every road, as yet, I have been astonished at the great movement and stir;the old coaches being invariably crammed, cars jingling about equally full, and no want of gentlemen's carriages to exercise the horses of the Royal Oak and similar establishments. In the time of the rebellion, the landlord of this Royal Oak, a great character in those parts, was a fierce United Irishman. One day it happened that Sir John Anderson came to the inn, and was eager for horses on. The landlord, who knew Sir John to be a Tory, vowed and swore he had no horses; that the judges had the last going to Kilkenny; that the yeomanry had carried off the best of them; that he could not give a horse for love or money. 'Poor Lord Edward!' said Sir John, sinking down in a chair, and clasping his hands, 'my poor dear misguided friend, and must you die for the loss of a few hours and the want of a pair of horses?'

'Lord *What*?' says the landlord.

'Lord Edward Fitzgerald,' replied Sir John. 'The Government has seized his papers, and got scent of his hiding-place. If I can't get to him before two hours, Sirr will have him.' 'My dear Sir John,' cried the landlord, 'it's not two horses but it's eight I'll give you, and may the judges go hang for me! Here, Larry! Tim! First and second pair for Sir John Anderson: and long life to you, Sir John, and the Lord reward you for your good deed this day.'

Sir John, my informant told me, had invented this predicament of Lord Edward's in order to get the horses; and by way of corroborating the whole story, pointed out an old chaise which stood at the inn-door with its window broken, a great crevice in the panel, some little wretches crawling underneath the wheels, and two huge blackguards lolling against the pole. 'And that,' says he, 'is no doubt the very post-chaise Sir John Anderson had.' It certainly looked ancient enough.

Of course, as we stopped for a moment in the place, troops of slatternly ruffianly-looking fellows assembled round the carriage, dirty heads peeped out of all the dirty windows, beggars came forward with a joke and a prayer, and troops of children raised their shouts and halloos. I confess, with regard to the beggars, that I have never yet had the slightest sentiment of compassion for the very oldest or dirtiest of them, or been inclined to give them a penny: they come crawling round you with lying prayers and loathsome compliments, that make the stomach turn; they do not even disguise that they are lies; for, refuse them, and the wretches turn off with a laugh and a joke, a miserable grinning cynicism that creates distrust and indifference, and must be, one would think, the very best way to close the purse, not to open it, for objects so unworthy.

How do all these people live? one can't help wondering;—these multifarious vagabonds, without work or workhouse, or means of subsistence? The Irish Poor Law Report says that there are twelve hundred thousand people in Ireland—a sixth of the population—who have no means of livelihood but charity, and whom the State, or individual members of it, must maintain. How *can* the State support such an enormous burden; or the twelve hundred thousand be supported? What a strange history it would be, could one but get it true,—that of the manner in which a score of these beggars have maintained themselves for a fortnight past!

Soon after quitting the Royal Oak our road branches off to the hospitable house where our party, consisting of a dozen persons, was to be housed and fed for the night. Fancy the look which an English gentleman of moderate means would assume, at being called on to receive such a company! A pretty road of a couple of miles, thickly grown with ash and oak trees, under which the hats of coach-passengers suffered some danger, leads to the house of D—. A young son of the house, on a white pony, was on the look-out, and great cheering and shouting took place among the young people as we came in sight.

Trotting away by the carriage-side, he brought us through a gate with a pretty avenue of trees leading to the pleasure-grounds of the house—a handsome building commanding noble views of river, mountains, and plantations. Our entertainer only rents the place; so I may say, without any imputation against him, that the house was by no means so handsome within as without,—not that the want of finish in the interior made our party the less merry, or the host's entertainment less hearty and cordial.

The gentleman who built and owns the house, like many other proprietors in Ireland, found his mansion too expensive for his means and has relinquished it. I asked what his income might be, and no wonder that he was compelled to resign his house; which a man with four times the income in England would scarcely venture to inhabit. There were numerous sitting-rooms below; a large suite of rooms above, in which our large party, with their servants, disappeared without any seeming inconvenience, and which already accommodated a family of at least a dozen persons, and a numerous train of domestics. There was a great courtyard surrounded by capital offices, with stabling and coach-houses sufficient for a half-dozen of country gentlemen. An English squire of ten thousand a year might live in such a place—the original owner, I am told, had not many more hundreds.

Our host has wisely turned the chief part of the pleasure-ground round the house into a farm; nor did the land look a bit the worse, as I thought, for having rich crops of potatoes growing in place of grass, and fine plots of waving wheat and barley. The care, skill, and neatness everywhere exhibited, and the immense luxuriance of the crops, could not fail to strike even a cockney; and one of our party, a very well-known practical farmer, told me that there was at least five hundred pounds' worth of produce upon the little estate of some sixty acres, of which only five-and-twenty were under the plough.

As at H— town, on the previous day, several men and women appeared sauntering in the grounds, and as the master came up, asked for work, or sixpence, or told a story of want. There are lodge-gates at both ends of the demesne; but it appears the good-natured practice of the country admits a beggar as well as any other visitor. To a couple our landlord gave money, to another a little job of work; another he sent roughly out of the premises: and I could judge thus what a continual tax upon the Irish gentleman these travelling paupers must be, of whom his ground is never free.

There, loitering about the stables and outhouses, were several people who seemed to have acquired a sort of right to be there: women and children who had a claim upon the buttermilk; men who did an odd job now and then; loose hangers-on of the family: and in the lodging-houses and inns I have entered, the same sort of ragged vassals are to be found; in a house however poor, you are sure to see some poorer dependant who is a stranger, taking a meal of potatoes in the kitchen; a Tim or Mike loitering hard by, ready to run on a message, or carry a bag. This is written, for instance, at a lodging over a shop at Cork. There sits in the shop a poor old fellow quite past work, but who totters up and down stairs to the lodgers, and does what little he can for his easily-won bread. There is another fellow outside who is sure to make his bow to anybody issuing from the lodging, and ask if his honour wants an errand done? Neither class of such dependants exists with us. What housekeeper in London is there will feed an old man of seventy that's good for nothing, or encourage such a disreputable hanger-on as yonder shuffling smiling cad?

Nor did Mr. M.—'s ' irregulars' disappear with the day; for when, after a great deal of merriment, and kind happy dancing and romping of young people, the fineness of the night suggested the propriety of smoking a certain cigar (it is never more acceptable than at that season), the young squire voted that we should adjourn to the stables for the purpose, where accordingly the cigars were discussed. There were still the inevitable half-dozen hangers-on: one came grinning with a lantern, all nature being in universal blackness except his grinning face: another ran obsequiously to the stables to show a favourite mare—I think it was a mare—though it may have been a mule, and your humble errant not much the wiser. The cloths were taken off; the fellows with the candles crowded about; and the young squire bade me admire the beauty of her fore-leg, which I did with the greatest possible gravity. '*Did* you ever see such a fore-leg as that in your life?' says the young squire, and further discoursed upon the horse's points, the amateur grooms joining in chorus.

There was another young squire of our party, a pleasant gentlemanlike young fellow, who danced as prettily as any Frenchman, and who had ridden over from a neighbouring house: as I went to bed, the two lads were arguing whether young Squire B— should go home or stay at D— that night. There was a bed for him—there was a bed for everybody, it seemed, and a kind welcome too. How different was all this to the ways of a severe English house!

Next morning the whole of our merry party assembled round a long jovial breakfast-table, stored with all sorts of good things; and the biggest and jovialest man of all, who had just come in fresh from a walk in the fields, and vowed that he was as hungry as a hunter, and was cutting some slices out of an inviting ham on the side-table, suddenly let fall his knife and fork with dismay. 'Sure, John, don't you know it's Friday?' cried a lady from the table; and back John came with a most lugubrious queer look on his jolly face, and fell to work upon bread-and-butter, as resigned as possible, amidst no small laughter, as may be well imagined. On this I was bound, as a Protestant, to eat a large slice of pork, and discharged that duty nobly, and with much self-sacrifice.

The famous 'drag' which had brought us so far, seemed to be as hospitable and elastic as the house which we now left, for the coach accommodated, inside and out, a considerable party from the house; and we took our road leisurely, in a cloudless scorching day, towards Waterford. The first place we passed through was the little town of Gowran, near which is a grand well-ordered park, belonging to Lord Clifden, and where his mother resides, with whose beautiful face, in Lawrence's pictures, every reader must be familiar. The kind English lady has done the greatest good in the neighbourhood, it is said, and the little town bears marks of her beneficence, in its neatness, prettiness, and order. Close by the church there are the ruins of a fine old abbey here, and a still finer one a few miles on, at Thomastown, most picturesquely situated amidst trees and meadow, on the river Nore. The place within, however, is dirty and ruinous—the same wretched suburbs, the same squalid congregation of beggarly loungers, that are to be seen elsewhere. The monastic ruin is very fine, and the road hence to Thomastown rich with varied cultivation and beautiful verdure, pretty gentlemen's mansions shining among the trees on either side of the way. There was one place along this rich tract that looked very strange and ghastly—a huge old pair of gate pillars, flanked by a ruinous lodge, and a wide road winding for a mile up a hill. There had been a park once, but all the trees were gone; thistles were growing in the yellow sickly land, and rank thin grass on the road. Far away you saw in this desolate tract a ruin of a house: many a butt of claret has been emptied there, no doubt, and many a merry party come out with hound and horn. But what strikes the Englishman with wonder is not so much, perhaps, that an owner of the place should have "been ruined and a spendthrift, as that the land should lie there useless ever since. If one is not successful with us another man will be, or another will try, at least. Here lies useless a great capital of hundreds of acres of land; barren, where the commonest effort might make it productive, and looking as if for a quarter of a century past no soul ever looked or cared for it. You might travel five hundred miles through England and not see such a spectacle.

A short distance from Thomastown is another abbey; and presently, after passing through the village of Knocktopher, we came to a posting-place called Ballyhale.

A dirty, old, contented, decrepit idler was lolling in the sun at a shop-door, and hundreds of the population of the dirty, old, decrepit, contented place were employed in the like way. A dozen of boys were playing at pitch-and-toss; other male and female beggars were sitting on a wall looking into a stream; scores of ragamuffins, of course, round the carriage; and beggars galore at the door of the little alehouse or hotel. A gentleman's carriage changed horses as we were baiting here. It was a rich sight to see the cattle, and the way of starting them:

'Halloo! Yoop-hoop!' a dozen of ragged ostlers and amateurs running by the side of the miserable old horses, the postillion shrieking, yelling, and belabouring them with his whip. Down goes one horse among the new-laid stones; the postillion has him up with a cut of the whip and a curse, and takes advantage of the start caused by the stumble to get the brute into a gallop, and to go down the hill. 'I know it for a fact,' a gentleman of our party says, 'that no horses *ever* got out of Ballyhale without an accident of some kind.'

'Will your honour like to come and see a big pig?' here asked a man of the above gentleman, well known as a great farmer and breeder. We all went to see the big pig, not very fat as yet, but, upon my word, it is as big as a pony. The country round is, it appears, famous for the breeding of such, especially a district called the Welsh mountains, through which we had to pass on our road to Waterford.

This is a curious country to see, and has curious inhabitants: for twenty miles there is no gentleman's house: gentlemen dare not live there. The place was originally tenanted by a clan of Welshes; hence its name; and they maintain themselves in their occupancy of the farms in Tipperary fashion, by simply putting a ball into the body of any man who would come to take a farm over any one of them. Some of the crops in the fields of the Welsh country seemed very good, and the fields well tilled; but it is common to see, by the side of one field that is well cultivated, another that is absolutely barren; and the whole tract is extremely wretched. Appropriate histories and reminiscences accompany the traveller: at a chapel near Mullinavat is the spot where sixteen policemen were murdered in the tithe-campaign; farther on you come to a limekiln, where the guard of a mail-coach was seized and *roasted alive.* I saw here the first hedge-school I have seen: a crowd of half-savage-looking lads and girls looked up from their studies in the ditch, their college or lecture-room being in a mud cabin hard by.

And likewise, in the midst of this wild tract, a fellow met us who was trudging the road with a fish-basket over his shoulder, and who stopped the coach, hailing two of the gentlemen in it by name, both of whom seemed to be much amused by his humour. He was a handsome rogue, a poacher, or salmon-taker, by profession, and presently poured out such a flood of oaths, and made such a monstrous display of grinning wit and blackguardism, as I have never heard equalled by the best Billingsgate practitioner, and as it would be more than useless to attempt to describe. Blessings, jokes, and curses trolled off the rascal's lips with a volubility which caused his Irish audience to shout with laughter, but which were quite beyond a cockney. It was a humour so purely national as to be understood by none but natives, I should think. I recollect the same feeling of perplexity while sitting, the only Englishman, in a company of jocular Scotchmen. They bandied about puns, jokes, imitations, and applauded with shrieks of laughter what, I confess, appeared to me the most abominable dullness; nor was the salmon-taker's jocularity any better. I think it rather served to frighten than to amuse; and I am not sure but that I looked out for a band of jocular cut-throats of this sort to come up at a given guffaw, and playfully rob us all round. However, he went away quite peaceably, calling down for the party the benediction of a great number of saints, who must have been somewhat ashamed to be addressed by such a rascal.

Presently we caught sight of the valley through which the Suir flows, and descended the hill towards it, and went over the thundering old wooden bridge to Waterford.

CHAPTER IV: FROM WATERFORD TO CORK

The view of the town from the bridge and the heights above it is very imposing; as is the river both ways. Very large vessels sail up almost to the doors of the houses, and the quays are flanked by tall red warehouses, that look at a little distance as if a world of business might be doing within them. But as you get into the place, not a soul is there to greet you except the usual society of beggars, and a sailor or two, or a green-coated policeman sauntering down the broad pavement. We drove up to the Coach Inn, a huge, handsome, dirty building, of which the discomforts have been pathetically described elsewhere. The landlord is a gentleman and considerable horse-proprietor, and though a perfectly well-bred, active, and intelligent man, far too much of a gentleman to play the host well: at least as an Englishman understands that character.

Opposite the town is a tower of questionable antiquity and undeniable ugliness; for though the inscription says it was built in the year one thousand and something, the same document adds that it was rebuilt in 1819—to either of which dates the traveller is thus welcomed. The quays stretch for a considerable distance along the river, poor patched-windowed mouldy-looking shops forming the basement-story of most of the houses. We went into one, a jeweller's, to make a purchase—it might have been of a gold watch for anything the owner knew; but he was talking with a friend in his back-parlour, gave us a look as we entered, allowed us to stand some minutes in the empty shop, and at length to walk out without being served. In another shop a boy was lolling behind a counter, but could not say whether the articles we wanted were to be had; turned out a heap of drawers, and could not find them; and finally went for the master, who could not come. True commercial independence, and an easy way enough of life.

In one of the streets leading from the quay is a large dingy Catholic chapel, of some pretensions within; but, as usual, there had been a failure for want of money, and the front of the chapel was unfinished, presenting the butt-end of a portico, and walls on which the stone coating was to be laid. But a much finer ornament to the church than any of the questionable gewgaws which adorned the ceiling was the piety, stern, simple, and unaffected, of the people within. Their whole soul seemed to be in their prayers, as rich and poor knelt indifferently on the flags. There is of course an episcopal cathedral, well and neatly kept, and a handsome Bishop's palace: near it was a convent of nuns, and a little chapel-bell clinking melodiously. I was prepared to fancy something romantic of the place; but as we passed the convent gate, a shoeless slattern of a maid opened the door—the most dirty and unpoetical of housemaids.

Assizes were held in the town, and we ascended to the court-house through a steep street, a sort of rag-fair, but more villainous and miserable than any rag-fair in St. Giles's: the houses and stock of the Seven Dials look as if they belonged to capitalists when compared with the scarecrow wretchedness of the goods here hung out for sale. Who wanted to buy such things? I wondered. One would have thought that the most part of the articles had passed the possibility of barter for money, even out of the reach of the half-farthings coined of late. All the street was lined with wretched hucksters and their merchandise of gooseberries, green apples, children's dirty cakes, cheap crockeries, brushes, and tinware; among which objects the people were swarming about busily. Before the court is a wide street, where a similar market was held, with a vast number of donkey-carts urged hither and thither, and great shrieking, chattering, and bustle. It is five hundred years ao since a poet who accompanied Richard II. in his voyage hither spoke of '*Watreforde ou moult vilaine et orde y sont la gente.*' They don't seem to be much changed now, but remain faithful to their ancient habits.

About the court-house swarms of beggars of course were collected, varied by personages of a better sort: grey-coated farmers, and women with their picturesque blue cloaks, who had trudged in from the country probably. The court-house is as beggarly and ruinous as the rest of the neighbourhood; smart-looking policemen kept order about it, and looked very hard at me as I ventured to take a sketch.

The figures were thus disposed. The man in the dock, the policeman seated easily above him, the woman looking down from a gallery. The man was accused of stealing a sack of wool, and, having no counsel, made for himself as adroit a defence as any one of the counsellors (they are without robes or wigs here, by the way) could have made for him. He had been seen examining a certain sack of wool in a coffee-shop at Dungarvan, and next day was caught sight of in Waterford Market, standing under an archway from the rain, with the sack by his side.

'Wasn't there twenty other people under the arch?' said he to a witness, a noble-looking beautiful girl—the girl was obliged to own there were. 'Did you see me touch the wool, or stand nearer to it than a dozen of the dacent people there?' and the girl confessed she had not. 'And this it is, my Lord,' says he to the bench; 'they attack me because I am poor and ragged, but they never think of charging the crime on a rich farmer.'

But alas for the defence! another witness saw the prisoner with his legs round the sack, and being about to charge him with the theft, the prisoner fled into the arms of a policeman, to whom his first words were, 'I know nothing about the sack.' So, as the sack had been stolen, as he had been seen handling it four minutes before it was stolen, and holding it for sale the day after, it was concluded that Patrick Malony had stolen the sack, and he was accommodated with eighteen months accordingly.

In another case we had a woman and her child on the table; and others followed, in the judgment of which it was impossible not to admire the extreme leniency, acuteness, and sensibility of the judge presiding, Chief Justice Pennefather:—the man against whom all the Liberals in Ireland, and every one else who has read his charge too, must be angry, for the ferocity of his charge against a Belfast newspaper editor. It seems as if no parties here will be dispassionate when they get to a party question, and that natural kindness has no claim when Whig and Tory come into collision.

The witness is here placed on a table instead of a witness-box; nor was there much further peculiarity to remark, except in the dirt of the court, the absence of the barristerial wig and gown, and the great coolness with which a fellow who seemed a sort of clerk, usher, and Irish interpreter to the court, recommended a prisoner, who was making rather a long defence, to be quiet. I asked him why the man might not have his say. 'Sure,' says he, 'he's said all he has to say, and there's no use in any more.' But there was no use in attempting to convince Mr. Usher that the prisoner was the best judge on this point: in fact the poor devil shut his mouth at the admonition, and was found guilty with perfect justice.

A considerable poor-house has been erected at Waterford, but the beggars of the place as yet prefer their liberty, and less certain means of gaining support. We asked one who was calling down all the blessings of all the saints and angels upon us, and telling a most piteous tale of poverty, why she did not go to the poor-house. The woman's look at once changed from a sentimental whine to a grin. 'Dey owe two hundred pounds at dat house,' said she, 'and faith, an honest woman can't go dere.' With which wonderful reason ought not the most squeamish to be content?

* * * * *

After describing, as accurately as words may, the features of a landscape, and stating that such a mountain was to the left, and such a river or town to the right, and putting down the situations and names of the villages, and the bearings of the roads, it has no doubt struck the reader of books of travels that the writer has not given him the slightest idea of the country, and that he would have been just as wise without perusing the letterpress landscape through which he has toiled. It will be as well then, under such circumstances, to spare the public any lengthened description of the road from Waterford to Dungarvan; which was the road we took, followed by benedictions delivered gratis from the beggarhood of the former city. Not very far from it you see the dark plantations of the magnificent domain of Curraghmore, and pass through a country blue, hilly, and bare, except where gentlemen's seats appear with their ornaments of wood. Presently, after leaving Waterford, we came to a certain town called Kilmacthomas, of which all the information I have to give is, that it is situated upon a hill and river, and that you may change horses there. The road was covered with carts of seaweed, which the people were bringing for manure from the shore some four miles distant; and beyond Kilmacthomas we beheld the Cummeragh Mountains, 'often named in maps the Nennavoulagh,' either of which names the reader may select at pleasure.

Thence we came to 'Cushcam,' at which village be it known that the turnpike-man kept the drag a very long time waiting. 'I think the fellow must be writing a book,' said the coachman, with a most severe look of drollery at a cockney tourist, who tried, under the circumstances, to laugh, and not to blush. I wish I could relate or remember half the mad jokes that flew about among the jolly Irish crew on the top of the coach, and which would have made a journey through the Desert jovial. When the 'pike-man had finished his composition (that of a turnpike-ticket, which he had to fill), we drove on to Dungarvan; the two parts of which town, separated by the river Colligan, have been joined by a causeway three hundred yards along, and a bridge erected at an enormous outlay by the Duke of Devonshire. In former times, before his Grace spent his eighty thousand pounds upon the causeway, this wide estuary was called 'Dungarvan Prospect,' because the ladies of the country, walking over the river at low water, took off their shoes and stockings (such as had them), and tucking up their clothes, exhibited,—what I have never seen, and cannot therefore be expected to describe. A large and handsome Catholic chapel, a square with some pretensions to regularity of building, a very neat and comfortable inn, and beggars and idlers still more numerous than at Waterford, were what we had leisure to remark in half-an-hour's stroll through the town.

Near the prettily situated village of Cappoquin is the Trappist House of Mount Meilleraie, of which we could only see the pinnacles. The brethren were presented some years since with a barren mountain, which they have cultivated most successfully. They have among themselves workmen to supply all their frugal wants: ghostly tailors and shoemakers, spiritual gardeners and bakers, working in silence, and serving Heaven after their way. If this reverend community, for fear of the opportunity of sinful talk, choose to hold their tongues, the next thing will be to cut them out altogether, and so render the danger impossible: if, being men of education and intelligence, they incline to turn butchers and cobblers, and smother their intellects by base and hard menial labour, who knows but one day a sect may be more pious still, and rejecting even butchery and bakery, as savouring too much of worldly convenience and pride, take to a wild-beast life at once? Let us concede that suffering, and mental and bodily debasement, are the things most agreeable to Heaven, and there is no knowing where such piety may stop. I was very glad we had not time to see the grovelling place; and as for seeing shoes made or fields tilled by reverend amateurs, we can find cobblers and ploughboys to do the work better.

By the way, the Quakers have set up in Ireland a sort of monkery of their own. Not far from Carlow we met a couple of cars drawn by white horses, and holding white Quakers and Quakeresses, in white hats, clothes, shoes, with wild maniacal-looking faces, bumping along the road. Let us hope that we may soon get a community of Fakeers and howling Dervishes into the country. It would be a refreshing thing to see such ghostly men in one's travels, standing at the corners of roads and praising the Lord by standing on one leg, or cutting and hacking themselves with knives like the prophets of Baal. Is it not as pious for a man to deprive himself of his leg as of his tongue, and to disfigure his body with the gashes of a knife, as with the hideous white raiment of the illuminated Quakers?

While these reflections were going on, the beautiful Blackwater river suddenly opened before us, and driving along it for three miles through some of the most beautiful rich country ever seen, we came to Lismore. Nothing can be certainly more magnificent than this drive. Parks and rocks covered with the grandest foliage; rich handsome seats of gentlemen in the midst of fair lawns and beautiful bright plantations and shrubberies; and at the end, the graceful spire of Lismore church, the prettiest I have seen in, or, I think, out of Ireland. Nor in any country that I have visited have I seen a view more noble—it is too rich and peaceful to be what is called romantic, but lofty, large, and *generous,* if the term may be used; the river and banks as fine as the Rhine; the castle not as large, but as noble and picturesque as Warwick. As you pass the bridge, the banks stretch away on either side in amazing verdure, and the castle-walks remind one somewhat of the dear old terrace of St. Germains, with its groves, and long grave avenues of trees.

The salmon-fishery of the Blackwater is let, as I hear, for a thousand a year. In the evening, however, we saw some gentlemen who are likely to curtail the profits of the farmer of the fishery—a company of ragged boys, to wit—whose occupation, it appears, is to poach. These young fellows were all lolling over the bridge, as the moon rose rather mistily, and pretended to be deeply enamoured of the view of the river. They answered the questions of one of our party with the utmost innocence and openness, and one would have supposed the lads were so many Arcadians, but for the arrival of an old woman, who suddenly coming up among them poured out, upon one and all, a volley of curses, both deep and loud, saving that perdition would be their portion, and calling them 'shchamers' at least a hundred times. Much to my wonder, the young men did not reply to the voluble old lady for some time, who then told us the cause of her anger. She had a son,—'Look at him there, the villain.' The lad was standing, looking very unhappy. 'His father, that's now dead, paid a fistful of money to bind him 'prentice at Dungarvan: but these shchamers followed him there; made him break his indentures, and go poaching and thieving and shchaming with them.' The poor old woman shook her hands in the air, and shouted at the top of her deep voice; there was something very touching in her grotesque sorrow; nor did the lads make light of it at all, contenting themselves with a surly growl, or an oath, if directly appealed to by the poor creature.

So, cursing and raging, the woman went away. The son, a lad of fourteen, evidently the fag of the big bullies round about him, stood dismally away from them, his head sunk down. I went up and asked him 'Was that his mother?' He said, 'Yes.' 'Was she good and kind to him when he was at home?' He said 'Oh yes.' 'Why not come back to her?' I asked him; but he said 'he couldn't.' Whereupon I took his arm, and tried to lead him away by main force; but he said, 'Thank you, sir, but I can't go back,' and released his arm. we stood on the bridge some minutes longer, looking at the view; but the boy, though he kept away from his comrades, would not come. I wonder what they have done together, that the poor boy is past going home? The place seemed to be so quiet and beautiful, and far away from London, that I thought crime couldn't have reached it; and yet here it lurks somewhere among six boys of sixteen, each with a stain in his heart, and some black history to tell. The poor widow's yonder was the only family about which I had a chance of knowing anything in this remote place; nay, in all Ireland: and God help us, hers was a sad lot!—A husband gone dead,—an only child gone to ruin. It is awful to think that there are eight millions of stories to be told in this island. Seven million nine hundred and ninety-nine thousand nine hundred and ninety-eight more lives that I, and all brother cockneys, know nothing about. Well, please God, they are not all like this.

That day, I heard *another* history. A little old disreputable man in tatters, with a huge steeple of a hat, came shambling down the street, one among the five hundred blackguards there. A fellow standing under the 'Sun' portico (a sort of swaggering, chattering, cringing *touter*, and master of ceremonies to the gutter) told us something with regard to the old disreputable man. His sou had been hanged the day before at Clonmel, for one of the Tipperary murders. That blackguard in our eyes instantly looked quite different from all other blackguards: I saw him gesticulating at the corner of a street, and watched him with wonderful interest.

The church with the handsome spire, that looks so graceful among the trees, is a cathedral church, and one of the neatest-kept and prettiest edifices I have seen in Ireland. In the old graveyard Protestants and Catholics lie together—that is, not together; for each has a side of the ground where they sleep, and, so occupied, do not quarrel. The sun was shining down upon the brilliant grass—and I don't think the shadows of the Protestant graves were any longer or shorter than those of the Catholics. Is it the right or the left side of the graveyard which is nearest heaven I wonder? Look, the sun shines upon both alike, 'and the blue sky bends over all.'

Raleigh's house is approached by a grave old avenue, and well-kept wall, such as is rare in this country; and the court of the castle within has a solid, comfortable, quiet look, equally rare. It is like one of our colleges at Oxford: there is a side of the quadrangle with pretty ivy-covered gables; another part of the square is more modern; and by the main body of the castle is a small chapel exceedingly picturesque. The interior is neat and in excellent order; but it was unluckily done up some thirty years ago (as I imagine from the style), before our architects had learned Gothic, and all the ornamental work is consequently quite ugly and out of keeping. The church has probably been arranged by the same hand. In the castle are some plainly-furnished chambers, one or two good pictures, and a couple of oriel windows, the views from which up and down the river are exceedingly lovely. You hear praises of the Duke of Devonshire as a landlord wherever you go among his vast estates: it is a pity that, with such a noble residence as this, and with such a wonderful country round about it, his Grace should not inhabit it more.

Of the road from Lismore to Fermoy it does not behove me to say much, for a pelting rain came on very soon after we quitted the former place, and accompanied us almost without ceasing to Fermoy. Here we had a glimpse of a bridge across the Blackwater, which we had skirted in our journey from Lismore. Now enveloped in mist and cloud, now spanned by a rainbow, at another time basking in sunshine, Nature attired the charming prospect for us in a score of different ways; and it appeared before us like a coquettish beauty who wag trying what dress in her wardrobe might most become her. At Fermoy we saw a vast barrack, and an overgrown inn, where, however, good fare was provided; and thence hastening came by Rathcormack, and Watergrass Hill, famous for the residence of Father Prout, whom my friend the Reverend Francis Sylvester has made immortal; from which descending we arrived at the beautiful wooded village of Glanmire, with its mills, and steeples, and streams, and neat school-houses, and pleasant country residences. This brings us down upon the superb stream which leads from the sea to Cork.

The view for three miles on both sides is magnificently beautiful Fine gardens, and parks, and villas cover the shore on each bank; the river is full of brisk craft moving to the city or out to sea; and the city, finely ends the view, rising upon two hills on either side of the stream. I do not know a town to which there is an entrance more beautiful, commodious, and stately.

Passing by numberless handsome lodges, and, nearer the city, many terraces in neat order, the road conducts us near a large tract of some hundred acres which have been reclaimed from the sea, and are destined to form a park and pleasure-ground for the citizens of Cork. In the river, and up to the bridge, some hundreds of ships were lying; and a fleet of steamboats opposite the handsome house of the St. George's Steam-Packet Company. A church stands prettily on the hill above it, surrounded by a number of new habitations very neat and white. On the road is a handsome Roman Catholic chapel, or a chapel which will he handsome so soon as the necessary funds are raised to complete it. But, as at Waterford, the chapel has been commenced, and the money has failed, and the fine portico which is to decorate it one day, as yet only exists on the architect's paper. Saint Patrick's Bridge, over which we pass, is a pretty building; and Patrick Street, the main street of the town, has an air of business and cheerfulness, and looks densely thronged.

As the carriage drove up to those neat, comfortable, and extensive lodgings which Mrs. MacO'Boy has to let, a magnificent mob was formed round the vehicle, and we bad an opportunity of at once making acquaintance with some of the dirtiest rascally faces that all Ireland presents. Besides these professional rogues and beggars, who make a point to attend on all vehicles, everybody else seemed to stop too, to see that wonder, a coach and four horses. People issued from their shops, heads appeared at windows. I have seen the Queen pass in state in London, and not bring together a crowd near so great as that which assembled in the busiest street of the second city of the kingdom, just to look at a green coach and four bay-horses. Have they nothing else to do?—or is it that they *will* do nothing but stare, swagger, and be idle in the streets?

CHAPTER V: CORK—THE AGRICULTURAL SHOW—FATHER MATHEW

A MAN has no need to be an agriculturist in order to take a warm interest in the success of the Irish Agricultural Society, and to see what vast, good may result from it to the country. The National Education scheme—a noble and liberal one, at least as far as a stranger can see, which might have united the Irish people, and brought peace, into this most distracted of; all countries—failed unhappily of one of its greatest, ends. The Protestant clergy have always treated the plan with bitter hostility: and I do believe, in withdrawing, from it, have struck the greatest blow to themselves as a body, and to their own influence in the country, which has been dealt to: them for many a year. Rich, charitable, pious, well-educated, to be found in every parish in Ireland, had they chosen to fraternise with the people and the plan, they might have directed the educational movement; they might have attained the influence which is now given; over entirely to the priest; and when the present generation, educated in the National Schools, were grown up to manhood,, they might have had an interest, in almost every man in Ireland. Are they as pious, and more polished, and better educated than their neighbours the priests? There is. no doubt of it; and by, constant communion with, the people, they would have gained all the benefits of the comparison, and advanced the interests of their religion far more than now they can hope to do. Look, at the National School: throughout the country it is commonly by the chapel side—it is a Catholic school, directed and fostered, by the priest; and as no people are more eager for learning, more apt to receive it, or more grateful for kindness than the Irish, he gets all the gratitude of the scholars who flock to the school, and all the future influence over. them, which naturally and justly comes to him. The Protestant wants to better the condition of these people; he says that the woes of the country are owing to its prevalent religion; and in order to carry his plans of amelioration into effect, he obstinately refuses to hold communion with those whom,he is desirous to convert to what he believes are sounder principles and purer doctrines. The clergyman will reply, that points of principle prevented him: with,this fatal doctrinal objection, it is not. of course; the province of a layman to meddle; but this is clear, that the. parson might have had an influence over the country, and he would not; that he might have rendered the Catholic population friendly to him, and he would not; but, instead, has added one cause of estrangement and hostility more to the many which already existed against him. This is one of the attempts at union in Ireland, and one can't but think with the deepest regret and sorrow of its failure.

Mr. O'Connell and his friends set going another scheme for advancing the prosperity of the country,—the notable project of home manufactures, and of a coalition against foreign importation. This was a union certainly, but a union of a different sort to that noble and peaceful one which the National Education Board proposed. It was to punish England, while it pretended to secure the independence of Ireland, by shutting out our manufactures from the Irish markets; which were one day or other, it was presumed, to be filled by native produce. Large bodies of tradesmen and private persons in Dublin and other towns in Ireland associated together, vowing to purchase no articles of ordinary consumption or usage but what were manufactured in the country. This bigoted old-world scheme of restriction—not much more liberal than Swing's crusade against the threshing-machines or the coalitions in England against machinery—failed, as it deserved to do. For the benefit of a few tradesmen, who might find their account in selling at dear rates their clumsy and imperfect manufactures, it was found impossible to tax a people that are already poor enough; nor did the party take into account the cleverness of the merchants across sea, who were by no means disposed to let go their Irish customers. The famous Irish frieze uniform which was to distinguish these patriots, and which Mr. O'Connell lauded so loudly and so simply, came over made at half-price from Leeds and Glasgow, and was retailed as real Irish by many worthies who had been first to join the union. You may still see shops here and there with their pompous announcement of 'Irish Manufactures'; but the scheme is long gone to ruin: it could not stand against the vast force of English and Scotch capital and machinery, any more than the Ulster spinning-wheel against the huge factories and steam-engines which one may see about Belfast.

The scheme of the Agricultural Society is a much more feasible one; and if, please God, it can be carried out, likely to give not only prosperity to the country, but union likewise in a great degree. As yet Protestants and Catholics concerned in it have worked well together; and it is a blessing to see them meet upon *any* ground without heartburning and quarrelling. Last year, Mr. Purcell, who is well known in Ireland as the principal mail-coach contractor for the country,—who himself employs more workmen in Dublin than perhaps any other person there, and has also more land under cultivation than most of the great landed proprietors in the country,—wrote a letter to the newspapers, giving his notions of the fallacy of the exclusive-dealing system, and pointing out at the same time how he considered the country might be benefited—by agricultural improvement, namely. He spoke of the neglected state of the country, and its amazing natural fertility; and, tor the benefit of all, called upon the landlords and landholders to use their interest and develop its vast agricultural resources. Manufactures are at best but of slow growth, and demand not only time, but capital; meanwhile, until the habits of the people should grow to be such as to render manufactures feasible, there was a great neglected treasure, lying under their feet, which might be the source of prosperity to all. He pointed out the superior methods of husbandry employed in Scotland and England, and the great results obtained upon soils naturally much poorer; and, taking the Highland Society for an example, the establishment of which had done so much for the prosperity of Scotland, he proposed the formation in Ireland of a similar association.

The letter made an extraordinary sensation throughout the country. Noblemen and gentry of all sides took it up; and numbers of these wrote to Mr. Purcell, and gave him their cordial adhesion to the plan. A meeting was held, and the Society formed: subscriptions were set on foot, headed by the Lord Lieutenant (Fortescue) and the Duke of Leinster, each with a donation of £200; and the trustees had soon £5000 at their disposal: with, besides, an annual revenue of £1000. The subscribed capital is funded; and political subjects strictly excluded. The Society has a show yearly in one of the principal towns of Ireland: it corresponds with the various local agricultural associations throughout the country; encourages the formation of new ones; and distributes prizes and rewards. It has further in contemplation to establish a large Agricultural School for farmers' sons; and has formed in Dublin an Agricultural Bazaar and Museum.

* * * * *

It was the first meeting of the Society which we were come to see at Cork. Will it be able to carry its excellent intentions into effect? Will the present enthusiasm of its founders and members continue? Will one political party or another get the upper hand in it? One can't help thinking of these points with some anxiety—of the latter especially: as yet, happily, the clergy of either side have kept aloof, and the union seems pretty cordial and sincere.

There are in Cork, as no doubt in every town of Ireland sufficiently considerable to support a plurality of hotels, some especially devoted to the Conservative and Liberal parties. Two dinners were to be given *à propos* of the Agricultural meeting; and in order to conciliate all parties, it was determined that the Tory landlord should find the cheap ten-shilling dinner for one thousand, the Whig landlord the genteel guinea dinner for a few select hundreds.

I wish Mr. Cuff, of the Freemasons' Tavern, could have been at Cork to take a lesson from the latter gentleman: for he would have seen that there are means of having not merely enough to eat, but enough of the very best, for the sum of a guinea; that persons can have not only wine, but good wine, and if inclined (as some topers are on great occasions) to pass to another bottle,—a second, a third, or a fifteenth bottle for what I know, is very much at their service. It was a fine sight to see Mr. MacDowall presiding over an ice-well and extracting the bottles of champagne. With what calmness he did it! How the corks popped, and the liquor fizzed, and the agriculturists drank the bumpers off! And how good the wine was too—the greatest merit of all! Mr. MacDowall did credit to his liberal politics by his liberal dinner.

'Sir,' says a waiter whom I had asked for currant-jelly for the haunch (there were a dozen such smoking on various parts of the. table—think of that, Mr. Cuff!)—'Sir, says the waiter, 'there's no jelly, but I've brought you *some very fine lobster-sauce*.' I think this was the most remarkable speech of the evening; not excepting that of my Lord Bernard, who, to three hundred gentlemen more or less connected with farming, had actually, the audacity to quote the words of the great agricultural poet of Rome—

'O fortunatos nimium sua si,' etc.

How long are our statesmen in England to continue to back their opinions by the Latin grammar'? Are the Irish agriculturists so *very* happy, if they did but know it—at least those out of doors? Well, those within were jolly enough. Champagne and claret, turbot and haunch, are gifts of the *justissima tellus*, with which few husbandmen will be disposed to quarrel:—no more let us quarrel either with eloquence after dinner.

If the Liberal landlord had shown his principles in his dinner, the Conservative certainly showed his—by conserving as much profit as possible for himself. We sat down one thousand to some two hundred and fifty cold joints of meat. Every man was treated with a pint of wine, and very bad too, so that there was the less cause to grumble because more was not served. Those agriculturists who had a mind;to drink whisky-and-water had, to pay extra for their punch. Nay, after shouting in vain for half-an-hour to a waiter for some cold water, the unhappy writer could only get it by promising a shilling. The sum was paid on delivery of the article; but as everybody round was thirsty too, I got but a glassful from the decanter, which, only served to make me long for more. The waiter (the rascal!), promised more, but never came near us afterwards: he had got his shilling, and so he left us in a hot room, surrounded by a thousand hot fellow-creatures, one of them making a dry speech. The agriculturists were not on this occasion *nimium fortunati.*

To have heard a nobleman, however, who discoursed to the meeting, you would have fancied that we. were the luckiest mortals under the broiling July sun. He said he could conceive nothing more delightful than to see, 'on proper occasions'—(mind, *on proper occasions*!)—'the landlord mixing with, his tenantry; and to look around him at a scene like this, and see *the condescension* with which the gentry mingled with the farmers!' Prodigious condescension truly! This neat speech seemed to me an oratorio slap on the face to about nine hundred and seventy persons present; and being one of the latter, I began to hiss by way of acknowledgment of the compliment, and hoped that a strong party would have destroyed the harmony of the evening, and done likewise. But not one hereditary bondsman would join in the compliment—and they were quite right too. The old lord who talked about condescension is one of the greatest and kindest landlords in Ireland. If he thinks he condescends by doing his duty and mixing with men as good as himself, the fault lies with the latter. Why are they so ready to go down on their knees to my Lord? A man can't help 'condescending' to another who will persist in kissing his shoestrings. They respect rank in England—the people seem almost to adore it here.

As an instance of the intense veneration for lords which distinguishes this county of Cork, I may mention what occurred afterwards. The members of the Cork Society gave a dinner to their guests of the Irish Agricultural Association. The founder of the latter, as Lord Downshire stated, was Mr. Purcell: and as it was agreed on all hands that the Society so founded was likely to prove of the greatest benefit to the country, one might have supposed that any compliment paid to it might have been paid to it through its founder. Not so. The Society asked the lords to dine, and Mr. Purcell to meet the lords.

After the grand dinner came a grand ball, which was indeed one of the gayest and prettiest sights ever seen; nor was it the less agreeable, because the ladies of the city mixed with the ladies from the country, and vied with them in grace and beauty. The charming gaiety and frankness of the Irish ladies have been noted and admired by every foreigner who has had the good fortune to mingle in their society; and I hope it is not detracting from the merit of the upper classes to say that the lower are not a whit less pleasing. I never saw in any country-such a general grace of manner and *ladyhood.* In the midst of their gaiety, too, it must be remembered that they are the chastest of women, and that no country in Europe can boast of such a general purity.

In regard of the Munster ladies, I had the pleasure to be present at two or three evening-parties at Cork, and must say that they seem to excel the English ladies not only in wit and vivacity, but in the still more important article of the toilette. They are as well dressed as Frenchwomen, and incomparably handsomer; and if ever this book reaches a thirtieth edition, and I can find out better words to express admiration, they shall be inserted here. Among the ladies' accomplishments, I may mention that I have heard in two or three private families such fine music as is rarely to be met with out of a capital. In one house we had a supper and songs afterwards, in the old honest fashion. Time was in Ireland when the custom was a common one; but the world grows languid as it grows genteel; and I fancy it requires more than ordinary spirit and courage now for a good old gentleman, at the head of his kind family table, to strike up a good old family song.

The delightful old gentleman who sang the song here mentioned could not help talking of the Temperance movement with a sort of regret, and said that all the fun had gone out of Ireland since Father Mathew banished the whisky from it. Indeed, any stranger going amongst the people can perceive that they are now anything but gay. I have seen a great number of crowds and meetings of people in all parts of Ireland, and found them all gloomy. There is nothing like the merry-making one reads of in the Irish novels. Lever and Maxwell must be taken as chroniclers of the old times—the pleasant but wrong old times—for which one can't help having an antiquarian fondness.

On the day we arrived at Cork, and as the passengers descended from 'the drag,' a stout, handsome, honest-looking man, of some two-and-forty years, was passing by, and received a number of bows from the crowd around. It was

THEOBALD MATHEW

with whose face a thousand little print-shop windows had already rendered me familiar. He shook hands with the master of the carriage very cordially, and just as cordially with the master's coachman, a disciple of temperance, as at least half Ireland is at present. The day after the famous dinner at MacDowall's, some of us came down rather late, perhaps in consequence of the events of the night before (I think it was Lord Bernard's quotation from Virgil, or else the absence of the currant-jelly for the venison, that occasioned a slight headache among some of us, and an extreme longing for soda-water),—and there was the Apostle of Temperance seated at the table drinking tea. Some of us felt a little ashamed of ourselves, and did not like to ask somehow for the soda-water in such an awful presence as that. Besides, it would have been a confession to a Catholic priest, and, as a Protestant, I am above it.

The world likes to know how a great man appears even to a valet-de-chambre, and I suppose it is one's vanity that is flattered in such rare company to find the great man quite as unassuming as the very smallest personage present; and so like to other mortals, that we would not know him to be a great man at all, did we not know his name, and what he had done. There is nothing remarkable in Mr. Mathew's manner, except that it is exceedingly simple, hearty, and manly, and that he does not wear the downcast demure look which, I know not why, certainly characterises the chief part of the gentlemen of his profession. Whence comes that general scowl which darkens the faces of the Irish priesthood? I have met a score of these reverend gentlemen in the country, and not one of them seemed to look or speak frankly, except Mr. Mathew, and a couple more. He is almost the only man, too, that I have met in Ireland, who, in speaking of public matters, did not talk as a partisan. With the state of the country, of landlord, tenant, and peasantry, he seemed to be most curiously and intimately acquainted; speaking of their wants, differences, and the means of bettering them, with the minutest practical knowledge. And it was impossible in hearing him to know, but from previous acquaintance with his character, whether he was Whig or Tory, Catholic or Protestant.

Why does not Government make a Privy Councillor of him?—that is, if he would honour the Right Honourable body by taking a seat amongst them. His knowledge of the people is prodigious, and their confidence in him as great; and what a touching attachment that is which these poor fellows show to any one who has their cause at heart—even to any one who says he has.

Avoiding all political questions, no man seems more eager than he for the practical improvement of this country. Leases and rents, farming improvements, reading-societies, music-societies—he was full of these, and of his schemes of temperance above all. He never misses a chance of making a convert, and has his hand ready and a pledge in his pocket for rich or poor. One of his disciples in a livery-coat came into the room with a tray—Mr. Mathew recognised him, and shook him by the hand directly; so he did with the strangers who were presented to him; and not with a courtly popularity-hunting air, but, as it seemed, from sheer hearty kindness, and a desire to do every one good.

When breakfast was done—(he took but one cup of tea, and says that, from having been a great consumer of tea and refreshing liquids before, a small cup of tea, and one glass of water at dinner, now serve him for his day's beverage)—he took the ladies of our party to see his burying-ground—a new and handsome cemetery, lying a little way out of the town, and where, thank God! Protestants and Catholics may lie together, without clergymen quarrelling over their coffins.

It is a handsome piece of ground, and was formerly a botanic garden; but the funds failed for that undertaking, as they have for a thousand other public enterprises in this poor disunited country; and so it has been converted into a *hortus siccus* for us mortals. There is already a pretty large collection. In the midst is a place for Mathew himself—honour to him living or dead! Meanwhile, numerous stately monuments have been built, flowers planted here and there over dear remains, and the garden in which they lie is rich, green, and beautiful. Here is a fine statue, by Hogan, of a weeping genius that broods over the tomb of an honest merchant and clothier of the city. He took a liking to the artist, his fellow-townsman, and ordered his own monument, and had the gratification to see it arrive from Rome a few weeks before his death. A prettier thing even than the statue is the tomb of a little boy, which has been shut in by a large and curious *grille* of ironwork. The father worked it, a blacksmith, whose darling the child was, and he spent three years in hammering out this mausoleum. It is the beautiful story of the pot of ointment told again at the poor blacksmith's anvil; and who can but like him for placing this fine gilded cage over the body of his poor little one? Presently you come to a Frenchwoman's tomb, with a French epitaph by a French husband, and a pot of artificial flowers in a niche—a wig, and a pot of rouge, as it were, just to make the dead look passably well. It is *his* manner of showing his sympathy for an immortal soul that has passed away. The poor may be buried here for nothing; and here, too, once more thank God! each may rest without priests or parsons scowling hell-fire at his neighbour unconscious under the;grass.

CHAPTER VI: CORK—THE URSTTLINE CONVENT

THERE is a large Ursuline convent at Blackrock, near Cork, and a lady who had been educated there was kind enough to invite me to join a party to visit the place. Was not this a great privilege for a heretic? I have peeped into convent chapels abroad, and occasionally caught glimpses of a white veil or black gown; but to see the pious ladies in their own retreat was quite a novelty—much more exciting than the exhibition of Long Horns and Short Horns by which we had to pass on our road to Blackrock.

The three miles' ride is very pretty. As far as nature goes, she has done her best for the neighbourhood; and the noble hills on the opposite coast of the river, studded with innumerable pretty villas and garnished with fine trees and meadows, the river itself dark blue under a brilliant cloudless heaven, and lively with its multiplicity of gay craft, accompany the traveller along the road; except here and there where the view is shut out by fine avenues of trees, a beggarly row of cottages, or a villa wall. Rows of dirty cabins, and smart bankers' country-houses, meet one at every turn, nor do the latter want for fine names, you may be sure. The Irish grandiloquence displays itself finely in the invention of such and, to the great inconvenience, I should think, of the postman, the names of the houses appear to change with the tenants: for I saw many old houses with new placards in front, setting forth the *last* title of the house.

I had the box of the carriage (a smart vehicle that would have done credit to the ring), and found the gentleman by my side very communicative. He named the owners of the pretty mansions and lawns visible on the other side of the river: they appear almost all to be merchants, who have made their fortunes in the city. In the like manner, though the air of the town is extremely fresh and pure to a pair of London lungs, the Cork shopkeeper is not satisfied with it, but contrives for himself a place (with an euphonious name, no doubt) if the suburbs of the city. These stretch to a great extent along the beautiful liberal-looking banks of the stream.

I asked the man about the Temperance, and whether he was a temperance man? He replied by pulling a medal out of his waistcoat pocket, saying that he always carried it about with him for fear of temptation. He said that he took the pledge two years ago, before which time, as he confessed, he had been a sad sinner in the way of drink. 'I used to take,' said he, 'from eighteen to twenty glasses of whisky a day; I was always at the drink; I'd be often up all night at the public: I was turned away by my present master on account of it;'—and all of a sudden be resolved to break it off. I asked him whether he had not at first experienced ill-health from the suddenness of the change in his habits: but he said—and let all persons meditating a conversion from liquor remember the fact—that the abstinence never affected him in the least, but that he went on growing better and better in health every day, stronger and more able of mind and body.

The man was a Catholic, and in speaking of the numerous places of worship along the road as we passed, I'm sorry to confess, dealt some rude cuts with his whip regarding the Protestants. Coachman as he was, the fellow's remarks seemed to be correct: for it appears that the religious world of Cork is of so excessively enlightened a kind, that one church will not content one pious person; but that, on the contrary, they will be at church of a morning, at Independent church of an afternoon, at a Darbyite congregation of an evening, and so on, gathering excitement or information from all sources which they could come at. Is not this the case? are not some of the ultra-serious as eager after a new preacher, as the ultra-worldly for a new dancer? don't they talk and gossip about him as much? Though theology from the coachbox is rather questionable (after all, the man was just as much authorised to propound his notions as many a fellow from an amateur pulpit), yet he certainly had the right here as far as his charge against certain Protestants went.

The reasoning from it was quite obvious, and I'm sure was in the man's mind, though he did not utter it, as we drove by this time into the convent gate. 'Here,' says coachman, 'is *our* church. *I* don't drive my master and mistress from church to chapel, from chapel to conventicle, hunting after new preachers every Sabbath. I bring them every Sunday and set them down at the same place, where they know that everything they hear must be right. Their fathers have done the same thing before them; and the young ladies and gentlemen will come here too; and all the new-fangled doctors and teachers may go roaring through the land, and still here we come regularly, not caring a whit for the vagaries of others, knowing that we ourselves are in the real old right original way.'

I am sure this was what the fellow meant by his sneer at the Protestants, and their gadding from one doctrine to another; but there was no call and no time to have a battle with him, as by this time we had entered a large lawn covered with haycocks, and prettily, as I think, ornamented with a border of blossoming potatoes, and drove up to the front door of the convent. It is a huge old square house, with many windows, having probably been some flaunting squire's residence; but the nuns have taken off somewhat from its rakish look, by flinging out a couple of wings with chapels, or buildings like chapels, at either end.

A large, lofty, clean, trim hall was open to a flight of steps, and we found a young lady in the hall, playing, instead of a pious sonata— which I vainly thought was the practice in such godly seminaries of learning—that abominable rattling piece of music called 'La Violette,' which it has been my lot to hear executed by other young ladies; and which (with its like) has always appeared to me to be constructed upon this simple fashion—to take a tune, and then, as it were, to fling it down and up stairs. As soon as the young lady playing 'The Violet' saw us, she quitted the hall and retired to an inner apartment, where she resumed the delectable piece at her leisure. Indeed there were pianos all over the educational part of the house.

We were shown into a gay parlour (where hangs a pretty drawing representing the melancholy old convent which the Sisters previously inhabited in Cork), and presently Sister No. Two-Eight made her appearance—a pretty and graceful lady.

"Tis the prettiest nun of the whole house,' whispered the lady who had been educated at the convent; and I must own that slim, gentle, and pretty, as this young lady was, and calculated with her kind smiling face and little figure to frighten no one in the world, a great six-foot Protestant could not help looking at her with a little tremble. I had never been in a nun's company before.; I'm afraid of such—I don't care to own—in their black mysterious robes and awful veils. As priests in gorgeous vestments, and little rosy incense-boys in red, bob their heads and knees up and down before altars, or clatter silver pots full of smoking odours, I feel I don't know what sort of thrill and secret creeping terror. Here I was in a room with a real live nun, pretty and pale—I wonder has she any of her sisterhood immured in *oubliettes* down below; is her poor little weak delicate body scarred all over with scourgings, iron-collars, hair-shirts? What has she had for dinner to-day?—as we passed the refectory there was a faint sort of vapid nun-like vegetable smell, speaking of fasts and wooden platters; and I could picture to myself silent sisters eating their meal—a grim old yellow one in the reading-desk, croaking out an extract from a sermon for their edification.

But is it policy, or hypocrisy, or reality? These nuns affect extreme happiness and content with their condition: a smiling beatitude, which they insist belongs peculiarly to them, and about which the only doubtful point is the manner in which it is produced before strangers. Young ladies educated in convents have often mentioned this fact—how the nuns persist in declaring and proving to them their own extreme enjoyment of life.

Were all the smiles of that kind-looking Sister Two-Eight perfectly sincere? Whenever she spoke her face was lighted up with one. She seemed perfectly radiant with happiness, tripping lightly before us, and distributing kind compliments to each, which made me in a very few minutes forget the introductory fright which her poor little presence had occasioned.

She took us through the hall (where was the vegetable savour before mentioned) and showed us the contrivance by which the name of Two-Eight was ascertained. Each nun has a number, or a combination of numbers, prefixed to her name; and a bell is pulled a corresponding number of times, by which each sister knows when she is wanted. Poor souls! are they always on the look-out for that bell, that the ringing of it should be supposed infallibly to awaken their attention?

From the hall the sister conducted us through ranges of apartments, and I had almost said avenues of pianofortes, whence here and there a startled pensioner would rise, *hinnuleo similis*, at our approach, seeking a *pavidam matrem* in the person of a demure old stout mother hard by. We were taken through a hall decorated with a series of pictures of Pope Pius VI.,—wonderful adventures, truly, in the life of the gentle old man. In one you see him gracefully receiving a Prince and Princess of Russia (tremendous incident!). The Prince has a pigtail, the Princess powder and a train, the Pope a— but never mind, we shall never get through the house at this rate.

Passing through Pope Pius's gallery, we came into a long, clean, lofty passage, with many little doors on each side; and here I confess my heart began to thump again. These were the doors of the cells of the Sisters. *Bon Dieu*! and is it possible that I shall see a nun's cell? Do I not recollect the nun's cell in 'The Monk,' or in 'The Romance of the Forest'? or, if not there, at any rate in a thousand noble romances, read in early days of half-holiday perhaps—romances at twopence a volume.

Come in, in the name of the saints! Here is the cell. I took off my hat and examined the little room with much curious wonder and reverence. There was an iron bed, with comfortable curtains of green serge. There was a little clothes-chest of yellow wood, neatly cleaned, and a wooden chair beside it, and a desk on the chest, and about six pictures on the wall,—little religious pictures: a saint with gilt paper round him; the Virgin showing on her breast a bleeding heart, with a sword run through it; and other sad little subjects, calculated to make the inmate of the cell think of the sufferings of the saints and martyrs of the Church. Then there was a little crucifix, and a wax-candle on the ledge; and here was the place where the poor black-veiled things were to pass their lives for ever!

After having seen a couple of these little cells, we left the corridors in which they were, and were conducted, with a sort of pride on the nun's part, I thought, into the grand room of the convent—a parlour with pictures of saints and a gay paper, and a series of small fineries, such only as women very idle know how to make. There were some portraits in the room, one an atrocious daub of an ugly old woman, surrounded by children still more hideous. Somebody had told the poor nun that this was a fine thing, and she believed it—Heaven bless her!—quite implicitly: nor is the picture of the ugly old Canadian woman the first reputation that has been made this way.

Then from the fine parlour we went to (the museum. I don't know how we should be curious of such trifles; but the chronicling of small-beer is the main business of life—people only differing, as Tom Moore wisely says in one of his best poems, about their own peculiar tap. The poor nun's little collection of gimcracks was displayed in great state: there were spars in one drawer; and, I think, a Chinese shoe and some Indian wares in another; and some medals of the Popes, and a couple of score of coins; and a clean glass case, full of antique- works of French theology of the distant period of Louis XV., to judge by the bindings—and this formed the main part of the museum. 'The chief objects were gathered together by a single nun,' said the sister with a look of wonder, as she went prattling on, and leading us hither and thither, like a child showing her toys.

What strange mixture of pity and pleasure is it which comes over you sometimes when a child takes you by the hand, and leads you up solemnly to some little treasure of its own—a feather or a string of glass beads. I declare I have often looked at such with more delight than at diamonds; and felt the same sort of soft wonder examining the nuns' little treasure-chamber. There was something touching in the very poverty of it;—had it been finer it would not have been half so good.

And now we had seen all the wonders of the house but the chapel, and thither we were conducted; all the ladies of our party kneeling down as they entered the building, and saying a short prayer.

This, as I am on sentimental confessions, I must own affected me too. It was a very pretty and tender sight. I should have liked to kneel down too, but was ashamed; our northern usages not encouraging—among men at least—that sort of abandonment of dignity. Do any of us dare to sing psalms at church? and don't we look with rather a sneer at the man who does?

The chapel had nothing remarkable in it except a very good organ, as I was told; for we were allowed only to see the exterior of that instrument, our pious guide with much pleasure removing an oil-cloth which covered the mahogany. At one side of the altar is a long high *grille,* through which you see a hall, where the nuns have their stalls, and sit in chapel time; and beyond this hall is another small chapel, with a couple of altars, and one beautiful print in one of them—a German Holy Family—a prim, mystical, tender piece, just befitting the place.

In the *grille* is a little wicket and a ledge before it. It is to this wicket that women are brought to kneel; and a bishop is in the chapel on the other side, and takes their hands in his, and receives their vows. I had never seen the like before, and own that I felt a sort of shudder at looking at the place. There rest the girl's knees as she offers herself up, and forswears the sacred affections which God gave her; there she kneels and denies for ever the beautiful duties of her being:—no tender maternal yearnings, no gentle attachments are to be had for her or .from her—there she kneels and commits suicide upon her heart: O honest Martin Luther! thank God, you came to pull that infernal, wicked, unnatural altar down—that cursed Paganism;! Let people, solitary, worn out by sorrow or oppressed with extreme remorse, retire to such places; fly and beat your breasts in caverns and wildernesses, O women, if you will, but be Magdalens first. It is shameful that any young girl, with any vocation however seemingly strong, should be allowed to bury herself in this small tomb of a few acres. Look at yonder nun—pretty, smiling, graceful, and young—what has God's world done to *her*, that she should run from it, or she- done to the world, that she should avoid it? What call has she to give up all her duties and affections? and would she not be best serving God with a husband at her side, and a. child on her knee?

The sights in the house having been seen, the nun led us through the grounds and gardens. There was the hay in front, a fine yellow cornfield at the back of the house, and a large, melancholy-looking kitchen-garden; in all of which places the nuns, for certain hours in the day, are allowed to take recreation. 'The nuns here are allowed to amuse themselves more than ours at New Hall,' said a little girl who is educated, at that English convent: 'do you know that here the nuns may make hay?' What a privilege is this! We saw none of the black sisterhood availing themselves of it, however: the hay was neatly piled into cocks and ready for housing; so the poor souls must wait until next year before they can enjoy this blessed sport once more.

Turning into a narrow gate with the nun at our head, we found ourselves in a little green quiet enclosure—it was the burial-ground of the convent. The poor things know the places where they are to lie: she who was with us talked smilingly of being stretched there one day, and pointed out the resting-place of a favourite old sister who had died three months; back, and been buried in the very, midst of the little ground. And here they come to live and die.. The gates are open, but they never go out. All their; world lies in a: dozen, acres of ground; and they sacrifice their, lives in early youth, many, of them passing from the grave, upstairs in the house to the one scarcely narrower in; the churchyard here; and are seemingly not unhappy.

I came out of the place quite sick; and looking before me,—there, thank God! was the blue spire of Monkstown church soaring up into the free sky—a river in front rolling away to the sea—liberty, sunshine, all sorts of glad, life and motion round about: and I couldn't but thank Heaven for it, and the Being whose service is freedom, and who has given us affections that we may use them—not smother and kill them; and a noble world to live in, that we may admire it and Him, who made it—not shrink from it, as though we dared not live there, but must turn our backs upon it and its bountiful Provider.

And in conclusion, if that most cold-blooded and precise of all personages, the respectable and respected English reader, may feel disposed to sneer at the above sentimental homily, or to fancy that it has been written for effect—let him go and see a convent for himself. I declare I think for my part that we have as much right to permit Sutteeism in India as to allow women in the United Kingdom to take these wicked vows, or Catholic bishops to receive them; and that Government has as good a right to interpose in such cases, as the police have to prevent a man from hanging himself, or the doctor to refuse a glass of prussic-acid to any one who may have a wish to go out of the world.

CHAPTER VII: CORK

AMIDST the bustle and gaieties of the Agricultural meeting, the working day aspect of the city was not to be judged of: but I passed a fortnight in the place afterwards, during which time it settled down to its calm and usual condition. The flashy French and plated goods shops, which made a show for the occasion of the meeting, disappeared; you were no longer crowded and jostled by smart male and female dandies in walking down Patrick Street or the Mall; the poor little theatre had scarcely a soul on its bare benches: I went once, but the dreadful brass-band of a dragoon regiment blew me out of doors. This music could be heard much more pleasantly at some distance off in the street.

One sees in this country many a grand and tall iron gate leading into a very shabby field covered with thistles; and the simile of the gate will in some degree apply to this famous city of Cork,—which is certainly not a city of palaces, but of which the outlets are magnificent. That towards Killarney leads by the Lee, the old Avenue of Mardyke, and the rich green pastures stretching down to the river; and as you pass by the portico of the county gaol, as fine and as glancing as a palace, you see the wooded heights on the other side of the fair stream, crowded with a thousand pretty villas and terraces, presenting every image of comfort and prosperity. The entrance from Cove has been mentioned before; nor is it easy to find anywhere a nobler, grander, and more cheerful scene.

Along the quays up to Saint Patrick's Bridge there is a certain bustle. Some forty ships may be lying at anchor along the walls of the quay, and its pavements are covered with goods of various merchandise: here a cargo of hides; yonder a company of soldiers, their kits, and their Dollies, who are taking leave of the red-coats at the steamer's side. Then you shall see a fine, squeaking, shrieking drove of pigs embarking by the same conveyance, and insinuated into the steamer by all sorts of coaxing, threatening, and wheedling. Seamen are singing and yeehoing on board; grimy colliers smoking at the liquor-shops along the quay; and as for the bridge—there is a crowd of idlers on *that,* you may be sure, sprawling over the balustrade for ever and, ever, with long ragged coats, steeple-hats, and stumpy-doodeens.

Then along the Coal Quay you may see a clump of jingle-drivers, who have all a word for your honour; and in Patrick Street, at three o'clock, when 'The Rakes of Mallow' gets under way (a cracked old coach with the paint rubbed off, some smart horses, and an exceedingly dingy harness)—at three o'clock, you will be sure to see at least forty persons waiting to witness the departure of the said coach: so that the neighbourhood of the inn has an air of some bustle.

At the other extremity of the town, if it be assize time, you will see some five hundred persons squatting by the court-house, or buzzing and talking within. The rest of the respectable quarter of the city is pretty free from anything like bustle: there is no more life in Patrick Street than in Russell Square of a sunshiny day; and as for the Mall, it is as lonely as the chief street of a German Residenz.

I have mentioned the respectable quarter of the city—for there are quarters in it swarming with life, but of such a frightful kind as no pen need care to describe: alleys where the odours and rags and darkness are so hideous, that one runs frightened away from them. In some of them, they say, not the policeman, only the priest, can penetrate. I asked a Roman Catholic clergyman of the city to take me into some of these haunts, but he refused very justly; and indeed a man may be quite satisfied with what he can see in the mere outskirts of the districts, without caring to penetrate farther. Not far from the quays is an open space where the poor hold a market or bazaar. Here is liveliness and business enough: ragged women chattering and crying their beggarly wares; ragged boys gloating over dirty apple-and pie-stalls; fish frying, and raw and stinking; clothes-booths, where you might buy a wardrobe for scarecrows; old nails, hoops, bottles, and marine-wares; old battered furniture, that has been sold against starvation. In the streets round about this place, on a sunshiny day, all the black gaping windows and mouldy steps are covered with squatting lazy figures—women, with bare breasts, nursing babies, and leering a joke as you pass by —ragged children paddling everywhere. It is but two minutes' walk out of Patrick Street, where you' come upon a fine flashy shop of plated goods, or a grand French emporium of dolls, walking-sticks, carpet-bags, and perfumery. The markets hard by have a rough, old-fashioned, cheerful look; it's a comfort after the misery to hear a red butcher's wife crying after you to buy an honest piece of meat.

The poor-house, newly established, cannot hold a fifth part of the poverty of this great town: the richer inhabitants are untiring in their charities, and the Catholic clergyman before mentioned took me to see a delivery of rice, at which he presides every day until the potatoes shall come in. This market, over which he presides so kindly, is held in an old bankrupt warehouse, and the rice is sold considerably under the prime cost to hundreds of struggling applicants who come when lucky enough to have wherewithal to pay.

That the city contains much wealth is evidenced by the number of handsome villas round; about it, where the rich merchants dwell;. but the warehouses, of the wealthy provision-merchants make no show to the stranger walking the streets; and of the retail-shops, if some are spacious and handsome, most look as if too big for the business carried on within. The want of ready-money was quite curious. In three of the principal shops I purchased articles, and tendered a pound in exchange—not one of them had silver enough; and as for a five-pound note, which I presented at one of the topping booksellers', his boy went round to various places in vain, and finally set forth to the Bank, where: change was got. In, another small shop I offered half-a-crown to pay for a sixpenny article—it was all the same. 'Tim,' says the good woman, 'run out in a hurry and fetch the gentleman change.' Two of the shopmen, seeing an Englishman, were very particular to tell me in what years they themselves had been in London. It seemed a merit in these gentlemen's eyes to have once dwelt in that city; and I see in the papers continually ladies advertising as governesses, and specifying; particularly that they are 'English ladies.'

I received six £5 post-office orders; I called four times on as many different days at the Post Office before the capital could be forth coming, getting on the third application ,£20 (after making a great clamour, and vowing that such things were unheard of in England), and on the fourth call the remaining £10. I saw poor people, who. may have come from the country with their orders, refused payment of an order of some 40s.; and a gentleman who tendered a. pound-note in payment, of a foreign letter, was told to 'leave his letter and pay some other time.' Such things could not take place in the hundred-and-second city in England; and as I do not pretend to doctrinise at all, I leave the reader to draw his own deductions with regard to the commercial condition and prosperity of the second city in Ireland.

Half-a-dozen of the public buildings I saw were spacious and shabby beyond all cockney belief. Adjoining the Imperial Hotel is a great, large, handsome, desolate reading-room, which was founded by a body of Cork merchants and tradesmen, and is the, very picture of decay. Not Palmyra—not the Russell Institution in Great Coram Street-presents a more melancholy appearance of faded greatness. Opposite this is: another institution, called the Cork Library, where there are plenty of books and plenty of kindness to the stranger;. but the shabbiness and faded splendour of the place are quite painful. There are three, handsome Catholic churches commenced of late years; not one of them is complete: two want their porticoes; the other is not more than thirty feet from the ground, and according to the architectural plan was to rise as high as a cathedral. There is an Institution, with a fair library of scientific works, a museum, and a drawing-school with a supply of casts. The place is in yet more dismal condition than the Library: the plasters are spoiled incurably for want of a sixpenny feather-brush; the dust lies on the walls, and nobody seems to heed it. Two shillings a year would have repaired much of the evil which has happened to this institution; and it is folly to talk of inward dissensions and political differences as causing the ruin of such institutions. Kings or laws don't cause or cure dust and cobwebs, but indolence leaves them to accumulate, and imprudence will not calculate its income, and vanity exaggerates its own powers, and the fault is laid upon that tyrant of a sister kingdom. The whole country is filled with such failures: swaggering beginnings that could not be carried through; grand enterprises begun dashingly, and ending in shabby compromises or downright ruin.

I have said something in praise of the manners of the Cork ladies: in regard of the gentlemen, a stranger too must remark the extraordinary degree of literary taste and talent amongst them, and the wit and vivacity of their conversation. The love for literature seems to an Englishman doubly curious. What, generally speaking, do a company of grave gentlemen and ladies in Baker Street know about if? Who ever reads books in the City, or how often does one hear them talked about at a Club? The Cork citizens are the most book-loving men I ever met. The town has sent to England a number of literary men, of reputation too, and is not a little proud of their fame. Everybody seemed to know what Maginn was doing, and that Father Prout had a third volume ready, and what was Mr. Croker's last article in the *Quarterly*. The young clerks and shopmen seemed as much *au fait* as their employers, and many is the conversation I heard about the merits of this writer or that—Dickens, Ainsworth, Lover, Lever.

I think, in walking the streets, and looking at the ragged urchins crowding there, every Englishman must remark that the superiority of intelligence is here, and not with us. I never saw such a collection of bright-eyed, wild, clever, eager faces. Mr. Maclise has carried away a number of them in his memory; and the lovers of his admirable pictures will find more than one Munster countenance under a helmet in company of Macbeth, or in a slashed doublet alongside of Prince Hamlet, or in the very midst of Spain in company with Señor Gil Blas. Gil Blas himself came from Cork, and not from Oviedo.

I listened to two boys almost in rags: they were lolling over the quay balustrade, and talking about *one of the Ptolemys*! and talking very well too. One of them had been reading in 'Rollin,' and was detailing his information with a great deal of eloquence and fire. Another day, walking in the Mardyke, I followed three boys, not half so well dressed as London errand-boys: one was telling the other about Captain Ross's voyages, and spoke with as much brightness and intelligence as the best-read gentleman's son in England could do. He was as much of a gentleman too, the ragged young student; his manner as good, though perhaps more eager and emphatic; his language was extremely rich, too, and eloquent. Does the reader remember his schooldays, when half-a-dozen lads in the bedrooms took it by turns to tell stories? how poor the language generally was, and how exceedingly poor the imagination! Both of those ragged Irish lads had the making of gentlemen, scholars, orators, in them. *À propos* of love of reading, let me mention here a Dublin story. Doctor Lever, the celebrated author of 'Harry Lorrequer,' went into Dycer's stables to buy a horse. The groom who brought the animal out, directly he heard who the gentleman was, came out and touched his cap, and pointed to a little book in his pocket in a pink cover. '*I can't do without it, sir,*' says the man. It was 'Harry Lorrequer.' I wonder does any one of Mr. Rymell's grooms take in 'Pickwick,' or would they have any curiosity to see Mr. Dickens, should he pass that way?

The Corkagians are eager for a Munster University; asking for, and having a very good right to, the same privilege which has been granted to the chief city of the North of Ireland. It would not fail of being a great benefit to the city and to the country too, which would have no need to go so far as Dublin for a school of letters and medicine; nor, Whig and Catholic for the most part, to attend a Tory and Protestant University. The establishing of an open college in Munster would bring much popularity to any Ministry that should accord such a boon. People would cry out, 'Popery and

Infidelity,' doubtless, as they did when the London University was established; as the same party in Spain would cry out, 'Atheism and Heresy.' But the time, thank God! is gone by in England when it was necessary to legislate for *them*; and Sir Robert Peel, in giving his adherence to the National Education scheme, has sanctioned the principle of which this so much longed-for college would only be a consequence.

The medical charities and hospitals are said to be very well arranged, and the medical men of far more than ordinary skill. Other public institutions are no less excellent. I was taken over the Lunatic Asylum, where everything was conducted with admirable comfort, cleanliness, and kindness; and as for the county gaol, it is so neat, spacious, and comfortable, that we can only pray to see every cottager in the country as cleanly, well lodged, and well fed as the convicts are. They get a pound of bread and a pint of milk twice a day: there must be millions of people in this wretched country, to whom such food would be a luxury that their utmost labours can never by possibility procure for them; and in going over this admirable institution, where everybody is cleanly, healthy, and well clad, I could not but think of the rags and filth of the horrid starvation market before mentioned; so that the prison seemed almost a sort of premium for vice. But the people like their freedom, such as it is, and prefer to starve and be ragged as they list. They will not go to the poor-houses, except at the greatest extremity, and leave them on the slightest chance of existence elsewhere.

Walking away from this palace of a prison, you pass amidst all sorts of delightful verdure, cheerful gardens, and broad green luscious pastures, down to the beautiful River Lee. On one side, the river shines away towards the city with its towers and purple steeples; on the other it is broken by little waterfalls and bound in by blue hills, an old castle towering in the distance, and innumerable parks and villas lying along the pleasant wooded banks. How beautiful the scene is, how rich and how happy! Yonder, in the old Mardyke Avenue, you hear the voices of a score or children, and along the bright green meadows, where the cows are feeding, the gentle shadows of the clouds go playing over the grass. Who can look at such a charming scene but with a thankful swelling heart?

In the midst of your pleasure, three beggars have hobbled up, and are howling supplications to the Lord. One is old and blind, and so diseased and hideous, that straightway all the pleasure of the sight round about vanishes from you—that livid ghastly face interposing between you and it. And so it is throughout the south and west of Ireland; the traveller is haunted by the face of the popular starvation. It is not the exception, it is the condition of the people. In this fairest and richest of countries, men are suffering and starving by millions. There are thousands of them at this minute stretched in the sunshine at their cabin doors with no work, scarcely any food, no hope seemingly. Strong countrymen are lying in bed *'for the hunger'*—because a man lying on his back does not need so much food as a person afoot. Many of them have torn up the unripe potatoes from their little gardens, to exist now, and must look to winter, when they shall have to suffer starvation and cold too. The epicurean, and traveller for pleasure, had better travel anywhere than here: where there are miseries that one does not dare to think of; where one is always feeling how helpless pity is, and how hopeless relief, and is perpetually made ashamed of being happy.

I have just been strolling up a pretty little height called Grattan's Hill, that overlooks the town and the river, and where the artist that comes Cork-wards may find many subjects for his pencil. There is a kind of pleasure-ground at the top of this eminence —a broad walk that draggles up to a ruined wall, with a ruined niche in it, and a battered stone bench. On the side that shelves down to the water are some beeches, and opposite them a row of houses from which you see one of the prettiest prospects possible—the shining river with the craft along the quays, and the busy city in the distance, the active little steamers puffing away towards Cove, the farther bank crowned with rich woods, and pleasant-looking country-houses: perhaps they are tumbling, rickety, and ruinous, as those houses close by us, but you can't see the ruin from here.

What a strange air of forlorn gaiety there is about the place!—the sky itself seems as if it did not know whether to laugh or cry, so full is it of clouds and sunshine. Little fat, ragged, smiling children are clambering about the rocks, and sitting on mossy doorsteps, tending other children yet smaller, fatter, and more dirty. 'Stop till I get you a posy' (pronounced *pawawawsee),* cries one urchin to another. 'Tell me who is it ye love, Jooly?' exclaims another, cuddling a red-faced infant with a very dirty nose. More of the same race are perched about the summer-house, and two wenches with large purple feet are flapping some carpets in the air. It is a wonder the carpets will bear this kind of treatment at all, and do not be off at once to mingle with the elements: I never saw things that hung to life by such a frail thread.

This dismal pleasant place is a suburb of the second city in Ireland, and one of the most beautiful spots about the town. What a prim, bustling, active, green-railinged, tea-gardened, gravel-walked place would it have been in the five-hundredth town in England!—but you see the people can be quite as happy in the rags and without the paint, and I hear a great deal more heartiness and affection from these children than from their fat little brethren across the Channel.

If a man wanted to study ruins, here is a house close at hand, not forty years old no doubt, but yet as completely gone to wreck as Netley Abbey. It is quite curious to study that house; and a pretty ruinous fabric of improvidence, extravagance, happiness, and disaster may the imagination build out of it! In the first place, the owners did not wait to finish it before they went to inhabit it! This is written in just such another place: a handsome drawing-room with a good carpet, a lofty marble mantelpiece, and no paper to the walls. The door is prettily painted white and blue, and though not six weeks old, a great piece of the woodwork is off already (Peggy uses it to prevent the door from banging to); and there are some fine chinks in every one of the panels, by which my neighbour may see all my doings.

A couple of score of years, and this house will be just like yonder place on Grattan's Hill.

Like a young prodigal, the house begins to use its constitution too early; and when it should yet (in the shape of carpenters and painters) have all its masters and guardians to watch and educate it, my house on Grattan's Hill must be a man at once, and enjoy all the privileges of strong health! I would lay a guinea they were making punch in that house before they could keep the rain out of it; that they had a dinner-party and ball before the floors were firm or the wainscots painted, and a fine tester-bed in the best room, where my lady might catch cold in state, in the midst of yawning chimneys, creaking window-sashes, and smoking plaster.

Now look at the door of the coach-house, with its first coat of paint seen yet, and a variety of patches to keep the feeble barrier together. The loft was arched once, but a great corner has tumbled at one end, leaving a gash that unites the windows with the coach-house door. Several of the arch-stones are removed, and the whole edifice is about as rambling and disorderly as—as the arrangement of this book, say. Very tall tufts of mouldy moss are on the drawing-room windows, with long white heads of grass. As I am sketching this—*honk!*—a great lean sow comes trampling through the slush within the courtyard, breaks down the flimsy apparatus of rattling boards and stones which had passed for the gate, and walks with her seven squeaking little ones to disport on the grass on the hill.

The drawing-room of the tenement mentioned just now, with its pictures, and pulleyless windows and lockless doors, was tenanted by a friend who lodged there with a sick wife and a couple of little children; one of whom was an infant in arms. It is not, however, the lodger—who is an Englishman—but the kind landlady and her family who may well be described here—for their like are hardly to be found on the other side of the Channel. Mrs. Fagan is a young widow who has seen better days, and that portrait over the grand mantelpiece is the picture of her husband that is gone, a handsome young man, and well to do at one time as a merchant. But the widow (she is as pretty, as ladylike, as kind, and as neat as ever widow could be) has little left to live upon but the rent of her lodgings and her furniture; of which we have seen the best in the drawing-room.

She has three fine children of her own: there is Minny, and Katey, and Patsey, and they occupy indifferently the dining-room on the ground-floor or the kitchen opposite; where in the midst of a great smoke sits an old nurse, by a copper of potatoes which is always bubbling and full. Patsey swallows quantities of them, that's clear: his cheeks are as red and shining as apples, and when he roars, you are sure that his lungs are in the finest condition. Next door to the kitchen is the pantry, and there is a bucketful of the before-mentioned fruit, and a grand service of china for dinner and dessert. The kind young widow shows them with no little pride, and says with reason that there are few lodging-houses in Cork that can match such china as that. They are relics of the happy old times when Fagan kept his gig and horse, doubtless, and had his friends to dine—the happy prosperous days which she has exchanged for poverty and the sad black gown.

Patsey, Minny, and Katey have made friends with the little English people upstairs; the elder of whom, in the course of a month, has as fine a Munster brogue as ever trolled over the lips of any born Corkagian. The old nurse carries out the whole united party to walk, with the exception of the English baby, that jumps about in the arms of a countrywoman of her own. That is, unless one of the four Miss Fagans takes her; for four of them there are, four *other* Miss Fagans, from eighteen downwards to fourteen:—handsome, fresh, lively, dancing, bouncing girls. You may always see two or three of them smiling at the parlour-window, and they laugh and turn away their heads when any young fellow looks at and admires them.

Now, it stands to reason that a young widow of five-and-twenty can't be the mother of four young ladies of eighteen downwards; and, if anybody wants to know how they come to be living with the poor widow their cousin, the answer is, they are on a visit. Peggy the maid says their papa is a gentleman of property, and can 'spend his eight hundred a year.'

Why don't they remain with the old gentleman then, instead of quartering on the poor young widow, who has her own little mouths to feed? The reason is, the old gentleman has gone and *married his cook;* and the daughters have quitted him in a body, refusing to sit down to dinner with a person who ought by rights to be in the kitchen. The whole family (the Fagans are of good family) take the quarrel up, and here are the young people under shelter of the widow.

Four merrier tenderer-hearted girls are not to be found in all Ireland; and the only subject of contention amongst them is, which shall have the English baby: they are nursing it, and singing to it, and dandling it by turns all day long. When they are not singing to the baby, they are singing to an old piano: such an old wiry, jingling, wheezy piano! It has plenty of work, playing jigs and song accompaniments between meals, and acting as a sideboard at dinner. I am not sure that it is at rest at night either; but have a shrewd suspicion that it is turned into a four-post bed. And for the following reason:—

Every afternoon, at four o'clock, you see a tall old gentleman walking leisurely to the house. He is dressed in a long great-coat with huge pockets, and in the huge pockets are sure to be some big apples for all the children—the English child amongst the rest, and she generally has the biggest one. At seven o'clock, you are sure to hear a deep voice shouting 'Paggy!' in an awful tone—it is the old gentleman calling for his 'materials'; which Peggy brings without any farther ado; and a glass of punch is made, no doubt, for everybody. Then the party separates: the children and the old nurse have long since tramped upstairs; Peggy has the kitchen for her sleeping-apartment, and the four young ladies make it out somehow in the back drawing-room. As for the old gentleman, he reposes in the parlour; and it must be somewhere about the piano, for there is no furniture in the room except that, a table, a few old chairs, a workbox, and a couple of albums.

The English girl's father met her in the street one day, talking confidentially with a tall old gentleman in a great-coat. 'Who's your friend?' says the Englishman afterwards to the little girl. 'Don't you know him, papa?' said the child in the purest brogue. 'Don't you know him?—That's Uncle James!' And so it was: in this kind, poor, generous, barebacked house, the English child found a set of new relations: little rosy brothers and sisters to play with, kind women to take the place of the almost dying mother, a good old Uncle James to bring her home apples and care for her—one and all ready to share their little pittance with her, and to give her a place in their simple friendly hearts. God Almighty bless the widow and her mite, and all the kind souls under her roof!

How much goodness and generosity—how much purity, fine feeling-nay, happiness —may dwell amongst the poor whom we have been just looking at! Here, thank God, is an instance of this happy and cheerful poverty: and it is good to look, when one can, at the heart that beats under the threadbare coat, as well as the tattered old garment itself. Well, please Heaven, some of those people whom we have been looking at are as good, and not much less happy: but though they are accustomed to their want, the stranger does not reconcile himself to it quickly; and I hope no Irish reader will be offended at my speaking of this poverty, not with scorn or ill-feeling, but with hearty sympathy and good-will.

* * * * *

One word more regarding the Widow Fagan's house. When Peggy brought in coals for the drawing-room fire, she carried them—in what do you think? 'In a coal-scuttle, to be sure,' says the English reader, down on you as sharp as a needle.

No, you clever Englishman, it wasn't a coal-scuttle.

'Well, then, it was in a fire-shovel,' says that brightest of wits, guessing again.

No, it *wasn't* a fire-shovel, you heaven-born genius; and you might guess from this until Mrs. Snooks called you up to coffee, and you would never find out. It was in something which I have already described in Mrs. Fagan's pantry.

'Oh, I have you now: it was the bucket where the potatoes were; the thlatternly wetch!' says Snooks.

Wrong again! Peggy brought up the coals—in a china plate!

Snooks turns quite white with surprise, and almost chokes himself with his port. 'Well,' says he, ' of all the *wum* countwith that I ever wead of, hang me if Ireland ithn't the *wummetht.* Coalth in a plate! Mawyann, do you hear that? In Ireland they alwayth thend up their coalth in a plate!'

CHAPTER VIII: FROM CORK TO BANTRY; WITH AN ACCOUNT OF THE CITY OF SKIBBEREEN

THAT light four-inside, four-horse coach, the 'Skibbereen Perseverance,' brought me fifty-two miles to-day, for the sum of three-and-sixpence, through a country which is, as usual, somewhat difficult to describe. We issued out of Cork by the western road, in which, as the Guide-book says, there is something very imposing. 'The magnificence of the county court-house, the extent, solidity, and characteristic sternness of the county gaol,' were visible to us for a few minutes; when, turning away southward from the pleasant banks of the stream, the road took us towards Bandon, through a country that is bare and ragged-looking, but yet green and pretty; and it always seems to me, like the people, to look cheerful in spite of its wretchedness, or, more correctly, to look tearful and cheerful at the same time.

The coach, like almost every other public vehicle I have seen in Ireland, was full to the brim and over it. What can send these restless people travelling and hurrying about from place to place as they do? I have heard one or two gentlemen hint that they had 'business' at this place or that; and found afterwards that one was going a couple of score of miles to look at a mare, another to examine a setter-dog, and so on. I did not make it my business to ask on what errand the gentlemen on the coach were bound; though two of them, seeing an Englishman, very good-naturedly began chalking out a route for him to take, and showing a sort of interest in his affairs, which is not with us generally exhibited. The coach, too, seemed to have the elastic hospitality of some Irish houses; it accommodated an almost impossible number. For the greater part of the journey the little guard sat on the roof among the carpet-bags, holding in one hand a huge tambour-frame, in the other a bandbox marked 'Foggarty, Hatter.' (What is there more ridiculous in the name of Foggarty than in that of Smith? and yet, had Smith been the name, I never should have laughed at or remarked it.) Presently by bis side clambered a green-coated policeman with his carbine, and we had a talk about the vitriol-throwers at Cork, and the sentence just passed upon them. The populace has decidedly taken part with the vitriol-throwers: parties of dragoons were obliged to surround the avenues of the court; and the judge who sentenced them was abused as he entered his carriage, and called an old villain, and many other opprobrious names.

This case the reader very likely remembers. A saw-mill was established at Cork, by which some four hundred sawyers were thrown out of employ. In order to deter the proprietors of this and all other mills from using such instruments further, the sawyers determined to execute a terrible vengeance, and cast lots among themselves which of their body should fling vitriol into the faces of the mill-owners. The men who were chosen by the lot were to execute this horrible office on pain of death, and did so,—

frightfully burning and blinding one of the gentlemen owning the mill. Great rewards were offered for the apprehension of the criminals, and at last one of their own body came forward as an approver, and the four principal actors in this dreadful outrage were sentenced to be transported for life. Crowds of the ragged admirers of these men were standing round 'the magnificent county court-house' as we passed the budding. Ours is a strange life indeed. What a history of poverty and barbarity, and crime, and even kindness, was that by which we passed before the magnificent county court-house, at eight miles an hour! What a chapter might a philosopher write on them! Look yonder at those two hundred ragged fellow-subjects of yours: they are kind, good, pious, brutal, starving. If the priest tells them, there is scarce any penance they will not perform; there is scarcely any pitch of misery which they have not been known to endure, nor any degree of generosity of which they are not capable: but if a man comes among these people, and can afford to take land over their heads, or if he invents a machine which can work more economically than their labour, they will shoot the man down without mercy, murder him, or put him to horrible tortures, and glory almost in what they do. There stand the men; they are only separated from us by a few paces: they are as fond of their mothers and children as we are; their gratitude for small kindnesses shown to them is extraordinary; they are Christians as we are; but interfere with their interests, and they will murder you without pity.

It is not revenge so much which these poor fellows take, as a brutal justice of their own. Now, will it seem a paradox to say, in regard to them and their murderous system, that the way to put an end to the latter is to *kill them no more*? Let the priest be able to go amongst them and say, The law holds a man's life so sacred that it will on *no account* take it away. No man, nor body of men, has a right to meddle with human life: not the Commons of England any more than the Commons of Tipperary. This may cost two or three lives, probably, until such time as the system may come to be known and understood: but which will be the greatest economy of blood in the end?

By this time the vitriol-men were long passed away, and we began next to talk about the Cork and London steamboats; which are made to pay, on account of the number of paupers whom the boats bring over from London at the charge of that city. The passengers found here, as in everything else almost which I have seen as yet, another instance of the injury which England inflicts on them. 'As long as these men are strong and can work,' says one, 'you keep them; when they are in bad health, you fling them upon us.' Nor could I convince him that the agricultural gentlemen were perfectly free to stay at home if they liked: that we did for them what was done for English paupers—sent them, namely, as far as possible on the way to their parishes; nay, that some of them (as I have seen with my own eyes) actually saved a bit of money during the harvest, and took this cheap way of conveying it and themselves to their homes again. But nothing would convince the gentleman that there was not some wicked scheming on the part of the English in the business; and, indeed, I find upon almost every other subject a peevish and puerile suspiciousness which is worthy of France itself.

By this time we came to a pretty village called Innishannon, upon the noble banks of the Bandon river; leading for three miles by a great number of pleasant gentlemen's seats to Bandon town. A good number of large mills were on the banks of the stream; and the chief part of them, as in Carlow, useless. One mill we saw was too small for the owner's great speculations; and so he built another and larger one: the big mill cost him £10,000, for which his brothers went security; and, a lawsuit being given against the mill-owner, the two mills stopped, the two brothers went off, and yon fine old house, in the style of Anne, with terraces and tall chimneys—one of the oldest country-houses I have seen in Ireland—is now inhabited by the natural son of the mill-owner, who has more such interesting progeny. Then we came to a tall comfortable house, in a plantation; opposite to which was a stone castle, in its shrubberies on the other side of the road. The tall house in the plantation shot the opposite side of the road in a duel, and nearly killed him; on which the opposite side of the road built this castle, *in order to plague* the tall house. They are good friends now; but, the opposite, side of the road ruined himself in building his house. I asked, 'Is the house finished ?'—'*A good deal of it is*,' was the answer.—And then we came to a brewery, about which was a similar story of extravagance and ruin; but, whether before or after entering Bandon, does not matter.

We did not, it appears, pass through the best part of Bandon: I looked along one side of the houses in the long street through which we went to see if there was a window without a broken pane of glass, and can declare on my conscience that every single window had three broken panes. There we changed horses, in a market place surrounded, as usual, by beggars; then we passed through a suburb still more wretched and ruinous than the first street, and which, in very large letters, is called Doyle Street: and the next stage was at a place called Dunmanway.

Here it was market day, too, and, as usual, no lack of attendants; swarms of peasants in their blue cloaks, squatting by their stalls here and there. There is a little miserable old market house, where a few women were selling buttermilk; another, bullocks' hearts, liver, and such like scraps of meat; another had dried mackerel on a board; and plenty of people huckstering, of course. Hound the coach came crowds of raggery, and blackguards fawning for money. I wonder who gives them any! I have never seen any one give yet; and were they not even so numerous that it. would be impossible to gratify them all, there is something in their cant and supplications to the Lord so disgusting to me, that I could not give a halfpenny.

In regard of pretty faces, male or female, this road is very unfavourable. I have not seen one for fifty miles; though, as it was market-day all along the. road, we have had the opportunity to examine vast numbers of countenances. The women are, for the most, part, stunted, short, with flat Tartar faces; and the men no handsomer. Every woman has bare legs, of course; and as the weather is fine, they are sitting outside their cabins, with the pig, and the geese, and the children sporting around.

Before many doors we saw a little flock of these useful animals, and the family pig almost everywhere: you might see him browsing and poking along the hedges, his fore and hind leg attached with a wisp of hay to cheek his propensity to roaming. Here and there were a small brood of turkeys; now and then a couple of sheep or a single cow grazing upon a scanty field, of which the chief crop seemed to be thistles and stones; and, by the side of the cottage, the potato field always.

The character of the landscape for the most part is bare and sad; except here and there in the. neighbourhood of the towns, where people have taken a fancy to plant, and where nature has helped them, as it almost always will in this country. If we saw a field with a good hedge to it, we were sure to see a good crop inside. Many a field was there that had neither crop nor hedge. We passed by and over many pretty streams, running bright, through brilliant emerald meadows: and I saw a thousand charming pictures, which want as yet an Irish Berghem. A bright road winding up a hill; on it a country cart, with its load, stretching a huge shadow; the before-mentioned emerald pastures and silver rivers in the foreground; a noble sweep of hills rising up from them, and contrasting their magnificent purple with the green; in the extreme distance the clear cold outline of some far-off mountains, and the white clouds tumbled about in the blue sky overhead. It has no doubt struck all persons who love to look at nature, how different the skies arc in different countries. I fancy Irish or French clouds are as characteristic as Irish or French landscapes. It would be well to have a daguerreotype and get a series of each. Some way beyond Dunmanway the road takes us through a noble savage country of rooks and heath. Nor must the painter forget long black tracts of bog here and there, and the water glistening brightly at the places whore the turf has been cut away. Add to this, and chiefly by the banks of rivers, a ruined old castle or two: some were built by the Danes, it. is said. The O'Connors, the O'Mahonys, the O'Driscolls, were lords of many others, and their ruined towers may be seen here and along the sea.

Near Dunmanway that great coach, 'The Skibbereen Industry,' dashed by us at seven miles an hour; a wondrous vehicle: there were gaps between every one of the panels; you could see daylight through-and-through it. Like our machine, it was full, with throe complementary sailors on the roof, as little harness as possible to the horses, and as long stages as horses can well endure; ours were each eighteen-mile stages. About eight miles from Skibbereen a one-horse car met us, and carried away an offshoot of passengers to Bantry. Five passengers and their luggage, and a very wild steep road: all this had one poor little pony to overcome! About the towns there were some show of gentlemen's cars, smart and well appointed, and on the road great, numbers of country carts; an army of them met us coming from Skibbereen, and laden with grey sand for manure.

.Before you enter the city of Skibebereen, the tall new poorhouse presents itself to the eye of the traveller; of the common model, being a bastard-Gothic edifice, with a profusion of cottage-ornée (is cottage masculine or feminine in French?)—of cottage-ornée roofs, and pinnacles, and insolent looking stacks of chimneys. It is built for nine hundred people, but as yet not more than four hundred have been induced to live in it; the beggars preferring the freedom of their precarious trade to the dismal certainty within its walls. Next we come to the chapel, a very large respectable-looking building of dark-grey stone; and presently, behold, by the crowd of blackguards in waiting, 'The Skibbereen Perseverance' has found its goal, and you are inducted to the 'hotel' opposite.

Some gentlemen were at the coach, besides those of lower degree. Here was a fat fellow with large whiskers, a geranium, and a cigar; yonder a tall handsome old man that I would swear was a dragoon on half-pay. He had a little cap, a Taglioni coat, a pair of beautiful spaniels, and a pair of knee-breeches which showed a very handsome old leg; and his object seemed to be to invite everybody to dinner as they got off the coach. No doubt he has seen the 'Skibbereen Perseverance' come in ever since it was a 'Perseverance.' It is wonderful to think what will interest men in prisons or country towns!

There is a dirty coffee-room, with a strong smell of whisky; indeed three young 'materialists' are employed at the moment: and I hereby beg to offer an apology to three other gentlemen—the captain, another, and the gentleman of the geranium, who had caught hold of a sketching-stool which is my property, and were stretching it, and sitting upon it, and wondering, and talking of it, when the owner came in, and they bounced off to their seats like so many schoolboys. Dirty as the place was, this was no reason why it should not produce an exuberant dinner of trouts and Kerry mutton; after which Dan the waiter, holding up a dingy decanter, asks how much whisky I'd have.

That calculation need not be made here; and if a man sleeps well, has he any need to quarrel with the appointments of his bedroom, and spy out the deficiencies of the land? As it was Sunday, it was impossible for me to say what sort of shops 'the active and flourishing town' of Skibbereen contains. There were some of the architectural sort,—viz. with gilt letters and cracked mouldings, and others into which I thought I saw the cows walking; but it was only into their little cribs and paddocks at the back of the shops. There is a trim Wesleyan chapel, without any broken windows; a neat church standing modestly on one side. The Lower Street crawls along the river to a considerable extent, having by-streets and boulevards of cabins here and there.

The people came flocking into the place by hundreds, and you saw their blue cloaks dotting the road and the bare open plains beyond. The men came with shoes and stockings to-day, the women all barelegged, and many of them might be seen washing their feet in the stream before they went up to the chapel. The street seemed to be lined on either side with blue cloaks, squatting along the doorways as is their wont. Among these, numberless cows were walking to and fro, and pails of milk passing, and here and there a hound or two went stalking about. Dan the waiter says they are hunted by the handsome old captain who was yesterday inviting everybody to dinner.

Anybody at eight o'clock of a Sunday morning in summer may behold the above scene from a bridge just outside the town. He may add to it the river, with one or two barges lying idle upon it; a flag flying at what looks like a custom-house; bare country all around; and the chapel before him, with a swarm of the dark figures round about it.

I went into it, not without awe (for, as I confessed before, I always feel a sort of tremor on going into a Catholic place of worship: the candles, and altars, and mysteries, the priest and his robes, and nasal chanting, and wonderful genuflections, will frighten me as long as I live). The chapel-yard was filled with men and women: a couple of shabby old beadles were at the gate, with copper shovels to collect money; and inside the chapel four or five hundred people were on their knees, and scores more of the blue-mantles came in, dropping their curtseys as they entered, and then taking their places on the flags.

And now the pangs of hunger beginning to make themselves felt, it became necessary for your humble servant (after making several useless applications to a bell, which properly declined to work on Sundays) to make a personal descent to the inn-kitchen, where was not a bad study for a painter. It was a huge room, with a peat fire burning, and a staircase walking up one side of it, on which stair was a damsel in a partial though by no means picturesque dishabille. The cook had just come in with a great frothing pail of milk, and sat with her arms folded; the ostler's boy sat dangling his legs from the table; the ostler was dandling a noble little boy of a year old, at whom Mrs. Cook likewise grinned delighted. Here, too, sat Mr. Dan the waiter; and no wonder breakfast was delayed, for all three of these worthy domestics seemed delighted with the infant.

He was handed over to the gentleman's arms for the space of thirty seconds; the gentleman being the father of a family, and of course an amateur.

'Say Dan for the gentleman,' says the delighted cook.

'Dada,' says the baby; at which the assembly grinned with joy: and Dan promised I should have my breakfast 'in a hurry.'

But of all the wonderful things to be seen in Skibbereen, Dan's pantry is the most wonderful: every article within is a makeshift, and has been ingeniously perverted from its original destination. Here lie bread, blacking, fresh butter, tallow-candles, dirty knives—all in the same cigar-box with snuff, milk, cold bacon, brown sugar, broken teacups, and bits of soap. No pen can describe that establishment as no English imagination could have conceived it. But lo! the sky has cleared after a furious fall of rain—-in compliance with Dan's statement to that effect, 'that the weather would be fine,'—and a car is waiting to carry us to Loughine.

Although the description of Loughine can make but a poor figure in a book, the ride thither is well worth the traveller's short labour. You pass by one of the cabin-streets out of the town into a country which for a mile is rich with grain, though bare of trees; then through a boggy bleak district, from which you enter into a sort of sea of rocks, with patches of herbage here and there. Before the traveller, almost all the way, is a huge pile of purple mountain, on which, as one comes nearer, one perceives numberless waves and breaks, as you see small waves on a billow in the sea; then clambering up a hill, we look down upon a bright green flat of land, with the lake beyond it, girt round by grey melancholy hills. The water may be a mile in extent; a cabin tops the mountain here and there; gentlemen have erected one or two anchorite pleasure-houses on the banks, as cheerful as a summer-house would be on Salisbury Plain. I felt not sorry to have seen this lonely lake, and still happier to leave it. There it lies with crags all round it, in the midst of desolate plains; it escapes somewhere to the sea; its waters are salt; half-a-dozen boats lie here and there upon its banks, and we saw a small crew of boys plashing about and swimming in it, laughing and yelling. It seemed a shame to disturb the silence so.

The crowd of swaggering 'gents' (I don't know the corresponding phrase in the Anglo-Irish vocabulary to express a shabby dandy) awaiting the Cork mail, which kindly goes twenty miles out of its way to accommodate the town of Skibbereen, was quite extraordinary. The little street was quite blocked up with shabby gentlemen, and shabby beggars, awaiting this daily phenomenon. The man who had driven us to Loughine did not fail to ask for his fee as driver; and then, having received it, came forward in his capacity of boots and received another remuneration. The ride is desolate, bare, and yet beautiful. There are a set of bills that keep one company the whole way; they were partially hidden in a grey sky, which flung a general hue of melancholy too over the green country through which we passed. There was only one wretched village along the road, but no lack of population: ragged people who issued from their cabins as the coach passed, or were sitting by the wayside. Everybody seems sitting by the wayside here: one never sees this general repose in England—a sort of ragged lazy contentment. All the children seem to be on the watch for the coach; waited very knowingly and carefully their opportunity, and then hung on by scores behind. What a pleasure to run over flinty roads with bare feet, to be whipped off, and to walk back to the cabin again! These were very different cottages to those neat ones I had seen in Kildare. the wretchedness of them is quite painful to look at; many of the potato-gardens were half dug up, and it was only the first week in August, near three months before the potato is ripe and at full growth; and the winter still six months away. There were chapels occasionally, and smart new-built churches —one of them has a congregation of ten souls, the coachman told me. Would it not be better that the clergyman should receive them in his room, and that the church-building money should be bestowed otherwise?

At length, after winding up all sorts of dismal hills speckled with wretched hovels, a ruinous mill every now and then, black bog-lands, and small winding streams, breaking here and there into little falls, we come upon some ground well tilled and planted, and descending (at no small rink from stumbling horses) a bleak long hill, we see the water before us, and turning to the right by the handsome little park of Lord Bearhaven, enter Ba,,try. The harbour is beautiful. Small mountains in pretty green undulations rising on the opposite side; great grey ones farther back; a pretty island in the midst of the water, which is wonderfully bright and calm. A handsome yacht, and two or three vessels with their Sunday colours out, were lying in the bay. It looked like a seaport scene at a theatre, gay, cheerful, neat, and picturesque. At a little distance the town, too, is very pretty. There are some smart houses on the quays, a handsome court-house as usual, a fine large hotel, and plenty of people flocking round the wonderful coach.

The town is most picturesquely situated, climbing up a wooded hill, with numbers of neat cottages here and there, an ugly church with an air of pretension, and a large grave Roman Catholic chapel the highest point of the place. The main street was as usual thronged with the squatting blue cloaks, carrying on their eager trade of butter-milk and green apples, and such cheap wares. With the exception of this street and the quay, with their whitewashed and slated houses, it is a town of cabins. The wretchedness of some of them is quite curious: I tried to make a sketch of a row which lean against an old wall, and are built upon a rock that tumbles about in the oddest and most fantastic shapes, with a brawling waterfall dashing down a channel in the midst. These are, it appears, the beggars' houses: any one may build a lodge against that wall, rent-free; and such places were never seen! As for drawing them, it was in vain to try; one might as well make a sketch of a bundle of rags. An ordinary pig-sty in England is really more comfortable. Most of them were not six feet long or five feet high, built of stones huddled together, a hole being left for the people to creep in at, a ruined thatch to keep out some little portion of the rain. The occupiers of these places sat at their doors in tolerable contentment, or the children came down and washed their feet in the water. I declare I believe a Hottentot kraal has more comforts in it; even to write of the place makes one unhappy, and the words move slow. But in the midst of all this misery there is an air of actual cheerfulness; and go but a few score yards off, and these wretched hovels lying together look really picturesque and pleasing.

CHAPTER IX: RAINY DAYS AT GLENGARIFF

A SMART two-horse car takes the traveller thrice a week from Bantry to Killarney, by way of Glengariff and Kenmare. Unluckily, the rain was pouring down furiously as we passed to the first-named places, and we had only opportunity to see a part of the astonishing beauties of the country. What sends picturesque tourists to the Rhine and Saxon Switzerland? within five miles round the pretty inn of Glengariff there is a country of the magnificence of which no pen can give an idea. I would like to be a great prince, and bring a train of painters over to make, if they could, and according to their several capabilities, a set of pictures of the place. Mr. Creswick would find such rivulets and waterfalls, surrounded by a luxuriance of foliage and verdure that only his pencil can imitate. As for Mr. Cattermole, a red-shanked Irishman should carry his sketching-books to all sorts of wild noble heights, and vast rocky valleys, where he might please himself by piling crag upon crag, and by introducing, if he had a mind, some of the wild figures which peopled this country in old days. There is the Eagle's Nest, for instance, regarding which the Guide-book gives a pretty legend. The Prince of Bantry being conquered by the English soldiers, fled away, leaving his Princess and children to the care of a certain faithful follower of his, who was to provide them with refuge and food. But the whole country was overrun by the conquerors; all the flocks driven away by them, all the houses ransacked, and the crops burnt off the ground, and the faithful servitor did not know where he should, find a meal or a resting-place for the unhappy Princess O'Donovan.

He made, however, a sort of shed by the side of a mountain, composing it of sods and stones so artfully that no one could tell but that it. was a part of the hill itself; and here, having speared or otherwise obtained a salmon, he fed their Highnesses for the first day; trusting to Heaven for a meal when the salmon should be ended.

The Princess O'Donovan and her princely family soon came to an end of the fish; and cried out for something more.

So the faithful servitor, taking with him a rope and his little son Shamus, mounted up to the peak where the eagles rested; and, from the spot to which he climbed, saw their nest, and the young eaglets in it, in a cleft below the precipice.

'Now,' said he, 'Shamus my son, you must take these thongs with you, and I will let you down by the rope' (it was a straw-rope, which he had made himself, and though it might be considered a dangerous thread to hang by in other countries, you'll see plenty of such contrivances in Ireland to the present day).

'I will let you down by the rope, and you must tie the thongs round the necks of the eaglets, not so as to choke them, but to prevent them from swallowing much.' So

Shamus went down and did as his father bade him, and came up again when the eaglets were doctored.

Presently the eagles came home: one bringing a rabbit and the other a grouse. These they dropped into the nest for the young ones; and soon after went away in quest of other adventures.

Then Shamus went down into the eagles' nest again, gutted the grouse and rabbit, and left the garbage to the eaglets (as was their right), and brought away the rest. And so the Princess and Princes had game that night for their supper. How long they lived in this way, the Guide-book does not say: but let us trust that the Prince, if he did not come to his own again, was at least restored to his family and decently mediatised: and, for my part, I have very little doubt but that Shamus, the gallant young eagle-robber, created a favourable impression upon one of the young princesses, and (after many adventures in which he distinguished himself), was accepted by her Highness for a husband and her princely parents for a gallant son-in-law.

And here, while we are travelling to Glengariff, and ordering painters about with such princely liberality (by the way, Mr. Stanfield should have a boat in the bay, and paint both rock and sea at his ease), let me mention a wonderful awful incident of real life which occurred on the road. About four miles from Bantry, at a beautiful wooded place, hard by a mill and waterfall, up rides a gentleman to the car with his luggage, going to Killarney races. The luggage consisted of a small carpet-bag and a pistol-case. About two miles farther on, a fellow stops the car: 'Joe,' says he, 'my master is going to ride to Killarney, so you please to take his luggage.' The luggage consisted of a small carpet-bag, and—a pistol-case as before. Is this a gentleman's usual travelling baggage in Ireland?

As there is more rain in this country than in any other, and as, therefore, naturally the inhabitants should be inured to the weather, and made to despise an inconvenience which they cannot avoid, the travelling conveyances are arranged so that you may get as much practice in being wet as possible. The traveller's baggage is stowed in a place between the two rows of seats, and which is not inaptly called the well, as in a rainy season you might possibly get a bucketful of water out of that orifice. And I confess I saw, with a horrid satisfaction, the pair of pistol-cases lying in this moist aperture, with water pouring above them and lying below them; nay, prayed that all such weapons might one day be consigned to the same fate. But as the waiter at Bantry, in his excessive zeal to serve me, had sent my portmanteau back to Cork by the coach, instead of allowing me to carry it with me to Killarney, and as the rain had long since begun to insinuate itself under the seat-cushion, and through the waterproof apron of the car, I dropped off at Glengariff, and dried the only suit of clothes I had by the kitchen-fire. The inn is very pretty: Borne thorn-trees stand before it, where many bare-legged people were lolling, in spite of the weather. A beautiful bay stretches out before the house, the full tide washing the thorn-trees; mountains rise on either side of the little bay, and there is an island, with a castle on it in the midst, near which a yacht was moored. But the mountains were hardly visible for the mist, and the yacht, island, and castle looked as if they had been washed against the flat grey sky in India-ink.

The day did not clear up sufficiently to allow me to make any long excursion about the place, or indeed to see a very wide prospect round about it: at a few hundred yards, most of the objects were enveloped in mist; but even this, for a lover of the picturesque, had its beautiful effect, for you saw the hills in the foreground pretty clear, and covered with their wonderful green, while immediately behind them rose an immense blue mass of mist and mountain that served to *relieve* (to use the painter's phrase) the nearer objects. Annexed to the hotel is a flourishing garden, where the vegetation is so great that the landlord told me it was all he could do to check the trees from growing; round about the bay, in several places, they come clustering down to the water's edge, nor does the salt-water interfere with them.

Winding up a hill to the right, as you quit the inn, is the beautiful road to the cottage and park of Lord Bantry. One or two parties on pleasure bent went so far as the house, and were partially consoled for the dreadful rain which presently poured down upon them, by wine, whisky, and refreshments which the liberal owner of the house sent out to them. I myself had only got a few hundred yards when the rain overtook me, and sent me for refuge into a shed, where a blacksmith had arranged a rude furnace and bellows, and where he was at work, with a rough gilly to help him, and of course a lounger or two to look on.

The scene was exceedingly wild and picturesque, and I took out a sketch-book and began to draw. The blacksmith was at first very suspicious of the operation which I had commenced, nor did the poor fellow's sternness at all yield until I made him a present of a shilling to buy tobacco—when he, his friend, and his son became good-humoured, and said their little say. This was the first shilling he had earned these three years: he was a small farmer, but was starved out, and had set up a forge here, and was trying to get a few pence. What struck me was the great number of people about the place. We had at least twenty visits while the sketch was being made: cars, and single and double horsemen, were continually passing: between the intervals of the shower a couple of ragged old women would creep out from some hole and display baskets of green apples for sale: wet or not, men and women were lounging up and down the road. You would have thought it was a fair, and yet there was not even a village at this place, only the inn and post-house, by which the cars to Tralee pass thrice a week.

The weather, instead of mending, on the second day was worse than ever. All the view had disappeared now under a rushing rain, of which I never saw anything like the violence. We were visited by five maritime—nay, buccaneering-looking gentlemen in moustaches, with fierce caps and jackets, just landed from a yacht: and then the car brought us three Englishmen wet to the skin and thirsting for whisky-and-water.

And with these three Englishmen a great scene occurred, such as we read of in Smollett's and Fielding's inns. One was a fat old gentleman from Cambridge—who, I was informed, was a Fellow of a College in that University, but whom I shrewdly suspect[x] to be butler or steward of the same. The younger men, burly, manly, good-humoured fellows of seventeen stone, were the nephews of the elder,—who, says one, 'could draw a cheque for his thousand pounds.'

Two-and-twenty years before, on landing at the Pigeon-House at Dublin, the old gentleman had been cheated by a carman, and his firm opinion seemed to be that all carmen—nay, all Irishmen—were cheats.

And a sad proof of this depravity speedily showed itself: for having hired a three-horse car at Killarney, which was to carry them to Bantry, the Englishmen saw, with immense indignation, after they had drunk a series of glasses of whisky, that the three-horse car had been removed, a one-horse vehicle standing in its stead.

Their wrath no pen can describe. ' Itell you they are all so!' shouted the elder. 'When I landed at the Pigeon-House—' 'Bring me a post-chaise!' roars the second. 'Waiter, get some more whisky!' exclaims the third. 'If they don't send us on with three horses, I'll stop here for a week.' Then issuing, with his two young friends, into the passage to harangue the populace assembled there, the elder Englishman began a speech about dishonesty, 'd—d rogues and thieves, Pigeon-House: he was a gentleman, and wouldn't be done, d—n his eyes and everybody's eyes.' Upon the affrighted landlord, who came to interpose, they all fell with great ferocity: the elder man swearing, especially, that he 'would write to Lord Lansdowne regarding his conduct, likewise to Lord Bandon, also to Lord Bantry: he was a gentleman; he'd been cheated in the year 1815, on his first landing at the Pigeon-House: and, d-n the Irish, they were all alike.' After roaring and cursing for half-an-hour, a gentleman at the door, seeing the meek bearing of the landlord—who stood quite lost and powerless in the whirlwind of rage that had been excited about his luckless ears— said, 'If men cursed and swore in that way in his house, he would know how to put them out.'

'Put *me* out!' says one of the young men, placing himself before the fat old blasphemer his relative. 'Put *me* out, my fine fellow!' But it was evident the Irishman did not like his customer. 'Put *me* out!' roars the old gentleman, from behind his young protector; '— my eyes, who are *you*, sir? who *are* you, sir? I insist on knowing who you are?'

'And who are you?' asks the Irishman.

'Sir, I'm a gentleman, and *pay my way*! and as soon as I get into Bantry, I swear I'll write a letter to Lord Bandon Bantry, and complain of the treatment I have received here.'

Now, as the unhappy landlord had not said one single word, and as, on the contrary, to the annoyance of the whole house, the stout old gentleman from Cambridge had been shouting, raging, and cursing for two hours, I could not help, like a great ass as I was, coming forward and (thinking the landlord might be a tenant of Lord Bantry's) saying, 'Well, sir, if you write and say the landlord has behaved ill, I will write to say that he has acted with extraordinary forbearance and civility.'

O fool! to interfere in disputes where one set of the disputants have drunk half-a-dozen glasses of whisky in the middle of the day! No sooner had I said this than the other young man came and fell upon me, and in the course of a few minutes found leisure to tell me 'that I was no gentleman; that I was ashamed to give my name, or say where I lived; that I was a liar, and didn't live in London, and couldn't mention the name of a single respectable person there; that he was a merchant and tradesman, and hid his quality from nobody'; and, finally, 'that though bigger than himself, there was nothing he would like better than that I should come out on the green and stand to him like a man.'

This invitation, although repeated several times, I refused with as much dignity as I could assume; partly because I was sober and cool, while the other was furious and drunk; also because I felt a strong suspicion that in about ten minutes the man would manage to give me a tremendous beating, which I did not merit in the least; thirdly, because a victory over him would not have been productive of the least pleasure to me; and lastly, because there was something really honest and gallant in the fellow coming out to defend his old relative. Both of the younger men would have fought like tigers for this disreputable old gentleman, and desired no better sport. The last I heard of the three was that they and the driver made their appearance before a magistrate in Bantry; and a pretty story will the old man have to tell to his club at the 'Hoop,' or the 'Red Lion,' of those swindling Irish, and the ill-treatment he met with in their country.

As for the landlord, the incident will be a blessed theme of conversation to him for a long time to come. I heard him discoursing of it in the passage during the rest of the day; and next morning when I opened my window and saw with much delight the bay clear and bright as silver—except where the green hills were reflected in it. the blue sky above, and the purple mountains round about with only a few clouds veiling their peaks—the first thing I heard was the voice of Mr. Eccles repeating the story to a new customer.

'I thought thim couldn't be gintlemin,' was the appropriate remark of Mr. Tom the waiter, 'from the way in which they took their whishky—raw with cold wather, widout *mixing or inything.'* Could an Irish waiter give a more excellent definition of the ungenteel?

At nine o'clock in the morning of the next day, the unlucky car which had carried the Englishmen to Bantry came back to Glengariff, and as the morning was very fine, I was glad to take advantage of it, and travel some five-and-thirty English miles to Killarney.

CHAPTER X: FROM GLENGARIFF TO KILLARNEY

THE Irish car seems accommodated for any number of persons: it appeared to be full when we left Glengariff, for a traveller from Bearhaven, and the five gentlemen from the yacht, took seats upon it with myself, and we fancied it was impossible more than seven should travel by such a conveyance; but the driver showed the capabilities of his vehicle presently. The journey from Glengariff to Kenmare is one of astonishing beauty; and I have seen Killarney since, and am sure that Glengariff loses nothing by comparison with this most famous of lakes. Rock, wood, and sea stretch around the traveller—a thousand delightful pictures: the landscape is at first wild without being fierce, immense woods and plantations enriching the valleys—beautiful streams to be seen everywhere.

Here again I was surprised at the great population along the road; for one saw but few cabins, and there is no village between Glengariff and Kenmare. But men and women were on banks and in fields; children, as usual, came trooping up to the car; and the jovial men of the yacht had long conversations with most of the persons whom we met on the road. A merrier set of fellows it were hard to meet. 'Should you like anything to drink, sir?' says one, commencing the acquaintance. 'We have the best whisky in the world, and plenty of porter in the basket.' Therewith the jolly seamen produced a long bottle of grog, which was passed round from one to another; and then began singing, shouting, laughing, roaring, for the whole journey. 'British sailors have a knack, pull away—ho, boys!' 'Hurroo, my fine fellow! does your mother know you're out?' 'Hurroo, Tim Herlihy! you 're *a fluke*, Tim Herlihy.' One man sang on the roof, one *hurroo'd* to the echo, another apostrophised the aforesaid Herlihy as he passed grinning on a car; a third had a pocket-handkerchief flaunting from a pole, with which he performed exercises in the face of any horseman whom we met; and great were their yells as the ponies shied off at the salutation and the riders swerved in their saddles. In the midst of this rattling chorus we went along: gradually the country grew wilder and more desolate, and we passed through a grim mountain region, bleak and bare, the road winding round some of the innumerable hills, and once or twice by means of a tunnel rushing boldly through them. One of these tunnels, they say, is a couple of hundred yards long; and a pretty howling, I need not say, was made through that pipe of rock by the jolly yacht's crew. 'We saw you sketching in the blacksmith's shed at Glengariff,' says one, 'and we wished we had you on board. Such a jolly life we led of it!'—They roved about the coast, they said, in their vessel; they feasted off the best of fish, mutton, and whisky; they had Gamble's turtle-soup on board, and fun from morning till night, and *vice versâ.* Gradually it came out that there was not, owing to the tremendous rains, a dry corner in their ship: that they slung two in a huge hammock in the cabin, and that one of their crew had been ill, and shirked off. What a wonderful thing pleasure is! To be wet all day and night; to be scorched and blistered by the sun and rain; to beat in and out of little harbours, and to exceed diurnally upon whisky-punch—'faith, London, and an arm-chair at the club, are more to the tastes of some men.

After much mountain-work of ascending and descending (in which latter operation, and by the side of precipices that make passing cockneys rather squeamish, the carman drove like mad to the whooping and screeching of the red-rovers), we at length came to Kenmare, of which all that I know is that it lies prettily in a bay or arm of the sea; that it is approached by a little hanging-bridge, which seems to be a wonder in these parts; that it is a miserable little place when you enter it; and that, finally, a splendid luncheon of all sorts of meat and excellent cold salmon may sometimes be had for a shilling at the hotel of the place. It is a great vacant house, like the rest of them, and would frighten people in England; but after a few days one grows used to the Castle Rackrent style., I am not sure that there is not a certain sort of comfort to be had in these rambling rooms, and among these bustling blundering waiters, which one does not always meet with in an orderly English house of entertainment.

After discussing the luncheon, we found the car with fresh horses, beggars, idlers, policemen, etc., standing round, of course; and now the miraculous vehicle, which had held hitherto seven with some difficulty, was called upon to accommodate thirteen.

A pretty noise would our three Englishmen of yesterday—nay, any other Englishmen for the matter of that—have made, if coolly called upon to admit an extra party of four into a mail-coach! The yacht's crew did not make a single objection; a couple clambered up on the roof, where they managed to locate themselves with wonderful ingenuity, perched upon hard wooden chests, or agreeably reposing upon the knotted ropes which held them together: one of the new passengers scrambled between the driver's legs, where he held on somehow, and the rest were pushed and squeezed astonishingly in the car.

Now the fact must be told, that five of the new passengers (I don't count a little boy besides) were women, and very pretty, gay, frolicsome, lively, kind-hearted, innocent women too; and for the rest of the journey there was no end of laughing and shouting, and singing, and hugging, so that the caravan presented the appearance which is depicted in the opposite engraving.

Now it may be a wonder to some persons, that with such a cargo the carriage did not upset, or some of us did not fall off; to which the answer is that we *did* fall off. A very pretty woman fell off, and showed a pair of never-mind-what-coloured garters, and an interesting English traveller fell off too: but Heaven bless you! these cars are made to fall off from; and considering the circumstances of the case, and in the same company, I would rather fall off than not. A great number of polite allusions and genteel inquiries were, as may be imagined, made by the jolly boat's crew. But though the lady affected to be a little angry at first, she was far too good-natured to be angry long, and at last fairly burst out laughing with the passengers. We did not fall off again, but held on very tight, and just as we were reaching Killarney, saw somebody else fall off from another car. But in this instance the gentleman had no lady to tumble with.

For almost half the way from Kenmare, this wild beautiful road commands views of the famous lake and vast blue mountains about Killarney. Turk, Tomies, and Mangerton were clothed in purple like kings in mourning; great heavy clouds were gathered round their heads, parting away every now and then, and leaving their noble features bare. The lake lay for some time underneath us, dark and blue, with dark misty islands in the midst. On the right-hand side of the road would be a precipice covered with a thousand trees, or a green rocky flat, with a reedy mere in the midst, and other mountains rising as far as we could see. I think of that diabolical tune in 'Der Freischütz' while passing through this sort of country. Every now and then, in the midst of some fresh country or enclosed trees, or at a turn of the road, you lose the sight of the great big awful mountain: but, like the aforesaid tune in ' Der Freischütz,' it is always there close at hand. You feel that it keeps you company. And so it was that we rode by dark old Mangerton, then presently past Mucross, and then through two miles of avenues of lime-trees, by numerous lodges and gentlemen's seats, across an old bridge, where you see the mountains again and the lake, until, by Lord Kenmare's house, a hideous row of houses informed us that we were at Killarney.

Here my companion suddenly let go my hand, and by a certain uneasy motion of the waist, gave me notice to withdraw the other too; and so we rattled up to the Kenmare Arms: and so ended, not without a sigh on my part, one of the merriest six-hour rides that five yachtsmen, one cockney, five women and a child, the carman, and a countryman with an alpeen, ever took in their lives.

As for my fellow-companion, she would hardly speak the next day; but all the five maritime men made me vow and promise that I would go and see them at Cork, where I should have horses to ride, the fastest yacht out of the harbour to sail in, and the best of whisky, claret, and welcome. Amen, and may every single person who buys a copy of this book meet with the same deserved fate!

The town of Killarney was in a violent state of excitement with a series of horse-races, hurdle-races, boat-races, and stag-hunts by land and water, which were taking-place, and attracted a vast crowd from all parts of the kingdom. All the inns were full, and lodgings cost five shillings a day—nay, more in some places; for though my landlady, Mrs. Macgillicuddy, charges but that sum, a leisurely old gentleman whom I never saw in my life before made my acquaintance by stopping me in the street yesterday, and said he paid a pound a day for his two bedrooms. The old gentleman is eager for company; and indeed, when a man travels alone, it is wonderful how little he cares to select his society; how different company pleases him; how a good fellow delights him: how sorry he is when the time for parting comes, and he has to walk off alone, and begin the friendship hunt over again.

The first sight I witnessed at Killarney was a race-ordinary, where, for a sum of twelve shillings, any man could take his share of turbot, salmon, venison, and beef, with port, and sherry, and whisky-punch at discretion. Here were the squires of Cork and Kerry, one or two Englishmen, whose voices amidst the rich humming brogue round about sounded quite affected (not that they were so, but there seems a sort of impertinence in the shrill, high-pitched tone of the English voice here). At the head of the table, near the chairman, sat some brilliant young dragoons, neat, solemn, dull, with huge moustaches, and boots polished to a nicety.

And here of course the conversation was of the horse horsey: how Mr. This had refused fifteen hundred guineas for a horse which he bought for a hundred; how Bacchus was the best horse in Ireland; which horses were to run at Something races; and how the Marquis of Waterford gave a plate or a purse. We drank 'the Queen,' with hip! hip! hurrah! the 'winner of the Kenmare stakes'—hurrah! Presently the gentleman next me rose and made a speech: he had brought a mare down and won the stakes—a hundred and seventy guineas—and I looked at him with a great deal of respect. Other toasts ensued, and more talk about horses. Nor am I in the least disposed to sneer at gentlemen who like sporting and talk about it: for I do believe that the conversation of a dozen fox-hunters is just as clever as that of a similar number of merchants, barristers, or literary men. But to this trade, as to all others, a man must be bred; if he has not learnt it thoroughly or in early life, he will not readily become a proficient afterwards, and when therefore the subject is broached, had best maintain a profound silence.

A young Edinburgh cockney, with an easy self-confidence that the reader may have perhaps remarked in others of his calling and nation, and who evidently knew as much of sporting matters as the individual who writes this, proceeded nevertheless to give the company his opinions, and greatly astonished them all; for these simple people are at first willing to believe that a stranger is sure to be a knowing fellow, and did not seem inclined to be undeceived even by this little pert grinning Scotchman. It was good to hear him talk of Haddington, Musselburgh—and Heaven knows what strange outlandish places, as if they were known to all the world. And here would be a good opportunity to enter into a dissertation upon national characteristics: to show that the bold swaggering Irishman is really a modest fellow, while the canny Scot is a most brazen one; to wonder why the inhabitant of one country is ashamed of it—which is in itself so fertile and beautiful, and has produced more than its fair proportion of men of genius, valour, and wit; whereas it never enters into the head of a Scotchman to question his own equality (and something more) at all: but that such discussions are quite unprofitable; nay, that exactly the contrary propositions may be argued to just as much length. Has the reader ever tried with a dozen of Mr. Tocqueville's short crisp philosophic apophthegms and taken the converse of them? The one or other set of propositions will answer equally well; and it is the best way to avoid all such. Let the above passage, then, simply be understood to say, that on a certain day the writer met a vulgar little Scotchman—not that all Scotchmen are vulgar;—that this little pert creature prattled about his country as if he and it were ornaments to the world—which the latter is no doubt; and that one could not but contrast his behaviour with that of great big stalwart simple Irishmen, who asked your opinion of their country with as much modesty as if you—because an Englishman—must be somebody, and they the dust of the earth.

Indeed this want of self-confidence at times becomes quite painful to the stranger. If, in reply to their queries, you say you like the country, people seem really quite delighted. Why should they? Why should a stranger's opinion who doesn't know the country be more valued than a native's who does?—Suppose an Irishman in England were to speak in praise or abuse of the country, would one be particularly pleased or annoyed? One would be glad that the man liked his trip; but as for his good or bad opinion of the country, the country stands on its own bottom, superior to any opinion of any man or men.

I must beg pardon of the little Scotchman for reverting to him (let it be remembered that there were *two* Scotchmen at Killarney, and that I speak of the other one); but I have seen no specimen of that sort of manners in any Irishman since I have been in the country. I have met more gentlemen here than in any place I ever saw: gentlemen of high and low ranks, that is to say: men shrewd and delicate of perception, observant of society, entering into the feelings of others, and anxious to set them at ease or to gratify them; of course exaggerating their professions of kindness, and in so far insincere; but the very exaggeration seems to be a proof of a kindly nature, and I wish in England we were a little more complimentary. In Dublin, a lawyer left his chambers, and a literary man his books, to walk the town with me—the town, which they must know a great deal too well: for, pretty as it is, it is but a small place after all, not like that great bustling, changing, struggling world, the Englishman's capital. Would a London man leave his business to trudge to the Tower or the Park with a stranger? We would ask him to dine at the club, or to eat whitebait at Lovegrove's, and think our duty done, neither caring for him, nor professing to care for him; and we pride ourselves on our honesty accordingly. Never was honesty more selfish. And so a vulgar man in England disdains to flatter his equals, and chiefly displays his character of snob by assuming as much as he can for himself, swaggering and showing off in his coarse, dull, stupid way.

'I am a gentleman, and pay my way,' as the old fellow said at Glengariff. I have not heard a sentence near so vulgar from any man in Ireland. Yes, by the way, there was another Englishman at Cork: a man in a middling, not to say humble, situation of life. When introduced to an Irish gentleman, his formula seemed to be, 'I think, sir, I have met you somewhere before.' 'I am sure, sir, I have met you before,' he said, for the second time in my hearing, to a gentleman of great note in Ireland. 'Yes, I have met you at Lord X—'s.' 'I don't know my Lord X—,' replied the Irishman. 'Sir,' says the other, '*I shall have great pleasure in introducing you to him*.' Well, the good-natured simple Irishman thought this gentleman a very fine fellow. There was only one, of some dozen who spoke about him, that found out Snob. I suppose the Spaniards lorded it over the Mexicans in this way: their drummers passing for generals among the simple red men, their glass beads for jewels, and their insolent bearing for heroic superiority.

Leaving, then, the race-ordinary (that little Scotchman with his airs has carried us the deuce knows how far out of the way), I came home just as the gentlemen of the race were beginning to 'mix,' that is, to forsake the wine for the punch. At the lodgings I found my five companions of the morning with a bottle of that wonderful whisky of which they spoke; and which they had agreed to exchange against a bundle of Liverpool cigars: so we discussed them, the whisky, and other topics in common. Now there is no need to violate the sanctity of private fife, and report the conversation which took place, the songs which were sung, the speeches which were made, and the other remarkable events of the evening. Suffice it to say, that the English traveller gradually becomes accustomed to whisky-punch (in moderation of course), and finds the beverage very agreeable at Killarney; against which I recollect a protest was entered at Dublin.

But after we had talked of hunting, racing, regatting, and all other; sports, I came to a discovery which astonished me, and for which these honest kind fellows are mentioned publicly here. The portraits, or a sort of resemblance of four of them, may be seen in the foregoing drawing of the car. The man with the straw-hat and handkerchief tied over it is the captain of an Indiaman; three others, with each a pair of moustaches, sported yacht-costumes, jackets, club anchor-buttons, and so forth; and, finally, one on the other side of the car (who cannot be seen on account of the portmanteaus, otherwise the likeness would be perfect) was dressed with a coat and a hat in the ordinary way. One with the gold band and moustaches is a gentleman of property; the other three are attorneys every man of them: two in large practice in Cork and Dublin; the other, and owner of the yacht, under articles to the attorney of Cork. Now did any Englishman ever live with three attorneys for a whole day without hearing a single syllable of law spoken? Did we ever see in our country attorneys with moustaches; or, above all, an attorney's clerk the owner of a yacht of thirty tons? He is a gentleman of property too—the heir, that is, to a good estate; and has had a yacht of his own, he says, ever since he was fourteen years old. Is there any English boy of fourteen who commands a ship with a crew of five men under him? We all agreed to have a boat for the stag-hunt on the lake next day; and I went to bed wondering at this strange country more than ever. An attorney with moustaches! What would they say of him in Chancery Lane?

CHAPTER XI: KILLARNEY—STAG-HUNTING ON THE LAKE

MRS. MACGILLICUDDY'S house is at the comer of the two principal streets of Killarney town, and the drawing-room windows command each a street. Before one window is a dismal, rickety building, with a slated face, that looks like an ex-town-hall. There is a row of arches to the ground-floor, the angles at the base of which seem to have mouldered or to have been kicked away. Over the centre arch is a picture with a flourishing yellow inscription above, importing that it is the meeting-place of the Total Abstinence Society. Total abstinence is represented by the figures of a gentleman in a blue coat and drab tights, with gilt garters, who is giving his hand to a lady; between them is an escutcheon, surmounted with a cross and charged with religious emblems. Cupids float above the heads and between the legs of this happy pair, while an exceedingly small tea-table with the requisite crockery reposes against the lady's knee; a still, with death's-head and bloody-bones, filling up the vacant corner near the gentleman. A sort of market is held here, and the place is swarming with blue cloaks and groups of men talking; here and there is a stall with coarse linens, crockery, a cheese; and crowds of egg- and milk-women are squatted on the pavement, with their ragged customers or gossips; and the yellow-haired girl, with a barrel containing nothing at all, has been sitting, as if for her portrait, this hour past.

Carts, cars, jingles, barouches, horses and vehicles of all descriptions rattle presently through the streets: for the town is crowded with company for the races and other sports, and all the world is bent to see the stag-hunt on the lake. "Where the ladies of the Macgillicuddy family have slept, Heaven knows, for their house is full of lodgers. What voices you hear! 'Bring me some hot water,' says a genteel high-piped English voice. 'Hwhere's me hot wather?′ roars a deep-toned Hibernian. See, over the way, three ladies in ringlets and green tabinet taking their 'tay' preparatory to setting out. I wonder whether they heard the sentimental songs of the law-marines last night? They must have been edified if they did.

My companions came, true to their appointment, and we walked down to the boats, lying at a couple of miles from the town, near the Victoria Inn, a handsome mansion, in pretty grounds, close to the lake, and owned by the patriotic Mr. Finn. A nobleman offered Finn eight hundred pounds for the use of his house during the races, and, to Finn's eternal honour be it said, he refused the money, and said he would keep his house for his friends and patrons, the public. Let the Cork Steam-Packet Company think of this generosity on the part of Mr. Finn, and blush for shame: at the Cork Agricultural Show they raised their fares, and were disappointed in their speculation, as they deserved to be, by indignant Englishmen refusing to go at all.

The morning had been bright enough; but for fear of accidents we took our mackintoshes, and at about a mile from the town found it necessary to assume those garments and wear them for the greater part of the day. Passing by the Victoria, with its beautiful walks, park, and lodge, we came to a little creek where the boats were moored; and there was the wonderful lake before us, with its mountains, and islands, and trees. Unluckily, however, the mountains happened to be invisible; the islands looked like grey masses in the fog, and all that we could see for some time was the grey silhouette of the boat ahead of us, in which a passenger was engaged in a witty conversation with some boat still farther in the mist.

Drumming and trumpeting was heard at a little distance, and presently we found ourselves in the midst of a fleet of boats upon the rocky shores of the beautiful little Innisfallen.

Here we landed for a while, and the weather clearing up allowed us to see this charming spot: rocks, shrubs, and little abrupt rises and falls of ground, covered with the brightest emerald grass; a beautiful little ruin of a Saxon chapel, lying gentle, delicate, and plaintive on the shore; some noble trees round about it, and beyond, presently, the tower of Ross Castle: island after island appearing in the clearing sunshine, and the huge hills throwing their misty veils off, and wearing their noble robes of purple. The boats' crews were grouped about the place, and one large barge especially had landed some sixty people, being the Temperance band, with its drums, trumpets, and wives. They were marshalled by a grave old gentleman with a white waistcoat and queue, a silver medal decorating one side of his coat, and a brass heart reposing on the other flap. The horns performed some Irish airs prettily; and at length, at the instigation of a fellow who went swaggering about with a pair of whirling drumsticks, all formed together and played 'Garryowen'—the active drum of course most dreadfully out of time.

Having strolled about the island for a quarter of an hour, it became time to take to the boats again, and we were rowed over to the wood opposite Sullivan's cascade, where the hounds had been laid in in the morning, and the stag was expected to take water. Fifty or sixty men are employed on the mountain to drive the stag lakewards, should he be inclined to break away: and the sport generally ends by the stag—a wild one—making for the water with the pack swimming afterwards; and here he is taken and disposed of: how I know not. It is rather a parade than a stag-hunt; but, with all the boats around and the noble view, must be a fine thing to see.

Presently, steering his barge, the *Erin,* with twelve oars and a green flag sweeping the water, came by the president of the sports, Mr. John OOonnell, a gentleman who appears to be liked by rich and poor here, and by the latter especially is adored. 'Sure we'd dhrown ourselves for him,' one man told me; and proceeded to speak eagerly in his praise, and to tell numberless acts of his generosity and justice. The justice is rather rude in this wild country sometimes, and occasionally the judges not only deliver the sentence but execute it; nor does any one think of appealing to any more regular jurisdiction. The likeness of Mr. O'Connell to his brother is very striking: one might have declared it was the Liberator sitting at the stern of the boat.

Some scores more boats were there, darting up and down in the pretty busy waters. Here came a Cambridge boat; and where, indeed, will not the gentlemen of that renowned University be found1? Yonder were the dandy dragoons, stiff, silent, slim, faultlessly appointed, solemnly puffing cigars. Every now and then a hound would be heard in the wood, whereon numbers of voices, right and left, would begin to yell in chorus—'Hurroo! Hoop! Yow—yow—yow!' in accents the most shrill or the most melancholious. Meanwhile the sun had had enough of the sport, the mountains put on their veils again, the islands retreated into the mist, the word went through the fleet to spread all umbrellas, and ladies took shares of mackintoshes and disappeared under the flaps of silk cloaks.

The wood comes down to the very edge of the water, and many of the crews thought fit to land and seek this green shelter. There you might see how the *dandium summâ genus hæsit ulmo*, clambering up thither to hide from the rain, and many 'membra' in dabbled russia-ducks cowering *viridi sub arbuto ad aquæ lene caput*. To behold these moist dandies the natives of the country came eagerly. Strange savage faces might be seen peering from out of the trees: long-haired bare-legged girls came down the hill, some with green apples and very sickly-looking plums; some with whisky and goat's-milk: a ragged boy had a pair of stag's horns to sell: the place swarmed with people. We went up the hill to see the noble cascade, and when you say that it comes rushing down over rocks and through tangled woods, alas! one has said all the dictionary can help you to, and not enough to distinguish this particular cataract from any other. This seen and admired, we came back to the harbour where the boats lay, and from which spot the reader might have seen a view of the lake—that is, you would see the lake, if the mist would only clear away.

But this for hours it did not seem inclined to do. We rowed up and down industriously for a period of time which seemed to me atrociously long. The bugles of the *Erin* had long since sounded 'Home, sweet home!' and the greater part of the fleet had dispersed. As for the stag-hunt, all I saw of it was four dogs that appeared on the shore at different intervals, and a huntsman in a scarlet coat, who similarly came and went: once or twice we were gratified by hearing the hounds: but at last it was agreed that there was no chance for the day, and we rowed off to Kenmare Cottage—where, on the lovely lawn, or in a cottage adjoining, the gentry picnic, and where, with a handkerchief-ful of potatoes, we made as pleasant a meal as ever I recollect. Here a good number of the boats were assembled; here you might see cloths spread and dinner going on; here were those wonderful officers, looking as if they had just stepped from bandboxes, with—by heavens!—not a shirt-collar disarranged nor a boot dimmed by the wet. An old piper was making a very feeble music, with a handkerchief spread over his face; and, farther on, a little smiling German boy was playing an accordion and singing a ballad of Hauff s. I had a silver medal in my pocket, with Victoria on one side and Britannia on the other, and gave it him, for the sake of old times and his round friendly face. Oh, little German boy, many a night as you trudge lonely through this wild land, must you yearn after *Brüderlein and Schwesterlein* at home—yonder in stately Frankfurt city that lies by silver Mayn. I thought of vineyards and sunshine, and the greasy clock in the theatre, and the railroad all the way to Wiesbaden, and the handsome Jew country-houses by the Bockenheimer-Thor...'Come along,' says the boatman. 'All the gintlemin are waiting for your honour.' And I found them finishing the potatoes, and we all had a draught of water from the lake, and so pulled to the Middle or Turk Lake through the picturesque green rapid that floats under Brickeen Bridge.

What is to be said about Turk Lake? When there, we agreed that it was more beautiful than the large lake, of which it is not one-fourth the size; then, when we came back, we said, 'No, the large lake is the most beautiful.' And so, at every point we stopped at, we determined that that particular spot was the prettiest in the whole lake. The fact is—and I don't care to own it—they are too handsome. As for a man coming from his desk in London or Dublin and seeing 'the whole lakes in a day,' he is an ass for his pains; a child doing sums in addition might as well read the whole multiplication-table, and fancy he had it by heart. We should look at these wonderful things leisurely and thoughtfully; and even then, blessed is he who understands them. I wonder what impression the sight made upon the three tipsy Englishmen at Glengariff? What idea of natural beauty belongs to an old fellow who says he is 'a gentleman, and pays his way'? What to a jolly fox-hunter, who had rather see a good 'screeching' run with the hounds than the best landscape ever painted? And yet they all come hither, and go through the business regularly, and would not miss seeing every one of the lakes and going up every one of the hills. By which circumlocution the writer wishes ingenuously to announce that he will not see any more lakes, ascend any mountains or towers, visit any gaps of Dunloe, or any prospects whatever, except such as nature shall fling in his way in the course of a quiet reasonable walk.

In the Middle Lake we were carried to an island where a ceremony of goat's-milk and whisky is performed by some travellers, and where you are carefully conducted to a spot that 'Sir Walter Scott admired more than all.' Whether he did or not, we can only say on the authority of the boatman; but the place itself was a quiet nook, where three waters meet, and indeed of no great picturesqueness when compared with the beauties around. But it is of a gentle homely beauty—not like the lake, which is as a princess dressed out in diamonds and velvet for a drawing-room, and knowing herself to be faultless too. As for Innisfallen, it was just as if she gave one smiling peep into the nursery before she went away, so quiet, innocent, and tender is that lovely spot; but, depend on it, if there is a lake fairy or princess, as Crofton Oroker and other historians assert, she is of her nature a vain creature, proud of her person, and fond of the finest dresses to adorn it. May I confess that I would rather, for a continuance, have a house facing a paddock, with a cow in it, than be always looking at this immense overpowering splendour. You would not, my dear brother cockney from Tooley Street? No, those brilliant eyes of thine were never meant to gaze at anything less bright than the sun. Your mighty spirit finds nothing too vast for its comprehension, spurns what is humble as unworthy, and only, like Foote's bear, dances to 'the genteelest of tunes.'

The long and short of the matter is, that on getting off the lake, after seven hours' rowing, I felt as much relieved as if I had been dining for the same length of time with her Majesty the Queen, and went jumping home as gaily as possible; but those marine-lawyers insisted so piteously upon seeing Ross Castle, close to which we were at length landed, that I was obliged (in spite of repeated oaths to the contrary) to ascend that tower, and take a bird's-eye view of the scene. Thank Heaven, I have neither tail nor wings, and have not the slightest wish to be a bird: that continual immensity of prospect which stretches beneath those little wings of theirs must deaden their intellects, depend on it. Tomkins and I are not made for the immense: we can enjoy a little at a time, and enjoy that little very much; or if like birds, we are like the ostrich—not that we have fine feathers to our backs, but because we cannot fly. Press us too much, and we become flurried, and run off and bury our heads in the quiet bosom of dear mother earth, and so get rid of the din, and the dazzle, and the shouting.

Because we dined upon potatoes, that was no reason we should sup on buttermilk. Well, well! salmon is good, and whisky is good too.

CHAPTER XII: KILLARNEY—THE RACES—MUCROSS

THE races were as gay as races could be, in spite of one or two untoward accidents that arrived at the close of the day's sport. Where all the people came from that thronged out of the town was a wonder; where all the vehicles, the cars, barouches and shandrydans, the carts, the horse- and donkey-men could have found stable and shelter, who can tell? Of all these equipages and donkeypages I had a fine view from Mrs. Macgillicuddy's window, and it was pleasant to See the happy faces shining under the blue cloaks as the carts rattled by. A very handsome young lady—I presume Miss MacG.—who gives a hand to the drawing-room and comes smiling in with the teapot—Miss MacG., I say, appeared to-day in a silk bonnet and stiff silk dress, with a brooch and a black mantle, as smart as any lady in the land, and looking as if she was accustomed to her dress too, which the housemaid on the banks of Thames does not. Indeed, I have not met a more ladylike young person in Ireland than Miss MacG.; and when I saw her in a handsome car on the course, I was quite proud of a bow.

Tramping thither, too, as hard as they could walk, and as happy and smiling as possible, were Mary the coachman's wife of the day before, and Johanna with the child, and presently the other young lady: the man with the stick, you may be sure: he would toil a year for that day's pleasure. They are all mad for it: people walk for miles and miles round to the race; they come without a penny in their pockets often, trusting to chance and charity, and that some worthy gentleman may fling them a sixpence. A gentleman told me that he saw on the course persons from his part of the country, who must have walked eighty miles for the sport.

For a mile and a half to the racecourse there could be no pleasanter occupation than looking at the happy multitudes who were thronging thither; and I am bound to say that on rich or poor shoulders I never saw so many handsome faces in my life. In the carriages, among the ladies of Kerry, every second woman was handsome; and there is something peculiarly tender and pleasing in the looks of the young female peasantry that is perhaps even better than beauty. Beggars had taken their stations along the road in no great numbers, for I suspect they were most of them on the ground, and those who remained were consequently of the oldest and ugliest. It is a shame that such horrible figures are allowed to appear in public as some of the loathsome ones which belong to these unhappy people. On went the crowd, however, laughing and as gay as possible; all sorts of fun passing from car to foot passengers as the pretty girls came clattering by, and the 'boys' had a word for each. One lady with long flowing auburn hair, who was turning away her head from some 'boys' very demurely, I actually saw, at a pause of the cart, kissed by one of them. She gave the fellow a huge box on the ear, and he roared out 'O murther!' and she frowned for some time as hard as she could, whilst the ladies in the blue cloaks at the back of the car uttered a shrill rebuke in Irish. But in a minute the whole party was grinning, and the young fellow who had administered the salute may, for what I know, have taken another without the slap on the face by way of exchange.

And here, lest the fair public may have a bad opinion of the personage who talks of kissing with such awful levity, let it be said that with all this laughing, romping, kissing, and the like, there are no more innocent girls in the world than the Irish girls; and that the women of our squeamish country are far more liable to err. One has but to walk through an English and Irish town, and see how much superior is the morality of the latter. That great terror-striker, the Confessional, is before the Irish girl, and sooner or later her sins must be told there.

By this time we are got upon the course, which is really one of the most beautiful spots that ever was seen: the lake and mountains lying along two sides of it, and of course visible from all. They were busy putting up the hurdles when we arrived: stiff bars and poles, four feet from the ground, with furze-bushes over them. The grand stand was already full; along the hedges sat thousands of the people, sitting at their ease doing nothing, and happy as kings. A daguerreotype would have been of great service to have taken their portraits, and I never saw a vast multitude of heads and attitudes so picturesque and lively. The sun lighted up the whole course and the lakes with amazing brightness, though behind the former lay a huge rack of the darkest clouds, against which the cornfields and meadows shone in the brightest green and gold, and a row of white tents was quite dazzling.

There was a brightness and intelligence about this immense Irish crowd, which I don't remember to have seen in an English one. The women in their blue cloaks, with red smiling faces peering from one end, and bare feet from the other, had seated themselves in all sorts of pretty attitudes of cheerful contemplation; -and the men, who are accustomed to lie about, were doing so now with all their might— sprawling on the banks, with as much ease and variety as club-room loungers on their soft cushions—or squatted leisurely among the green potatoes. The sight of so much happy laziness did one good to look on. Nor did the honest fellows seem to weary of this amusement. Hours passed on, and the gentlefolks (judging from our party) began to grow somewhat weary; but the finest peasantry in Europe never budged from their posts, and continued to indulge in talk, indolence, and conversation.

When we came to the row of white tents, as usual it did not look so brilliant or imposing as it appeared from a Little distance, though the scene around them was animating enough. The tents were long humble booths stretched on hoops, each with its humble streamer or ensign without, and containing, of course, articles of refreshment within. But Father Mathew has been busy among the publicans, and the consequence is that the poor fellows are now condemned for the most part to sell 'tay' in place of whisky; for the concoction of which beverage huge cauldrons were smoking, in front of each hut-door, in round graves dug for the purpose and piled up with black smoking sod.

Behind this camp were the carts of the poor people, which were not allowed to penetrate into the quarter where the quality cars stood. And a little way from the huts, again, you might see (for you could scarcely hear) certain pipers executing their melodies and inviting people to dance.

Anything more lugubrious than the drone of the pipe, or the jig danced to it, or the countenances of the dancers and musicians, I never saw. Round each set of dancers the people formed a ring, in the which the figurantes and coryphees went through their operations. The toes went in and the toes went out; then there came certain mystic figures of hands across, and so forth. I never saw less grace or seemingly less enjoyment—no, not even in a. quadrille. The people, however, took a great interest, and it was 'Well done, Tim!' 'Step out, Miss Brady!' and so forth during the dance.

Thimble-rig too obtained somewhat, though in a humble way. A ragged scoundrel—the image of Hogarth's Bad Apprentice—went bustling and shouting through the crowd with his dirty tray and thimble, and as soon as he had taken his post, stated that this was the 'royal game of thimble,' and called upon 'gintlemin' to come forward. And then a ragged fellow would be seen to approach, with as innocent an air as he could assume, and the bystanders might remark that the second ragged fellow almost always won. Nay, he was so benevolent, in many instances, as to point out to various people who had a mind to bet, under which thimble the pea actually was. Meanwhile, the first fellow was sure to be looking away and talking to some one in the crowd; but somehow it generally happened—and how of course I can't tell—that any man who listened to the advice of rascal No. 2 lost his money. I believe it is so even in England.

Then you would see gentlemen with halfpenny roulette-tables; and, again, here were a pair who came forward disinterestedly with a table and a pack of cards, and began playing against each other for ten shillings a game, betting crowns as freely as possible.

Gambling, however, must have been fatal to both of these gentlemen, else might not one have supposed that, if they were in the habit of winning much, they would have treated themselves to better clothes? This, however, is the way with all gamblers, as the reader has no doubt remarked: for, look at a game of loo or *vingt-et-un* played in a friendly way, and where you, and three or four others, have certainly lost three or four pounds,—well, ask at the end of the game who has won, and you invariably find that nobody has. Hopkins has only covered himself; Snooks has neither lost nor won; Smith has won four shillings; and so on. Who gets the money? The devil gets it, I dare say; and so, no doubt, he has laid hold of the money of yonder gentleman in the handsome great-coat.

But, to the shame of the stewards be it spoken, they are extremely averse to this kind of sport; and presently comes up one, a stout old gentleman on a bay horse, wielding a huge hunting-whip, at the sight of which all fly, amateurs, idlers, professional men, and all. He is a rude customer to deal with, that gentleman with the whip: just now he was clearing the course, and cleared it with such a vengeance that a whole troop on a hedge retreated backwards into a ditch opposite, where was rare kicking, and sprawling, and disarrangement of petticoats, and cries of 'O murther!' 'Mother of God! I'm kilt!' and so on. But as soon as the horsewhip was gone, the people clambered out of their ditch again, and were as thick as ever on the bank.

The last instance of the exercise of the whip shall be this. A groom rode insolently after a gentleman, calling him names, and inviting him to fight. This the great flagellator hearing, rode up to the groom, lifted him gracefully off his horse into the air, and on to the ground, and when there administered to him a severe and merited fustigation; after which he told the course-keepers to drive the fellow off the course, and enjoined the latter not to appear again at his peril.

As for the races themselves, I won't pretend to say that they were better or worse than other such amusements; or to quarrel with gentlemen who choose to risk their lives in manly exercise. In the first race there was a fall: one of the gentlemen was carried off the ground, and it was said *he was dead.* In the second race, a horse and man went over and over each other, and the fine young man (we had seen him five minutes before, full of life and triumph, clearing the hurdles on his grey horse, at the head of the race):—in the second heat of the second race the poor fellow missed his leap, was carried away stunned and dying, and the bay horse won.

I was standing, during the first heat of this race (this is the second man the grey has killed—they ought to call him the Pale Horse), by half-a-dozen young girls from the gentleman's village, and hundreds more of them were there, anxious for the honour of their village, the young squire, and the grey horse. Oh, how they hurrah'd as he rode ahead! I saw these girls—they might be fourteen years old—after the catastrophe. 'Well,' says I, 'this is a sad end to the race.' '*And is it the pink jacket or the blue has won this time?*' says one of the girls. It was poor Mr. O-'s only epitaph: and wasn't it a sporting answer? That girl ought to be a hurdle-racer's wife; and I would like, for my part, to bestow her upon the groom who won the race.

I don't care to confess that the accident to the poor young gentleman so thoroughly disgusted my feelings as a man and a cockney, that I turned off the racecourse short, and hired a horse for sixpence to carry me back to Miss Macgillicuddy. In the evening, at the inn (let no man who values comfort go to an Irish inn in race-time), a blind old piper, with silvery hair, and of a most respectable bard-like appearance, played a great deal too much for us after dinner. He played very well, and with very much feeling, ornamenting the airs with flourishes and variations that were very pretty indeed, and his pipe was by far the most melodious I have heard; but honest truth compels me to say that the bad pipes are execrable, and the good inferior to a clarionet.

Next day, instead of going back to the racecourse, a car drove me out to Mucross, where, in Mr. Herbert's beautiful grounds, lies the prettiest little *bijou* of a ruined abbey ever seen—a little chapel with a little chancel, a little cloister, a little dormitory, and in the midst of the cloister a wonderful huge yew-tree which darkens the whole place. The abbey is famous in book and legend; nor could two young lovers, or artists in search of the picturesque, or picnic-parties with the cold chicken and champagne in the distance, find a more charming place to while away a summer's day than in the park of Mr. Herbert. But depend on it, for show-places and the due enjoyment of scenery, that distance of cold chicken and champagne is the most pleasing perspective one can have. I would have sacrificed a mountain or two for the above, and would have pitched Mangerton into the lake for. the sake of a friend with whom to enjoy the rest of the landscape.

The walk through Mr. Herbert's domain carries you, through all sorts of beautiful avenues, by a fine house which he is building in the Elizabethan style, and from which, as from the whole road, you command the most wonderful rich views of the lake. The shore breaks into little bays, which the water washes; here and there are picturesque grey rocks to meet it, the bright grass as often, or the shrubs of every kind which bathe their roots in the lake. It was August, and the men before Turk Cottage were cutting a second crop of clover, as fine, seemingly, as a first crop elsewhere: a short walk from it brought us to a neat lodge, whence issued a keeper with a key, quite willing, for the consideration of sixpence, to conduct us to Turk waterfall.

Evergreens and other trees, in their brightest livery; blue sky; roaring water, here black, and yonder foaming of a dazzling white; rocks shining in the dark places, or frowning black against the light, all the leaves and branches keeping up a perpetual waving and dancing round about the cascade: what is the use of putting down all this? A man might describe the cataract of the Serpentine in exactly the same terms, and the reader be no wiser. Suffice it to say, that the Turk cascade is even handsomer than the before-mentioned waterfall of O'Sullivan, and that a man may pass half-an-hour there, and look, and listen, and muse, and not even feel the want of a companion, or so much as think of the iced champagne. There is just enough of savageness in the Turk cascade to make the view *piquante*. It is not, at this season at least, by any means fierce, only wild; nor was the scene peopled by any of the rude red-shanked figures that clustered about the trees of O'Sullivan's waterfall—savages won't pay sixpence for the prettiest waterfall ever seen—so that this only was for the best of company.

The road hence to Killarney carries one through Mucross village, a pretty cluster of houses, where the sketcher will find abundant materials for exercising his art and puzzling his hand. There are not only noble trees, but a green common and an old water-gate to a river, lined on either side by beds of rushes and discharging itself beneath an old mill-wheel. But the old mill-wheel was perfectly idle, like most men and mill-wheels in this country: by it is a ruinous house, and a fine garden of stinging-nettles; opposite it, on the common, is another ruinous house, with another garden containing the same plant; and far away are sharp ridges of purple hills, which make as pretty a landscape as the eye can see. I don't know how it is, but throughout the country the men and the landscapes seem to be the same, and one and the other seem rugged, ruined, and cheerful.

Having been employed all day (making some abominable attempts at landscape-drawing, which shall not be exhibited here), it became requisite, as the evening approached, to recruit an exhausted cockney stomach—which, after a very moderate portion of exercise, begins to sigh for beefsteaks in the most peremptory manner. Hard by is a fine hotel with a fine sign stretching along the road for the space of a dozen windows at least, and looking inviting enough. All the doors were open, and I walked into a great number of rooms, but the only person I saw was a woman with trinkets of arbutus, who offered me, by way of refreshment, a walking-stick or a card-rack. I suppose everybody was at the races; and an evilly-disposed person might have laid *main-basse* upon the great-coats which were there, and the silver spoons, if by any miracle such things were kept:—but Britannia-metal is the favourite composition in Ireland; or else iron by itself; or else iron that has been silvered over, but that takes good care to peep out at all the corners of the forks: and blessed is the traveller who has not other observations to make regarding his fork, besides the mere abrasion of the silver.

This was the last day's race, and on the next morning (Sunday), all the thousands who had crowded to the race seemed trooping to the chapels, and the streets were blue with cloaks. Walking in to prayers, and without his board, came my young friend of the thimble-rig, and presently after sauntered in the fellow with the long coat, who had played at cards for sovereigns. I should like to hear the confession of himself and friend the next time they communicate with his reverence.

The extent of this town is very curious, and I should imagine its population to be much greater than five thousand, which was the number, according to Miss Macgillicuddy. Along the three main streets are numerous arches, down every one of which runs an alley, intersected by other alleys, and swarming with people. A stream or gutter runs commonly down these alleys, in which the pigs and children are seen paddling about. The men and women loll at their doors or windows, to enjoy the detestable prospect. I saw two pigs under a fresh-made deal staircase in one of the main streets near the Bridewell: two very well-dressed girls, with their hair in ringlets, were looking out of the parlour-window: almost all the glass in the upper rooms was of course smashed, the windows patched here and there (if the people were careful), the woodwork of the door loose, the whitewash peeling off,—and the house evidently not two years old.

By the Bridewell is a busy potato-market, picturesque to the sketcher, if not very respectable to the merchant: here were the country carts and the country cloaks, and the shrill beggarly bargains going on— a world of shrieking, and gesticulating, and talk, about a pennyworth of potatoes.

All round the town miserable streets of cabins are stretched. You see people lolling at each door, women staring and combing their hair, men with their little pipes, children whose rags hang on by a miracle, idling in a gutter. Are we to set all this down to absenteeism, and pity poor injured Ireland? Is the landlord's absence the reason why the house is filthy, and Biddy lolls in the porch all day? Upon my word, I have heard people talk as if, when Pat's thatch was blown off, the landlord ought to go fetch the straw and the ladder, and mend it himself. People need not be dirty if they are ever so idle; if they are ever so poor, pigs and men need not live together. Half-an-hour's work, and digging a trench, might remove that filthy dunghill from that filthy window. The smoke might as well come out of the chimney as out of the door. Why should not Tim do that, instead of walking a hundred-and-sixty miles to a race? The priests might do much more to effect these reforms than even the landlords themselves: and I hope now that the excellent Father Mathew has succeeded in arraying his clergy to work with him in the abolition of drunkenness, they will attack the monster Dirt, with the same good-will, and surely with the same success.

CHAPTER XIII: TRALEE—LISTOWEL—TARBERT

I MADE the journey to Tralee next day, upon one of the famous Bianconi cars—very comfortable conveyances too, if the booking officers would only receive as many persons as the car would hold, and not have too many on the seats. For half-an-hour before the car left Killarney, I observed people had taken their seats: and, let all travellers be cautious to do likewise, lest, although they have booked their places, they be requested to mount on the roof, and accommodate themselves on a bandbox, or a pleasant deal trunk with a knotted rope, to prevent it from being slippery, while the corner of another box jolts against your ribs for the journey. I had put my coat on a place, and was stepping to it, when a lovely lady with great activity jumped up and pushed the coat on the roof, and not only occupied my seat, but insisted that her husband should have the next one to her. So there was nothing for it but to make a huge shouting with the book-keeper and call instantly for the taking down of my luggage, and vow my great gods that I would take a postchaise and make the office pay: on which, I am ashamed to say, some other person was made to give up a decently comfortable seat on the roof, which I occupied, the former occupant hanging on—Heaven knows where or how.

A company of young squires were on the coach, and they talked of horse-racing and hunting punctually for three hours, during which time I do believe they did not utter one single word upon any other subject. What a wonderful faculty it is! The writers of Natural Histories, in describing the noble horse, should say he is made not only to run, to carry burdens, etc., but to be talked about. What would hundreds of thousands of dashing young fellows do with their tongues, if they had not this blessed subject to discourse on?

As far as the country went, there was here, to be sure, not much to be said. You pass through a sad-looking, bare, undulating country, with few trees, and poor stone-hedges, and poorer crops; nor have I yet taken in Ireland so dull a ride. About half-way between Tralee and Killarney is a wretched town, where horses are changed, and where I saw more hideous beggary than anywhere else, I think. And I was glad to get over this gloomy tract of country, and enter the capital of Kerry.

It has a handsome description in the guide-books; but, if I mistake not, the English traveller will find a stay of a couple of hours in the town quite sufficient to gratify his curiosity with respect to the place. There seems to be a great deal of poor business going on; the town thronged with people as usual; the shops large and not too splendid. There are two or three rows of respectable houses, and a mall and the townspeople have the further privilege of walking in the neighbouring grounds of a handsome park, which the proprietor has liberally given to their use. Tralee has a newspaper, and boasts of a couple of clubs: the one I saw was a big white house, no windows broken, and looking comfortable. But the most curious sight of the town was the chapel, with the festival held there. It was the feast of the Assumption of the Virgin (let those who are acquainted with the calendar and the facts it commemorates say what the feast was, and when it falls), and all the country seemed to be present on the occasion: the chapel and the large court leading to it were thronged with worshippers, such as one never sees in our country, where devotion is by no means so crowded as here. Here, in the courtyard, there were thousands of them on their knees, rosary in hand, for the most part praying, and mumbling, and casting a wistful look round as the strangers passed. In a corner was an old man groaning in the agonies of death or colic, and a woman got off her knees to ask us for charity for the unhappy old fellow. In the chapel the crowd was enormous: the priest and his people were kneeling, and bowing, and humming and chanting, and censer-rattling; the ghostly crew being attended by a fellow that I don't remember to have seen in Continental churches, a sort of Catholic clerk, a black shadow to the parson, bowing his head when his reverence bowed, kneeling when he knelt, only three steps lower.

But we who wonder at copes and candlesticks, see nothing strange in surplices and beadles. A Turk, doubtless, would sneer equally at each, and have you to understand that the only reasonable ceremonial was that which took place at his mosque.

Whether right or wrong in point of ceremony, it was evident the heart of devotion was there: the immense dense crowd moaned and swayed, and you heard a hum of all sorts of wild ejaculations, each man praying seemingly for himself, while the service went on at the altar. The altar candles flickered red in the dark steaming place, and every now and then from the choir you heard a sweet female voice chanting Mozart's music, which swept over the heads of the people a great deal more pure and delicious than the best incense that ever smoked out of pot.

On the chapel-floor, just at the entry, lay several people moaning, and tossing, and telling their beads. Behind the old woman was a font of holy water, up to which little children were clambering; and in the chapel-yard were several old women, with tin cans full of the same sacred fluid, with which the people, as they entered, aspersed themselves with all their might, flicking a great quantity into their faces, and making a curtsey and a prayer at the same time. 'A pretty prayer, truly!' says the parson's wife. 'What sad sad benighted superstition!' says the Independent minister's lady. Ah! ladies, great as your intelligence is, yet think, when compared with the Supreme One, what a little difference there is after all between your husbands' very best extempore oration and the poor Popish creatures'! One is just as far off Infinite Wisdom as the other: and so let us read the story of the woman and her pot of ointment, that most noble and charming of histories; which equalises the great and the small, the wise and the poor in spirit, and shows that their merit before Heaven lies *in doing their best.*

When I came out of the chapel, the old fellow on the point of death was still howling and groaning in so vehement a manner, that I heartily trust he was an impostor, and that on receiving a sixpence he went home tolerably comfortable, having secured a maintenance for that day. But it will be long before I can forget the strange wild scene, so entirely different was it from the decent and comfortable observances of our own Church.

Three cars set off together from Tralee to Tarbert: three cars full to overflowing. The vehicle before us contained nineteen persons, half-a-dozen being placed in the receptacle called the well, and one clinging on as if by a miracle at the bar behind. What can people want at Tarbert? I Wondered; or anywhere else, indeed, that they rush about from one town to another in this inconceivable way? All the cars in all the towns seem to be thronged: people are perpetually hurrying from one dismal tumble-down town to another; and yet no business is done anywhere that I can see. The chief part of the contents of our three cars was discharged at Listowel, to which, for the greater part of the journey, the road was neither more cheerful nor picturesque than that from Killarney to Tralee. As, however, you reach Listowel, the country becomes better cultivated, the gentlemen's seats are more frequent, and the town itself, as seen from a little distance, lies very prettily on a river, which is crossed by a handsome bridge, which leads to a neat-looking square, which contains a smartish church, which is flanked by a big Roman Catholic chapel, etc. An old castle, grey and ivy-covered, stands hard by. It was one of the strongholds of the lords of Kerry, whose burying-place (according to the information of the coachman) is seen at about a league from the town.

But pretty as Listowel is from a distance, it has, on a more intimate acquaintance, by no means the prosperous appearance which a first glance gives it. The place seemed like a scene at a country theatre, once smartly painted by the artist; but the paint has cracked in many places, the lines are worn away, and the whole piece only looks more shabby for the flaunting strokes of the brush which remain. And here, of course, came the usual crowd of idlers round the car: the epileptic idiot holding piteously out his empty tin snuff-box; the brutal idiot, in an old soldier's coat, proffering his money-box, and grinning, and clattering the single halfpenny it contained; the old man with no eyelids, calling upon you in the name of the Lord; the woman with a child at her hideous wrinkled breast; the children without number. As for trade, there seemed to be none: a great Jeremy-Diddler kind of hotel stood hard by, swaggering and out-at-elbows, and six pretty girls were smiling out of a beggarly straw-bonnet shop, dressed as smartly as any gentleman's daughters of good estate. It was good, among the crowd of bustling shrieking fellows, who were 'jawing' vastly and doing nothing, to see how an English bagman, with scarce any words, laid hold of an ostler, carried him off, *vi et armis,* in the midst of a speech, in which the latter was going to explain his immense activity and desire to serve, pushed him into a stable, from which he issued in a twinkling leading the ostler and a horse, and had his bag on the car and his horse off in about two minutes of time, while the natives were still shouting round about other passengers' portmanteaus.

Some time afterwards, away we rattled on our own journey to Tarbert, having a postillion on the leader, and receiving, I must say, some graceful bows from the young bonnet-makeresses. But of all the roads over which human bones were ever jolted, the first part of this from Listowel to Tarbert deserves the palm. It shook us all into headaches; it shook some nails out of the side of a box I had; it shook all the cords loose in a twinkling, and sent the baggage bumping about the passengers' shoulders. The coachman at the call of another English bagman, who was a fellow-traveller,—the postillion at the call of the coachman, descended to re-cord the baggage. The English bagman had the whole mass of trunks and bags stoutly corded and firmly fixed in a few seconds; the coachman helped him as far as his means allowed; the postillion stood by with his hands in his pockets, smoking his pipe, and never offering to stir a finger. I said to him that I was delighted to see in a youth of sixteen that extreme activity and willingness to oblige, and that I would give him a handsome remuneration for his services at the end of the journey: the young rascal grinned with all his might, understanding the satiric nature of the address perfectly well; but he did not take his hands out of his pockets for all that, until it was time to get on his horse again, and then, having carried us over the most difficult part of the journey, removed his horse and pipe, and rode away, with a parting grin.

The cabins along the road were not much better than those to be seen south of Tralee, but the people were far better clothed, and indulged in several places in the luxury of pigsties. Near the prettily situated village of Ballylongford, we came in sight of the Shannon mouth; and a huge red round moon, that shone behind an old convent on the banks of the bright river, with dull green meadows between it and us, and wide purple flats beyond, would be a good subject for the pencil of any artist whose wrist had not been put out of joint by the previous ten miles' journey.

The town of Tarbert, in the guide-books and topographical dictionaries, nourishes considerably. You read of its port, its corn and provision stores, etc., and of certain good hotels; for which as travellers we were looking with a laudable anxiety. The town, in fact, contains about a dozen of houses, some hundreds of cabins, and two hotels; to one of which we were driven, and a kind landlady, conducting her half-dozen guests into a snug parlour, was for our ordering refreshment immediately, — which I certainly should have done, but for the ominous whisper of a fellow in the crowd as we descended (of course a disinterested patron of the other house), who hissed into my ears, '*Ask to see the beds*': which proposal, accordingly, I made before coming to any determination regarding supper.

The worthy landlady eluded my question several times with great skill and good-humour, but it became at length necessary to answer it; which she did by putting on as confident an air as possible, and leading the way upstairs to a bedroom, where there was a good large comfortable bed certainly.

The only objection to the bed, however, was that it contained a sick lady, whom the hostess proposed to eject without any ceremony, saying that she was a great deal better, and going to get up that very evening. However, none of us had the heart to tyrannise over lovely woman in so painful a situation, and the hostess had the grief of seeing four out of her five guests repair across the way to Brallaghan's or Gallagher's Hotel,—the name has fled from my memory, but it is the big hotel in the place; and unless the sick lady has quitted the other inn, which most likely she has done by this time, the English traveller will profit by this advice, and on arrival at Tarbert will have himself transported to Gallagher's at once.

The next morning a car carried us to Tarbert Point, where there is a pier not yet completed, and a Preventive station, and where the Shannon steamers touch, that ply between Kilrush and Limerick. Here lay the famous river before us, with low banks and rich pastures on either side.

CHAPTER XIV: LIMERICK

A CAPITAL steamer, which on this day was thronged with people, carried us for about four hours down the noble stream and landed us at Limerick quay. The character of the landscape on either side the stream is not particularly picturesque, but large, liberal, and prosperous. Gentle sweeps of rich meadows and cornfields cover the banks, and some, though not too many, gentlemen's parks and plantations rise here and there. But the landscape was somehow more pleasing than if it had been merely picturesque; and, especially after coming out of that desolate county of Kerry, it was pleasant for the eye to rest upon this peaceful, rich, and generous scene. The first aspect of Limerick is very smart and pleasing: fine neat quays with considerable liveliness and bustle, a very handsome bridge (the Wellesley Bridge) before the spectator; who, after a walk through two long and flourishing streets, stops at length at one of the best inns in Ireland—the large, neat, and prosperous one kept by Mr. Cruise. Except at Youghal, and the poor fellow whom the Englishman belaboured at Glengariff, Mr. Cruise is the only landlord of an inn I have had the honour to see in Ireland. I believe these gentlemen commonly (and very naturally) prefer riding with the hounds, or manly sports, to attendance on their guests; and the landladies, if they prefer to play the piano, or to have a game of cards in the parlour, only show a taste at which no one can wonder: for who can expect a lady to be troubling herself with vulgar chance-customers, or looking after Molly in the bedroom or waiter Tim in the cellar?

Now, beyond this piece of information regarding the excellence of Mr. Cruise's hotel, which every traveller knows, the writer of this doubts very much whether he has anything to say about Limerick that is worth the trouble of saying or reading. I can't attempt to describe the Shannon, only to say that on board the steamboat there was a piper and a bugler, a hundred of genteel persons coming back from donkey-riding and bathing at Kilkee, a couple of heaps of raw hides that smelt very foully, a score of women nursing children, and a lobster-vendor, who vowed to me on his honour that he gave eightpence apiece for his fish, and that he had boiled them only the day before; but when I produced the Guide-book, and solemnly told him to swear upon that to the truth of his statement, the lobster-seller turned away quite abashed, and would not be brought to support his previous assertion at all. Well, this is no description of the Shannon, as you have no need to be told, and other travelling cockneys will, no doubt, meet neither piper nor lobster-seller nor raw hides; nor, if they come to the inn where this is written, is it probable that they will hear, as I do at this present moment, two fellows with red whiskers, and immense pomp and noise and blustering with the waiter, conclude by ordering a pint of ale between them. All that one can hope to do is, to give a sort of notion of the movement and manners of the people; pretending by no means to offer a description of places, but simply an account of what one sees in them.

So that if any traveller after staying two days in Limerick should think fit to present the reader with forty or fifty pages of dissertation upon the antiquities and history of the place, upon the state of commerce, religion, education, the public may be pretty well sure that the traveller has been at work among the guide-books, and filching extracts from the topographical and local works.

They say there are three towns to make one Limerick: there is the Irish Town on the Clare side; the English Town with its old castle (which has sustained a deal of battering and blows from Danes, from fierce Irish kings, from English warriors who took an interest in the place, Henry Secundians, Elizabethians, Cromwellians, and, *vice versâ,* Jacobites, King Williamites,—and nearly escaped being in the hands of the Robert Emmettites); and finally the district called Newtown-Pery. In walking through this latter tract, you are at first half led to believe that you are arrived in a second Liverpool, so tall are the warehouses and broad the quays; so neat and trim a street of near a mile which stretches before you. But even this mile-long street does not, in a few minutes, appear to be so wealthy and prosperous as it shows at a first glance; for of the population that throng the streets, two-fifths are barefooted women, and two-fifths more ragged men: and the most part of the shops which have a grand show with them appear, when looked into, to be no better than they should be, being empty makeshift-looking places with their best goods outside.

Here, in this handsome street too, is a handsome club-house, with plenty of idlers, you may be sure, lolling at the portico; likewise you see numerous young officers, with very tight waists and absurd brass shell-epaulettes to their little absurd frock-coats, walking the pavement—the dandies of the street. Then you behold whole troops of pear-, apple-, and plum-women, selling very raw green-looking fruit, which, indeed, it is a wonder that any one should eat and live. The houses are bright red—the street is full and gay, carriages and cars in plenty go jingling by—dragoons in red are every now and then clattering up the street, and as upon every car which passes with ladies in it you are sure (I don't know how it is) to see a pretty one, the great street of Limerick is altogether a very brilliant and animated sight.

If the ladies of the place are pretty, indeed the vulgar are scarcely less so. I never saw a greater number of kind, pleasing, clever-looking faces among any set of people. There seem, however, to be two sorts of physiognomies which are common: the pleasing and somewhat melancholy one before mentioned, and a square, high-cheeked, flat-nosed physiognomy not uncommonly accompanied by a hideous staring head of dry red hair. Except, however, in the latter case, the hair flowing loose and long is a pretty characteristic of the women of the country; many a fair one do you see at the door of the cabin, or the poor shop in the town, combing complacently that 'greatest ornament of female beauty,' as Mr. Rowland justly calls it.

The generality of the women here seem also much better clothed than in Kerry; and I saw many a one going barefoot whose gown was nevertheless a good one, and whose cloak was of fine cloth. Likewise it must be remarked that the beggars in Limerick were by no means so numerous as those in Cork, or in many small places through which I have passed. There were but five, strange to say, round the mail-coach as we went away; and, indeed, not a great number in the streets.

The belles-lettres seem to me by no means so well cultivated here as in Cork. I looked in vain for a Limerick guide-book: I saw but one good shop of books, and a little trumpery circulating library, which seemed to be provided with those immortal works of a year old—which, having been sold for half-a-guinea the volume at first, are suddenly found to be worth only a shilling. Among these, let me mention, with perfect resignation to the decrees of fate, the works of one Tit-marsh: they were rather smartly bound by an enterprising publisher, and I looked at them in Bishop Murphy's Library at Cork, in a bookshop in the remote little town of Ennis, and elsewhere, with a melancholy tenderness. Poor flowerets of a season! (and a very short season too), let me be allowed to salute your scattered leaves with a passing sigh!...Besides the book-shops, I observed in the long best street of Limerick a half-dozen of what are called French shops, with nicknacks, German-silver chimney ornaments, and paltry finery. In the windows of these you saw a card with 'Cigars'; in the book-shop, 'Cigars'; at the grocer's, the whisky-shop, 'Cigars': everybody sells the noxious weed, or makes believe to sell it, and I know no surer indication of a struggling uncertain trade than that same placard of 'Cigars.' I went to buy some of the pretty Limerick gloves (they are chiefly made, as I have since discovered, at Cork). I think the man who sold them had a patent from the Queen, or his Excellency, or both, in his window: but, seeing a friend pass just as I entered the shop, he brushed past, and held his friend in conversation for some minutes in the street,—about the Killarney races no doubt, or the fun going on at Kilkee. I might have swept away a bagful of walnut-shells containing the flimsy gloves: but instead walked out, making him a low bow, and saying I would call next week. He said 'wouldn't I wait?' and resumed his conversation; and, no doubt, by this way of doing business, is making a handsome independence. I asked one of the ten thousand fruit-women the price of her green pears. 'Twopence apiece,' she said; and there were two little ragged beggars standing by, who were munching the fruit. A book-shopwoman made me pay threepence for a bottle of ink which usually costs a penny; a potato-woman told me that her potatoes cost fourteenpence a stone: and all these ladies treated the stranger with a leering wheedling servility which made me long to box their ears, were it not that the man who lays his hand upon a woman is an etc., whom 'twere gross flattery to call a what-d'ye-call-'em. By the way, the man who played Duke Aranza at Cork delivered the celebrated claptrap above alluded to as follows:—

'The man who lays a hand upon a woman,
Save in the way of kindness, is a villain,
Whom 'twere *a gross piece* of flattery to call a coward;'

and looked round calmly for the applause, which deservedly followed his new reading of the passage.

To return to the apple-women:—legions of ladies were employed through the town upon that traffic; there were really thousands of them, clustering upon the bridges, squatting down in doorways and vacant sheds for temporary markets, marching and crying their bout goods in all the crowded lanes of the city. After you get out of the main street the handsome part of the town is at an end, and you suddenly find yourself in such a labyrinth of busy swarming poverty and squalid commerce as never was seen—no, not in Saint Giles's, where Jew and Irishman side by side exhibit their genius for dirt. Here every house almost was a half ruin, and swarming with people: in the cellars you looked down and saw a barrel of herrings, which a merchant was dispensing; or a sack of meal, which a poor dirty woman sold to people poorer and dirtier than herself: above was a tinman, or a shoemaker, or other craftsman, his battered ensign at the door, and his small wares peering through the cracked panes of his shop. As for the ensign, as a matter of course the name is never written in letters of the same size. High and low, in this country, they begin things on too large a scale. They begin churches too big and can't finish them; mills and houses too big, and are ruined before they are done; letters on signboards too big, and are up in a corner before the inscription is finished. There is something quite strange, really, in this general consistency.

Well, over James Hurley, or Pat Hanlahan, you will most likely see another board of another tradesman, with a window to the full as curious. Above Tim Carthy evidently lives another family. There are long-haired girls of fourteen at every one of the windows, and dirty children everywhere. In the cellars, look at them in dingy white nightcaps over a bowl of stirabout; in the shop, paddling up and down the ruined steps, or issuing from beneath the black counter; up above, see the girl of fourteen is tossing and dangling one of them; and a pretty tender sight it is, in the midst of this filth and wretchedness, to see the women and children together. It makes a sunshine in the dark place, and somehow half reconciles one to it. Children are everywhere. Look out of the nasty streets into the still more nasty black lanes: there they are, sprawling at every door and court, paddling in every puddle; and in about a fair proportion to every six children an old woman—a very old, bleared-eyed, ragged woman—who makes believe to sell something out of a basket, and is perpetually calling upon the name of the Lord. For every three ragged old women you will see two ragged old men, praying and moaning like the females. And there is no lack of young men, either, though I never could make out what they were about: they loll about the street, chiefly conversing in knots; and in every street you will be pretty sure to see a recruiting sergeant, with gay ribbons in his cap, loitering about with an eye upon the other loiterers there. The buzz and hum and chattering of this crowd is quite inconceivable to us in England, where a crowd is generally silent. As a person with a decent coat passes, they stop in their talk and say, 'God bless you for a fine gentleman!' In these crowded streets, where all are beggars, the beggary is but small:

only the very old and hideous venture to ask for a penny, otherwise the competition would be too great.

As for the buildings that one lights upon every now and then in the midst of such scenes as this, they are scarce worth the trouble to examine: occasionally you come on a chapel with sham Gothic windows and a little belfry, one of the Catholic places of worship; then, placed in some quiet street, a neat-looking Dissenting meeting-house. Across the river yonder, as you issue out from the street, is a handsome hospital; near it the old cathedral, a barbarous old turreted edifice—of the fourteenth century it is said: how different to the sumptuous elegance which characterises the English and Continental churches of the same period! Passing by it, and walking down other streets,— black, ruinous, swarming, dark, hideous,—you come upon the barracks and the walks of the old castle, and from it on to an old bridge, from which the view is a fine one. On one side are the grey bastions of the castle; beyond them, in the midst of the broad stream, stands a huge mill that looks like another castle; further yet is the handsome new Wellesley Bridge, with some little craft upon the river, and the red warehouses of the New Town looking prosperous enough. The Irish Town stretches away to the right; there are pretty villas beyond it; and on the bridge are walking twenty-four young girls, in parties of four and five, with their arms round each other's waists, swaying to and fro, and singing or chattering, as happy as if they had shoes to their feet. Yonder you see a dozen pair of red legs glittering in the water, their owners being employed in washing their own or other people's rags.

The Guide-book mentions that one of the aboriginal forests of the country is to be seen at a few miles from Limerick, and thinking that an aboriginal forest would be a huge discovery, and form an instructive and delightful feature of the present work, I hired a car in order to visit the same, and pleased myself with visions of gigantic oaks, Druids, Norma, wildernesses and awful gloom, which would fill the soul with horror. The romance of the place was heightened by a fact stated by the carman, viz., that until late years robberies were very frequent about the wood; the inhabitants of the district being a wild lawless race. Moreover, there are numerous castles round about,—and for what can a man wish more than robbers, castles, and an aboriginal wood?

The way to these wonderful sights lies through the undulating grounds which border the Shannon; and though the view is by no means a fine one, I know few that are pleasanter than the sight of these rich, golden, peaceful plains, with the full harvest waving on them and just ready for the sickle. The hay harvest was likewise just being concluded, and the air loaded with the rich odour of the hay. Above the trees, to your left, you saw the mast of a ship, perhaps moving along, and every now and then caught a glimpse of the Shannon, and the low grounds and plantations of the opposite county of Limerick. Not an unpleasant addition to the landscape, too, was a sight which I do not remember to have witnessed often in this country—that of several small and decent farmhouses, with their stacks and sheds and stables, giving an air of neatness and plenty that the poor cabin with its potato-patch does not present. Is it on account of the small farms that the land seems richer and better cultivated here than in most other parts of the country? Some of the houses in the midst of the warm summer landscape had a strange appearance, for it is often the fashion to whitewash the roofs of the houses, leaving the slates of the walls of their natural colour: hence, and in the evening especially, contrasting with the purple sky, the house-tops often looked as if they were covered with snow.

According to the Guide-book's promise, the castles began soon to appear; at one point we could see three of these ancient mansions in a line, each seemingly with its little grove of old trees, in the midst of the bare but fertile country. By this time,.too, we had got into a road so abominably bad and rocky, that I began to believe more and more with regard to the splendour of the aboriginal forest, which must be most aboriginal and ferocious indeed when approached by such a savage path. After travelling through a couple of lines of wall with plantations on either side, I at length became impatient as to the forest, and, much to my disappointment, was told this was it. For the fact is, that though the forest has always been there, the trees have not, the proprietors cutting them regularly when grown to no great height, and the monarchs of the woods which I saw round about would scarcely have afforded timber for a bed-post. Nor did any robbers make their appearance in this wilderness: with which disappointment, however, I was more willing to put up than with the former one.

But if the wood and the robbers did not come up to my romantic notions, the old Castle of Bunratty fully answered them, and indeed should be made the scene of a romance, in three volumes at least.

'It is a huge, square tower, with four smaller ones at each angle; and you mount to the entrance by a steep flight of steps, being commanded all the way by the crossbows of two of the Lord De Clare's retainers, the points of whose weapons may be seen lying upon the ledge of the little narrow *meurtrière* on each side of the gate. A venerable seneschal, with the keys of office, presently opens the little back postern, and you are admitted to the great hall—a noble chamber, *pardi*! some seventy feet in length and thirty high. 'Tis hung round with a thousand trophies of war and chase,—the golden helmet and spear of the Irish king, the long yellow mantle he wore, and the huge brooch that bound it. Hugo De Clare slew him before the castle in 1305, when he and his kernes attacked it. Less successful in 1314, the gallant Hugo saw his village of Bunratty burned round his tower by the son of the slaughtered O'Neil; and, sallying out to avenge the insult, was brought back—a corpse! Ah! what was the pang that shot through the fair bosom of the *Lady Adela* when she knew that 'twas the hand of *Redmond O'Neil* sped the shaft which slew her sire!

'You listen to this sad story, reposing on an oaken settle (covered with deer's-skin taken in the aboriginal forest of Carclow hard by) and placed at the enormous hall-fire. Here sits Thonom an Diaoul, "Dark Thomas," the blind harper of the race of De Clare, who loves to tell the deeds of the lordly family. "Penetrating in disguise," he continues, "into the castle, Redmond of the golden locks sought an interview with the

Lily of Bunratty; but she screamed when she saw him under the disguise of the gleeman, and said, 'My father's blood is in the hall!' At this, up started fierce Sir Ranulph. 'Ho, Bludyer!' he cried to his squire, 'call me the hangman and Father John; seize me, vassals, yon villain in gleeman's guise, and hang him on the gallows on the tower!'"

'"Will it please ye walk to the roof of the old castle and see the beam on which the lords of the place execute the refractory?" "Nay, marry," say you, "by my spurs of knighthood, I have seen hanging enough in merry England, and care not to see the gibbets of Irish kernes." The harper would have taken fire at this speech reflecting on his country; but luckily here G—ulph, your English squire, entered from the pantler (with whom he had been holding a parley), and brought a manchet of bread, and bade ye, in the Lord De Clare's name, crush a cup of Ypocras, well spiced, *pardi,* and by the fair hands of the Lady Adela.

'"The Lady Adela!" say you, starting up in amaze. "Is not this the year of grace 1600, and lived she not three hundred years syne?"

'"Yes, Sir Knight, but Bunratty tower hath *another Lily*: will it please you see your chamber?"

'So saying, the seneschal leads you up a winding stair in one of the turrets, past one little dark chamber and another, without a fireplace, without rushes (how different from the stately houses of Nonsuch or Audley End!), and, leading you through another vast chamber above the baronial hall, similar in size, but decorated with tapestries and rude carvings, you pass the little chapel ("Marry," says the steward, "many would it not hold, and many do not come!") until at last you are located in the little cell appropriated to you. Some rude attempts have been made to render it fitting for the stranger; but, though more neatly arranged than the hundred other little chambers which the castle contains, in sooth 'tis scarce fitted for the serving-man, much more for Sir Reginald, the English knight.

'While you are looking at a bouquet of flowers, which lies on the settle—magnolias, geraniums, the blue flowers of the cactus, and in the midst of the bouquet, *one lily*; whilst you wonder whose fair hands could have culled the flowers—hark! the horns are blowing at the drawbridge and the warder lets the portcullis down. You rush to your window, a stalwart knight rides over the gate, the hoofs of his black courser clanging upon the planks. A host of wild retainers wait round about him: see, four of them carry a stag, that hath been slain no doubt in the aboriginal forest of Carclow. "By my fay!" say you, "'tis a stag of ten."

'But who is that yonder on the grey palfrey, conversing so prettily, and holding the sportive animal with so light a rein?—a light green riding-habit and ruff, a little hat with a green plume—sure it must be a lady, and a fair one. She looks up. O blessed Mother of Heaven, that look! those eyes that smile, those sunny golden ringlets! It is —*it is* the Lady Adela: the Lily of Bunrat—'

If the reader cannot finish the other two volumes for him or herself, he or she never deserves to have a novel from a circulating library again: for my part, I will take my affidavit the English knight will marry the Lily at the end of the third volume, having previously slain the other suitor at one of the multifarious sieges of Limerick. And I beg to say that the historical part of this romance has been extracted carefully from the Guide-book: the topographical and descriptive portion being studied on the spot. A policeman shows you over it, halls, chapels, galleries, gibbets and all. The huge old tower was, until late years, inhabited by the family of the proprietor, who built himself a house in the midst of it: but he has since built another in the park opposite, and half-a-dozen 'Peelers,' with a commodity of wives and children, now inhabit Bunratty. On the gate where we entered were numerous placards offering rewards for the apprehension of various country offenders; and a turnpike, a bridge, and a quay have sprung up from the place which Red Redmond (or anybody else) burned.

* * * * *

On our road to Galway the next day, we were carried once more by the old tower, and for a considerable distance along the fertile banks of the Fergus lake, and a river which pours itself into the Shannon. The first town we come to is Castle Clare, which lies conveniently on the river, with a castle, a good bridge, and many quays and warehouses, near which a small ship or two were lying. The place was once the chief town of the county, but is wretched and ruinous now, being made up for the most part of miserable thatched cots, round which you see the usual dusky population. The drive hence to Ennis lies through a country which is by no means so pleasant as that rich one we have passed through, being succeeded 'by that craggy, bleak, pastoral district which occupies so large a portion of the limestone district of Clare.' Ennis, likewise, stands upon the Fergus—a busy little narrow-streeted, foreign-looking town, approached by half-a-mile of thatched cots, in which I am not ashamed to confess that I saw some as pretty faces as over any half-mile of country I ever travelled in my life.

A great light of the Catholic Church, who was of late a candlestick in our own communion, was on the coach with us, reading devoutly out of a breviary on many occasions along the road. A crowd of black coats and heads, with that indescribable look which belongs to the Catholic clergy, were evidently on the look-out for the coach; and as it stopped, one of them came up to me with a low bow, and asked if I was the Honourable and Reverend Mr. S—? How I wish I had answered him I was! It would have been a grand scene. The respect paid to this gentleman's descent is quite absurd: the papers bandy his title about with pleased emphasis—the Galway paper calls him the *very* reverend. There is something in the love for rank almost childish: witness the adoration of George IV.; the pompous joy with which John Tuam records his correspondence with a great man; the continual My-Lording of the Bishops, the Right-Honourabling of Mr. O'Connell— which title his party papers delight on all occasions to give him—nay, the delight of that great man himself when first he attained the dignity: he figured in his robes in the most good-humoured simple delight at having them, and went to church forthwith in them. As if such a man wanted a title before his name!

At Ennis, as well as everywhere else in Ireland, there were of course the regular number of swaggering-looking buckeens and shabby-genteel idlers to watch the arrival of the mail-coach. A poor old idiot, with his grey hair tied up in bows, and with a ribbon behind, thrust out a very fair soft hand with taper fingers, and told me, nodding his head very wistfully, that he had no father nor mother: upon which score he got a penny. Nor did the other beggars round the carriage who got none seem to grudge the poor fellow's good fortune. I think when one poor wretch has a piece of luck, the others seem glad here: and they promise to pray for you just the same if you give as if you refuse.

The town was swarming with people: the little dark streets, which twist about in all directions, being full of cheap merchandise and its vendors. Whether there are many buyers, I can't say. This is written opposite the market-place in Galway, where I have watched a stall a hundred times in the course of the last three hours and seen no money taken: but at every place I come to, I can't help wondering at the numbers; it seems market-day everywhere—apples, pigs, and potatoes being sold all over the kingdom. There seem to be some good shops in those narrow streets: among others, a decent little library, where I bought, for eighteenpence, six volumes of works strictly Irish, that will serve for a half-hour's gossip on the next rainy day.

The road hence to Gort carried us at first by some dismal, lonely-looking, reedy lakes, through a melancholy country; an open village standing here and there, with a big chapel in the midst of it, almost always unfinished in some point or other. Crossing at a bridge near a place called Tubbor, the coachman told us we were in the famous county of Galway, which all readers of novels admire in the warlike works of Maxwell and Lever; and, dismal as the country had been in Clare, I think on the northern side of the bridge it was dismaller still— the stones not only appearing in the character of hedges, but strewing over whole fields, in which sheep were browsing as well as they could.

We rode for miles through this stony dismal district, seeing more lakes now and anon, with fellows spearing eels in the midst. Then we passed the plantations of Lord Gort's Castle of Loughcooter, and presently came to the town which bears his name, or *vice versâ*. It is a regularly built little place, with a square and street: but it looked as if it wondered how the deuce it got into the midst of such a desolate country, and seemed to *bore* itself there considerably. It had nothing to do, and no society.

A short time before arriving at Oranmore, one has glimpses of the sea, which comes opportunely to relieve the dulness of the land. Between Gort and that place we passed through little bat the most woeful country, in the midst of which was a village, where a horse-fair was held, and where (upon the word of the coachman) all the bad horses of the country were to be seen. The man was commissioned, no doubt, to buy for his employers, for two or three merchants were on the look-out for him, and trotted out their cattle by the side of the coach. A very good, neat-looking, smart-trotting chestnut horse, of seven years old, was offered by the owner for £8; a neat brown mare for £10, and a better (as I presume) for £14; but all *looked* very respectable, and I have the coachman's word for it that they were good serviceable horses. Oranmore, with an old castle in the midst of the village, woods, and park plantations round about, and the bay beyond it, has a pretty and romantic look; and the drive of about four miles thence to Galway is the most picturesque part perhaps of the fifty miles' ride from Limerick. The road is tolerably wooded. You see the town itself, with its huge old church-tower, stretching along the bay, 'backed by hills linking into the long chain of mountains which stretch across Connemara and the Joyce country.' A suburb of cots that seems almost endless has, however, an end at last among the houses of the town: and a little fleet of a couple of hundred fishing-boats was manoeuvring in the bright waters of the bay.

CHAPTER XV: GALWAY—KILROY'S HOTEL—GALWAY NIGHTS' ENTERTAINMENTS—FIRST NIGHT: AN EVENING WITH CAPTAIN FREENY

WHEN it is stated that, throughout the town of Galway, you cannot get a cigar which costs more than twopence, Londoners may imagine the strangeness and remoteness of the place. The rain poured down for two days after our arrival at Kilroy's Hotel. An umbrella under such circumstances is a poor resource: self-contemplation is far more amusing; especially smoking, and a game at cards, if any one wIll be so good as to play.

But there was no one in the hotel coffee-room who was inclined for the sport. The company there, on the day of our arrival, consisted of two coach-passengers,—a Frenchman who came from Sligo, and ordered mutton-chops and *fraid potatoes* for dinner by himself; a turbot which cost two shillings, and in Billingsgate would have been worth a guinea; and a couple of native or inhabitant bachelors who frequented the *table d'hôte.*

By the way, besides these there were at dinner two turkeys (so that Mr. Kilroy's two-shilling ordinary was by no means ill supplied); and, as a stranger, I had the honour of carving these animals, which were dispensed in rather a singular way. There are, as it is generally known, to two turkeys four wings. Of the four passengers, one ate no turkey, one had a pinion, another the remaining part of the wing, and the fourth gentleman took the other three wings for his share. Does everybody in Galway eat three wings when there are two turkeys for dinner? One has heard wonders of the country,—the dashing, daring, duelling, desperate, rollicking, whisky-drinking people: but this wonder beats all. When I asked the Galway turkiphagus (there is no other word, for Turkey was invented long after Greece) 'if he would take a third wing?' with a peculiar satiric accent on the words *third wing,* which cannot be expressed in writing, but which the occasion fully merited, I thought perhaps that, following the custom of the country, where everybody, according to Maxwell and Lever, challenges everybody else,—I thought the Galwagian would call me out; but no such thing. He only said, 'If you plase, sir,' in the blandest way in the world; and gobbled up the limb in a twinkling.

As an encouragement, too, for persons meditating that important change of condition, the gentleman was a teetotaller: he took but one glass of water to that intolerable deal of bubblyjock. Galway must be very much changed since the days when Maxwell and Lever knew it. Three turkey-wings and a glass of water! But the man cannot be the representative of a class, that is clear: it is physically and arithmetically impossible. They can't *all* eat three wings of two turkeys at dinner: the turkeys could not stand it, let alone the men. These wings must have been 'non usitafce (nee tenues) penna.' But no more of these flights; let us come to sober realities.

The fact is, that when the rain is pouring down in the streets the traveller has little else to remark except these peculiarities of his fellow-travellers and inn-sojournera; and, lest one should be led into further personalities, it is best to quit that water-drinking gormandizer at once, and retiring to a private apartment, to devote one's self to quiet observation and the acquisition of knowledge, either by looking out of the window and examining mankind, or by perusing books, and so living with past heroes and ages.

As for the knowledge to be had by looking out of window, it is this evening not much. A great, wide, blank, bleak, water-whipped square lies before the bedroom window; at the opposite side of which is to be seen the opposition hotel, looking even more bleak and cheerless than that over which Mr. Kilroy presides. Large dismal warehouses and private houses form three sides of the square; and in the midst is a hare pleasure-ground surrounded by a growth of gaunt iron railings, the only plants seemingly in the place. Three triangular edifices that look somewhat like gibbets stand in the paved part of the square, but the victims that are consigned to their fate under these triangles are only potatoes, which are weighed there; and, in spite of the torrents of rain, a crowd of barefooted red-petticoated women, and men in grey coats and flower-pot hats, are pursuing their little bargains with the utmost calmness. The rain seems to make no impression on the males; nor do the women guard against it more than by flinging a petticoat over their heads, and so stand bargaining and chattering in Irish, their figures indefinitely reflected in the shining, varnished pavement. Donkeys and pony-carts innumerable stand around, similarly reflected; and in the baskets upon these vehicles you see shoals of herrings lying. After a short space this prospect becomes somewhat tedious, and one looks to other sources of consolation.

The eighteenpennyworth of little books purchased at Ennis in the morning came here most agreeably to my aid; and indeed they afford many a pleasant hour's reading. Like the 'Bibliotheque Grise,' which one sees in the French cottages in the provinces, and the German 'Volksbücher,' both of which contain stores of old legends that are still treasured in the country, these yellow-covered books are prepared for the people chiefly; and have been sold for many long years before the march of knowledge began to banish Fancy out of the world, and gave us, in place of the old fairy tales, Penny Magazines and similar wholesome works. Where are the little harlequin-backed story-books that used to be read by children in England some thirty years ago? Where such authentic narratives as 'Captain Bruce's Travels,' 'The Dreadful Adventures of Sawney Bean,' etc., which were commonly supplied to little boys at school by the same old lady who sold oranges and alicompayne?—they are all gone out of the world, and replaced by such books as 'Conversations on Chemistry,' 'The Little Geologist,' 'Peter Parley's Tales about the Binomial Theorem,' and the like. The world will be a dull world some hundreds of years hence, when Fancy shall be dead, and ruthless Science (that has no more bowels than a steam-engine) has killed her.

It is a comfort, meanwhile, to come on occasions on some of the good old stories and biographies. These books were evidently written before the useful had attained its present detestable popularity. There is nothing useful *here,* that's certain: and a man will be puzzled to extract a precise moral out of the 'Adventures of Mr. James Freeny'; or out of the legends in the 'Hibernian Tales'; or out of the lamentable tragedy of the 'Battle of Aughrim,' writ in most doleful Anglo-Irish verse. But are we to reject all things that have not a moral tacked to them? 'Is there any moral shut within the bosom of the rose?' And yet, as the same noble poet sings (giving a smart slap to the utility people the while), 'useful applications lie in art and nature,' and every man may find a moral suited to his mind in them; or, if not a moral, an occasion for moralising.

Honest Freeny's adventures (let us begin with history and historic tragedy, and leave fancy for future consideration), if they have a moral, have that dubious one which the poet admits may be elicited from a rose; and which every man may select according to his mind. And surely this is a far better and more comfortable system of moralising than that in the fable-books, where you are obliged to accept the story with the inevitable moral corollary that *will* stick close to it.

Whereas, in Freeny's life, one man may see the evil of drinking, another the harm of horse-racing, another the danger attendant on early marriage, a fourth the exceeding inconvenience as well as hazard of the heroic highwayman's life—which a certain Ainsworth, in company with a certain Cruikshank, has represented as so poetic and brilliant, so prodigal of delightful adventure, so adorned with champagne, gold lace, and brocade.

And the best part of worthy Freeny's tale is the noble *naiveté* and simplicity of the hero as he recounts his own adventures, and the utter unconsciousness that he is narrating anything wonderful. It is the way of all great men, who recite their great actions modestly, and as if they were matters of course; as indeed to them they are. A common tyro, having perpetrated a great deed, would be amazed and flurried at his own action; whereas I make no doubt the Duke of Wellington, after a great victory, took his tea and went to bed just as quietly as he would after a dull debate in the House of Lords. And so with Freeny,—his great and charming characteristic is grave simplicity: he does his work; he knows his danger as well as another; but he goes through his fearful duty quite quietly and easily, and not with the least air of bravado, or the smallest notion that he is doing anything uncommon.

It is related of Carter, the Lion-King, that when he was a boy, and exceedingly fond of gingerbread-nuts, a relation gave him a parcel of those delicious cakes, which the child put in his pocket just as he was called on to go into a cage with a very large and roaring lion. He had to put his head into the forest-monarch's jaws, and leave it there for a considerable time, to the delight of thousands: as is even now the case; and the interest was so much the greater, as the child was exceedingly innocent, rosy-cheeked, and pretty. To have seen that little flaxen head bitten off by the lion would have been a far more pathetic spectacle than that of the decapitation of some grey-bearded old unromantic keeper, who had served out raw meat and stirred up the animals with a pole any time these twenty years: and the interest rose in consequence.

While the little darling's head was thus enjawed, what was the astonishment of everybody to see him put his hand into his little pocket, take out a paper—from the paper a gingerbread-nut—pop that gingerbread-nut into the lion's mouth, then into his own, and so finish at least twopennyworth of nuts!

The excitement was delirious: the ladies, when he came out of chancery, were for doing what the lion had not done, and eating him up—with kisses. And the only remark the young hero made was, 'Uncle, them nuts wasn't so crisp as them I had t'other day.' He never thought of the danger,—he only thought of the nuts.

Thus it is with Feeeny. It is fine to mark his bravery, and to see how he cracks his simple philosophic nuts in the jaws of innumerable lions.

At the commencement of the last century, honest Freeny's father was house-steward in the family of Joseph Robbins, Esq., of Ballyduff; and, marrying Alice Phelan, a maid-servant in the same family, had issue James, the celebrated Irish hero. At a proper age James was put to school; but being a nimble active lad, and his father's mistress taking a fancy to him, he was presently brought to Ballyduff, where she had a private tutor to instruct him during the time which he could spare from his professional duty, which was that of pantry-boy in Mr. Robbins's establishment. At an early age he began to neglect his duty; and although his father, at the excellent Mrs. Robbins's suggestion, corrected him very severely, the bent of his genius was not to be warped by the rod, and he attended 'all the little country dances, diversions, and meetings, and became what is called a good dancer; his own natural inclinations hurrying him' (as he finely says) 'into the contrary diversions.'

He was scarce twenty years old when he married (a frightful proof of the wicked recklessness of his former courses), and set up in trade in Waterford; where, however, matters went so ill with him, that he was speedily without money, and £50 in debt. He had, he says, not any way of paying the debt, except by selling his furniture or his *riding-mare*, to both of which measures he was averse: for where is the gentleman in Ireland that can do without a horse to ride? Mr. Freeny and his riding-mare became soon famous, insomuch that a thief in gaol warned the magistrates of Kilkenny to beware of a one-eyed man with a *mare.*

These unhappy circumstances sent him on the highway to seek a maintenance, and his first exploit was to rob a gentleman of £50; then to attack another, against whom he 'had *a secret disgust,* because this gentleman had prevented his former master from giving him a suit of clothes!'

Urged by a noble resentment against this gentleman, Mr. Freeny, in company with a friend by the name of Reddy, robbed the gentleman's house, taking therein £70 in money, which was honourably divided among the captors.

'We then,' continues Mr. Freeny, 'quitted the house with the booty, and came to Thomastown; but not knowing how to dispose of the plate, left it with Reddy, who said he had a friend from whom he would get cash for it. In some time afterwards I asked him for the dividend of the cash he got for the plate, but all the satisfaction he gave me was, that it was lost, which occasioned me *to have my own opinion of him*.'

Mr. Freeny then robbed Sir William Fownes's servant of £14, in such an artful manner that everybody believed the servant had himself secreted the money; and no doubt the rascal was turned adrift, and starved in consequence—a truly comic incident, and one that could be used, so as to provoke a great deal of laughter, in an historical work of which our champion should be the hero.

The next enterprise of importance is that against the house of Colonel Palliser, which Freeny thus picturesquely describes. Coming with one of his spies close up to the house, Mr. Freeny watched the Colonel lighted to bed by a servant; and thus, as he cleverly says, could judge ' of the room the Colonel lay in.'

'Some time afterwards,' says Freeny, 'I observed a light up-stairs, by which I judged the servants were going to bed, and soon after observed that the candles were all quenched, by which I assured myself they were all gone to bed. I then came back to where the men were, and appointed Bulger, Motley, and Commons to go in along with me; but Commons answered that he never had been in any house before where there were arms: upon which I asked the coward what business he had there, and swore I would as soon shoot him as look at him, and at the same time cocked a pistol to his breast; but the rest of the men prevailed upon me to leave him at the back of the house, where he might run away when he thought proper.

'I then asked Grace where did he choose to be posted: he answered "that he would go where I pleased to order him," for which I thanked him. We then immediately came up to the house, lighted our candles, put Houlahan at the back of the house to prevent any person from coming out that way, and placed Hacket on my mare, well armed, at the front; and I then broke one of the windows with a sledge, whereupon Bulger, Motley, Grace, and I got in; upon which I ordered Motley and Grace to go upstairs, and Bulger and I would stay below, where we thought the greatest danger would be; but I immediately, upon second consideration, for fear Motley or Grace should be daunted, desired Bulger to go up with them, and when he had fixed matters above, to come down, as I judged the Colonel lay below. I then went to the room where the Colonel was, and burst open the door; upon which he said, "Odds-wounds! who's there?" to which I answered, "A friend, sir;" upon which he said, "You lie! by G—d, you are no friend of mine!" I then said that I was, and his relation also, and that if he viewed me close he would know me, and begged of him not to be angry; upon which I immediately seized a bullet-gun and case of pistols, which I observed hanging up in his room; I then quitted his room, and walked round the lower part of the house, thinking to meet some of the servants, *whom* I thought would strive to make their escape from the men who were above, and meeting none of them, I immediately returned to the Colonel's room; where I no sooner entered than he desired me to go out for a villain, and asked why I bred such disturbance in his house at that time of night. At the same time I snatched his breeches from under his head, wherein I got a small purse of gold, and said that abuse was not fit treatment for me who was his relation, and that it would hinder me of calling to see him again. I then demanded the key of his desk which stood in his room; he answered he had no key; upon which I said I had a very good key; at the same time giving it a stroke with the sledge, which burst it open, wherein I got a purse of ninety guineas, a four-pound piece, two moidores, some small gold, and a large glove with twenty-eight guineas in silver.

'By this time Bulger and Motley came downstairs to me, after rifling the house above. We then observed a closet inside his room, which we soon entered, and got therein a basket wherein there was plate to the value of three hundred pounds.'

And so they took leave of Colonel Palliser, and rode away with their earnings.

The story, as here narrated, has that simplicity which is beyond the reach of all except the very highest art; and it is not high art certainly which Mr. Freeny can be said to possess, but a noble nature rather, which leads him thus grandly to describe scenes wherein he acted a great part. With what a gallant determination does he inform the coward Commons that he would shoot him *'as soon as look at him';* and how dreadful he must have looked (with his one eye) as he uttered that sentiment! But he left him, he says, with a grim humour, at the back of the house, 'where he might run away when he thought proper.' The Duke of Wellington must have read Mr. Freeny's history in his youth (his Grace's birthplace is not far from the scene of the other gallant Irishman's exploit), for the Duke acted in precisely a similar way by a Belgian Colonel at Waterloo.

It must be painful to great and successful commanders to think how their gallant comrades and lieutenants, partners of their toil, their feelings, and their fame, are separated from them by time, by death, by estrangement—nay, sometimes by treason. Commons is off, disappearing noiseless into the deep night, whilst his comrades perform the work of danger; and Bulger,—Bulges, who in the above scene acts so gallant a part, and in whom Mr. Freeny places so much confidence— actually went away to England, carrying off 'some plate, some shirts, a gold watch, and a diamond ring' of the Captain's; and, though he returned to his native country, the valuables did not return with him, on which the Captain swore he would blow his brains out. As for poor Grace, he was hanged, much to his leader's sorrow, who says of him that he was 'the faithfullest of his spies.' Motley was sent to Naas gaol for the very robbery: and though Captain Freeny does not mention his ultimate fate, 'tis probable he was hanged too. Indeed, the warrior's life is a hard one, and over misfortunes like these the feeling heart cannot but sigh.

But, putting out of the question the conduct and fate of the Captain's associates, let us look to his own behaviour as a leader. It is impossible not to admire his serenity, his dexterity, that dashing impetuosity in the moment of action, and that aquiline *coup d'œil* which belongs to but few generals. He it is who leads the assault, smashing in the window with a sledge; he bursts open the Colonel's door, who says (naturally enough), 'Odds-wounds! who's there'? 'A friend, sir,' says Freeny. 'You lie! by G—d, you are no friend of mine!' roars the military blasphemer. 'I then said that I was, *and his relation also*, and that if he viewed me close he would know me, and begged of him not to be angry: *upon which I immediately seized* a brace of pistols which I observed hanging up in his room.' That is something like presence of mind: none of your brutal braggadocio work, but neat, wary—nay, sportive bearing in the face of danger. And again, on the second visit to the Colonel's room, when the latter bids him 'go out for a villain, and not breed a disturbance,' what reply makes Freeny? '*At the same time I snatched his breeches* from under his head.' A common man would never have thought of looking for them in such a place at all. The difficulty about the key he resolves in quite an Alexandrian manner; and, from the specimen we already have had of the Colonel's style of speaking, we may fancy how ferociously he lay in bed and swore, after Captain Freeny and his friends had disappeared with the ninety guineas, the moidores, the four-pound piece, and the glove with twenty-eight guineas in silver.

As for the plate, he hid it in a wood; and then, being out of danger, he sat down and paid everybody his deserts. By the way, what a strange difference of opinion is there about a man's *deserts*! Here sits Captain Freeny with a company of gentlemen, and awards them a handsome sum of money for an action which other people would have remunerated with a halter. Which are right? perhaps both: but at any rate it will be admitted that the Captain takes the humane view of the question.

The greatest enemy Captain Freeny had was Counsellor Bobbins, a son of his old patron, and one of the most determined thief-pursuers the country ever knew. But though he was untiring in his efforts to capture (and of course to hang) Mr. Freeny, and though the latter was strongly urged by his friends to blow the Counsellor's brains out: yet, to his immortal honour be it said, he refused that temptation, agreeable as it was, declaring that he had eaten too much of that family's bread ever to take the life of one of them, and being besides quite aware that the Counsellor was only acting against him in a public capacity. He respected him, in fact, like an honourable though terrible adversary.

How deep a stratagem-inventor the Counsellor was, may be gathered from the following narration of one of his plans:—

'Counsellor Robbins finding his brother had not got intelligence that was sufficient to carry any reasonable foundation for apprehending us, walked out as if merely for exercise, till he met with a person whom he thought he could confide in, and desired the person to meet him at a private place appointed for that purpose, which they did;

and he told that person he had a very good opinion of him, from the character received from his father of him, and from his own knowledge of him, and hoped that the person would then show him that such opinion was not ill founded. The person assuring the Counsellor he would do all in his power to serve and oblige him, the Counsellor told him how greatly he was concerned to hear the scandalous character that part of the country (which had formerly been an honest one) had lately fallen into; that it was said that a gang of robbers who disturbed the country lived thereabouts. The person told him he was afraid what he said was too true; and, on being asked whom he suspected, he named the same four persons Mr. Robbins had, but said he dare not, for fear of being murdered, be too inquisitive, and therefore could not say anything material. The Counsellor asked him if he knew where there was any private ale to be sold; and he said Moll Burke, who lived near the end of Mr. Robbins's avenue, had a barrel or half a barrel. The Counsellor then gave the person a moidore, and desired him to go to Thomastown and buy two or three gallons of whisky, and bring it to Moll Burke's, and invite as many as he suspected to be either principals or accessories to take a drink, and make them drink very heartily, and when he found they were fuddled, and not sooner, to tell some of the hastiest that some other had said some bad things of them, so as to provoke them to abuse and quarrel with each other; and then, probably, in their liquor and passion, they might make some discoveries of each other, as may enable the Counsellor to get some one of the gang to discover and accuse the rest.

'nThe person accordingly got the whisky and invited a good many to drink; but the Counsellor being then at his brother's, a few only went to Moll Burke's, the rest being afraid to venture while the Counsellor was in the neighbourhood: among those who met there was one Moll Brophy, the wife of Mr. Robbins's smith, and one Edmund or Edward Stapleton, otherwise Gaul, who lived thereabouts; and when they had drunk plentifully, the Counsellor's spy told Moll Brophy that Gaul had said she had gone astray with some persons or other: she then abused Gaul, and told him he was one of Freeny's accomplices, for that he, Gaul, had told her he had seen Colonel Palliser's watch with Freeny, and that Freeny had told him, Gaul, that John Welsh and the two Graces had been with him at the robbery.

'The company on their quarrel broke up, and the next morning the spy met the Counsellor at the place appointed, at a distance from Mr. Robbins's house, to prevent suspicion, and there told the Counsellor what intelligence he had got. The Counsellor not being then a justice of the peace, got his brother to send for Moll Brophy to be examined; but when she came, she refused to be sworn or to give any evidence, and thereupon the Counsellor had her tied and put on a car in order to be carried to gaol on a mittimus from Mr. Robbins's, for refusing to give evidence on behalf of the Crown. When she found she would really be sent to gaol, she submitted to be sworn, and the Counsellor drew from her what she had said the night before, and something further, and desired her not to tell anybody what she had sworn.'

But if the Counsellor was acute, were there not others as clever as he? For when, in consequence of the information of Mrs. Brophy, some gentlemen who had been engaged in the burglarious enterprises in which Mr. Freeny obtained so much honour were seized and tried, Freeny came forward with the best of arguments in their favour. Indeed, it is fine to see these two great spirits matched one against the other, —the Counsellor, with all the regular force of the country to back him; the Highway General, with but the wild resources of his gallant genius, and with cunning and bravery for his chief allies.

'I lay by for a considerable time after, and concluded within myself to do no more mischief till after the assizes, when I would hear how it went with the men who were then in confinement. Some time before the assizes Counsellor Bobbins came to Ballyduff, and told his brother that he believed Anderson and Welsh were guilty, and also said he would endeavour to have them both hanged: of which I was informed.

'Soon after, I went to the house of one George Roberts, who asked me if I had any regard for those fellows who were then confined (meaning Anderson and Welsh). I told him I had a regard for one of them: upon which he said he had a friend who was a man of power and interest—that he would save either of them, provided I would give him five guineas. I told him I would give him ten, and the first gold watch I could get; whereupon he said that it was of no use to speak to his friend without the money or value, for that he was a mercenary man: on which I told Roberts I had not so much money at that time, but that I would give him my watch as a pledge to give his friend. I then gave him my watch, and desired him to engage that I would pay the money which I promised to pay, or give value for it in plate, in two or three nights after; upon which, he engaged that his friend would act the needful; when we appointed a night to meet, and we accordingly met; and Roberts told me that his friend agreed to save Anderson and Welsh from the gallows; whereupon I gave him a plate tankard, value £10, a large ladle, value £4, with some table-spoons; and the assizes of Kilkenny, in spring 1748, coming on soon after, Counsellor Robbins had Welsh transmitted from Naas to Kilkenny, in order to give evidence against Anderson and Welsh; and they were tried for Mrs. Mounford's robbery, on the evidence of John Welsh and others. The physic working well, six of the jury were for finding them guilty, and six more for acquitting them; and the other six finding them peremptory, and that they were resolved to starve the others into compliance, as they say they may do by law, were for their own sakes obliged to comply with them, and they were acquitted. On which Counsellor Robbins began to smoke the affair, and suspect the operation of gold dust, which was well applied for my comrades, and thereupon left the court in a rage, and swore he would for ever quit the country, since he found people were not satisfied with protecting and saving the rogues they had under themselves, but must also show that they could and would oblige others to have rogues under them whether they would or no.'

Here Counsellor Robbins certainly loses that greatness which has distinguished him in his former attack on Freeny; the Counsellor is defeated and loses his temper. Like

Napoleon, he is unequal to reverses, but in adverse fortune his presence of mind deserts him.

But what call had he to be in a passion at all? It may be very well for a man to be, in a rage because he is disappointed of his prey: so is the hawk, when the dove escapes, in a rage; but let us reflect that, had Counsellor Robbins had his will, two honest fellows would have been hanged; and so let us be heartily thankful that he was disappointed, and that these men were acquitted by a jury of their countrymen. What right had the Counsellor, forsooth, to interfere with their verdict? Not against Irish juries at least does the old satire apply, 'And culprits hang that jurymen may dine.' At Kilkenny, on the contrary, the jurymen starved in order that the culprits might be saved—a noble and humane act of self-denial.

In another case, stern justice, and the law of self-preservation, compelled Mr. Freeny to take a very different course with respect to one of his ex-associates. In the former instance we have seen him pawning his watch, giving up tankard, tablespoons—all, for his suffering friends; here we have his method of dealing with traitors.

One of his friends, by the name of Dooling, was taken prisoner, and condemned to be hanged, which gave Mr. Freeny, he says, 'a great shock'; but presently this Dooling's fears were worked upon by some traitors within the gaol, and—

'He then consented to discover; but I had a friend in gaol at the same time, one Patrick Healy, who daily insinuated to him that it was of no use or advantage to him to discover anything, as he had received sentence of death; and that, after he had made a discovery, to leave him as he was, without troubling themselves about a reprieve. But notwithstanding, he told the gentlemen that there was a man *blind of an eye who had a bay mare*, that lived at the other side of Thomastown bridge, *whom* he assured them would be very troublesome in that neighbourhood after his death. When Healy discovered what he told the gentlemen, he one night took an opportunity and made Dooling fuddled, and prevailed upon him to take his oath he never would give the least hint about me any more. He also told him the penalty that attended infringing upon his oath—but more especially as he was at that time near his end—which had the desired effect; for he never mentioned my name, nor even anything relative to me,' and so went out of the world repenting of his meditated treason.

What further exploits Mr. Freeny performed may be learned by the curious in his history: they are all, it need scarcely be said, of a similar nature to that noble action which has already been described. His escapes from his enemies were marvellous; his courage in facing them equally great. He is attacked by whole 'armies,' through which he makes his way; wounded, he lies in the woods for days together with three bullets in his leg, and in this condition manages to escape several ' armies' that have been marched against him. He is supposed to be dead, or travelling on the Continent, and suddenly makes his appearance in his old haunts, advertising his arrival by robbing ten men on the highway in a single day. And so terrible is his courage, or so popular his manners, that he describes scores of labourers looking on while his exploits were performed, and not affording the least aid to the roadside traveller whom he vanquished.

But numbers always prevail in the end; what could Leonidas himself do against an army? The gallant band of brothers led by Freeny were so pursued by the indefatigable Bobbins and his myrmidons, that there was no hope left for them, and the Captain saw that he must succumb.

He reasoned, however, with himself (with his usual keen logic), and said:—

'My men must fall,—the world is too strong for us, and to-day, or to-morrow—it matters scarcely when—they must yield. They will be hanged for a certainty, and thus will disappear the noblest company of knights the world has ever seen.

'But as they will certainly be hanged, and no power of mine can save them, is it necessary that I should follow them too to the tree? and will James Bulger's fate be a whit more agreeable to him, because James Freeny dangles at his side? To suppose so, would be to admit that he was actuated by a savage feeling of revenge, which I know belongs not to his generous nature.'

In a word, Mr. Freeny resolved to turn King's evidence; for though he swore (in a communication with the implacable Bobbins) that he would rather die than betray Bulger, yet when the Counsellor stated that he must then die, Freeny says, 'I promised to submit, and *understood that Bulger should be set.'*

Accordingly some days afterwards (although the Captain carefully avoids mentioning that he had met his friend with any such intentions as those indicated in the last paragraph) he and Mr. Bulger came together; and, strangely enough, it was agreed that the one was to sleep while the other kept watch; and, while thus employed, the enemy came upon them. But let Freeny describe for himself the last passages of his history:—

'We then went to Welsh's house, with a view not to make any delay there; but, taking a glass extraordinary after supper, Bulger fell asleep. Welsh, in the meantime, told me his house was the safest place I could get in that neighbourhood, and while I remained there I would be very safe, provided that no person knew of my coming there (I had not acquainted him that Breen knew of my coming that way). I told Welsh that, as Bulger was asleep, I would not go to bed till morning: upon which Welsh and I stayed up all night, and in the morning Welsh said that he and his wife had a call to Callen, it being market-day. About nine o'clock I went and awoke Bulger, desiring him to get up and guard me whilst I slept, as I guarded him all night; he said he would, and then I went to bed charging him to watch close, for fear we should be surprised. I put my blunderbuss and two cases of pistols under my head, and soon fell fast asleep. In two hours after the servant-girl of the house, seeing an enemy coming into the yard, ran up to the room where we were, and said that there were an hundred men coming into the yard; upon which Bulger immediately awoke me, and, taking up my blunderbuss, he fired a shot towards the door, which wounded

Mr. Burgess, one of the sheriffs of Kilkenny, of which wound he died. They concluded to set the house on fire about us, which they accordingly did; upon which I took my fusee in one hand, and a pistol in the other, and Bulger did the like, and as we came out of the door, we fired on both sides, imagining it to be the best method of dispersing the enemy, who were on both sides of the door. We got through them, but they fired after us, and as Bulger was leaping over a ditch he received a shot in the small of the leg, which rendered him incapable of running; but, getting into a field, where I had the ditch between me and the enemy, I still walked slowly with Bulger, till I thought the enemy were within shot of the ditch, and then wheeled back to the ditch and presented my fusee at them. They all drew back and went for their horses to ride round, as the field was wide and open, and without cover except the ditch When I discovered their intention I stood in the middle of the field, and one of the gentlemen's servants (there were fourteen in number) rode foremost towards me; upon which I told the son of a coward I believed he had no more than five pounds a year from his master, and that I would put him in such a condition that his master would not maintain him afterwards. To which he answered that he had no view of doing us any harm, but that he was commanded by his master to ride so near us; and then immediately rode back to the enemy, who were coming towards him. They rode almost within shot of us, and I observed they intended to surround us in the field, and prevent me from having any recourse to the ditch again. Bulger was at this time so bad with the wound, that he could not go one step without leaning on my shoulder. At length, seeing the enemy coming within shot of me, I laid down my fusee and stripped off my coat and waistcoat, and running towards them, cried out, "You sons of cowards, come on, and I will blow your brains, out!" On which they returned back, and then I walked easy to the place where I left my clothes, and put them on, and Bulger and I walked leisurely some distance further. The enemy came a second time, and I occasioned them to draw back as before, and then we walked to Lord Dysart's deer-park wall. I got up the wall and helped Bulger up. The enemy, who still pursued us, though not within shot, seeing us on the wall, one of them fired a random shot at us to no purpose. We got safe over the wall, and went from thence into my Lord Dysart's wood, where Bulger said he would remain, thinking it a safe place; but I told him he would be safer anywhere else, for the army of Kilkenny and Callen would be soon about the wood, and that he would be taken if he stayed there. Besides, as I was very averse to betraying him at all, I could not bear the thoughts of his being taken in my company by any party but Lord Carrick's. I then brought him about half a mile beyond the wood, and left him there in a brake of briars, and looking towards the wood I saw it surrounded by the army. There was a cabin near that place where I fixed Bulger: he said he would go to it at night, and he would send for some of his friends to take care of him. It was then almost two o'clock, and we were four hours going to that place, which was about two miles from Welsh's house. Imagining that there were spies fixed on all the fords and by-roads between that place and the mountain, I went towards the bounds of the county Tipperary, where I arrived about nightfall, and going to a cabin, I asked whether there was any drink sold near that place? The man of the house said there was not; and as I was very much fatigued, I sat down, and there refreshed myself with what the cabin afforded. I then begged of the man to sell me a pair of his brogues and stockings, as I was then barefooted, which he accordingly did. I quitted the house, went through Kinsheenah and Poulacoppal, and having so many thorns in my feet, I was obliged to go barefooted, and went to Sleedelagh, and through the mountains, till I came within four miles of Waterford, and going into a cabin, the man of the house took eighteen thorns out of the soles of my feet, and I remained in and about that place for some time after.

'In the meantime a friend of mine was told that it was impossible for me to escape death, for Bulger had turned against me, and that his friends and Stack were resolved upon my life; but the person who told my friend so, also said, that if my friend would set Bulger and Breen, I might get a pardon through the Earl of Carrick's means and Counsellor Robbins's interest. My friend said that he *was sure I would not consent to such a thing, but the best way was to do it unknown to me*; and my friend accordingly set Bulger, who was taken by the Earl of Carrick and his party, and Mr Fitzgerald, and six of Counsellor Robbins's soldiers, and committed to Kilkenny gaol. He was three days in gaol before I heard he was taken, being at that time twenty miles distant from the neighbourhood; nor did I hear from him or see him since I left him near Lord Dysart's wood, *till a friend* came and told me it was to preserve my life and to fulfil my articles that Bulger was taken.'

* * * * *

'Finding I was suspected, I withdrew to a neighbouring wood and concealed myself there till night, and then went to Ballyduff to Mr. Fitzgerald and surrendered myself to him, till I could write to my Lord Carrick; which I did immediately, and gave him an account of what I escaped, or that I would have gone to Ballilynch and surrendered myself there to him, and begged his Lordship to send a guard for me to conduct me to his house—which he did, and I remained there for a few days.

'He then sent me to Kilkenny gaol; and at the summer assizes following, James Bulger, Patrick Hacket otherwise Bristeen, Martin Millea, John Stack, Felix Donelly, Edmund Kenny, and James Larrassy were tried, convicted, and executed; and at spring assizes following, George Roberts was tried for receiving Colonel Palliser's gold watch knowing it to be stolen, but was acquitted on account of exceptions taken to my pardon, which prevented my giving evidence. At the following assizes, when I had got a new pardon, Roberts was again tried for receiving the tankard, ladle, and silver spoons from me knowing them to be stolen, and was convicted and executed. At the same assizes, John Reddy, my instructor, and Martin Millea were also tried, convicted, and executed.'

And so they were all hanged: James Bulger, Patrick Hacket or Bristeen, Martin Millea, John Stack and Felix Donelly, and Edmund Kenny and James Larrassy, with Roberts, who received the Colonel's watch, the tankard, ladle, and the silver spoons, were all convicted and all executed. Their names drop naturally into blank verse. It is hard upon poor George Roberts too: for the watch he received was no doubt in the very inexpressibles which the Captain himself took from the Colonel's head.

As for the Captain himself, he says that, on going out of gaol, Counsellor Robbins and Lord Carrick proposed a subscription for him—in which, strangely, the gentlemen of the county would not join, and so that scheme came to nothing; and so he published his memoirs in order to get himself a little money. Many a man has taken up the pen under similar circumstances of necessity.

But what became of Captain Freeny afterwards does not appear. Was he an honest man ever after? Was he hanged for subsequent misdemeanours? It matters little to him now; though, perhaps, one cannot help feeling a little wish that the latter fate may have befallen him.

Whatever his death was, however, the history of his life has been one of the most popular books ever known in this country. It formed the class-book in those rustic universities which are now rapidly disappearing from among the hedges of Ireland. And lest any English reader should, on account of its lowness, quarrel with the introduction here of this strange picture of wild courage and daring, let him be reconciled by the moral at the end, which, in the persons of Bulger and the rest, hangs at the beam before Kilkenny gaol.

CHAPTER XVI: MORE RAIN IN GALWAY—A WALK THERE—AND THE SECOND GALWAY NIGHT'S ENTERTAINMENT

'Seven hills has Rome, seven mouths has Nilus' stream,
    Around the Pole seven burning planets gleam.
Twice equal these is Galway, Connaught's Rome:
    Twice seven illustrious tribes here find their home.[xi]
Twice seven fair towers the city's ramparts guard:
    Each house within is built of marble hard.
With lofty turret flanked, twice seven the gates,
    Through twice seven bridges water permeates.
In the High Church are twice seven altars raised,
    At each a holy saint and patron's praised.
Twice seven the Convents dedicate to Heaven,—
    Seven for the female sex—for Godly fathers seven.'[xii]

HAVING read in Hardiman's History the quaint inscription in Irish Latin, of which the above lines are a version, and looked admiringly at the old plans of Galway which are to be found in the same work, I was in hopes to have seen in the town some considerable remains of its former splendour, in spite of a warning to the contrary which the learned historiographer gives.

The old city certainly has some relics of its former stateliness; and, indeed, is the only town in Ireland I have seen, where an antiquary can find much subject for study, or a lover of the picturesque an occasion for using his pencil. It is a wild, fierce, and most original old town. Joyce's Castle in one of the principal streets, a huge square grey tower, with many carvings and ornaments, is a gallant relic of its old days of prosperity, and gives one an awful idea of the tenements which the other families inhabited, and which are designed in the interesting plate which Mr. Hardiman gives in his work. The Collegiate Church, too, is still extant, without its fourteen altars, and looks to be something between a church and a castle, and as if it should be served by Templars with sword and helmet in place of mitre and crosier. The old houses in the Main Street are like fortresses: the windows look into a court within; there is but a small low door, and a few grim windows peering suspiciously into the street.

Then there is Lombard Street, otherwise called Deadman's Lane, with a raw-head and cross-bones and a 'memento mori' over the door where the dreadful tragedy of the Lynches was acted in 1493. If Galway is the Rome of Connaught, James Lynch Fitzstephen, the Mayor, may be considered as the Lucius Junius Brutus thereof. Lynch had a son who went to Spain as master of one of his father's ships, and being of an extravagant wild turn, there contracted debts, and drew bills, and alarmed his father's correspondent, who sent a clerk and nephew of his own back in young Lynch's ship to Galway to settle accounts. On the fifteenth day, young Lynch threw the Spaniard overboard. Coming back to his own country, he reformed his life a little, and was on the point of marrying one of the Blakes, Burkes, Bodkins, or others, when a seaman who had sailed with him, being on the point of death, confessed the murder in which he had been a participator.

Hereon the father, who was chief magistrate of the town, tried his son, and sentenced him to death; and when the clan Lynch rose in a body to rescue the young man, and avert such a disgrace from their family, it is said that Fitzstephen Lynch hanged the culprit with his own hand. A tragedy called 'The Warden of Galway' has been written on the subject, and was acted a few nights before my arrival.

The waters of Lough Corrib, which 'permeate' under the bridges of the town, go rushing and roaring to the sea with a noise and eagerness only known in Galway; and along the banks you see all sorts of strange figures washing all sorts of wonderful rags, with red petticoats and redder shanks standing in the stream. Pigs are in every street: the whole town shrieks with them. There are numbers of idlers on the bridges, thousands in the streets, humming and swarming in and out of dark old ruinous houses; congregated round numberless apple-stalls, nail-stalls, bottle-stalls, pigsfoot-stalls; in queer old shops, that look to be two centuries old; loitering about warehouses, ruined or not; looking at the washerwomen washing in the river, or at the fish-donkeys, or at the potato-stalls, or at a vessel coming into the quay, or at the boats putting out to sea.

That boat at the quay, by the little old gate, is bound for Arran-more; and one next to it has a freight of passengers for the cliffs of Mohir on the Clare coast; and as a sketch is taken, a hundred of people have stopped in the street to look on; and are buzzing behind in Irish, telling the little boys in that language—who will persist in placing themselves exactly in front of the designer—to get out of his way; which they do for some time; but at length curiosity is so intense that you are entirely hemmed in and the view rendered quite invisible. A sailor's wife Comes up—who speaks English—with a very wistful face, and begins to hint that them black pictures are very bad likenesses, and very dear too for a poor woman, and how much would a painted one cost does his honour think? And she has her husband that is going to sea to the West Indies to-morrow, and she'd give anything to have a picture of him. So I made bold to offer to take his likeness for nothing. But he never came, except one day at dinner, and not at all on the next day, though I stayed on purpose to accommodate him. It is true that it was pouring with rain; and as English waterproof coats are not waterproof in *Ireland*, the traveller who has but one coat must of necessity respect it, and had better stay where he is, unless he prefers to go to bed while he has his clothes dried at the next stage.

The houses in the fashionable street where the club-house stands (a strong building, with an agreeable Old Bailey look) have the appearance of so many little Newgates. The Catholic chapels are numerous, unfinished, and ugly. Great warehouses and mills rise up by the stream, or in the midst of unfinished streets here and there; and handsome convents with their gardens; justice-houses, barracks, and hospitals adorn the large, poor, bustling, rough-and-ready-looking town. A man who sells hunting-whips, gunpowder, guns, fishing-tackle, and brass and iron ware, has a few books on his counter; and a lady in a by-street, who carries on the profession of a milliner, ekes out her stock in a similar way. But- there were no regular book-shops that I saw, and when it came on to rain I had no resource but the hedge-school volumes again. They, like Patrick Spelman's sign, present some very rude flowers of poetry and 'entertainment' of an exceedingly humble sort; but such shelter is not to be despised when no better is to be had; nay, possibly its novelty may be piquant to some readers, as an admirer of Shakespeare will occasionally condescend to listen to Mr. Punch, or an epicure to content himself with a homely dish of beans and bacon.

When Mr. Kilroy's waiter has drawn the window-curtains, brought the hot water for the whisky-negus, and a pipe and a 'screw' of tobacco, and two huge old candlesticks that were plated once, the audience may be said to be assembled, and after a little overture performed! on the pipe, the second night's entertainment begins with the historical tragedy of the 'Battle of Aughrim.'

Though it has found its way to the West of Ireland, the 'Battle of Aughrim' is evidently by a Protestant author, a great enemy of Popery and wooden shoes: both of which principles incarnate in the person of St. Ruth, the French General commanding the troops sent by Louis XIV. to the aid of James II., meet with a woeful downfall at the conclusion of the piece. It must have been written in the reign of Queen Anne, judging from some loyal compliments which are paid to that sovereign in the play; which is also modelled upon 'Cato.'

The 'Battle of Aughrim' is written from beginning to end in decasyllabic verse of the richest sort; and introduces us to the chiefs of William's and James's armies. On the English side we have Baron Ginckle, three Generals, and two Colonels; on the Irish, Monsieur St. Ruth, two Generals, two Colonels, and an English gentleman of fortune, a volunteer, and son of no less a person than Sir Edmonbury Godfrey.

There are two ladies—Jemima, the Irish Colonel Talbot's daughter, in love with Godfrey; and Lucinda, lady of Colonel Herbert, in love with her lord. And the deep nature of the tragedy may be imagined when it is stated that Colonel Talbot is killed, Colonel Herbert is killed, Sir Charles Godfrey is killed, and Jemima commits suicide, as resolved not to survive her adorer. St. Ruth is also killed, and the remaining Irish heroes are taken prisoners or run away. Among the supernumeraries there is likewise a dreadful slaughter.

The author, however, though a Protestant, is an Irishman (there are peculiarities in his pronunciation which belong only to that nation), and as far as courage goes, he allows the two parties to be pretty equal. The scene opens with a martial sound of kettle-drums and trumpets in the Irish camp, near Athlone. That town is besieged by Ginckle, and Monsieur St. Ruth (despising his enemy with a confidence often fatal to Generals) meditates an attack on the besiegers' lines, if, by any chance, the besieged garrison be not in a condition to drive them off. After discoursing on the posture of affairs, and letting General Sarsfield and Colonel O'Neil know his hearty contempt of the English and their General, all parties, after protestations of patriotism, indulge in hopes of the downfall of William. St. Ruth says he will drive the wolves' and lions' cubs away. O'Neil declares he scorns the Revolution, and, like great Cato, smiles at persecution. Sarsfield longs for the day 'when our Monks and Jesuits shall return, and holy incense on our altars burn.' When

'*Enter* a Post.

Post. With important news I from Athlone am sent,
Be pleased to lead me to the General's tent.
Sars. Behold the General there. Your message tell.
St. Ruth. Declare your message. Are our friends all well?
Post. Pardon me, sir, the fatal news I bring
Like vulture's poison every heart shall sting.
Athlone is lost without your timely aid.
At six this morning an assault was made,
When, under shelter of the British cannon,
Their grenadiers in armour took the Shannon,
Led by brave Captain Sandys, who with fame
Plunged to his middle in the rapid stream.
He led them through, and with undaunted ire
He gained the bank in spite of all our fire;
Being bravely followed by his grenadiers
Though bullets flew like hail about their ears,
And by this time they enter uncontrolled.
St. Ruth. Dare all the force of England be so bold
T'attempt to storm so brave a town, when I
With all Hibernia's sons of war am nigh?
Return: and if the Britons dare pursue,
Tell them St. Ruth is near, and that will do.
Post. Your aid would do much better than your name.
St. Ruth. Bear back this answer, friend, from whence you came.
[*Exit* Post.'

The picture of brave Sandys, 'who with fame, plunged to his middle in the rapid strame,' is not a bad image on the part of the Post; and St. Ruth's reply, 'Tell them St. Ruth is near, and *that will do,'* characteristic of the vanity of his nation. But Sarsfield knows Britons better, and pays a merited compliment to their valour:

'*Sars.* Send speedy succours and their fate prevent,

You know not yet what Britons dare attempt.
I know the English fortitude is such,
To boast of nothing, though they hazard much.
No force on earth their fury can repel,
Nor would they fly from all the devils in hell.'

Another officer arrives: Athlone is really taken, St. Ruth gives orders to retreat to Aughrim, and Sarsfield, in a rage, first challenges him, and then vows he will quit the army. 'A *gleam* of horror does my vitals *damp*,' says the Frenchman (in a figure of speech more remarkable for vigour than logic): 'I fear Lord Lucan has forsook the camp!' But not so: after a momentary indignation, Sarsfield returns to his duty, and ere long is reconciled with his vain and vacillating chief.

And now the love-intrigue begins. Godfrey enters, and states Sir Charles Godfrey is his lawful name: he is an Englishman, and was on his way to join Ginckle's camp, when Jemima's beauty overcame him: he asks Colonel Talbot to bestow on him the lady's hand. The Colonel consents, and in Act h., on the plain of Aughrim, at five o'clock in the morning, Jemima enters and proclaims her love. The lovers have an interview, which concludes by a mutual confession of attachment, and Jemima says, 'Here, take my hand. 'Tis true the gift is small, but when I can I'll give you heart and all.' The lines show finely the agitation of the young person. She meant to say, Take *my heart,* but she is longing to be married to him, and the words slip out as it were unawares. Godfrey cries in raptures—

'Thanks to the gods! who such a present gave:
Such radiant graces ne'er could man *receive* (*resave*);
For who on earth has e'er such transports known?
What is the Turkish monarch on his throne,
Hemmed round *with rusty swords* in pompous state?
Amidst his Court no joys can be so great.
Retire with me, my soul, no longer stay
In public view, the General moves this way.'

'Tis, indeed, the General, who, reconciled with Sarsfield, straightway, according to his custom, begins to boast about what he will do:—

'Thrice welcome to my heart, thou best of friends!
The rock on which our holy faith depends!
May this our meeting as a tempest make
The vast foundations of Britannia shake,
Tear up their orange plant, and overwhelm
The strongest bulwarks of the British realm!
Then shall the Dutch and Hanoverian fall,
And James shall ride in triumph to Whitehall,
Then to protect our faith he will maintain
An Inquisition here like that in Spain.

*S*ars. Most bravely urged, my Lord! your skill, I own,
Would be *unparalleled*—had you saved Athlone.'

—'Had you saved Athlonc!' Sarsfield. has him there. And the contest of words might have provoked quarrels still more fatal, but alarms are heard: the battle begins, and St. Ruth (still confident) goes to meet the enemy, exclaiming, 'Athlone was sweet, but Aughrim shall be sour.' The fury of the Irish is redoubled on hearing of Talbot's heroic death. The Colonel's corpse is presently brought in, and to it enters Jemima, who bewails her loss in the following pathetic terms:—

'*Jemima*. Oh!—he is dead!—my soul is all on fire,
Witness ye gods!—he did with fame expire.
For Liberty a sacrifice was made,
And fell, like Pompey, by some *villain's* blade.
There lies a breathless corse, whose soul ne'er knew
A thought but what was always just and true;
Look down from heaven, God of peace and love,
Waft him with triumph to the throne above;
And Oh! ye winged guardians of the skies!
Tune your sweet harps and sing his obsequies!
Good friends, stand off—whilst I embrace the ground
Whereon he lies—and bathe each mortal wound
With brinish tears, that like to torrents run
From these sad eyes. O heavens! I'm undone.
[Falls down on the body.
Enter Sir Charles Godfrey. He raises her.
Sir Char. Why do these precious eyes like fountains flow,
To drown the radiant heaven that lies below?
Dry up your tears, I trust his soul ere this
Has reached the mansions of eternal bliss.
Soldiers! bear hence the body out of sight.
[They bear him off.
Jem. Oh, stay—ye murderers, cease to kill me quite:
See how he glares!-and see again he flies!
The clouds fly open, and he mounts the skies.
O! see his blood, it shines refulgent bright,
I see him yet—I cannot lose him quite,
But still pursue him on—and—*lose my sight*.'

The gradual disappearance of the Colonel's soul is now finely indicated, and so is her grief: when showing the body to Sir Charles, she says, 'Behold the mangled cause of all my woes.' The sorrow of youth, however, is but transitory; and when her lover bids her dry her *gushish* tears, she takes out her pocket-handkerchief with the elasticity of youth, and consoles herself for the father in the husband.

Act in. represents the English camp: Ginckle and his Generals discourse; the armies are engaged. In Act IV. the English are worsted in spite of their valour, which Sarsfield greatly describes. 'View,' says he—

'View how the foe like an impetuous flood
Breaks through the smoke, the water, and—the mud!'
It becomes exceedingly hot. Colonel Earles says—
'In vain Jove's lightnings issue from the sky,
For death more sure from British *ensigns* fly.
Their messengers of death much blood have spilled,
And full three hundred of the Irish killed.'
(A description of war.—Herbert).
'Now bloody colours wave in their pride,
And each proud hero does his beast bestride.'

General Dorrington's description of the fight is, if possible, still more noble:—

'*Lor*. Haste, noble friends, and save your lives by flight,
For 'tis but madness if you stand to fight.
Our cavalry the battle have forsook,
And death appears in each dejected look;
Nothing but dread confusion can be seen,
For severed heads and trunks o'erspread the green;
The fields, the vales, the hills, and vanquished plain,
For five miles round are covered with the slain.
Death in each quarter does the eye alarm,
Here lies a leg, and there a shattered arm.
There heads appear, which, cloven by mighty bangs,
And severed quite, on either shoulder hangs:
This is the awful scene, my Lords! Oh, fly
The impending danger, for your fate is nigh!'

Which party, however, is to win—the Irish or English? Their heroism is equal, and young Godfrey especially, on the Irish side, is carrying all before him—when he is interrupted in the slaughter by *the ghost of his father;* of old Sir Edmonbury, whose monument we may see in Westminster Abbey. Sir Charles, at first, doubts about the genuineness of this venerable old apparition; and thus puts a case to the ghost:—

'Were ghosts in heaven, in heaven they there would stay,
Or if in hell, *they could not get away.*'

A clincher, certainly, as one would imagine: but the ghost jumps over the horns of the fancied dilemma, by saying that he is not at liberty to state where he comes from.

'*Ghost.* Where visions rest, or souls imprisoned dwell,
By Heaven's command, we are forbid to tell;
But in the obscure grave—where corpse decay,

Moulder in dust and putrefy away,—
No rest is there; for the immortal soul
Takes its full flight and flutters round the Pole;
Sometimes I hover over the Euxine sea—
From Pole to Sphere, until the judgment day—
Over the Thracian Bosphorus do I float,
And pass the Stygian lake in Charon's boat,
O'er Vulcan's fiery court and sulph'rous cave,
And ride like Neptune on a briny wave;
List to the blowing noise of Etna's flames,
And court the shades of Amazonian dames;
Then take my flight up to the gleamy moon:
Thus do I wander till the day of doom.
Proceed I dare not, or I would unfold
A horrid tale would make your blood run cold,
Chill all your nerves and sinews in a trice
Like whispering rivulets congealed to ice.
Sir Char. Ere you depart me, ghost, I here demand
You'd let me know your last divine command!'

The ghost says that the young man must die in the battle; that it will go ill for him if he die in the wrong cause; and, therefore, that he had best go over to the Protestants—which poor Sir Charles (not without many sighs for Jemima) consents to do. He goes off then, saying—

'I'll join my countrymen, and yet proclaim
Nassau's great title to the *crimson plain.'*

In Act V., that desertion turns the fate of the day. Sarsfield enters with his sword drawn, and acknowledges his fate. 'Aughrim,' exclaims Lord Lucan,

'Aughrim is now no more, St. Ruth is dead,
And all his guards are from the battle fled.
As he rode down the hill he met his fall,
And died a victim to a cannon ball.'

And bids the Frenchman's body to

'—lie like Pompey in his gore,
Whose hero's blood encircles the Egyptian shore.'

'Four hundred Irish prisoners we have got,' exclaims an English General, 'and seven thousand lyeth on the spot.' In fact, they are entirely discomfited, and retreat off the stage altogether; while, in the moment of victory, poor Sir Charles Godfrey enters, wounded to death, according to the old gentleman's prophecy. He is racked by bitter remorse: he tells his love of his treachery, and declares 'no crocodile was ever more unjust.' His agony increases, the 'optic nerves grow dim and lose their sight, and all his veins are now exhausted quite'; and he dies in the arms of his Jemima, who stabs herself in the usual way.

And so every one being disposed of, the drums and trumpets give a great peal, the audience huzzas, and the curtain falls on Ginckle and his friends exclaiming—

'May all the gods th' auspicious evening bless,
Who crowns Great Britain's *arrums* with success!'

And questioning the prosody, what Englishman will not join in the sentiment?

In the interlude the band (the pipe) performs a favourite air. Jack the waiter and candle-snuffer looks to see that all is ready; and after the dire business of the tragedy, comes in to sprinkle the stage with water (and perhaps a little whisky in it). Thus all things being arranged, the audience takes its seat again and the afterpiece begins.

Two of the little yellow volumes purchased at Ennis are entitled 'The Irish and Hibernian Tales.' The former are modern, and the latter of an ancient sort; and so great is the superiority of the old stories over the new, in fancy, dramatic interest, and humour, that one can't help fancying Hibernia must have been a very superior country to Ireland.

These Hibernian novels, too, are evidently intended for the hedge-school universities. They have the old tricks and some of the old plots that one has read in many popular legends of almost all countries, European and Eastern: successful cunning is the great virtue applauded; and the heroes pass through a thousand wild extravagant dangers, such as could only have been invented when art was young and faith was large. And as the honest old author of the tales says 'they are suited to the meanest as well as the highest capacity, tending both to improve the fancy and enrich the mind,' let us conclude the night's entertainment by reading one or two of them, and reposing after the doleful tragedy which has been represented. The 'Black Thief' is worthy of the 'Arabian Nights,' I think,—as wild and odd as an Eastern tale.

It begins, as usual, with a King and Queen who lived once on a time in the South of Ireland, and had three sons; but the Queen being on her death-bed, and fancying her husband might marry again, and unwilling that her children should be under the jurisdiction of any other woman, besought his Majesty to place them in a tower at her death, and keep them there safe until the young Princes should come of age.

The Queen dies: the King of course marries again, and the new Queen, who bears a son too, hates the offspring of the former marriage, and looks about for means to destroy them.

'At length the Queen, *having got some business with the hen-wife,* went herself to her, and after a long conference passed, was taking leave of her, when the hen-wife prayed that if ever she should come back to her again she might break her neck. The Queen, greatly incensed at such a daring insult from one of her meanest subjects, to make such a prayer on her, demanded immediately the reason, or she would have her put to death. "It was worth your while, madam," says the hen-wife, "to pay me well for it, for the reason I prayed so on you concerns you much." "What must I pay you?" asked the Queen. "You must give me," says she, "the full of a pack of wool: and I have an ancient crock which you must fill with butter; likewise a barrel which you must fill for me full of wheat." "How much wool will it take to the pack?" says the Queen. "It will take seven herds of sheep," said she, "and their increase for seven years." "How much butter will it take to fill your crock?" " Seven dairies," said she, "and the increase for seven years." "And how much will it take to fill the barrel you have?" says the Queen. "It will take the increase of seven barrels of wheat for seven years." "That is a great quantity," says the Queen, "but the reason must be extraordinary, and before I want it I will give you all you demand."'

The hen-wife acquaints the Queen with the existence of the three sons, and giving her Majesty an enchanted pack of cards, bids her to get the young men to play with her with these cards, and on their losing, to inflict upon them such a task as must infallibly end in their ruin. All young princes are set upon such tasks, and it is a sort of opening of the pantomime, before the tricks and activity begin. The Queen went home, and 'got speaking' to the King 'in regard of his children, and *she broke it off* to him in a very polite and engaging manner, so that he could see no muster or design in it.' The King agreed to bring his sons to Court, and at night, when the Royal party 'began to sport, and play at all kinds of diversions,' the Queen cunningly challenged the three Princes to play cards. They lose, and she sends them in consequence to bring her back the Knight of the Glen's wild steed of bells.

On their road (as wandering young princes, Indian or Irish, always do) they meet with the Black Thief of Sloan, who tells them what they must do. But they are caught in the attempt, and brought 'into that dismal part of the palace where the Knight kept a furnace always boiling, in which he threw all offenders that ever came in his way, which in a few minutes would entirely consume them. "Audacious villains!" says the Knight of the Glen, "how dare you attempt so bold an action as to steal my steed? See now the reward of your folly: for your greater punishment, I will not boil you all together, but one after the other, so that he that survives may witness the dire afflictions of his unfortunate companions." So saying, he ordered his servants to stir up the fire. "We will boil the eldest-looking of these young men first," says he, "and so on to the last, which will be this *old champion* with the black cap. He seems to be the captain, and looks as if he had come through many toils."—"I was as near death once as this Prince is yet," says the Black Thief, "and escaped: and so will he too." "No, you never were," said the Knight, "for he is within two or three minutes of his latter end." "But," says the Black Thief, "I was within one moment of my death, and I am here yet." "How was that?" says the Knight. "I would be glad to hear it, for it seems to be impossible." "If you think, Sir Knight," says the Black Thief, "that the danger I was in surpassed that of this young man, will you pardon him his crime?" "I will," says the Knight, "so go on with your story."

'"I was, sir," says he, "a very wild boy in my youth, and came through many distresses: once in particular, as I was on my rambling, I was benighted, and could find no lodging. At length I came to an old kiln, and being much fatigued, I went up and lay on the ribs. I had not been long there, when I saw three witches coming in with three bags of gold. Each put their bags of gold under their heads as if to sleep. I heard the one say to the other that if the Black Thief came on them while they slept he would not leave them a penny. I found by their discourse that everybody had got my name into their mouth, though I kept silent as death during their discourse. At length they fell fast asleep, and then I stole softly down, and seeing some turf *convenient,* I placed one under each of their heads, and off I went with their gold as fast as I could.

'"I had not gone far," continued the Thief of Sloan, "until I saw a greyhound, a hare, and a hawk in pursuit of me, and began to think it must be the witches that had taken that metamorphosis, in order that I might not escape them unseen either by land or water. Seeing they did not appear in any formidable shape, I was more than once resolved to attack them, thinking that with my broadsword I could easily destroy them. But considering .again that it was perhaps still in their power to become so, I gave over the attempt, and climbed with difficulty up a tree, bringing my sword in my hand, and all the gold along with me. However, when they came to the tree they found what I had done, and, making further use of their hellish art, one of them was changed into a smith's anvil, and another into a piece of iron, of which the third one soon made a hatchet. Having the hatchet made, she fell to cutting down the tree, and in course of an hour it began to shake with me."'

This is very good and original. The 'boiling' is in the first fee-faw-fum style, and the odd allusion to 'the old champion in the black cap' has the real Ogresque humour. Nor is that simple contrivance of the honest witches without its charm; for if, instead of wasting their time, the one in turning herself into an anvil, the other into a piece of iron, and so hammering out a hatchet at considerable labour and expense—if either of them had turned herself into a hatchet at once, they might have chopped down the Black Thief before cock-crow, when they were obliged to fly off and leave him in possession of the bags of gold.

The eldest Prince is ransomed by the Knight of the Glen in consequence of this story; and the second Prince escapes on account of the merit of a second story; but the great story of all is of course reserved for the youngest Prince.

'I was one day on my travels,' says the Black Thief, 'and I came into a large forest, where I wandered a long time and could not get out of it. At length I came to a large castle, and fatigue obliged me to call into the same, where I found a young woman, and a child sitting on her knee, and she crying. I asked her what made her cry, and where the lord of the castle was, for I wondered greatly that I saw no stir of servants or any person about the place. "It is well for you," says the young woman, "that the lord of this castle is not at home at present; for he is a monstrous giant, with but one eye on his forehead, who lives on human flesh. He brought me this child," says she —"I do not know where he got it—and ordered me to make it into a pie, and I cannot help crying at the command." I told her that if she knew of any place convenient that I could leave the child safely, I would do it, rather than that it should be buried in the bowels of such a monster. She told of a house a distance off, where I would get a woman who would take care of it. "But what will I do in regard of the pie?" "Cut a finger off it," said I, "and I will bring you in a young wild pig out of the forest, which you may dress as if it was the child, and put the finger in a certain place, that if the giant doubts anything about it, you may know where to turn it over at first, and when he sees it he will be fully satisfied that it is made of the child." She agreed to the plan I proposed; and, cutting off the child's finger, by her direction I soon had it at the house she told me of, and brought her the little pig in the place of it. She then made ready the pie; and, after eating and drinking heartily myself, I was just taking my leave of the young woman when we observed the giant coming through the castle-gates. "Lord bless me!" said she, " what will you do now? Run away, and lie down among the dead bodies that he has in the room" (showing me the place), "and strip off your clothes that he may not know you from the rest if he has occasion to go that way." I took her advice, and laid myself down among the rest, as if dead, to see how he would behave. The first thing I heard was him calling for his pie. When she set it down before him, he swore it smelt like swine's flesh: but, knowing where to find the finger, she immediately turned it up—which fairly convinced him of the contrary. The pie only served to sharpen his appetite, and I heard him sharpen his knife, and saying be must have a collop or two, for he was not near satisfied. But what was my terror when I heard the giant groping among the bodies, and, fancying myself, cut the half of my hip off, and took it with him to be roasted. You may be certain I was in great pain; but the fear of being killed prevented me from making any complaint. However, when he had eat all, he began to drink hot liquors in great abundance, so that in a short time he could not hold up his head, but threw himself on a large creel he had made for the purpose, and fell fast asleep. Whenever I heard him snoring, bad as I was, I went up and caused the woman to bind my wound with a handkerchief; and taking the giant's spit, I reddened it in the fire, and ran it through the eye, but was not able to kill him. However, I left the spit sticking in his head and took to my heels; but I soon found he was in pursuit of me, although blind; and, having an enchanted ring, he threw it at me, and it fell on my big toe and remained fastened to it. The giant then called to the ring, "Where it was?" and to my great surprise it made him answer, "On my foot," and he, guided by the same, made a leap at me—which I had the good luck to observe, and fortunately escaped the danger. However, I found running was of no use in saving me as long as I had the ring on my foot; so I took my sword and cut off the toe it was fastened on, and threw both into a large fish-pond that was convenient. The giant called again to the ring, which, by the power of enchantment, always made answer; but he, not knowing what I had done, imagined it was still on some part of me, and made a violent leap to seize me—when he went into the pond over head and ears and was drowned. Now, Sir Knight,' said the Thief of Sloan, 'you see what dangers I came through and always escaped; but indeed I am lame for want of my toe ever since.'

And now remains but one question to be answered, viz. How is the Black Thief himself to come off? This difficulty is solved in a very dramatic way and with a sudden turn in the narrative that is very wild and curious.

'My lord and master,' says an old woman that was listening all the time, 'that story is but too true, as I well know: *for I am the very woman that was in the giant's castle, and you, my lord, the child that I was to make into a pie;* and this is the very man that saved your life, which you may know by the want of your finger that was taken off, as you have heard, to deceive the giant.'

That fantastical way of bearing testimony to the previous tale by producing an old woman who says the tale is not only true, but she was the very old woman who lived in the giant's castle, is almost a stroke of genius. It is fine to think that the simple chronicler found it necessary to have a proof for his story, and he was no doubt perfectly contented with the proof found.

'The Knight of the Glen, greatly surprised at what he had heard the old woman tell, and knowing he wanted his finger from his childhood, began to understand that the story was true enough. "And is this my dear deliverer?" says he. "O brave fellow, I not only pardon you all, but I will keep you with myself while you live; where you shall feast like princes and have every attendance that I have myself." They all returned thanks on their knees, and the Black Thief told him the reason they attempted to steal the steed of bells, and the necessity they were under of going home. "Well," says the Knight of the Glen, "if that's the case, I bestow you my steed rather than this brave fellow should die: so you may go when you please: only remember to call and see me betimes, that we may know each other well." They promised they would, and with great joy they set off for the King their father's palace, and the Black Thief along with them. The wicked Queen was standing all this time on the tower, and hearing the bells ringing at a great distance off, knew very well it was the Princes coming home, and the steed with them, and through spite and vexation precipitated herself from the tower and was shattered to pieces. The three Princes lived happy and well during their father's reign, always keeping the Black Thief along with them; but how they did after the old King's death is not known.'

Then we come upon a story that exists in many a European language—of the man cheating Death: then to the history of the Apprentice Thief, who of course cheated his masters: which, too, is an old tale, and may have been told very likely among those Phoenicians who were the fathers of the Hibernians, for whom these tales were devised. A very curious tale is there concerning Manus O'Malaghan and the Fairies: —

'In the parish of Ahoghill lived Manus O'Malaghan. *As he ms searching for a calf that had strayed*, he heard many people talking. Drawing near, he distinctly heard them repeating, one after the other, "Get me a horse, get me a horse"; and "Get me a horse too," says Manus. Manus was instantly mounted on a steed, surrounded with a vast crowd, who galloped off, taking poor Mauus with them. In a short time they suddenly stopped in a large wide street, asking Manus if he knew where he was? "Faith," says he, "I do not." "You are *in Spain*," said they.'

Here we have again the wild mixture of the positive and the fanciful. The chronicler is careful to tell us why Manus went out searching for a calf, and this positiveness prodigiously increases the reader's wonder at the subsequent events. And the question and answer of the mysterious horsemen is fine: 'Don't you know where you are? *In Spain*.' A vague solution, such as one has of occurrences in dreams sometimes.

The history of Robin the Blacksmith is full of these strange flights of poetry. He is followed about 'by a little boy in a green jacket,' who performs the most wondrous feats of the blacksmith's art, as follows:—

Robin was asked to do something, who wisely shifted it, saying he would be very sorry not to give the honour of the first trick to his Lordship's smith—at which he was called forth to the bellows.

When the fire was well kindled, to the great surprise of all present, he blew a great shower of wheat out of the fire, which fell through all the shop. They then demanded of Robin to try what he could do. "Pho!" said Robin, as if he thought nothing of what was done. "Come," said he to the boy, "I think I showed you something like that." The boy goes then to the bellows and blew out a great flock of pigeons, who soon devoured all the grain and then disappeared.

'The Dublin smith, sorely vexed that such a boy as him should outdo him, goes a second time to the bellows and blew a fine trout out of the hearth, who jumped into a little river that was running by the shop-door, and was seen no more at that time.

'Robin then said to the boy, "Come, you must bring us yon trout back again, to let the gentlemen see we can do something." Away the boy goes and blew a large otter out of the hearth, who immediately leaped into the river and in a short time returned with the trout in his mouth, and then disappeared. All present allowed that it was a folly to attempt a competition any further.'

The boy in the green jacket was one 'of a kind of small beings called fairies'; and not a little does it add to the charm of these wild tales to feel, as one reads them, that the writer must have believed in his heart a great deal of what he told. You see the tremor as it were, and a wild look of the eyes, as the story-teller sits in his nook and recites, and peers wistfully round lest the beings he talks of be really at hand.

Let us give a couple of the little tales entire. They are not so fanciful as those before mentioned, but of the comic sort, and suited to the first kind of capacity mentioned by the author in his preface.

Donald and his Neighbours

'Hudden and Dudden and Donald O'Neary were near neighbours in the barony of Ballinconlig, and ploughed with three bullocks; but the two former, envying the present prosperity of the latter, determined to kill his bullock to prevent his farm being properly cultivated and laboured—that, going back in the world, he might be induced to sell his lands, which they meant to get possession of. Poor Donald, finding his bullock killed, immediately skinned it, and throwing the skin over his shoulder, with the fleshy side out, set off to the next town with it, to dispose of it to the best advantage. Going along the road a magpie flew on the top of the hide, and began picking it, chattering all the time. This bird had been taught to speak and imitate the human voice, and Donald, thinking he understood some words it was saying, put round his hand and caught hold of it. Having got possession of it, he put it under his greatcoat, and so went on to the town. Having sold the hide, he went into an inn to take a dram; and, following the landlady into the cellar, he gave the bird a squeeze, which caused it to chatter some broken accents that surprised her very much. "What is that I hear?" said she to Donald: " I think it is talk, and yet I do not understand." "Indeed," said Donald, "it is a bird I have that tells me everything, and I always carry it with me to know when there is any danger. Faith," says he, "it says you have far better liquor than you are giving me." "That is strange," said she, going to another cask of better quality, and asking him if he would sell the bird. "I will," said Donald, "if I get enough for it." "I will fill your hat with silver if you leave it with me." Donald was glad to hear the news, and, taking the silver, set off, rejoicing at his good luck. He had not been long home when he met with Hudden and Dudden. "Ha!" said he, "you thought you did me a bad turn, but you could not have done me a better: for, look here, what I have got for the hide," showing them the hatful of silver. "You never saw such a demand for hides in your life as there is at present." Hudden and Dudden that very night killed their bullocks, and set out the next morning to sell their hides. On coming to the place they went to all the merchants, but could only get a trifle for them. At last they had to take what they could get, and came home in a great rage and vowing revenge on poor Donald. He had a pretty good guess how matters would turn out, and his bed being under the kitchen-window, he was afraid they would rob him, or perhaps kill him when asleep; and on that account, when he was going to bed, he left his old mother in his bed, and lay down in her place, which was in the other side of the house, and, taking the old woman for Donald, choked her in the bed; but he making some noise, they had to retreat and leave the money behind them, which grieved them very much. However, by daybreak, Donald got his mother on his back, and carried her to town. Stopping at a well, he fixed his mother with her staff as if she was stooping for a drink, and then went into a public-house convenient and called for a dram. "I wish," said he to a woman that stood near him, "you would tell my mother to come in. She is at yon well trying to get a drink, and she is hard in hearing: if she does not observe you, give her a little shake, and tell her that I want her." The woman called her several times, but she seemed to take no notice: at length she went to her and shook her by the arm; but when she let her go again, she tumbled on her head into the well, and, as the woman thought, was drowned. She, in great fear and surprise at the accident, told Donald what had happened. "O mercy," said he, "what is this?" He ran and pulled her out of the well, weeping and lamenting all the time, and acting in such a manner that you would imagine that he had lost his senses. The woman, on the other hand, was far worse than Donald: for his grief was only feigned, but she imagined herself to be the cause of the old woman's death. The inhabitants of the town, hearing what had happened, agreed to make Donald up a good sum of money for his loss, as the accident happened in their place; and Donald brought a greater sum home with him than he got for the magpie. They buried Donald's mother; and as soon as he saw Hudden and Dudden, he showed them the last purse of money he had got. "You thought to kill me last night," said he; "but it was good for me it happened on my mother, for I got all that purse for her to make gunpowder."

'That very night Hudden .and Dudden killed their mothers, and the next morning set off with them to town. On coming to the town with their burden on their backs, they went up and down crying, "Who will buy old wives for gunpowder?" so that every one laughed at them, and the boys at last clodded them out of the place. They then saw the cheat, and vowing revenge on Donald, buried the old women and set off in pursuit of him. Coming to his house, they found him sitting at his breakfast, and seizing him, put him in a sack, and went to drown him in a river at some distance. As they were going along the highway they raised a hare, which they saw had but three feet, and, throwing off the sack, ran after her, thinking by appearance she would be easily taken. In their absence there came a drover that way, and hearing Donald singing in the sack, wondered greatly what could be the matter. "What is the reason," said he, "that you are singing, and you confined?" "Oh, I am going to heaven," said Donald: "and in a short time I expect to be free from trouble." "Oh dear," said the drover, "what will I give you if you let me to your place?" "Indeed I do not know," said he: "it would take a good sum." "I have not much money," said the drover; "but I have twenty head of fine cattle, which I will give you to exchange places with me." "Well, well," says Donald, "I don't care if I should: loose the sack and I will come out." In a moment the drover liberated him, and went into the sack himself: and Donald drove home the fine heifers and left them in his pasture.

'Hudden and Dudden having caught the hare, returned, and getting the sack on one of their backs, carried Donald, as they thought, to the river, and threw him in, where he immediately sank. They then marched home, intending to take immediate possession of Donald's property; but how great was their surprise, when they found him safe at home before them, with such a fine herd of cattle, whereas they knew he had none before! "Donald," said they, "what is all this? We thought you were drowned, and yet you are here before us?" "Ah!" said he, "if I had but help along with me when you threw me in, it would have been the best job ever I met with; for of all the sight of cattle and gold that ever was seen, is there, and no one to own them; but I was not able to manage more than what you see, and I could show you the spot where you might get hundreds." They both swore they would be his friends, and Donald accordingly led them to a very deep part of the river, and lifting up a stone, " Now," said he, "watch this," throwing it into the stream. "There is the very place, and go in, one of you, first, and if you want help you have nothing to do but call." Hudden jumping in, and sinking to the bottom, rose up again, and making a bubbling noise as those do that are drowning, seemed trying to speak but could not. "What is that he is saying now?" says Dudden. "Faith," says Donald, "he is calling for help —don't you hear him? Stand about," said he, running back, "till I leap in. I know how to do better than any of you." Dudden, to have the advantage of him, jumped in off the bank, and was drowned along with Hudden. And this was the end of Hudden and Dudden.'

The Spaeman

'A poor man in the North of Ireland was under the necessity of selling his cow to help to support his family. Having sold his cow, he went into an inn and called for some liquor. Having drunk pretty heartily, he fell asleep, and when he awoke he found he had been robbed of his money. Poor Roger was at a loss to know how to act; and, as is often the case, when the landlord found that his money was gone, he turned him out of doors. The night was extremely dark, and the poor man was compelled to take up his lodging in an old uninhabited house at the end of the town.

'Roger had not remained long here until he was surprised by the noise of three men, whom he observed making a hole, and, depositing something therein, closing it carefully up again and then going away. The next morning, as Roger was walking towards the town, he heard that a cloth-shop had been robbed to a great amount, and that a reward of thirty pounds was offered to any person who could discover the thieves. This was joyful news to Roger, who recollected what he had been witness to the night before. He accordingly went to the shop and told the gentlemen that for the reward he would recover the goods, and secure the robbers, provided he got six stout men to attend him. All which was thankfully granted him.

'At night Roger and his men concealed themselves in the old house, and in a short time after the robbers came to the spot for the purpose of removing their booty; but they were instantly seized and carried into the town prisoners, with the goods. Roger received the reward and returned home, well satisfied with his good luck. Not many days after, it was noised over the country that this robbery was discovered by the help of one of the best Spaemen to be found—insomuch that it reached the ears of a worthy gentleman of the county of Deny, who made strict inquiry to find him out. Having at length discovered his abode, he sent for Roger, and told him he was every day losing some valuable article, and as he was famed for discovering lost things, if he could find out the same, he should be handsomely rewarded. Poor Roger was put to a stand, not knowing what answer to make, as he had not the smallest knowledge of the like. But recovering himself a little, he resolved to humour the joke; and, thinking he would make a good dinner and some drink of it, told the gentleman he would try what he could do, but that he must have a room to himself for three hours, during which time he must have three bottles of strong ale and his dinner. All which the gentleman told him he should have. No sooner was it made known that the Spaeman was in the house than the servants were all in confusion, wishing to know what would be said.

'As soon as Roger had taken his dinner, he was shown into an elegant room, where the gentleman sent him a quart of ale by the butler. No sooner had he set down the ale than Roger said, "There comes one of them" (intimating the bargain he had made with the gentleman for the three quarts), which the butler took in a wrong light and imagined it was himself. He went away in great confusion and told his wife. "Poor fool," said she, "the fear makes you think it is you he means; but I will attend in your place, and hear what he will say to me." Accordingly she carried the second quart: but no sooner had she opened the door than Roger cried, "There comes two of them." The woman, no less surprised than her husband, told him the Spaeman knew her too, "And what will we do?" said he. "We will be hanged." "I will tell you what we must do," said she: "we must send the groom the next time; and if he is known, we must offer him a good sum not to discover on us." The butler went to William and told him the whole story, and that he must go next to see what he would say to him, telling him at the same time what to do in case he was known also. When the hour was expired, William was sent with the third quart of ale—which when Roger observed, he cried out, "There is the third and last of them!" At which he changed colour, and told him "that if he would not discover on them, they would show him where they were all concealed and give him five pounds besides." Roger, not a little surprised at the discovery he had made, told him "if he recovered the goods, he would follow them no further."

'By this time the gentleman called Roger to know how he had succeeded. He told him "he could find the goods, but that the thief was gone." "I will be well satisfied," said he, "with the goods, for some of them are very valuable." "Let the butler come along with me, and the whole shall be recovered." He accordingly conducted Roger to the back of the stables, where the articles were concealed— such as silver cups, spoons, bowls, knives, forks, and a variety of other articles of great value.

'When the supposed Spaeman brought back the stolen goods, the gentleman was so highly pleased with Roger that he insisted on his remaining with him always, as he supposed he would be perfectly safe as long as he was about his house. Roger gladly embraced the offer, and in a few days took possession of a piece of land which the gentleman had given to him in consideration of his great abilities.

'Some time after this, the gentleman was relating to a large company the discovery Roger had made, and that he could tell anything. One of the gentlemen said he would dress a dish of meat, and bet for fifty pounds that he could not tell what was in it, and he would allow him to taste it. The bet being taken and the dish dressed, the gentleman sent for Roger and told the bet that was depending on him. Poor Roger did not know what to do; at last he consented to the trial. The dish being produced, he tasted it, but could not tell what it was. At last, seeing he was fairly beat, he said, "Gentlemen, it is folly to talk: the fox may run awhile, but he is caught at last"—allowing with himself that he was found out. The gentleman that had made the bet then confessed that it was a fox he had dressed in the dish: at which they all shouted out in favour of the Spaeman—particularly his master, who had more confidence in him than ever.

'Roger then went home, and so famous did he become, that no one dared take anything but what belonged to them, fearing that the Spaeman would discover on them.'

* * * * *

And so we shut up the Hedge-school Library, and close the Galway Nights' Entertainments. They are not quite so genteel as Almack's to be sure; but many a lady who has her opera-box in London has listened to a piper in Ireland.

A propos of pipers, I caught and copied a young one to-day. He was paddling in the mud, shining in the sun careless of his rays, and playing his little tin music as happy as Mr. Cooke with his oboe.

Perhaps the above verses and tales are not unlike my little Galway musician. They are grotesque and rugged; but they are pretty and innocent-hearted too; and as such, polite persons may deign to look at them for once in a way. While we have Signor Costa in a white neckcloth ordering opera-bands to play for us the music of Donizetti, which is not only sublime but genteel: of course such poor little operatives as he who plays the wind-instrument yonder cannot expect to be heard often. But is not this Galway? And how far is Galway from the Haymarket?

CHAPTER XVII: FROM GALWAY TO BALLYNAHINCH

THE Clifden car, which carries the Dublin letters into the heart of Connemara, conducts the passenger over one of the most wild and beautiful districts that it is ever the fortune of a traveller to examine; and I could not help thinking, as we passed through it, at how much pains and expense honest English cockneys are to go and look after natural beauties far inferior, in countries which, though more distant, are not a whit more strange than this one. No doubt, ere long, when people know how easy the task is, the rush of London tourism will come this way; and I shall be very happy if these pages shall be able to awaken in one bosom beating in Tooley Street or the Temple the desire to travel towards Ireland next year.

After leaving the quaint old town behind us, and ascending one or two small eminences to the north-westward, the traveller, from the car, gets a view of the wide sheet of Lough Corrib shining in the sun, as we saw it, with its low dark banks stretching round it. If the view is gloomy, at least it is characteristic: nor are we delayed by it very long; for though the lake stretches northwards into the very midst of the Joyce country (and is there in the close neighbourhood of another huge lake, Lough Mask, which again is near to another sheet of water), yet from this road henceforth, after keeping company with it for some five miles, we only get occasional views of it, passing over hills and through trees, by many rivers and small lakes, which are dependent upon that of Corrib. Gentlemen's seats, on the road from Galway to Moycullen, are scattered in great profusion. Perhaps there is grass growing on the gravel-walk, and the iron gates of the tumble-down old lodges are rather rickety; but, for all that, the places look comfortable, hospitable, and spacious. As for the shabbiness and want of finish here and there, the English eye grows quite accustomed to it in a month; and I find the bad condition of the Galway houses by no means so painful as that of the places near Dublin. At some of the lodges, as we pass, the mail-carman, with a warning shout, flings a bag of letters. I saw a little party looking at one which lay there in the road crying, 'Come, take me!' but nobody cares to steal a bag of letters in this country, I suppose, and the carman drove on without any alarm. Two days afterwards a gentleman with whom I was in company left on a rock his book of fishing-flies; and I can assure you there was a very different feeling expressed about the safety of *that.*

In the first part of the journey, the neighbourhood of the road seemed to be as populous as in other parts of the country; troops of red-petticoated peasantry peering from their stone-cabins; yelling children following the car, and crying, 'Lash, lash!' It was Sunday, and you would see many a white chapel among the green bare plains to the right of the road, the courtyard blackened with a swarm of cloaks. The service seems to continue (on the part of the people) all day. Troops of people issuing from the chapel met us at Moycullen; and ten miles farther on, at Oughterard, their devotions did not yet seem to be concluded.

A more beautiful village can scarcely be seen than this. It stands upon Lough Corrib, the banks of which are here, for once at least, picturesque and romantic: and a pretty river, the Feogh, comes rushing over rocks and by woods until it passes the town and meets the lake. Some pretty buildings in the village stand on each bank of this stream: a Roman Catholic chapel with a curate's neat lodge; a little church on one side of it, a fine court-house of grey stone on the other. And here it is that we get into the famous district of Connemara, so celebrated in Irish stories, so mysterious to the London tourist.

'It presents itself,' says the Guide-book, 'under every possible combination of heathy moor, bog, lake, and mountain. Extensive mossy plains and wild pastoral valleys lie embosomed among the mountains, and support numerous herds of cattle and horses, for which the district has been long celebrated. These wild solitudes, which occupy by far the greater part of the centre of the county, are held by a hardy and ancient race of grazing farmers, who live in a very primitive state, and, generally speaking, till little beyond what supplies their immediate wants. For the first ten miles the country is comparatively open; and the mountains on the left, which are not of great elevation, can be distinctly traced as they rise along the edge of the heathy plain.

'Our road continues along the Feogh river, which expands itself into several considerable lakes, and at five miles from Oughterard we reach Lough Bonn, which the road also skirts. Passing in succession Lough-a-Preaghan, the lakes of Anderran and Shindella, at ten miles from Oughterard we reach Slyme and Lynn's Inn, or Halfway House, which is near the shore of Loughonard. Now, as we advance towards the group of Binabola, or the Twelve Pins, the most gigantic scenery is displayed.'

But the best guide-book that ever was written cannot set the view before the mind's eye of the reader, and I won't attempt to pile up big words in place of these wild mountains, over which the clouds as they passed, or the sunshine as it went and came, cast every variety of tint, light, and shadow; nor can it be expected that long level sentences, however smooth and shining, can be made to pass as representations of those calm lakes by which we took our way. All one can do is to lay down the pen and ruminate, and cry, 'Beautiful!' once more; and to the reader say, 'Come and see!'

Wild and wide as the prospect around us is, it has somehow a kindly friendly look; differing in this from the fierce loneliness of some similar scenes in Wales that I have viewed. Bagged women and children come out of rude stone-huts to see the car as it passes. But it is impossible for the pencil to give due raggedness to the rags, or to convey a certain picturesque mellowness of colour that the garments assume. The sexes, with regard to raiment, do not seem to be particular. There were many boys on the road in the national red petticoat, having no other covering for their lean brown legs. As for shoes, the women eschew them almost entirely; and I saw a peasant trudging from mass in a handsome scarlet cloak, a fine blue-cloth gown, turned up to show a new lining of the same colour, and a petticoat quite white and neat—in a dress of which the cost must have been at least £10; and her husband walked in front carrying her shoes and stockings.

The road had conducted us for miles through the vast property of the gentleman to whose house I was bound, Mr. Martin, the Member for the county; and the last and prettiest part of the journey was round the Lake of Ballynahinch, with tall mountains rising immediately above us on the right, pleasant woody hills on the opposite side of the lake, with the roofs of the houses rising above the trees; and in an island in the midst of the water a ruined old castle that cast a long white reflection into the blue waters where it lay. A land-pirate used to live in that castle, one of the peasants told me, in the time of 'Oliver Cromwell.' And a fine fastness it was for a robber, truly; for there was no road through these wild countries in his time—nay, only thirty years since, this lake was at three days' distance of Galway. Then comes the question, What, in a country where there were no roads and no travellers, and where the inhabitants have been wretchedly poor from time immemorial,—what was there for the land-pirate to rob? But let us not be too curious about times so early as those of Oliver Cromwell. I have heard the name many times from the Irish peasant, who still has an awe of the grim resolute Protector.

The builder of Ballynahinch House has placed it to command a view of a pretty melancholy river that runs by it, through many green flats and picturesque rocky grounds; but from the lake it is scarcely visible. And so, in like manner, I fear it must remain invisible to the reader too, with all its kind inmates, and frank cordial hospitality; unless he may take a fancy to visit Galway himself, when, as I can vouch, a very small pretext will make him enjoy both.

It will, however, be only a small breach of confidence to say that the major-domo of the establishment (who has adopted accurately the voice and manner of his master with a severe dignity of his own which is quite original) ordered me on going to bed 'not to move in the morning till he called me,' at the same time expressing a hearty hope that I should 'want nothing more that evening.' Who would dare, after such peremptory orders, not to fall asleep immediately, and in this way secure the repose of Mr. J—n M-ll-y?

There may be many comparisons drawn between English and Irish gentlemen's houses; but perhaps the most striking point of difference between the two is the immense following of the Irish house, such as would make an English housekeeper crazy almost. Three comfortable, well-clothed, good-humoured fellows walked down with me from the car, persisting in carrying one a bag, another a sketching-stool, and so on. Walking about the premises in the morning, sundry others were visible in the courtyard, and near the kitchen-door; in the grounds a gentleman, by name Mr. Marcus C-rr, began discoursing to me regarding the place, the planting, the fish, the grouse, and the Master; being himself, doubtless, one of the irregulars of the house. As for maids, there were half-a-score of them skurrying about the house; and I am not ashamed to confess that some of them were exceedingly good-looking. And if I might venture to say a word more, it would be respecting Connemara breakfasts; but this would be an entire and flagrant breach of confidence; and, to be sure, the dinners were just as good.

One of the days of my three days' visit was to be devoted to the lakes j and as a party had been arranged for the second day after my arrival, I was glad to take advantage of the society of a gentleman staying in the house, and ride with him to the neighbouring town of Clifden.

The ride thither from Ballynahinch is surprisingly beautiful; and as you ascend the high ground from the two or three rude stone-huts which face the entrance-gates of the house, there are views of the lakes and the surrounding country, which the best parts of Killarney do not surpass, I think; although the Connemara lakes do not possess the advantage of wood which belongs to the famous Kerry landscape.

But the cultivation of the country is only in its infancy as yet, and it is easy to see how vast its resources are, and what capital and cultivation may do for it. In the green patches among the rocks, and on the mountain-sides, wherever crops were grown, they flourished; plenty of natural wood is springing up in various places; and there is no end to what the planter may do and to what time and care may effect. The carriage-road to Clifden is but ten years old: as it has brought the means of communication into the country, the commerce will doubtless follow it; and in fact, in going through the whole kingdom, one can't but be struck with the idea that not one-hundredth part of its capabilities are yet brought into action, or even known perhaps, and that by the easy and certain progress of time, Ireland will be poor Ireland no longer. For instance, we rode by a vast green plain, skirting a lake and river, which is now useless almost for pasture, and which a little draining will convert into thousands of acres of rich productive land. Streams and falls of water dash by one everywhere—they have only to utilise this water-power for mills and factories; and hard by are some of the finest bays in the world, where ships can deliver and receive foreign and home produce. At Roundstone especially, where a little town has been erected, the bay is said to be unexampled for size, depth, and shelter; and the Government is now, through the rocks and hills on their wild shore, cutting a coast-road to Bunown, the most westerly part of Connemara, whence there is another good road to Clifden. Among the charges which the 'Repealers' bring against the Union, they should include at least this—they would never have had these roads but for the Union; roads which are as much at the charge of the London taxpayer as of the most ill-used Milesian in Connaught.

A string of small lakes follow the road to Olifden, with mountains on the right of the traveller for the chief part of the way. A few figures at work in the bog-lands, a red petticoat passing here and there, a goat or two browsing among the stones, or a troop of ragged whitey-brown children who came out to gaze at the car, form the chief society on the road. The first house at the entrance to Clifden is a gigantic poorhouse

—tall, large, ugly, comfortable; it commands the town, and looks almost as big as every one of the houses therein. The town itself is but of a few years' date, and seems to thrive in its small way. Clifden Castle is a fine château in the neighbourhood, and belongs to another owner of immense lands in Galway—Mr. D'Arcy.

Here a drive was proposed along the coast to Bunown, and I was glad to see some more of the country, and its character. Nothing can be wilder. We passed little lake after lake, lying a few furlongs inwards from the shore. There were rocks everywhere, some patches of cultivated land here and there, nor was there any want of inhabitants along this savage coast. There were numerous cottages, if cottages they may be called, and women and, above all, children in plenty. To depict the multiplicity of their rags would require a month's study.

At length we came in sight of a half-built edifice which is approached by a rocky, dismal, grey road, guarded by two or three broken gates, against which rocks and stones were piled, which were to be removed to give an entrance to our car. The gates were closed so laboriously, I presume, to prevent the egress of a single black consumptive pig, far gone in the family way—a teeming skeleton—that was cropping the thin dry grass that grew upon a round hill which rises behind this most dismal castle of Bunown.

If the traveller only seeks for strange sights, this place will repay his curiosity. Such a dismal house is not to be seen in all England: or, perhaps, such a dismal situation. The sea lies before and behind; and on each side, likewise, are rocks and copper-coloured meadows, by which a few trees have made an attempt to grow. The owner of the house had, however, begun to add to it; and there, unfinished, is a whole apparatus of turrets, and staring raw stone and mortar, and fresh ruinous carpenters' work. And then the courtyard!—tumble-down outhouses, staring empty pointed windows, and new-smeared plaster cracking from the walls—a black heap of turf, a mouldy pump, a wretched old coal-scuttle, emptily sunning itself in the midst of this cheerful scene! There was an old Gorgon who kept the place, and who was in perfect unison with it: Venus herself would become bearded, blear-eyed, and haggard if left to be the housekeeper of this dreary place.

In the house was a comfortable parlour, inhabited by the priest who has the painful charge of the district. Here were his books and his breviaries, his reading-desk with the cross engraved upon it, and his portrait of Daniel O'Connell the Liberator to grace the walls of his lonely cell. There was a dead crane hanging at the door on a gaff: his red fish-like eyes were staring open, and his eager grinning bill. A rifle-ball had passed through his body. And this was doubtless the only game about the place; for we saw the sportsman who had killed the bird hunting vainly up the round hill for other food for powder. This gentleman had had good sport, he said, shooting seals upon a neighbouring island, four of which animals he had slain.

Mounting up the round hill, we had a view of the Sline Lights—the most westerly point in Ireland.

Here too was a ruined sort of summer-house, dedicated 'DEO HIBERNIÆ LIBERATORI.' When these lights were put up, I am told the proprietor of Bunown was recommended to apply for compensation to Parliament, inasmuch as there would be no more *wrecks* on the coast: from which branch of commerce the inhabitants of the district used formerly to derive a considerable profit. Between these Sline Lights and America nothing lies but the Atlantic. It was beautifully blue and bright on this day, and the sky almost cloudless; but I think the brightness only made the scene more dismal, it being of that order of beauties which cannot bear the full light, but require a cloud or a curtain to set them off to advantage. A pretty story was told me by the gentleman who had killed the seals. The place where he had been staying for sport was almost as lonely as this Bunown, and inhabited by a priest too—a young, lively, well-educated man. 'When I came here first,' the priest said, *'I cried for two days'*: but afterwards he grew to like the place exceedingly, his whole heart being directed towards it, his chapel, and his cure. Who would not honour such missionaries—the virtues they silently practise, and the doctrines they preach? After hearing that story, I think Bunown looked not quite so dismal, as it is inhabited, they say, by such another character. What a pity it is that John Tuam, in the next county of Mayo, could not find such another hermitage to learn modesty in, and forget his Graceship, his Lordship, and the sham titles by which he sets such store.

A moon as round and bright as any moon that ever shone, and riding in a sky perfectly cloudless, gave us a good promise of a fine day for the morrow, which was to be devoted to the lakes in the neighbourhood of Ballynahinch: one of which, Lough Ina, is said to be of exceeding beauty. But no man can speculate upon Irish weather. I have seen a day beginning with torrents of rain that looked as if a deluge was at hand, clear up in a few minutes, without any reason, and against the prognostications of the glass and all other weather-prophets. So in like manner, after the astonishingly fine night, there came a villainous dark day: which, however, did not set in fairly for rain until we were an hour on our journey, with a couple of stout boatmen rowing us over Ballynahinch Lake. Being, however, thus fairly started, the water began to come down, not in torrents certainly, but in that steady, creeping, insinuating mist, of which we scarce know the luxury in England; and which, I am bound to say, will wet a man's jacket as satisfactorily as a cataract would do.

It was just such another day as that of the famous stag-hunt at Killarney, in a word; and as, in the first instance, we went to see the deer killed, and saw nothing thereof, so, in the second case, we went to see the landscape with precisely the same good fortune. The mountains covered their modest beauties in impenetrable veils of clouds; and the only consolation to the boat's crew was, that it was a remarkably good day for trout-fishing—which amusement some people are said to prefer to the examination of landscapes, however beautiful.

0 you who laboriously throw flies in English rivers, and catch, at the expiration of a hard day's walking, casting, and wading, two or three feeble little brown trouts of two or three ounces in weight, how would you rejoice to have but an hour's sport in

Derryclear or Ballynahinch; where you have but to cast, and lo! a big trout springs at your fly, and, after making a vain struggling, splashing, and plunging for a while, is infallibly landed in the net and thence into the boat! The single rod in the boat caught enough fish in an hour to feast the crew, consisting of five persons, and the family of a herd of Mr. Martin's, who has a pretty cottage on Derryclear Lake, inhabited by a cow and its calf, a score of fowls, and I don't know how many sons and daughters.

Having caught enough trout to satisfy any moderate appetite, like true sportsmen the gentlemen on board our boat became eager to hook a salmon. Had they hooked a few salmon, no doubt they would have trolled for whales, or for a mermaid, one of which finny beauties the waterman swore he had seen on the shore of Derryclear—he with Jim Mullen being above on a rock, the mermaid on the shore directly beneath them, visible to the middle, and as usual 'racking her hair.' It was fair hair, the boatman said; and he appeared as convinced of the existence of the mermaid as he was of the trout just landed in the boat.

In regard of mermaids, there is a gentleman living near Killala Bay, whose name was mentioned to me, and who declares solemnly that one day, shooting on the sands there, he saw a mermaid, and determined to try her with a shot. So he drew the small-shot charge from his gun and loaded with a ball—that he always had by him for seal-shooting— fired, and hit the mermaid through the breast. The screams and moans of the creature—whose person he describes most accurately—were the most horrible heart-rending noises that he ever, he said, heard: and not only were they heard by him, but by the fishermen along the coast, who were furiously angry against Mr. A—n, because, they said, the injury done to the mermaid would cause her to drive all the fish away from the bay for years to come.

But we did not, to my disappointment, catch a single glimpse of one of these interesting beings, nor of the great sea-horse which is said to inhabit these waters, nor of any fairies (of whom the stroke-oar, Mr. Marcus, told us not to speak, for they didn't like bein' spoken of); nor even of a salmon, though the fishermen produced the most tempting flies. The only animal of any size that was visible we saw while lying by a swift black river that comes jumping with innumerable little waves into Derryclear, and where the salmon are especially suffered to ' stand': this animal was an eagle—a real wild eagle, with grey wings and a white head and belly: it swept round us, within gunshot reach, once or twice, through the leaden sky, and then settled on a grey rock, and began to scream its shrill ghastly aquiline note.

The attempts on the salmon having failed, the rain continuing to fall steadily, the herd's cottage before-named was resorted to; when Marcus, the boatman, commenced forthwith to gut the fish, and taking down some charred turf-ashes from the blazing fire, on which about a hundredweight of potatoes were boiling, he—Marcus—proceeded to grill on the floor some of the trout, which we afterwards ate with immeasurable satisfaction. They were such trouts as, when once tasted, remain for ever in the recollection of a commonly grateful mind—rich, flaky, creamy, full of flavour. A Parisian *gourmand* would have paid ten francs for the smallest *cooleen* among them; and, when transported to his capital, how different in flavour would they have been!—how inferior to what they were as we devoured them, fresh from the fresh waters of the lake, and jerked as it were from the water to the gridiron! The world had not had time to spoil those innocent beings before they were gobbled up with pepper and salt, and missed, no doubt, by their friends. I should like to know more of their 'set.' But enough of this: my feelings overpower me: suffice it to say, they were red or salmon trouts—none of your white-fleshed brown-skinned river fellows.

When the gentlemen had finished their repast, the boatmen and the family set to work upon the potatoes, a number of the remaining fish, and a store of other good things; then we all sat round the turf-fire in the dark cottage, the rain coming down steadily outside, and veiling everything except the shrubs and verdure immediately about the cottage. The herd, the herd's wife, and a nondescript female friend, two healthy young herdsmen in corduroy rags, the herdsman's daughter paddling about with bare feet, a stout black-eyed wench with her gown over her head, and a red petticoat not quite so good as new, the two boatmen, a badger just killed and turned inside out, the gentlemen, some hens cackling and flapping about among the rafters, a calf in a corner cropping green meat and occasionally visited by the cow her mamma, formed the society of the place. It was rather a strange picture; but as for about two hours we Bat there, and maintained an almost unbroken silence, and as there was no other amusement but to look at the rain, I began, after the enthusiasm of the first half-hour, to think that after all London was a bearable place, and that for want of a turf-fire and a bench in Connemara, one *might* put up with a sofa and a newspaper in Pall Mall.

This, however, is according to tastes; and I must say that Mr. Marcus betrayed a most bitter contempt for all cockney tastes, awkwardness, and ignorance: and very right too. The night, on our return home, all of a sudden cleared; but though the fishermen, much to my disgust—at the expression of which, however, the rascals only laughed—persisted in making more casts for trout, and trying back in the dark upon the spots which we had visited in the morning, it appeared the fish had been frightened off by the rain; and the sportsmen met with such indifferent success that at about ten o'clock we found ourselves at Ballynahinch. Dinner was served at eleven; and, I believe, there was some whisky-punch afterwards, recommended medicinally and to prevent the ill effects of the wetting: but that is neither here nor there.

The next day the petty sessions were to be held at Roundstone, a little town which has lately sprung up near the noble bay of that name. I was glad to see some specimens of Oonnemara litigation, as also to behold at least one thousand beautiful views that lie on the five miles of road between the town and Ballynahinch. Rivers and rocks, mountains and sea, green plains and bright skies, how (for the hundred-and-fiftieth time) can pen-and-ink set you down? But if Berghem could have seen those blue mountains, and Karel Dujardin could have copied some of these green airy plains, with their brilliant little coloured groups of peasants, beggars, horsemen, many an Englishman would know Connemara upon canvas as he does Italy or Flanders now.

CHAPTER XVIII: ROUNDSTONE PETTY SESSIONS

'THE temple of august Themis,' as a Frenchman would call the sessions-room at Roundstone, is an apartment of some twelve feet square, with a deal table and a couple of chairs for the accommodation of the magistrates, and a Testament with a paper cross pasted on it to be kissed by the witnesses and complainants who frequent the court. The law-papers, warrants, etc., are kept on the sessions-clerk's bed in an adjoining apartment, which commands a fine view of the courtyard—where there is a stack of turf, a pig, and a shed beneath which the magistrates' horses were sheltered during the sitting. The sessions-clerk is a gentleman 'having,' as the phrase is here, both the English and Irish languages, and interpreting for the benefit of the worshipful bench.

And if the cockney reader supposes that in this remote country spot, so wild, so beautiful, so distant from the hum and vice of cities, quarrelling is not, and litigation never shows her snaky head, he is very much mistaken. From what I saw, I would recommend any ingenious young attorney whose merits are not appreciated in the metropolis, to make an attempt upon the village of Roundstone; where as yet, I believe, there is no solicitor, and where an immense and increasing practice might speedily be secured. Mr. O'Connell, who is always crying out 'Justice for Ireland,' finds strong supporters among the Roundstonians, whose love of justice for themselves is inordinate. I took down the plots of the five first little litigious dramas which were played before Mr. Martin and the stipendiary magistrate.

Case 1.—A boy summoned a young man for beating him so severely that he kept his bed for a week, thereby breaking an engagement with his master, and losing a quarter's wages.

The defendant stated, in reply, that the plaintiff was engaged—in a field through which defendant passed with another person—setting two little boys to fight; on which defendant took plaintiff by the collar and turned him out of the field. A witness who was present swore that defendant never struck plaintiff at all, nor kicked him, nor ill-used him, further than by pushing him out of the field.

As to the loss of his quarter's wages, the plaintiff ingeniously proved that he had afterwards returned to his master, that he had worked out his time, and that he had in fact received already the greater part of his hire. Upon which the case was dismissed, the defendant quitting court without a stain upon his honour.

Case 2 was a most piteous and lamentable case of killing a cow. The plaintiff stepped forward with many tears and much gesticulation to state the fact, and also to declare that she was in danger of her life from the defendant's family.

It appeared on the evidence that a portion of the defendant's respectable family are at present undergoing the rewards which the law assigns to those who make mistakes in fields with regard to the ownership of sheep which sometimes graze there. The defendant's father, O'Damon, for having appropriated one of the fleecy bleaters of O'Melibœus, was at present passed beyond sea to a country where wool, and consequently mutton, is so plentiful, that he will have the less temptation. Defendant's brothers tread the Ixionic wheel for the same offence. Plaintiff's son had been the informer in the case: hence the feud between the families, the threats on the part of the defendant, the murder of the innocent cow.

But upon investigation of the business, it was discovered, and on the plaintiff's own testimony, that the cow had not been killed, nor even been injured; but that the defendant had flung two stones at it, which *might* have inflicted great injury had they hit the animal with greater force in the eye or in any delicate place.

Defendant admitted flinging the stones, but alleged as a reason that the cow was trespassing on his grounds; which plaintiff did not seem inclined to deny. Case dismissed.—Defendant retires with unblemished honour; on which his mother steps forward, and lifting up her hands with tears and shrieks, calls upon God to witness that the defendant's own brother-in-law had sold to her husband the very sheep on account of which he had been transported.

Not wishing probably to doubt the justice of the verdict of an Irish jury, the magistrate abruptly put an end to the lamentation and oaths of the injured woman by causing her to be sent out of court, and called the third cause on.

This was a case of thrilling interest and a complicated nature, involving two actions, which ought each perhaps to have been gone into separately, but were taken together. In the first place Timothy Horgan brought an action against Patrick Dolan for breach of contract in not remaining with him for the whole of six months during which Dolan had agreed to serve Horgan. Then Dolan brought an action against Horgan for not paying him his wages for six months' labour done—the wages being two guineas.

Horgan at once, and with much candour, withdrew his charge against Dolan, that the latter had not remained with him for six months; nor can I understand to this day why in the first place he swore to the charge, and why afterwards he withdrew it. But immediately advancing another charge against his late servant, he pleaded that he had given him a suit of clothes, which should be considered as a set-off against part of the money claimed.

Now such a suit of clothes as poor Dolan had was never seen—I will not say merely on an English scarecrow, but on an Irish beggar. Strips of rags fell over the honest fellow's great brawny chest, and the covering on his big brown legs hung on by a wonder. He held out his arms with a grim smile, and told his worship to look at the clothes! The argument was irresistible; Horgan was ordered to pay forthwith. He ought to have been made to pay another guinea for clothing a fellow-creature in rags so abominable.

And now came a case of trespass, in which there was nothing interesting but the attitude of the poor woman who trespassed, and who meekly acknowledged the fact. She stated, however, that she only got over the wall as a short cut home; but the wall was eight feet high, with a ditch too; and I fear there were cabbages or potatoes in the enclosure. They fined her a sixpence, and she could not pay it, and went to gaol for three days—where she and her baby at any rate will get a meal.

Last on the list which I took down came a man who will make the fortune of the London attorney that I hope is on his way hither: a rather old curly-headed man, with a sly smile perpetually lying on his face (the reader may give whatever interpretation he please to the ' lying'). He comes before the court almost every fortnight, they say, with a complaint of one kind or other. His present charge was against a man for breaking into his courtyard, and wishing to take possession of the same. It appeared that he, the defendant, and another lived in a row of houses: the plaintiff's house was, however, first built, and as his agreement specified that the plot of ground behind his house should be his likewise, he chose to imagine that the plot of ground behind all the three houses was his, and built his turf-stack against his neighbour's window. The magistrates of course pronounced against this ingenious discoverer of wrongs, and he left the court still smiling and twisting round his little wicked eyes, and declaring solemnly that he would put in an *appale.* If one could have purchased a kicking at a moderate price off that fellow's back, it would have been a pleasant little piece of self-indulgence, and I confess I longed to ask him the price of the article.

And so, after a few more such great cases, the court rose, and I had leisure to make moral reflections, if so minded—and sighing to think that cruelty and falsehood, selfishness and rapacity, dwell not in crowds alone, but flourish all the world over: sweet flowers of human nature, they bloom in all climates and seasons, and are just as much at home in a hot-house in Thavies' Inn as on a lone mountain or a rocky sea-coast in Ireland, where never a tree will grow!

We walked along this coast, after the judicial proceedings were over, to see the country, and the new road that the Board of Works is forming. Such a wilderness of rocks I never saw! The district for miles is covered with huge stones, shining white in patches of green, with the Binabola on one side of the spectator, and the Atlantic running in and out of a thousand little bays on the other. The country is very hilly, or wavy rather, being a sort of ocean petrified; and the engineers have hard work with these numerous abrupt little ascents and descents, which they equalise as best they may—by blasting, cutting, filling cavities, and levelling eminences. Some hundreds of men were employed at this work, busy with their hand-barrows, their picking and boring. Their pay is eighteenpence a day.

There is little to see in the town of Roundstone, except a Presbyterian chapel in process of erection—that seems big enough to accommodate the Presbyterians of the county—and a sort of a lay convent, being a community of brothers of the third order of Saint Francis. They are all artisans and workmen, taking no vows, but living together in common, and undergoing a certain religious regimen. Their work is said to be very good, and all are employed upon some labour or other. On the front of this unpretending little dwelling is an inscription with a great deal of pretence, stating that the establishment was founded with the approbation of 'his Grace the Most Reverend the Lord Archbishop of Tuam.'

The Most Reverend Doctor MacHale is a clergyman of great learning, talents, and honesty; but his Grace the Lord Archbishop of Tuam strikes me as being no better than a mountebank; and some day I hope even his own party will laugh this humbug down. It is bad enough to be awed by big titles at all; but to respect sham ones! stars and garters! We shall have his Grace the Lord Chief Rabbi next, or his Lordship the Arch-Imaum!

CHAPTER XIX: CLIFDEN TO WESTPORT

ON leaving Ballynahinch (with sincere regret, as any lonely tourist may imagine, who is called upon to quit the hospitable friendliness of such a place and society), my way lay back to Clifden again, and thence through the Joyce country, by the Killery mountains, to Westport in Mayo. The road, amounting in all to four-and-forty Irish miles, is performed in cars, in different periods of time, according to your horse and your luck. Sometimes, both being bad, the traveller is two days on the road; sometimes a dozen hours will suffice for the journey—which was the case with me, though I confess to having found the twelve hours long enough. After leaving Clifden, the friendly look of the country seemed to vanish; and though picturesque enough, was a thought too wild and dismal for eyes accustomed to admire a hopgarden in Kent, or a view of rich meadows in Surrey, with a clump of trees and a comfortable village spire. 'Inglis,' the Guide-book says, 'compares the scenes to the Norwegian Fiords.' Well, the Norwegian Fiords must, in this case, be very dismal sights; and I own that the wildness of Hampstead Heath (with the imposing walls of 'Jack Straw's Castle' rising stern in the midst of the green wilderness) is more to my taste than the general views of yesterday.

We skirted by lake after lake, lying lonely in the midst of lonely bog-lands, or bathing the sides of mountains robed in sombre rifle green. Two or three men, and as many huts, you see in the course of each mile perhaps, as toning up the bleak hills, or jingling more rapidly down them, you pass through this sad region. In the midst of the wilderness a chapel stands here and there, solitary, on the hillside; or a ruinous useless school-house, its pale walls contrasting with the general surrounding hue of sombre purple and green. But though the country looks more dismal than Connemara, it is clearly more fertile: we passed miles of ground that evidently wanted but bttle cultivation to make them profitable; and along the mountain-sides, in many places, and over a great extent of Mr. Blake's country especially, the hills were covered with a thick natural plantation, that may yield a little brushwood now, but might in fifty years' time bring thousands of pounds of revenue to the descendants of the Blakes. This spectacle of a country going to waste is enough to make the cheerfullest landscape look dismal: it gives this wild district a woeful look indeed. The names of the lakes by which we came I noted down in a pocket-book as we passed along; but the names were Irish, the car was rattling, and the only name readable in the catalogue is Letterfrack.

The little hamlet of Leenane is at twenty miles' distance from Clifden; and to arrive at it, you skirt the mountain along one side of a vast pass, through which the ocean runs from Killery Bay, separating the mountains of Mayo from the mountains of Galway. Nothing can be more grand and gloomy than this pass; and as for the character of the scenery, it must, as the Guide-book says, 'be seen to be understood.' Meanwhile, let the reader imagine huge dark mountains in their accustomed livery of purple and green, a dull grey sky above them, an estuary silver-bright below: in the water lies a fisherman's boat or two; a pair of seagulls undulating with the little waves of the water; a pair of curlews wheeling overhead and piping on the wing; and on the hillside a jingling car, with a cockney in it, oppressed by and yet admiring all these things. Many a sketcher and tourist, as I found, has visited this picturesque spot: for the hostess of the inn had stories of English and American painters, and of illustrious book-writers, too, travelling in the service of our Lords of Paternoster Row.

The landlord's son of Clifden, a very intelligent young fellow, was here exchanged for a new carman in the person of a raw Irisher of twenty years of age, 'having' little English, and dressed in that very pair of pantaloons which Humphrey Clinker was compelled to cast off some years since on account of the offence which they gave to Mrs. Tabitha Bramble. This fellow, emerging from among the boats, went off to a field to seek for the black horse, which the landlady assured me was quite fresh and had not been out all day, and would carry me to Westport in three hours. Meanwhile I was lodged in a neat little parlour, surveying the Mayo side of the water, with some cultivated fields and a show of a village at a spot where the estuary ends, and above them lodges and fine dark plantations climbing over the dark hills that lead to Lord Sligo's seat of Delphi. Presently, with a curtsey, came a young woman who sold worsted socks at a shilling a pair.

It required no small pains to entice this rustic beauty to stand while a sketch should be made of her. Nor did any compliments or cajolements, on my part or the landlady's, bring about the matter: it was not until money was offered that the lovely creature consented. I offered (such is the ardour of the real artist) either to give her sixpence, or to purchase two pairs of her socks, if she would stand still for fire minutes. On which she said she would prefer selling the socks. Then she stood still for a moment in the corner of the room; then she turned her face towards the corner and the other part of her person towards the artist, and exclaimed in that attitude, 'I must have a shilling more.' Then I told her to go to the deuce. Then she made a proposition, involving the stockings and sixpence, which was similarly rejected; and, finally, the design was completed at the price first stated.

However, as we went off, this timid little dove barred the door for a moment, and said that 'I ought to give her another shilling; that a gentleman would give her another shilling,' and so on. She might have trod the London streets for ten years and not have been more impudent and more greedy.

By this time the famous fresh horse was produced, and the driver, by means of a wraprascal, had covered a great part of the rags of his lower garment. He carried a whip and a stick, the former lying across his knees ornamentally, the latter being for service; and as his feet were directly under the horse's tail, he had full command of the brute's back, and belaboured it for six hours without ceasing.

What little English the fellow knew he uttered with a howl, roaring into my ear answers—which, for the most part, were wrong—to various questions put to him. The lad's voice was so hideous, that I asked him if he could sing; on which forthwith he began yelling a most horrible Irish ditty—of which he told me the title, that I have forgotten. He sang three stanzas, certainly keeping a kind of tune, and the latter lines of each verse were in rhyme; but when I asked him the meaning of the song, he only roared out its Irish title.

On questioning the driver further, it turned out that the horse, warranted fresh, had already performed a journey of eighteen miles that morning, and the consequence was that I had full leisure to survey the country through which we passed. There were more lakes, more mountains, more bog, and an excellent road through this lonely district, though few only of the human race enlivened it. At ten miles from Leenane, we stopped at a roadside hut, where the driver pulled out a bag of oats, and borrowing an iron pot from the good people, half filled it with corn, which the poor tired, galled, bewhipped black horse began eagerly to devour. The young charioteer himself hinted very broadly his desire for a glass of whisky, which was the only kind of refreshment that this remote house of entertainment supplied.

In the various cabins I have entered, I have found talking a vain matter; the people are suspicious of the stranger within their wretched gates, and are shy, sly, and silent. I have, commonly, only been able to get half-answers in reply to my questions, given in a manner that seemed plainly to intimate that the visit was unwelcome. In this rude hostel, however, the landlord was a little less reserved, offered a seat at the turf-fire, where a painter might have had a good subject for his skill. There was no chimney, but a hole in the roof, up which a small portion of the smoke ascended (the rest preferring an egress by the door, or else to remain in the apartment altogether); and this light from above lighted up as rude a set of figures as ever were seen. There were two brown women with black eyes and locks, the one knitting stockings on the floor, the other 'racking' (with that natural comb which five horny fingers supply) the elf-locks of a dirty urchin between her knees. An idle fellow was smoking his pipe by the fire; and by his side sat a stranger, who had been made welcome to the shelter of the place—a sickly well-looking man, whom I mistook for a deserter at first, for he had evidently been a soldier.

But there was nothing so romantic as desertion in his history. He had been in the Dragoons, but his mother had purchased his discharge: he was married, and had lived comfortably in Cork for some time, in the glass-blowing business. Trade failing at Cork, he had gone to Belfast to seek for work. There was no work at Belfast; and he was so far on his road home again: sick, without a penny in the world, a hundred and fifty miles to travel, and a starving wife and children to receive him at his journey's end. He had been thrown off a caravan that day, and had almost broken his back in the fall. Here was a cheering story! I wonder where he is now: how far has the poor starving lonely man advanced over that weary desolate road, that in good health, and with a horse to carry me, I thought it a penalty to cross? What would one do under such circumstances, with solitude and hunger for present company, despair and starvation at the end of the vista? There are a score of lonely lakes along the road which he has to pass: would it be well to stop at one of them, and fling into it the wretched load of cares which that poor broken back has to carry? Would the world he would light on *then* be worse for him than that he is pining in now? Heaven help us! and on this very day, throughout the three kingdoms, there are a million such stories to be told! Who dare doubt of heaven after that? of a place where there is at last a welcome to the heart-stricken prodigal and a happy home to the wretched?

The crumbs of oats which fell from the mouth of the feasting Dives of a horse were battled for outside the door by a dozen Lazaruses in the shape of fowls; and a lanky young pig, who had been grunting in an old chest in the cabin, or in a miserable recess of huddled rags and straw which formed the couch of the family, presently came out and drove the poultry away, picking up, with great accuracy, the solitary grains lying about, and more than once trying to shove his snout into the corn-pot, and share with the wretched old galled horse. Whether it was that he was refreshed by his meal, or that the car-boy was invigorated by his glass of whisky, or inflamed by the sight of eighteen-pence—which munificent sum was tendered to the soldier—I don't know; but the remaining eight miles of the journey were got over in much quicker time, although the road was exceedingly bad and hilly for the greatest part of the way to Westport. However, by running up the hills at the pony's side, the animal, fired with emulation, trotted up them too—descending them with the proverbial surefootedness of his race, the car and he bouncing over the rocks and stones at the rate of at least four Irish miles an hour.

At about five miles from Westport the cultivation became much more frequent. There were plantations upon the hills, yellow corn and potatoes in plenty in the fields, and houses thickly scattered. We had the satisfaction, too, of knowing that future tourists will have an excellent road to travel over in this district: for by the side of the old road, which runs up and down a hundred little rocky steeps, according to the ancient plan, you see a new one running for several miles,—the latter way being conducted, not over the hills, but around them, and, considering the circumstances of the country, extremely broad and even. The car-boy presently yelled out 'Reek, Reek!' with a shriek perfectly appalling. This howl was to signify that we were in sight of that famous conical mountain so named, and from which St. Patrick, after inveigling thither all the venomous reptiles in Ireland, precipitated the whole noisome race into Clew Bay. The road also for several miles was covered with people, who were flocking in hundreds from West-port market, in cars and carts, on horseback single and double, and on foot.

And presently, from an eminence, I caught sight not only of a fine view, but of the most beautiful .view I ever saw in the world, I think; and to enjoy the splendour of which I would travel a hundred miles in that car with that very horse and driver. The sun was just about to set, and the country round about and to the east was almost in twilight. The mountains were tumbled about in a thousand fantastic ways, and swarming with people. Trees, cornfields, cottages, made the scene indescribably cheerful; noble woods stretched towards the sea, and abutting on them, between two highlands, lay the smoking town. Hard by was a large Gothic building—it is but a poor-house; but it looked like a grand castle in the grey evening. But the Bay—and the Reek which sweeps down to the sea—and a hundred islands in it, were dressed up in gold and purple and crimson, with the whole cloudy west in a flame. Wonderful, -wonderful!...The valleys in the road to Leenane have lost all glimpses of the sun ere this; and I suppose there is not a soul to be seen in the black landscape, or by the shores of the ghastly lakes, where the poor glass-blower from the whisky-shop is faintly travelling now.

CHAPTEE XX: WESTPORT

NATURE has done much for this pretty town of Westport; and after Nature, the traveller ought to be thankful to Lord Sligo, who has done a great deal too. In the first place, ho has established one of the prettiest, comfortablest inns in Ireland, in the best part of his little town, stocking the cellars with good wines, filling the house with neat furniture, and lending, it is said, the whole to a landlord gratis, on condition that he should keep the house warm, and furnish the larder, and entertain the traveller. Secondly, Lord Sligo has given up, for the use of the townspeople, a beautiful little pleasure-ground about his house. 'You may depand upon it,'said a Scotchman at the inn, 'that they've right of pathway through the groonds, and that the marquess couldn't shut them oot.' Which is a pretty fair specimen of charity in this world—this kind world, that is always ready to encourage and applaud good actions, and find good motives for the same. I wonder how much would induce that Scotchman to allow poor people to walk in *his* park, if he had one!

In the midst of this pleasure-ground, and surrounded by a thousand fine trees, dressed up in all sorts of verdure, stands a pretty little church; paths through the wood lead pleasantly down to the bay; and, as we walked down to it on the day after our arrival, one of the green fields was suddenly black with rooks, making a huge cawing and clanging as they settled down to feed. The house, a handsome massive structure, must command noble views of the bay, over which all the colours of Titian were spread as the sun set behind its purple islands.

Printer's ink will not give these wonderful hues; and the reader will make his picture at his leisure. That conical mountain to the left is Croaghpatrick: it is clothed in the most magnificent violet colour, and a couple of round clouds were exploding as it were from the summit, that part of them towards the sea lighted up with the most delicate gold and rose colour. In the centre is the Clare island, of which the edges were bright cobalt, whilst the middle was lighted up with a brilliant scarlet tinge, such as I would have laughed at in a picture, never having seen in nature before, but looked at now with wonder and pleasure until the hue disappeared as the sun went away. The islands in the bay (which was of a gold colour) looked like so many dolphins and whales basking there. The rich park-woods stretched down to the shore; and the immediate foreground consisted of a yellow cornfield, whereon stood innumerable shocks of corn, casting immense long purple shadows over the stubble. The farmer, with some little ones about him, was superintending his reapers; and I heard him say to a little girl, 'Norey, I love you the best of all my children!' Presently, one of the reapers coming up, says, 'It's always the custom in these parts to ask strange gentlemen to give something to drink the first day of reaping; and we'd like to drink your honour's health in a bowl of coffee.' *O fortunatos nimium*! The cockney takes out sixpence, and thinks that he never passed such a pleasant half-hour in all his life as in that cornfield, looking at that wonderful bay.

A car which I had ordered presently joined me from the town, and going down a green lane very like England, and across a causeway near a building where the carman proposed to show me 'me Lard's caffin that he brought from Rome, and a mighty big caffin entirely,' we came close upon the water and the port. There was a long handsome pier (which, no doubt, remains at this present minute), and one solitary cutter lying alongside it; which may or may not be there now. There were about three boats lying near the cutter, and six sailors, with long shadows, lolling upon the pier. As for the warehouses, they are enormous; and might accommodate, I should think, not only the trade of Westport, but of Manchester too. There are huge streets of these houses, ten stories high, with cranes, owners' names, etc., marked Wine Stores, Flour Stores, Bonded Tobacco Warehouses, and so forth. The six sailors that were singing on the pier no doubt are each admirals of as many fleets of a hundred sail that bring wines and tobacco from all quarters of the world to fill these enormous warehouses. These dismal mausoleums, as vast as pyramids, are the places where the dead trade of Westport lies buried—a trade that, in its lifetime, probably was about as big as a mouse. Nor is this the first nor the hundredth place to be seen in this country, which sanguine builders have erected to accommodate an imaginary commerce. Mill-owners over-mill themselves, merchants over-warehouse themselves, squires over-castle themselves, little tradesmen about Dublin and the cities over-villa and over-gig themselves, and we hear sad tales about hereditary bondage and the accursed tyranny of England.

Passing out of this dreary pseudo-commercial port, the road lay along the beautiful shores of Clew Bay, adorned with many a rickety villa and pleasure-house, from the cracked windows of which may be seen one of the noblest views in the world. One of the villas the guide pointed out with peculiar exultation: it is called by a grand name-Waterloo Park, and has a lodge, and a gate, and a field of a couple of acres, and belongs to a young gentleman who, being able to write Waterloo Park on his card, succeeded in carrying off a young London heiress with a hundred thousand pounds. The young couple had just arrived, and one of them must have been rather astonished, no doubt, at the 'park.' But what will not love do? With love and a hundred thousand pounds, a cottage may be made to look like a castle, and a park of two acres may be brought to extend for a mile. The night began now to fall, wrapping up in a sober grey livery the bay and mountains, which had just been so gorgeous in sunset; and we turned our backs presently upon the bay, and the villas with the cracked windows, and scaling a road of perpetual ups and downs, went back to Westport. On the way was a pretty cemetery, lying on each side of the road, with a ruined chapel for the ornament of one division, a holy well for the other. In the holy well lives a sacred trout, whom sick people come to consult, and who operates great cures in the neighbourhood. If the patient see the trout floating on his back, he dies; if on his belly, he lives; or *vice versâ.* The little spot is old, ivy-grown, and picturesque, and I can't fancy a better place for a pilgrim to kneel and say his beads at.

But considering the whole country goes to mass, and that the priests can govern it as they will, teaching what shall be believed and what shall be not credited, would it not be well for their reverences, in the year eighteen hundred and forty-two, to discourage these absurd lies and superstitions, and teach some simple truths to their flock? Leave such figments to magazine-writers and ballad-makers; but, *corbleu*! it makes one indignant to think that people in the United Kingdom, where a press is at work, and good sense is abroad, and clergymen are eager to educate the people, should countenance such savage superstitions and silly grovelling heathenisms.

The chapel is before the inn where I resided, and on Sunday, from a very early hour, the side of the street was thronged with worshippers, who came to attend the various services. Nor are the Catholics the only devout people of this remote district. There is a large Presbyterian church very well attended, as was the Established Church service in the pretty church in the park. There was no organ, but the clerk and a choir of children sang hymns sweetly and truly; and a charity sermon being preached for the benefit of the diocesan schools, I saw many pound-notes in the plate, showing that the Protestants here were as ardent as their Roman Catholic brethren. The sermon was extempore, as usual, according to the prevailing taste here. The preacher by putting aside his sermon-book, may gain in warmth, which we don't want, but lose in reason, which we do. If I were Defender of the Faith, I would issue an order to all priests and deacons to take to the book again; weighing well, before they uttered it, every word they proposed to say upon so great a subject as that of religion; and mistrusting that dangerous facility given by active jaws and a hot imagination. Reverend divines have adopted this habit, and keep us for an hour listening to what might well be told in ten minutes. They are wondrously fluent, considering all things; and though I have heard many a sentence begun whereof the speaker did not evidently know the conclusion, yet, somehow or other, he has always managed to get through the paragraph without any hiatus, except perhaps in the sense. And as far as I can remark, it is not calm, plain, downright preachers who preserve the extemporaneous system for the most part, but pompous orators indulging in all the cheap graces of rhetoric—exaggerating words and feelings to make effect, and dealing in pious caricature. Church-goers become excited by this loud talk and captivating manner, and can't go back afterwards to a sober discourse read out of a grave old sermon-book, appealing to the reason and the gentle feelings, instead of to the passions and the imagination. Beware of too much talk, O parsons! If a man is to give an account of every idle word he utters, for what a number of such loud nothings, windy emphatic tropes and metaphors, spoken, not for God's glory, but the preacher's, will many a cushion-thumper have to answer! And this rebuke may properly find a place here, because the clergyman by whose discourse it was elicited is not of the eloquent dramatic sort, but a gentleman, it is said, remarkable for old-fashioned learning and quiet habits that do not seem to be to the taste of the many boisterous young clergy of the present day.

The Catholic chapel was built before their graces the most reverend lord archbishops came into fashion. It is large and gloomy, with one or two attempts at ornament byway of pictures at the altars, and a good inscription warning the incomer, in a few bold words, of the sacredness of the place he stands in. Bare feet bore away thousands of people who came to pray there; there were numbers of smart equipages for the richer Protestant congregation. Strolling about the town in the balmy summer evening, I heard the sweet tones of a hymn from the people in the Presbyterian praying-house. Indeed, the country is full of piety, and a warm, sincere, undoubting devotion.

On week-days the street before the chapel is scarcely less crowded than on the Sabbath: but it is with women and children merely; for a stream bordered with lime-trees runs pleasantly down the street, and hither come innumerable girls to wash, while the children make dirt-pies and look on. Wilkie was here some years since, and the place affords a great deal of amusement to the painter of character. Sketching, *tant ben que mal,* the bridge and the trees, and some of the nymphs engaged in the stream, the writer became an object of no small attention; and at least a score of dirty brats left their dirt-pies to look on, the bare-legged washing-girls grinning from the water.

One, a regular rustic beauty, whose face and figure would have made the fortune of a frontispiece, seemed particularly amused and *agacante;* and I walked round to get a drawing of her fresh jolly face: but directly I came near she pulled her gown over, her head, and resolutely turned round her back; and, as that part of her person did not seem to differ in character from the backs of the rest of Europe, there is no need of taking its likeness.

CHAPTER XXI: THE PATTERN AT CROAGHPATRICK

ON the Pattern day, however, the washerwomen and children had all disappeared—nay, the stream, too, seemed to be gone out of town. There was a report current, also, that on the occasion of the Pattern, six hundred teetotallers had sworn to revolt; and I fear that it was the hope of witnessing this awful rebellion which induced me to stay a couple of days at Westport. The Pattern was commenced on the Sunday, and the priests, going up to the mountain, took care that there should be no sports nor dancing on that day; but that the people should only content themselves with the performance of what are called religious duties. Religious duties! Heaven help us! If these reverend gentlemen were worshippers of Moloch or Baal, or any deity whose honour demanded bloodshed, and savage rites, and degradation, and torture, one might fancy them encouraging the people to the disgusting penances the poor things here perform. But it's too hard to think that in our days any priests of any religion should be found superintending such a hideous series of self-sacrifices as are, it appears, performed on this hill.

A friend who ascended the hill brought down the following account of it. The ascent is a very steep and hard one, he says; but it was performed in company of thousands of people who were making their way barefoot to the several ' stations' upon the hill.

'The first station consists of one heap of stones, round which they must walk seven times, casting a stone on the heap each time, and before and after every stone's throw saying a prayer.

'The second station is on the top of the mountain. Here there is a great altar—a shapeless heap of stones. The poor wretches crawl *on their knees* into this place, say fifteen prayers, and after going round the entire top of the mountain fifteen times, say fifteen prayers again.

'The third station is near the bottom of the mountain at the farther side from Westport. It consists of three heaps. The penitents must go seven times round these collectively, and seven times afterwards round each individually, saying a prayer before and after each progress.'

My informant describes the people as coming away from this 'frightful exhibition suffering severe pain, wounded and bleeding in the knees and feet, and some of the women shrieking with the pain of their wounds.' Fancy thousands of these bent upon their work, and priests standing by to encourage them!—For shame, for shame! If all the popes, cardinals, bishops, hermits, priests, and deacons that ever lived were to come forward and preach this as a truth—that to please God you must macerate your body, that the sight of your agonies is welcome to Him, and that your blood, groans, and degradation find favour in His eyes, I would not believe them. Better have over a company of Fakeers at once, and set the Suttee going.

Of these tortures, however, I had not the fortune to witness a sight: for going towards the mountain for the first four miles, the only conveyance I could find was half the pony of an honest sailor, who said, when applied to, 'I tell you what I do wid you: I give you a spell about.' But, as it turned out we were going different ways, this help was but a small one. A car with a spare seat, however (there were hundreds of others quite full, and scores of rattling country-carte covered with people, and thousands of bare legs trudging along the road)—a car with a spare seat passed by at two miles from the Pattern, and that just in time to get comfortably wet through on arriving there. The whole mountain was enveloped in mist; and we could nowhere see thirty yards before us. The women walked forward, with their gowns over their heads; the men sauntered on in the rain, with the utmost indifference to it. The car presently came to a cottage, the court in front of which was black with two hundred horses, and where as many drivers were jangling and bawling; and here we were told to descend. You had to go over a wall and across a brook, and behold the Pattern.

The pleasures of the poor people—for after the business on the mountain came the dancing and love-making at its foot;—were woefully spoiled by the rain, which rendered dancing on the grass impossible; nor were the tents big enough for that exercise. Indeed, the whole sight was as dismal and half-savage a one as I have seen. There may have been fifty of these tents squatted round a plain of the most brilliant green grass, behind which the mist-curtains seemed to rise immediately; for you could not even see the mountain-side beyond them. Here was a great crowd of men and women, all ugly, as the fortune of the day would have it (for the sagacious reader has, no doubt, remarked that there are ugly and pretty days in life). Stalls were spread about, whereof the owners were shrieking out the praises of their wares—great coarse damp-looking bannocks of bread for the most part, or, mayhap, a dirty collection of pigs'-feet and such refreshments. Several of the booths professed to belong to 'confectioners' from Westport or Castlebar, the confectionery consisting of huge biscuits and doubtful-looking ginger-beer—ginger-ale or gingeretta it is called in this country, by a fanciful people who love the finest titles. Add to these, caldrons containing water for 'tay' at the doors of the booths, other pots full of masses of pale legs of mutton (the owner 'prodding,' every now and then, for a bit, and holding it up and asking the passenger to buy). In the booths it was impossible to stand upright, or to see much, on account of smoke. Men and women were crowded in these rude tents, huddled together, and disappearing in the darkness. Owners came bustling out to replenish the emptied water-jugs: and landladies stood outside in the rain calling strenuously upon all passers-by to enter.

Meanwhile, high up on the invisible mountain, the people were dragging their bleeding knees from altar to altar, flinging stones, and muttering some endless litanies, with the priests standing by. I think I was not sorry that the rain, and the care of my precious health, prevented me from mounting a severe hill to witness a sight that could only have caused one to be shocked and ashamed that servants of God should encourage it. The road home was very pleasant; everybody was wet through, but everybody was happy, and by some miracle we were seven on the car. There was the honest Englishman in the military cap, who sang 'The sea, the hopen sea's my 'ome,' although not any one of the company called upon him for that air. Then the music was taken up by a good-natured lass from Castlebar; then the Englishman again, 'With burnished brand and musketoon'; and there was no end of pushing, pinching, squeezing, and laughing. The Englishman, especially, had a favourite yell, with which he saluted and astonished all cottagers, passengers, cars, that we met or overtook. Presently came prancing by two dandies, who were especially frightened by the noise. 'Thim's two tailors from Westport,' said the carman, grinning with all his might. 'Come, gat out of the way there, gat along!' piped a small English voice from above somewhere, I looked up, and saw a little creature perched on the top of a tandem, which he was driving with the most knowing air—a dreadful young hero, with a white hat, and a white face, and a blue bird's-eye neckcloth. He was five feet high, if an inch, an ensign, and sixteen; and it was a great comfort to think, in case of danger or riot, that one of his years and personal strength was at hand to give help.

'Thim's the afficers,' said the carman, as the tandem wheeled by, a small groom quivering on behind—and the carman spoke with the greatest respect this time. Two days before, on arriving at Westport, I had seen the same equipage at the door of the inn—where for a moment there happened to be no waiter to receive me. So, shouldering a carpet-bag, I walked into the inn-hall, and asked a gentleman standing there where was the coffee-room? It was the military tandem-driving youth, who with much grace looked up in my face, and said calmly, '*I dawnt knaw*.' I believe the little creature had just been dining in the very room—and so present my best compliments to him.

The Guide-book will inform the traveller of many a beautiful spot which lies in the neighbourhood of Westport, and which I had not the time to visit; but I must not take leave of the excellent little inn without speaking once more of its extreme comfort; nor of the place itself, without another parting word regarding its beauty. It forms an event in one's life to have seen that place, so beautiful is it, and so unlike all other beauties that I know of. Were such beauties lying upon English shores it would be a world's wonder: perhaps, if it were on the Mediterranean, or the Baltic, English travellers would flock to it

by hundreds; why not come and ffee it in Ireland? Remote as the spot is, Westport is only two days' journey from London now, and lies in a country far more strange to most travellers than France or Germany can be.

CHAPTER XXII: FROM WESTPORT TO BALLINASLOE

THE mail-coach took us next day by Castlebar and Tuam to Ballinasloe, a journey of near eighty miles. The country is interspersed with innumerable seats belonging to the Blakes, the Browns, and the Lynches; and we passed many large domains belonging to bankrupt lords and fugitive squires, with fine lodges adorned with moss and battered windows, and parks where, if the grass was growing on the roads, on the other hand the trees had been weeded out of the grass. About these seats and their owners the guard—an honest shrewd fellow—had all the gossip to tell. The jolly guard himself was a ruin, it turned out: he told me his grandfather was a man of large property; his father, he said, kept a pack of hounds, and had spent everything by the time he, the guard, was sixteen: so the lad made interest to get a mail-car to drive, whence he had been promoted to the guard's seat, and now for forty years had occupied it, travelling eighty miles, and earning seven-and-twopence every day of his life. He had been once ill, he said, for three days; and if a man may be judged by ten hours' talk with him, there were few more shrewd, resolute, simple-minded men to be found on the outside of any coaches or the inside of any houses in Ireland.

During the first five-and-twenty miles of the journey,—for the day was very sunny and bright, Croaghpatrick kept us company; and, seated with your back to the horses, you could see, 'on the left, that vast aggregation of mountains which stretches southwards to the Bay of Galway; on the right, that gigantic assemblage which sweeps in circular outline northward to Killule.' Somewhere amongst those hills the great John Tuam was born, whose mansion and cathedral are to be seen in Tuam town, but whose fame is spread everywhere. To arrive at Castlebar, we go over the undulating valley which lies between the mountains of Joyce country and Erris; and the first object which you see on entering the town is a stately Gothic castle that stands at a short distance from it.

On the gate of the stately Gothic castle was written an inscription not very hospitable: 'without beware, within amend';—just beneath which is an iron crane of neat construction. The castle is the county gaol, and the iron crane is the gallows of the district. The town seems neat and lively; there is a fine church, a grand barracks (celebrated as the residence of the young fellow with the bird's-eye neckcloth), a club, and a Whig and Tory newspaper. The road hence to Tuam is very pretty and lively, from the number of country seats along the way, giving comfortable shelter to more Blakes, Browns, and Lynches.

In the cottages, the inhabitants looked healthy and rosy in their rags, and the cots themselves in the sunshine almost comfortable. After a couple of months in the country, the stranger's eye grows somewhat accustomed to the rags: they do not frighten him as at first; the people who wear them look for the most part healthy enough: especially the small children—those who can scarcely totter, and are sitting shading their eyes at the door, and leaving the unfinished dirt-pie to shout as the coach passes by—are as healthy a looking race as one will often see. Nor can any one pass through the land without being touched by the extreme love of children among the people: they swarm everywhere, and the whole country rings with cries of affection towards the children, with the songs of young ragged nurses dandling babies on their knees, and warnings of mothers to Patsey to come out of the mud, or Norey to get off the pig's back.

At Tuam the coach stopped exactly for fourteen minutes and a half, during which time those who wished might dine: but instead, I had the pleasure of inspecting a very mouldy dirty town, and made my way to the Catholic cathedral—a very handsome edifice indeed; handsome without and within, and of the Gothic sort. Over the door is a huge coat of arms, surmounted by a cardinal's hat—the arms of the see, no doubt, quartered with John Tuam's own patrimonial coat; and that was a frieze coat, from all accounts, passably ragged at the elbows. Well, he must be a poor wag who could sneer at an old coat, because it was old and poor; but if a man changes it for a tawdry gimcrack suit bedizened with twopenny tinsel, and struts about calling himself his Grace and my Lord, when may we laugh if not then? There is something simple in the way in which these good people belord their clergymen, and respect titles real or sham. Take any Dublin paper,—a couple of columns of it are sure to be filled with movements of the small great men of the world. Accounts from Derrynane state that the 'Right Honourable the Lord Mayor is in good health—his Lordship went out with his beagles yesterday'; or 'his Grace the Most Reverend the Lord Archbishop of Ballywhack, assisted by the Right Reverend the Lord Bishops of Trincomalee and Hippopotamus, assisted,' etc.; or 'Colonel Tims, of Castle Tims, and lady, have quitted the Shelburne Hotel, with a party for Kilballybathershins, where the august party[xiii] propose to enjoy a few days' shrimp-fishing,'—and so on. Our people are not witty and keen of perceiving the ridiculous, like the Irish; but the bluntness and honesty of the English have well-nigh kicked the fashionable humbug down; and except, perhaps, among footmen and about Baker Street, this curiosity about the aristocracy is wearing fast away. Have the Irish so much reason to respect their lords that they should so chronicle all their movements; and not only admire real lords, but make sham ones of their own to admire *them*?

There is no object of special mark upon the road from Tuam to Ballinasloe—the country being flat for the most part, and the noble Galway and Mayo mountains having disappeared at length—until you come to a glimpse of old England in the pretty village of Ahascragh. An old oak-tree grows in the neat street, the houses are as trim and white as eye can desire, and about the church and the town are handsome plantations, forming on the whole such a picture of comfort and plenty as is rarely to be seen in the part of Ireland I have traversed. All these wonders have been wrought by the activity of an excellent resident agent. There was a countryman on the coach deploring that, through family circumstances, this gentleman should have been dispossessed of his agency, and declaring that the village had already begun to deteriorate in consequence. The marks of such decay were not, however, visible—at least to a new-comer; and, being reminded of it, I indulged, in many patriotic longings for England: as every Englishman does when he is travelling out of the country which he is always so willing to quit.

That a place should instantly begin to deteriorate because a certain individual was removed from it—that cottagers should become thriftless, and houses dirty, and house-windows cracked,—all these are points which public economists may ruminate over, and can't fail to give the carelessest traveller much matter for painful reflection. How is it that the presence of one man more or less should affect a set of people come to years of manhood, and knowing that they have their duty to do?—Why should a man at Ahascragh let his home go to ruin and stuff his windows with ragged breeches instead of glass, because Mr. Smith is agent in place of Mr. Jones? Is he a child, that won't work unless the schoolmaster be at hand? or are we to suppose, with the 'Repealers,' that the cause of all this degradation and misery is the intolerable tyranny of the sister country, and the pain which poor Ireland has been made to endure? This is very well at the Corn Exchange, and among patriots after dinner; but, after all, granting the grievance of the franchise (though it may not be unfair to presume that a man who has not strength of mind enough to mend his own breeches or his own windows will always be the tool of one party or another), there is no Inquisition set up in the country: the law tries to defend the people as much as they will allow; the odious tithe has even been whisked off from their shoulders to the landlords'; they may live pretty much as they like. Is is not too monstrous to howl about English tyranny and suffering Ireland, and call for a Stephen's Green Parliament to make the country quiet and the people industrious? The people are not politically worse treated than their neighbours in England. The priests and the landlords, if they chose to co-operate, might do more for the country now than any kings or laws could. What you want here is not a Catholic or Protestant party, but an Irish party.

In the midst of these reflections, and by what the reader will doubtless think a blessed interruption, we came in sight of the town of Ballinasloe and its 'gash-lamps,' which a fellow-passenger did not fail to point out with admiration. The road-menders, however, did not appear to think that light was by any means necessary: for, having been occupied, in the morning, in digging a fine hole upon the highway, previous to some alterations to be effected there, they had left their work at sundown, without any lamp to warn coming travellers of the hole—which we only escaped by a wonder. The papers have much such another story. In the Galway and Ballinasloe coach a horse on the road suddenly fell down and died: the coachman drove his coach unicorn-fashion into town; and, as for the dead horse, of course he left it on the road at the place where it fell, and where another coach coming up was upset over it, bones broken, passengers maimed, coach smashed. By heavens! the tyranny of England is unendurable; and I have no doubt it had a hand in upsetting that coach.

CHAPTER XXIII: BALLINASLOE TO DUBLIN

DURING the cattle-fair the celebrated town of Ballinasloe is thronged with farmers from all parts of the kingdom—the cattle being picturesquely exhibited in the park of the noble proprietor of the town, Lord Clancarty. As it was not fair-time the town did not seem particularly busy, nor was there much to remark in it, except a church, and a magnificent lunatic asylum, that lies outside the town on the Dublin road, and is as handsome and stately as a palace. I think the beggars were more plenteous and more loathsome here than almost anywhere. To one hideous wretch I was obliged to give money to go away, which he did for a moment, only to obtrude his horrible face directly afterwards half eaten away with disease. 'A penny for the sake of poor little Mery,' said another woman, who had a baby sleeping on her withered breast; and how can any one who has a little Mery at home resist such an appeal? 'Pity the poor blind man!' roared a respectably dressed grenadier of a fellow. I told him to go to the gentleman with a red neckcloth and fur cap (a young buck from Trinity College)—to whom the blind man with much simplicity immediately stepped over; and as for the rest of the beggars, what pen or pencil could describe their hideous leering flattery, their cringing swindling humour!

The inn, like the town, being made to accommodate the periodical crowds of visitors who attended the fair, presented in their absence rather a faded and desolate look; and in spite of the live-stock for which the place is famous, the only portion of their produce which I could get to my share, after twelve hours' fasting and an hour's bell-ringing awl scolding, was one very lean mutton-chop and one very small damp kidney, brought in by an old tottering waiter to a table spread in a huge black coffee-room, dimly lighted by one little jet of gas.

As this only served very faintly to light up the above banquet, the waiter, upon remonstrant, proceeded to light the other *bec*; but the lamp was sulky, and upon this attempt to force it, as it were, refused to act altogether, and went out. The big room was then accommodated with a couple of yellow mutton-candles. There was a neat, handsome, correct young English officer warming his slippers at the fire, and opposite him sat a worthy gentleman, with a glass of 'mingled materials,' discoursing to him in a very friendly and confidential way.

As I don't know the gentleman's name, and as it is not at all improbable, from the situation in which he was, that he has quite forgotten the night's conversation, I hope there will be no breach of confidence in recalling some part of it. The speaker was dressed in deep black— worn, however, with that *dégagé* air peculiar to the votaries of Bacchus, or that nameless god, offspring of Bacchus and Ceres, who may have invented the noble liquor called whisky. It was fine to see the esay folds in which his neckcloth confined a shirt collar moist with the generous drops that trickled from the chin above,—its little percentage upon the punch. There was a fine dashing black-satin waistcoat that called for its share, and generously disdained to be buttoned. I think this is the only specimen I have seen yet of the personage still so frequently described in the Irish novels—the careless drinking squire—the Irish Will Whimble.

'Sir,'says he, 'as I was telling you before this gentleman came in (from Westport, I preshume, sir, by the mail? (and my service to you!), the butchers in Chume (Tuam)—where I live, and shall be happy to see you and give you a shakedown, a cut of mutton, and the use of as good a brace of pointers as ever you shot over—the butchers say to me, whenever I look in at their shops and ask for a joint of meat—they say: "Take down that quarther o' mutton, boy; IT'S NO USE WEIGHING IT for Mr. Bodkin. He can tell with an eye what's the weight of it to an ounce!" And so, sir, I can; and I'd make a bet to into any market in Dublin, Tchume, Ballinasloe, where you please, and just by looking at the meat decide its weight.'

At the pause, during which the gentleman here designated Bodkin drank off his 'materials,' the young officer said gravely that this was a very rare and valuable accomplishment, and thanked him for the invitation to Tchume.

The honest gentleman proceeded with bis personal memoirs; and (with a charming modesty that authenticated his talc, while it interested his hearers for the teller) he called for a fresh tumbler, and began discoursing about horses. 'Them I don't know,' says he, confessing the fact at once; 'or, if I do, I've been always so unlucky with them that it's as good as if I didn't.

'To give you an idea of my ill fortune: Me brother 'n law Burke once sent me three colts of his to sell at this very fair of Ballinasloe, and for all I could do I could only get a bid for one of 'em, and sold her for sixteen pound. And d'ye know what that mare was, sir?' says Mr. Bodkin, giving a thump that made the spoon jump out of the punch-glass for fright. 'D' ye know who she was? she was Water-Wagtail, sir,—WATER-WAGTAIL! She won fourteen cups and plates in Ireland before she went to Liverpool; and you know what she did *there*?' (We said, 'Oh! of course.') 'Well, sir, the man who bought her from me sold her for four hunder' guineas; and in England she fetched eight hunlder' pounds.

'Another of them very horses, gentlemen (Tim, some hot wather-screeching hot, you divil—and a sthroke of the limin)—another of them horses that I was refused fifteen pound for, me brother-in-law sould to Sir Rufford Bufford for a hunder'-and-fifty guineas. Wasn't *that* luck?'

'Well, sir, Sir Rufford gives Burke his bill at six months, and don't pay it when it come jue. A pretty pickle Tom Burke was in, as I leave ye to fancy, for he'd paid away the bill, which ho thought as good as goold; and sure it ought to be, for Sir Rufford had come of age since the bill was drawn, and before it was due, and, as I needn't tell you, had slipped into a very handsome property.

'On the protest of the bill, Burke goes in a fury to Gresham's in Sackville Street, where the Baronet was living, and (would ye believe it?) the latter says he doesn't intend to meet the bill, on the score that he was a minor when he gave it. On which Burke was in such a rage that he took a horsewhip and vowed he'd beat the baronet to a jelly, and post him in every club in Dublin, and publish every circumstance of the transaction.'

'It *does* seem rather a queer one,' says one of Mr. Bodkin's hearers.

'Queer indeed: but that's not it, you see; for Sir Rufford is as honourable a man as ever lived; and after the quarrel he paid Burke his money, and they've been warm friends ever since. But what I want to show ye is our infernal luck. *Three months before, Sir Rufford had sold that very horse for three hunder' guineas.'*

The worthy gentleman had just ordered in a fresh tumbler of his favourite liquor, when we wished him good-night, and slept by no means the worse, because the bedroom candle was carried by one of the prettiest young chambermaids possible.

Next morning, surrounded by a crowd of beggars more filthy, hideous, and importunate than any I think in the most favoured towns of the south, we set off, a coach-load, for Dublin. A clergyman, a guard, a Scotch farmer, a butcher, a bookseller's hock, a lad bound for Maynooth and another for Trinity, made a varied pleasant party enough, where each, according to his lights, had something to say,

I have seldom seen a more dismal and uninteresting road than that which we now took, and which brought us through the 'old inconvenient, ill-built, and ugly town of Athlone.' The painter would find here, however, some good subjects for his sketch-book, in spite of the commination of the Guide-book. Here, too, great improvements are taking place for the Shannon navigation, which will render the town not so inconvenient as at present it is stated to be; and hard by lies a little village that is known and loved by all the world where English is spoken. It is called Lishoy, but its real name is Auburn, and it gave birth to one Noll Goldsmith, whom Mr. Boswell was in the habit of despising very heartily. At the Quaker town of Moate, the butcher and the farmer dropped off, the clergyman went inside, and their places were filled by four Maynoothians, whose vacation was just at an end. One of them, a freshman, was inside the coach with the clergyman, and told him, with rather a long face, of the dismal discipline of his college. They are not allowed to quit the gates (except on general walks); they are expelled if they read a newspaper; and they begin term with 'a retreat' of a week, which time they are made to devote to silence, and, as it is supposed, to devotion and meditation.

I must say the young fellows drank plenty of whisky on the road to prepare them for their year's abstinence; and, when at length arrived in the miserable village of Maynooth, determined not to go into college that night, but to devote the evening to 'a lark.' They were simple kind-hearted young men, sons of farmers or tradesmen seemingly; and, as is always the case here, except among some of the gentry, very gentlemanlike and pleasing in manners. Their talk was of this companion and that; how one was in rhetoric, and another in logic, and a third had got his curacy. Wait for a while; and with the happy system pursued within the walls of their college, those smiling good-humoured faces will come out with a scowl, and downcast eyes that seem afraid to look the world in the face. When the time comes for them to take leave of yonder dismal-looking barracks, they will be men no longer, but bound over to the Church, body and soul; their free thoughts chained down and kept in darkness, their honest affections mutilated. Well, I hope they will be happy to-night at any rate, and talk and laugh to their hearts' content. The poor freshman, whose big chest is carried off by the porter yonder to the inn, has but twelve hours more of hearty, natural human life. To-morrow, they will begin their work upon him; cramping his mind, and bitting his tongue, and firing and cutting at his heart,—breaking him to pull the Church chariot. Ah! why didn't he stop at home, and dig potatoes and get children?

Part of the drive from Maynooth to Dublin is exceedingly pretty: you are carried through Leixlip, Lucan, Chapelizod, and by scores of parks and villas, until the gas-lamps come in sight. Was there ever a cockney that was not glad to see them; and did not prefer the sight of them, in his heart, to the best lake or mountain ever invented? Pat the waiter comes jumping down to the car and says, 'Welcome back, sir!' and bustles the trunk into the queer little bedroom, with all the cordial hospitality imaginable.

CHAPTER XXIV: TWO DAYS IN WICKLOW

THE little tour we have just been taking has been performed., not only by myriads of the 'car-drivingest, tay-drinkingest, say-bathingest people in the world,' the inhabitants of the city of Dublin, but also by all the tourists who have come to discover this country for the benefit of the English nation. 'Look here!' says the ragged bearded genius of a guide at the Seven Churches. 'This is the spot which Mr. Henry Inglis particularly admired, and said it was exactly like Norway. Many's the song I've heard Mr. Sam Lover sing here—a pleasant gentleman entirely. Have you seen my picture that's taken off in Mrs. Hall's book? All the strangers know me by it, though it makes me much cleverer than I am.' Similar tales has he of Mr. Barrow, and the Transatlantic Willis, and of Crofton Croker, who has been everywhere.

The guide's remarks concerning the works of these gentlemen inspired me, I must confess, with considerable disgust and jealousy. A plague take them! What remains for me to discover after the gallant adventurers in the service of Paternoster Row have examined every rock, lake, and ruin of the district, exhausted it of all its legends, and 'invented new' most likely, as their daring genius prompted? Hence it follows that the description of the two days' jaunt must of necessity be short; lest persons who have read former accounts should be led to refer to the same, and make comparisons which might possibly be unfavourable to the present humble pages.

Is there anything new to be said regarding the journey? In the first place, there's the railroad: it's no longer than the railroad to Greenwich, to be sure, and almost as well known: but has it been *done*? that's the question; or has anybody discovered the dandies on the railroad?

After wondering at the beggars and carmen of Dublin, the stranger can't help admiring another vast and numerous class of inhabitants of the city—namely, the dandies. Such a number of smartly-dressed young fellows I don't think any town possesses; no, not Paris, where the young shopmen, with spurs and stays, may be remarked strutting abroad on fête-days; nor London, where on Sundays, in the Park, you see thousands of this cheap kind of aristocracy parading; nor Liverpool, famous for the breed of commercial dandies, desk and counter Dorsays, and cotton and sugar-barrel Brummels, and whom one remarks pushing on to business with a brisk determined air. All the above races are only to be encountered on holidays, except by those persons whose affairs take them to shops, docks, or counting-houses, where these fascinating young fellows labour during the week.

But the Dublin breed of dandies is quite distinct from those of the various cities above named, and altogether superior: for they appear every day, and all day long, not once a week merely, and have an original and splendid character and appearance of their own, very hard to describe, though no doubt every traveller, as well as myself, has admired and observed it. They assume a sort of military and ferocious look, not observable in other cheap dandies, except in Paris perhaps now and then; and are to be remarked not so much for the splendour of their ornaments as for the profusion of them. Thus, for instance, a hat which is worn straight over the two eyes costs very likely more than one which hangs upon one ear; a great oily bush of hair to balance the hat (otherwise the head no doubt would fall hopelessly on one side) is even more economical than a crop which requires the barber's scissors oft-times; also a tuft on the chin may be had at a small expense of bear's-grease by persons of a proper age; and although big pins are the fashion, I am bound to say I have never seen so many or so big as here. Large agate marbles or 'taws,' globes terrestrial and celestial, pawnbrokers' balls,—I cannot find comparisons large enough for these wonderful ornaments of the person. Canes also should be mentioned, which are sold very splendid, with gold or silver heads, for a shilling on the Quays; and the dandy not uncommonly finishes off with a horn quizzing-glass, which being stuck in one eye contracts the brows and gives a fierce determined look to the whole countenance.

In idleness at least these young men can compete with the greatest lords; and the wonder is, how the city can support so many of them, or they themselves; how they manage to spend their time: who gives them money to ride hacks in the 'Phaynix' on field and race days; to have boats at Kingstown during the summer; and to be crowding the railway-coaches all the day long? Cars go whirling about all day, bearing squads of them. You see them sauntering at all the railway-stations in vast numbers, and jumping out of the carriages as the trains come up, and greeting other dandies with that rich large brogue which some actor ought to make known to the English public: it being the biggest, richest, and coarsest of all the brogues of Ireland.

I think these dandies are the chief objects which arrest the stranger's attention as he travels on the Kingstown railroad, and I have always been so much occupied in watching and wondering at them as scarcely to have leisure to look at anything else during the pretty little ride of twenty minutes so beloved by every Dublin cockney. The waters of the bay wash in many places the piers on which the railway is built, and you see the calm stretch of water beyond, and the big purple hill of Howth, and the lighthouses, and the jetties, and the shipping. Yesterday was a boat-race (I don't know how many scores of such take place during the season), and you may be sure there were tens of thousands of the dandies to look on. There had been boat-races the two days previous: before that, had been a field day—before that, three days of garrison races—to-day, to-morrow, and the day after, there are races at Howth. There seems some sameness in the sports, but everybody goes; everybody is never tired; and then, I suppose, comes the punch-party, and the song in the evening—the same old pleasures, and the same old songs the next day, and so on to the end. As for the boat-race, I saw two little boats in the distance tugging away for dear life—the beach and piers swarming with spectators, the bay full of small yachts and innumerable row-boats, and in the midst of the assemblage a convict-ship lying ready for sail, with a black mass of poor wretches on her deck—who, too, were eager for pleasure.

Who is not, in this country? Walking away from the pier and King George's column, you arrive upon rows after rows of pleasure-houses, whither all Dublin flocks during the summer-time—for every one must have his sea-bathing; and they say that the country-houses to the west of the town are empty, or to be had for very small prices, while for those on the coast, especially towards Kingstown, there is the readiest sale at large prices. I have paid frequent visits to one, of which the rent is as great as that of a tolerable London house; and there seem to be others suited to all purses: for instance, there are long lines of two-roomed houses, stretching far back and away from the sea, accommodating, doubtless, small commercial men, or small families, or some of those travelling dandies we have just been talking about, and whose costume is so cheap and so splendid.

A two-horse car, which will accommodate twelve, or will condescend to receive twenty passengers, starts from the railway-station for Bray, running along the coast for the chief part of the journey, though you have but few views of the sea, on account of intervening woods and hills. The whole of this country is covered with handsome villas and their gardens and pleasure-grounds. There are round many of the houses parks of some extent, and always of considerable beauty, among the trees of which the road winds. New churches are likewise to be seen in various places; built like the poorhouses, that are likewise everywhere springing up, pretty much upon one plan—a sort of bastard or Vauxhall Gothic—resembling no architecture of any age previous to that when Horace Walpole invented the Castle of Otranto and the other monstrosity upon Strawberry Hill: though it must be confessed that those on the Bray line are by no means so imaginative. Well, what matters, say you, that the churches be ugly, if the truth is preached within? Is it not fair, however, to say that Beauty is the truth too, of its kind? and why should it not be cultivated as well as other truth? Why build these hideous barbaric temples, when at the expense of a little study and taste beautiful structures might be raised?

After leaving Bray, with its pleasant bay, and pleasant river, and. pleasant inn, the little Wicklow tour maybe said to commence properly; and, as that romantic and beautiful country has been described many times in familiar terms, our only chance is to speak thereof in romantic and beautiful language, such as no other writer can possibly have employed.

We rang at the gate of the steward's lodge and said, 'Grant us a pass, we pray, to see the parks of Powerscourt, and to behold the brown deer upon the grass, and the cool shadows under the whispering trees.'

But the steward's son answered, 'You may not see the parks of Powerscourt, for the lord of the castle comes home, and we expect him daily.' So, wondering at this reply, but not understanding the same, we took leave of the son of the steward and said, 'No doubt Powers-court is not fit to see. Have we not seen parks in England, my brother, and shall we break our hearts that this Irish one hath its gates closed to us?'

Then the car-boy said, 'My lords, the park is shut, but the waterfall runs for every man; will it please you see the waterfall?' 'Boy,' we replied, 'we have seen many waterfalls; nevertheless, lead on!' And the boy took his pipe out of his mouth and belaboured the ribs of his beast.

And the horse made believe, as it were, to trot, and jolted the ardent travellers; and we passed the green trees of Tinnehinch, which the grateful Irish nation bought and consecrated to the race of Grattan; and we said, 'What nation will spend fifty thousand pounds for our benefit?' and we wished we might get it; and we passed on. The birds were, meanwhile, chanting concerts in the woods; and the sun was double-gilding the golden corn.

And we came to a hill, which was steep and long of descent; and the car-boy said, 'My lords, I may never descend this hill with safety to your honours' bones: for my horse is not sure of foot, and loves to kneel in the highway. Descend therefore, and I will await your return here on the top of the hill.'

So we descended, and one grumbled greatly; but the other said, 'Sir, be of good heart! the way is pleasant, and the footman will not weary as he travels it.' And we went through the swinging gates of a park, where the harvestmen sate at their potatoes—a mealy meal.

The way was not short, as the companion said, but still it was a pleasant way to walk. Green stretches of grass were there, and a forest nigh at hand. It was but September: yet the autumn had already begun to turn the green trees into red; and the ferns that were waving underneath the trees were reddened and fading too. And as Dr. Jones's boys of a Saturday disport in the meadows after school-hours, so did the little clouds run races over the waving grass. And as grave ushers who look on smiling at the sports of these little ones, so stood the old trees around the green, whispering and nodding to one another.

Purple mountains rose before us in front, and we began presently to hear a noise and roaring afar off—not a fierce roaring, but one deep and calm, like to the respiration of the great sea, as he lies basking on the sands in the sunshine.

And we came Boon to a little hillock of green, which was standing before a huge mountain of purple black, and there were white clouds over the mountains, and some trees waving on the hillock, and between the trunks of them we saw the waters of the water-fall descending; and there was a snob on a rock, who stood and examined the same.

Then we approached the water, passing the clump of oak-trees. The waters were white, and the cliffs which they varnished were purple. But those round about were grey, tall, and gay with blue shadows, and ferns, heath, and rusty-coloured funguses sprouting here and there in the same. But in the ravine where the waters fell, roaring as it were with the fall, the rocks were dark, and the foam of the cataract was of a yellow ,colour. And we stood, and were silent, and wondered. And still the trees continued to wave, and the waters to roar and tumble, and the sun to shine, and the fresh wind to blow.

And we stood and looked: and said in our hearts it was beautiful, and bethought us how shall all this be set down in types and ink? (for our trade is to write books and sell the same—a chapter for a guinea, a line for a penny); and the waterfall roared in answer: 'For shame, O vain man: think not of thy books and of thy pence now; but look on, and wonder, and be silent. Can types or ink describe my beauty, though aided by thy small wit? I am made for thee to praise and wonder at: be content, and cherish thy wonder. It is enough that thou hast seen a great thing: is it needful that thou shouldst prate of all thou hast seen?'

So we came away silently, and walked through the park without looking back. And there was a man at the gate, who opened it and seemed to say, 'Give me a little sixpence.' But we gave nothing, and walked up the hill, which was sore to climb; and on the summit found the car-boy, who was lolling on his cushions and smoking, as happy as a lord.

Quitting the waterfall of Powerscourt (the grand style in which it has been described was adopted in order that the reader, who has probably read other descriptions of the spot, might have at least *something* new in this account of it), we speedily left behind us the rich and wooded tract of country about Powerscourt, and came to a bleak tract, which, perhaps by way of contrast to so much natural wealth, is not unpleasing, and began ascending what is very properly called the Long Hill. Here you see, in the midst of the loneliness, a grim-looking barrack, that was erected when, after the Rebellion, it was necessary for some time to occupy this most rebellious country; and a church, looking equally dismal, a lean-looking sham-Gothic building, in the midst of this green desert. The road to Luggala, whither we were bound, turns off the Long Hill, up auother hill, which seems still longer and steeper, inasmuch as it was ascended perforce on foot, and over lonely boggy moorlands, enlivened by a huge grey boulder plumped here and there, and come, one wonders how, to the spot. Close to this bill of Slievebuck is marked in the maps a district called 'the uninhabited country,' and these stones probably fell at a period of time when not only this district, but all the world, was uninhabited,—and in some convulsion of the neighbouring mountains this and other enormous rocks were cast abroad.

From behind one of them, or out of the ground somehow, as we went up the hill, sprang little ragged guides, who are always lurking about in search of stray pence from tourists; and we had three or four of such at our back by the time we were at the top of the hill. Almost the first sight we saw was a smart coach-and-four, with a loving wedding-party within, and a genteel valet and lady's-maid without. I wondered had they been burying their modest loves in the uninhabited district? But presently, from the top of the hill, I saw the place in which their honeymoon had been passed:

nor could any pair of lovers, nor a pious hermit bent on retirement from the world, have selected a more sequestered spot.

Standing by a big shining granite stone on the hill-top, we looked immediately down upon Lough Tay—a little round lake of half a mile in length, which lay beneath us as black as a pool of ink—a high, crumbling, white-sided mountain falling abruptly into it on the side opposite to us, with a huge ruin of shattered rocks at its base. Northwards, we could see between mountains a portion of the neighbouring lake of Lough Dan—which, too, was dark, though the Annamoe river, which connects the two lakes, lay coursing through the greenest possible flats and shining as bright as silver. Brilliant green shores, too, come gently down to the southern side of Lough Tay; through these runs another river, with a small rapid or fall, which makes a music for the lake; and here, amidst beautiful woods, lies a villa, where the four horses, the groom and valet, the postillions, and the young couple had no doubt been hiding themselves.

Hereabouts, the owner of the villa, Mr. Latouche, has a great grazing establishment; and some herd-boys, no doubt seeing strangers on the hill, thought proper that the cattle should stray that way, that they might drive them back again, and parenthetically ask the travellers for money,—everybody asks travellers for money, as it seems. Next day, admiring in a labourer's arms a little child—his master's son, who could not speak—the labourer, his he-nurse, spoke for him, and demanded a little sixpence to buy the child apples. One grows not a little callous to this sort of beggary: and the only one of our numerous young guides who got a reward was the raggedest of them. He and his companions had just come from school, he said,—not a Government school, but a private one, where they paid. I asked how much,—'Was it a penny a week?' 'No; not a penny a week, but so much at the end of the year.' 'Was it a barrel of meal, or a few stone of potatoes, or something of that sort?' ' Yes; something of that sort.'

The something must, however, have been a very small something on the poor lad's part. He was one of four young ones, who lived with their mother, a widow. He had no work; he could get no work; nobody had work. His mother had a cabin with no land—not a perch of land, no potatoes—nothing but the cabin. How did they live?—their mother knitted stockings. I asked had she any stockings at home?— the boy said, 'No.' How did he live?—he lived how he could; and we gave him threepence, with which, in delight, he went bounding off to the poor mother. Gracious heavens! what a history to hear, told by a child looking quite cheerful as he told it, and as if the story was quite a common one. And a common one, too, it is: and God forgive us.

Here is another, and of a similar low kind, but rather pleasanter. We asked the car-boy how much he earned. He said, ' Seven shillings a week, and his chances'—which, in the summer season, from the number of tourists who are jolted in his car, must be tolerably good— eight or nine shillings a week more, probably. But, he said, in winter his master did not hire him for the car; and he was obliged to look for work elsewhere: as for saving, he never had saved a shilling in his life.

We asked him was he married? and he said, No, but he was *as good as married*; for he had an old mother and four little brothers to keep, and six mouths to feed, and to dress himself decent to drive the gentlemen. Was not the 'as good as married' a pretty expression? and might not some of what are called their betters learn a little good from these simple poor creatures. There's many a young fellow who sets up in the world would think it rather hard to have four brothers to support; and I have heard more than one genteel Christian pining over five hundred a year. A few such may read this, perhaps: let them think of the Irish widow with the four children and *nothing,* and at least be more contented with their port and sherry and their leg of mutton.

This brings us at once to the subject of dinner and the little village, Roundwood, which was reached by this time, lying a few miles off from the lakes, and reached by a road not particularly remarkable for any picturesqueness in beauty; though you pass through a simple pleasing landscape, always agreeable as a repose, I think, after viewing a sight so beautiful as those mountain lakes we have just quitted. All the hills up which we had panted had imparted a fierce sensation of hunger; and it was nobly decreed that we should stop in the middle of the street of Roundwood, impartially between the two hotels, and solemnly decide upon a resting-place after having inspected the larders and bedrooms of each.

And here, as an impartial writer, I must say that the hotel of Mr. Wheatly possesses attractions which few men can resist, in the shape of two very handsome young ladies his daughters; whose faces, were they but painted on his signboard, instead of the mysterious piece which ornaments it, would infallibly draw tourists into the house, thereby giving the opposition inn of Murphy not the least chance of custom.

A landlord's daughters in England, inhabiting a little country inn, would be apt to lay the cloth for the traveller, and their respected father would bring in the first dish of the dinner; but this arrangement is never known in Ireland; we scarcely ever see the cheering countenance of my landlord. And as for the young ladies of Roundwood, I am bound to say that no young persons in Baker Street could be more genteel; and that our bill, when it was brought the next morning, was written in as pretty and fashionable a lady's hand as ever was formed in the most elegant finishing school at Pimlico.

Of the dozen houses of the little village, the half seem to be houses of entertainment. A green common stretches before these, with its rural accompaniments of geese, pigs, and idlers; a park and plantation at the end of the village, and plenty of trees round about it, give it a happy, comfortable, English look; which is, to my notion, the best compliment that can be paid to a hamlet; for where, after all, are villages so pretty?

Here, rather to one's wonder—for the district was not thickly enough populated to encourage dramatic exhibitions—a sort of theatre was erected on the common, a ragged cloth covering the spectators and the actors, and the former (if there were any) obtaining admittance through two doors on the stage in front, marked 'pit & galery.' Why should the word not be spelt with one l as with two?

The entrance to the 'pit' was stated to be threepence, and to the 'galery' twopence. We heard the drums and pipes of the orchestra as we sate at dinner: it seemed to be a good opportunity to examine Irish humour of a peculiar sort, and we promised ourselves a pleasant evening in the pit.

But although the drums began to beat at half-past six, and a crowd of young people formed round the ladder at that hour, to whom the manager of the troop addressed the most vehement invitations to enter, nobody seemed to be inclined to mount the steps: for the fact most likely was, that not one of the poor fellows possessed the requisite twopence which would induce the fat old lady who sate by it to fling open the gallery-door. At one time I thought of offering a half-crown for a purchase of tickets for twenty and so at once benefiting the manager and the crowd of ragged urchins who stood wistfully without his pavilion; but it seemed ostentatious, and we had not the courage to face the tall man in the greatcoat gesticulating and shouting in front of the stage and make the proposition.

Why not? It would have given the company potatoes at least for supper, and made a score of children happy. They would have seen 'the learned pig who spells your name, the feats of manly activity, the wonderful Italian vaulting'; and they would have heard the comic gongs by 'your humble servant.'

'Your humble servant' was the head of the troop: a long man, with a broad accent, a yellow topcoat, and a piteous lean face. What a speculation was this poor fellow's! he must have a company of at least a dozen to keep. There were three girls in trousers, who danced in front of the stage, in Polish caps, tossing their arms about to the tunes of three musicianers; there was a page, two young tragedy-actors, and a clown; there was the fat old woman at the gallery-door waiting for the twopences; there was the Jack Pudding; and it was evident that there must have been some one within, or else who would take care of the learned pig?

The poor manager stood in front, and shouted to the little Irishry beneath; but no one seemed to move. Then he brought forward Jack Pudding, and had a dialogue with him; the jocularity of which, by heavens! made the heart ache to hear. We had determined, at least, to go to the play before that, but the dialogue was too much: we were obliged to walk away, unable to face that dreadful Jack Pudding, and heard the poor manager shouting still for many hours through the night, and the drums thumping vain invitations to the people. O unhappy children of the Hibernian Thespis! it is my belief that they must have eaten the learned pig that night for supper.

It was Sunday morning when we left the little inn at Roundwood: the people were flocking in numbers to church, on cars and pillions, neat, comfortable, and well dressed. We saw in this country more health, more beauty, and more shoes than I have remarked in any quarter. That famous resort of sightseers, the Devil's Glen, lies at a few miles' distance from the little village; and, having gone on the car as near to the spot as the road permitted, we made across the fields—boggy, stony, ill-tilled fields they were—for about a mile, at the end of which walk we found ourselves on the brow of the ravine that has received so ugly a name.

Is there a legend about the place? No doubt for this, as for almost every other natural curiosity in Ireland, there is some tale of monk, saint, fairy, or devil; but our guide on the present day was a banister from Dublin, who did not deal in fictions by any means so romantic, and the history, whatever it was, remained untold. Perhaps the little breechesless cicerone who offered himself would have given us the story, but we dismissed the urchin with scorn, and had to find our own way through bush and bramble down to the entrance of the gully.

Here we came on a cataract, which looks very big in Messrs. Curry's pretty little Guide-book (that every traveller to Wicklow will be sure to have in his pocket); but the waterfall, on this shining Sabbath morning, was disposed to labour as little as possible, and indeed is a spirt of a very humble ordinary sort.

But there is a ravine of a mile and a half, through which a river runs roaring (a lady who keeps the gate will not object to receive a gratuity)—there is a ravine, or Devil's Glen, which forms a delightful wild walk, and where a Methuselah of a landscape-painter might find studies for all his life long. All sorts of foliage and colour, all sorts of delightful caprices of light and shadow—the river tumbling and frothing amidst the boulders—'raucum per lævia murmur saxa ciens,' and a chorus of 150,000 birds (there might be more), hopping, twittering, singing under the clear cloudless Sabbath scene, make this walk one of the most delightful that can be taken; and indeed I hope there is no harm in saying that you may get as much out of an hour's walk there as out of the best hour's extempore preaching. But this was as a salvo to our conscience for not being at church.

Here, however, was a long aisle, arched gothically overhead, in a much better taste than is seen in some of those dismal new churches; and, by way of painted glass, the sun lighting up multitudes of various-coloured leaves, and the birds for choristers, and the river by way of organ, and in it stones enough to make a whole library of sermons. No man can walk in such a place without feeling grateful, and grave, and humble; and without thanking Heaven for it as he comes away. And, walking and musing in this free happy place, one could not help thinking of a million and a half of brother cockneys shut up in their huge prison (the treadmill for the day being idle), and told by some legislators that relaxation is sinful, that works of art are abominations except on week-days, and that their proper place of resort is a dingy tabernacle, where a loud-voiced man is howling about hell-fire in bad grammar. Is not this beautiful world, too, a part of our religion? Yes, truly, in whatever way my Lord John Russell may vote; and it is to be learned without having recourse to any professor at any Bethesda, Ebenezer, or Jerusalem: there can be no mistake about it; no terror, no bigoted dealing of damnation to one's neighbour: it is taught without false emphasis or vain spouting on the preacher's part—how should there be such with such a preacher?

This wild onslaught upon sermons and preachers needs perhaps an explanation: for which purpose we must whisk back out of the Devil's Glen (improperly so named) to Dublin, and to this day week, when, at this very time, I heard one of the first preachers of the city deliver a sermon that lasted for an hour and twenty minutes—time enough to walk up the Glen and back, and remark a thousand delightful things by the way.

Mr. G-'s church (though there would be no harm in mentioning the gentleman's name, for a more conscientious and excellent man, as it is said, cannot be) is close by the Custom House in Dublin, and crowded morning and evening with his admirers. The service was beautifully read by him, and the audience joined in the responses, and in the psalms and hymns[xiv], with a fervour which is very unusual in England. Then came the sermon; and what more can be said of it than that it was extempore, and lasted for an hour and twenty minutes? The orator never failed once for a word, so amazing is his practice; though, as a stranger to this kind of exercise, I could not help trembling for the performer, as one has for Madame Saqui on the slack-rope, in the midst of a blaze of rockets and squibs, expecting every minute she must go over. But the artist was too skilled for that; and after some tremendous bound of a metaphor, in the midst of which you expect he must tumble neck and heels, and be engulfed in the dark abyss of nonsense, down he was sure to come, in a most graceful attitude too, in the midst of a fluttering 'Ah!' from a thousand wondering people.

But I declare solemnly that when I came to try and recollect of what the exhibition consisted, and gave an account of the sermon at dinner that evening, it was quite impossible to remember a word of it; although, to do the orator justice, he repeated many of his opinions a great number of times over. Thus, if he had to discourse of death to us, it was, 'At the approach of the Dark Angel of the Grave,' 'At the coming of the grim King of Terrors,' 'At the warning of that awful Power to whom all of us must bow down,' 'At the summons of that Pallid Spectre whose equal foot knocks at the monarch's tower or the poor man's cabin'—and so forth. There is an examiner of plays, and indeed there ought to be an examiner of sermons, by which audiences are to be fully as much injured or misguided as by the other named exhibitions. What call have reverend gentlemen to repeat their dicta half-a-dozen times over, like Sir Robert Peel when he says anything that he fancies to be witty? Why are men to be kept for an hour and twenty minutes listening to that which may be more effectually said in twenty?

And it need not be said here that a church is not a sermon-house— that it is devoted to a purpose much more lofty and sacred, for which has been set apart the noblest service, every single word of which latter has been previously weighed with the most scrupulous and thoughtful reverence. And after this sublime work of genius, learning, and piety is concluded, is it not a shame that a man should mount a desk, who has not taken the trouble to arrange his words beforehand, and speak thence his crude opinions in his doubtful grammar? It will be answered that the extempore preacher does not deliver crude opinions, but that he arranges his discourse beforehand: to all which it may be replied that Mr.— contradicted himself more than once in the course of the above oration, and repeated himself a half-dozen of times. A man in that place has no right to say a word too much or too little.

And it comes to this,—it is the preacher the people follow, not the prayers; or why is this church more frequented than any other? It is that warm emphasis, and word-mouthing, and vulgar imagery, and glib rotundity of phrase, which brings them together and keeps them happy and breathless. Some of this class call the Cathedral Service *Paddy's Opera;* they say it is Popish—downright scarlet—-they won't go to it. They will have none but their own hymns—and pretty they are—no ornaments but those of their own minister, his rank incense and tawdry rhetoric. Coming out of the church, on the Custom House steps hard by, there was a fellow with a bald large forehead, a new black coat, a little Bible, spouting—spouting *'in omne volubilis œvum'*—the very counterpart of the reverend gentleman hard by. It was just the same thing, just as well done: the eloquence quite as easy and round, the amplifications as ready, the big words rolling round the tongue just as within doors. But we are out of the Devil's Glen by this time; and perhaps, instead of delivering a sermon there, we had better have been at church hearing one.

The country people, however, are far more pious; and the road along which we went to Glendalough was thronged with happy figures of people plodding to or from mass. A chapel-yard was covered with grey cloaks; and at a little inn hard by, stood numerous carts, cars, shandrydans, and pillioned horses, awaiting the end of the prayers. The aspect of the country is wild, and beautiful of course; but why try to describe it? I think the Irish scenery just like the Irish melodies-sweet, wild, and sad even in the sunshine. You can neither represent one nor other by words; but I am sure if one could translate 'The Meeting of the Waters' into form and colours, it would fall into the exact shape of a tender Irish landscape. So take and play that tune upon your fiddle, and shut your eyes, and muse a little, and you have the whole scene before you.

I don't know if there is any tune about Glendalough; but if there be, it must be the most delicate, fantastic, fairy melody that ever was played. Only fancy can describe the charms of that delightful place. Directly you see it, it smiles at you as innocent and friendly as a little child; and once seen, it becomes your friend for ever, and you are always happy when you think of it. Here is a little lake, and little fords across it, surrounded by little mountains, and which lead you now to little islands where there are all sorts of fantastic little old chapels and graveyards; or, again, into little brakes and shrubberies where small rivers are crossing over little rocks, plashing and jumping, and singing as loud as ever they can. Thomas Moore has written rather an awful description of it; and it may indeed appear big to *him*, and to the fairies who must have inhabited the place in old days, that's clear. For who could be accommodated in it except the little people?

There are seven churches, whereof the clergy must have been the smallest persons, and have had the smallest benefices and the littlest congregations ever known. As for the cathedral, what a bishoplet it must have been that presided there! The place would hardly hold the Bishop of London, or Mr. Sydney Smith—two full-sized clergymen of these days—who would be sure to quarrel there for want of room, or for any other reason. There must have been a dean no bigger than Mr. Moore before mentioned, and a chapter no bigger than that chapter in 'Tristram Shandy' which does not contain a single word, and mere popguns of canons, and a beadle about as tall as Crofton Croker, to whip the little boys who were playing at taw (with peas) in the yard.

They say there was a university, too, in the place, with I don't know how many thousand scholars; but for accounts of this there is an excellent guide on the spot, who, for a shilling or two, will tell all he knows, and a great deal more too.

There are numerous legends, too, concerning Saint Kevin, and Fin MacCoul and the Devil, and the deuce knows what. But these stories are, I am bound to say, abominably stupid and stale; and some guide[xv] ought to be seized upon and choked, and flung into the lake, by way of warning to the others to stop their interminable prate. This is the curse attending curiosity, for visitors to almost all the show-places in the country: you have not only the guide—who himself talks too much—but a string of ragged amateurs, starting from bush and briar, ready to carry his honour's umbrella or my lady's cloak, or to help either up a bank or across a stream. And all the while they look wistfully in your face, saying, 'Give me sixpence!' as clear as looks can speak. The unconscionable rogues! how dare they, for the sake of a little starvation or so, interrupt gentlefolks in their pleasure!

A long tract of wild country, with a park or two here and there, a police-barrack perched on a hill, a half-starved-looking church stretching its long scraggy steeple over a wide plain, mountains whose base is richly cultivated while their tops are purple and lonely, warm cottages and farms nestling at the foot of the hills, and humble cabins here and there on the wayside, accompany the car, that jingles back over fifteen miles of ground through Inniskerry to Bray. You pass by wild gaps and Greater and Lesser Sugar Loaves; and about eight o'clock, when the sky is quite red with sunset, and the long shadows are of such a purple as (they may say what they like) Claude could no more paint than I can, you catch a glimpse of the sea beyond Bray, and crying out, 'Θάλαττα, Θάλαττα!' affect to be wondrously delighted by the sight of that element.

The fact is, however, that at Bray is one of the best inns in Ireland; and there you may be perfectly sure is a good dinner ready, five minutes after the honest car-boy, with innumerable hurroos and smacks of his whip, has brought up his passengers to the door with a gallop.

* * * * *

As for the Vale of Avoca, I have not described that: because (as has been before occasionally remarked) it is vain to attempt to describe natural beauties; and because, secondly (though this is a minor consideration), we did not go thither. But we went on another day to the Dargle, and to Shanganah, and the city of Cabinteely, and to the Scalp—that wild pass: and I have no more to say about them than about the Vale of Avoca. The Dublin cockney, who has these places at his door, knows them quite well; and as for the Londoner, who is meditating a trip to the Rhine for the summer, or to Brittany or Normandy, let us beseech him to see his *own country first* (if Lord Lyndhurst will allow us to call this a part of it); and if, after twenty-four hours of an easy journey from London, the cockney be not placed in the midst of a country as beautiful, as strange to him, as romantic as the most imaginative man on 'Change can desire,—may this work be praised by the critics all round and never reach a second edition!

CHAPTER XXV: COUNTRY MEETINGS IN KILDARE—MEATH—DROGHEDA

AN agricultural show was to be held at the town of Naas, and I was glad, after having seen the grand exhibition at Cork, to be present at a more homely, unpretending country festival, where the eyes of Europe, as the orators say, did not happen to be looking on. Perhaps men are apt, under the idea of this sort of inspection, to assume an air somewhat more pompous and magnificent than that which they wear every day. The Naas meeting was conducted without the slightest attempt at splendour or display—a hearty, modest, matter-of fact country meeting.

Market-day was fixed upon of course, and the town, as we drove into it, was thronged with frieze-coats, the market-place bright with a great number of apple-stalls, and the street filled with carts and vans of numerous small tradesmen, vending cheeses, or cheap crockeries, or ready-made clothes and such goods. A clothier, with a great crowd round him, had arrayed himself in a staring new waistcoat of his stock, and was turning slowly round to exhibit the garment, spouting all the while to his audience, and informing them that he could fit out any person, in one minute, 'in a complete new shuit from head to fut.' There seemed to be a crowd of gossips at every shop-door, and, of course, a number of gentlemen waiting at the inn-steps, criticising the cars and carriages as they drove up. Only those who hive in small towns know what an object of interest the street becomes, and the carriages and horses which pass therein. Most of the gentlemen had sent stock to compete for the prizes. The shepherds were tending the stock. The judges were making their award, and until their sentence was given, no competitors could enter the show-yard. The entrance to that, meanwhile, was thronged by a great posse of people, and as the gate abutted upon an old grey tower, a number of people had scaled that, and were looking at the beasts in the court below. Likewise, there was a tall haystack, which possessed similar advantages of situation, and was equally thronged with men and boys. The rain had fallen heavily all night, the heavens were still black with it, and the coats of the men, and the red feet of many ragged female spectators, were liberally spattered with mud.

The first object of interest we were called upon to see was a famous stallion; and passing through the little by-streets (dirty and small, but not so small and dirty as other by-streets to be seen in Irish towns) we came to a porte-cochère, leading into a yard filled with wet fresh hay, sinking juicily under the feet; and here in a shed was the famous stallion. His sire must have been a French diligence-horse; he was of a roan colour, with a broad chest, and short clean legs. His forehead was ornamented with a blue ribbon, on which his name and prizes were painted, and on his chest hung a couple of medals by a chain—a silver one awarded to him at Cork, a gold one carried off by superior merit from other stallions assembled to contend at Dublin. When the points of the animal were sufficiently discussed, a mare, his sister, was produced, and admired still more than himself. Any man who has witnessed the performance of the French horses in the Havre diligence, must admire the vast strength and the extraordinary swiftness of the breed; and it was agreed on all hands, that such horses would prove valuable in this country, where it is hard now to get a stout horse for the road, so much has the fashion for blood, and nothing but blood, prevailed of late.

By the time the stallion was seen, the judges had done their arbitration; and we went to the yard, where broad-backed sheep were resting peaceably in their pens; bulls were led about by the nose; enormous turnips, both Swedes and Aberdeens, reposed in the mud; little cribs of geese, hens, and peafowl were come to try for the prize; and pigs might be seen—some encumbered with enormous families, others with fat merely. They poked up one brute to walk for us: he made, after many futile attempts, a desperate rush forward, his legs almost lost in fat, his immense sides quivering and shaking with the exercise; he was then allowed to return to his straw, into which he sank panting. Let us hope that he went home with a pink ribbon round his tail that night, and got a prize for his obesity.

I think the pink ribbon was, at least to a cockney, the pleasantest sight of all: for on the evening after the show we saw many carts going away so adorned, having carried off prizes on the occasion. First came a great bull stepping along, he and his driver having each a bit of pink on their heads; then a cart full of sheep; then a car of good-natured-looking people, having a churn in the midst of them that sported a pink favour. When all the prizes were distributed, a select company sat down to dinner at Macavoy's Hotel; and no doubt a reporter who was present has given in the county paper an account of all the good things eaten and said. At our end of the table we had saddle-of-mutton, and I remarked a boiled leg of the same delicacy, with turnips, at the opposite extremity. Before the vice I observed a large piece of roast-beef, which I could not observe at the end of dinner, because it was all swallowed. After the mutton we had cheese, and were just beginning to think that we had dined very sufficiently, when a squadron of apple-pies came smoking in, and convinced us that, in such a glorious cause, Britons are never at fault. We ate up the apple-pies, and then the punch was called for by those who preferred that beverage to wine, and the speeches began.

The chairman gave 'The Queen,' nine times nine and one cheer more; 'Prince Albert and the rest of the Royal Family,' great cheering; ' The Lord-Lieutenant'—his Excellency's health was received rather coolly, I thought. And then began the real business of the night: health of the Naas Society, health of the Agricultural Society, and healths all round; not forgetting the Sallymount Beagles and the Kildare Foxhounds—which toasts were received with loud cheers and halloos by most of the gentlemen present, and elicited brief speeches from the masters of the respective hounds, promising good sport next season. After the Kildare Foxhounds, an old farmer in a gray coat got gravely up, and without being requested to do so in the least, sang a song, stating that—

'At seven in the morning by most of the clocks

We rode to Kilruddery in search of a fox;'

and at the conclusion of his song challenged a friend to give another song. Another old farmer, on this, rose and sang one of Morris's songs with a great deal of queer humour; and no doubt many more songs were sung during the evening, for plenty of hot-water jugs were blocking the door as we went out.

The jolly frieze-coated songster who celebrated the Kilruddery fox, sang, it must be confessed, most wofully out of tune; but still it was pleasant to hear him, and I think the meeting was the most agreeable one I have seen in Ireland: there was more good-humour, more cordial union of classes, more frankness and manliness, than one is accustomed to find in Irish meetings. All the speeches were kind-hearted, straightforward speeches, without a word of politics or an attempt at oratory: it was impossible to say whether the gentlemen present were Protestant or Catholic,—each one had a hearty word of encouragement for his tenant, and a kind welcome for his neighbour. There were forty stout well-to-do farmers in the room, renters of fifty, seventy, a hundred acres, of land. There were no clergymen present; though it would have been pleasant to have seen one of each persuasion to say grace for the meeting and the meat.

At a similar meeting at Ballytore the next day, I had an opportunity of seeing a still finer collection of stock than had been brought to Naas, and at the same time one of the most beautiful flourishing villages in Ireland. The road to it from H— town, if not remarkable for its rural beauty, is pleasant to travel, for evidences of neat and prosperous husbandry are around you everywhere: rich crops in the fields, and neat cottages by the roadside, accompanying us as far as Ballytore—a white straggling village, surrounding green fields of some five furlongs square, with a river running in the midst of them, and numerous fine cattle on the green. Here is a large windmill, fitted up like a castle, with battlements and towers: the castellan thereof is a good-natured old Quaker gentleman, and numbers more of his following inhabit the town.

The consequence was that the shops of the village were the neatest possible, though by no means grand or pretentious. Why should Quaker shops be neater than other shops? They suffer to the full as much oppression as the rest of the hereditary bondsmen; and yet, in spite of their tyrants, they prosper.

I must not attempt to pass an opinion upon the stock exhibited at Ballytore; but, in the opinion of some large agricultural proprietors present, it might have figured with advantage in any show in England, and certainly was finer than the exhibition at Naas; which, however, is a very young society. The best part of the show, however, to everybody's thinking (and it is pleasant to observe the manly fair-play spirit which characterises the society), was, that the prizes of the Irish Agricultural Society were awarded to two men—one a labourer, the other a very small holder, both having reared the best stock exhibited on the occasion. At the dinner, which took place in a barn of the inn, smartly decorated with laurels for the purpose, there was as good and stout a body of yeomen as at Naas the day previous, but only two landlords; and here, too, as at Naas, neither priest nor parson. Cattle-feeding of course formed the principal theme of the after-dinner discourse—not, however, altogether to the exclusion of tillage; and there was a good and useful prize for those who could not afford to rear fat oxen—for the best kept cottage and garden, namely—which was won by a poor man with a large family and scanty precarious earnings, but who yet found means to make the most of his small means and to keep his little cottage neat and cleanly. The tariff and the plentiful harvest together had helped to bring down prices, severely; and we heard from the farmers much desponding talk. I saw hay sold for £2 the ton, and oats for 8s. 3d. the barrel.

In the little village I remarked scarcely a single beggar, and very few bare feet indeed among the crowds who came to see the show. Here the Quaker village had the advantage of the town of Naas, in spite of its poorhouse, which was only half full when we went to see it; but the people prefer beggary and starvation abroad to comfort and neatness in the union-house.

A neater establishment cannot be seen than this; and liberty must be very sweet indeed, when people prefer it and starvation to the certainty of comfort in the union-house. We went to see it after the show at Naas.

The first persons we saw at the gate of the place were four buxom lasses in blue jackets and petticoats, who were giggling and laughing as gaily as so many young heiresses of a thousand a year, and who had a colour in their cheeks that any lady of Almack's might envy. They were cleaning pails and carrying in water from a green court or playground in front of the house, which some of the able-bodied men of the place were busy in enclosing. Passing through the large entrance of the house, a nondescript Gothic building, we came to a court divided by a road and two low walls: the right enclosure is devoted to the boys of the establishment, of whom there were about fifty at play: boys more healthy or happy it is impossible to see. Separated from them is the nursery; and here were seventy or eighty young children, a shrill clack of happy voices leading the way to the door where they were to be found. Boys and children had a comfortable little uniform, and shoes were furnished for all; though the authorities did not seem particularly severe in enforcing the wearing of the shoes, which most of the young persons left behind them.

In spite of all the *Times's* in the world, the place was a happy one. It is kept with a neatness and comfort to which, until his entrance into the union-house, the Irish peasant must perforce have been a stranger. All the rooms and passages are white, well scoured, and airy; all the windows are glazed; all the beds have a good store of blankets and sheets. In the women's dormitories there lay several infirm persons, not ill enough for the infirmary, and glad of the society of the common room: in one of the men's sleeping-rooms we found a score of old grey-coated men sitting round another who was reading prayers to them. And outside the place we found a woman starving in rags, as she had been ragged and starving for years; her husband was wounded, and lay in his house upon straw; her children were ill with a fever; she had neither meat, nor physic, nor clothing, nor fresh air, nor warmth for them;—and she preferred to starve on rather than enter the house!

The last of our agricultural excursions was to the fair of Castledermot, celebrated for the show of cattle to be seen there, and attended by the farmers and gentry of the neighbouring counties. Long before reaching the place we met troops of cattle coming from it—stock of a beautiful kind, for the most part large, sleek, white, long-backed, most of the larger animals being bound for England. There was very near as fine a show in the pastures along the road—which lies across a light green country with plenty of trees to ornament the landscape, and some neat cottages along the roadside.

At the turnpike of Castledermot the droves of cattle met us by scores no longer, but by hundreds, and the long street of the place was thronged with oxen, sheep, and horses, and with those who wished to see, to sell, or to buy. The squires were all together in a cluster at the police-house; the owners of the horses rode up and down, showing the best paces of their brutes; among whom you might see Paddy, in his ragged frieze-coat, seated on his donkey's bare rump, and proposing him for sale. I think I saw a score of this humble though useful breed that were brought for sale to the fair. 'I can sell him,' says one fellow, with a pompous air, 'wid his tackle or widout.' He was looking as grave over the negotiation as if it had been for a thousand pounds. Besides the donkeys, of course there was plenty of poultry, and there were pigs without number, shrieking and struggling and pushing hither and thither among the crowd, rebellious to the straw-rope. It was a fine thing to see one huge grunter and the manner in which he was landed into a cart. The cart was let down on an easy inclined plane to tempt him: two men ascending, urged him by the forelegs, other two entreated him by the tail. At length, when more than half of his body had been coaxed upon the cart, it was suddenly whisked up, causing the animal thereby to fall forward; a parting shove sent him altogether into the cart; the two gentlemen inside jumped out, and the monster is left to ride home.

The farmers, as usual, were talking of the tariff, predicting ruin to themselves, as farmers will, on account of the decreasing price of stock and the consequent fall of grain. Perhaps the person most to be pitied is the poor pig-proprietor yonder: it is his rent which he is carrying through the market squeaking at the end of the straw-rope, and Sir Robert's bill adds insolvency to that poor fellow's misery.

This was the last of the sights which the kind owner of H— town had invited me into his country to see; and I think they were among the most pleasing I witnessed in Ireland. Rich and poor were working friendlily together; priest and parson were alike interested in these honest, homely, agricultural festivals; not a word was said about hereditary bondage and English tyranny; and one did not much regret the absence of those patriotic topics of conversation. If but for the sake of the change, it was pleasant to pass a few days with people among whom there was no quarrelling: no furious denunciations against Popery on the part of the Protestants, and no tirades against the parsons from their bitter and scornful opponents of the other creed.

Next Sunday, in the county Meath, in a quiet old church lying amongst meadows and fine old stately avenues of trees, and for the benefit of a congregation of some thirty persons, I heard for the space of an hour and twenty minutes some thorough Protestant doctrine, and the Popish superstitions properly belaboured. Does it strengthen a man in his own creed to hear his neighbour's belief abused? One would imagine so: for though abuse converts nobody, yet many of our pastors think they are not doing their duty by their own fold unless they fling stones at the flock in the next field, and have, for the honour of the service, a match at cudgelling with the shepherd. Our shepherd to-day was of this pugnacious sort.

The Meath landscape, if not varied and picturesque, is extremely rich and pleasant; and we took some drives along the banks of the Boyne—to the noble park of Slane (still sacred to the memory of George IV., who actually condescended to pass some days there), and to Trim—of which the name occurs so often in Swift's Journals, and where stands an enormous old castle that was inhabited by Prince John. It was taken from him by an Irish chief, our guide said; and from the Irish chief it was taken by Oliver Cromwell. O'Thuselah was the Irish chief's name no doubt.

Here too stands, in the midst of one of the most wretched towns in Ireland, a pillar erected in honour of the Duke of Wellington by the gentry of his native country. His birthplace, Dangan, lies not far off, And as we saw the hero's statue, a flight of birds had hovered about it: there was one on each epaulette and two on his marshal's staff. Besides these wonders, we saw a certain number of beggars; and a madman, who was walking round a mound and preaching a sermon on grace; and a little child's funeral came passing through the dismal town, the only stirring thing in it (the coffin was laid on a one-horse country ear—a little deal box, in which the poor child lay—and a great troop of people followed the humble procession); and the innkeeper, who had caught a few stray gentlefolk in a town where travellers must be rare; and in his inn—which is more gaunt and miserable than the town itself, and which is by no means rendered more cheerful because sundry theological works are left for the rare frequenters in the coffee-room—the innkeeper brought in a bill which would have been worthy of Long's, and which was paid with much grumbling on both sides.

It would not be a bad rule for the traveller in Ireland to avoid those inns where theological works are left in the coffee-room. He is pretty sure to be made to pay very dearly for these religious privileges.

We waited for the coach at the beautiful lodge and gate of Annsbrook; and one of the sons of the house coming up, invited us to look at the domain, which is as pretty and neatly ordered as—as any in England. It is hard to use this comparison so often, and must make Irish hearers angry. Can't one see a neat house and grounds without instantly thinking that they are worthy of the sister country; and implying, in our cool way, its superiority to everywhere else? Walking in this gentleman's grounds, I told him, in the simplicity of my heart, that the neighbouring country was like Warwickshire, and the grounds as good as any English park. Is it the fact that English grounds *are* superior, or only that Englishmen are disposed to consider them so?

A pretty little twining river, called the Nanny's Water, runs through the park: there is a legend about that, as about other places. Once upon a time (ten thousand years ago), Saint Patrick being thirsty as he passed by this country, came to the house of an old woman, of whom he asked a drink of milk. The old woman brought it to his reverence with the best of welcomes, and-here it is a great mercy that the Belfast mail comes up, whereby the reader is spared the rest of the history.

The Belfast mail had only to carry us five miles to Drogheda, but, in revenge, it made us pay three shillings for the five miles; and again, by way of compensation, it carried us over five miles of a country that was worth at least five shillings to see—not romantic or especially beautiful, but having the best of all beauty—a quiet, smiling, prosperous, unassuming, *work-day* look, that in views and landscapes most good judges admire. Hard by Nanny's Water, we came to Duleek Bridge, where, I was told, stands an old residence of the De Bath family, who were, moreover, builders of the picturesque old bridge.

It leads over a wide green common, which puts one in mind of Eng— (a plague on it, there is the comparison again!), and at the end of the common lies the village among trees: a beautiful and peaceful sight. In the background there was a tall ivy-covered old tower, looking noble and imposing, but a ruin and useless; then there was a church, and next to it a chapel—the very same sun was shining upon both. The chapel and church were connected by a farmyard, and a score of golden ricks were in the background, the churches in unison, and the people (typified by the corn-ricks) flourishing at the feet of both. May one ever hope to see the day in Ireland when this little landscape allegory shall find a general application?

For some way after leaving Duleek the road and the country round continue to wear the agreeable cheerful look just now lauded. You pass by a house where James n. is said to have slept the night before the battle of the Boyne (he took care to sleep far enough off on the night after), and also by an old red-brick hall standing at the end of an old chace or terrace-avenue, that runs for about a mile down to the house, and finishes at a moat towards the road. But as the coach arrives near Drogheda, and in the boulevards of that town, all resemblance to England is lost. Up hill and down, we pass low rows of filthy cabins in dirty undulations. Parents are at the cabin-doors dressing the hair of ragged children; shockheads of girls peer out from the black circumference of smoke, and children inconceivably filthy yell wildly and vociferously as the coach passes by. One little ragged savage rushed furiously up the hill, speculating upon permission to put on the drag-chain at descending, and hoping for a halfpenny reward. He put on the chain, but the guard did not give a halfpenny. I flung him one, and the boy rushed wildly after the carriage, holding it up with joy. 'The man inside has given me one,' says he, holding it up exultingly to the guard. I flung out another (by-the-bye, and without any prejudice, the halfpence in Ireland *are* smaller than those of England), but when the child got this halfpenny, small as it was, it seemed to overpower him: the little man's look of gratitude was worth a great deal more than the biggest penny ever struck.

The town itself, which I had three-quarters of an hour to ramble through, is smoky, dirty, and lively. There was a great bustle in the black main street, and several good shops, though some of the houses were in a half state of ruin, and battered shutters closed many of the windows where formerly had been 'emporiums,' 'repositories,'and other grandly-titled abodes of small commerce. Exhortations to repeal were liberally plastered on the blackened walls, proclaiming Borne past or promised visit of the great agitator. From the bridge is a good bustling spectacle of the river and the craft; the quays were grimy with the discharge of the coal-vessels that lay alongside them; the warehouses were not less black; the seamen and porters loitering on the quay were as swarthy as those of Puddledock; numerous factories and chimneys were vomiting huge clouds of black smoke: the commerce of the town is stated by the Guide-book to be considerable, and increasing of late years. Of one part of its manufactures every traveller must speak with gratitude — of the ale namely, which is as good as the best brewed in the sister kingdom. Drogheda ale is to be drunk all over Ireland in the bottled state: candour calls for the acknowledgment that it is equally praiseworthy in draught. And while satisfying himself of this fact, the philosophic observer cannot but ask why ale should not be as good elsewhere as at Drogheda: is the water of the Boyne the only water in Ireland whereof ale can be made?

Above the river and craft, and the smoky quays of the town, the hills rise abruptly, up which innumerable cabins clamber; on one of them, by a church, is a round tower, or fort, with a flag: the church is the successor of one battered down by Cromwell in 1649, in his frightful siege of the place. The place of one of his batteries is still marked outside the town, and known as 'Cromwell's Mount': here he 'made the breach assaultable, and, by the help of God, stormed it.' He chose the strongest point of the defence for his attack.

After being twice beaten back, by the divine assistance he was enabled to succeed in a third assault: he ' knocked on the head' all the officers of the garrison; he gave orders that none of the men should be spared. 'I think,' says he, 'that night we put to the sword two thousand men; and one hundred of them having taken possession of Saint Peter's steeple and a round tower next the gate, called Saint Sunday's, I ordered the steeple of Saint Peter's to be fired, when one in the flames was heard to say, "God confound me, I burn, I burn!"' The Lord General's history of 'this great mercy vouchsafed to us' concludes with appropriate religious reflections: and prays Mr. Speaker of the House of Commons to remember that 'it is good that God alone have all the glory.' Is not the recollection of this butchery almost enough to make an Irishman turn rebel?

When troops march over the bridge, a young friend of mine (whom I shrewdly suspect to be an Orangeman in his heart) told me that their bands played the 'Boyne Water.' Here is another legend of defeat for the Irishman to muse upon; and here it was, too, that King Richard n. received the homage of four Irish kings, who flung their skenes or daggers at his feet and knelt to him, and were wonder-stricken by the richness of his tents and the garments of his knights and ladies. I think it is in Lingard that the story is told; and the antiquarian has no doubt seen that beautiful old manuscript at the British Museum where these yellow-mantled warriors are seen riding down to the King, splendid in his forked beard, and peaked shoes, and long dangling scolloped sleeves and embroidered gown.

The Boyne winds picturesquely round two sides of the town, and following it, we came to the Linen Hall,—in the days of the linen manufacture a place of note, now the place where Mr. O'Connell harangues the people; but all the windows of the house were barricaded when we passed it, and of linen or any other sort of merchandise there seemed to be none. Three boys were running past it with a mouse tied to a string and a dog galloping after; two little children were paddling down the street, one saying to the other, '*Once I had a halfpenny,* and bought apples with it.' The barges were lying lazily on the river, on the opposite side of which was a wood of a gentleman's domain, over which the rooks were cawing; and by the shore were some ruins— ' where Mr. Ball once had his kennel of hounds'—touching reminiscence of former prosperity!

There is a very large and ugly Roman Catholic chapel in the town, and a smaller one of better construction: it was so crowded, however, although on a week-day, that we could not pass beyond the chapel-yard—where were great crowds of people, some praying, some talking, some buying and selling. There were two or three stalls in the yard, such as one sees near Continental churches, presided over by old women, with a store of little brass crucifixes, beads, books, and bénitiers for the faithful to purchase. The church is large and commodious within, and looks (not like all other churches in Ireland) as if it were frequented. There is a hideous stone monument in the churchyard representing two corpses half rotted away: time or neglect had battered away the inscription, nor could we see the dates of some older tombstones in the ground, which were mouldering away in the midst of nettles and rank grass on the wall.

By a large public school of some reputation, where a hundred boys are educated (my young guide the Orangeman was one of them: he related with much glee how, on one of the Liberator's visits, a schoolfellow had waved a blue and orange flag from the window and cried, 'King William for ever, and to hell with the Pope!'), there is a fine old gate leading to the river, and in excellent preservation, in spite of time and Oliver Cromwell. It is a good specimen of Irish architecture. By this time that exceedingly slow coach the 'Newry Lark' had arrived at that exceedingly filthy inn where the mail had dropped us an hour before. An enormous Englishman was holding a vain combat of wit with a brawny grinning beggar-woman at the door. 'There's a *clever* gentleman,' says the beggar-woman. 'Sure he'll give me something.' 'How much should you like?' says the Englishman, with playful jocularity. 'Musha,' says she, 'many a *littler* man nor you has given me a shilling.' The coach drives away; the lady had clearly the best of the joking-match; but I did not see, for all that, that the Englishman gave her a single farthing.

From Castle Bellingham—as famous for ale as Drogheda, and remarkable likewise for a still better thing than ale, an excellent resident proprietress, whose fine park lies by the road, and by whose care and taste the village has been rendered one of the most neat and elegant I have yet seen in Ireland—the road to Dundalk is exceedingly picturesque, and the traveller has the pleasure of feasting his eye with the noble line of Mourne Mountains, which rise before him while he journeys over a level country for several miles. The 'Newry Lark,' to be sure, disdained to take advantage of the easy roads to accelerate its movements in any way; but the aspect of the country is so pleasant that one can afford to loiter over it. The fields were yellow with the stubble of the corn—which in this, one of the chief corn counties of Ireland, had just been cut down;' and a long straggling line of neat farmhouses and cottages runs almost the whole way from Castle Bellingham to Dundalk. For nearly a couple of miles of the distance the road runs along the picturesque flat called Lurgan Green; and gentlemen's residences and parks are numerous along the road, and one seems to have come amongst a new race of people, so trim are the cottages, so neat the gates and hedges, in this peaceful smiling district. The people, too, show signs of the general prosperity. A national-school had just dismissed its female scholars as we passed through Dunlar; and though the children had most of them bare feet, their clothes were good and clean, their faces rosy and bright, and their long hair as shiny and as nicely combed as young ladies' need to be. Numerous old castles and towers stand on the road here and there; and long before we entered Dundalk we had a sight of a huge factory-chimney in the town, and of the dazzling white walls of the Roman Catholic church lately erected there. The cabin-suburb is not great, and the entrance to the town is much adorned by the hospital—a handsome Elizabethan building—and a row of houses of a similar architectural style which lie on the left of the traveller.

CHAPTER XXVI: DUNDALK

THE stranger can't fail to be struck with the look of Dundalk, as he has been with the villages and country leading to it, when contrasted with places in the South and West of Ireland. The coach stopped at a cheerful-looking *Place*, of which almost the only dilapidated mansion was the old inn at which it discharged us, and which did not hold out much prospect of comfort. But in justice to the King's Arms, it must be said that good beds and dinners are to be obtained there by voyagers; and if they choose to arrive on days when his Grace the Most Reverend the Lord Archbishop of Armagh and R. C. Primate of Ireland is dining with his clergy, the house of course is crowded, and the waiters, and the boy who carries in the potatoes, a little hurried and flustered. When their reverences were gone, the laity were served; and I have no doubt, from the leg of a duck which I got, that the breast and wings must have been very tender.

Meanwhile the walk was pleasant through the bustling little town. A grave old church with a tall copper spire defends one end of the main street; and a little way from the inn is the superb new chapel, which the architect, Mr. Duff, has copied from King's College Chapel in Cambridge. The ornamental part of the interior is not yet completed; but the area of the chapel is spacious and noble, and three handsome altars of scagliola (or some composition resembling marble) have been erected, of handsome and suitable form. When by the aid of further subscriptions the church shall be completed, it will be one of the handsomest places of worship the Roman Catholics possess in this country. Opposite the chapel stands a neat low black building—the gaol: in the middle of the building, and over the doorway, is an ominous balcony and window, with an iron beam overhead. Each end of the beam is ornamented with a grinning iron skull! Is this the hanging-place? and do these grinning cast-iron skulls facetiously explain the business for which the beam is there? For shame! for shame! Such disgusting emblems ought no longer to disgrace a Christian land. If kill we must, let us do so with as much despatch and decency as possible,—not brazen out our misdeeds and perpetuate them in this frightful satiric way.

A far better cast-iron emblem stands over a handsome shop in the 'Place' hard by—a plough namely, which figures over the factory of Mr. Shekelton, whose industry and skill seem to have brought the greatest benefit to his fellow-townsmen—of whom he employs numbers in his foundries and workshops. This gentleman was kind enough to show me through his manufactories, where all sorts of iron-works are made, from a steam-engine to a door-key; and I saw everything to admire, and a vast deal more than I could understand, in the busy, cheerful, orderly, bustling, clanging place. Steam-boilers were hammered here, and pins made by a hundred busy hands in a manufactory above. There was the engine-room, where the monster was whirring his ceaseless wheels and directing the whole operations of the factory, fanning the forges, turning the drills, blasting into the pipes of the smelting-houses: he had a house to himself, from which his orders issued to the different establishments round about. One machine was quite awful to me, a gentle cockney, not used to such things: it was an iron-devourer, a wretch with huge jaws and a narrow mouth, ever opening and shutting—opening and shutting. You put a half-inch iron plate between his jaws, and they shut not a whit slower or quicker than before, and bit through the iron as if it were a sheet of paper. Below the monster's mouth was a punch that performed its duties with similar dreadful calmness.

I was so lucky as to have an introduction to the Vicar of Dundalk, which that gentleman's kind and generous nature interpreted into a claim for unlimited hospitality; and he was good enough to consider himself bound not only to receive me, but to give up previous engagements abroad in order to do so. I need not Bay that it afforded me sincere pleasure to witness, for a couple, of days, his labours among his people; and indeed it was a delightful occupation to watch both flock and pastor. The world is a wicked, selfish, abominable place, as the parson tells us: but his reverence comes out of his pulpit and gives the flattest contradiction to his doctrine: busying himself with kind actions from morning till night, denying to himself, generous to others, preaching the truth to young and old, clothing the naked, feeding the hungry, consoling the wretched, and giving hope to the sick;—and I do not mean to say that this sort of life is led by the Vicar of Dundalk merely, but do firmly believe that it is the life of the great majority of the Protestant and Roman Catholic clergy of the country. There will be no breach of confidence, I hope, in publishing here the journal of a couple of days spent with one of these reverend gentlemen, and telling some readers, as idle and profitless as the writer, what the clergyman's peaceful labours are.

In the first place, we set out to visit the church—the comfortable copper-spired old edifice that was noticed two pages back. It stands in a green churchyard of its own, very neat and trimly kept, with an old row of trees that were dropping their red leaves upon a flock of vaults and tombstones below. The building being much injured by flame and time, some hundred years back was repaired, enlarged, and ornamented—as churches in those days were ornamented—and has consequently lost a good deal of its Gothic character. There is a great mixture, therefore, of old style and new style and no style: but, with all this, the church is one of the most commodious and best appointed I have seen in Ireland. The vicar held a council with a builder regarding some ornaments for the roof of the church, which is, as it should be, a great object for his care and architectural taste, and on which he has spent a very large sum of money. To these expenses he is in a manner bound, for the living is a considerable one, its income being no less than two hundred and fifty pounds a year; out of which he has merely to maintain a couple of curates and a clerk and sexton, to contribute largely towards schools and hospitals, and relieve a few scores of pensioners of his own, who are fitting objects of private bounty.

We went from the church to a school, which has been long a favourite resort of the good vicar's: indeed, to judge from the schoolmaster's books, his attendance there is almost daily, and the number of the scholars some two hundred. The number was considerably greater until the schools of the Educational Board were established, when the Roman Catholic clergymen withdrew many of their young people from Mr. Thackeray's establishment.

We found a large room with sixty or seventy boys at work; in an upper chamber were a considerable number of girls, with their teachers, two modest and pretty young women; but the favourite resort of the vicar was evidently the Infant-School,—and no wonder: it is impossible to witness a more beautiful or touching sight.

Eighty of these little people, healthy, clean, and rosy—some in smart gowns and shoes and stockings, some with patched pinafores and little bare pink feet—sate upon a half-dozen low benches, and were singing, at the top of their four-score fresh voices, a song when we entered. All the voices were hushed as the vicar came in, and a great bobbing and curtseying took place; whilst a hundred and sixty innocent eyes turned awfully towards the clergyman, who tried to look as unconcerned as possible, and began to make his little ones a speech. 'I have brought,' says he, 'a gentleman from England, who has heard of my little children and their school, and hopes he will carry away a good account of it. Now, you know, we must all do our best to be kind and civil to strangers: what can we do here for this gentleman that he would like?—do you think he would like a song?'

(*All the Children.*)—'We'll sing to him!'

Then the schoolmistress, coming forward, sang the first words of a hymn, which at once eighty little voices took up, or near eighty—for some of the little things were too young to sing yet, and all they could do was to beat the measure with little red hands as the others sang. It was a hymn about heaven, with a chorus of 'Oh, that will be joyful, joyful!' and one of the verses beginning, 'Little children will be there.' Some of my fair readers (if I have the honour to find such) who have been present at similar tender charming concerts, know the hymn, no doubt. It was the first time I had ever heard it; and I do not care to own that it brought tears to my eyes, though it is ill to parade such kind of sentiment in print. But I think I will never, while I live, forget that little chorus, nor would any man who has ever loved a child or lost one. God bless you, O little happy singers! What a noble and useful life is his, who, in place of seeking wealth or honour, devotes his life to such a service as this! And all through our country, thank God! in quiet humble corners, that busy citizens and men of the world never hear of, there are thousands of such men employed in such holy pursuits, with no reward beyond that which the fulfilment of duty brings them. Most of these children were Roman Catholics. At this tender age the priests do not care to separate them from their little Protestant brethren: and no wonder. He must be a child-murdering Herod who would find the heart to do so.

After the hymn, the children went through a little Scripture catechism, answering very correctly, and all in a breath, as the mistress put the questions. Some of them were, of course, too young to understand the words they uttered; but the answers are so simple that they cannot fail to understand them before long; and they learn in spite of themselves.

The catechism being ended, another song was sung; and now the vicar (who had been humming the chorus along with his young singers, and, in spite of an awful and grave countenance, could not help showing his extreme happiness) made another oration, in which he stated that the gentleman from England was perfectly satisfied; that he would have a good report of the Dundalk children to carry home with him; that the day was very fine, and the schoolmistress would probably like to take a walk; and, finally, would the young people give her a holiday? 'As many,' concluded he, 'as will give the schoolmistress a holiday, hold up their hands!' This question was carried unanimously.

But I am bound to say, when the little people that as many as wouldn't like a holiday were to hold up *their* hands, all the little hands went up again exactly as before: by which it may be concluded either that the audience did not understand his reverence's speech, or that they were just as happy to stay at school as to go and play; and the reader may adopt whichever of the reasons he inclines to. It is probable that both are correct.

The little things are so fond of the school, the vicar told me as we walked away from it, that on returning home they like nothing better than to get a number of their companions who don't go to school, and to play at infant-school.

They may be heard singing their hymns in the narrow alleys and humble houses in which they dwell: and I was told of one dying who sang his song of: 'Oh, that will be joyful, joyful.!' to his poor mother weeping at his bedside, and promising her that they should meet where no parting should be.

'There was a child in the school,' said the vicar, 'whose father, a Roman Catholic, was a carpenter by trade, a good workman, and earning a considerable weekly sum, but neglecting his wife and children and spending his earnings in drink. We have a song against drunkenness that the infants sing; and one everiing, going home, the child found her father excited with liquor and ill-treating his wife. The little thing forthwith interposed between them, told her father what she had heard at school regarding the criminality of drunkenness and quarrelling, and finished her little sermon with the hymn. The father was first amused, then touched; and the end of it was that be kissed his wife, and asked her to forgive him, hugged his child, and from that day would always have her in the bed, made her sing to him morning and night, and forsook his old haunts for the sake of his little companion.'

He was quite sober and prosperous for eight months; but the vicar at the end of that time began to remark that the child looked ragged at school, and passing by her mother's house, saw the poor woman with a black eye. 'If it was any one but your husband, Mrs. C.—, who gave you that black eye,' says the vicar, 'tell me; but if be did it, don't say a word.' The woman was silent, and soon after, meeting her husband, the vicar took him to task. 'You were sober for eight months. No tell me fairly, C—.' says he, 'were you happier when you lived at home with your wife and child, or are you more happy now?' The man owned that he was much happier formerly, and the end of the conversation was that he promised to go home once more and try the sober life again, and he went home and succeeded.

The vicar continued to hear good accounts of him; but passing one day by the house he saw the wife there looking very sad. 'Had her husband relapsed?'—'No, he was dead,' she said—'dead of the cholera; but he had been sober ever since his last conversation with the clergyman, and had done his duty to his family up to the time of his death.' 'I said to the woman,' said the good old clergymand, in a grave low voice, '"Your .husband is gone now to the place where, according to his conduct here, an eternal reward will be assigned him; and let us be thankful to think what a different position he occupies now to that which he must have held had not the little girl been the means under God of converting him."'

Our next walk was to the County Hospital, the handsome edifice which ornaments the Drogheda entrance of the town, and which I had remarked on my arrival. Concerning this hospital, the governors were, when I passed through Dundalk, in a state of no small agitation, for a gentleman by the name of—, who, from being an apothecary's assistant in the place, had gone forth as a sort of amateur inspector of hospitals throughout Ireland, had thought fit to censure their extravagance in erecting the new building, stating that the old one was fully sufficient to hold fifty patients, and that the public money might consequently have been spared. Mr. —'s plan for the better maintenance of them in general is, that commissioners should be appointed to direct them, and not county gentlemen as heretofore; the discussion of which question does not need to be carried on in this humble work.

My guide, who is one of the governors of the new hospital, conducted me in the first place to the old one—a small dirty house in a damp and low situation, with but three rooms to accommodate patients, and these evidently not fit to hold fifty, or even fifteen patients. The new hospital is one of the handsomest buildings of the size and kind in Ireland—an ornament to the town, as the angry commissioner stated, but not after all a building of undue cost, for the expense of its erection was but £3000—and the sick of the county are far better accommodated in it than in the damp and unwholesome tenement regretted by the eccentric commissioner.

An English architect, Mr, Smith, of Hertford, designed and completed the edifice; strange to say, only exceeding his estimates by the sum of three-and-sixpence, as the worthy governor of the hospital with great triumph told me. The building is certainly a wonder of cheapness, and, what is more, so complete for the purpose for which it was intended, and so handsome in appearance, that the architect's name deserves to be published by all who hear it; and if any country newspaper editors should notice this volume, they are requested to make the fact known. The house is provided with every convenience for men and women, with all the appurtenances of baths, water, gas, airy wards, and a garden for convalescents; and, below, a dispensary, a handsome board-room, kitchen, and matron's apartments, etc. Indeed, a noble requiring a house for a large establishment need not desire a handsomer one than this, at its moderate price of £3000. The beauty of this building has, as is almost always the ease, created emulation, and a terrace in the same taste has been raised in the neighbourhood of the hospital.

From the hospital we bent our steps to the Institution; of which place I give below the rules, and a copy of the course of study, and the dietary: leaving English parents to consider the fact, that their children can be educated at this place for *thirteen pounds a year.* Nor is there anything in the establishment savouring of the Dotheboys Hall[xvi]. I never saw, in any public school in England, sixty cleaner, smarter, more gentlemanlike boys than were here at work. The upper class had been at work on Euclid as we came in, and were set, by way of amusing the stranger, to perform a sum of compound interest of diabolical complication, which, with its algebraic and arithmetical solution, was handed up to me by three or four of the pupils; and I strove to look as wise as I possibly could. Then they went through questions of mental arithmetic with astonishing correctness and facility; and finding from the master that classics were not taught in the school, I took occasion to lament this circumstance, saying, with a knowing air, that I would like to have examined the lads in a Greek play.

Classics, then, these young fellows do not get. Meat they get but twice a week. Let English parents bear this fact in mind; but that the lads are healthy and happy, anybody who sees them can have no question; furthermore, they are well instructed in a sound practical education—history, geography, mathematics, religion. What a place to know of would this be for many a poor half-pay officer, where he may put his children in all confidence that they will be well cared for and soundly educated! Why have we not State-schools in England, where, for the prime cost—for a sum which never need exceed for a young boy's maintenance *£25* a year—our children might be brought up? We are establishing national schools for the labourer: why not give education to the sons of the poor gentry—the clergyman whose pittance is small, and would still give his son the benefit of a public education; the artist, the officer, the merchant's office-clerk, the literary man? What a benefit might be conferred upon all of us if honest charter-schools could be established for our children, and where it would be impossible for Squeers to make a profit![xvii]

Arrangement of School Business in Dundalk Institution.			
Hours.	Monday, Wednesday, and Friday.	Tuesday and Thursday.	Saturday.

<table>
<tr><td>6 to 7</td><td>Rise, wash, etc.</td><td>Rise, wash, etc.</td><td>Rise, wash, etc.</td></tr>
<tr><td>7 to 7½</td><td>Scripture by the Master, and prayer.</td><td>Scripture by the Master, and prayer.</td><td>Scripture by the Master, and prayer.</td></tr>
<tr><td>7½ to 8½</td><td>Reading, History, etc.</td><td>Reading, History, etc.</td><td>Reading, History, etc.</td></tr>
<tr><td>8½ to 9</td><td>Breakfast.</td><td>Breakfast.</td><td>Breakfast.</td></tr>
<tr><td>9 to 10</td><td>Play.</td><td>Play.</td><td>Play.</td></tr>
<tr><td>10 to 10½</td><td>English Grammar.</td><td>Geography.</td><td rowspan="2">10 to 11, repetition.</td></tr>
<tr><td>10½ to 11¼</td><td>Algebra.</td><td>Euclid.</td></tr>
<tr><td>11¼ to 12</td><td>Scripture.</td><td>Lecture on principles of Arithmetic.</td><td>11 to 12, Use of Globes</td></tr>
<tr><td>12 to 12½</td><td>Writing.</td><td>Writing.</td><td rowspan="2">12 to 1, Catechism and Scripture by the Catechist.</td></tr>
<tr><td>12½ to 2</td><td>Arithmetic at Desks, and Book-keeping.</td><td>Mensuration.</td></tr>
<tr><td>2 to 2½</td><td>Dinner.</td><td>Dinner.</td><td>Dinner.</td></tr>
<tr><td>2½ to 5</td><td>Play.</td><td>Play.</td><td rowspan="6">The remainder of this day is devoted to exercise till the hour of Supper, after which the Boys assemble in the Schoolroom and hear a portion of Scripture read and explained by the Master, as on other days, and conclude with prayer.</td></tr>
<tr><td>5 to 7½</td><td>Spelling, Mental Arithmetic, and Euclid.</td><td>Spelling, Mental Arithmetic, and Euclid.</td></tr>
<tr><td>7½ to 8</td><td>Supper.</td><td>Supper.</td></tr>
<tr><td>8 to 8½</td><td>Exercise.</td><td>Exercise.</td></tr>
<tr><td>8½ to 9</td><td>Scripture by the Master, and prayer in Schoolroom.</td><td>Scripture by the Master, and prayer in Schoolroom.</td></tr>
<tr><td>9</td><td>Retire to bed.</td><td>Retire to bed.</td></tr>
<tr><td colspan="4">The sciences of Navigation and practical Surveying are taught in the Establishment: also a selection of the Pupils, who have a taste for it, are instructed in the art of Drawing.</td></tr>
</table>

Dietary.
BREAKFAST.—Stirabout and Milk, every Morning.
DINNER.—On Sunday and Wednesday, Potatoes and Beef: 10 ounces of the latter to each boy. On Monday and Thursday, Bread and Broth; ½ lb. of the former to each boy. On Tuesday, Friday, and Saturday, Potatoes and Milk; 2 lbs. of the former to each boy.
SUPPER.—½ lb. of Bread with Milk, uniformly, except on Monday and Thursday: on these days, Potatoes and Milk.

Our next day's journey led us, by half-past ten o'clock, to the ancient town of Louth, a little poor village now, but a great seat of learning and piety, it is said, formerly, where there stood a university and abbeys, and where Saint Patrick worked wonders. Here my kind friend the rector was called upon to marry a smart sergeant of police to a pretty lass, one of the few Protestants who attend his church; and, the ceremony over, we were invited to the house of the bride's father hard by, where the clergyman was bound to cut the cake and drink a glass of wine to the health of the new-married couple. There was evidently to be a dance and some merriment in the course of the evening; for the good mother of the bride (oh, blessed is he who has a good mother-in-law!) was busy at a huge fire in the little kitchen, and along the road we met various parties of neatly-dressed people, and several of the sergeant's comrades, who were hastening to the wedding. The mistress of the rector's darling Infant-School was one of the bridesmaids: consequently the little ones had a holiday.

But he was not to be disappointed of his Infant-School in this manner: so, mounting the car again, with a fresh horse, we went a very pretty drive of three miles to the snug lone schoolhouse of Glyde Farm—near a handsome park, I believe of the same name, where the proprietor is building a mansion of the Tudor order.

The pretty scene of Dundalk was here played over again; the children sang their little hymns, the good old clergyman joined delighted in the chorus, the holiday was given, and the little hands held up, and I looked at more clean bright faces and little rosy feet. The scene need not be repeated in print, but I can understand what pleasure a man must take in the daily witnessing of it, and in the growth of these little plants, which are set and tended by his care. As we returned to Louth, a woman met us with a curtsey and expressed her sorrow that she had been obliged to withdraw her daughter from one of the rector's schools, which the child was vexed at leaving too. But the orders of the priest were peremptory; and who can say they were unjust? The priest, on his side, was only enforcing the rule which the parson maintains as his:—the latter will not permit his young flock to be educated except upon certain principles and by certain teachers; the former has his own scruples unfortunately also

—and so that noble and brotherly scheme of National Education falls to the ground. In Louth, the national school was standing by the side of the priest's chapel; it is so almost everywhere throughout Ireland: the Protestants have rejected, on very good motives doubtless, the chance of union which the Education Board gave them. Be it so: if the children of either sect be educated apart, so that they *be* educated, the education scheme will have produced its good, and the union will come afterwards.

The church at Louth stands boldly upon a hill looking down on the village, and has nothing remarkable in it but neatness, except the monument of a former rector, Doctor Little, which attracts the spectator's attention from the extreme inappropriateness of the motto on the coat-of-arms of the reverend defunct. It looks rather unorthodox to read in a Christian temple, where a man's bones have the honour to lie—and where, if anywhere, humility is requisite—that there is *multum in Parvo,* 'a great deal in Little.' O Little, in life you were not much, and lo! you are less now: why should filial piety engrave that pert pun upon your monument, to cause people to laugh in a place where they ought to be grave? The defunct doctor built a very handsome rectory-house, with a set of stables that would be useful to a nobleman, but are rather too commodious for a peaceful rector who does not ride to hounds; and it was in Little's time, I believe, that the church was removed from the old abbey, where it formerly stood, to its present proud position on the hill.

The abbey is a fine ruin, the windows of a good style, the tracings of carvings on many of them; but a great number of stones and ornaments were removed formerly to build farm-buildings withal, and the place is now as rank and ruinous as the generality of Irish burying-places seem to be. Skulls lie in clusters amongst nettle-beds by the abbey-walls: graves are only partially covered with rude stones; a fresh coffin was lying broken in pieces within the abbey; and the surgeon of the dispensary hard by might procure subjects here, almost without grave-breaking. Hard by the abbey is a building; the legend in the country goes that the place was built for the accommodation of 'Saint Murtogh,' who lying down to sleep here in the open fields, not having any place to house under, found to his surprise, on waking in the morning, the above edifice, which the angels had built. The angelic architecture, it will be seen, is of rather a rude kind; and the village antiquary, who takes a pride in showing the place, says that the building was erected *two thousand years ago.* In the handsome grounds of the rectory is another spot visited by popular tradition—a fairy's ring: a regular mound of some thirty feet in height, flat and even on the top, and provided with a winding path for the foot-passenger to ascend. Some trees grew on the mound, one of which was removed in order to make the walk. But the country-people cried out loudly at this desecration, and vowed that the 'little people' had quitted the countryside for ever in consequence.

While walking in the town, a woman meets the rector with a number of curtseys and compliments, and vows that "tis your reverence is the friend of the poor, and may the Lord preserve you to us and lady'; and having poured out blessings innumerable, concludes by producing a paper for her son that's in throuble in England. The paper ran to the effect that 'We, the undersigned, inhabitants of the parish of Louth, have known Daniel Horgan ever since his youth, and can speak confidently as to his integrity, piety, and good conduct.' In fact, the paper stated that Daniel Horgan was an honour to his country, and consequently quite incapable of the crime of—sack-stealing, I think—with which at present he was charged, and lay in prison in Durham Castle. The paper had, I should think, come down to the poor mother from Durham, with a direction ready written to despatch it back again when signed, and was evidently the work of one of those benevolent individuals in assize-towns, who, following the profession of the law, delight to extricate unhappy young men of whose innocence (from various six-and-eightpenny motives) they feel convinced. There stood the poor mother, as the rector examined the document, with a huge wafer in her hand, ready to forward it as soon as it was signed: for the truth is that' We, the undersigned,' were as yet merely imaginary.

'You don't come to church,' says the rector. 'I know nothing of you or your son: why don't you go to the priest?'

'Oh, your reverence, my son's to be tried next Tuesday,' whimpered the woman. She then said the priest was not in the way, but, as we had seen him a few minutes before, recalled the assertion, and confessed that she *had* been to the priest and that he would not sign; and fell to prayers, tears, and unbounded supplications to induce the rector to give his signature. But that hard-hearted divine, stating that he had *not* known Daniel Horgan from his youth upwards, that he could not certify as to his honesty or dishonesty, enjoined the woman to make an attempt upon the R. C. curate, to whose handwriting he would certify if need were.

The upshot of the matter was that the woman returned with a certificate from the R. C. curate as to her son's good behaviour while in the village, and the rector certified that the handwriting was that of the R. C. clergyman in question, and the woman popped her big red wafer into the letter and went her way. Tuesday is passed long ere this: Mr. Horgan's guilt or innocence is long since clearly proved, and he celebrates the latter in freedom, or expiates the former at the mill. Indeed, I don't know that there was any call to introduce his adventures to the public, except perhaps it may be good to see how in this little distant Irish village the blood of life is running. Here goes a happy party to a marriage, and the parson prays a 'God bless you!' upon them, and the world begins for them. Yonder lies a stall-fed rector in his tomb, flaunting over his nothingness his pompous heraldic motto: and yonder lie the fresh fragments of a nameless deal coffin, which any foot may kick over. Presently you hear the clear voices of little children praising God; and here comes a mother wringing her hands and asking for succour for her lad, who was a child but the other day. Such *motus animorum atque hæc certamina tanta* are going in an hour of an October day in a little pinch of clay in the county Louth.

Perhaps—being in the moralising strain—the honest surgeon at the dispensary might come in as an illustration. He inhabits a neat humble house, a storey higher than his neighbours', but with a thatched roof. He relieves a thousand patients yearly at the dispensary, he visits seven hundred in the parish, he supplies the medicines gratis; and receiving for these services the sum of about one hundred pounds yearly, some county economists and calculators are loud against the extravagance of his salary, and threaten his removal. All these individuals and their histories we presently turn our backs upon, for, after all, dinner is at five o'clock, and we have to see the new road to Dundalk, which the county has lately been making.

Of this undertaking, which shows some skilful engineering—some gallant cutting of rocks and hills, and filling of valleys, with a tall and handsome stone bridge thrown across the river, and connecting the high embankments on which the new road at that place is formed—I can say little, except that it is a vast convenience to the county, and a great credit to the surveyor and contractor too; for the latter, though a poor man, and losing heavily by his bargain, has yet refused to mulct his labourers of their wages; and, as cheerfully as he can, still pays them their shilling a day.

CHAPTER XXVII: NEWRY, ARMAGH, BELFAST—FROM DUNDALK TO NEWRY

MY kind host gave orders to the small ragged boy that drove the car to take 'particular care of the little gentleman'; and the car-boy, grinning in appreciation of the joke, drove off at his best pace, and landed his cargo at Newry after a pleasant two hours' drive. The country for the most part is wild, but not gloomy; the mountains round about are adorned with woods and gentlemen's seats; and the car-boy pointed out one hill—that of Slievegullion, which kept us company all the way—as the highest hill in Ireland. Ignorant or deceiving car-boy! I have seen a dozen hills, each the highest in Ireland, in my way through the country, of which the inexorable Guide-book gives the measurement and destroys the claim. Well, it was the tallest hill, in the estimation of the car-boy; and in this respect the world is full of car-boys. Has not every mother of a family a Slievegullion of a son, who, according to her measurement, towers above all other sons? *I*s not the patriot, who believes himself equal to three Frenchmen, a car-boy in heart? There was a kind young creature, with a child in her lap, that evidently held this notion. She paid the child a series of compliments, which would have led one to fancy he was an angel from heaven at the least; and her husband sat gravely by, very silent, with his arms round a barometer.

Beyond these there were no incidents or characters of note, except an old ostler that they said was ninety years old, and watered the horse at a lone inn on the road. 'Stop!' cries this wonder of years and rags, as the ear, after considerable parley, got under way. The car-boy pulled up, thinking a fresh passenger was coming out of the inn.

'*Stop, till one of the gentlemen gives me something*,' says the old man, coming slowly up with us: which speech created a laugh, and got him a penny: he received it without the least thankfulness, and went away grumbling to his pail.

Newry is remarkable as being the only town I have seen which had no cabin suburb: strange to say, the houses begin all at once, handsomely coated and hatted with stone and slate; and if Dundalk was prosperous, Newry is better still. Such a sight of neatness and comfort is exceedingly welcome to an English traveller, who, moreover, finds himself, after driving through a plain bustling clean street, landed at a large plain comfortable inn, where business seems to be done, where there are smart waiters to receive him, and a comfortable warm coffee-room that bears no traces of dilapidation.

What the merits of the *cuisine* may be I can't say for the information of travellers; a gentleman to whom I had brought a letter from Dundalk taking care to provide me at his own table, accompanying me previously to visit the lions of the town. A river divides it, and the counties of Armagh and Down: the river runs into the sea at

Carling-ford Bay, and is connected by a canal with Lough Neagh, and thus with the North of Ireland. Steamers to Liverpool and Glasgow sail continually. There are mills, foundries, and manufactories, of which the Guide-book will give particulars; and the town of 13,000 inhabitants is the busiest and most thriving that I have yet seen in Ireland.

Our first walk was to the church: a large and handsome building, although built in the unlucky period when the Gothic style was coming into vogue. Hence one must question the propriety of many of the ornaments, though the whole is massive, well-finished, and stately. Near the church stands the Roman Catholic chapel, a very fine building, the work of the same architect, Mr. Duff, who erected the chapel at Dundalk; but, like almost all other edifices of the kind in Ireland that I have seen, the interior is quite unfinished, and already so dirty and ruinous, that one would think a sort of genius for dilapidation must have been exercised in order to bring it to its present condition. There are tattered green-baize doors to enter at, a dirty clay floor, and cracked plaster walls, with an injunction to the public not to spit on the floor. Maynooth itself is scarcely more dreary. The architect's work, however, does him the highest credit: the interior of the church is noble and simple in style; and one can't but grieve to see a fine work of art, that might have done good to the country, so defaced and ruined as this is.

The Newry poorhouse is as neatly ordered and comfortable as any house, public or private, in Ireland: the same look of health which was so pleasant to see among the Naas children of the union-house was to be remarked here: the same care and comfort for the old people. Of able-bodied there were but few in the house: it is in winter that there are most applicants for this kind of relief; the sunshine attracts the women out of the place, and the harvest relieves it of the men. Cleanliness, the matron said, is more intolerable to most of the inmates than any other regulation of the house; and instantly on quitting the house they relapse into their darling dirt, and of course at their periodical return are subject to the unavoidable initiatory lustration.

Newry has many comfortable and handsome public buildings: the streets have a business-like look, the shops and people are not too poor, and the southern grandiloquence is not shown here in the shape of fine words for small wares. Even the beggars are not so numerous, I fancy, or so coaxing and wheedling in their talk. Perhaps, too, among the gentry the same moral change may be remarked, and they seem more downright and plain in their manner; but one must not pretend to speak of national characteristics from such a small experience as a couple of evenings' intercourse may give.

Although not equal in natural beauty to a hundred other routes which the traveller takes in the South, the ride from Newry to Armagh is an extremely pleasant one, on account of the undeniable increase of prosperity which is visible through the country. Well-tilled fields, neat farmhouses, well-dressed people, meet one everywhere, and people and landscape alike have a plain, hearty, flourishing look.

The greater part of Armagh has the aspect of a good stout old English town, although round about the steep on which the cathedral stands (the Roman Catholics have taken possession of another hill, and are building an opposition cathedral on this eminence) there are some decidedly Irish streets, and that dismal combination of house and pigsty which is so common in Munster and Connaught.

But the main streets, though not fine, are bustling, substantial, and prosperous; and a fine green has some old trees and some good houses, and even handsome stately public buildings round about it, that remind one of a comfortable cathedral city across the water.

The cathedral service is more completely performed here than in any English town, I think. The church is small, but extremely neat, fresh, and handsome—almost too handsome; covered with spick-and-span gilding and carved-work in the style of the thirteenth century; every pew as smart and well-cushioned as my Lord's own seat in the country church; and for the clergy and their chief, stalls and thrones quite curious for their ornament and splendour. The Primate with his blue riband and badge (to whom the two clergymen bow reverently as, passing between them, he enters at the gate of the altar rail) looks like a noble Prince of the Church: and I had heard enough of his magnificent charity and kindness to look with reverence at his lofty handsome features.

Will it be believed that the sermon lasted only for twenty minutes? Can this be Ireland? I think this wonderful circumstance impressed me more than any other with the difference between North and South, and, having the Primate's own countenance for the opinion, may confess a great admiration for orthodoxy in this particular.

A beautiful monument to Archbishop Stuart, by Chantrey; a magnificent stained window, containing the arms of the clergy of the diocese (in the very midst of which I was glad to recognise the sober old family coat of the kind and venerable rector of Louth), and numberless carvings and decorations, will please the lover of church architecture here. I must confess, however, that in my idea the cathedral is quite too complete. It is of the twelfth century, but not the least venerable. It is as neat and trim as a lady's drawing-room. It wants a hundred years at least to cool the raw colours of the stones, and to dull the brightness of the gilding: all which benefits, no doubt, time will bring to pass, and future cockneys setting off from London Bridge after breakfast in an aerial machine may come to hear the morning service here, and not remark the faults which have struck a too susceptible tourist of the nineteenth century.

Strolling round the town after service, I saw more decided signs that Protestantism was there in the ascendant. I saw no less than three different ladies on the prowl, dropping religious tracts at various doors; and felt not a little ashamed to be seen by one of them getting into a car with bag and baggage, being bound for Belfast.

The ride of ten miles from Armagh to Portadown was not the prettiest, but one of the pleasantest drives I have had in Ireland, for the country is well cultivated along the whole of the road, the trees in plenty, and villages and neat houses always in sight. The little farms, with their orchards and comfortable buildings, were as clean and trim as could be wished; they are mostly of one storey, with long thatched roofs and shining windows, such as those that may be seen in Normandy and Picardy. As it was Sunday evening, all the people seemed to be abroad, some sauntering quietly down the roads, a pair of girls here and there pacing leisurely in a field, a little group seated under the trees of an orchard, which pretty adjunct to the farm is very common in this district; and the crop of apples seemed this year to be extremely plenty. The physiognomy of the people too has quite changed: the girls have their hair neatly braided up, not loose over their faces as in the South; and not only are bare feet very rare, and stockings extremely neat and white, but I am sure I saw at least a dozen good silk gowns upon the women along the road, and scarcely one which was not clean and in good order. The men for the most part figured in jackets, caps, and trousers, eschewing the old well of a hat which covers the popular head at the other end of the island, the breeches and the long ill-made tailcoat. The people's faces are sharp and neat, not broad, lazy, knowing-looking, like that of many a shambling Diogenes who may be seen lounging before his cabin in Cork or Kerry. As for the cabins, they have disappeared: and the houses of the people may rank decidedly as cottages. The accent, too, is quite different; but this is hard to describe in print. The people speak with a Scotch twang, and, as I fancied, much more simply and to the point. A man gives you a downright answer, without any grin or joke, or attempt at flattery. To be sure these are rather early days to begin to judge of national characteristics; and very likely the above distinctions have been drawn after profoundly studying a Northern and a Southern waiter at the inn at Armagh.

At any rate, it is clear that the towns are vastly improved, the cottages and villages no less so; the people look active and well-dressed; a sort of weight seems all at once to be taken from the Englishman's mind on entering the province, when he finds himself once more looking upon comfort and activity, and resolution. What is the cause of this improvement? *Protestantism* is, more than one Church-of-England man said to me; but for Protestantism, would it not be as well to read Scotchism?—meaning thrift, prudence, perseverance, boldness, and common sense: with which qualities any body of men, of any Christian denomination, would no doubt prosper.

The little brisk town of Portadown, with its comfortable unpretending houses, its squares and market-place, its pretty quay, with craft along the river,—a steamer building on the dock, close to mills and warehouses that look in a full state of prosperity,—was a pleasant conclusion to this ten miles' drive, that ended at the newly opened railway-station. The distance hence to Belfast is twenty-five miles; Lough Neagh may be seen at one point of the line, and the Guide-book says that the station towns of Lurgan and Lisburn are extremely picturesque; but it was night when I passed by them, and after, a journey of an hour and a quarter reached Belfast.

That city has been discovered by another eminent cockney traveller (for though born in America, the dear old Bow-bell blood must run in the veins of Mr. N. P. Willis), and I have met, in the periodical works of the country, with repeated angry allusions to his description of Belfast, the pink heels of the chambermaid who conducted him to bed (what business had he to be looking at the young woman's legs at all?), and his wrath at the beggary of the town and the laziness of the inhabitants, as marked by a line of dirt running along the walls, and showing where they were in the habit of lolling.

These observations struck me as rather hard when applied to Belfast, though possibly pink heels and beggary might be remarked in other cities of the kingdom; but the town of Belfast seemed to me really to be as neat, prosperous, and handsome a city as need be seen; and, with respect to the inn, that in which I stayed (Kearn's) was as comfortable and well-ordered an establishment as the most fastidious cockney can desire, and with an advantage which some people perhaps do not care for, that the dinners which cost seven shillings at London taverns are here served for half-a-crown; but I must repeat here, in justice to the public, what I stated to Mr. William the waiter, viz., that half-a-pint of port-wine *does* contain more than two glasses—at least it does in happy, happy England....Only, to be sure, here the wine is good, whereas the port-wine in England is not port, but for the most part an abominable drink of which it would be a mercy only to give us two glasses: which, however, is clearly wandering from the subject in hand.

They call Belfast the Irish Liverpool. If people are for calling names, it would be better to call it the Irish London at once—the chief city of the kingdom at any rate. It looks hearty, thriving, and prosperous, as if it had money in its pockets and roast-beef for dinner: it has no pretensions to fashion, but looks mayhap better in its honest broadcloth than *some people* in their shabby brocade. The houses are as handsome as at Dublin, with this advantage, that the people seem to live in them. They have no attempt at ornament for the most part, but are grave, stout, red-brick edifices, laid out at four angles in orderly streets and squares.

The stranger cannot fail to be struck (and haply a little frightened) by the great number of meeting-houses that decorate the town, and give evidence of great sermonising on Sundays. These buildings do not affect the Gothic, like many of the meagre edifices of the Established and the Roman Catholic churches, but have a physiognomy of their own—a thick-set citizen look. Porticoes have they, to be sure, and ornaments Doric, Ionic, and what not; but the meeting-house peeps through all these classical friezes and entablatures; and though one reads of ' Imitations of the Ionic Temple of Dissus, near Athens,' the classic temple is made to assume a bluff, downright, Presbyterian air, which would astonish the original builder, doubtless. The churches of the Establishment are handsome and stately. The Catholics are building a brick cathedral, no doubt of the Tudor style:—the present chapel, flanked by the national schools, is an exceedingly unprepossessing building of the Strawberry Hill or Castle of Otranto Gothic: the keys and mitre figuring in the centre—'The cross-keys and night-cap,' as a hardhearted Presbyterian called them to me, with his blunt humour.

The three churches are here pretty equally balanced: Presbyterians 25,000, Catholics 20,000, Episcopalians 17,000. Each party has two or more newspaper organs; and the wars between them are dire and unceasing, as the reader may imagine. For whereas in other parts of Ireland where Catholics and Episcopalians prevail, and the Presbyterian body is too small, each party has but one opponent to belabour: here the Ulster politician, whatever may be his way of thinking, has the great advantage of possessing two enemies on whom he may exercise his eloquence; and in this triangular duel all do their duty nobly. Then there are subdivisions of hostility. For the Church there is a High Church and a Low Church journal; for the Liberals there is a Repeal journal and a No-repeal journal; for the Presbyterians there are yet more varieties of journalistic opinion, on which it does not become a stranger to pass a judgment. If the *Northern Whig* says that the *Banner of Ulster* 'is a polluted rag, which has hoisted the red banner of falsehood' (which elegant words may be found in the first-named journal of the 13th October), let us be sure the *Banner* has a compliment for the *Northern Whig* in return; if the 'Repeal' *Vindicator* and the priests attack the Presbyterian journals and the 'home missions,' the reverend gentlemen of Geneva are quite as ready with the pen as their brethren of Rome, and not much more scrupulous in their language than the laity. When I was in Belfast, violent disputes were raging between Presbyterian and Episcopalian Conservatives with regard to the Marriage Bill; between Presbyterians and Catholics on the subject of the 'home missions'; between the Liberals and Conservatives, of course. 'Thank God,' for instance, writes a Repeal journal, 'that the honour and power *of Ireland* are not involved in the disgraceful Afghan war!'—a sentiment insinuating Repeal and something more; disowning, not merely this or that Ministry, but the Sovereign and her jurisdiction altogether. But details of these quarrels, religious or political, can tend to edify but few readers out of the country. Even in it, as there are some nine shades of politico-religious differences, an observer pretending to impartiality must necessarily displease eight parties, and almost certainly the whole nine; and the reader who desires to judge the politics of Belfast must study for himself. Nine journals, publishing four hundred numbers in a year, each number containing about as much as an octavo volume: these, and the back numbers of former years, sedulously read, will give the student a notion of the subject in question. And then, after having read the statements on either side, he must ascertain the truth of them, by which time more labour of the same kind will have grown upon him, and he will have attained a good old age.

Amongst the poor, the Catholics and Presbyterians are said to go in a pretty friendly manner to the national schools; but among the Presbyterians themselves it appears there are great differences and quarrels, by which a fine institution, the Belfast Academy, seems to have suffered considerably. It is almost the only building in this large and substantial place that bears, to the stranger's eye, an unprosperous air. A vast building, standing fairly in the midst of a handsome green and place, and with snug comfortable red-brick streets stretching away at neat right angles all around, the

Presbyterian College looks handsome enough at a short distance, but on a nearer view is found in a woful state of dilapidation. It does not possess the supreme dirt and filth of Maynooth—*that* can but belong to one place, even in Ireland; but the building is in a dismal state of unrepair, steps and windows broken, doors and stairs battered. Of scholars I saw but a few, and these were in the drawing academy. The fine arts do not appear as yet to flourish in Belfast. The models from which the lads were copying were not good: one was copying a bad copy of a drawing by Prout; one was colouring a print. The ragged children in a German national school have better models before them, and are made acquainted with truer principles of art and beauty.

Hard by is the Belfast Museum, where an exhibition of pictures was in preparation, under the patronage of the Belfast Art Union. Artists in all parts of the kingdom had been invited to send their works, of which the Union pays the carriage; and the porters and secretary were busy unpacking cases, in which I recognised some of the works which had before figured on the walls of the London Exhibition rooms.

The book-shops which I saw in this thriving town said much for the religious disposition of the Belfast public: there were numerous portraits of reverend gentlemen, and their works of every variety:—'The Sinner's Friend,' 'The Watchman on the Tower,' 'The Peep of Day,' 'Sermons delivered at Bethesda Chapel,' by So-and-so: with hundreds of the neat little gilt books with bad prints, Scriptural titles, and gilt edges, that come from one or two serious publishing houses in London, and in considerable numbers from the neighbouring Scotch shores. As for the theatre, with such a public the drama can be expected to find but little favour; and the gentleman who accompanied me in my walk, and to whom I am indebted for many kindnesses during my stay, said not only that he had never been in the playhouse, but that he never heard of any one going thither. I found out the place where the poor neglected Dramatic Muse of Ulster hid herself; and was of a party of six in the boxes, the benches of the pit being dotted over with about a score more. Well, it was a comfort to see that the gallery was quite full, and exceedingly happy and noisy: they stamped, and stormed, and shouted, and clapped, in a way that was pleasant to hear. One young god, between the acts, favoured the public with a song— extremely ill sung certainly, but the intention was everything; and his brethren above stamped in chorus with roars of delight.

As for the piece performed, it was a good old melodrama of the British sort, inculcating a thorough detestation of vice and a warm sympathy with suffering virtue. The serious are surely too hard upon poor playgoers. We never for a moment allow rascality to. triumph beyond a certain part of the third act; we sympathise with the woes of young lovers—her in ringlets and a Polish cap, him in tights and a Vandyke collar; we abhor avarice or tyranny in the person of ' the first old man' with the white wig and red stockings, or of the villain with the roaring voice and black whiskers; we applaud the honest wag (he is a good fellow in spite of his cowardice) in his hearty jests at the tyrant before mentioned; and feel a kindly sympathy with all mankind as the curtain falls over all the characters in a group, of which successful love is the happy centre. Reverend gentlemen in meeting-house and church, who shout against the immoralities of this poor stage, and threaten all playgoers with the fate which is awarded to unsuccessful plays, should try and bear less hardly upon us.

An artist—who, in spite of the Art Union, can scarcely, I should think, flourish in a place that seems devoted to preaching, politics, and trade—has somehow found his way to this humble little theatre, and decorated it with some exceedingly pretty scenery—almost the only indication of a taste for the fine arts which I have found as yet in the country.

A fine night-exhibition in the town is that of the huge spinning-mills which surround it, and of which the thousand windows are lighted up at nightfall, and may be seen from almost all quarters of the city.

A gentleman to whom I had brought an introduction good-naturedly left his work to walk with me to one of these mills, and stated by whom he had been introduced to me to the mill-proprietor, Mr. Mulholland. '*That* recommendation,' said Mr. Mulholland gallantly, 'is welcome anywhere.' It was from my kind friend Mr. Lever. What a privilege some men have, who can sit quietly in their studies and make friends all the world over!

There are nearly five hundred girls employed in the place. They work in huge long chambers, lighted by numbers of windows, hot with steam, buzzing and humming with hundreds of thousands of whirling wheels, that all take their motion from a steam-engine which lives apart in a hot cast-iron temple of its own, from which it communicates with the innumerable machines that the five hundred girls preside over. They have seemingly but to take away the work when done—the enormous monster in the cast-iron room does it all. He cards the flax, and combs it, and spins it, and beats it, and twists it: the five hundred girls stand by to feed him, or take the material from him, when he has had his will of it. There is something frightful in the vastness as in the minuteness of this power. Every thread writhes and twirls as the steam-fate orders it,—every thread, of which it would take a hundred to make the thickness of a hair.

I have seldom, I think, seen more good looks than amongst the young women employed in this place. They work for twelve hours daily, in rooms of which the heat is intolerable to a stranger; but in spite of it they looked gay, stout, and healthy; nor were their forms much concealed by the very simple clothes they wear while in the mill.

The stranger will be struck by the good looks not only of these spinsters, but of almost all the young women in the streets. I never saw a town where so many women are to be met—so many and so pretty—with and without bonnets, with good figures, in neat homely shawls and dresses. The grisettes of Belfast are among the handsomest ornaments of it; and as good, no doubt, and irreproachable in morals as their sisters in the rest of Ireland.

Many of the merchants' counting-houses are crowded in little old-fashioned 'entries,' or courts, such as one sees about the Bank in London. In and about these, and in the principal streets in the daytime, is a great activity, and homely unpretending bustle. The men have a business look, too; and one sees very few flaunting dandies, as in Dublin. The shopkeepers do not brag upon their signboards, or keep 'emporiums,' as elsewhere,—their places of business being for the most part homely; though one may see some splendid shops, which are not to be surpassed by London. The docks and quays are busy with their craft and shipping, upon the beautiful borders of the Lough; —the large red warehouses stretching along the shores, with ships loading, or unloading, or building, hammers clanging, pitch-pots flaming and boding, seamen cheering in the ships, or lolling lazily on the shore. The life and movement of a port here give the stranger plenty to admire and observe. And nature has likewise done everything for the place— surrounding it with picturesque hills and water;—for which latter I must confess I was not very sorry to leave the town behind me, and its mills, and its meeting-houses, and its commerce, and its theologians, and its politicians.

CHAPTER XXVIII: BELFAST TO TIIE CAUSEWAY

THE Lough of Belfast has a reputation for beauty almost as great as that of the Bay of Dublin; but though, on the day I left Belfast for Larne, the morning was fine, and the sky clear and blue above, an envious mist lay on the water, which hid all its beauties from the down of passengers on the Lame coach. All we could see were ghostly-looking silhouettes of ships gliding here and there through the clouds; and I am sure, the coachman's remark was quite correct that it was a pity the day was so misty. I found myself, before I was aware, entrapped into a theological controversy with two grave gentlemen outside the coach—another fog, which did not subside much before we reached Carrickfergus. The road from the Ulster capital to that little town seemed meanwhile to be extremely lively: cars and omnibuses passed thickly peopled. For some miles along the road is a string of handsome country-houses, belonging to the rich citizens of the town; and we passed by neat-looking churches and chapels, factories and rows of cottages clustered round them, like villages of old at the foot of feudal castles. Furthermore it was hard to see, for the mist which lay on the water had enveloped the mountains too, and we only had a glimpse or two of smiling comfortable fields and gardens.

Carrickfergus rejoices in a real romantic-looking castle jutting bravely into the sea, and famous as a background for a picture. It is of use for little else now, luckily; nor has it been put to any real warlike purposes since the day when honest Thurot stormed, took and evacuated it. Let any romancer who is in want of a hero peruse the second volume, or it may be the third, of the 'Annual Register,' where the adventures of that gallant fellow are related, He was a gentleman, a genius, and, to crown all, a smuggler. He lived for some time in Ireland, and in England, in disguise; he had love-passages and romantic adventures; he landed a body of his countrymen on these shores, and died in the third volume, after a battle gallantly fought on both sides, but in which victory rested with the British arms. What can a novelist want more? William III. also landed here; and as for the rest—M'Skimin, the accurate and laborious historian of the town, informs us that the founding of the castle is lost in the depths of antiquity:—It is pleasant to give a little historic glance at a place as one passes through. The above facts may be relied on as coming from Messrs. Curry's excellent new Guide-book; with the exception of the history of Monsieur Thurot, which is 'private information,' drawn years ago from the scarce work previously mentioned. By the way, another excellent companion to the traveller in Ireland is the collection of the 'Irish Penny Magazine,' which may be purchased for a guinea, and contains a mass of information regarding the customs and places of the country. Willis's work is amusing, as everything is, written by that lively author, and the engravings accompanying it as unfaithful as any ever made.

Meanwhile, asking pardon for this double digression, which has been made while the guard-coachman is delivering his mail-bags—while the landlady stands looking on in the sun, her hands folded a little below the waist—while a company of tall burly troops from the castle has passed by 'commanded' by a very mean, mealy-faced, uneasy-looking little subaltern—while the poor epileptic idiot of the town, wallowing and grinning in the road, and snorting out supplications for a halfpenny, has tottered away in possession of the coin:—meanwhile, fresh horses are brought out, and the small boy who acts behind the coach makes an unequal and disagreeable tootooing on a horn kept to warn sleepy carmen and celebrate triumphal entries into and exits from cities. As the mist clears up, the country shows round about wild but friendly: at one place we passed a village where a crowd of well-dressed people might be seen coming over the fields and issuing from the mist. The owner of the carts and machines is going to emigrate to America. Presently we come to the demesne of Red Hall, 'through which is a pretty drive of upwards of a mile in length: it contains a rocky glen, the bed of a mountain stream—which is perfectly dry, except in winter—and the woods about it are picturesque, and it is occasionally the resort of summer-parties of pleasure.' Nothing can be more just than the first part of the description, and there is very little doubt that the latter paragraph is equally faithful; with which we come to Larne, a 'most thriving two,' the same authority says, but a most dirty and narrow-streeted and ill-built one. Some of the houses reminded one of the South.

And here, after a drive of nineteen miles upon a comfortable coach, we were transferred with the mail-bags to a comfortable car that makes the journey to Ballycastle. There is no harm in saying that there was a very pretty smiling Buxom young lass for a travelling companion; and somehow, to a lonely person, the landscape always looks prettier in such society. The 'Antrim coast-road.' which we now, after a few miles, begin to follow, besides being one of the most noble and gallant works of art that is to be seen in any country, is likewise a route highly picturesque and romantic; the sea spreading wide before the spectator's eyes upon one side of the route, the tall cliffs of limestone rising abruptly above him on the other. There are in the map of Curry's Guide-book points indicating castles and abbey ruins in the vicinity of Glenarm; and the little place looked so comfortable, as we abruptly came upon it, round a rock, that I was glad to have an excuse for staying, and felt an extreme curiosity with regard to the abbey and the castle.

The abbey only exists in the unromantic shape of a wall; the castle, however, far from being a ruin, is an antique in the most complete order—an old castle repaired so as to look like new, and increased by modern wings, towers, gables, and terraces, so extremely old that the whole forms a grand and imposing-looking baronial edifice, towering above the little town which it seems to protect, and with which it is connected by a bridge and a severe-looking armed tower and gate. In the town is a town-house, with a campanile in the Italian taste, and a school or chapel opposite in the Early English; so that the inhabitants can enjoy a considerable architectural variety. A grave-looking church, with a beautiful steeple, stands amid some trees hard by a second handsome bridge and the little quay; and here, too, was perched a poor little wandering theatre (gallery 1d., pit 2d.), and proposing that night to play 'Bombastes Furioso, and the Comic Bally of Glenarm in an Uproar.' I heard the thumping of the drum in the evening; but, as at Roundwood, nobody patronised the poor players. At nine o'clock there was not a single taper lighted under their awning, and my heart (perhaps it is too susceptible) bled for Fusbos.

The severe gate of the castle was opened by a kind good-natured old porteress, instead of a rough gallowglass with a battle-axe and yellow shirt (more fitting guardian of so stern a postern), and the old dame insisted upon my making an application to see the grounds of the castle, which request was very kindly granted, and afforded a delightful half-hour's walk. The grounds are beautiful, and excellently kept; the trees in their autumn livery of red, yellow, and brown, except some stout ones that keep to their green summer clothes, and the laurels and their like, who wear pretty much the same dress all the year round. The birds were singing with the most astonishing vehemence in the dark glistening shrubberies; but the only sound in the walks was that of the rakes pulling together the falling leaves. There was of these walks one especially, flanked towards the river by a turreted wall covered with ivy, and having on the one side a row of lime-trees that had turned quite yellow, while opposite them was a green slope, and a quaint terrace-stair, and a long range of fantastic gables, towers, and chimneys there was, I say, one of these walks which Mr. Cattermole would hit off with a few strokes of his gallant pencil, and which I could fancy to he frequented by some of those long-trained, tender, gentle-looking young beauties whom Mr. Stone loves to design. Here they come, talking of love in a tone that is between a sigh and a whisper, and gliding in rustling shot silks over the fallen leaves.

There seemed to be a good deal of stir in the little port, where, says the Guide-book, a couple of hundred vessels take in cargoes annually of the produce of the district. Stone and lime are the chief articles exported, of which the cliffs for miles give an unfailing supply; and, as one travels the mountains at night, the kilns may be seen lighted up in the lonely places, and flaring red in the darkness.

If the road from Larne to Glenarm is beautiful, the coast route from the latter place to Cushendall is still more so; and, except peerless Westport, I have seen nothing in Ireland so picturesque as this noble line of coast scenery. The new road, luckily, is not yet completed, and the lover of natural beauties had better hasten to the spot in time, ere, by flattening and improving the road, and leading it along the sea-shore, half the magnificent prospects are shut out, now visible from along the mountainous old road; which, according to the good old fashion, gallantly takes all the hills in its course, disdaining to turn them. At three miles' distance, near the village of Cairlough, Glenarm looks more beautiful than when you are close upon it; and, as the car travels on to the stupendous Garron Head, the traveller, looking back, has a view of the whole line of coast southward as far as Isle Magee, with its bays and white villages, and tall precipitous cliffs, green, white, and grey. Eyes left, you may look with wonder at the mountains rising above, or presently at the pretty park and grounds of Drumnasole. Here, near the woods of Nappan, which are dressed in ten thousand colours—ash-leaves turned yellow, nut-trees red, birch-leaves brown, lime-leaves speckled over with black spots (marks of a disease which they will never get over)—stands a school-house that looks like a French château, having probably been a villa in former days, and discharges as we pass a cluster of fair-haired children that begin running madly down the hill, their fair hair streaming behind them. Down the hill goes the car, madly too, and you wonder and bless your stars that the horse does not fall or crush the children that are running before, or you that are sitting behind. Every now and then, at a trip of the horse, a disguised lady's-maid, with a canary-bird in her lap and a vast anxiety about her best bonnet in the bandbox, begins to scream: at which the car-boy grins, and rattles down the hill only the quicker. The road, which almost always skirts the hillside, has been torn sheer through the rock here and there: an immense work of levelling, shovelling, picking, blasting, filling, is going on along the whole line. As I was looking up a vast cliff, decorated with patches of green here and there at its summit, and at its base, where the sea had beaten until now, with long thin waving grass, that I told a grocer, my neighbour, was like mermaid's hair (though he did not in the least coincide in the simile)—as I was looking up the bill, admiring two goats that were browsing on a little patch of green, and two sheep perched yet higher (I had never seen such agility in mutton)—as, I say once more, I was looking at these phenomena, the grocer nudges me and says, '*Look on to this side—that's Scotland yon.*' If ever this book reaches a second edition, a sonnet shall be inserted in this place, describing the author's feelings on his first view op Scotland. Meanwhile, the Scotch mountains remain undisturbed, looking blue and solemn far away in the placid sea.

Rounding Garron Head, we come upon the inlet which is called Red Bay, the shores and sides of which are of red clay, that has taken the place of limestone, and towards which, between two noble ranges of mountains, stretches a long green plain, forming, together with the hills that protect it and the sea that washes it, one of the most beautiful landscapes of this most beautiful country. A fair writer, whom the Guide-book quotes, breaks out into strains of admiration in speaking of this district; calls it 'Switzerland in miniature,' celebrates its mountains of Glenariff and Lurgethan, and lauds, in terms of equal admiration, the rivers, waterfalls, and other natural beauties that lie within the glen.

The writers' enthusiasm regarding this tract of country is quite warranted, nor can any praise in admiration of it be too high; but alas! in calling a place 'Switzerland in miniature,' do we describe it? In joining together cataracts, valleys, rushing streams, and blue mountains, with all the emphasis and picturesqueness of which type is capable, we cannot get near to a copy of Nature's sublime countenance; and the writer can't hope to describe such grand sights so as to make them visible to the fireside reader, but can only, to the best of his taste and experience, warn the future traveller where he may look out for objects to admire. I think this sentiment has been repeated a score of times in this journal; but it comes upon one at every new display of beauty and magnificence, such as here the Almighty in His bounty has set before us; and every such scene seems to warn one, that it is not made to talk about too much, but to think of and love, and be grateful for.

Rounding this beautiful bay and valley, we passed by some caves that penetrate deep into the red rock, and are inhabited—one by a blacksmith, whose forge was blazing in the dark; one by cattle; and one by an old woman that has sold whisky here for time out of mind. The road then passes under an arch cut in the rock by the same spirited individual who has cleared away many of the difficulties in the route to Glenarm, and beside a conical hill, where for some time previous have been visible the ruins of the 'ancient auld castle' of Red Bay. At a distance, it looks very grand upon its height; but on coming close it has dwindled down to a mere wall, and not a high one. Hence quickly we reached Cushendall, where the grocer's family are on the look-out for him: the driver begins to blow his little bugle, and the disguised lady's-maid begins to smooth her bonnet and hair.

At this place a good dinner of fresh whiting, broiled bacon, and small beer was served up to me for the sum of eightpence, while the lady's-maid in question took her tea. 'This town is full of Papists,' said her ladyship, with an extremely genteel air; and, either in consequence of this, or because she ate up one of the fish, which she had clearly no right to, a disagreement arose between us, and we did not exchange another word for the rest of the journey. The road led us for fourteen miles by wild mountains, and across a fine aqueduct to Ballycastle; but it was dark as we left Cushendall, and it was difficult to see more in the grey evening but that the country was savage and lonely, except where the kilns were lighted up here and there in the hills, and a shining river might be seen winding in the dark ravines. Not far from Ballycastle lies a little old ruin, called the Abbey of Bonamargy: by it the Margy river runs into the sea, upon which you come suddenly; and on the shore are some tall buildings and factories, that looked as well in the moonlight as if they had not been in ruins: and hence a fine avenue of limes leads to Ballycastle. They must have been planted at the time recorded in the Guide-Book, when a mine was discovered near the town, and the works and warehouses on the quay erected. At present, the place has little trade, and half-a-dozen carts with apples, potatoes, dried fish, and turf, seem to contain the commerce of the market.

The picturesque sort of vehicle which is here designed,[xviii] is said to be going much out of fashion in the country, the solid wheels giving place to those common to the rest of Europe. A fine and edifying conversation took place between the designer and the owner of the vehicle. 'Stand still for a minute, you and the car, and I will give you twopence!' 'What do you want to do with it?' says the latter. 'To draw it.' 'To *draw* it!' says he, with a wild look of surprise. 'And is it you'll draw it?' 'I mean I want to take a picture of it: you know what a picture is!' 'No, I don't.' 'Here's one,' says I, showing him a book. 'Oh, faith, sir,' says the carman, drawing back rather alarmed, 'I'm no scholar!' And he concluded by saying, '*Will you buy the turf, or will you not*?' By which straightforward question he showed himself to be a real practical man of sense; and, as he got an unsatisfactory reply to this query, he forthwith gave a lash to his pony and declined to wait a minute longer. As for the twopence, he certainly accepted that handsome sum, and put it into his pocket, but with an air of extreme wonder at the transaction, and of contempt for the giver; which very likely was perfectly justifiable. I have seen men despised in genteel companies with not half so good a cause.

In respect to the fine arts, I am bound to say that the people in the South and West showed much more curiosity and interest with regard to a sketch and its progress than has been shown by the *badauds* of the North; the former looking on by dozens and exclaiming, 'That's Frank Mahony's house?' or 'Look at Biddy Mullins and the child!' or 'He's taking off the chimney now!' as the case may be; whereas, sketching in the North, I have collected no such spectators, the people not taking the slightest notice of the transaction.

The little town of Ballycastle does not contain much to occupy the traveller: behind the church stands a ruined old mansion with round turrets, that must have been a stately tower in former days. The town is more modern, but almost as dismal as the tower. A little street behind it slides off into a potatoe-field—the peaceful barrier of the place; and hence I could see the tall rock of Bengore, with the sea beyond it, and a pleasing landscape stretching towards it.

Dr. Hamilton's elegant and learned book has an awful picture of yonder head of Bengore; and hard by it the Guide-book says is a coalmine, where Mr. Barrow found a globular stone hammer, which, he infers, was used in the coal-mine before weapons of iron were invented. The former writer insinuates that the mine must have been worked more than a thousand years ago, 'before the turbulent chaos of events that succeeded the eighth century.' Shall I go and see a coal-mine that may have been worked a thousand years since? Why go see it? says idleness. To be able to say that I have seen it. Sheridan's advice to his son here came into my mind;[xix] and I shall reserve a description of the mine, and an antiquarian dissertation regarding it, for publication elsewhere.

Ballycastle must not be left without recording the fact that one of the snuggest inns in the country is kept by the postmaster there; who has also a stable full of good horses for travellers who take his little inn on the way to the Giant's Causeway.

The road to the Causeway is bleak, wild, and hilly. The cabins along the road are scarcely better than those of Kerry, the inmates as ragged, and more fierce and dark-looking. I never was so pestered by juvenile beggars as in the dismal village of Ballintoy. A crowd of them rushed after the car, calling for money in a fierce manner, as if it was their right; dogs as fierce as the children came yelling after the vehicle; and the faces which scowled out of the black cabins were not a whit more good-humoured. We passed by one or two more clumps of cabins, with their turf and corn-stacks lying together at the foot of the hills; placed there for the convenience of the children, doubtless, who can thus accompany the car either way, and shriek out their 'Bonny gantleman, gi'e us a ha'p'ny.' A couple of churches, one with a pair of its pinnacles blown off, stood in the dismal open country, and a gentleman's house here and there: there were no trees about them, but a brown grass round about—hills rising and falling in front, and the sea beyond. The occasional view of the coast was noble; wild Bengore towering eastwards as we went along; Baghery Island before us, in the steep rocks and caves of which Bruce took shelter when driven from yonder Scottish coast, that one sees stretching blue in the north-east.

I think this wild gloomy tract through which one passes is a good prelude for what is to be the great sight of the day, and got my mind to a proper state of awe by the time we were near the journey's end; and turning away shorewards by the fine house of Sir Francis Macnaghten, I went towards a lone handsome inn, that stands close to the Causeway. The landlord at Ballycastle had lent me Hamilton's book to read on the road; but I had not time then to read more than half-a-dozen pages of it. They described how the author, a clergyman distinguished as a man of science, had been thrust out of a friend's house by the frightened servants one wild night, and butchered by some Whiteboys who were waiting outside and called for his blood. I had been told at Belfast that there was a corpse in the inn: was it there now? It had driven off, the car-boy said, 'in a handsome hearse and four to Dublin the whole way.' It was gone, but I thought the house looked as if the ghost was there. See, yonder are the black rocks stretching to Port-rush: how leaden and grey the sea looks! how grey and leaden the sky! You hear the waters roaring evermore, as they have done since the beginning of the world. The car drives up with a dismal grinding noise of the wheels to the big lone house: there's no smoke in the chimneys; the doors are locked. Three savage-looking men rush after the car: are they the men who took out Mr. Hamilton —took him out and butchered him in the moonlight? Is everybody, I wonder, dead in that big house? Will they let us in before those men are up? Out comes a pretty smiling girl, with a curtsey, just as the savages are at the car, and you are ushered into a very comfortable room; and the men turn out to be guides. Well, thank Heaven it's no worse! I had fifteen pounds still left; and, when desperate, have no doubt should fight like a lion.

CHAPTER XXIX: THE GIANT'S CAUSEWAY—COLERAINE—PORTRUSH

THE traveller no sooner issues from the inn by a back door, which he is informed will lead him straight to the Causeway, than the guides pounce upon him, with a dozen rough boatmen who are likewise lying in wait; and a crew of shrill beggar boys, with boxes of spars, ready to tear him and each other to pieces seemingly, yell and bawl incessantly round him. 'I'm the guide Miss Henry recommends,' shouts one. 'I'm Mr. Macdonald's guide,' pushes in another. 'This way,' roars a third, and drags his prey down a precipice; the rest of them clambering and quarrelling after. I had no friends: I was perfectly helpless. I wanted to walk down to the shore by myself, but they would not let me, and I had nothing for it but to yield myself into the hands of the guide who had seized me, who hurried me down the steep to a little wild bay, flanked on each side by rugged cliffs and rocks, against which the waters came tumbling, frothing, and roaring furiously. Upon some of these black rocks two or three boats were lying: four men seized a boat, pushed it shouting into the water, and ravished me into it. We had slid between two rocks, where the channel came gurgling in: we were up one swelling wave that came in a huge advancing body ten feet above us, and were plunging madly down another (the descent causes a sensation in the lower regions of the stomach which it is not at all necessary here to describe), before I had leisure to ask myself why the deuce I was in that boat, with four rowers hurrooing and bounding madly from one huge liquid mountain to another—four rowers whom I was bound to pay. I say, the query came qualmishly across me why the devil I was there, and why not walking calmly on the shore.

The guide began pouring bis professional jargon into my ears. 'Every one of them bays,' says be, 'has a name (take my place, and the spray won't come over you): that is Port Noffer, and the next, Port na Gange; them rocks is the Stookawns (for every rock has its name as well as every bay); and yonder—give way, my boys,—hurray, we're over it now: has it wet you much, sir?—that's the little cave: it goes five hundred feet under ground, and the boats goes into it easy of a calm day.'

'Is it a fine day or a rough one now?' said I; the internal disturbance going on with more severity than ever.

'It's betwixt and between; or, I may say, neither one nor the other. Sit up, sir. Look at the entrance of the cave. Don't be afraid, sir: never has an accident happened in any one of these boats, and the most delicate ladies has rode in them on rougher days than this. Now, boys, pull to the big cave. That, sir, is six hundred and sixty yards in length, though some say it goes for miles inland, where the people sleeping in their houses hear the waters roaring under them.'

The water was tossing and tumbling into the mouth of the little cave. I looked,—for the guide would not let me alone till I did,—and saw what might be expected: a black hole of some forty feet high, into which it was no more possible to see than into a millstone. 'For Heaven's sake, sir,' says I, 'if you've no particular wish to see the mouth of the big cave, put about and let us see the Causeway and get ashore.' This was done, the guide meanwhile telling some story of a ship of the Spanish Armada having fired her guns at two peaks of rock, then visible, which the crew mistook for chimney-pots—what benighted fools these Spanish Armadilloes must have been; it is easier to see a rock than a chimney-pot; it is easy to know that chimney-pots do not grow on rocks.—'But where, if you please, is the Causeway?'

'That's the Causeway before you,' says the guide.

'Which?'

'That pier which you see jutting out into the bay right ahead.' *'Mon dieu*! and have I travelled a hundred and fifty miles to see *that*?'

I declare, upon my conscience, the barge moored at Hungerford Market is a more majestic object, and seems to occupy as much space. As for telling a man that the Causeway is merely a part of the sight; that he is there for the purpose of examining the surrounding scenery; that if he looks to the westward he will see Portrush and Donegal Head before him; that the cliffs immediately in his front are green in some places, black in others, interspersed with blotches of brown and streaks of verdure;—what is all this to a lonely individual lying sick in a boat, between two immense waves that only give him momentary glimpses of the land in question, to show that it is frightfully near, and yet you are an hour from it? They won't let you go away—that cursed guide *will* tell out his stock of legends and stories. The boatmen insist upon your looking at boxes of 'specimens,' which you must buy of them; they laugh as you grow paler and paler; they offer you more and more 'specimens'; even the dirty lad who pulls number three, and is not allowed by his comrades to speak, puts in *his* oar, and hands you over a piece of Irish diamond (it looks like half-sucked alicompayne), and scorns you. 'Hurray, lads, now for it, give way!' how the oars do hurtle in the rowlocks, as the boat goes up an aqueous mountain, and then down into one of those cursed maritime valleys where there is no rest as on shore!

At last, after they had pulled me enough about, and sold me all the boxes of specimens, I was permitted to land at the spot whence we set out, and whence, though we had been rowing for an hour, we had never been above five hundred yards distant. Let all cockneys take warning from this; let the solitary one caught issuing from the back door of the hotel, shout at once to the boatmen to be gone—that he will have none of them. Let him, at any rate, go first down to the water to determine whether it be smooth enough to allow him to take any decent pleasure by riding on its surface. For after all, it must be remembered that it *is* pleasure we come for—that we are not *obliged* to take those boats.— Well, well! I paid ten shillings for mine, and ten minutes before would cheerfully have paid five pounds to be allowed to quit it; it was no hard bargain after all. As for the boxes of spar and specimens, I at once, being on terra firma, broke my promise, and said I would see them all-first. It is wrong to swear, I know; but sometimes it relieves one *so* much!

The first act on shore was to make a sacrifice to Sanctissima Tellus; offering up to her a neat and becoming Taglioni coat, bought for a guinea in Covent Garden only three months back. I sprawled on my back on the smoothest of rocks that is, and tore the elbows to pieces: the guide picked me up; the boatmen did not stir, for they had had their will of me; the guide alone picked me up, I say, and bade me follow him. We went across a boggy ground in one of the little hays, round which rise the green walls of the cliff, terminated on either side By a black crag, and the line of the shore washed by the poluphloisboiotic, nay, the poluphloisboiotatotic sea. Two beggars stepped over the bog after us howling for money, and each holding up a cursed box of specimens. No oaths, threats, entreaties, would drive these vermin away; for some time the whole scene had been spoilt by the incessant and abominable jargon of them, the boatmen, and the guides. I was obliged to give them money to be left in quiet, and if, as no doubt will be the case, the Giant's Causeway shall be a still greater resort of travellers than ever, the county must put policemen on the rocks to keep the beggars away, or fling them in the water when they appear.

And now, by force of money, having got rid of the sea and land beggars, you are at liberty to examine at your leisure the wonders of the place. There is not the least need for a guide to attend the stranger, unless the latter have a mind to listen to a parcel of legends, which may be well from the mouth of a wild simple peasant who believes in his tales, but are odious from a dullard who narrates them at the rate of sixpence a lie. Fee him and the other beggars, and at last you are left tranquil to look at the strange scene with your own eyes and enjoy your own thoughts at leisure.

That is, if the thoughts awakened by such a scene may be called enjoyment; but for me, I confess, they are too near akin to fear to he pleasant; and I don't know that I would desire to change that sensation of awe and terror which the hour's walk occasioned, for a greater familiarity with this wild, sad, lonely place. The solitude is awful. 1 cant understand how those chattering guides dare to lift up their voices here, and cry for money.

It looks like the beginning of the world, somehow: the sea looks older than in other places, the hills and rocks strange, and formed differently from other rocks and hills —as those vast dubious monsters were formed who possessed the earth before man. The hill-tops are shattered into a thousand cragged fantastical shapes; the water comes swelling into scores of little strange creeks, or goes off with a leap, roaring into those mysterious caves yonder, which penetrate who knows how far into our common world. The savage rock-sides are painted of a hundred colours. Does the sun ever shine here? When the world was moulded and fashioned out of formless chaos, this must have been the *bit over*—a remnant of chaos! Think of that!—it is a tailor's simile. Well, I am a cockney: I wish I were in Pall Mall! Yonder is a kelp-burner: a lurid smoke from his burning kelp rises up to the leaden sky, and he looks as naked and fierce as Cain. Bubbling up out of the rocks at the very brim of the sea rises a little crystal spring: how comes it there? and there is an old grey hag beside it, who has been there for hundreds and hundreds of years, and there sits and sells whisky at the extremity of creation! How do you dare to sell whisky there, old woman? Did you serve old Saturn with a glass when he lay along the Causeway here? In reply, she says, she has no change for a shilling: she never has; but her whisky is good.

This is not a description of the Giant's Causeway (as some clever critic will remark), but of a Londoner there, who is by no means so interesting an object as the natural curiosity in question. That single hint is sufficient; I have not a word more to say. 'If,' says he, 'you cannot describe the scene lying before us—if you cannot state from your personal observation that the number of basaltic pillars composing the Causeway has been computed at about forty thousand, which vary in diameter, their surface presenting the appearance of a tesselated pavement of polygonal stones—that each pillar is formed of several distinct joints, the convex end of the one being accurately fitted in the concave of the next, and the length of the joints varying from five feet to four inches—that although the pillars are polygonal, there is but one of three sides in the whole forty thousand (think of that!), but three of nine sides, and that it may be safely computed that ninety-nine out of one hundred pillars have either five, six, or seven sides;—-if you cannot state something useful, you had much better, sir, retire and get your dinner.'

Never was summons more gladly obeyed. The dinner must be ready by this time; so, remain you, and look on at the awful scene, and copy it down in words if you can. If at the end of the trial you are dissatisfied with your skill as a painter, and find that the biggest of your words cannot render the hues and vastness of that tremendous swelling sea—of those lean solitary crags standing rigid along the shore, where they have been watching the ocean ever since it was made—of those grey towers of Dunluce standing upon a leaden rock, and looking as if some old old princess, of old old fairy times, were dragon-guarded within—of yon flat stretches of sand where the Scotch and Irish mermaids hold conference—come away, too, and prate no more about the scene! There is that in nature, dear Jenkins, which passes even our powers. We can feel the beauty of a magnificent landscape, perhaps: but we can describe a leg of mutton and turnips better. Come, then, this scene is for our betters to depict. If Mr. Tennyson were to come hither for a month, and brood over the place, he might, in some of those lofty heroic lines which the author of the 'Morte d'Arthur' knows how to pile up, convey to the reader a sense of this gigantic desolate scene. What! you, too, are a poet? Well, then, Jenkins, stay! but believe me, you had best take my advice, and come off.

The worthy landlady made her appearance with the politest of bows and an apology, —for what does the reader think a lady should apologise in the most lonely rude spot in the world?—because a plain servant-woman was about to bring in the dinner, the waiter being absent on leave at Coleraine! O heaven and earth! where will the genteel end? I replied philosophically that I did not care twopence for the plainness or beauty of the waiter, but that it was the dinner I looked to, the frying whereof made a great noise in the huge lonely house; and it must be said, that though the lady *was* plain, the repast was exceedingly good. 'I have expended my little all,' says the landlady, stepping in with a speech after dinner, 'in the building of this establishment; and though to a man its profits may appear small, to such a *being* as I am it will bring, I trust, a sufficient return;' and on my asking her why she took the place, she replied that she had always, from her earliest youth, a fancy to dwell in that spot, and had accordingly realised her wish by building this hotel—this mausoleum. In spite of the bright fire, and the good dinner, and the good wine, it was impossible to feel comfortable in the place; and when the car-wheels were heard, I jumped up with joy to take my departure and forget the awful lonely shore, and that wild, dismal, genteel inn. A ride over a wide gusty country, in a grey, misty, half-moonlight, the loss of a wheel at Bushmills, and the escape from a tumble, were the delightful varieties after the late awful occurrences. 'Such a being' as I am would die of loneliness in that hotel; and so let all brother cockneys be warned.

Some time before we came to it, we saw the long line of mist that lay above the Bann, and coming through a dirty suburb of low cottages, passed down a broad street with gas and lamps in it (thank Heaven, there are people once more!), and at length drove up in state, across a gas-pipe, in a market-place, before an hotel in the town of Coleraine, famous for linen and for Beautiful Kitty, who must be old and ugly now, for it's a good five-and-thirty years since she broke her pitcher, according to Mr. Moore's account of her. The scene as we entered the Diamond was rather a lively one —a score of little stalls were brilliant with lights; the people were thronging in the place making their Saturday bargains; the town clock began to toll nine; and hark! faithful to a minute, the horn of the Derry mail was heard tootooing, and four commercial gentlemen, with Scotch accents, rushed into the hotel at the same time with myself.

Among the beauties of Coleraine may be mentioned the price of beef, which a gentleman told me may be had for fourpence a pound; and I saw him purchase an excellent codfish for a shilling. I am bound, too, to state for the benefit of aspiring Radicals, what two Conservative citizens of the place stated to me, viz.:—that though there were two Conservative candidates then canvassing the town, on account of a vacancy in the representation, the voters were so truly liberal that they would elect any person of any other political creed, who would simply bring money enough to purchase their votes. There are 220 voters, it appears; of whom it is not, however, necessary to ' argue' with more than fifty, who alone are open to conviction; but as parties are pretty equally balanced, the votes of the quinquagint, of course, carry an immense weight with them. Well, this is all discussed calmly standing on an inn steps, with a jolly landlord and a professional man of the town to give the information. So, Heaven bless us, the ways of London are beginning to be known even here. Gentility has already taken up her seat in the Giant's Causeway, where she apologises for the plainness of her look: and, lo! here is bribery, as bold as in the most civilised places—hundreds and hundreds of miles away from St. Stephen's and Pall Mall. I wonder, in that little island of Raghery, so wild and lonely, whether civilisation is beginning to dawn upon them?—whether they bribe and are genteel? But for the rough sea of yesterday, I think I would have fled thither to make the trial.

The town of Coleraine, with a number of cabin suburbs belonging to it, lies picturesquely grouped on the Bann river; and the whole of the little city was echoing with psalms as I walked through it on the Sunday morning. The piety of the people seems remarkable; some of the inns even will not receive travellers on Sunday; and this is written in an hotel, of which every room is provided with a Testament, containing an injunction on the part of the landlord to consider this world itself as only a passing abode. Is it well that Boniface should furnish his guest with Bibles as well as bills, and sometimes shut his door on a traveller, who has no other choice but to reach it on a Sunday? I heard of a gentleman arriving from shipboard at Kilrush on a Sunday, when the pious hotel-keeper refused him admittance; and some more tales, which to go into would require the introduction of private names and circumstances, but would tend to show that the Protestant of the North is as much priest-ridden as the Catholic of the South:—priest and old-woman-ridden, for there are certain expounders of doctrine in our Church, who are not, I believe, to be found in the Church of Rome; and woe betide the stranger who comes to settle in these parts, if his 'seriousness' be not satisfactory to the heads (with false fronts to most of them) of the congregations.

Look at that little snug harbour of Portrush! a hideous new castle standing on a rock protects it on one side, a snug row of gentlemen's cottages curves round the shore facing northward, a bath-house, an hotel, more smart houses, face the beach westward, defended by another mound of rocks. In the centre of the little town stands a new-built church; and the whole place has an air of comfort and neatness which is seldom seen in Ireland. One would fancy that all the tenants of these pretty snug habitations, sheltered in this nook far away from the world, have nothing to do but to be happy, and spend their little comfortable means in snug little hospitalities among one another, and kind little charities among the poor. What does a man in active Life ask for more than to retire to such a competence, to such a snug nook of the world; and there repose with a stock of healthy children round the fireside, a friend within call, and the means of decent hospitality wherewith to treat him?

Let any one meditating this pleasant sort of retreat, and charmed with the look of this or that place as peculiarly suited to his purpose, take a special care to understand his neighbourhood first, before he commit himself, by lease-signing or house-buying. It is not sufficient that you should be honest, kind-hearted, hospitable, of good family: — what are your opinions upon religious subjects'? Are they such as agree with the notions of old Lady This, or Mrs. That, who are the patronesses of the village? If not, woe betide you! you will be shunned by the rest of the society, thwarted in your attempts to do good, whispered against over evangelical bohea and serious muffins.

Lady This will inform every new arrival that you are a reprobate, and lost: and Mrs. That will consign you and your daughters, and your wife (a worthy woman, but, alas! united to that sad worldly man!) to damnation. The clergyman who partakes of the muffins and bohea before mentioned, will very possibly preach sermons against you from the pulpit: this was not done at Portstewart to my knowledge, but I have had the pleasure of sitting under a minister in Ireland who insulted the very patron who gave him his living, discoursing upon the sinfulness of partridge-shooting, and threatening hell-fire as the last 'meet' for fox-hunters; until the squire, one of the best and most charitable resident landlords in Ireland, was absolutely driven out of the church where his fathers had worshipped for hundreds of years, by the insults of this howling evangelical inquisitor.

So much as this I did not hear at Portstewart; but I was told that at yonder neat-looking bath-house *a dying woman* was denied a bath on a Sunday. By a clause of the lease by which the bath-owner rents his establishment, he is forbidden to give baths to any one on the Sunday. The landlord of the inn, forsooth, shuts his gates on the same day, and his conscience on week-days will not allow him to supply his guests with whisky or ardent spirits. I was told by my friend, that because he refused to subscribe for some fancy charity, he received a letter to state that 'he spent more in one dinner than in charity in the course of the year.' My worthy friend did not care to contradict the statement, as why should a man deign to meddle with such a lie? But think how all the fishes, and all the pieces of meat, and all the people who went in and out of his snug cottage by the seaside must have been watched by the serious round about! The sea is not more constant roaring there, than scandal is whispering. How happy I felt, while hearing these histories (demure heads in crimped caps peering over the blinds at us as we walked on the beach), to think I am a cockney, and don't know the name of the man who lives next door to me.

I have heard various stories, of course from persons of various ways of thinking, charging their opponents with hypocrisy, and proving the charge by statements clearly showing that the priests, the preachers, or the professing religionists in question, belied their professions woefully by their practice. But in matters of religion, hypocrisy is so awful a charge to make against a man, that I think it is almost unfair to mention even the cases in which it is proven, and which,—as, pray God, they are but exceptional,—a person should be very careful of mentioning, lest they be considered to apply generally. 'Tartuffe' has been always a disgusting play to me to see, in spite of its sense and its wit; and so, instead of printing, here or elsewhere, a few stories of the Tartuffe kind which I have heard in Ireland, the best way will be to try and forget them. It is an awful thing to say of any man walking under God's sun by the side of us, 'You are a hypocrite, lying as you use the Most Sacred Name, knowing that you lie while you use it.' Let it be the privilege of any sect that is so minded, to imagine that there is perdition in store for all the rest of God's creatures who do not think with them: but the easy countercharge of hypocrisy, which the world has been in the habit of making in its turn, is surely just as fatal and bigoted an accusation as any that the sects make against the world.

What has this disquisition to do *a propos* of a walk on the beach at Portstewart? Why, it may be made here as well as in other parts of Ireland, or elsewhere as well, perhaps, as here. It is the most priest-ridden of countries: Catholic clergymen lord it over their ragged flocks, as Protestant preachers, lay and clerical, over their more genteel coreligionists. Bound to inculcate peace and goodwill, their whole life is one of enmity; and distrust.

Walking away from the little bay and the disquisition which has somehow been raging there, we went across some wild dreary highlands to the neighbouring little town of Portrush, where is a neat town and houses, and a harbour, and a new church too, so like the last-named place that I thought for a moment we had only made a round, and were back again at Portstewart. Some gentlemen of the place, and my guide, who had a neighbourly liking for it, showed me the new church, and seemed to be well pleased with the edifice; which is, indeed, a neat and convenient one, of a rather irregular Gothic. The best thing about the church, I think, was the history of it. The old church had lain some miles off, in the most inconvenient part of the parish, whereupon the clergyman and some of the gentry had raised a subscription in order to build the present church. The expenses had exceeded the estimates, or the subscriptions had fallen short of the sums necessary; and the church, in consequence, was opened with a debt on it, which the rector and two more of the gentry had taken on their shoulders. The living is a small one; the other two gentlemen going bail for the edifice not so rich as to think fight of the payment of a couple of hundred pounds beyond their previous subscriptions; the lists are therefore still open; and the clergyman expressed himself perfectly satisfied either that he would be reimbursed one day or other, or that he would be able to make out the payment of the money for which he stood engaged. Most of the Roman Catholic churches that I have seen through the country have been built in this way,—begun when money enough was levied for constructing the foundation, elevated by degrees as fresh subscriptions came in, and finished—by the way, I don't think I *have* seen one finished; but there is something noble in the spirit (however certain economists may cavil at it) that leads people to commence these pious undertakings with the firm trust that 'Heaven will provide.'

Eastwards from Portrush, we came upon a beautiful level sand which leads to the White Rocks, a famous place of resort for the frequenters of the neighbouring watering-places. Here are caves, and for a considerable distance a view of the wild and gloomy Antrim coast as far as Bengore. Midway, jutting into the sea (and I was glad it was so far off), was the Causeway; and nearer the grey towers of Dunluce.

Looking north, were the blue Scotch hills and the neighbouring Raghery Island. Nearer Portrush were two rocky islands, called the Skerries, of which a sportsman of our party vaunted the capabilities, regretting that my stay was not longer, so that I might land and shoot a few ducks there. This unlucky lateness of the season struck me also as a most afflicting circumstance. He said also that fish were caught off the island—not fish good to eat, but very strong at pulling, eager of biting, and affording a great deal of sport. And so we turned our backs once more upon the Giant's Causeway, and the grim coast on which it lies; and as my taste in life leads me to prefer looking at the smiling fresh face of a young cheerful beauty, rather than at the fierce countenance and high features of a dishevelled Meg Merrilies, I must say again that I was glad to turn my back on this severe part of the Antrim coast, and my steps towards Deny.

CHAPTER XXX: PEG OF LIMAVADDY

BETWEEN Coleraine and Derry there is a daily car (besides one or two occasional queer-looking coaches), and I had this vehicle, with an intelligent driver, and a horse with a hideous raw on his shoulder, entirely to myself for the five-and-twenty miles of our journey. The cabins of Coleraine are not parted with in a hurry, and we crossed the bridge, and went up and down the hills of one of the suburban streets, the Bann flowing picturesquely to our left; a large Catholic chapel, the before-mentioned cabins, and farther on, some neatlooking houses and plantations, to our right. Then we began ascending wild lonely hills, pools of bog shining here and there amongst them, with birds both black and white, both geese and crows, on the hunt. Some of the stubble was already ploughed up, but by the side of most cottages you saw a black potato-field that it was time to dig now, for the weather was changing and the winds beginning to roar. Woods, whenever we passed them, were flinging round eddies of mustard-coloured leaves; the white trunks of lime and ash trees beginning to look very bare.

Then we stopped to give the raw-backed horse water; then we trotted down a hill with a noble bleak prospect of Lough Foyle and the surrounding mountains before us, until we reached the town of Newton Limavaddy, where the raw-backed horse was exchanged for another not much more agreeable in his appearance, though, like his comrade, not slow on the road.

Newtown Limavaddy is the third town in the county of Londonderry. It comprises three well-built streets, the others are inferior; it is, however, respectably inhabited: all this may be true, as the well-informed Guide-book avers, but I am bound to say that I was thinking of something else as we drove through the town, having fallen eternally in love during the ten minutes of our stay. Yes, Peggy of Limavaddy, if Barrow and Inglis have gone to Connemara to fall in love with the Misses Flynn, let us be allowed to come to Ulster and offer a tribute of praise at your feet—at your stockingless feet, O Margaret! Do you remember the October day ('twas the first day of the hard weather), when the wayworn traveller entered your inn? But the circumstances of this passion had better be chronicled in deathless verse.

PEG OF LIMAVADDY

Riding from Coleraine
   (Famed for lovely Kitty),
Came a Cockney bound
   Unto Deny City;
Weary was his soul,
   Shivering and sad he

Bumped along the road
    Leads to Limavaddy.

Mountains stretch'd around,
    Gloomy was their tinting,
And the horses hoofs
    Made a dismal dinting;
Wind upon the heath
    Howling was and piping,
On the heath and bog,
    Black with many a snipe in;
'Mid the bogs of black
    Silver pools were flashing,
Crows upon their sides
    Picking were and splashing;
Cockney on the car
    Closer folds his plaidy,
Grumbling at the road
    Leads to Limavaddy.

Through the crashing woods
    Autumn brawl'd and bluster'd,
Tossing round about
    Leaves the hue of mustard;
Yonder lay Lough Foyle,
    Which a storm was whipping,
Covering with mist
    Lake, and shores, and shipping.
Up and down the hill
    (Nothing could be bolder),
Horse went with a raw,
    Bleeding on his shoulder.
'Where are horses changed?'
    Said I to the laddy
Driving on the box:
    'Sir, at Limavaddy.'

Limavaddy inn's
    But a humble baithouse,
Where you may procure
    Whisky and potatoes;
Landlord at the door
    Gives a smiling welcome
To the shivering wights
    Who to his hotel come.

Landlady within
  Sits and knits a stocking,
With a wary foot
  Baby's cradle rocking.
To the chimney nook
  Having found admittance,
There I watch a pup
  Playing with two kittens
(Playing round the fire,
  Which of blazing turf is,
Roaring to the pot
  Which bubbles with the murphies);
And the cradled babe
  Fond the mother nursed it!
Singing it a song
  As she twists the worsted!

Up and down the stair
  Two more young ones patter
(Twins were never seen
  Dirtier nor fatter);

Both have mottled legs,
  Both have snubby noses,
Both have—Here the Host
  Kindly interposes:
'Sure you must be froze
  With the sleet and hail, sir,
So will you have some punch,
  Or will you have some ale, sir?'

Presently a maid
  Enters with the liquor
(Half-a-pint of ale
  Frothing in a beaker).
Gods! I didn't know
  What my beating heart meant,
Hebe's self I thought
  Enter'd the apartment.

As she came she smiled,
  And the smile bewitching,
On my word and honour,
  Lighted all the kitchen!
With a curtsey neat

Greeting the new-comer,
Lovely, smiling Peg
Offers me the rummer;
But my trembling hand
Up the beaker tilted,
And the glass of ale
Every drop I spilt it:
Spilt it every drop
(Dames, who read my volumes,
Pardon such a word)
On my what-d' ye-call-'ems!

Witnessing the sight
Of that dire disaster,
Out began to laugh
Missis, maid, and master;
Such a merry peal,
'Specially Miss Peg's was
(As the glass of ale
Trickling down my legs was),
That the joyful sound
Of that ringing laughter
Echoed in my ears
Many a long day after.

Such a silver peal!
In the meadows listening,
You who've heard the bells
Ringing to a christening;
You who ever heard
Caradori pretty,
Smiling like an angel
Singing 'Giovinetti,'
Fancy Peggy's laugh,
Sweet, and clear, and cheerful,
At my pantaloons
With half-a-pint of beer full!

When the laugh was done,
Peg, the pretty hussy,
Moved about the room
Wonderfully busy;
Now she looks to see
If the kettle keep hot,
Now she rubs the spoons,

Now she cleans the teapot;
Now she sets the cups
Trimly and secure,
Now she scours a pot,
And so it was I drew her.

Thus it was I drew her
Scouring of a kettle.[xx]
(Faith! her blushing cheeks
Redden'd on the metal!)
Ah! but 'tis in vain
That I try to sketch it;
The pot perhaps is like,
But Peggy's face is wretched.
No: the best of lead,
And of Indian-rubber,
Never could depict
That sweet kettle-scrubber!
See her as she moves!
Scarce the ground she touches,
Airy as a fay,
Graceful as a duchess;
Bare her rounded arm,
Bare her little leg is,
Vestris never show'd
Ankles like to Peggy's;
Braided is her hair,
Soft her look and modest,
Slim her little waist
Comfortably boddiced.

This I do declare,
Happy is the laddy
Who the heart can share
Of Peg of Limavaddy;
Married if she were,
Blest would be the daddy
Of the children fair
Of Peg of Limavaddy;
Beauty is not rare
In the land of Paddy,
Fair beyond compare
Is Peg of Limavaddy.
Citizen or squire,

Tory, Whig, or Radi-
cal would all desire
Peg of Limavaddy.
Had I Homer's fire,
Or that of Sergeant Taddy,
Meetly I'd admire
Peg of Limavaddy.
And till I expire,
Or till I grow mad, I
Will sing unto my lyre
Peg of Limavaddy!

CHAPTER XXXI: TEMPLEMOYLE-DERRY

FROM Newtown Limavaddy to Deny the traveller has many wild and noble prospects of Lough Foyle and the plains and mountains round it, and of scenes which may possibly in this country be still more agreeable to him—of smiling cultivation, and comfortable well-built villages, such as are only too rare in Ireland. Of a great part of this district the London Companies are landlords— the best of landlords, too, according to the report I could gather; and their good stewardship shows itself especially in the neat villages of Muff and Ballikelly, through both of which I passed. In Ballikelly, besides numerous simple, stout, brick-built dwellings for the peasantry, with their shining windows and trim garden-plots, is a Presbyterian meeting-house, so well-built, substantial and handsome, so different from the lean, pretentious, sham-Gothic ecclesiastical edifices which have been erected of late years in Ireland, that it can't fail to strike the tourist who has made architecture his study or his pleasure. The gentlemen's seats in the district are numerous and handsome: and the whole movement along the road betokened cheerfulness and prosperous activity.

As the carman had no other passengers but myself, he made no objection to carry me a couple of miles out of his way, through the village of Muff, belonging to the Grocers of London (and so handsomely and comfortably built by them as to cause all cockneys to exclaim, 'Well done our side!'), and thence to a very interesting institution, which was established some fifteen years since in the neighbourhood—the Agricultural Seminary of Templemoyle. It bes on a hill in a pretty wooded country, and is most curiously secluded from the world by the tortuousness of the road which approaches it.

Of course it is not my business to report upon the agricultural system practised there, or to discourse on the state of the land or the crops; the best testimony on this subject is the fact, that the Institution hired, at a small rental, a tract of land, which was reclaimed and farmed, and that of this farm the landlord has now taken possession.

leaving the young farmers to labour on a new tract of land, for which they pay five times as much rent as for their former holding. But though a person versed in agriculture could give a far more satisfactory account of the place than one to whom such pursuits are quite unfamiliar, there is a great deal about the establishment which any citizen can remark on; and he must be a very difficult cockney indeed who won't be pleased here.

After winding in and out, and up and down, and round about the eminence on which the house stands, we at last found an entrance to it, by a courtyard, neat, well built, and spacious, where are the stables and numerous offices of the farm. The scholars were at dinner off a comfortable meal of boiled beef, potatoes, and cabbages, when I arrived; a master was reading a book of history to them; and silence, it appears, is preserved during the dinner. Seventy scholars were here assembled, some young, and some expanded into six feet and whiskers—all, however, are made to maintain exactly the same discipline, whether whiskered or not.

The 'head farmer' of the school, Mr. Campbell, a very intelligent Scotch gentleman, was good enough to conduct me over the place and the farm, and to give a history of the establishment and the course pursued there. The Seminary was founded in 1827, by the North-West of Ireland Society, by members of which and others about three thousand pounds were subscribed, and the buildings of the school erected. These are spacious, simple, and comfortable; there is a good stone house, with airy dormitories, schoolrooms, etc., and large and convenient offices. The establishment had, at first, some difficulties to contend with, and for some time did not number more than thirty pupils. At present, there are seventy scholars, paying *ten pounds* a year, with which sum, and the labour of the pupils on the farm, and the produce of it, the school is entirely supported. The reader will, perhaps, like to see an extract from the Report of the school, which contains more details regarding it.

'TEMPLEMOYLE WORK AND SCHOOL TABLE

'From 20th March to 23rd September

'Boys divided into two classes, A and B

Hours.		At work.	At school.
5½	All rise.		
6—8		A	B
8—9	Breakfast.		
9—1		A	B
1—2	Dinner and recreation.		
2—6		B	A
6—7	Recreation.		
7—9	Prepare lessons for next day.		
9	To bed.		

'On Tuesday B commences work in the morning and A at school, and so on alternate days.

'Each class is again subdivided into three divisions, over each of which is placed a monitor, selected from the steadiest and best-informed boys; he receives the Head Farmer's directions as to the work to be done, and superintends his party while performing it.

'In winter the time of labour is shortened according to the length of the day, and the hours at school increased.

'In wet days, when the boys cannot work out, all are required to attend school.

'Dietary

'Breakfast.—Eleven ounces of oatmeal made in stirabout, one pint of sweet milk.

'Dinner.—Sunday—Three-quarters of a pound of beef stewed with pepper and onions, or one half-pound of corned beef with cabbage, and three and a half pounds of potatoes.

'Monday—One half-pound of pickled beef, three and a half pounds of potatoes, one pint of buttermilk.

'Tuesday—Broth made of one half-pound of beef, with leeks, cabbage, and parsley, and three and a half pounds of potatoes.

'Wednesday—Two ounces of butter, eight ounces of oatmeal made into bread, three and a half pounds of potatoes, and one pint of sweet milk.

'Thursday—Half-a-pound of pickled pork, with cabbage or turnips, and three and a half pounds of potatoes.

'Friday—Two ounces of butter, eight ounces wheatmeal made into bread, one pint of sweet milk or fresh buttermilk, three and a half pounds of potatoes.

'Saturday—Two ounces of butter, one pound of potatoes mashed, eight ounces of wheatmeal made into bread, two and a half pounds of potatoes, one pint of buttermilk.

'Supper.—In summer, flummery made of one pound of oatmeal seeds, and one pint of sweet milk. In winter, three and a half pounds of potatoes, and one pint of buttermilk or sweet milk.

'Rules for the Templemoyle School

'1. The pupils are required to say their prayers in the morning, before leaving the dormitory, and at night, before retiring to rest, each separately, and after the manner to which he has been habituated.

'2. The pupils are required to wash their hands and faces before the commencement of business in the morning, on returning from agricultural labour, and after dinner.

'3. The pupils are required to pay the strictest attention to their instructors, both during the hours of agricultural and literary occupation.

'4. Strife, disobedience, inattention, or any description of riotous or disorderly conduct, is punishable by extra labour or confinement, as directed by the Committee, according to circumstances.

'5. Diligent and respectful behaviour, continued for a considerable time, will be rewarded by occasional permission for the pupil so distinguished to visit his home.

'6. No pupil, on obtaining leave of absence, shall presume to continue it for a longer period than that prescribed to him on leaving the Seminary.

'7. During their rural labour, the pupils are to consider themselves amenable to the authority of their Agricultural Instructor alone, and during their attendance in the schoolroom, to that of their Literary Instructor alone.

'8. Non-attendance during any part of the time allotted either for literary or agricultural employment, will be punished as a serious offence.

'9. During the hours of recreation the pupils are to be under the superintendence of their Instructors, and not suffered to pass beyond the limits of the farm, except under their guidance, or with a written permission from one of them.

'10. The pupils are required to make up their beds, and keep those clothes not in immediate use neatly folded up in their trunks, and to be particular in never suffering any garment, book, implement, or other article belonging to or used by them, to lie about in a slovenly or disorderly manner.

'11. Respect to superiors, and gentleness of demeanour, both among the pupils themselves and towards the servants and labourers of the establishment, are particularly insisted upon, and will be considered a prominent ground of approbation and reward.

'12. On Sundays the pupils are required to attend their respective places of worship, accompanied by their Instructors or Monitors; and it is earnestly recommended to them to employ a part of the remainder of the day in sincerely reading the Word of God, and in such other devotional exercises as their respective ministers may point out.'

At certain periods of the year, when all hands are required, such as harvest, etc., the literary labours of the scholars are stopped, and they are all in the field. On the present occasion we followed them into a potato-field, where an army of them were employed digging out the potatoes; while another regiment were trenching-in elsewhere for the winter: the boys were leading the carts to and fro. To reach the potatoes we had to pass a field, part of which was newly ploughed: the ploughing was the work of the boys, too; one of them being left with an experienced ploughman for a fortnight at a time, in which space the lad can acquire some practice in the art. Amongst the potatoes and the boys digging them, I observed a number of girls taking them up as dug and removing the soil from the roots. Such a society for seventy young men would, in any other country in the world, be not a little dangerous; but Mr. Campbell said that no instance of harm had ever occurred in consequence, and I believe his statement may be fully relied on: the whole country bears testimony to this noble purity of morals. Is there any other in Europe which in this point can compare with it?

In winter the farm-works do not occupy the pupils so much, and they give more time to their literary studies. They get a good English education; they are grounded in arithmetic and mathematics; and I saw a good map of an adjacent farm, made from actual survey by one of the pupils. Some of them are good draughtsmen likewise, but of their performances I could see no specimen, the artists being abroad, occupied wisely in digging the potatoes.

And here, *à propos,* not of the school but of potatoes, let me tell a potato story, which is, I think, to the purpose, wherever it is told. In the county of Mayo a gentleman by the name of Crofton is a landed proprietor, in whose neighbourhood great distress prevailed among the peasantry during the spring and summer, when the potatoes of the last year were consumed, and before those of the present season were up. Mr. Crofton, by liberal donations on his own part, and by a subscription which was set on foot among his friends in England as well as in Ireland, was enabled to collect a sum of money sufficient to purchase meal for the people, which was given to them, or sold at very low prices, until the pressure of want was withdrawn, and the blessed potato-crop came in. Some time in October, a smart night's frost made Mr. Crofton think that it was time to take in and pit his own potatoes, and he told his steward to get labourers accordingly.

Next day, on going to the potato-grounds, he found the whole fields swarming with people; the whole crop was out of the ground, and again under it, pitted and covered, and the people gone, in a few hours. It was as if the fairies that we read of in the Irish legends, as coming to the aid of good people and helping them in their labours, had taken a liking to this good landlord, and taken in his harvest for him. Mr. Crofton, who knew who his helpers had been, sent the steward to pay them their day's wages, and to thank them at the same time for having come to help him at a time when their labour was so useful to him. One and all refused a penny; and their spokesman said, 'They wished they could do more for the likes of him or his family.' I have heard of many conspiracies in this country; is not this one as worthy to be told as any of them?

Round the house of Templemoyle is a pretty garden, which the pupils take pleasure in cultivating, filled not with fruit (for this, though there are seventy gardeners, the superintendent said somehow seldom reached a ripe state), but with kitchen herbs, and a few beds of pretty flowers, such as are best suited to cottage horticulture. Such simple carpenters' and masons' work as the young men can do is likewise confided to them; and though the dietary may appear to the Englishman as rather a scanty one, and though the English lads certainly make at first very wry faces at the stirabout porridge (as they naturally will when first put in the presence of that abominable mixture), yet after a time, strange to say, they begin to find it actually palatable; and the best proof of the excellence of the diet is, that nobody is ever ill in the institution; colds and fevers and the ailments of lazy gluttonous gentility, are unknown; and the doctor's bill for the last year, for seventy pupils, amounted to thirty-five shillings. O *beati agricoliculæ*! I You do not know what it is to feel a little uneasy after half-a-crown's worth of raspberry-tarts, as lads do at the best public schools; you don't know in what majestic polished hexameters the Roman poet has described your pursuits; you are not fagged and flogged into Latin and Greek at the cost of two hundred pounds a year. Let these be the privileges of your youthful betters; meanwhile content yourselves with thinking that you *are* preparing for a profession, while they are *not*; that you are learning something useful, while they, for the most part, are not: for after all, as a man grows old in the world, old and fat, cricket is discovered not to be any longer very advantageous to him—even to have pulled in the Trinity boat does not in old age amount to a substantial advantage; and though to read a Greek play be an immense pleasure, yet it must be confessed few enjoy it. In the first place, of the race of Etonians, and Harrovians, and Carthusians that one meets in the world, very few *can* read the Greek; of those few—there are not, as I believe, any considerable majority of poets. Stout men in the bow-windows of clubs (for such young Etonians by time become) are not generally remarkable for a taste for Æschylus.[xxi] You do not hear much poetry in Westminster Hall, or I believe at the bar-tables afterwards; and if occasionally, in the House of Commons, Sir Robert Peel lets off a quotation—a pocket-pistol wadded with a leaf torn out of Horace—depend on it, it is only to astonish the country gentlemen who don't understand him: and it is my firm conviction that Sir Robert no more cares for poetry than you or I do.

Such thoughts will suggest themselves to a man who has had the benefit of what is called an education at a public school in England, when he sees seventy lads from all parts of the empire learning what his Latin poets and philosophers have informed him is the best of all pursuits,—finds them educated at one-twentieth part of the cost which has been bestowed on his own precious person; orderly without the necessity of submitting to degrading personal punishment; young, and full of health and blood, though vice is unknown among them; and brought up decently and honestly to know the things which it is good for them in their profession to know. So it is, however: all the world is improving except the gentlemen. There are at this present writing five hundred boys at Eton, kicked, and licked, and bullied by another hundred—scrubbing shoes, running errands, making false concords, and (as if that were a natural consequence!) putting their posteriors on a block for Dr. Hawtrey to lash at; and still calling it education. They are proud of it—good heavens!—absolutely vain of it; as what dull barbarians are not proud of their dulness and barbarism? They call it the good old English system: nothing like classics, says Sir John, to give a boy a taste, you know, and a habit of reading—(Sir John, who reads the 'Racing Calendar,' and belongs to a race of men of all the world the least given to reading)—it's the good old

English system; every boy fights for himself—hardens 'em, eh, Jack? Jack grins, and helps himself to another glass of claret, and presently tells you how Tibbs and Miller fought for an hour and twenty minutes 'like good uns.'....Let us come to an end, however, of this moralising; the car-driver has brought the old raw-shouldered horse out of the stable, and says it is time to be off again.

Before quitting Templemoyle, one thing more may be said in its favour. It is one of the very few public establishments in Ireland where pupils of the two religious denominations are received, and where no religious disputes have taken place. The pupils are called upon, morning and evening, to say their prayers privately. On Sunday, each division, Presbyterian, Roman Catholic, and Episcopalian, is marched to its proper place of worship. The pastors of each sect may visit their young flock when so inclined; and the lads devote the Sabbath evening to reading the books pointed out to them by their clergymen.

Would not the Agricultural Society of Ireland, of the success of whose peaceful labours for the national prosperity every Irish newspaper I read brings some new indication, do well to show some mark of its sympathy for this excellent institution of Templemoyle? A silver medal given by the Society to the most deserving pupil of the year, would be a great object of emulation amongst the young men educated at the place, and would be almost a certain passport for the winner in seeking for a situation in after life. I do not know if similar seminaries exist in England. Other seminaries of a like nature have been tried in this country, and have failed: but English country gentlemen cannot, I should think, find a better object of their attention than this school; and our farmers would surely find such establishments of great benefit to them: where their children might procure a sound literary education at a small charge, and at the same time be made acquainted with the latest improvements in their profession. I can't help saying here, once more, what I have said *à propos* of the excellent school at Dundalk, and begging the English middle classes to think of the subject. If Government will not act (upon what never can be effectual, perhaps, until it become a national measure), let small communities act for themselves, and tradesmen and the middle classes set up cheap proprietary schools. Will country newspaper editors, into whose hands this book may fall, be kind enough to speak upon this hint, and extract the tables of the Templemoyle and Dundalk establishments, to show how, and with what small means, boys may be well, soundly, and humanely educated—not brutally, as some of us have been, under the bitter fagging and the shameful rod? It is no plea for the barbarity that use has made us accustomed to it; and in seeing these institutions for humble lads, where the system taught is at once useful, manly, and kindly, and thinking of what I had undergone in my own youth,—of the frivolous monkish trifling in which it was wasted, of the brutal tyranny to which it was subjected,—I could not look at the lads but with a sort of envy. Please God, there lot will be shared by thousands of their equals and their betters before long!

It was a proud day for Dundalk, Mr. Thackeray well said, when, at the end of one of the vacations there, fourteen English boys, and an Englishman with his little son in his hand, landed from the Liverpool packet, and, walking through the streets of the town, went into the schoolhouse quite happy. That *was* a proud day in truth for a distant Irish town, and I can't help saying that I grudge them the cause of their pride somewhat. Why should there not be schools in England as good, and as cheap, and as happy?

With this, shaking Mr. Campbell gratefully by the hand, and begging all English tourists to go and visit his establishment, we trotted off for Londonderry, leaving at about a mile's distance from the town, and at the pretty lodge of Saint Columb's, a letter, which was the cause of much delightful hospitality.

Saint Columb's Chapel, the walls of which still stand picturesquely in Sir George Hill's park, and from which that gentleman's seat takes its name, was here since the sixth century. It is but fair to give precedence to the mention of the old abbey, which was the father, as it would seem, of the town. The approach to the latter from three quarters, certainly, by which various avenues I had occasion to see it, is always noble. We had seen the spire of the cathedral peering over the hills for four miles on our way; it stands, a stalwart and handsome building, upon an eminence, round which the old-fashioned stout red houses of the town cluster, girt in with the ramparts and walls that kept out James's soldiers of old. Quays, factories, huge red warehouses, have grown round this famous old barrier, and now stretch along the river. A couple of large steamers and other craft lay within the bridge; and, as we passed over that stout wooden edifice, stretching eleven hundred feet across the noble expanse of the Foyle, we heard along the quays a great thundering and clattering of iron-work in an enormous steam frigate which has been built in Derry, and seems to lie alongside a whole street of houses. The suburb, too, through which we passed was bustling and comfortable; and the view was not only pleasing from its natural beauties, but has a manly, thriving, honest air of prosperity, which is no bad feature, surely, for a landscape.

Nor does the town itself, as one enters it, belie, as many other Irish towns do, its first flourishing look. It is not splendid, but comfortable; a brisk movement in the streets; good downright shops, without particularly grand titles; few beggars. Nor have the common people, as they address you, that eager smile,—that manner of compound fawning and swaggering, which an Englishman finds in the townspeople of the West and South. As in the North of England, too, when compared with other districts, the people are greatly more familiar, though by no means disrespectful to the stranger.

On the other hand, after such a commerce as a traveller has with the race of waiters, postboys, porters, and the like (and it may be that the vast race of postboys, etc., whom I did not see in the North, are quite unlike those unlucky specimens with whom I came in contact), I was struck by their excessive greediness after the traveller's gratuities, and their fierce dissatisfaction if not sufficiently rewarded. To the gentleman who brushed my clothes at the comfortable hotel at Belfast, and carried my bags to the coach, I tendered the sum of two shillings, which seemed to me quite a sufficient reward for his services: he battled and brawled with me for more, and got it too; for a street-dispute with a porter calls together a number of delighted bystanders, whose remarks and company are by no means agreeable to a solitary gentleman. Then, again, there was the famous case of Boots of Ballycastle, which, being upon the subject, I may as well mention here: Boots of Ballycastle, that romantic little village near the Giant's Causeway, had cleaned a pair of shoes for me certainly, but declined either to brush my clothes, or to carry down my two carpet-bags to the car; leaving me to perform those offices for myself, which I did: and indeed they were not very difficult. But immediately I was seated on the car, Mr. Boots stepped forward and wrapped a mackintosh very considerately round me, and begged me at the same time to 'remember him.'

There was an old beggar-woman standing by, to whom I had a desire to present a penny: and having no coin of that value, I begged Mr. Boots, out of sixpence which I tendered to him, to subtract a penny, and present it to the old lady in question. Mr. Boots took the money, looked at me, and his countenance, not naturally good-humoured, assumed an expression of the most indignant contempt and hatred as he said, 'I'm thinking I've no call to give my money away. Sixpence is my right for what I've done.'

'Sir,' says I, 'you must remember that you did but black one pair of shoes, and that you blacked them very badly too.'

'Sixpence is my right,' says Boots; 'a *gentleman* would give me sixpence!' and though I represented to him that a pair of shoes might be blacked in a minute—that fivepence a minute was not usual wages in the country—that many gentlemen, half-pay officers, briefless barristers, unfortunate literary gentlemen, would gladly black twelve pairs of shoes per diem if rewarded with five shillings for so doing, there was no means of convincing Mr. Boots. I then demanded back the sixpence, which proposal, however, he declined, saying, after a struggle, he would give the money, but a gentleman would have given sixpence; and so left me with furious rage and contempt.

As for the city of Deny, a carman who drove me one mile out to dinner at a gentleman's house, where he himself was provided with a comfortable meal, was dissatisfied with eighteenpence, vowing that a 'dinner job' was always paid half-a-crown, and not only asserted this, but continued to assert it for a quarter of an hour with the most noble though unsuccessful perseverance. A second car-boy, to whom I gave a shilling for a drive of two miles altogether, attacked me because I gave the other boy eighteenpence; and the porter who brought my hags fifty yards from the coach, entertained me with a dialogue that lasted at least a couple of minutes, and said, 'I should have had sixpence for carrying one of 'em.'

For the car which carried me two miles the landlord of the inn made me pay the sum of five shillings. He is a godly landlord, has Bibles in the coffee-room, the drawing-room, and every bedroom in the house, with this inscription—

'UT MIGRATURUS HABITA

THE TRAVELLER'S TRUE REFUGE

Jones's Hotel, Londonderry.'

This pious double or triple entendre, the reader will, no doubt, admire—the first simile establishing the resemblance between this life and an inn; the second allegory showing that the inn and the Bible are both the traveller's refuge.

In life we are in death—the hotel in question is about as gay as a family vault: a severe figure of a landlord, in seedy black, is occasionally seen in the dark passages or on the creaking old stairs of the black inn. He does not bow to you—very few landlords in Ireland condescend to acknowledge their guests—he only warns you:—a silent solemn gentleman who looks to be something between a clergyman and a sexton—'ut migraturus habita!'—the 'migraturus' was a vast comfort in the clause.

It must, however, be said, for the consolation of future travellers, that when at evening, in the old lonely parlour of the inn, the great gaunt fireplace is filled with coals, two dreary funereal candles and sticks glimmering upon the old-fashioned round table, the rain pattering fiercely without, the wind roaring and thumping in the streets, this worthy gentleman can produce a pint of port^wine for the use of his migratory guests, which causes the latter to be almost reconciled to the cemetery in which he is resting himself, and he finds himself, to his surprise, almost cheerful. There is a mouldy-looking old kitchen, too, which, strange to say, sends out an excellent comfortable dinner, so that the sensation of fear gradually wears off.

As in Chester, the ramparts of the town form a pleasant promenade; and the batteries, with a few of the cannon, are preserved, with which the stout 'prentice boys of Derry beat off King James in '88. The guns bear the names of the London Companies—venerable cockney titles! It is pleasant for a Londoner to read them, and see how, at a pinch, the sturdy citizens can do their work.

The public buildings of Derry are, I think, among the best I have seen in Ireland; and the Lunatic Asylum, especially, is to be pointed out as a model of neatness and comfort. When will the middle classes be allowed to send their own afflicted relatives to public institutions of this excellent kind, where violence is never practised—where it is never to the interest of the keeper of the asylum to exaggerate his patient's malady, or to retain him in durance, for the sake of the enormous sums which the sufferer's relatives are made to pay? The gentry of three counties which contribute to the Asylum have no such resource for members of their own body, should any be so afflicted—the condition of entering this admirable asylum is, that the patient must be a pauper, and on this account he is supplied with every comfort and the best curative means, and his relations are in perfect security. Are the rich in any way so lucky?—and if not, why not?

The rest of the occurrences at Derry belong, unhappily, to the domain of private life, and though very pleasant to recall, are not honestly to be printed. Otherwise, what popular descriptions might be written of the hospitalities of St. Columb's, of the jovialities of the mess of the —th Regiment, of the speeches made and the songs sung, and the devilled turkey at twelve o'clock, and the headache afterwards; all which events could be described in an exceedingly facetious manner. But these amusements are to be met with in every other part of her Majesty's dominions; and the only point which may be mentioned here as peculiar to this part of Ireland, is the difference of the manner of the gentry to that in the South. The Northern manner is far more *English* than that of the other provinces of Ireland—whether it is *better* for being English is a question of taste, of which an Englishman can scarcely be a fair judge.

CHAPTER XXXII: DUBLIN AT LAST

A WEDDING-PARTY that went across Derry Bridge to the sound of bell and cannon, had to flounder through a thick coat of frozen snow, that covered the slippery planks, and the hills round about were whitened over by the same inclement material. Nor was the weather, implacable towards young lovers and unhappy buckskin postillions shivering in white favours, at all more polite towards the passengers of her Majesty's mail that runs from Derry to Ballyshannon.

Hence the aspect of the country between those two places can only be described at the rate of nine miles an hour, and from such points of observation as may be had through a coach window, starred with ice and mud. While horses were changed we saw a very dirty town, called Strabane; and bad to visit the old house of the O'Donnels in Donegal during a quarter of an hour's pause that the coach made there—and with an umbrella overhead. The pursuit of the picturesque under umbrellas let us leave to more venturesome souls: the fine weather of the finest season known for many long years in Ireland was over, and I thought with a great deal of yearning of Pat the waiter, at the Shelburne Hotel, Stephen's Green, Dublin, and the gas-lamps, and the covered cars, and the good dinners to which they take you.

Farewell, then, O wild Donegal! and ye stern passes through which the astonished traveller windeth! Farewell, Ballyshannon, and thy salmon-leap, and thy bar of sand, over which the white head of the troubled Atlantic was peeping! Likewise, adieu to Lough Erne, and its numberless green islands, and winding river-lake, and wavy fir-clad hills! Good-bye, moreover, neat Enniskillen, over the bridge and churches whereof the sun peepeth as the coach starteth from the inn! See, how he shines now on Lord Belmore's stately palace and park, with gleaming porticoes and brilliant grassy chases: now, behold he is yet higher in the heavens, as the twanging horn proclaims the approach to beggarly Cavan, where a beggarly breakfast awaits the hungry voyager.

Snatching up a roll wherewith to satisfy the pangs of hunger, sharpened by the mockery of breakfast, the tourist now hastens in his arduous course, through Virginia, Kells, Navan, by Tara's threadbare mountain, and Skreen's green hill; day darkens, and a hundred thousand lamps twinkle in the grey horizon—see above the darkling trees a stumpy column rise, see on its base the name of Wellington (though this, because 'tis night, thou canst not see), and cry, 'It is the *Phaynix!'*— On and on, across the iron bridge, and through the streets (dear streets, though dirty, to the citizen's heart how dear you be!), and lo, now, with a bump, the dirty coach stops at the seedy inn, six ragged porters battle for the bags, six wheedling carmen recommend their cars, and (giving first the coachman eighteenpence) the cockney says, 'Drive, car-boy, to the Shelburne.'

And so having reached Dublin, it becomes necessary to curtail the observations which were to be made upon that city; which surely ought to have a volume to itself: the humours of Dublin at least require so much space. For instance, there was the dinner at the Kildare Street Club, or the hotel opposite,—the dinner in the Trinity College Hall,—that at Mr.—, the publisher's, where a dozen of the literary men of Ireland were assembled,—and those (say fifty) with Harry Lorrequer himself, at his mansion of Templeogue. What a favourable opportunity to discourse upon the peculiarities of Irish character! to describe men of letters, of fashion, and University dons!

Sketches of these personages may be prepared, and sent over, perhaps, in confidence to Mrs. Sigourney in America—(who will of course not print them)—but the English habit does not allow of these happy communications between writers and the public; and the author who wishes to dine again at his friend's cost, must needs have a care how he puts him in print.

Suffice it to say, that at Kildare Street we had white neckcloths, black waiters, wax-candles, and some of the best wine in Europe; at Mr.—, the publisher's, wax-candles, and some of the best wine in Europe; at Mr. Lever's, wax-candles, and some of the best wine in Europe; at Trinity College—but there is no need to mention what took place at Trinity College; for, on returning to London, and recounting the circumstances of the repast, my friend B—, a Master of Arts of that University, solemnly declared the thing was impossible:—no stranger *could* dine at Trinity College; it was too great a privilege—in a word, he would not believe the story, nor will he to this day; and why, therefore, tell it in vain? I am sure if the fellows of Colleges in Oxford and Cambridge were told that the Fellows of T. C. D. only drink beer at dinner, they would not believe *that.* Such, however, was the fact: or may-be it was a dream, which was followed by another dream of about four-and-twenty gentlemen seated round a common-room table after dinner; and, by a subsequent vision of a tray of oysters in the apartments of a tutor of the University, some time before midnight. Did we swallow them or not?—the oysters are an open question.

Of the Catholic College of Maynooth, I must likewise speak briefly, for the reason that an accurate description of that establishment would be of necessity so disagreeable, that it is best to pass it over in a few words. An Irish union-house is a palace to it. Ruin so needless, filth so disgusting, such a look of lazy squalor, no Englishman who has not seen can conceive. Lecture-room and dining-hall, kitchen and students' room, were all the same. I shall never forget the sight of scores of shoulders of mutton lying on the filthy floor in the former, or the view of a bed and dressing-table that I saw in the other. Let the next Maynooth grant include a few shillings'-worth of whitewash and a few hundredweights of soap; and if to this be added a half-score of drill-sergeants, to see that the students appear clean at lecture, and to teach them to keep their heads up and to look people in the face, Parliament will introduce some cheap reforms into the seminary, which were never needed more than here. Why should the place be so shamefully ruinous and foully dirty? Lime is cheap, and water plenty at the canal hard by. Why should a stranger, after a week's stay in the country, be able to discover a priest by the scowl on his face, and his doubtful downcast manner? Is it a point of discipline that his reverence should be made to look as ill-humoured as possible? And I hope these words will not be taken hostilely. It would have been quite as easy, and more pleasant, to say the contrary, had the contrary seemed to me to have been the fact; and to have declared that the priests were remarkable for their expression of candour, and their college for its extreme neatness and cleanliness.

This complaint of neglect applies to other public institutions besides Maynooth. The Mansion-house, when I saw it, was a very dingy abode for the Right Honourable Lord Mayor, and that Lord Mayor Mr. O'Connell. I saw him in full council, in a brilliant robe of crimson velvet, ornamented with white satin bows and sable collar, in an enormous cocked-hat, like a slice of an eclipsed moon.

The Aldermen and Common Council, in a black oak parlour and at a dingy green table, were assembled around him, and a debate of thrilling interest to the town ensued; it related, I think, to water-pipes. The great man did not speak publicly, but was occupied chiefly at the end of the table, giving audiences to at least a score of clients and petitioners.

The next day I saw him in the famous Corn Exchange. The building without has a substantial look, but the hall within is rude, dirty, and ill kept. Hundreds of persons were assembled in the black steaming place; no inconsiderable share of frieze-coats were among them; and many small Repealers, who could but lately have assumed their breeches, ragged as they were. These kept up a great chorus of shouting, and 'hear, hear!' at every pause in the great Repealer's address. Mr. O'Connell was reading a report from his Repeal-wardens; which proved that when Repeal took place, commerce and prosperity would instantly flow into the country; its innumerable harbours would be filled with countless ships, its immense water-power would be directed to the turning of myriads of mills; its vast energies and resources brought into full action. At the end of the report three cheers were given for Repeal, and in the midst of a great shouting Mr. O'Connell leaves the room.

'Mr. Quiglan, Mr. Quiglan!' roars an active aide-de-camp to the doorkeeper, 'a covered kyar for the Lard Mayre.' The covered car came; I saw his Lordship get into it. Next day he was Lord Mayor no longer; but Alderman O'Connell in his state-coach, with the handsome greys whose manes were tied up with green ribbon, following the new Lord Mayor to the right honourable inauguration. Javelin-men, city-marshals (looking like military undertakers), private carriages, glass coaches, cars, covered and uncovered, and thousands of yelling ragamuffins, formed the civic procession of that faded, worn-out, insolvent old Dublin Corporation.

The walls of this city had been placarded with huge notices to the public, that O'Connell's rent-day was at hand; and I went round to all the chapels in town on that Sunday (not a little to the scandal of some Protestant friends), to see the popular behaviour. Every door was barred, of course, with plate-holders; and heaps of pence at the humble entrances, and bank-notes at the front gates, told the willingness of the people to reward their champion. The car-boy who drove me had paid his little tribute of fourpence at morning mass; the waiter who brought my breakfast had added to the national subscription with his humble shilling; and the Catholic gentleman with whom I dined, and between whom and Mr. O'Connell there is no great love lost, pays his annual donation, out of gratitude for old services, and to the man who won Catholic Emancipation for Ireland. The piety of the people at the chapels is a sight, too, always well worthy to behold. Nor indeed is this religious fervour less in the Protestant places of worship: the warmth and attention of the congregation, the enthusiasm with which hymns are sung and responses uttered, contrast curiously with the cool formality of worshippers at home.

The service at Saint Patrick's is finely sung; and the shameless English custom of retreating after the anthem, is properly prevented by locking the gates, and having the music after the sermon. The interior of the cathedral itself, however, to an Englishman who has seen the neat and beautiful edifices of his own country, will be anything but an object of admiration. The greater part of the huge old building is suffered to remain in gaunt decay, and with its stalls of sham Gothic, and the tawdry old rags and gimcracks of the 'most illustrious order of Saint Patrick' (whose pasteboard helmets, and calico banners, and lath swords, well characterise the humbug of chivalry which they are made to represent), looks like a theatre behind the scenes. 'Paddy's Opera,' however, is a noble performance; and the Englishman may here listen to a half-hour sermon, and in the anthem to a bass singer whose voice is one of the finest ever heard.

The Drama does not flourish much more in Dublin than in any other part of the country. Operatic stars make their appearance occasionally, and managers lose money. I was at a fine concert, at which Lablache and others performed, where there were not a hundred people in the pit of the pretty theatre, and where the only encore given was to a young woman in ringlets and yellow satin, who stepped forward and sang 'Coming through the rye,' or some other scientific composition, in an exceedingly small voice. On the nights when the regular drama was enacted, the audience was still smaller. The theatre of Fishamble Street was given up to the performances of the Rev. Mr. Gregg and his Protestant company, whose soirées I did not attend; and, at the Abbey Street Theatre, whither I went in order to see, if possible, some specimens of the national humour, I found a company of English people ranting through a melodrama, the tragedy whereof was the only laughable thing to be witnessed.

Humbler popular recreations may be seen by the curious. One night I paid twopence to see a puppet-show—such an entertainment as may have been popular a hundred and thirty years ago, and is described in the *Spectator*. But the company here assembled were not, it scarcely need be said, of the genteel sort. There were a score of boys, however, and a dozen of labouring men, who were quite happy and contented with the piece performed, and loudly applauded. Then in passing homewards of a night, you hear, at the humble public-houses, the sound of many a fiddle, and the stamp of feet dancing the good old jig, which is still maintaining a struggle with teetotalism, and, though vanquished now, may rally some day and overcome the enemy. At Kingstown, especially, the old ' fire-worshippers' yet seem to muster pretty strongly; loud is the music to be heard in the taverns there, and the cries of encouragement to the dancers.

Of the numberless amusements that take place in the *Phaynix,* it is not very necessary to speak. Here you may behold garrison races, and reviews; lord-lieutenants in brown greatcoats; aides-de-camp scampering about like mad in blue; fat colonels roaring 'charge' to immense heavy dragoons; dark riflemen lining woods and firing; galloping cannoneers banging and blazing right and left. Here comes his Excellency the Commander-in-Chief, with his huge feathers, and white hair, and hooked nose; and yonder sits his Excellency the Ambassador from the republic of Topinambo in a glass coach, smoking a cigar. The honest Dublinites make a great deal of such small dignitaries as his Excellency of the glass coach; you hear everybody talking of him, and asking which is he; and when presently one of Sir Robert Peel's sons makes bis appearance on the course, the public rush delighted to look at him.

They love great folks, those honest Emerald Islanders, more intensely than any people I ever heard of, except the Americans. They still cherish the memory of the sacred George IV. They chronicle genteel small beer with never-failing assiduity. They go in long trains to a sham Court—simpering in tights and bags, with swords between their legs. O heaven and earth, what joy! Why are the Irish noblemen absentees? If their lordships like respect, where would they get it so well as in their own country?

The Irish noblemen are very likely going through the same delightful routine of duty before their real sovereign—in *real* tights and bagwigs, as it were, performing their graceful and lofty duties, and celebrating the august service of the throne. These, of course, the truly loyal heart can only respect: and I think a drawing-room at St. James's the grandest spectacle that ever feasted the eye or exercised the intellect. The crown, surrounded by its knights and nobles, its priests, its sages, and their respective ladies; illustrious foreigners, men learned in the law, heroes of land and sea, beef-eaters, gold-sticks, gentlemen-at-arms rallying round the throne and defending it with those swords which never knew defeat (and would surely, if tried, secure victory): these are sights and characters which every man must look upon with a thrill of respectful awe, and count amongst the glories of his country. What lady that sees this will not confess that she reads every one of the drawing-room costumes, from Majesty down to Miss Ann Maria Smith; and all the names of the presentations, from

Prince Baccabocksky (by the Russian Ambassador) to Ensign Stubbs on his appointment?

We are bound to read these accounts. It is our pride, our duty as Britons. But though one may honour the respect of the aristocracy of the land for the sovereign, yet there is no reason why those who are not of the aristocracy should be aping their betters; and the Dublin Castle business has, I cannot but think, a very high-life-below-stairs look There is no aristocracy in Dublin. Its magnates are tradesmen—Sir Fiat Haustus, Sir Blacker Dosy, Mr. Serjeant Bluebag, or Mr. Counsellor O'Fee. Brass-plates are their titles of honour, and they live by their boluses or their briefs. What call have these worthy people to be dangling and grinning at lord-lieutenants' levées, and playing sham aristocracy before a sham sovereign? Oh that old humbug of a Castle! It is the greatest sham of all the shams in Ireland.

Although the season may be said to have begun, for the Courts are opened, and the *noblesse de la robe* have assembled, I do not think the genteel quarters of the town look much more cheerful. They still, for the most part, wear their faded appearance and lean half-pay look. There is the beggar still dawdling here and there. Sounds of carriages or footmen do not deaden the clink of the burly policeman's boot-heels. You may see, possibly, a smutty-faced nursemaid leading out her little charges to walk; or the observer may catch a glimpse of Mick the footman lolling at the door, and grinning as he talks to some dubious tradesman. Mick and John are very different characters externally and inwardly;—profound essays (involving the histories of the two countries for a thousand years) might be written regarding Mick and John, and the moral and political influences which have developed the flunkeys of the two nations. The friend, too, with whom Mick talks at the door is a puzzle to a Londoner. I have hardly ever entered a Dublin house without meeting with some such character on my way in or out. He looks too shabby for a dun, and not exactly ragged enough for a beggar—a doubtful, lazy, dirty family vassal—a guerilla footman. I think it is he who makes a great noise, and whispering, and clattering, handing in the dishes to Mick from outside of the dining-room door. When an Irishman comes to London he brings Erin with him; and ten to one you will find one of these queer retainers about his place.

London one can only take leave of by degrees: the great town melts away into suburbs, which- soften, as it were, the parting between the cockney and his darling birthplace. But you pass from some of the stately fine Dublin streets straight into the country. After No. 46 Eccles Street, for instance, potatoes begin at once. You are on a wide green plain, diversified by occasional cabbage-plots, by drying-grounds white with chemises, in the midst of which the chartered wind is revelling; and though in the map some fanciful engineer has laid down streets and squares, they exist but on paper; nor, indeed, can there be any need of them at present, in a quarter where houses are not wanted so much as people to dwell in the same.

If the genteel portions of the town look to the full as melancholy as they did, the downright poverty ceases. I fear, to make so strong an impression as it made four months ago. Going over the same ground again, places appear to have quite a different aspect; and, with their strangeness, poverty and misery have lost much of their terror. The people, though dirtier and more ragged, seem certainly happier than those in London.

Near to the King's Court, for instance (a noble building, as are almost all the public edifices of the city), is a straggling green suburb, containing numberless little shabby, patched, broken-windowed huts, with rickety gardens dotted with rags that have been washed, and children that have not; and thronged with all sorts of ragged inhabitants. Near to the suburb, in the town, is a dingy old mysterious district, called Stoney-batter, where some houses have been allowed to reach an old age, extraordinary in this country of premature ruin, and look as if they had been built some six score years since. In these and the neighbouring tenements, not so old, but equally ruinous and mouldy, there is a sort of vermin swarm of humanity: dirty faces at all the dirty windows; children on all the broken steps; smutty slipshod women clacking and bustling about, and old men dawdling. Well, only paint and prop the tumbling gates and huts in the suburb, and fancy the Stoney-batterites clean, and you would have rather a gay and agreeable picture of human life—of workpeople and their families reposing after their labours. They are all happy, and sober, and kind-hearted,—they seem kind, and play with the children—the young women having a gay good-natured joke for the passer-by; the old seemingly contented, and buzzing to one another. It is only the costume, as it were, that has frightened the stranger, and made him fancy that people so ragged must be unhappy. Observation grows used to the rags as much as the people do, and my impression of the walk through this district, on a sunshiny clear autumn evening, is that of a fête. I am almost ashamed it should be so.

Near to Stoney-batter lies a group of huge gloomy edifices—an hospital, a penitentiary, a madhouse, and a poorhouse. I visited the latter of these, the North Dublin Union-house, an enormous establishment, which accommodates two thousand beggars. Like all the public institutions of the country, it seems to be well conducted, and is a vast, orderly, and cleanly place, wherein the prisoners are better clothed, better fed, and better housed than they can hope to be when at liberty. We were taken into all the wards in due order: the schools and nursery for the children; the dining-rooms, day-rooms, etc., of the men and women. Each division is so accommodated, as also with a large court or ground to walk and exercise in.

Among the men, there are very few able-bodied; the most of them, the keeper said, having gone out for the harvest-time, or as soon as the potatoes came in. If they go out, they cannot return before the expiration of a month: the guardians have been obliged to establish this prohibition, lest the persons requiring relief should go in and out too frequently. The old men were assembled in considerable numbers in a long day-room that is comfortable and warm. Some of them were picking oakum by way of employment, but most of them were past work; all such inmates of the house as are able-bodied being occupied upon the premises. Their hall was airy and as clean as brush and water could make it: the men equally clean, and their grey jackets and Scotch caps stout and warm. Thence we were led, with a sort of satisfaction, by the guardian, to the kitchen—a large room, at the end of which might be seen certain coppers, emitting, it must be owned, a very faint inhospitable smell. It was Friday, and rice-milk is the food on that day, each man being served with a pint-canful, of which cans a great number stood smoking upon stretchers—the platters were laid, each with its portion of salt, in the large clean dining-room hard by. 'Look at that rice,' said the keeper, taking up a bit; 'try it, sir, it's delicious.' I'm sure I hope it is.

The old women's room was crowded with, I should think, at least four hundred old ladies—neat and nice, in white clothes and caps—sitting demurely on benches, doing nothing for the most part; but some employed, like the old men, in fiddling with the oakum. 'There's tobacco here,' says the guardian, in a loud voice; 'who's smoking tobacco'?' 'Fait, and I wish dere *was* some tabaccy here,' says one old lady, 'and my service to you, Mr. Leary, and I hope one of the gentlemen has a snuff-box, and a pinch for a poor old woman.' But we had no boxes; and if any person who reads this visit, goes to a poorhouse or lunatic asylum, let him carry a box, if for that day only—a pinch is like Dives's drop of water to those poor limboed souls. Some of the poor old creatures began to stand up as we came in—I can't say how painful such an honour seemed to me.

There was a separate room for the able-bodied females; and the place and courts were full of stout, red-cheeked, bouncing women. If the old ladies looked respectable, *I* cannot say the young ones were particularly good-looking; there were some Hogarthian faces amongst them—sly, leering, and hideous. I fancied I could see only too well what these girls had been. Is it charitable or not to hope that such bad faces could only belong to bad women?

'Here, sir, is the nursery,' said the guide, flinging open the door of a long room. There may have been eighty babies in it, with as many nurses and mothers. Close to the door sat one with as beautiful a face as I almost ever saw: she had at her breast a very sickly and puny child, and looked up, as we entered, with a pair of angelical eyes, and a face that Mr. Eastlake could paint—a face that *had* been angelical that is; for there was the snow still, as it were, but with the footmark on it. I asked her how old she was—she did not know. She could not have been more than fifteen years, the poor child. She said she had been a servant—and there was no need of asking anything more about her story. I saw her grinning at one of her comrades as we went out of the room; her face did not look angelical then. Ah, young master or old, young or old villain, who did this!—have you not enough wickedness of your own to answer for, that you must take another's sins upon your shoulders; and be this wretched child's sponsor in crime?...

But this chapter must be made as short as possible: and so I will not say how much prouder Mr. Leary, the keeper, was of his fat pigs than of his paupers—how he pointed us out the burial-ground of the family of the poor—their coffins were quite visible through the niggardly mould; and the children might peep at their fathers over the burial-ground-playground wall—nor how we went to see the Linen Hall of Dublin —that huge, useless, lonely, decayed place, in the vast windy solitudes of which stands the simpering statue of George IV., pointing to some bales of shirting, over which he is supposed to extend his august protection.

The cheers of the rabble hailing the new Lord Mayor were the last sounds that I heard in Dublin: and I quitted the kind friends I had made there with the sincerest regret. As for forming 'an opinion of Ireland,' such as is occasionally asked from a traveller on his return— that is as difficult an opinion to form as to express; and the puzzle which has perplexed the gravest and wisest, may be confessed by a humble writer of light literature, whose aim it only was to look at the manners and the scenery of the country, and who does not venture to meddle with questions of more serious import.

To have 'an opinion about Ireland,' one must begin by getting at the truth: and where is it to be had in the country? Or rather, there are two truths, the Catholic truth and the Protestant truth. The two parties do not see things with the same eyes. I recollect, for instance, a Catholic gentleman telling me that the Primate had forty-three thousand *five hundred* a year; a Protestant clergyman gave me, chapter and verse, the history of a shameful perjury and malversation of money on the part of a Catholic priest; nor was one tale more true than the other. But belief is made a party business; and the receiving of the archbishop's income would probably not convince the Catholic, any more than the clearest evidence to the contrary altered the Protestant's opinion. Ask about an estate: you may be sure almost that people will make misstatements, or volunteer them if not asked. Ask a cottager about his rent, or his landlord: you cannot trust him. I shall never forget the glee with which a gentleman in Munster told me how he had sent off MM. Tocqueville and Beaumont 'with *such* a set of stories.' Inglis was seized, as I am told, and mystified in the same way. In the midst of all these truths, attested with 'I give ye my sacred honour and word,' which is the stranger to select? And how are we to trust philosophers who make theories upon such data?

Meanwhile it is satisfactory to know, upon testimony so general as to be equivalent almost to fact, that, wretched as it is, the country is steadily advancing, nor nearly so wretched now as it was a score of years since; and let us hope that the *middle class,* which this increase of prosperity must generate (and of which our laws have hitherto forbidden the existence in Ireland, making there a population of Protestant aristocracy and Catholic peasantry), will exercise the greatest and most beneficial influence over the country. Too independent to be bullied by priest or squire—having their interest in quiet, and alike indisposed to servility or to rebellion; may not as much be hoped from the gradual formation of such a class, as from any legislative meddling? It is the want of the middle class that has rendered the squire so arrogant, and the clerical or political demagogue so powerful; and I think Mr. O'Connell himself would say that the existence of such a body would do more for the steady acquirement of orderly freedom, than the occasional outbreak of any crowd, influenced by any eloquence from altar or tribune.

i Saint Paul speaking from the Areopagus, and rebuking these superstitions away, yet speaks tenderly to the people before him, whose devotions he had marked; quotes their poets, to bring them to think of the God unknown, whom they had ignorantly worshipped; and says, that the times of this ignorance God winked at, but that now it was time to repent. No rebuke can surely be more gentle than this delivered by the upright Apostle.

ii Thackeray's sketch is reproduced in the centrefold following page 122.

iii Thackeray's sketch is reproduced in the centrefold following page 122.

iv Thackeray's sketch is reproduced in the centrefold following page 122.

v At Derrynane Beg, for instance.

vi Thackeray's sketch is reproduced in the centrefold following page 122.

vii The two men were executed pursuant to sentence, and both persisted solemnly in denying their guilt. There can be no doubt of it: but it appears to be a point of honour with these unhappy men to make no statement which may incriminate the witnesses who appeared on their behalf, and on their part perjured themselves equally.

viii Thackeray's sketch is reproduced in the centrefold following page 122.

ix The only instances of intoxication that I have heard of as yet, have been on the part of two 'cyouncillors,' undeniably drunk and noisy yesterday after the bar dinner at Waterford.

x The suspicion turned out to be very correct. The gentleman is the respected cook of C—, as I learned afterwards from a casual Cambridge man.

xi By the help of an Alexandrine, the names of these famous families may also be accommodated to verse.

'Athey, Blake, Bodkin, Browne, Deane, Dorsey, Frinche,
Joyce, Moreeh, Skereth, Fonte, Kirowan, Martin, Lyncho.'

xii If the rude old verses are not very remarkable in quality, in quantity they are still more deficient, and take some dire liberties with the laws laid down in the Gradus and the Grammar:—

'Septom ornant montes Romam, septem ostia Nilum,
    Tot rutilis stellis splendet in axe Polus.
Galvia, Polo Niloque bis æquas. Roma Conachtæ,
    Bis septem illustres has colit illa tribus.
Bis urbis septem defendunt mœnia turres,
    Intus et en duro est marmore quæque domus.
Bis septem portæ sunt, castra et culmina circum,
    Per totidem pontum permeat unda vias.
Principo bis septem fulgent altaria templo,

Quævis patronæ est ara dicata suo,
Et septem sacrata Deo cœnobia, patrum
Fœminei et sexus, tot pia tecta tenet.'

xiii This epithet is applied to the party of a Colonel somebody, in a Dublin paper.

xiv Here is an extract from one of the latter—

'Hasten to some distant isle,
In the bosom of the deep,
Where the skies for ever smile,
And the blacks for ever weep!'

Is it not a shame that such nonsensical false twaddle should be sung in a house of the Church of England, by people assembled for grave and decent worship?

xv It must be said, for the worthy fellow who accompanied us, and who acted as cicerone previously to the great Willis, the great Hall, the great Barrow, that though he wears a ragged coat his manners are those of a gentleman, and his conversation evinces no small talent, taste, and scholarship.

xvi 'Boarders are received from the age of eight to fourteen at £12 per annum, and £1 for washing, paid quarterly in advance.

'Day scholars are received from the age of ten to twelve at £2, paid quarterly in advance.

'The Incorporated Society have abundant cause for believing that the introduction of Boarders into their Establishments has produced far more advantageous results to the public than they could, at so early a period, have anticipated; and that the election of boys to their Foundations only after a fair competition with others of a given district, has had the effect of stimulating masters and scholars to exertion and study, and promises to operate most beneficially for the advancement of religious and general knowledge.

'The districts for eligible Candidates are as follow:—

Dundalk Institution embraces the counties of Louth and Down, because the properties which support it lie in this district.

'The Pococke Institution, Kilkenny, embraces the counties of Kilkenny and Waterford, for the same cause.

'The Ranelagh Institution, the towns of Athlone and Roscommon, and three districts in the counties of Galway and Roscommon, which the Incorporated society hold in fee, or from which they receive impropriate tithes.

(Signed) 'Cæsar Otway, Secretary.'

xvii The Proprietary Schools of late established have gone far to protect the interests of parents and children; but the masters of these schools take boarders, and of course draw profits from them. Why make the learned man a beef-and-mutton contractor? It would be easy to arrange the economy of a school so that there should be no possibility of a want of confidence, or of peculation, to the detriment of the pupil.

xviii Thackeray's sketch is reproduced in the centrefold following page 122.

xix 'I want to go into a coal-mine,' says Tom Sheridan, 'in order to say I have been there.' 'Well, then, say so,' replied the admirable father.

xx The late Mr. Pope represents Camilla as 'scouring the plain,' an absurd and useless task. Peggy's occupation with the kettle is much more simple and noble. The second line of this verse (whereof the author scorns to deny an obligation) is from the celebrated 'Frithiof' of Esaias Tigner. A maiden is serving warriors to drink, and is standing by a shield—'Und die Runde des Schildes ward wie das Mägdelein roth,'—perhaps the above is the best thing in both poems.

xxi And then, how much Latin and Greek does the public schoolboy know? Also, does he know anything else, and what? Is it history, or geography, or mathematics, or divinity?